YANKEES IN THE LAND
OF THE GODS

BOOKS BY PETER BOOTH WILEY

Empires in the Sun: The Rise of the New American West
(WITH ROBERT GOTTLIEB)

America's Saints: The Rise of Mormon Power
(WITH ROBERT GOTTLIEB)

YANKEES IN THE LAND

 OF THE

GODS

COMMODORE PERRY AND THE

OPENING OF JAPAN

PETER BOOTH WILEY

WITH

KOROGI ICHIRO

VIKING

G

enguin Group

Penguin Books USA Inc.,

New York, New York 10014, U.S.A.
Penguin Books Ltd, 27 Wrights Lane, London W8 5TZ, England
Penguin Books Australia Ltd, Ringwood, Victoria, Australia
Penguin Books Canada Ltd, 2801 John Street,
Markham, Ontario, Canada L3R 1B4
Penguin Books (N.Z.) Ltd, 182–190 Wairau Road,
Auckland 10, New Zealand

Penguin Books Ltd, Registered Offices:
Harmondsworth, Middlesex, England

First published in 1990 by Viking Penguin,
a division of Penguin Books USA Inc.

1 3 5 7 9 10 8 6 4 2

Illustration credits appear on page 579.

Maps on pages 90–91 and 236 by Virginia Norey. Copyright © Viking
Penguin, a division of Penguin Books USA Inc., 1990.

Maps on pages 133, 170, 206–7, and 285 adapted by Virginia Norey
from the book *"Old Bruin," Commodore Matthew C. Perry, 1794–1858*,
by Samuel Eliot Morison. Copyright © 1967 by Samuel Eliot Morison.
By permission of Little, Brown and Company.

LIBRARY OF CONGRESS CATALOGING IN PUBLICATION DATA
Wiley, Peter Booth.
Yankees in the land of the gods: Commodore Perry and the opening of
Japan / Peter Booth Wiley with Ichiro Korogi.
p. cm.
Includes bibliographical references.
ISBN 0-670-81507-1
1. United States Naval Expedition to Japan, 1852–1854. 2. United
States—Foreign relations—Japan. 3. Japan—Foreign relations—
United States. 4. Perry, Matthew Calbraith, 1794–1858.
I. Korogi, Ichiro. II. Title.
DS8818.W55 1990
952'.025—dc20
90-50066

Printed in the United States of America
Set in DeVinne
Designed by Francesca Belanger

In memory of
ESTHER BOOTH WILEY

Driven by
an insatiable curiosity,
she loved people and
the world of books.

ACKNOWLEDGMENTS

I could not have written this book, which describes the first serious diplomatic contact between the United States and Japan from the perspective of both participants, without the assistance of Korogi Ichiro. Without his knowledge of Japanese, Chinese, and classical Japanese, we would not have had access to the documents that portray the Japanese side of the story. In working together our discussions ranged around the globe and through many historical eras, and we became fast friends.

My first help came from two old friends I knew from graduate school, Professor Naganuma Hideyo of Tsuda College and Professor Shinkawa Kensaburo of the University of Tokyo. They pointed me in the direction of Japanese sources, introduced me to others who are interested in the Perry expedition, were my hosts in Japan, and did everything that they could to make my work there easier. Professor Herbert P. Bix of the Asian Studies Centre at the University of Sheffield in Sheffield, England, also helped start me on the scholarly path and then later read and critiqued the manuscript. His assistance was invaluable. Captain Roger Pineau, USNR (Ret.), the foremost Perry scholar in the United States, provided me with ideas, documents, and help along the way. I am indebted to William Haver, Professor Marius B. Jansen of Princeton University, and Professor Irwin Scheiner of the University of California, Berkeley, for suggestions about the study of Japanese history. During a long conversation translated by Professor Shinkawa, Professor Mitani Hiroshi helped me understand Abe Masahiro's activities before Perry's arrival. On a trip to Mito, Japan, Dr. Yoshida

Toshizumi of the Ibarakiken Ritsu Rekishikan provided me with a better sense of Tokugawa Nariaki as a historical personality. Ito Hisako, archivist at the Yokohama Archives of History, was very helpful in collecting material for the illustrations. I was also assisted in Japan by Saito Setsuko, Hamaya Misaki, Professor Yui Daizaburo of Hitotsubashi University, Araki Shigeyoshi of the Foreign Press Center/Japan, and Kawamura Kinji, its former president.

In Hong Kong, Martha Avery and John Stevenson were both hosts and guides. They also critiqued the manuscript while Betty Peh-T'i Wei provided me with a number of helpful suggestions after reading an early version of Chapter 4. At Hong Kong University I was assisted by Dr. Elizabeth Sinn. In Shanghai I benefited from a discussion about the Small Knife Society with Zu-An Cheng of the Institute of History at the Academy of Social Science. Lo Chao Tien of the Shanghai Translation Publishing House arranged the interview and translated.

Bradford Wiley, Bradford Wiley II, Nancy Wolfberg, and Richard Haver provided me with a number of suggestions after reading the manuscript. In my research I was assisted by James W. Cheevers of the United States Naval Academy Museum, Alice Creighton of the Nimitz Library at the Naval Academy, Bernard R. Crystal of the Butler Library at Columbia University, Judith Downie of the Old Dartmouth Historical Society, Elizabeth A. Falsey of the Houghton Library at Harvard University, Abbot Fletcher, Roy Kiplinger of the William L. Clements Library at the University of Michigan, Kobayashi Yoshiko of San Francisco State University, James W. Lee of the Naval Historical Foundation, Alton E. Peters, Professor John Curtis Perry of Tufts University, Marion T. Saportas, Patricia Shaw, Professor Teruya Yoshihiko of the University of the Ryukyus, George Tilton, Richard A. Von Doenhoff of the National Archives, Professor Bob Tadashi Wakabayashi of Yorke University, and Xiao-Min Lu. I would also like to thank Madeleine Gleason for ideas about sources and an introduction to the Harvard libraries and Emily Morison Beck for permission to use the papers of Samuel Eliot Morison in the Harvard Archives.

I was assisted in compiling the illustrations by Captain Pineau,

Peter Carlson, Chong Lee, Richard Bancroft of the Pierce Studio, Judith Brisker and Maja Falaco of the Library of Congress, Marion Campbell of the Honolulu Academy of Art, Delphine Castel of the Provincial Archives of British Columbia, Christina K. L. Chu of the Hong Kong Museum of Art, Peter Drummey of the Massachusetts Historical Society, Harold Ellis of the American History Museum at the Smithsonian Institution, Susan Y. Elter of the Franklin D. Roosevelt Library, Ikeya Harumi of the Tokugawa Remeikan Foundation, Marguerite Lavin of the Brooklyn Museum, Lois Oglesby of the Mariners' Museum, Ono Masao of the Historiographical Institute at the University of Tokyo, Bill Peterson and Peggy Tate Smith of the Mystic Seaport Museum, Irene Roughton of the Chrysler Museum, Tokugawa Tunenari, Gretchen K. Viehman of the Museum of the City of New York, and Mary E. Winter of the Kentucky Historical Society.

I would be remiss in not mentioning the excellence of the libraries and staff at the University of California, Berkeley, particularly the Bancroft, Doe, and East Asiatic libraries, where I did the bulk of my research.

Finally I would like to thank my agent Robert Cornfield, who went about finding a publisher and supporting this project with his usual genial enthusiasm, Dan Frank, of Viking, who signed the book, and Michael Millman, who proved to be a good listener and a forceful editor.

CONTENTS

PART
I

PROLOGUE

THE UNITED STATES' VICTORY over Mexico in 1848 was a victory with epic implications. It virtually doubled the size of the United States and was the culmination of a headlong expansionist rush with the battle cry "Manifest Destiny." The United States became a continental power, albeit an underdeveloped one, with both a Pacific littoral and global pretensions.

Since the dawning days of the republic, Americans, particularly the merchants and whalers of New England, had cast their eyes toward the Pacific. Sea captains, often men barely out of their teens who commanded crews younger still, navigated perilously small sailing ships into every nook and corner of the Great Western Ocean looking for whales, seals, sea otters, and opportunities for trade. Missionaries, the proper offspring of proper Puritans, followed in their wake. Some of the first fortunes made in Salem, Boston, and Providence were garnered in the fabled China trade: the skins of seals and sea otters were bought from the great native trading nations of the Northwest coast and taken to Canton, where they were exchanged for tea, silks, and nankeens or sold outright for cash.

During their travels these shrewd and adventurous traders and their missionary cousins inevitably would skirt the shores of Japan and hear strange tales of a powerful nation ruled by two emperors. Some two centuries earlier this nation had attempted to wipe out Christianity among its people, banned all foreign missionaries, and shut itself off from the outside world, barring any contact with the Western trading nations. There was, the stories

went, one exception: each year at Nagasaki a Dutch ship and sometimes two were permitted to make port and trade.

In crossing the North Pacific heading toward China, these
American Magellans thrust their bows against the mighty Black
Current, which the Japanese called Kura Siwo. It surged past
Japan in a northeasterly direction and then curved southward
through the Gulf of Alaska, brushing the shores of the Pacific
Northwest. This current brought with it strange messengers, Japanese sailors from tiny coastal vessels that had been blown off the
shores of their native land in one storm or another. Then they were
either picked up by American whalers or cast on the shores of the
Northwest Territories. They were envoys from a different world,
maybe even from some prehistoric era, their facial features suggesting a distant tie to the Indians of the Pacific Coast. Though
lost at sea, these sailors were barred by the shogun's law from
returning to their native land. In a wildly expansionist era, these
messengers, the lure of trade, the conversion of lost souls, and maybe
even gold sang a siren song that inspired numerous Americans to
think of being the first to cross the threshold of Japan and open it
to the outside world.

In the aftermath of the Mexican War, the United States pushed
new lines of communication through the Caribbean across the isth-
muses of Panama and Nicaragua and into the Pacific. The primary
means of transportation were the steamship and railroad, driven
by engines of progress, which promised to link all of Asia to the
United States and even to propel the United States past Great
Britain as the dominant power in the Pacific. No less a dream than
this brought the Americans to Edo, the capital city of the shoguns.

1

A GOOD CAUSE FOR
A QUARREL

I flatter myself that I was the instigator of Commodore Perry's expedition to Japan.[1] —RANALD MACDONALD

If that double-bolted land, Japan, is ever to become hospitable, it is the whale-ship alone to whom the credit will be due; for already she is on the threshold.[2] —HERMAN MELVILLE, *Moby-Dick,* 1851

So long as the Sun shall warm the earth, let no Christian dare to come to Japan; and, let all know that the King of Spain himself, or the Christian's God, . . . if he violates this command shall pay for it with his head.[3] —Shogun's Edict of 1638

IN THE SPRING OF 1847 Ranald MacDonald, who was then wandering the beaches of Hawaii, signed before the mast on the whaler *Plymouth* out of Sag Harbor, New York. It was MacDonald's second voyage on the *Plymouth*; two years earlier he had sailed aboard her from New York to these same islands. Now, MacDonald had a proposition for Captain Laurence Edwards. He would ship aboard the *Plymouth* to the Japan whaling grounds and work until her hold was filled with barrels of whale oil. Then he wanted Edwards to leave him in a small boat off the coast of Japan. At first Edwards objected; the idea was crazy. But after a time he gave in. He knew that MacDonald was a good sailor and a strong harpooner, and as MacDonald tells the tale, Edwards thought that MacDonald would surely change his mind.[4]

The *Plymouth* followed the trade winds westward on the first leg of a voyage then being made by dozens of whaling ships that were combing the seas of East Asia from Japan to the Arctic Circle for their prey. The *Plymouth*'s first landfall was a coral atoll in the Marianas where the crew discovered a polyglot community of native and American castaways. From there Edwards sailed to the Bonin Islands, which would figure prominently six years later in the American expedition to Japan. (See map, pages 206–7.) From the Bonins the ship moved on to the Bashis, south of Taiwan, where the crew killed their first sperm whales, and from there through heavy gales in the China Sea to Hong Kong, the recently established outpost of the British Empire in China. After a month spent refitting, the *Plymouth* headed north, finally entering the Sea of Japan in March 1848.[5]

For three months, the *Plymouth* encountered mild weather, light breezes interspersed with periods of calm and then dense fog as Edwards worked his way north into the Tatar Strait between the Sakhalin Peninsula and the Russian mainland. "Whaling was so easy in the Japan Sea," MacDonald later wrote, "the fish were so numerous that we had no occasion to chase them with our ship: we had nothing to do but to lower our boats, harpoon them, and bring them alongside for stripping." During their last hunt near the northern coast of Japan, the *Plymouth* encountered more than twenty-five whaling ships, most of them American owned. By June, the *Plymouth*'s hold was packed with hogsheads of whale oil, a cargo that might net the ship's owners something between fifty and seventy-five thousand dollars.[6] Already two and a half years at sea, Captain Edwards was eager to head for home, but Ranald MacDonald was ready to begin his great adventure.

Edwards and the crew pleaded with MacDonald not to go, but seeing that he was determined they ultimately agreed to his hare-brained scheme. With the funds that he had earned as a harpooner, MacDonald bought a small boat from Edwards, rigged it with a sail and equipped it with a quadrant, nautical almanac, books, and provisions for thirty-six days. Assigning his remaining six hundred dollars in trust to Edwards, MacDonald clambered into his boat. But the crew, as one companion offered to join him, refused to untie the last knot that bound him to the ship. MacDonald pulled his clasp knife and saying his final farewell, cut the line, setting himself adrift in a dense fog some five miles, he thought, from an uninhabited island near the northern tip of Ezo (Hokkaido), the northernmost part of Japan.

"We parted!" MacDonald wrote. "They 'Homeward bound!' I, for the mysterious dread Japan! But my mind was fixed; as the needle to the pole; and my hot heart, full of its purpose of years, rose to swell in unison with the Pacific billow. There I floated!—like a bird on the ocean of fathomless chance: wild and free as the roving sea gull; at home on its heaving bosom."[7]

Photograph of Ranald MacDonald

How had Ranald MacDonald, a twenty-four-year-old, half Chinook Indian, half Scot, conceived of the extravagant notion then being pondered by a handful of American diplomats, naval officers, whaling captains, merchants, and missionaries of journeying to Japan?

MacDonald's maternal grandfather was the powerful chieftain Comcomly, who headed the Chinook federation, whose villages dotted the northern banks of the Columbia River from its mouth to the Cascade Mountains. A formidable figure, Comcomly owned a large entourage of slaves and claimed numerous brides in marriages, which tied him to the lesser tribes in the federation.[8] In 1792 Captain Robert Gray brought the eighty-three-foot *Columbia* to the mouth of the mighty river where Comcomly reigned. Two years earlier Gray had journeyed from Boston around Cape Horn to Nootka Sound, on Vancouver Island. Here he had bought sea otter furs from the Indians and then taken the furs to Canton, China, where he had bought tea and silks to be sold in Boston after a three-year voyage that covered 41,899 miles. Gray thus became one of the principal navigators of the Canton trade, a lucrative enterprise that would lay the foundation of merchant wealth in Boston, New York, and a dozen other seaports along the northeastern coast of the United States. America's new gentry wanted Chinese silks and tea, fine porcelain, lacquer ware, rosewood, and camphor wood furniture to decorate their homes.[9] But as citizens of a poor nation recovering from the commercial ravages of the Revolution, they lacked the specie and exotic Asian products, such as sharks' fins and birds' nests, that the Chinese merchants demanded in exchange. Gray had found a commodity that would ultimately tie the Pacific Northwest to China with sinews of trade, establish a powerful American claim to the Pacific littoral, and link the ports of the northeast with those of East Asia.

The Indians of the Pacific Northwest were more than eager to trade furs for goods such as shoes, mirrors, nails, chisels, copper, clothing, buttons, and muskets that the "Boston men" had to offer. In short order, Comcomly's people became major suppliers on an important new trade route. "It was as if a new gold coast had been discovered," Washington Irving wrote in 1836 in *Astoria*, his history of the early fur trade.[10] And it was natural enough that Ranald MacDonald, growing up among the Boston men and their competitors, who worked for the Montreal-based North West Company and the British-owned Hudson's Bay Company, would hear and learn about Japan. For in these higher latitudes, Asia and North America inclined their headlands toward each other and were separated by a scant fifty miles at the Bering Straits. "Japan was our next neighbor across the way," MacDonald wrote, "only the placid sea, the Pacific between us."[11]

MacDonald's father, Archibald, was a Scot who went to work

as a clerk for the Hudson's Bay Company at the age of twenty-two. He rose to be a chief trader and one of the most respected men in the Pacific Northwest. Archibald MacDonald came to the Pacific Coast in the early 1820s at the end of a decade of desultory trade along the coast.[12] Gray's two visits in the 1790s had triggered a boom that brought many ships to the Northwest Coast despite a number of violent attacks by the Indians. In 1811 explorers working

Chinook Indians; drawing by George Catlin

for the New York merchant John Jacob Astor built a fort and called it Astoria. Astor's men, as well as the American explorers Meriwether Lewis and William Clark, were greeted warmly by Comcomly. The fur boom did not last, however. When the United States and England clashed in the War of 1812, Astor's men surrendered Astoria to the British, sold their business to the rival North West Company, and returned to the States. The Boston men had come close to monopolizing the fur trade, and Astor had become the wealthiest parvenu in New York. But the fur trade all but disappeared as a result of the U.S. embargo of overseas trade that preceded the War of 1812 and the collapse of oceangoing commerce that followed the British blockade of the East Coast.[13]

The Hudson's Bay men came to the Northwest in the 1820s to revive the fur trade after their company had devoured—not merged with—the rival North West Company. It was an established policy of the Hudson's Bay Company to encourage marriages between its employees and native women. Archibald MacDonald had already married one Indian woman, or "country wife," who bore him a son before he came to Astoria, now known as Fort George. At Fort George, MacDonald married Comcomly's youngest daughter, Koale' xoa (Raven), who in February 1824 bore him a son named Ranald. A few days after giving birth, she died, and Archibald MacDonald soon moved farther up the Columbia and remarried.[14]

The MacDonalds lived a nomadic life, moving from trading post to trading post throughout the Northwest. In 1834, when the MacDonalds were living at Fort Vancouver on the Columbia River, Ranald chanced to meet three Japanese sailors. They were part of a crew of seventeen men who had started on a voyage from Owari to Edo (as Tokyo was then known) with a load of rice. Their junk was disabled at sea, and they were caught up in the great Black Current that ran from Japan into the Gulf of Alaska and southward to the shores of the Pacific Northwest. Seventeen months later, their junk was dashed to pieces on the beaches of the Olympic Peninsula. The three survivors were enslaved by the local Indians but were later freed by a Hudson's Bay sea captain, who brought them to Fort Vancouver.[15]

The Hudson's Bay officials were well aware of Japan's self-imposed isolation, as were all those who traded in the North Pacific. MacDonald later recalled frequent speculative conversations about the Japanese.

What, of such people?—What of their manner of life?—What of their unrivalled wealth with its gleam of gold and things most precious?— What of their feelings and tendencies—if any—towards association or friendly relations with other peoples, especially us, neighbors of their East? These and such like questions and considerations ever recurring; the subject, oft, of talk amongst my elders . . . entering deeply into my young, and naturally receptive mind; breeding, in their own way, thoughts and aspirations which dominated me, as a soul possessed.[16]

MacDonald befriended the Japanese sailors. An impressiona-ble ten-year-old, he noted that the Japanese looked very much like the Indians he had grown up with. The Japanese sailors soon left for China in hopes of returning safely home. And Ranald MacDonald, after moving again, was sent east by his father to get him away from the libertine, liquor-dominated culture of the frontier fur trading posts.

Ranald's father and some of his friends saw something unique in Ranald. One spoke of "certain indescribable qualities." These Hudson's Bay men predicted great things for the boy. "Bear in mind he [Ranald] is of a particular race," his anxious father wrote a friend, "and who knows but that a kinsman of King Comcomly is ordained to make a great figure in the new world; as yet he bears an excellent character."[17]

Ranald's first encounter with school at Fort Vancouver had not been altogether enjoyable. "I attended the school to learn my A.B.C. and English," he wrote. "The big boys had a medal put over their necks, if caught speaking French or Chinook, and when school was out had to remain and learn a task. I made no progress."[18] At the Red River missionary school, however, Ranald appeared to be making progress. After six years of schooling, he went to work in St. Thomas, Ontario, as a clerk in a bank that belonged to a friend of his father. Outwardly Ranald seemed to be conforming to the desires of his father and the demands of civilization.

It was at this time, Ranald wrote later, that he began to conceive of his plan to go to Japan or at least to follow some inner calling that he could not quite fathom. At sixteen, he was a handsome young man about five foot seven, thick set, dark complected with straight black hair and gray eyes. His broad face, particularly his nose, revealed his Indian heritage. He had a friendly, almost courtly way of speaking. But all his personal qualities did little to endear him to the life of the wealthy citizens of St. Thomas, particularly after he fell in love and was rebuffed because of his mixed blood—his first real confrontation with his Indian heritage.

MacDonald found banking or dealing with money in any way highly distasteful. Instead he yearned for the Arcadian life he had spent wandering about the frontier with his father. "I felt, ever, and uncontrollably in my blood, the wild strain for wandering freedom," he later wrote, "*in primis* of my Highland father of Glencoe; secondly, and possibly more so (though unconsciously) of my

Indian mother, of the Pacific Shore, Pacific Seas, in boundless dominion."[19]

One day MacDonald simply walked away from the bank and headed on foot for the Mississippi River, where he worked his way south on a steamer. From New Orleans he sailed to New York and then to London. For the next four years he wandered the globe. Eager to find his son, his father followed his trail to New York. The Oregon boundary dispute between England and the United States would soon be settled, and he wanted Ranald to press his claim to land as a direct descendant of Comcomly. But Ranald had vanished, gone to sea, and ultimately to Japan, one of the colorful romantics who followed their instincts into the Pacific.[20]

As the *Plymouth* glided into the cool fog off northern Japan leaving MacDonald in its wake, Captain Edwards dipped the stars and stripes several times in salute, and MacDonald responded with the little white flag he carried with him. Heading north and east toward an island that appeared on his chart, MacDonald could see a line of breakers and then islands looming out of the damp, gray shroud. Landing on one of the islands, he found it uninhabited.

That night he slept in his boat, and after a breakfast of salt beef, biscuits, and chocolate, explored the island so as to allow time for the *Plymouth* to get well away. Seeing another island, Rishiri, to the north with a snow-capped peak, he decided to head for it. Before departing, he brought his supplies ashore and practiced capsizing his boat in the frigid water. MacDonald had heard stories of the Japanese cruelty toward shipwrecked sailors. It was said that they had even killed a man the year before off the whaler *Lawrence*. Thus he wanted to appear to the Japanese as a sailor in distress, hoping that his plight would warm their hearts or at least soften the expected blows. After another night on the island, he sailed for the snow-capped peak and assuming that the island was inhabited, capsized his boat. However, there was no response from the beach. To his chagrin, MacDonald had to right his boat, but he had lost his clothing, bedding, pistols, bailer, and some books. To his further horror he now saw another ship approaching. In his later years, MacDonald found out that the whaler was the *Uncas* out of Falmouth, Massachusetts. No one aboard the *Uncas* spotted MacDonald, but a crew member did recover the rudder from his capsized craft. In time the story spread that MacDonald had been lost at sea.[21]

After falling overboard and losing more of his provisions, MacDonald spent another wet, uncomfortable night in his boat, awake and fearful that he would end up in the surf. At dawn he spotted smoke on the beach of the island with the snowy peak. Soon a group of men launched a skifflike boat and headed in his direction. MacDonald pulled the plug, and his boat filled rapidly with water. About a hundred yards from him, the boat stopped, and its four occupants, shaggy beings with long black matted hair and beards and uttering guttural sounds, began to bow to him with their palms up. MacDonald attached his swamped craft to their boat and was towed toward the shore in the direction of a large wooden house surrounded by ramshackle huts.[22]

MacDonald was greeted ashore with more bows by at least a hundred people from a nearby village and led gently to the large house. "We were met by a Japanese whose exterior denoted consequence," MacDonald later described the scene. "The front part of his head was shaved, and the hair was gathered into a top knot or queue which projected slightly over the forehead." MacDonald had reached the village of Notsuka and had fallen in among the Ainus, a tribal people who had been conquered and cruelly subjugated by the Japanese. The remnants of the Ainu people lived on Ezo (Hokkaido) under Japanese occupation. To MacDonald, the Ainus resembled the Haida and Bella Coola Indians who lived along the coast of British Columbia. His host, a local official called Tangaro, offered MacDonald food and drink, calling the sake "grog-yes." MacDonald puzzled over this English-sounding word and found later that it had originated from earlier contact with shipwrecked whalers, in fact those from the *Lawrence*.[23]

After a restful night, MacDonald was visited by two more Japanese officials, who conducted a careful inventory of his effects. They exclaimed over each of his possessions, excited by his books and letters but horrified by his supply of beef and pork, deigning to touch the meat only with a long fork. The Japanese shunned the barbarian custom of eating meat, and animals, slaughtered to make leather, were touched only by outcasts. MacDonald remained in the village for ten days with Tangaro as his constant companion. They explored the vicinity and exchanged Japanese and English lessons as MacDonald occupied himself writing Ainu and Japanese words on his slate. MacDonald noted that his companion's desire to learn English "seemed to be intense." At one point Tangaro produced a map of Japan after checking carefully to see that no one was looking. Like all Japanese, Tangaro had been warned against providing any barbarians who landed with information about Japan.[24] So far MacDonald's sojourn had been idyllic. Tangaro was a gracious host, lavishing attention and small gifts on him. Was this the dreaded Japan that he had heard so much about?

After about two weeks, two junks arrived, and a group of Japanese came to find MacDonald, bringing him a gift of sweetmeats. The next day they warned him to stay indoors and hung mats over his windows so that he could not see out. Soon a contingent of soldiers led by six officers appeared and began interrogating MacDonald. MacDonald, with gestures and the help of Tangaro, told them the same story that he had told his Japanese companion: he had jumped ship after a disagreement with the captain. The ship, he explained, was headed back to its home port. This delegation also carefully examined MacDonald's possessions, making drawings of many items, such as his quadrant and the boat, and measuring everything with great care, including MacDonald himself.

The soldiers accompanied MacDonald to another village, where he was marched down a street bordered with curtains of striped material to prevent him from seeing or being seen from the adjacent houses. He was taken to the principal house in town and confined in a room with wooden bars.[25]

Events now took a more ominous turn; MacDonald seemed to have seen the last of his freedom. He was confined for thirty days, though still treated with great kindliness. From his island prison he was taken by junk to Soya (now Wakkanai) at the extreme northern tip of Ezo, where he was imprisoned in what he thought was a government building. When asked if his new abode was satisfactory, he answered in sign language and the smattering of Japanese he knew that he did not like being imprisoned and had no intention of greeting anyone through his bars. His captors were extremely solicitous, allowing him to exercise outside his barred room and making every effort to fulfill his needs with food, tobacco, and other items. During his stay in Soya, MacDonald, undoubtedly quite an attraction, was visited by numerous samurai—distinguished by their two swords—and a doctor. All of them were anx-

Japanese junk; *Narrative of the Expedition*

ious to interrogate him about the outside world. The doctor took his pulse, but when MacDonald, in a cooperative mood, stuck out his tongue, the doctor recoiled in fright. MacDonald gathered from his visitors that Soya was a small military outpost with five cannon manned by one hundred men and officers under the jurisdiction of a local lord, or daimyo.[26]

After an extended stay and a tearful departure from Tangaro, MacDonald was placed aboard another junk and told that in eight to ten days they expected to be in Matsumae, the castle town of the daimyo of Matsumae, which was located on the southern tip of the island. The junk was a colorful craft of about two hundred tons with a high sharp bow and a higher stern with a huge rudder affixed to a twenty-foot-long tiller. The sides of the craft were hung with white cotton sheeting with portholes painted on it. On the quarterdeck stood rows of spears with shining shafts ornamented with gold and mother of pearl, each with a sheath made of fine fur. At the bow hung a huge black hair or fibre swab MacDonald described as "a veritable Neptune's shaving brush."[27]

Fifteen days later, in Matsumae, MacDonald was again visited by a large group of officials, whose leader, mistaking MacDonald for a native, exclaimed, "Niponjin!" meaning "Japanese!" During his first interview, MacDonald was made to understand that they were finishing work on a ship to convey him to Nagasaki. Why bother, responded MacDonald, who was increasingly impatient with his status as a prisoner. Why not let him live there? His interrogators laughed loudly and said, "No, no—Nagasaki!—go away!"[28]

MacDonald was taken by palanquin through a gathering crowd, which appeared to regard him as some kind of wild beast, to a house outside of Matsumae. To his surprise he found here the letters *J* and *C* written on the wall with charcoal. There were other words in English, his host pointed out. On the post that held up the ridge pole of the small building were written the names Robert McCoy, John Brady, and John ———, the last name being indecipherable. Pointing to a freshly boarded-over hole in the ceiling, the Japanese official repeated the word "America," and then in sign language indicated that fifteen Americans had escaped through the hole but had been caught and bound. Drawing the longer of his two swords, he pantomimed the cutting of their throats. "All this made me reflect," MacDonald wrote in his account of the trip. "The reported murder or at least death of the captain of the *Lawrence* recurred to me, and I believed that my 'fifteen' predecessors had shared the same fate."[29] Despite this threat, the Japanese continued to treat MacDonald with the greatest kindness during his voyage to Nagasaki, confining him in a cage but permitting him the run of space below decks when he complained.

After a ten-day trip along the west coast of Honshu and Kyushu, the junk anchored in the harbor at Nagasaki, the one port that maintained legal contact with the world beyond Japan. It was here that the annual Dutch trading ship brought goods and information from the outside world. It was also here that Chinese junks came on a regular basis with reports of the comings and goings of West-

erners and their naval ships along the Chinese coast, of the debilitating impact of "foreign mud," as opium was called, and of the
defeat of the Chinese at the hands of the British in a war initiated
by the British to protect and extend the opium trade.

MacDonald's junk was visited by a contingent of officials, one
of whom was described as a close aide to the governor of Nagasaki.
The officials were accompanied by Moryama Einosuke, who spoke
some English and acted as interpreter.* Again they questioned
MacDonald about his place of birth, his citizenship, his family, his
religious beliefs, and the circumstances that led to his arrival in
Japan. Two days later, MacDonald was brought ashore and got a
quick look at Nagasaki. He saw a city that he estimated contained
ten thousand houses, houses he thought seemed smaller but better
built than others he had seen in the north. Most of them were a
single story of unpainted wood with shingled or red-tiled roofs that
projected out over the street. The windows were of oiled paper on
sliding frames. There were a number of large, two-storied houses
made of brick or stone with gardens in front separated from the
street by walls topped with broken glass. The streets were wide and
paved with stones. In the harbor he noted a Dutch ship tied up
near the small, fenced-off island of De-shima, where the Dutch
factory (a trading settlement maintained by factors), the sole link
between Japan and the Western nation, was located. Also in the
harbor were three large armed junks from China and a huge fleet
of Japanese junks.

MacDonald was escorted to the governor's residence by a large
crowd. Led through lines of soldiers, he was confined in a filthy
shed and offered something to eat. Moryama came in to tell him
that in a short time he would be taken before the governor. Before
he saw the governor, Moryama explained, he would be shown an
image on the floor, the image of the devil of Japan. He was to put
his foot on the image. MacDonald agreed, saying that he did not
believe in images. Finally MacDonald was led to a large neatly
graveled courtyard where magistrates appeared to be trying prisoners. Before entering the courtyard, he was told to remove his

---

* Japanese names are written in Japanese fashion, family name first and given
name last.

boots and replace them with sandals. Then he was taken before what appeared to be a copper image of the Virgin and Child about six inches in diameter lying on the floor. "Told to put my foot on it," MacDonald later recalled, "being a Protestant, I unhesitatingly did so."

MacDonald faced an elevated platform on which sat a number of Japanese officials dressed in stiff silk gowns with projecting shoulder pieces. Moryama knelt nearby on a platform slightly lower than that of the governor and his entourage. MacDonald was taken to a dirty mat marked *O*. Incensed at the filthy mat, he kicked at it while complaining to Moryama that there was no chair for him to sit on. Moryama insisted that MacDonald was to kneel with his feet under him, as the Japanese officials were doing, and that he was to bow low but not look at the governor when he entered. MacDonald heard a low rustling sound, and as the governor, Ido Tsushima, entered preceded by an attendant carrying a sword by the point with the hilt in the air, all in attendance—officials, interpreter, soldiers—fell flat on their faces with their arms outstretched and their heads resting on their hands—all, that is, except MacDonald. MacDonald looked full in the governor's face, and he and the governor continued to stare at each other while all those around them remained bowed to the floor. Ido Tsushima was a portly man of about thirty-five dressed in wide greenish trousers of flowered silk, white socks, no sandals, an open silk gown that hung down to his ankles, and a belt. He wore an overgarment of stiffened cotton material with projecting shoulder pieces that stood out like enormous epaulettes. His expression seemed not unfriendly despite MacDonald's impudence. Finally MacDonald relented, bowing without touching his head to the floor.

Again the oft-repeated questions: his place of birth, his family, his home, and finally the governor came to questions about his religion. Did he believe in God in Heaven? Yes, MacDonald responded. What did he believe about this God in Heaven? After some confusion about the question, MacDonald began to recite the Apostles' Creed from the Anglican church service, but when he came to the words "and in Jesus Christ, his only Son, born of the Virgin Mary," Moryama suddenly stopped him saying, "That will do, that will do." Moryama, who had already become quite fond of his strange charge, blithely turned to the governor and proceeded to translate his own version of MacDonald's answer: "There are no gods nor buddhas. [I] merely cultivate mind and will and reverence heaven in order to obtain clear understanding and to secure happiness. [I have] nothing else to declare."[30]

The interview over, MacDonald was conveyed by palanquin to his new place of confinement, a seven-by-nine-foot room in a small house within the grounds of a Buddhist temple on the outskirts of Nagasaki. Though his room was barred along one wall and the house was screened off in front by very high walls, he was allowed to use a nearby bathhouse and was treated kindly, with four or more waiters serving his four meals a day.

Over the next seven months, MacDonald was interrogated two more times by the governor. The Japanese appeared to be probing for specific information about MacDonald's intentions—especially in the forbidden area of commerce—and more generally about the affairs of the outside world. They wanted to know where he had traveled, what were the people and products of these places like, and what were the particulars of the whaling industry. For his part, MacDonald, the less than dutiful son, but son nevertheless, of a Hudson's Bay trader, made his own inquiries about Japan's receptiveness to becoming a supply depot for whalers and to opening trade with the West. The Japanese response was a definitive, "No! It is against the law!" Not satisfied with MacDonald's answers, the Japanese officials sent the superintendent of the Dutch factory to ask the same questions. To his sorrow, the superintendent told MacDonald that the Dutch ship for that year had just departed; he would have to wait another year to leave.[31]

Once MacDonald had established some rapport with his captors, his humble room became the gathering place and then classroom for the interpreters who dealt with the Dutch and with the increasing number of shipwrecked and marooned sailors, mostly whalemen, who were brought to Nagasaki for repatriation. Moryama Einosuke became MacDonald's especial friend. MacDonald found this young man with "piercing black eyes which seemed to search into the very soul, and read its every emotion" the most intelligent person he had ever met as well as a lovable companion. Early on, Moryama explained how he had reinterpreted

Moryama Einosuke (LEFT) and fellow interpreter;
Narrative of the Expedition

MacDonald's recitation of the Apostles' Creed so as to placate the governor, and this must have bound MacDonald all the more firmly to his new friend. Under MacDonald's tutelage, Moryama learned to speak English fluently, using correct grammar and with a facility for those letters and syllables that were most difficult for the Japanese. In addition to English, Moryama, according to the Dutch superintendent, spoke Dutch better than the superintendent himself.[32]

During their regular visits, the interpreters would read to MacDonald in English, and he would correct their grammar and pronunciation. He, in turn, worked on his own command of Japanese. From time to time, one of the interpreters would use a nautical term in English or they would ask MacDonald what such terms meant. Were there other sailors being held captive in the city, he wondered.

There was always one exception to the free flow of knowledge that suffused his growing friendship with the interpreters. When MacDonald made inquiries about Japan, his companions offered him very little. He did pick up some information about the state of affairs in Japan. The country was governed by what appeared to be two monarchs: one religious and one secular, who was the shogun. The country seemed to be under some kind of feudal regime, with the shogun ruling a group of lords, or daimyo. This regime had grown out of efforts to curb the internecine warfare of an earlier time.[33]

On April 17, 1849, after seven months in captivity, one of MacDonald's gatherings with his interpreter friends was interrupted by the sound of cannon fire. His students and the guards rushed from his prison and soon returned to say that a foreign ship had arrived and that the cannon shots were summoning troops from the interior. The next morning a pile of papers was left beside the single guard outside his door. When he inquired, the guard told him it was a list of the 3,500 Japanese soldiers who had arrived the night before. MacDonald found this very peculiar. Why was he being informed about the movement of troops around Nagasaki, unless the Japanese were hoping that in the event that he went aboard the foreign ship, he would impress its officers with the number of troops deployed in the event of an attack?

Three days later MacDonald was told that his deliverance was at hand, for the foreign ship was the 18-gun American naval corvette *Preble* under Commander James Glynn. Glynn, knowing nothing of MacDonald, had come to Nagasaki to demand the release of the surviving sailors from a shipwrecked American whaler.

MacDonald had thought that there might be other sailors, perhaps American or British, in Nagasaki, but he knew nothing of the flurry of diplomatic correspondence that had resulted in the *Preble*'s arrival in Nagasaki. After another five days, MacDonald was carried to the governor's mansion to pay his final respects. To his surprise MacDonald was joined by thirteen American sailors, looking very pale and thin.[34]

The bedraggled sailors were part of the crew of a whaler, and they had a very different, more harrowing tale to tell of their captivity in Japan. In the very month that MacDonald had gone ashore on an island off Ezo, fifteen sailors from the whaler *Lagoda* out of New Bedford had decided that they could no longer take the harsh treatment of their captain. The mutineers, who ranged in age from nineteen to forty, included the first and second mates and thirteen seamen, nine of whom were Hawaiians. They had seized three boats and gone ashore on the southwest coast of Ezo, some miles to the north of Matsumae. Ashore they were greeted by a scene out of another era: soldiers armed with swords and ancient matchlocks who ordered them to return to their boats and leave. Moving up and down the shore, the whalemen tried to avoid the soldiers, but finally the soldiers, after offering them a ship in which to leave, confined them in a large house, which it soon became apparent was meant to serve as a prison.[35]

After forty days of captivity, Robert McCoy, a twenty-two-year-old sailor from Philadelphia, and three others cut their way through the roof of the privy and escaped into the nearby woods. They were captured the next day in a nearby village and returned to their original place of confinement. McCoy and another sailor again tried to escape by cutting their way through the roof of the house. This was the house where MacDonald was held on his way to Nagasaki, and the hole in the ceiling, subsequently boarded over, was the one pointed out by the guard. Indeed, MacDonald had seen McCoy's and two other names scrawled on the wall and had thought them dead. The escapees were discovered almost immediately and imprisoned in a cage with one of the men who had participated in the first escape attempt.

After ten days, the three men were taken aboard a junk, but not before they had gotten into a fight among themselves when their guards tried to remove them from their cages on shore. In response, the guards tied one of the men, John Martin, a nineteen-year-old seaman from New York, to a post and beat him about the face and body with a length of rope in front of his fellow prisoners. This enraged his companions so much that they stripped down and vowed they would die before they allowed the guards to continue beating Martin. There was little, however, that the men could do. Finally, all the men were taken aboard a junk and confined in cages below deck.[36]

After a voyage that lasted almost a month, the men arrived in Nagasaki. Aboard the junk they were visited by Moryama Einosuke, MacDonald's boon companion. Moryama explained that they would be held in a comfortable house ashore and sent away in a Dutch ship in a month and a half. After being ordered to walk on the image of the Virgin and Child imbedded in the floor, the men, like MacDonald, were taken before Ido Tsushima. McCoy was told that if the men did not go through with this ceremony, they would be thrown into a prison from which death would be the only exit. Again like MacDonald, the sailors walked upon the image but refused to bow before Ido. When the governor asked how they came to be in Japan, the men replied that their ship had run on a shoal and gone to pieces, they had saved themselves in the ship's boats, the rest of the crew was lost. Some time after their interview, a Dutch ship arrived, but the Dutch superintendent wrote the prisoners, saying that he had not received permission to take the men out of the country. This sorry situation led to another fight among the men and another unsuccessful escape attempt by McCoy. McCoy, now desperate, refused to eat. The superintendent tried to encourage him, saying that he had written to the U.S. consul in

Batavia about their situation. After waiting for five days for permission to take the men out of the country, the Dutch ship finally sailed without them.

Within a month McCoy and two other men again escaped, this time by burning a hole through the floor. Again they were captured and returned to their prison. They were bound so tightly, with their hands pulled up behind their backs, that the ropes broke the skin. After four hours of this, they were confined overnight out of doors in stocks. Taken before the governor, they again were accused of being spies and were consigned with the rest of the crew to a Japanese prison. Irate, the men warned the Japanese that if the Americans ever found out about their treatment, they would come to Japan and punish them.[37]

The sailors from the *Lagoda* now faced a grim future, confined in filthy cages in the open, exposed to the elements without proper clothing and with nothing but lice-infested mats to sleep on. No fires or lights were allowed. There was no way to wash or mend their clothes, and it took three months just to get two combs for all of them. During the second night in the prison, one of the Hawaiians hanged himself. The Japanese left the body in the cage for two days. Because of the constant exposure to rain and snow that blew into the open-sided cages, one of the sailors became sick, his throat turning black and his tongue swelling up until it cracked. Finally he became delirious. After a short time, he died, frothing at the mouth. Until then the Japanese had refused to provide proper clothing for the men, but when the sailor became ill, they returned some of the sailors' clothes and provided a blanket for a second sick man. The sailors, however, grew suspicious, thinking perhaps that because the skin on the dead man's stomach turned black and blue soon after he died, he had been poisoned. Their suspicions seemed to be confirmed when another man became sick and then delirious after he took medicine provided by a Japanese doctor. When his shipmates withheld the medicine, the man recovered.

After a time the Japanese announced that the men had been condemned to having their heads cut off. When a group of guards assembled, the miserable company of lice-infested, filth-encrusted men feared the worst. But the guards had come for a Japanese prisoner, who was led away. Soon after they heard a scream, and a boy passed their cages carrying a head. There were no executions, but they did hear that there was another sailor confined somewhere in Nagasaki.[38]

Some four months after they were moved to the Japanese prison, the men of the *Lagoda* heard a single cannon fired. The cannon signaled the approach of a foreign vessel, a friendly guard explained. More guns would be fired to alert the city. Soon after, sure enough, they heard more cannon fire, and the men began to cheer, alarming the guard, who feared that he would be singled out as an informer. For six days, the prisoners waited in suspense, knowing only what the friendly guard told them of the progress of the negotiations with the foreign ship, which appeared to be American. Finally Moryama and a group of officials arrived at the prison to tell them that in two days they would be delivered to the Dutch factory to be taken to the ship. On the appointed day the prisoners were taken before the governor and a number of other officials, where for the first time they met Ranald MacDonald. From there they went to the Dutch factory for a sumptuous dinner—"with a parting cup of [the] best Dutch Java coffee," according to MacDonald—while they waited to be taken aboard the *Preble*.[39]

News about the mutineers from the crew of the *Lagoda*, still believed to have been shipwrecked, had been sent to the American commissioner in China via the Dutch East India Company in Batavia aboard the annual Dutch trading ship, which had left Nagasaki in November 1848 after waiting for the release of the sailors. The American commissioner quickly conferred with Commodore David Geisinger, the commander of the U.S. East India Squadron, which consisted of only two ships. Geisinger in turn dispatched Commander James Glynn, aboard the *Preble*, to demand the release of the sailors. Glynn's orders called for him to approach the Japanese in "a conciliatory, but firm" manner and not to violate the laws or customs of the country. If the Japanese authorities claimed that the decision had to be made in Edo, he was to proceed to Edo and communicate to the imperial court "a firm, temperate, and respectful demand" for the sailors' release. Because a number of fierce typhoons had lashed the Chinese coast during the monsoon season, Glynn was also to inquire about other shipwrecked sailors. "The protection of our valuable whaling fleet, and the encouragement of the whale fishery, are objects of deep interest to our government," Geisinger concluded.[40]

When Glynn and the 123-foot *Preble* sailed into Nagasaki harbor, Moryama Einosuke was the first to board the ship. He informed Glynn that he was there to acquaint the commander with the laws of Japan and to point out where he would be permitted to anchor. Glynn immediately objected to Moryama's request that the *Preble* anchor outside the harbor. He also informed Moryama that the manner in which the Japanese had greeted the *Preble*—by throwing a bamboo stick with a document attached aboard the ship—was not the proper way to begin discussions.

The notice attached to the stick warned foreign ships on or near the coast of Japan to behave properly and civilly toward Japanese citizens. It went on to state that "No one may leave the vessel, or use her boats for cruising or landing on the islands, or on the main coast." Foreigners were also told not to fire guns or use firearms either aboard ship or in its boats. "Very disagreeable consequences might result in case the aforesaid should not be strictly observed," the message from the governor of Nagasaki warned.

Glynn's response was to throw the stick with the message overboard. And when Moryama asked to accompany the American warship to its anchorage, Glynn firmly but politely ordered him off the ship.

Glynn was eager to present a respectful but no-nonsense demeanor to the Japanese. There was truth to the jeers that the Japanese guards had hurled at the sailors from the *Lagoda* as they carried them off to a common prison in Nagasaki. A Japanese soldier had indeed knocked down the commander of a two-ship naval squadron three years earlier during attempted negotiations in Edo Bay, and the United States had not responded.

Determined to avoid a repeat of this unfortunate confrontation, Glynn insisted that he deal directly with a Japanese official high enough in rank to show respect for his own stature as a naval commander. He also asked for provisions but insisted that if they were provided he would pay for them, thereby hoping to force the Japanese into de facto commercial relations. Glynn too objected to the guardboats that surrounded the *Preble*. Their number had grown daily. At night the *Preble* was an eerie sight, surrounded by a cordon of guardboats lit with torches placed in pans at the end of long poles to illuminate the water around the ship. Glynn, however, had little to fear. Through his glass, he noted the poorly constructed stone fortress that commanded the harbor and the placement of its light guns in such a way that they would be blown over backward in the event that they were fired.[41]

But since Glynn's instructions were to deal peacefully with the Japanese, he did nothing to disperse the guardboats. The Japanese official and his interpreter, for their part, tried to solicit as much information as possible from Glynn about his mission, his previous ports of call, and even the dimensions and armament of the *Preble*. Asked why an American warship was so far from home, Glynn responded that "wherever [we] have merchant ships or citizens, [we] send the men-of-war to protect them from injustice or oppression, and to relieve their necessities, if necessary." Asked how many ships there were in the U.S. Navy, Glynn answered with a great deal of exaggeration, sixty, seventy, or a hundred. Glynn was particularly amused by the Japanese response to his efforts to procure some coal. When he took them to the *Preble*'s forge to show them what he wanted, the Japanese official exclaimed, "What a curious stone it is!" saying that they had no such mineral in Japan.[42]

After four days without a response to his requests, Glynn explained that if the sailors were released to him, he would depart immediately. If they weren't, he went on cryptically, he was ordered "to do something else." The Japanese officials, like their counterparts in China with whom Americans had been dealing for more than forty years, were masters of the temporizing and evasive answer. When Glynn, for instance, asked whether the *Lagoda* sailors were in prison, the Japanese said they did not know what the word meant, but the men were "in a place by themselves." The negotiations dragged on for yet another day and then another, with the Japanese finally saying that the response to Glynn's demands had to come from Edo, that it would take thirty or forty days, and that it was customary to send sailors away in either Dutch or Chinese ships. Meanwhile Glynn tried to get a copy of the laws that governed foreign commerce and the treatment of shipwrecked sailors. No, he was told, the Japanese officials were not permitted to give copies of their laws to representatives of foreign nations.[43]

Finally, Glynn insisted on a response within three days. By now, the Dutch superintendent had been brought into the negotiations by the Japanese. Glynn objected to his presence but accepted a report from him saying that the sailors' needs had been taken care of and that they were receiving medical attention. After a week of fruitless negotiations, the Japanese finally capitulated and sent the men aboard the *Preble* along with a demand forwarded via the Dutch superintendent that American whalers cease their operations in Japanese coastal waters. The men were returned to the *Preble* in such a way, Glynn noted, that the Japanese officials were well away from the ship before the men had a chance to relate what had really happened to them in captivity.[44]

With the sailors and MacDonald aboard, the *Preble* returned to Hong Kong. During the voyage, a number of sailors from the *Lagoda* gave depositions about their treatment at the hands of the Japanese and finally admitted that they had not been shipwrecked but had mutinied. MacDonald too gave a deposition detailing his experiences in Japan. He told of his lessons with the interpreters and concluded that "the common people appeared to be amiable and friendly, but the government agents were the reverse." In later years, when he wrote of his experiences, he reached more favorable conclusions. He noted that he made friends easily and that this was made simpler by the fact that the Japanese were "naturally chatty; always in a vein of good humor . . . I never had a cross word with any of them; and I think I passed rather as a favorite amongst them." He found that his captors exhibited markedly militaristic instincts, were tolerant of all creeds except Christianity, and despite their placid appearance, showed "the inner working of aspirations for a higher life amongst the nations of the earth." This, he felt, was particularly true of the interpreter Moryama Einosuke. Like his other pupils, he showed a "quick and comprehensive attitude in learning" that MacDonald found extraordinary, if not phenomenal. Above all, MacDonald concluded, he was "served with almost lordly state."[45]

From China, MacDonald was once again lured by the siren

call of adventure. He departed for Australia's newly discovered gold fields while the sailors from the *Lagoda* were returned to the United States. Because MacDonald did not return with them, it was the experiences of the men of the *Lagoda* that would help shape American attitudes toward Japan and contribute to plans to send a naval expedition to Japan. Ultimately, MacDonald's sojourn in Japan, despite his claim, would only marginally affect the events unfolding between Japan and the United States. The Americans, aroused by the treatment of the sailors from the *Lagoda*, were now prepared to take a hard line in future dealings with the Japanese. In an official account of the *Preble*'s rescue mission, the author (most likely Glynn) wrote that "one could have a little more patience with a people like the Japanese, if, to their cruelty in carrying out regulations which they suppose necessary to the national safety, they did not add such gratuitous mendacity, to delude the unfortunates in their power. . . . The narrative of the imprisonment of these unhappy mariners," the report concluded, "shows the cruelty of the Japanese government, and the necessity of making some arrangement with it, involving the better usage of those who are cast upon its shores."[46]

In the last year that MacDonald and the *Lagoda* mutineers languished in Nagasaki, Herman Melville began to write what he described as "a strange sort of book." It was a saga of the whaling industry and Ahab, a monomaniacal sea captain who had lost his leg—"dismasted off Japan," as Melville put it—to a demonic white whale. Bedeviled by the dark forces at the heart of the universe, Ahab pursued his vengeance across the Atlantic and the Indian oceans, through the Straits of Sunda, and into the Pacific, where he met his death off the eastern coast of Japan.

Melville, more than any other American writer, brought the world of the Pacific, which he called "the tide-beating heart of the earth," to the hearthside of the American reader. As a young man very much in the romantic mold of Ranald MacDonald, he had wandered the Pacific, sailing aboard two whalers and living in captivity with a tribe of benevolent cannibals in the Marquesa Islands, where he loved the beauteous Fayaway, and then returning

to Boston aboard a U.S. man-of-war. His two books about his Pacific
adventures, *Typee* and *Omoo*, were very popular and introduced
Americans to the new world that they had inherited as recent
conquerors of the Pacific littoral. This was a world of seaborn traders, beachcombers, whale men, and missionaries whose work, Melville argued, was contributing to the destruction of native cultures.

In *Moby-Dick* Melville turned to whaling, one of the twin
engines, along with the lucrative China trade, that drove America
into the Pacific Basin. The first American killed a whale in the
Pacific in 1788. By the 1820s, when the whale population in the
Atlantic was already showing signs of depletion, there were five
established whaling grounds in the Pacific, and one of them, soon
to be the most productive, was "on Japan," as the whalers said.
Whaling became a multimillion-dollar business, a major component
of the American economy. Melville, in his exhaustive description
of the industry, estimated that the United States, with the largest
whaling industry in the world, employed 18,000 men aboard 700
ships that reaped a harvest of $7 million annually. The *Lagoda*
turned a ninety-eight percent profit on six voyages between 1841
and 1860, including the one during which its men mutinied. In
1846, out of the 945 American vessels that sailed the Pacific, 736
were whalers. Whaling, Melville argued with remarkable presci-
ence, inevitably would bring the United States to Japan: "If that
double-bolted land, Japan, is ever to become hospitable, it is the
whale-ship alone to whom the credit will be due; for already she is
on the threshold."[47]

More than whaling and Ranald MacDonald brought the United
States to Japan, however. The Pacific had become the object of
many ambitions. During the time between MacDonald's conceiving
his plans to go to Japan and his rescue by Commander Glynn, the
United States, in the most spectacular burst of expansionism since
the Louisiana Purchase, had become a continental power. With the
defeat of Mexico in 1848, it acquired California. Two years earlier
England had relinquished its claim to the Oregon Territory, which
included MacDonald's own native soil, so that MacDonald left home
a British subject and eventually returned as an American. Though
the new clipper ships dashed around Cape Horn, other American
merchant and naval vessels still preferred to reach the Orient by

way of the Cape of Good Hope, which was a less hazardous route. But this route took one along the southern reaches of the British Empire. British-controlled ports such as Cape Town, Aden, Trincomalee, and Singapore only reminded brashly nationalistic Americans of their decidedly junior status in the world of global power politics. Now the Americans were looking for new routes, via Panama and Nicaragua and across the continent, to their recently acquired territory on the West Coast and on to the tantalizing markets of China and the whaling grounds of the Pacific Basin.

Japan would eventually figure in these ambitions. The first American to reach Japan, John Kendrick of Boston, aboard the brigantine *Lady Washington*, is thought to have arrived in 1791. Kendrick remained only long enough to leave a note in Dutch and Chinese announcing: "This ship belongs to the Red Hairs from a land called America." For a time during the Napoleonic Wars, American ships traded directly, though covertly, with Japan. At least eight American ships sailed there under the Dutch flag between 1797 and 1809, when the Hollanders' fear of hostile British cruisers that were preying on Dutch merchantmen in East Asia led the Dutch East India Company to charter American ships to carry on its annual trade with Nagasaki.[48]

In his reports of a raiding cruise into the Pacific directed at British whalers during the War of 1812, Commodore David Porter proposed sending an expedition to Japan. Almost twenty years later, the State Department sent Edmund Roberts, a failed merchant from Portsmouth, New Hampshire, on an open-ended mission to sign treaties "with some of the native powers bordering on the Indian Ocean." Roberts sailed with the first U.S. naval ships to cruise Asian waters. Roberts negotiated a treaty with Siam in 1833 but failed in his effort to open the country to the opium trade. Though under the escort of the U.S.S. *Peacock*, he was to proceed to Japan aboard a foreign ship because, as Secretary of State Edmund Livingston wrote, an American naval vessel "cannot submit to the indignity of being disarmed," as all foreign vessels were when they entered Japanese ports. Roberts, however, died before he could follow out his orders.[49]

The next effort to negotiate with Japan involved an attempt to return three of the Japanese fishermen whom Ranald MacDonald had befriended at Fort Vancouver. The voyage was financed by D. W. C. Olyphant, a New York merchant who funded early missionary efforts in China, and was led by his partner Charles W. King, another missionary-merchant. Seeking trade and the conversion of pagan souls, King and Olyphant argued that the return of the shipwrecked sailors would provide a perfect opportunity to impress the Japanese with foreigners' good intentions. "Since it was the misconduct of foreigners which closed their ports," wrote Samuel Wells Williams, a young American missionary who sailed with King aboard the *Morrison*, "it in fairness belongs to the same source to disabuse them of their misanthropy. Free trade begets a free interchange of thought; with the goods, the civilization and Christianity of foreign nations will extend."[50]

The *Morrison* first sailed to Naha on Okinawa in the Ryukyu Islands, and then continued northward to Japan. Rain rattling on its sails, the ship rounded Cape Sagami, on the island of Honshu, on July 30, 1837, and beat up the Uraga Channel toward Edo, the capital city of the shoguns. Greeted by a warning shot, the ship was boarded by numerous Japanese, who examined everything with minute attention, exclaiming over the height of the masts and the complexity of the rigging. The Japanese were friendly but "much surprised," Williams wrote, "that not any one of us was able to converse with them; some would seize the arm, enter into earnest discourse, and then, after a few unsuccessful sentences, leave us, seemingly amazed at our doltishness and the ill success of their eloquence."[51] The shipwrecked Japanese were kept out of sight; they had explained to King that by law they were barred from returning to their native land once they had left by whatever means, death being the penalty for an infraction.

Without warning, the *Morrison* was fired upon the next day. Weighing anchor, the dispirited missionaries headed back out of the bay stopping only long enough to throw over a piece of canvas with a plea written in Chinese for the Japanese to visit the ship and bring water and provisions. The *Morrison* sailed southwestward to Kagoshima, the castle town of the Shimazu clan. King hoped that the daimyo of Satsuma, who controlled the Ryukyus and had a reputation for being independent and a supporter of maritime trade, illicit though it was, would be more amenable to their overtures. In Kagoshima Bay, the *Morrison* was greeted warmly by local villagers and fishermen, who eventually warned them of rumors of an attack. Again the *Morrison* was fired upon and left with little recourse but to return to China.

In his account of the voyage, Williams noted "how gradually the Japanese government has gone on in perfecting its system of seclusion, and how the mere lapse of time has indurated, instead of disintegrating, the wall of prejudice and misanthropy which surrounds their policy." He concluded that the Japanese government, based on what he knew of European wars, "must congratulate themselves on their seclusion from such contests." Since they must now "regard foreigners as ready to pounce upon their country the moment it should be opened," he suggested that those seeking ports had to assure them they could be "peaceable friends." It was worth investigating, Williams concluded, if this hardening of Japanese attitudes was caused by whalers who might have visited the coast of Japan and engaged in "conduct unworthy of Christians."[52]

Charles W. King, the leader of the undertaking, was less sympathetic in his evaluation of the Japanese and more strident in his call for a renewed diplomatic effort directed at Japan. In 1839 he published a book concluding that the next move "had better be left to the stronger and wiser action of the American government." He noted that the American flag had been fired on, and it was the flag of "the only nation which maintains no church establishment; forms no offensive leagues; holds no foreign colonies; grasps at no Asiatic territory; and whose citizens represent themselves, for the first time, at the gates of the capital [of Japan], unarmed, and with every pledge of peaceful, humane, and generous intentions." King was afraid that what had happened to the *Morrison* would tempt the Japanese to attack every ship that approached the coast showing any sign of distress. For this reason, he recommended that the U.S. government dispatch two war sloops and a tender to Japan that very summer, when they should issue an ultimatum demanding diplomatic relations and humane treatment of each others' sailors. A discussion of commercial relations should follow this initial humanistic plea. If the Japanese failed to respond, King suggested that the Americans should blockade Edo Bay. If the Japanese were still obdurate, King proposed the freeing of all Japanese dependencies south and west of Satsuma. If that should happen, America would be hailed as an emancipator and "every friend of Eastern Asia, and of man will celebrate the day of [the Japanese empire's] dissolution." The United States, King concluded, was the hope of all Asia east of the Malay peninsula.[53]

King's call for the dispatch of a naval force to blockade Edo Bay and threaten the dismemberment of the Japanese empire, though steeped in the patriotic bombast of the day, fell on deaf ears. In fact, almost no one in the United States paid much attention to Japan for the next five years. Then for the five years after that, beginning in 1844, there were almost annual encounters with the Japanese. As American whalers poured into the Pacific, growing contact with Japan was inevitable. The curtain of seclusion was being drawn aside, whether the Japanese liked it or not.

In 1844 Caleb Cushing, the first American commissioner in China, while negotiating the Treaty of Wanghia, which opened five Chinese ports to American trade, was sent a dispatch giving him full powers to negotiate with the Japanese government. Cushing, however, returned to the States before his instructions reached him. Accordingly, his successor, Alexander Everett, was conveyed to China by the East India Squadron under Commodore James Biddle. Everett was also authorized to negotiate with the Japanese. If he decided not to, Biddle could go in his place "to ascertain if the ports of Japan are accessible." Everett never went. Meanwhile, unknown to Everett and Biddle, an American whaler, the *Manhattan* under Captain Mercator Cooper, had made a visit to Edo Bay in a futile attempt to return eleven Japanese sailors he had picked up on an island who were from a shipwrecked junk.[54] The year after Cooper's visit, 1846, Biddle departed for Edo with two U.S. warships, one a formidable, 74-gun ship of the line.

Biddle anchored where the *Morrison* had been fired upon nine years before, and his two ships were likewise surrounded by guardboats. Biddle, to establish his peaceful intentions, allowed the Japanese to swarm aboard the American ships. He refused, however, a Japanese official's demand that he send his armament ashore. After a week of fruitless conversations, Biddle went unannounced to a Japanese barge to receive a response to his inquiries about Japanese ports, having earlier told the Japanese that he expected them to bring the response to his ship. When he went to climb aboard the barge, he was pushed back into his boat by a Japanese guard. Biddle was outraged. He demanded that the Japanese authorities, who were extremely apologetic, arrest the man immediately and deal with him according to Japanese law. The Japanese explanation for the incident: they had misunderstood the outcome of the conversations about where Biddle would be to receive the Japanese response. They had not been prepared for Biddle to approach their barge. Though apologetic, Biddle considered the Japanese response to his request for negotiations blunt to the point of insult. He was told that the Japanese only traded with the Dutch and Chinese and was ordered to "depart as quick[ly] as possible and not come any more to Japan." Biddle, having completed his mission, prepared to depart. But his ships were becalmed and, as a final humiliation, had to be towed to sea by the Japanese guardboats.[55]

The insult to Biddle plus the cruel treatment that the crew of the *Lagoda* had received from the Japanese prison guards added to the accumulated feeling that something had to be done to chasten the Japanese, to "bring them fully into the family of nations." Upon Biddle's return to China, Everett wrote to Secretary of State James Buchanan to explain, somewhat elliptically, that "the attempt of the commodore to open a negociation [sic] was perhaps not made with all the discretion that might have been desired, and has placed the subject in rather less favorable position than that in which it stood before." He suggested that another opportunity to approach the Japanese might present itself while he was in China.[56] But it did not.

The Americans were greatly annoyed when they later found out that while Biddle was in the Uraga Channel attempting to negotiate with the Japanese, seven survivors from the shipwrecked whaler *Lawrence*, out of Poughkeepsie, New York, were languishing in a Nagasaki prison while waiting their repatriation via the annual Dutch trading ship. The Japanese never mentioned the whalers to Biddle. One of the men wrote an account of "the bad treatment we met with from our guards, who frequently struck us, and insulted us in every possible way they could."[57] The wreck of the *Lawrence*, Cooper's visit to Edo Bay, and Biddle's ill-fated mission were followed by Ranald MacDonald's adventure, the *Lagoda* mutiny, and the marooning of three more American sailors, who were imprisoned for fifteen months before being sent home aboard the Dutch trading ship.

At first little notice was taken in the United States of these semihostile encounters with the Japanese. But with the arrival in Washington in 1850 of Commander Glynn's reports about MacDonald and the *Lagoda* mutineers, Congress turned its attention to this remote corner of the Pacific. Resolutions were introduced in both houses calling on the president to provide information about what was happening in Japan. Glynn in one of his reports spoke boldly of "a good cause of a quarrel" and proposed yet another expedition to Japan. The Japanese officials at Nagasaki could send an order to Glynn barring all whaling ships from Japanese waters, but the Japanese were working against a rising tide, stronger than the mighty Black Current that swept their coast, a tide that would inevitably carry Americans toward that doubled-bolted land. And the experiences of MacDonald and the numerous other Americans who had reached Japan would ultimately shape the plans of Captain Matthew Calbraith Perry, the leader of the first official U.S. expedition to Japan.

2

PERRY GROWS UP
WITH THE NAVY

I have found the strongest interest existing on the prospect of estab-
lishing a line of steamers between Asia and America. . . . The island
of Nipshon [sic] (in Japan) lies directly on the line from San Francisco
to Shanghai. —COMMANDER JAMES GLYNN to Howland
and Aspinwall, February 24, 1851

The facts of that case [the Lagoda] *are of a character to excite the*
indignation of the people of the United States.[1]   —GLYNN, Ibid.

For a ship is a bit of terra firma cut off from the main; it is a state in
itself; and the captain is its king.
—HERMAN MELVILLE, *White-Jacket,* 1850

The Navy is the asylum for the perverse, the home of the unfortunate.
Here the sons of adversity meet the children of calamity, and here the
children of calamity meet the offspring of sin.[2]
—HERMAN MELVILLE, Ibid.

Those who are unacquainted with the Navy cannot understand the
transition that takes place in a poor half-fed and half-clad boy, when
taken from the streets and wharfs of our great cities and entered on
board a man-of-war. . . . There is, perhaps, no pleasure which the
benevolent officer experiences in a man-of-war greater than that which
he feels in watching the growth and daily improvement, in appearance,
character and usefulness of an active lad, aspiring to the dignity of an
able seaman, with an ambition unsurpassed by any thing that we see
in the loftier walks of life.[3]
—A.S. [ALEXANDER SLIDELL MACKENZIE and
MATTHEW CALBRAITH PERRY], January 1837

On January 7, 1851, the *Preble,* under Commander James Glynn, entered New York harbor having sailed nearly 100,000 miles in the four years and four months since she had left her native land. The cruise of the *Preble* had begun with service off California in the Mexican War, already a fleeting memory, and was now ending after a tour of the western Pacific and a visit to Nagasaki. Glynn brought home with him fresh news of the rescue of the whalemen from the *Lagoda.* The report of his trip to Japan had already been published the summer before. Between Hong Kong and Honolulu, the ship had been swept by dysentery, and thirty-one sailors and officers, a full twenty percent of the ship's complement, had died. From Honolulu, the *Preble* limped toward San Francisco with a skeleton crew of 35 men, her normal complement being 145. For a time the *Preble* lay abandoned at Benicia, on the Sacramento River, the copper worn from her bottom, her hull and spars eaten by decay, and her sails barely fit to spread before a moderate breeze. Her crew was either in the hospital or off to the gold diggings. Somehow Glynn recruited a new crew—a nearly impossible task when the mines offered sixteen dollars a day and the U.S. Navy thirty cents— and sailed for home.[4]

In recounting the tale of the *Lagoda* whalemen and their harrowing sojourn in Japan, the reporter for the *New York Herald* noted that they had experienced at the hands of the Japanese "an ignominious and cruel imprisonment of nearly seventeen months" during which they were treated with "inhuman barbarity." The rescue was achieved, the reporter went on, only after Glynn's demand to turn the whalemen over to him was first received "with well-affected haughty indifference" followed by "evasive diplomacy."

With the *Lagoda* episode now before the public, Glynn moved quickly to capitalize on his encounter with the Japanese. In February, he released to the press a copy of a letter that he had written to the New York merchant firm of Howland and Aspinwall. It may have seemed strange that a naval officer chose to discuss a rescue mission in Japan with a merchant firm, but Glynn had chosen his correspondents carefully. Howland and Aspinwall was the largest and most influential merchant house in the city, a firm that could boast of extensive ties to the Pacific. Among its achievements, Howland and Aspinwall had paved the way for American domination of the China carrying trade by building the first American clipper ship, in 1842, and dispatching it to the Orient. Through the Pacific Mail Steamship Company, Howland and Aspinwall also enjoyed a government-subsidized monopoly of the steamship route from Panama to California. Thus the company was already an important presence in the quickly thrown-together boom town of San Francisco. And having secured a strategic and lucrative route to the goldfields, Howland and Aspinwall was at that very moment pushing a new railroad line across the swamps of Panama in an effort to extend their monopoly backward toward the ports of the east coast.

To assure their right of way, William Aspinwall had generously donated six hundred thousand gold francs to the general from New Granada, who claimed sovereignty over the isthmus. Moreover, both William Aspinwall and John Howland were prominent Whigs, and as such were part of the group of wealthy New York businessmen who contributed freely to paying the extravagant expenses of Daniel Webster, the bon vivant secretary of state, as well as being major backers of Millard Fillmore, the Whig lawyer from Buffalo who had moved into the White House upon the death of President Zachary Taylor less than a year before.[5] If anyone could increase the prospects of sending an expedition to Japan, Howland and Aspinwall could.

About his two-year tour of the Pacific, Glynn reported to Howland and Aspinwall, "I have found the strongest interest existing on the prospect of establishing a line of steamers between Asia and America." He himself, Glynn explained, was deeply interested in the development of such a line and was eager to contribute his "mite of opinion to aid others." He knew of no one who could make better use of the information than their firm. Glynn estimated that there were three problems to consider in establishing such a line: its terminus in China, a fuel supply, and the best route. Having visited both Canton and Shanghai, he thought Shanghai the better location for a western terminus, given its greater proximity to California, its central location on the China coast, and its closeness to the tea-producing regions of China—tea being the major export from China to the United States. Moreover, in Shanghai the local populace was less hostile to foreigners. As for fuel, Glynn reported that there were unlimited supplies available in northern Taiwan and probably an abundant supply in Japan. Despite Japan's seclusion policy and the seeming ignorance of the Japanese official in Nagasaki when Glynn asked about coal, he was confident that through diplomatic intervention—"if the business was properly managed"—coal could be bought in Japan.

The most important question, Glynn went on, was the route to be taken across the Pacific. The United States would have to build fuel depots at ports along the route across the Pacific to provide coal for the steamers, since they gobbled up fuel at the rate of more than a ton an hour. Hawaii was the first logical place for a fuel depot. Glynn then reviewed a number of other possible island stopovers, including the Bonin Islands, some one thousand miles east of Okinawa. To go by a more northern route would take the steamers into fog-bound areas that would be dangerous to navigate and uncomfortable for passengers—like "the disagreeable atmosphere" for which San Francisco was so notorious. This left only one logical stopover place: "the island of Nipshon [sic] (in Japan) lies directly on the line from San Francisco to Shanghai." All the European commentators on Japan and the best maps by Philipp Franz von Siebold, the German physician and naturalist, indicated that there were abundant and excellent harbors in Japan. For this reason, Glynn thought, any convenient point on the coast would be likely to have a good harbor.

The problem, thus, became one of "the diplomatic influence of our government," Glynn concluded. The time had come for something to be done. A resolution had been introduced in Congress calling for an investigation of the circumstances surrounding the imprisonment of the men from the *Lagoda*. "The facts of that case are of a character to excite the indignation of the people of the United States," Glynn wrote. He had hoped to be in Washington in time to influence this investigation, but unfortunately he was not. No matter, "the nation stands upon strong vantage ground; we want accommodations for fuel and a depot for our steamers; we have a good cause of a quarrel, and as I told the Japanese officer who received my demand, 'they have no friends in the wide world;' we ask for redress—are willing to take it out in the facilities they can afford for the navigation of our steamers. They won't willingly come to terms—make them; we could convert their selfish government into a liberal republic in a short time; such an unnatural system would at the present day fall to pieces upon the slightest concussion. But it is better to go to work peacefully with them if we can."

After these stirring words, Glynn returned to stroking the egos of Messrs. Howland and Aspinwall, concluding in a flight of hyperbole and a clarion call for action. Glynn hoped, he wrote, "to see you executing one of the most magnificent and perhaps profitable projects that has ever entered into the mind of a practical man—that of directing the commerce of half the human family from its foreign channels into the bosom of his own country."[6]

Glynn was hoping for more than that. He had already proposed an expedition to Japan to a member of the Fillmore cabinet. Now he was undoubtedly hoping that men as well connected as Howland and Aspinwall would back his bid to lead the expedition. Events, however, were moving too fast for the dashing commander, and Glynn, despite the sophistication of his grasp of the importance of Japan, lacked the connections and distinguished record that were needed to secure command of an expedition that was already beginning to take shape. True, his voyage to Nagasaki to rescue the mutinous sailors from the *Lagoda* was just one more proof that something had to be done about Japan as soon as possible. But as it turned out, a handful of influential merchants, experienced sea captains, and well-connected politicians had already been approached for advice and support.

By a remarkable coincidence, exactly one month before Glynn's letter Captain Matthew Calbraith Perry had written a private letter to Secretary of the Navy William A. Graham outlining his own ideas for a full-scale naval expedition to Japan, an expedition that Perry did not expect to lead.[7] And during the next year, Perry began collecting information that could be used in preparing for the expedition. At fifty-seven years of age Perry was one of the navy's most competent and well-connected officers. He was the senior member of a large and famous—infamous, James Fenimore

Cooper would claim—naval clan. It was really two intermarried naval clans when one included the Rodgers, the relatives and descendants of John Rodgers, the navy's ranking officer from the War of 1812 until his death, in 1838. Perry's brother-in-law, Alexander Slidell MacKenzie, could also claim clan allegiance, since he entered the navy under the sponsorship of Perry's famous brother, Oliver Hazard Perry, the hero of the Battle of Lake Erie in the War of 1812.

Matthew Calbraith Perry had already proven his mettle as a sailor, diplomat, naval reformer, and advocate of the new steam navy. Perry, too, was personally acquainted with many if not all of the most powerful men in the New York merchant community. His daughter Caroline was married to August Belmont, one of the wealthiest businessmen in New York, and he had supervised, as a representative of the Navy Department, the construction of the mail steamers subsidized by the federal government. This job had brought him into regular contact with merchants such as Howland and Aspinwall. Perry, moreover, was an avid expansionist who had commanded the Home Squadron, the largest ever assembled, that blockaded and shelled Vera Cruz and ranged up and down the Gulf Coast of Mexico during the Mexican War. Now he was at work under Millard Fillmore's Whig administration, which was doing its best to promote more legal and less abrasive forms of expansion while heading off the aggressive schemes of Manifest Destiny Democrats, filibusteros, and slave owners, all of whom were casting covetous eyes on Cuba, Mexico, and parts of Central America.

By the time Perry began to work on the Japan expedition, he was the epitome of the crusty old salt. The Perry clan had literally grown up with the American navy, its family history intertwined with the service to which it was devoted. Perry himself had served for forty-two years, having gone to sea in 1809 at the age of fifteen. These famous naval warriors were, ironically, of Quaker stock. It is thought that Edward Perry was the first Perry to have come from England to Sandwich on Cape Cod in or about 1639. Edward Perry's Quakerism kept him in constant trouble with the Puritan authorities. In time two of his sons moved to Rhode Island because of its more tolerant atmosphere.[8]

The Perrys settled in the swampy and wooded lowlands that

adjoined the western shore of Narragansett Bay. Here the colonists carved a uniquely prosperous and genteel society from the wilderness. Their slaves worked large farms that produced excellent milch cows, a popular cheddar cheese, corn that was ground into johnny-cake meal, and the Narragansett pacer, a well-known breed of horse. Matthew Calbraith Perry's grandfather, Freeman Perry, served this community as a doctor, land surveyor, chief justice of the county court, and in numerous other elected and appointed posts. Freeman's son, Christopher, fled to sea in the early years of the Revolution, after an incident in which he shot a farmer while his militia unit was attempting to requisition the farmer's cattle. Christopher Perry served on a number of privateers and spent time imprisoned in and escaping from both a British hulk in New York harbor and the Newry barracks in Ireland. In Ireland, he met the black-haired, blue-eyed daughter of the commandant of the barracks. Perry immediately vowed that he would marry her but escaped before pursuing his courtship. After the war, he returned to Dublin on a merchant ship, where by chance the orphaned Sarah Wallace Alexander, the young lady of the prison barracks, was waiting to board a ship for Philadelphia in the company of her guardian, a Mr. Calbraith, and his son Matthew. Christopher and Sarah were married in Philadelphia. Having settled his wife in Newport, Perry went back to sea as a merchant captain. Matthew Calbraith Perry, Sarah and Christopher's fourth child, was born in Newport on April 10, 1794.[9]

"No land force can act decisively," George Washington had written a month after Yorktown, "unless it is accompanied by a maritime superiority." During the Revolution, that superiority had been provided, alas, by the French navy. Christopher Perry had fought in the first American navy, but the navy emerged from the Revolution with little popular renown, and by 1785 Congress had either sold or given away its few remaining ships.[10] By virtue of its history and its seaboard, the United States was destined, however, to become an oceangoing commercial power in a world of European empires that boasted great navies. Within a decade of the dissolution of the Revolutionary navy, American merchantmen were ranging from Latin America to the Mediterranean and from Africa to China. So no matter how often American statesmen emphasized the country's geographical isolation and independence from the affairs of Europe, the United States ultimately had no choice but to become a naval power.

It would, however, take many years of a seesaw battle between the political spokesmen of the seaboard states and those of the interior before the U.S. government would commit itself to the strategic projection of naval power. The coastal states of the Northeast, led by the Federalists, argued that international commerce demanded naval protection. The rural areas, led in Congress by James Madison of Virginia and backed by Thomas Jefferson, responded that a permanent navy was an unwarranted and costly expansion of governmental power. A permanent navy reflected hated aristocratic pretensions and imperial ambitions, would draw the country into the "mischievous politics of Europe," and would work to the detriment of farmers, who were the mainstay of the economy. "What has reduced a great portion of the British nation to a state of misery unequaled?" asked a Kentucky congressman during the perennial debate on the future of the navy. "Her navy. What has kept the British nation perpetually at war for half a century past? Her navy.... What enabled her to commit enormities in Hindostan, the bare relation of which would add gloom to the regions of the dead? Her navy."[11]

The young republic paid a heavy price for its lack of a navy: depredations and kidnappings for ransom by the piratic regimes of North Africa, an undeclared naval war with France, and the constant bullying of the British navy, which made a practice of stopping American ships and pressing her sailors into its own naval service. Ultimately the country's seaports were blockaded during the War of 1812, Washington itself was attacked and burned, and seaborne commerce was all but destroyed because of a lack of ships to keep the British at bay.

The undeclared war with France, in 1798, provided the impetus for the establishment of a Navy Department under President John Adams and the construction, purchase, and renting of enough ships to provide a fifty-ship navy. Christopher Perry, with his thirteen-year-old-son Oliver serving as midshipman, commanded one of the new frigates, the 124-foot, 32-gun *General Greene*. The *General Greene* made two cruises to the Caribbean to look for French privateers and to support Toussaint L'Ouverture, the leader of a Haitian revolt against the French. The elder Perry was eventually suspended from the navy without pay. He had gained a reputation for spending too much time in port and had employed some novel forms of discipline. During one cruise a sailor who missed his watch and was found below in a drunken stupor was laid out on deck where three boys urinated into his mouth. Perry was also charged with using his ship to transport livestock to his father's farm in Narragansett.[12]

With the victory of Thomas Jefferson and the antinavy Democratic Republicans in 1800, the navy was reduced in size to thirteen ships. Christopher Perry at the age of forty was furloughed; his son Oliver, deemed good officer material, continued in the navy, serving in the Mediterranean Squadron in the war against Tripoli. In 1809 fifteen-year-old Matthew Calbraith Perry went to sea as a midshipman aboard the 12-gun schooner *Revenge* commanded by his twenty-four-year-old brother. In time all of Christopher Perry's sons served in the navy and three of his daughters married naval officers. During these years, the jerry-built U.S. navy was assigned the task of protecting American shipping from the search and seizure tactics of British vessels cruising off the Atlantic coast. From the *Revenge* Perry was transferred to the new, 44-gun frigate *President* under Commodore John Rodgers. Perry first saw action under Rodgers in May, 1811, when the *President*, cruising off the entrance to the Chesapeake Bay looking for British ships, decimated the smaller British sloop *Little Belt* in a bloody incident that contributed to the outbreak of war.[13]

The War of 1812, at least in the naval arena, had all the characteristics of a flea fighting a mastodon. The British navy totaled 600 fighting ships including 124 ships of the line. The American navy was made up of 16 oceangoing vessels. With the British fleet tied up fighting the French in European waters, the Americans won some significant victories in the first year of the war. Perry's sea duty under Commodore Rodgers, who commanded a four-ship squadron, was less satisfying. Rodgers did fire the first shot of the real war, chasing a British frigate into Halifax, Nova Scotia, but on three cruises in the Atlantic Rodgers never saw action and could only claim a handful of prizes. Both Rodgers and Perry were wounded by an exploding cannon in their first and last encounter, but after that, Perry's sea diary was salted with the refrain, "No remarkable occurrence this day." In the second year of the war, the British were able to concentrate more and more ships in American waters, eventually driving all but a handful of American fighting ships from the sea and successfully blockading the coast. As a result, Perry spent the rest of the war after August 1813 aboard a ship bottled up in New York harbor.[14]

The War of 1812, despite its anticlimactic ending for the navy, produced many a saga of sea fighting and a generation of naval heroes. The navy was celebrated in song and verse. The war even led to a grudging acceptance of the navy's permanence as a military institution. The Americans had demonstrated the superiority of native shipbuilding and had won most of their encounters with British ships, capturing over a thousand British merchant vessels. And all of this with no overall strategic goals, no specific instructions issued to American commanders, and no shoreside support organization.

Among the most prominent naval heroes was Perry's handsome older brother, Oliver Hazard. His victory over the British at the Battle of Lake Erie was the decisive factor in securing the country's northern frontier against a British invasion. It literally saved the nation, since the British had planned to march south and sever the western frontier from the eastern seaboard, establishing a new colony in the west.

The Americans' initial stunning naval victories produced a pronavy majority in Congress. In the last of three successive acts, the Naval Act of 1816, Congress authorized the expenditure of a million dollars a year for eight years and the construction of nine ships of the line and nine frigates. But with the end of the war, intentions fell prey to indolence, and the first of the ships of the line, meant to be the core of a peacetime navy, was not finished until 1825. Two more were built in the 1830s while five built even later were obsolete by the time they were launched. When the Civil War began, two were still in construction. America was destined to remain for years the fifth-ranked (or lower) naval power in the world.[15]

Twenty-year-old Matthew Calbraith Perry married on Christmas Eve 1814, the very day that the Treaty of Ghent ending the War of 1812 was signed. His bride was Jane Slidell, the daughter of a well-to-do New York shipowning merchant and banker. Perry's marriage put him on intimate terms with New York's merchant community, a group of men that in the prosperous years to come would build the city into a great international commercial center. His new brother-in-law John Slidell, a local ne'er-do-well, left New York for a successful career as a lawyer in New Orleans after a duel. A Southern moderate, Slidell became an important member of the new Democratic Party in the Jackson era, providing Perry with another connection that worked to his advantage. John Slidell's brother, the eleven-year-old Alexander Slidell (he later added his mother's name to become Alexander Slidell MacKenzie), was appointed an acting midshipman by Oliver Hazard Perry and went on to become a friend, a fellow naval officer, and Oliver Hazard Perry's biographer.[16] Soon after Perry's own marriage, his sister Anna Maria married George Rodgers, the younger brother of his wartime commander, John Rodgers. Perry's new ties with the Rodgers family, reinforced some years later when his own daughter married John Rodgers's son, assured that there would be a firm protective hand in the Navy Department as Perry advanced through the ranks.

Portrait of
Oliver Hazard Perry

Immediately after the war, John Rodgers was appointed to the Navy Department's board of commissioners, which he served as president during two separate terms, making him the ranking naval officer and the highest authority in the Navy Department below the secretary. The Perrys and the Rodgers looked after each other's interests. Perry maintained a regular correspondence with Rodgers, seeking advice and an occasional favor from his first naval mentor, and through the years he repeatedly asked for assignments for members of both the Perry and Rodgers families aboard ships that he commanded.[17] It was an era of extended family ties, and such were the customs of the day.

After the war, Matthew Perry, surely aware of the waning enthusiasm for the navy, considered a civilian career, as the captain

of one of his father-in-law's merchant-men. The Navy Department, however, refused to grant him a furlough. The United States was back at war almost immediately, again with the dey of Algiers, and Lieutenant Perry served as second in command on the man-of-war brig *Chippewa*. After this cruise, which produced a new treaty with Algiers, Perry went to sea as a merchant captain until 1819. In 1819 he was back in the navy serving at the Brooklyn Navy Yard, where he was appointed first lieutenant aboard the *Cyane*.

Portrait of
Commodore John Rodgers

The *Cyane* was ordered to escort a ship full of blacks who were looking for a site for a permanent colony on the west coast of Africa. Since Congress had outlawed the slave trade, the *Cyane* was also to be on the lookout for slavers. As second in command of the *Cyane*, Lieutenant Commandant Perry played a prominent role in locating the site for a colony for repatriated slaves, which eventually became Liberia. He returned again to Africa, in 1821, this time aboard his first command, the schooner *Shark*. While off Africa, Perry gained a reputation for employing systematic measures to protect the health of his crew from scurvy and malaria and for enforcing what was known as the Rodgers system of discipline. This called for a minimum of shore leave, a rigorous shipboard work routine, and judicious use of the lash.[18]

Back in the States Perry received another command, at a time when appointments were increasingly difficult to come by. This time he shipped out to the Caribbean, still commanding the *Shark*, as part of a concerted effort to put an end to piracy. Matthew Perry was aggressive in his pursuit of pirate vessels, but the war against the pirates in the Caribbean cost Oliver Hazard Perry his life. He died of yellow fever in Venezuela at the age of thirty-four.

In time, the American navy restored a measure of order to the Caribbean, and Perry was assigned again to the Brooklyn Navy Yard under his brother-in-law George Rodgers. Two years later, 1825, Perry went to sea as first lieutenant aboard the ship of the line *North Carolina*, the flagship of the Mediterranean fleet under Commodore John Rodgers. The magnificent *North Carolina*, which sported a three-tiered battery of 102 guns and was sailed by a crew of 832, was completed that year, the first of the ships of the line authorized in 1816. After twenty-eight months protecting American shipping during the Greek war of independence, Perry returned to the States, where he served as commander of the Boston Navy Yard for the next two years.[19]

After three commands, a brief stint as acting commodore of the Mediterranean Squadron, and an unhappy voyage delivering the American ambassador to Russia, the thirty-nine-year-old Perry was destined for a decade of shore duty at the Brooklyn Navy Yard, where he served first as captain of the yard in charge of naval recruiting and then commandant. A portrait painted at the time shows a man of stocky build and medium height with curly brown hair, mutton chop sideburns, brown eyes, and a large nose. Though imposing, Perry was not a handsome man, and he was inevitably compared negatively to his late brother, Oliver Hazard, who was known for his dashing good looks. During his years of command, Perry had gained a reputation as a competent skipper who insisted on strict discipline. He was old school in his belief in discipline but he insisted that corporal punishment be administered in a "more formal and consequently less frequent manner."[20] Perry was very much an autocrat of the quarterdeck, a martinet, one of his officers reported, aware of the prerogatives of command and the subordinate status of his officers and men. Stern and aloof, even dour, he nevertheless was absorbed by his crews' welfare—witness his struggle against malaria, scurvy, and yellow fever.[21]

"The captain's word is law," wrote Herman Melville in *White-*

Matthew Calbraith Perry, 1834;
portrait by William Sidney Mount

Jacket, his account of his cruise aboard the man-of-war *United States,* "he never speaks but in the imperative mood. When he stands on his Quarter-deck at sea, he absolutely commands as far as eye can reach. Only the moon and stars are beyond his jurisdiction. He is lord and master of the sun." Melville noted that the captain was a figure of such remote authority that when he appeared on the quarterdeck, his officers moved aside in silent deference. "At the first sign of those epaulets of his on the weather side of the poop," Melville wrote, "the officers there congregated invariably shrunk over to the leeward, and left him alone."[22] And according to his officers Perry fit very much in this mold.

"He was bluff, positive and stern on duty, and a terror to the ignorant and lazy, but the faithful ones who performed their duties with intelligence and zeal held him in the highest estimation, for they knew his kindness and consideration," said Silas Bent, who served under him in Mexico and Japan. Tightly wound, Perry hesitated when he spoke, often reaching for the right word. But though his penmanship, for which he apologized, was often close to undecipherable, he was a fluid writer and his letters and journals were thoughtful, even on occasion poetic. A religious man who enjoyed a good sermon, he was known for his sulfurous tongue and enjoyed a good drink. Perry had always shown a strong intellectual drive and interest in science. On his first cruise to the Mediterranean, he spent his spare time translating a Spanish book and later became fluent in Spanish. He was also a careful student of the weather, winds, and currents, as well as botany and conchology. At sea he made sure that the midshipmen under him were given as full an education as shipboard life permitted. While on shore duty he turned his mental energies toward the improvement of the navy, organizing a naval lyceum, museum, library, and a naval journal at the Brooklyn Navy Yard.[23]

Perry had grown up in a navy where members of a small clique of senior officers scrambled for the limited command opportunities, where feuding, backbiting, and even dueling were a way of life. During the navy's first fifty years, thirty-three officers were killed in duels.[24] There was a compulsive (and often alcoholic) quality to a naval officer's inflated (and often infantile) sense of honor. And it took very little to trigger a feud. Perry, for instance, spent weeks trying to track down the source of a story that a marine lieutenant had called him "a damned rascal." The remark, he wrote John Rodgers, reflected on "his conduct as an officer and a gentleman." Perry eventually enlisted the support of the Rodgers clan, sending his brother-in-law George Rodgers to ask the alleged culprit if he had made the remark. Perry also wrote to John Rodgers to make sure that his reputation was not hurt at the department. While fanning the flames of petty acrimony, Perry complained to the secretary of the navy that "the evils and injuries arising to the service from these frequent calumnies and unfounded reports generally put in circulation to answer some malignant motive have become seriously prejudicial to the prosperity, harmony and high standing of the corps."[25]

Andrew Jackson's threat to go to war with the French over claims from the Napoleonic Wars and the rumors that a French fleet was headed for the United States triggered a debate on naval strategy while Perry was at the Brooklyn Navy Yard. Many old-line naval officers still clung to the romance of the wooden sailing ship operating as a lone cruiser. John Quincy Adams, an expansion-minded New Englander who preceded Jackson as president, had argued that the United States was destined to become a great naval power. But though Jackson came into office with scant regard for the navy, he left as a convert to the necessity of having a big navy. Building up the navy year by year in peacetime "is your true policy," Jackson said on the day that he retired from office, "for your Navy will not only protect your rich and flourishing commerce in distant seas, but it will enable you to reach and annoy the enemy and will give to defense its greatest efficiency by meeting danger at a distance from home."[26] Jackson's call for a *projection of naval power* beyond coastal waters put him in step with the most forward-thinking of his own naval officers, and it echoed the arguments of Perry and his brother-in-law Alexander Slidell MacKenzie that were presented in the second issue of the new *Naval Magazine*.

Perry and MacKenzie, using "A.S." as a pseudonymn, argued that the United States had been from its colonial days a naval power by reason of its history and geography. A review of American history showed that "all of our misfortunes as a nation"—two wars with England and the quasi-wars with Barbary pirates and the French—were because of "the want of a sufficient navy." As a result, the navy was "the victim of inveterate and unmeaning routine" with "a system of death-like stagnation among officers." Worse, naval architecture had regressed to the point where the government had "launched some ships that would be a disgrace to the Chinese navy."[27]

The two authors suggested naïvely that the root of the problem was a lack of information. To be sure, the old regional antagonisms toward the navy had broken down to a certain degree during Jackson's presidency, but Perry and MacKenzie glossed over the historic hostility centered in the interior and western parts of the country toward a big navy. The United States had chosen "safety by shutting itself up like a tortoise within its shell" and now possessed only the seventh or eighth largest navy in the world. Instead the nation needed "an adequate force, stationed at every point where our interests may be assailed, . . . a force sufficient to extend effectual protection to our commerce in every sea." To create this capability, Perry and MacKenzie recommended a major naval construction program. They called for a five-year program that would lead to the construction of forty ships of the line and forty frigates. Perry and MacKenzie went on to advocate a complete reorganization of the officers corps, the creation of a naval academy, and new methods of recruiting sailors.[28]

The Perry-MacKenzie call for a big navy and naval reform had little immediate impact. They did, however, set the reform agenda for the next decade and more, little knowing that Slidell MacKenzie would become a target of reformers, though of a different stripe. Some of the measures that they recommended, as others had earlier, such as the creation of a naval academy, were eventually carried out. But the country was still not ready and would not be for years to make a major investment in naval forces. Disregard, even disdain, for the navy was nothing new. In this situation Perry chose to focus on what could be accomplished, and he spent his next few years promoting the development of steam war vessels.

During the War of 1812, Robert Fulton had conducted the

first experiment with a steam warship. Fulton designed the *De-mologos*, an elliptical, double-keeled floating battery powered by a single steam engine located in a slot between two joined hulls. The *Demologos* was squat and bulky, a strange-looking craft 156 feet long and 56 feet wide displacing an unheard of 2,475 tons. With her armament of twenty cannon aboard, she still averaged an amazing five and a half knots on one trial run. Fulton died before she was launched, and the renamed *Fulton* ended her days as a receiving ship in the Brooklyn Navy Yard until she blew up in an accident.[29] By the 1830s, although steam transportation was common in coastal and inland waters and steamships had crossed the Atlantic and visited India and China, nothing further had been done to develop steam war vessels. There were numerous objections to steam war vessels. They lacked maneuverability, they were unreliable and too vulnerable, since their side paddle wheels required that the engine be placed above the water line where it or the paddle wheels could easily be crippled by enemy gunners. Besides, their range was limited by the huge amount of coal required for a long voyage.

Still there was the Naval Act of 1816, the source of sporadic efforts to build large-scale fighting ships. Buried in its fine print was an authorization never acted on that provided for the construction of another steam battery. So in 1835, a year in which there were seven hundred steam vessels in use in American waters, the navy began work under Perry's supervision on the *Fulton*, a 130-foot, 700-ton ship to be powered by two engines that drove side paddle wheels. The *Fulton* was rigged as a three-masted sailing ship, since it was still not clear whether steam would be the prime motive force or an auxiliary to wind power. Perry took command when the *Fulton* was launched in 1837. On her first run she made ten knots, blithely steaming past the huge Cunard liner, the *Great Western*, in a race in New York Harbor.[30]

Perry quickly grasped the implications of a steam navy. Steam vessels, he wrote in 1838 on a trip to France and England to survey their accomplishments in this area, "will soon become a necessary arm of our naval strength to enable the country to sustain with . . . dignity its maritime rights." The British, eager to patronize a naval officer from their former colony and principal commercial rival, gave Perry a thorough demonstration of their superiority in the construction of steam engines. Perry concluded that the British would soon have an overwhelming advantage in naval power with "a preponderating steamer force." He noted that official encouragement had been given "to all those who have made the slightest improvement in the massive engine so that almost every ingenious mechanic throughout the Kingdom is exercising his skill to discover

The U.S. steam frigate *Fulton*

some new step to perfection." Perry was particularly interested to find out that the British government was subsidizing the construction of private steamers on the condition that they would be armed and used as naval vessels in the event of a war.[31]

How different was the situation at home in the United States! President Martin Van Buren, Jackson's successor, was doing his best to ignore the navy and was reported to have said that "this country required no navy at all, much less a steam navy" while his secretary of the navy swore he "would never consent to see our grand old ships supplanted by these new and ugly sea-monsters."[32] Still, in 1838 Congress appropriated funds for three steam warships. One of them, the *Mississippi*, turned out to be the finest and largest of her type ever built, demonstrating her capabilities on a three-year cruise of East Asian waters including two trips to Japan under Perry's command.

During his years at the Brooklyn Navy Yard, Perry was gaining recognition as an aggressive advocate of a reorganized and powerful navy. But he was also courting notoriety as the head, after John Rodgers's death, of a naval clan whose members were dogged by controversy. In an age of reform the navy was increasingly being scrutinized and attacked as a quaint but cruel autocracy whose treatment of its recruits was out of step with ebullient Jacksonian democracy.[33]

With his sense of pride and authority, it was perhaps inevitable that Calbraith Perry, as he was known to his friends, would come into conflict over these same issues with James Fenimore Cooper, who also moved in naval circles. Cooper had made his mark as America's first widely acclaimed novelist, even winning accolades in the mother country. After returning from an extended stay in Europe in the early 1830s, Cooper retired to his expansive estate at Cooperstown where he sang the praise of a landed aristocracy—"what is most needed for a higher order of civilization"—and decried the provincial crudities and prejudices of his fellow Americans.[34] None of this, naturally

Portrait of
James Fenimore Cooper

enough, endeared him to his American friends. Cooper, however, was busily enhancing his reputation as a cranky and disputatious loner with a penchant for pursuing his journalistic critics with libel suits and a knack for winning them.

Perry and Cooper started off on a friendly enough basis. Cooper joined the Naval Lyceum at the Brooklyn Navy Yard, contributed to *The Naval Magazine*, and socialized with Perry. Cooper, after all, had some knowledge of the sea. After being expelled from Yale, he went to sea before the mast, a favored rite of passage among the gentry, and then served in the navy as a midshipman for two years before the War of 1812. But when Cooper published his *Naval History of the United States*, the Perry clan objected to his description of the late Oliver Hazard Perry's role in the Battle of Lake Erie. Cooper had stepped into one of those peculiar naval feuds that went back years and years, and as far as Perry was concerned he had not tread lightly enough.

Jesse Elliott, an unpopular officer with a long history of duels, courts-martial, and other unpleasant confrontations, had been publicly shamed by his role in the battle that won Oliver Hazard Perry accolades as a national hero. When the Americans bore down on the British squadron in a light southeast wind on the morning of August 6, 1813, Elliott in command of the *Niagara* remained to the windward. Perry had ordered his officers to closely engage their counterparts in the British line of battle, and he proceeded to do so aboard the *Lawrence*. But without the support of Elliott aboard the *Niagara*, the British were able to concentrate their fire on the *Lawrence*. The *Lawrence* was hammered into a splintered hulk with most of its crew dead or wounded and bits of flesh and bone hanging in the rigging. After more than three hours of pounding, Perry abandoned the *Lawrence*, which was now a dismasted hulk with all its guns out of commission and blood running so thick on its decks that it dripped through the planking onto the dead and wounded below. Perry had himself rowed under heavy fire to the *Niagara*, where he took command and brought Elliott's ship into combat against the British. In the end the Americans prevailed, and the Battle of Lake Erie entered naval mythology as the greatest sea fight of the war.

In his reports of the battle, Perry praised Elliott while attempting to squelch the inevitable stories that portrayed Elliott as a malingerer. But Elliott, as the story of his actions circulated in wider and wider circles, became obsessed with the affair, continuing to press Perry for further public statements condoning his behavior. In the end Perry drew the line, eventually pressing charges against Elliott after Elliott challenged him to a duel. President Monroe quashed Perry's legal efforts, and Perry turned down Elliott's challenge because duels, he implied in a letter to Elliott, could only be fought between gentlemen.[35]

In his account of the battle, Cooper was fulsome in his praise of Perry's conduct. He did note that Perry was criticized at the time for the way in which he brought his squadron into the battle. Perry had gone out ahead of his line of battle, thus leaving the rest of the squadron to catch up to him while he took the brunt of the British attack. But Cooper dismissed this as an accident, describing Perry's battle plan as "highly judicious." The problem was that Cooper chose not to take the side of the Perry clan and did not portray Elliott as a coward.[36]

Incensed by Cooper's description of the battle, the Perry clan cleared for action. Slidell MacKenzie attacked Cooper in a long article in the *North American Review*. William Duer, Slidell MacKenzie's uncle and the president of Columbia University, took after him in a personally abusive manner in a New York newspaper. (Cooper sued the editor of the paper for slander and won.) Cooper responded with a long pamphlet in which he complained that the attacks on his book had led to its being excluded from district school libraries in favor of Slidell MacKenzie's bombastic and highly lau-datory biography of Oliver Hazard Perry.[37]

While this controversy was raging, the Perry clan found them-selves embroiled in an even more troublesome misadventure, the first "mutiny" in U.S. naval history.[38] In the summer of 1842 Perry was supervising the final construction of a graceful new sailing machine, the man-of-war brig *Somers*. Built along the lines of a Baltimore clipper, this sleek 103-foot craft sported two raking masts and a long bowsprit that could carry as many as four jibs. The *Somers* was fitted out for a mission that was central to the reform program of Perry and Alexander Slidell MacKenzie. It was to serve as a school ship for naval apprentices. Perry and Slidell MacKenzie had argued in their 1837 article that the navy took the flotsam and jetsam that haunted the wharves and alleys of the big cities, sent them to sea, and returned them as well-dressed, well-disciplined young men.

Perry assigned Slidell MacKenzie to command the *Somers*. He appointed his twenty-one-year-old son, Matthew C. Perry, Jr., third in command and his seventeen-year-old son, Oliver H. Perry II, captain's clerk. The family complement was rounded out by Henry Rodgers, a midshipman who was John Rodgers's youngest son, and

Adrien Deslonde, Slidell MacKenzie's brother-in-law. Second in command was Herman Melville's cousin, Lieutenant Guert Ganesvoort. Perry's fatal mistake was the recruitment of Philip Spencer as a midshipman. The nineteen-year-old Spencer was a hard-drinking college dropout, who was appointed a midshipman through the good offices of his father, the secretary of war in the

The U.S. brig-of-war *Somers*, with the bodies
of three alleged mutineers hanging from the yardarm

Tyler cabinet. Perry chose to overlook Spencer's naval record, which was spotted with charges of fighting and drunkenness. After all, Perry was a firm believer that naval discipline would provide an opportunity to improve an erring youth.

After a shakedown cruise the *Somers*, with its youthful crew— seventy percent under the age of nineteen—set off for the coast of Africa. One hundred and ten men and boys were crowded into a space designed for about seventy-five. Until the return voyage, the cruise was a routine one. A number of boys were flogged with the colt, a one-stranded, less damaging version of the dreaded cat-o'-

nine-tails. Spencer, for his part, avoided his fellow midshipmen, preferring to fraternize with the crew, for some of whom he illegally provided cigars and liquor.

On the return voyage from Monrovia to St. Thomas in the Caribbean, the crew's attitude became sullen, the officers later claimed. Fifteen days out of Monrovia one of the sailors approached the ship's purser to report that Spencer had come to him with a plan for murdering the officers, seizing the ship, and transforming the *Somers* into a pirate vessel. MacKenzie, when he first heard this tale, refused to believe it. Then he confronted Spencer. Spencer said that it was only a joke. It was a joke that "may cost you your life," MacKenzie responded.[39] MacKenzie had Spencer chained to the bulkhead on the quarterdeck. In Spencer's sea chest was found a list in awkward Greek lettering with the names of five crew members who were "certain," ten who were "doubtful," and eighteen who were "to be kept *nolens volens*." The next day there was an accident that carried away part of the rigging. The officers, already nervous, decided that it was part of a plot to free Spencer and seize the ship. Accordingly, two more men, Ned Cromwell, an abusive boatswain's mate, and Elisha Small, a senior petty officer, were arrested.

Now the *Somers* officers were increasingly wary of what they perceived as a hostile crew infiltrated by would-be mutineers. They went fully armed at all times and stood "watch and watch," four hours on and four hours off. After another mishap with the rigging seemed to lead to a second rush toward the quarterdeck, four more suspects were arrested. MacKenzie asked four of the officers, including Matthew Perry, Jr., and three of the midshipmen, to deliberate and make a recommendation about what to do with the prisoners, all seven of whom were chained to the quarterdeck bulkheads. Twenty-four hours later the group came back with a verdict: Spencer, Cromwell, and Small were "guilty of a full and determined intention to commit mutiny" and should be hanged.

MacKenzie was planning to make a brief call at St. Thomas within a few days, but he concluded that it was inappropriate to seek foreign assistance by jailing the men there until they could be safely transported for trial to the United States. Faced with the noose, Spencer and Small confessed their guilt, but Spencer ex-

onerated Cromwell, the bullying boatswain's mate. Cromwell protested his innocence to the end. Nonetheless all three were strung
up from the main yardarm. MacKenzie ended the macabre affair
by lecturing the crew and calling for three cheers for the flag. Then
the men were piped to dinner as the three bodies dangled from the
yardarms.[40]

When the *Somers* reached New York, she was anchored in a
remote corner of the harbor and no communications were allowed
with the shore. Young Matthew Perry
was dispatched to Washington with Slidell MacKenzie's report of the alleged
mutiny and executions. Soon enough,
news of what had happened leaked out
under the shroud of secrecy with which
the navy surrounded its inquiry.
MacKenzie was at first treated sympa-
thetically in the newspapers. But as the
press began to turn up real and imagined information here and there, the
tide of opinion shifted against Mac-
Kenzie. The navy, certain papers now
said, had lived up to its reputation as
a cruel and anachronistic autocracy.

Portrait of Alexander
Slidell MacKenzie

With two sons deeply involved in the
alleged mutiny, Calbraith Perry, Sr., was appalled. He went to
work immediately, rallying support for his brother-in-law. His sons,
he assured his congressman in a letter backing MacKenzie, had his
"unmeasured approbation." A court of inquiry made up of three
commodores was convened, and after an inquiry, the naval officers
ruled that "the immediate execution of the prisoners was demanded
by duty and justified by necessity."[41]

Exonerated by the inquiry, Slidell MacKenzie immediately
asked to be court-martialed, hoping to irrevocably clear his name
and head off a civilian murder trial being sought by Spencer's
father, the secretary of war, and Cromwell's widow. After a lengthy
hearing, which was highly publicized and well attended, MacKenzie
was acquitted of the five charges against him—murder, oppression,
illegal punishment, conduct unbecoming an officer, and cruelty.

MacKenzie had his prominent supporters, including Richard Henry Dana, author of *Two Years Before the Mast*, and Charles Sumner, then a young Boston lawyer, and his supporters made every effort to manipulate public opinion through the press. His critics, led by Cooper but including a number of prominent naval officers, were equally vociferous. To them it was a case of the despotic powers of the quarterdeck versus the "sacred principle" of due process. MacKenzie had hanged the three on the basis of circumstantial evidence without a proper trial. Worse, the men could only be tried for their offenses by a general court-martial, and MacKenzie, as captain of a ship, did not have the power to convene such a court. Then when the *Somers* returned to New York, MacKenzie remained in command of the ship, and the crew remained aboard, providing an opportunity to apply pressure to the young witnesses. Further suspicion was aroused when MacKenzie pushed for the promotion of a number of the officers, who were key witnesses and who testified in his support.[42]

Cooper described the Somers affair as "one of the most discreditable events that ever occurred in the service, since it exhibits a *demoralized quarterdeck*." He went on to publish and then rehash the entire court-martial proceedings in a book-length attack on the verdict. Cooper ascribed the verdict to the influence of New York's merchant class. They controlled the newspapers, and they were concerned about the impact of the trial on insurance rates. In private he noted that two close associates of the late Oliver Hazard Perry sat on the court-martial. One of them he described as "to all intents and purposes" a member of the Perry family. As for the *Somers*, "she went to sea with too much of the character of a family yacht, to come within the usual category of a regular cruiser."[43]

Since it was their family yacht, the Perry clan came under sustained attack. MacKenzie had promoted Oliver Perry to midshipman to replace Spencer. Oliver Perry, Cooper noted, was reprimanded for giving an incorrect order that resulted in the accident which was interpreted by the officers as part of a plot to free Spencer. And MacKenzie had either committed "the darkest and most revolting crime" or had demonstrated "gross deficiency of judgment." It was Cooper's opinion, after a long and detailed analysis of the evidence, that MacKenzie was "beyond a question

. . . guilty of murder." In the end, Cooper felt that his conclusion was justified when the remaining "mutineers" were released, and no charges were ever preferred against them.[44]

The *Somers* affair proved to be little more than a minor setback for Matthew Calbraith Perry, though one of his and Slidell MacKenzie's choice reform ideas, the training of naval apprentices, was scuttled for more than two decades. Perry went on, however, to participate in drawing up the plans for a new naval academy. The *Somers* affair was a case study in the hazards of naval favoritism. The wags were often heard to say about the navy that a cruise in Washington was worth two around Cape Horn. Young Spencer would never have been aboard the *Somers* if it had not been for his father's political influence. And the Perry-Rodgers-Slidell-MacKenzie clique might not have been in command without their ability to shape the decisions of the naval brass. The navy had proven incapable of making certain fundamental reforms from within, at least in the area of discipline. Now the public began to clamor for reforms that would curtail the "despotism of the quarterdeck." As for Perry, within three weeks of MacKenzie's acquittal, he departed for Africa as commander of the Africa Squadron. With him aboard the flagship he took two nephews as captain's clerk and midshipman.[45]

The naval establishment that Perry left behind as he sailed off to pursue slavers along the coast of Africa came under increasing attack from civilian reformers. The charge was that sailors, particularly sailors in the navy, were horribly exploited and little better than slaves, in some instances worse off. As a young apprentice printer of thirteen, Charles Nordhoff, the grandfather of the Charles Nordhoff who co-wrote *Mutiny on the Bounty*, decided to go to sea aboard a man-of-war to improve his health. He knew the infamous Commodore Jesse Elliott, who was then commandant of the Philadelphia Navy Yard. When Nordhoff asked his advice, Elliott told him, "If you go to sea, you will be nothing all your life but a vagabond, drunken sailor—a dog for everyone to kick at."[46] Nonetheless, Nordhoff went to sea under Commodore James Biddle aboard the *Columbus* and ended up accompanying Biddle to Edo

Bay on his ill-fated mission of 1846. Elliott's comments reflected an officer's opinion of the common sailor.

Herman Melville's sympathies lay with the sailor. He had sailed before the mast on merchantmen, whalers, and a man-of-war, but he had little better to say. "The Navy is the asylum for the perverse, the home of the unfortunate," he wrote in *White-Jacket*. "Here the sons of adversity meet the children of calamity, and here the children of calamity meet the offspring of sin. Bankrupt brokers, boot-blacks, blacklegs, and blacksmiths here assemble together; and castaway tinkers, watch-makers, quill-drivers, cobblers, doctors, farmers, and lawyers compare past experiences of old times."[47]

There is no doubt that sailors were a cruelly exploited lot, a pariah class that languished somewhere between the slave and the unskilled worker. Sailors were recruited along the wharves and in the slums of the major port cities by crimps and the landlords of the cheap sailors' boarding houses, often the same people who were paid to bring live bodies to naval recruiters. Often, the would-be sailors were misled into signing up by being brought aboard a ship on a tour of inspection and then denied the right to leave. Others were brought aboard semiconscious from drugs and alcohol. Having offered liberal credit terms, landlords would lend money to a sailor and then get hold of the sailor's advance pay. When vessels returned to port, the same landlords swarmed over the vessel—hence the term landshark—looking to reestablish the cycle of debt peonage. Once aboard ship, the sailor fell easy prey to the purser, who was in the business (for his own profit until 1842) of selling him supplies at inflated prices in lieu of pay to be received later. The result: more debt peonage.[48]

Discipline aboard naval vessels ranged from strict to grossly brutal. The cat-o'-nine-tails was the dreaded instrument of enforcement. To many, flogging was a sickening affair. The offenses for which flogging was administered ranged from mutinous conduct (a hundred lashes) to being slow in getting into a boat (six lashes) and getting in debt ashore (twelve lashes). After a hearing, all hands were called to witness punishment, and the guilty party's hands were tied over his head to the hammock netting or some other part of the rigging and his feet to a grate on the deck. He was then stripped to the waist and struck with full force across his back with a devilish instrument that consisted of a handle with nine strands of rope attached to it. The ropes were knotted at the end and sometimes tipped with lead or leather. The first blows raised purple welts; next the blood began to flow.[49] The navy produced its share of sadistic officers, and some ships were hellholes of discipline. On others, flogging was rarely employed, particularly since a growing number of naval officers opposed it.

Living and working conditions were little better than the rigid

Punishment by flogging; drawing by William H. Myers

discipline. "The living on board a man-of-war," Melville wrote, "is like living in a market; where you dress on the doorsteps, and sleep in the cellar. No privacy can you have; hardly one moment's seclusion." Aboard the *United States*, the men were allowed a scant eighteen inches to swing their hammocks. "Dreadful! they give you more swing than that at the gallows," was Melville's reaction. Food was poor and hard on the stomach, largely hard biscuits, boiled salt beef or pork, and coffee, tea, and cocoa in rotation with occasional servings of beans, rice, a few raisins, and small amounts of butter and cheese. There was little rest at sea. Sailors stood watch and watch, meaning that they were on and off duty every four hours. Since their hammocks were stored away from eight in the morning to sunset, they averaged about three hours' sleep a night. All in all it was a miserable life, and it was little wonder that the

navy had continual difficulties recruiting sailors and was so dependent on foreigners to fill out its crews, particularly in the rel-
atively high-wage economy of pre–Civil War America.[50]

Grog, or the spirit ration, was the sailor's favorite solace. At
first grog was a mixture of a half cup of rum (four ounces) mixed
with water and served twice daily. By 1805 annual rum consumption in the U.S. navy equaled forty-five thousand gallons. At about
this time rum was replaced with whiskey. In 1842, because of the
protests of naval reformers and the growing temperance movement,
the grog ration was cut in half and could no longer be served to
minors. Still, the distribution of grog remained an important event
that took on all the elements of a quasi-ceremony as the sailors
gathered at the roll of a drum around a wooden barrel to receive
their daily tot.[51]

To the reformers grog and flogging were twin evils that fed
on each other. Grog might not get a sailor drunk, the argument
went, but it increased his appetite for liquor. And sailors became
experts at smuggling liquor aboard their ships. "It is hardly to be
doubted," Melville wrote *after* the spirit ration was cut in half,
"that the controlling inducement which keeps many men in the
Navy, is the unbounded confidence they have in the ability of the
United States government to supply them, regularly and unfail-
ingly, with their daily allowance of this beverage." Charles Nordhoff
was amazed at "the scenes of drunkenness and riotous debauchery
of which I had been a witness almost constantly since my entry
into the Navy."[52] Liquor, the reformers argued, led to infractions
of the rules, and infractions led to flogging. It was a tight and
vicious circle of inhumanity.

The movement to improve the lives of sailors gained impetus
in the United States in the Jackson administration with its intense
interest in the plight of the common man. Matthew Calbraith Perry's unhappy diplomatic mission to Russia was the cause of the first
government investigation of flogging. "The scenes which I witnessed
on board the *Concord*," John Randolph, the U.S. ambassador to
Russia, reported to President Jackson, "were so revolting, that I
made up my mind never to take passage again on board of a vessel
of War." The four floggings administered were an "odious spectacle
that surprised and shocked my negroe [sic] slaves. In seven years

the same quantity of punishment would not be distributed among the same number of slaves as was inflicted in a voyage of three weeks from Hampton Roads to Portsmouth."[53] And recall that Perry was very circumspect in his use of the lash.

In response Congress authorized a revision of the navy's thirty-two-year-old rules and regulations. But nothing came of this effort until after the *Somers* affair. Then sea-borne quill pushers, such as Melville, turned their reformist zeal on the navy. Even the navy's own officers took up the call for reform. "Never before has the spirit of discontent, among all grades in the navy, walked forth in the broad light of day, with half such restive but determined steps," wrote Lieutenant Matthew Maury, the noted oceanographer, under the pseudonym Harry Bluff. "The period is fast approaching, when something must be done to stay the evils of the deranged system."[54]

Finally, in 1844, amendments to abolish flogging and the spirit ration were attached to bills in Congress. It would take another six years before flogging was abolished. The spirit ration would last until the Civil War. The reformist sentiment of the Jacksonian years finally swept through the navy, but except for some minor changes, the storm passed over doing very little damage. The navy remained a tight little autocracy living by its own rules and its own neo-feudalistic behavioral code.

In the aftermath of the *Somers* affair, Perry's African cruise appeared to be a mild form of exile. "I am no favorite with the present administration for reasons with which you and many others are acquainted," Perry wrote from Africa to his brother-in-law John Slidell, who was then a Democratic congressman from Louisiana.[55] The mission of the three-ship African Squadron was to suppress the slave trade. It was an onerous, even dangerous business because of the dangers of disease in a tropical climate. Rather than catching slavers, Perry found himself settling conflicts that had developed between the coastal tribes and the new colonies of former American slaves, which he had helped establish on his last voyage to Africa some twenty years earlier, and between the tribesmen and American trading vessels invariably out of Salem, Massachusetts. One attempt at negotiations with a tribe on the Ivory Coast, which had murdered an American sea captain and his crew, led to bloodshed, and Perry and his men ended up burning the native village and killing its leader.

Two years later, in 1845, Perry was back in New York. A new administration was in power, one with which he and his extended family were in much greater favor. President James Polk was in the process of annexing Texas, a move that would provoke a war with Mexico. Polk had already dispatched John Slidell to Mexico as his special commissioner to negotiate with the Mexicans. His brother, Alexander Slidell MacKenzie, resurrected after the *Somers* affair, was sent to negotiate with General Santa Anna. In the summer of 1846, four months after the first shots were fired near the Rio Grande, Perry was given orders to assume command of the Home Squadron. The Home Squadron, with twenty-seven ships, was the largest American fleet ever assembled. It was charged with blockading the Gulf Coast of Mexico. Based near Vera Cruz, smaller detachments of vessels were sent to raid a number of coastal towns. And ultimately the squadron participated in the week-long bombardment and capture of Vera Cruz, an event that opened the way for General Winfield Scott and his troops to march on to Mexico City.

The Mexican War made of Perry a zealous convert to Manifest Destiny expansionism; it also brought the Pacific for the first time into his purview. After an incursion into Tabasco, Perry wrote to the secretary of the navy that the United States, not Great Britain, should build a canal across the Isthmus of Tehuantepec. "Destiny has doubtless decided," he wrote, "that the vast Continent of North America from Davis' Straits to the Isthmus of Darien shall in the course of time fall under the influence of the Laws and institutions of the United States, hence the impolicy of permitting any European Power or interest to obtain a footing within the prescribed Latitudes."

For this reason, Perry explained, he had taken possession of the Coatzacoalcos River as far up as his ships had traveled. Perry was suggesting that the United States could use control of the river as the basis for demanding at the peace talks an exclusive right of way across the isthmus. Perry admitted that his idea might be "visionary and chimerical." And indeed nothing ever came of either

Perry's proposal or of his backing in the Yucatán civil war of a group of Mexicans of European extraction who were fighting a native uprising and asking to be annexed by the United States. But Perry was clearly attuned to the next wave of expansion, which would bring an American steamship line to Panama within a year, lead to the construction of an American-owned railroad across the Isthmus of Panama, and the start of another steamship line up the West Coast to the new state of California, a thrust that led the United States relentlessly in the direction of Japan.[56]

Perry returned to New York in July 1848 a hero. He was feted at a civic reception, presented with a gilt key to the city, and praised along with his officers and men for their "gallantry and good conduct in the late war with Mexico." He continued to serve for a short time as commodore of the Home Squadron, but in November, he was appointed to the newly created position of General Superintendent of Mail Steamers. A decade before Perry had noted on a trip to England that the British were subsidizing the construction of steamers by awarding mail contracts to private citizens. In the event of a war, these steamers could then be taken over by the government. The idea had caught on in the United States where it satisfied, to a certain extent, the advocates of a big navy, and Perry was given the job of supervising their construction. It was a responsibility that would carry him one step closer to Japan.

Since Perry's new job kept him at work in and around the shipyards of New York, he was able to settle into domestic life in Tarrytown, up the Hudson River. In 1839 he had bought a farm on the banks of the Hudson near the Slidell MacKenzie farm. On his farm he built a comfortable stone house, described by one visitor as a beautiful cottage. Besides the Slidell MacKenzies, Perry counted among his neighbors James Watson Webb, his friend who edited the *Morning Courier and New York Enquirer*, and Washington Irving. Perry aspired to the life of the gentry, but could barely afford it on a naval officer's salary. As a captain, he made $3,500 a year, and when he had to entertain aboard ship while on diplomatic missions, as happened, for example, when he was in the Mediterranean during the Greek war of independence, he had to pay for entertainment out of his own pocket. This along with his large family of seven children (three more had died in infancy)

kept him in financial straits. He borrowed money from his daughters' husbands (the Rodgers brothers), from Webb, and from another wealthy neighbor to build his farmhouse. This arrangement
made him extremely sensitive about his financial situation, to the
point where he considered selling the farm. Finally, his son-in-law
arranged for him to sell a right-of-way over his property to the
Hudson River Railroad (another Aspinwall venture). With this
money, $800 in prize money from Mexico, and some other funds,
Perry managed to pay off his debts.[57]

When the Hudson River Railroad reached Tarrytown, Perry
began to commute to New York and spend more time at home. He
had always enjoyed his children. The domestic scene seemed to
soften the edges of his personality. He worked at making his children laugh and often entertained them by playing tunes on the
flute. Once when he had returned after a long absence at sea, he
was held up at the Brooklyn Navy Yard for an extra day. A friend
noted that he cried openly because he was being kept from his
family.[58] By the time that he returned from Mexico, Perry was
fifty-four years old, and only his two youngest daughters remained
at home. One daughter was married to Robert S. Rodgers, a naval
officer. His son William Frederick was a marine lieutenant. Another
daughter, Jane, was married to John Hone. Oliver Hazard II had
spent some time in California prospecting for gold while Matthew
Jr. was still in the navy.

A little more than a year after his return, Perry's twenty-year-
old-daughter, Caroline, married August Belmont, one of the wealthiest and most eligible bachelors in the city. Belmont was a German
Jew who had come to New York on behalf of his distant relatives,
the Rothschild banking family, arriving just in time to witness the
devastation of the Panic of 1837. In the city's depressed economy,
Belmont was one of the few men with cash and reputable credit.
He built a fortune buying up whatever he could lay his hands on—
building lots, bank notes, commodities—at rock bottom prices, and
was soon one of the three most important bankers in the city. Belmont was a sophisticated European who spoke English with an
accent and enjoyed a reputation for extravagant living. He walked
with a permanent limp, the result of a duel fought with a man who
had accused him of having an affair with a very beautiful married

woman. Belmont was also a staunch Democrat, whose support for Polk led to his financing both loans to the United States government and to the Mexican government to pay for reparations growing out of the recent war. Belmont's marriage to Caroline Perry was hailed by the press and the social arbiters of the city; it was a match between a man of astounding wealth and "the beautiful daughter of a well-known and gallant naval officer." For a wedding present, Belmont gave his wife more than two city blocks of prime New York real estate.[59]

Well-established and, if not wealthy, at least surrounded by wealth, Calbraith Perry appeared to be settling comfortably into old age. His years of active sea duty were more than likely behind him. If he was called upon to go to sea, he would undoubtedly, as a very senior officer with excellent connections in the Navy Department, have his choice of assignments. But then some time in 1850, the exact circumstances are unknown, Perry was called to Washington to begin research for a new undertaking, a major diplomatic expedition to Japan.

3

THE COMMODORE
IN THE CITY OF
MAGNIFICENT
INTENTIONS

The real object of the expedition should be concealed from public view, under a general understanding, that its main purpose will be to examine the usual resorts of our whaling ships, with special reference to their protection, and the opening to them of new ports of refuge and refreshment.[1] —MATTHEW CALBRAITH PERRY to Secretary of the Navy William A. Graham, January 1851

We are aspiring to the first place among the nations of the earth, in a commercial point of view—a place which belongs to us as a matter of right—and are we to suffer ourselves to be overcome by British commercial capitalists under the auspices of the British crown?[2] —THOMAS RUSK, Committee on the Post Office and Post Roads, Report, June 15, 1852

When I look at the position in which we stand in relation to the Pacific and the East, and consider we have advanced our posts to the coast of the Pacific ocean; that the trade of the East is in the hands of European powers, who have been for two hundred years engaged by commercial treaties, by naval expeditions, and by armed power, in securing and parcelling out the vast trade of the East among themselves; and that one nation alone has a monopoly of the trade of Japan, I think that, instead of inquiring why an expedition is now ordered

by the Government of the United States to Japan, the question naturally arises, Why have not the United States before sent an expedition to the East?[3]
—SENATOR WILLIAM SEWARD of New York, April 1, 1852

IN THE WINTER OF 1850–1851, while Perry worked in Washington, a measure of tranquillity had returned to the capital after the histrionic and near violent debates over the slavery issue, which at last produced the Compromise of 1850. After a decade of land acquisition by war with Mexico and by treaty with England, the United States, having devoured 1,204,896 square miles of new territories, was threatened with a case of terminal indigestion. The unsettling question, which was settled at least temporarily by the Compromise, was should the South, home of the Democratic advocates of militant expansionism, be allowed to extend slavery into the newly acquired territories or should it be banned? Now that the United States was a continental power would it extend democracy or slavery to the shores of the Pacific?

During the debates on the Compromise of 1850 President Zachary Taylor—old "Rough and Ready," the hero of the Mexican War—died in the second year of his Whig administration. Taylor had been a likeable soul with a folksy manner, the kind of straightforward man that was valued for his Republican plainness, but hardly a politician. When the weather permitted, Taylor could be seen strolling along the streets of Washington on his morning walk, his thin gray hair disheveled, dressed in an oversized suit and a tobacco-stained shirt, a black silk hat perched on the back of his head.[4] His successor, Millard Fillmore, another less than dynamic leader, was at least a seasoned politician. Fillmore, a Buffalo lawyer, even looked and sounded like a statesman with his stalwart, portly figure, placid pink face, quiet dignified bearing, and his deep-voiced deliberate manner of speaking. The new president had made a good part of his respectable fortune representing New York businessmen in their dealings with Buffalo's merchants, an unpleasant task that often involved suing his neighbors on behalf of his clients. Mixing law with politics and the perfect embodiment of the Whig business ethic, Fillmore and his former law partners controlled the Whig Party in western New York.[5]

The Washington of Millard Fillmore and the Whigs—with a population of 40,000, including 1,700 slaves and 4,800 freemen— was hardly more than a large town. It was marked by the noticeable contrast between its elegant buildings—stately private homes, such as the one Webster had built on the north side of Lafayette Square in the 1840s, and a few public buildings, such as the White House,

View of Washington, D.C., 1852

the Capitol, the Smithsonian, the Patent Office, with its portico modeled after the Parthenon, and the City Hall—and the half- finished squalor of much of the city. The streets were unpaved; cows, goats, pigs, and chickens wandered freely along garbage- strewn thoroughfares that were alternately dusty in the summer and muddy in the winter. Wide expanses of swampy lands and open meadow bordered the Washington Canal, which had been cut earlier in the century eastward from the Potomac River along what would become the Mall, turning southward at the foot of Capitol Hill.

When the sewage did not simply accumulate on low ground, the city's open sewers drained along a number of creeks and ditches and into the canal, whose odiferous waters rose and fell with the Potomac. In the summer the marshlands along the Potomac produced clouds of mosquitoes, an unhealthy, malaria-breeding complement to the hordes of fleas, bedbugs, and cockroaches that plagued the populace and kept the infant mortality rate high, particularly among the poor. While the Capitol stood in isolated splendor on the top of a hill with a few houses nearby, the half-constructed Treasury Department on Pennsylvania Avenue and the Washington Monument, which was then a sixty-five-foot granite stump topped by wooden construction cranes, contributed to the sense of some future city of grandiose design.[6]

After a visit a decade earlier, Charles Dickens dubbed Washington "the headquarters of tobacco-tinctured saliva." "It is sometimes called the City of Magnificent Distances," he wrote in his *American Notes*, "but it might with greater propriety be termed the city of magnificent intentions; for it is only on taking a bird's-eye view of it from the top of the Capitol, that one can at all comprehend the vast designs of its projector, an aspiring Frenchman. Spacious avenues, that begin in nothing, and lead nowhere, streets, mile-long, that only want houses, roads and inhabitants; public buildings that need but a public to be complete; and ornaments of great thoroughfares which only lack great thoroughfares to ornament—are its leading features. One might fancy the season over, and most of the houses gone out of town forever with their masters."[7]

Many of the 1,533 full-time federal employees rented rooms while members of Congress lived in boarding houses and a handful of hotels, the Willard House and the National Hotel being the best known of these. The focus of nightlife for those so inclined was a raucous string of fifty gambling saloons that lined Pennsylvania Avenue between the Capitol and the half-finished Treasury Building. For the more genteel and the well-connected, there were the weekly levees and dinner parties held at the White House. These were judged rather dull affairs, in part because Mrs. Fillmore's health made it difficult for her to set a social standard for the city. The city's doyennes expected little more of the First Lady because, they noted, she had been nothing but a poor school teacher before she married the president. These gatherings did provide an opportunity for one to talk to an important Cabinet member or draw the president aside for a brief chat. Beyond this, there was an

The Washington Monument under construction, 1851

endless whirl of dinners, tea parties, and hops organized at the better hotels by the city's young ladies. Respectable working hours were from 9:30 A.M. to 4:30 P.M., and the social whirl was enough to keep the most coveted guests out every night.[8]

In early 1851, the hot embers of the slavery issue still smoldered beneath the surface despite the compromise worked out the year before. It was like a fire in a coal vein. From time to time, the flames would force their way into the air, flaring up but then subsiding as the fire still burned underground. The nation, however, was entering a golden interregnum, a period of prosperity when most minds turned from sectional rivalries to grand schemes. With the settlement of the Oregon boundary dispute with England in 1846 and the victory over Mexico in 1848, the United States was now a continental power with hundreds of miles of coastline facing China and Japan across the Pacific Ocean. Gold flowed in freely from the mines of California. On one day alone a steamer from Panama brought $2.5 million in bullion into the port of New York. American goods flowed out in all directions from eastern and southern ports—with cotton and tobacco leading the list. The government enjoyed a surplus of almost five million dollars on a total budget of forty-eight million dollars. America was at peace with everyone, including itself.

The U.S. Navy was only the fifth largest in the world, but American shipping dominated world trade. American shipbuilders made the finest wooden sailing ships, the graceful and very fast clipper ships, which ruled the China trade. And virtually all the Atlantic sailing packets were American owned. During the summer of 1851 American ascendancy in the world of shipbuilders was underlined by the fact that the steamers of the Collins line outpaced the rival Cunard line, setting a transatlantic record of nine days, thirteen hours, and thirty minutes. To add insult to injury, the schooner yacht *America* in the same summer vanquished the British-owned *Titania* in a race around the Isle of Wight, thereby winning what became known as the America's Cup. Not surprisingly the British, the dominant commercial power in the world and the possessor of the world's largest navy, agonized over the growing number of American ships that were being bought by British companies. And even the U.S. Navy, kept small and understaffed during most of its history by its sectional opponents in the western and interior states, had money to spend on new ships, bigger shipyards—particularly in cities that supported the Whigs—and expeditions to farflung corners of the globe.

Though tempers flared over competition with England for control of Central America and the Canadian fisheries, most of the issues that made relations with England difficult had been settled to the satisfaction of the Americans. Washington might be a crude frontier town by European standards, but it was, as Dickens said, a city of magnificent intentions, the capital of a brash and newly continental empire, a town where, improbable as it might seem, a handful of men working at the Navy Department were making plans to confront an ancient empire, a vast bureaucratic family dictatorship whose capital city of Edo was the largest in the world.

Calbraith Perry had never been any closer to the Pacific than Mexico's Isthmus of Tehuantepec, but he was quickly developing ideas about how to deal with the Japanese, ideas drawn largely from the reports of previous visitors to Japan, like Commander James Glynn and Charles King, the merchant missionary who tried to open trade with Japan in 1837. For months Perry had been poring over the written record of earlier encounters with the Japanese. He found key documents in the files of the State and Navy departments and quite a number of books in the Congressional Library, more than might be expected about a country as unvisited as Japan. These accounts told the story of forty years of haphazard diplomacy, if it could even be called diplomacy, a story of stray encounters, private initiatives, and ambassadorial intentions gone astray.

Glynn's reports of the ill treatment of the *Lagoda* crew had reached Washington some time during 1850. In response, both houses of Congress introduced resolutions calling on the executive branch to provide information about what was happening in Japan. At the same time Aaron Haight Palmer, a New York businessman, had been running a one-man campaign trying to interest the State

Department in his plan for an expedition to Japan. He solicited memorials from chambers of commerce in eastern cities and sent a steady stream of information about Japan to members of Congress.[9] The question arose again whether it was time to send a diplomat to Japan to open commercial relations. But this question came up during the acrimonious debates over slavery and the admission of California into the union, and Japan dropped for a time from public view.

It is more than likely that the *Lagoda* affair triggered renewed interest in establishing relations with Japan. So in some sense, Ranald MacDonald was at least connected with the events that led to the organization of a Japan expedition. Whatever the case, at some point in 1850, Commodore Perry began to outline a plan for a major diplomatic undertaking. On his periodic trips to the capital, Perry was working closely with Secretary of the Navy William A. Graham, a North Carolina lawyer who had served as governor of his state for two terms. Graham, brought into the cabinet to provide regional balance, represented the pro-Union southerners in the Whig alliance. A capable administrator, he knew almost nothing about naval or diplomatic affairs. But a Japan expedition fit into the overall Whig strategy of pursuing foreign commerce by peaceful means.

In late January 1851, Perry wrote privately to Graham laying out his preliminary ideas about a strategy for dealing with the Japanese. "The real object of the expedition," he explained, "should be concealed from public view, under a general understanding, that its main purpose will be to examine the usual resorts of our whaling ships, with special reference to their protection, and the opening to them of new ports of refuge and refreshment." Perry described Nagasaki as the only port at which foreign vessels were admitted, but noted that the Dutch "through their intrigues" had enough influence to frustrate any other nation's attempts to enter into negotiations there. For this reason he proposed selecting as a destination for an expedition one or two ports at the other end of the country, but within communicating distance from Edo, such as Matsumae, Hakodate, or both. At one of these ports, a squadron should suddenly appear and then demand free access for American ships seeking provisions and repair.

Perry thought that the sudden arrival of an American squadron "would doubtless produce great surprise, and confusion, and every means, including force, would be devised by the Japanese (for they are a shrewd and cunning people) to get rid of the intruders." The Americans, however, should remain on the defensive, responding with force only as circumstances demanded. In this way, Perry was confident that "a favourable issue to the enterprise might reasonably be expected."

Perry called Graham's attention to a map of Japan noting that the islands of "Yesso" (Hokkaido) and "Niphon" (Honshu) were located in relation to each other somewhat like Ireland and Great Britain. He asked Graham to imagine a situation where a strong naval force from a powerful foreign nation occupied two ports in Ireland and cut off communications with Great Britain. In this way and by establishing friendly relations with the people of Yesso-Ireland, who were already disaffected with their conquerors, the naval force could force the Japanese-English to negotiate.

Perry went on to say that according to his research the Japanese were superior to the Chinese. Though treacherous, Perry wrote, "they have many redeeming traits . . . [being] brave, generous and humane, inordinately curious and fond of pleasure, giving importance to form and ceremonies beyond any people in the world, and spending half their lives in attendance upon the capricious edicts of the Court, which exercises an extraordinary influence over the people by a system of perfectly organized *espionage*, extending to every individual, however obscure, one half the population being employed to watch the other half." For this reason people lived in dread and "are constantly engaged in plots, and counterplots."

Perry thought that the accounts of prejudice against foreigners were highly exaggerated. He assigned blame for the lack of trade with the outside world to the intrigues of the Dutch, "who have stopped at nothing, however dishonorable, or degrading to their national character, to effect their object." Perry agreed with the assessment of a British doctor who had visited Japan in the early part of the century that the Japanese hated "the restrictions of their political institutions" and were a people "who seem inclined to throw themselves into the hands of any nation of superior intelligence." From his research, he doubted that "the Supreme Government at Yedo" was strong enough to prevent a well-organized resistance to its authority that originated at a point distant from the capital.

For a naval force, Perry requested three first-class steamers and a sloop of war. Since the Japanese had never seen a steamer before, he could imagine "the astonishment and consternation that would be produced by the sudden, and to them mysterious, approach of these vessels towards their ports, moving silently, and to all appearance stealthily along, without sails, and without regard to wind or tide." He thought that the steamers plus a display of their heavy-caliber guns, explosive shells, rockets, and other equipment on the ships "would do more to command their fears, and secure their friendship, than all that the diplomatic missions have accomplished in the last one hundred years."

Perry argued that an expedition could be justified on the basis of "the maxim, universally practised in this Country, that the few must give way to the many." If this was not sufficient, then the treatment of foreigners and the two occasions in which the Japanese fired on the *Morrison*, albeit some fourteen years earlier, were. They were grounds, Perry felt, not only for investigation of the situation in Japan, but for "signal punishment."

Finally, Perry advised that the expedition be "strictly naval, untrammelled by the interference of diplomatic agents." Then once a show of force had led to an opening, trade and diplomatic relations, the responsibilities of a diplomat, could follow.[10]

While Perry was laying out a preliminary scenario for the Japan expedition, he sought more information on whaling in the Pacific, writing confidentially to one of the most distinguished American sea captains, Joseph C. Delano of New Bedford, Massachusetts. Delano was an influential figure in this capital city of whaling. He, like so many sons of prominent New England families, had gone to New York as a young man and for a time had captained sailing ships for one of the American-owned packet lines that ran monthly between New York and Liverpool. As the skipper of a packet, Delano had worked for the merchant house of Fish and Grinnell, later Grinnell, Minturn and Company, a firm that was a major force in foreign trade with Latin America and China. Grinnell, Minturn and Company was one of the handful of merchant houses that dominated the China trade, ranking in New York merchant circles with Howland and Aspinwall. Joseph Delano's kinsman, Amasa Delano, had been one of the first sea captains to write of his voyages in the Pacific. His brother Warren Jr. was the principal partner in China of Russell and Company, the leading American firm trading with that country and the largest of the American firms that participated in the opium trade.[11]

Perry explained in his letter to Delano that he was collecting information about whaling in the Pacific. His inquiries, Perry went on, were a strict secret, and for that reason he asked Delano not to connect his (Perry's) name with them. Perry wanted to know some basic facts about the industry: the number and value of American vessels engaged in Pacific whaling, the number of men involved, the best fishing grounds in the Pacific, ports that whaling ships entered along the Russian coast and among the Japanese dependencies, and the need for additional ports of call. Specifically Perry wanted to know if whaling ships were ever allowed to enter any Japanese ports. Had any ever entered Nagasaki? Did they anchor along the coast and trade with the natives? Did Delano know anything about Captain Mercator Cooper's visit aboard the *Manhattan* to Edo Bay? Finally he asked for details about the weather, facilities, inconveniences, and dangers that one might encounter in that part of the Pacific.[12]

Delano's response to Perry has been lost, but in 1851 New Bedford was the premier metropolis of the whale trade, and whaling was one of New England's leading industries, important enough to make New Bedford the fifth largest port in the United States. England had already begun to use other forms of oil for lubricating machinery, but Americans, in the early years of the industrial revolution, were still using whale oil as well as spermaceti for candles, which were known for their clear, bright light, and whale bone, or baleen, for umbrellas and for the stiffening substance that gave women's skirts their rounded look.[13]

A month later, Delano forwarded a letter from Mercator Cooper, the one whaling captain who had actually entered a Japanese port other than Nagasaki. Cooper had been to the very gates of Edo, something no other American had ever accomplished. But the city—it was April 1845—was so overgrown with trees that he could see little of its buildings except that they were low, numerous, and white. The harbor, which was filled with a large number of junks, was easy of access, safe, and a bustle of commercial activity. Cooper was given all the supplies that he needed without charge.

The natives were quiet & friendly & intelligent all the sailors I picked up could write & read their own language fluently & they had a great many books with them, their government is an absolute one, very strict with its subjects, in regard to foriners [sic] entering their dominions, they seem to have more knowledge of the world than we have of them as the interpreter spoke of Washington, Bonepart [sic], Wellington, & several other distinguished men which proves they know more about us than we know about them.[14]

By the end of February, Perry was writing more confidently and openly to Delano about plans for a Japan expedition. "Something will doubtless be done with regard to Japan," he confided to Delano, "but not as much as I fear I would desire." Perry and Graham had already accomplished one of their major objectives. Daniel Webster, Fillmore's secretary of state, "has taken the matter up, and is making inquiries." For his part Perry preferred, he explained to Delano, to play a background role in promoting an expedition—"acting in some measure sub rosa preferring to let the members of the Gov't and the merchants take the lead," as he put it. He had already talked with four members of Congress from New York as well as some of the city's merchants. He had had a friendly talk with Joseph Grinnell, New Bedford's congressman. Grinnell was also Delano's partner in the Wamsutta Mills, a New Bedford textile factory, a former partner in Minturn and Grinnell, and brother of Moses Grinnell, the head of Grinnell, Minturn and Company and another of the small but powerful group of New York merchants. Joseph Grinnell, to Perry's surprise, showed very little interest, although Perry was not able to explain "the particulars of the proposition." Only Webster could do that. So Delano, Perry suggested, should get Grinnell to talk to Webster.

Perry had received assurances that the leading merchants from the major maritime cities, especially the chambers of commerce and insurance companies, would back the expedition. But first it was necessary to get the president and the Cabinet to support the plan. For this reason men like Grinnell and "other influential men of the East" should be encouraged to use their connections with Webster to assure his backing.[15]

Webster, as the dominant member of the Cabinet, was the key to administration support. A friend wrote that among his fellow Cabinet members, Webster was like "a father teaching his listening children." But Webster's powers were waning, and he was coming under increasing attack even from his own allies. The major issue was his support of the Fugitive Slave Law, which was bitterly opposed by abolitionists and a growing number of moderate northerners. Then there was the old issue of his friends—the Whig merchants, manufacturers, and lawyers of New York and Massachusetts—providing the funds that supported his gentlemanly lifestyle. Webster had agreed to return to the Senate in 1844 only if a group of Massachusetts businessmen would provide him with an annuity that totaled at least $37,000. When he joined Fillmore's Cabinet, he got a $20,000 payment from a group of forty New York bankers and businessmen, each of whom put up $500.

By 1851 Webster, whose commanding presence was reinforced by his fiery black eyes and his prominent forehead, was a shadow of his former self. His love of the abundant provender of his native land—Maryland oysters, Virginia ham, Maine salmon, Illinois prairie chickens—and his heavy drinking—he was portrayed in one cartoon as "The Great Ornament of the Bar"—were taking their toll. His face was sallow and shrunken, his steps faltering, and his eyes rheumy and bloodshot. The godlike Daniel, in the eyes of both his former friends and his longtime enemies, had become Black Dan. As cirrhosis ate into Webster's liver, Fillmore allowed him to spend more and more time at Marshfield, his estate south of Boston. But when he had to, Webster could still muster his talents. He worked hard at the State Department, when his health permitted, often drafting his own correspondence and researching diplomatic documents from his own library.[16]

It was Fillmore, not Webster, who had set the diplomatic tone of his administration when he declared, "I rejoice in all measures which extend and increase our means of intercourse with foreign

Daguerreotype of Daniel Webster, 1850

countries, and strengthen and enlarge our foreign commerce." The Caribbean and Central America were the immediate focuses of Fillmore and Webster's foreign policy, but the whole thrust of American expansionism to the south was part of a concerted effort to tie the country, East and West, together and to reach beyond to the markets of China and the Pacific. Since the end of the Mexican War, the United States had established Panama as the boulevard to the Pacific. It was the route across which American gold flowed from California, the connecting artery to the West Coast and the untapped markets of the Pacific. George Law's mail steamers called at Chagres from New York, Havana, and New Orleans while William Aspinwall's sailed from the Pacific side of the isthmus for San Francisco and Oregon. Simultaneously Aspinwall was building a railroad into the impenetrable swamps along the Caribbean coast from a new town to be named Aspinwall.[17]

And there were other expansionist initiatives that kept U.S. relations with England, the other major power in the Caribbean, on edge. Nicaragua was "the most delicate and important point in our foreign relations," Webster wrote a friend in February 1851.[18] Both England and the United States were maneuvering for control of Nicaragua's Mosquito Coast, where William Vanderbilt, the illiterate Staten Island ferryman, was building a new cross-isthmus transportation system to rival Howland and Aspinwall's and was talking about building a canal. In Mexico, an American held title to a million acres of land that spanned the Isthmus of Tehuantepec, another site being promoted as possible for a canal and railroad.[19]

Fillmore and Webster were committed to expansionism, but it must be peaceful expansionism. "We instigate no revolutions, nor suffer any hostile military expeditions to be fitted out in the United States to invade the territory or provinces of a friendly nation," said Fillmore in his first address to Congress.[20] Fillmore directed his remarks at the southern Democrats and filibusteros who were actively plotting to launch a private invasion of Cuba to bring it into the union as a slave state. There had already been one invasion attempt, led by a Venezuelan adventurer named Narciso Lopez, and there were rumors of another, which Fillmore and Webster intended to prevent.

Webster's vision ran beyond the Caribbean to China. His merchant friends in New York and Boston controlled the China trade, and his son Fletcher had assisted Caleb Cushing in negotiating the Treaty of Wanghia in 1844 when Webster had served as John Tyler's secretary of state. Moreover, Webster and Fillmore shared the view that the establishment of steamship lines was the best and most peaceful way to advance American commerce into the Pacific. Thus for Perry, Webster's support was decisive when it came to support for a Japan expedition.

In February 1851, Congress was approaching adjournment, and Perry was appalled by the melee of favor seekers forcing themselves upon the government. "Great crowds," he wrote to Delano, "from all parts of the U.S. [are] in this city at present most of them engaged in lobbying for a portion of the public patrimony, schemes for steam mail routes have been proposed, some of them involving vast outlays and not infrequently by men known to be without a cent of means." Some of the schemes were so preposterous, Perry complained, that they called for the government to advance all the money to build new lines.[21]

Perry knew when to speak—and when to remain silent—with regard to mail steamship lines. He had been intimately involved with the government subsidization of the construction of mail steamers in New York's shipyards since 1848, when he was appointed general superintending agent of mail steamers. From then on, he identified personally with the fate of the program. "I feel that my official reputation is largely involved in the success of these lines," he wrote to the secretary of the navy when he accepted his new assignment.[22]

From the start, the subsidization of mail steamship lines had been a volatile issue in the halls of Congress. In time, the government's largesse in backing the construction of the mail steamers had become a politically dangerous issue. Just the year before, the Senate had called for an investigation of the program, and Perry's name had appeared on many of the key documents. More recently, the House Committee on Naval Affairs began backing the subsidization of a mail steamship line from San Francisco to China proposed by a Philadelphia businessman, and the proposal had renewed the fight over subsidies in Congress.[23]

Perry was eager to keep his plans for an expedition to Japan out of the acrimonious debate about subsidizing a new steamship line across the Pacific. Besides if such a line was to be built, Perry had his own connections with William Aspinwall, the man whose company already controlled the steamship line from Panama to the West Coast. In this political climate, Perry, who knew Washington all too well, chose to conceal "the real object of the expedition"— the search for coal and a coal depot for a trans-Pacific steamship line. Instead he carefully selected a more palatable issue—the treatment of American whalemen and the needs of the whaling industry—when he began to outline the reasons for a Japan expedition. Too, there was always the danger that an attack on postal subsidies, which came out of the navy budget, would carry over into a general attack on the navy's funding, thereby threatening the prospects for the Japan expedition.

The original idea of subsidizing steamship lines had been proposed as a solution to two interrelated problems: British domination of the international mail service, and the weakness of the American navy in comparison to the navy of England. In the early 1840s U.S. relations with England became increasingly tense as John Bull and Cousin Jonathan wrangled over control of the Oregon territory, and tempers continued to flare over incidents along the Canadian border. In 1842 reports reached the United States, inaccurate as they turned out, that the British government was going to subsidize the extension of mail steamship service to a number of eastern and southern American ports. This was considered triply threatening: in an emergency, the ships could be converted to warships; England appeared to be planning to extend its near monopoly control of the international mail service to the United States; and British naval officers, who commanded the privately owned mail steamers, could be gathering military intelligence when they brought their ships into American ports.[24]

In response to the rumors, the secretary of the navy recommended the formation of a Home Squadron to supplement the thirty-six commissioned ships that made up the tiny U.S. Navy. (England, in comparison, had eight times as many naval ships and 141 war steamers compared with the United States' 7.)[25] Big navy advocates in Congress wanted more ships, and especially steamships. The problem was that despite the efforts of advocates like Perry of a steam navy, there were doubts about whether steam war vessels represented the navy of the future. The construction of three steam warships had been authorized in 1839. By 1844 only one of them, the *Princeton*, had been built. And it hardly enhanced the reputation of the new navy when a gun blew up during a gathering held aboard the ship for the president, members of Congress, and other prominent Washingtonians, killing six people, including the secretary of state and the secretary of the navy.

In the early 1840s, as the hysteria that surrounded relations between the United States and England subsided, plans to build up the navy languished. Then in 1845 a law was passed without debate that called for subsidization of the mail service by ship, preferably steamship, or railroad. The first contract was awarded to Edward Mills, a New Yorker with little experience in shipping, for a line that would go from New York to Bremerhaven and would be subsidized at the rate of $400,000 a year. The contract was immediately attacked in Congress and the press. Even the administration's own Washington newspaper described Mills and his supporters as "a nest of Wall Street stock-jobbers."[26]

Thomas Butler King of Georgia, chairman of the House Committee on Naval Affairs, saw subsidization as an alternative to a big navy. Under his skillful guidance, a bill was put together in 1847, again with almost no debate, that provided for the construction of four naval steamers and the addition of three more subsidized steamship lines: from New York to Liverpool ($385,000 a year), from New York to New Orleans, Havana, and Chagres, Panama ($230,000 a year), and from Panama to Oregon ($199,000 a year). The Pacific Mail Steamship Company won the contract to take the mails from Panama to Oregon. William Aspinwall was the major investor in the company.

Construction of the steamers for these lines was to be carried out under naval supervision so that they could be converted for

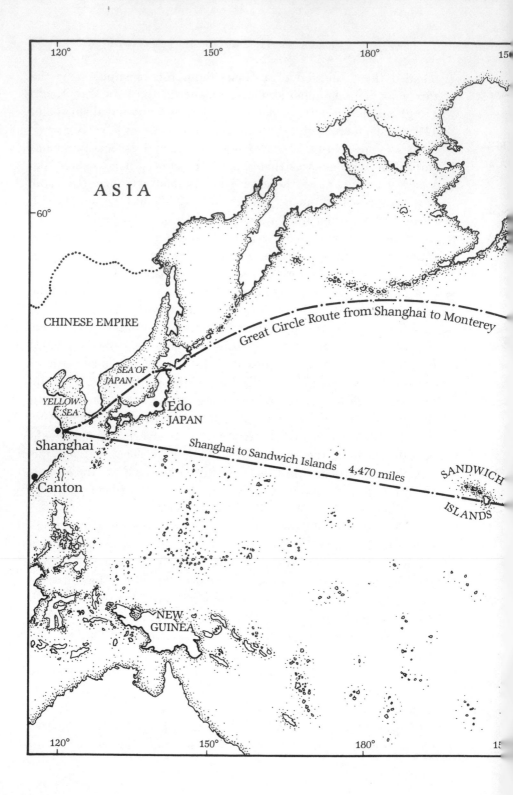

RUSSIAN
AMERICA

120°   90°   60°

60°

NORTH

AMERICA

5,400 miles

Memphis to Monterey
1,500 miles
New York

Monterey

New York to
Panama
2,500 miles

Memphis

New Orleans

30°

Monterey to Panama
3,000 miles

GULF OF
MEXICO

WEST INDIES

Panama to Sandwich Islands   4,780 miles

Shanghai to Panama   9,250 miles

New Orleans to Panama
1,600 miles

PANAMA

SOUTH

0°

THE GREAT CIRCLE ROUTE
TO JAPAN

AFTER CHART PREPARED BY
LIEUTENANT M. F. MAURY, U.S.N.,
MAY 1848

AMERICA

120°   90°

war use in the event of an emergency. King claimed that "no government has hitherto ever had presented for its acceptance a system so cheap and efficient as that now under construction. In time of peace it will aid in promoting the commercial intercourse and prosperity of the country, and in time of war form a most powerful offensive force or defensive force."[27]

The new mail steamship lines were intimately linked in the minds of merchants and advocates of a bigger navy to American expansion into the Pacific. And in this context the strategic location of Japan again came into focus. In 1848, a year after the funding of the first four steamship lines, Congressman King called for a fifth line to run from California to China. Lieutenant Matthew Maury, the navy's famed oceanographer, had suggested a very simple but at that time startling idea to King's House Committee on Naval Affairs. Placing one end of a piece of string on the Monterey-San Francisco area of a globe, he traced a great circle route through the northern Pacific. Maury concluded that it was a journey of 10,950 miles if one traveled from New York to Shanghai via Panama, San Francisco, and the northern Pacific via a great circle route. The same voyage via the Cape of Good Hope was approximately 18,000 to 20,000 miles. If a steamer averaged ten knots, this meant that it would take a little over forty-five days to get from New York to Shanghai via the northern Pacific great circle route, a remarkable feat at a time when the fastest clipper ship could only make the trip in eighty plus days.[28]

The implications of this simple exercise for the global commercial competition between the United States and England were staggering, King suggested. Since it took the British overland mail sixty-five days to reach Canton from London, the United States had "it in our power ultimately to establish and control the most rapid means of communication with all India as well as China." This was particularly true if the United States abandoned the idea of building a canal across one of the three locations then being considered in Mexico and Central America, and instead built a railroad from Memphis to the West Coast. King's committee concluded that time is money, and the United States by establishing the quickest lines of communication with the Orient "could break up the old thoroughfares and channels of commerce through the

Pacific, and turn them through the United States."[29] The United States was bidding for no less a prize than the commercial domination of the Pacific. American steamers following Maury's great circle would have to pass by Japan on their way to Shanghai, and Japan, it was noted, could be a source of coal for the steamers.

The plans to use the tax dollar to establish American steamship lines was a tremendous coup for New York City, which was locked in an intense rivalry with a fast-closing Boston for commercial leadership of the nation. The Naval Affairs Committee's promise to make New York "the great settling house of the world" was a bit premature. But New York had drawn together into its own grasp all the strands of a new communications system that stretched from Europe to the Oregon territory. Ahead, as King had pointed out, lay the problem of spanning the Pacific and bringing it under American influence. For his efforts, King was feted at the Astor House in New York at an appropriately lavish banquet given by New York's business elite. And for Captain Perry, 1848 marked the beginning of a new assignment that would soon ally him closely with the plans of the city's leading shipbuilders and merchant houses.

Despite King's claim that the subsidized steamship lines would be cheap and efficient, the contractors were back in Washington in the summer of 1848 asking for additional funds before the first ship was even off the ways. The steamers had turned out to be more costly than they originally estimated, and the contractors were seeking advances against their annual subsidies so that they could complete construction on the vessels.

When the contractors asked for a $25,000-a-month advance for each steamer, to be paid between the time of launching and completion of the vessels, their request was attacked bitterly in the House. Ultimately, the advocates of an additional subsidy prevailed, although in the House by only one vote. Meanwhile, the Pacific Mail Steamship Company was launching its three steamers. These steamers fit the terms of their contracts more accurately than their expensive counterparts. Thus Perry approved them, with only minor reservations about their engines and boilers, and the first steamer, the *California*, sailed for the Pacific in October 1848.[30]

Howland and Aspinwall may have been the wealthiest New

York merchant house, but members of the business community were puzzled by their involvement in the mail steamship business. True, they were active in both the South American and China trade. Howland and Aspinwall had, in fact, built the famed clipper ship *Sea Witch*, which sailed from New York to Hong Kong in 104 days and then returned, Canton to New York, in 81 days, moving at a faster pace than any existing steamship. But in 1847 when William Aspinwall and his partners bought the contract for the Pacific Coast mail line from speculators, there was little money to be made along the West Coast. California did have deep and impressive harbors in San Diego and San Francisco, but these cities of the future were little more than clusters of shacks and humble adobes built near decaying missions. The Oregon territory was if anything an even more rudimentary community.

This situation was to change dramatically almost overnight. The month before the *California* sailed, a navy officer arrived in Washington with 230 ounces of gold in a tea caddy. Gold had been discovered in California in April, and now word had reached the East Coast. In a desperate frenzy, gold seekers headed for the West Coast, taking with them one of Perry's sons. When the *California* reached the Pacific Coast of Panama after a voyage marred by recurrent breakdowns, it was swamped by 726 frantic passengers angrily vying for the ship's 250 berths. After forcing 17 Peruvians, who had been picked up in Callao, out of their cabins into makeshift berths, 365 argonauts crowded aboard the *California*. Arriving in San Francisco, the ship was abandoned by passengers and crew alike, leaving only the captain and an engine room boy. Meanwhile back in New York, Howland and Aspinwall's business associates were puzzled. Were these powerful merchants clairvoyant, lucky, or privy to some secret source of information about the gold strike?[31]

With the hothouse growth of the California economy and the United States' bid for domination of the China carrying trade, the question of a subsidized steamship line from San Francisco to Shanghai naturally enough surfaced once again while Perry was in Washington in February 1851 planning the Japan expedition. Before the news of gold in California reached Washington, Congressman King's vision of America straddling the Pacific seemed chimerical. Now it seemed imperative.

The year before, Perry's name had come up frequently in a Senate investigation of the mail subsidies. The investigation was triggered by reports of lavish expenditures with public funds and of continued delays in the construction of a number of the steamers in New York, despite the advance of government funds. The Collins Line's *Arctic*, for example, was to be built for the New York to

Howland and Aspinwall's U.S. mailship *California*

Liverpool run for less than $500,000 and was to be completed by 1849. The *Arctic*, launched in late 1850, was the epitome of ocean-going luxury and ended up costing $700,000. The ship boasted ornamental woodwork of satinwood, rosewood, and white holly, a number of staterooms with double beds, French bedsteads, and ornate curtains, a ladies' salon with a carved and gilded ceiling, walls of highly polished precious woods, numerous mirrors and luxurious furnishings, and a grand saloon with stained glass, silver plate, costly carpets, and marble center tables.[32]

The mail steamships, despite Congressman King's claim, were turning out to be neither cheap nor efficient. Nor in the opinion of the secretary of the navy and a number of naval inspectors working under Perry were they contributing to the strengthening of the U.S. Navy. William Ballard Preston, Zachary Taylor's secretary of the navy, was so exasperated with the mail steamship scheme

that he had fired a broadside against the project in his first annual
report. Preston denounced the mail steamer scheme as "entirely
subversive of the object which it intends to promote" and "fraught
with incalculable mischief to the navy, and involving immense expenditures of public money." While arguing that mail steamers
should be built by private enterprise, Preston preferred a steam
navy built solely for military purposes.[33]

And where did Perry stand with regard to a project that he
had once described as reflecting upon his "official reputation"?
Though generally enthusiastic about the new steamers that were
built under his supervision and supportive of their challenge to
their British competitors, Perry offered a wide variety of opinions
about the convertibility and cost of conversion of the mail steamers.
In his first year on the job, he routinely reported that the ships he
inspected could be "easily converted into war vessels," although he
noted that they did not conform to every particular of the contracts.
The next year he informed the Navy Department that "the form
and dimensions best adapted to a war steamer would not be the
most suitable for a commercial vessel" and that "the cost of converting them to war purposes would be large, and in no respect
would they be as economical." At that time Perry hazarded the
opinion that the construction of these steamers should not "interfere
with the organization and gradual increase of an efficient and permanent steam navy." But then when the department ordered him
to respond to the Senate call for an investigation, he reported that
"considerable alteration would be required" for conversion, although "without any great disbursement of money."[34]

Nothing came of the 1850 investigation of the mail contracts
because, soon after the investigation, President Taylor died. His
Cabinet, including the combative Secretary of the Navy Preston,
resigned, and William Graham succeeded Preston. Graham, it
turned out, was much more amenable to the demands of the steamship company owners. He was also a backer of expanded steamship
service in the Pacific, both through a new line across the Pacific
and expanded service from Panama to the West Coast. In early
March 1851, while Perry was still in Washington, Congress appropriated $874,000 for the mail steamship lines. The funding provided
for expanded service from Panama to the West Coast, for which

Aspinwall and the Pacific Mail Steamship Company would receive an additional $149,250 a year.[35] The mail steamship subsidies (and Perry) had survived their first serious challenge, and though bloodied in congressional infighting, both had come out better than winners.

Perry knew the difference between a mail steamer, built in a private shipyard for commercial use, and a war steamer, built in a naval shipyard for combat. After all he was a passionate supporter of a steam navy made up of vessels constructed solely for military purposes. But since it was impossible to secure funding for a real steam navy, for now the idea of converting mail steamers to war vessels would have to do. Perry was also aware of the danger to his own reputation that lingered around the edges of the mail steamship controversy because, as he once wrote Preston, "of the extensive interests involved, public as well as private."[36] For this reason he was careful, despite his own doubts about the mail steamers' convertibility, to keep his name from being associated with his fellow officers' criticisms of the mail steamship system. Both his professional reputation *and* the future of the Japan expedition depended on his connections with what he had described as "influential men of the East," that is, the New York merchants, steamship company owners, shipbuilders, and their congressional backers. His relations with this powerful clique could at any moment embroil him in the controversy over more mail lines that still festered quietly in Washington. Perry's connections with these "extensive interests" were also the key to getting support among the northeastern business and political elite for the Japan expedition.

Besides, Perry and the Japan expedition faced an even more serious challenge as Congress adjourned in early March. In line with Secretary Graham's recommendation, Congress had appropriated $8.1 million for the navy, a million-plus dollars *less* than the year before. In asking for this sum, Graham had made brave statements about the nation arriving at the beginning of a new era with the country's expansion to the Pacific. He had asked for the appointment of two rear admirals, one to command a naval force based on the California coast that would encourage and protect American whalers and other commercial shipping. He had noted that the American merchant marine, with three million tons of shipping and an estimated 180,000 seamen, was the largest in the world. Recognizing that a big navy lacked political support, he left it up to some future statesman to decide the appropriate size of the navy that was required to protect this huge merchant marine. Instead, in a decided anticlimax to what had sounded like a clarion call for a big navy, he recommended that the navy "need not be immediately augmented in any great degree." And then in an afterthought, Graham concluded that war steamers would serve as valuable auxiliaries, but would not replace sailing vessels in the navy as ships of war.[37]

As former Secretary of the Navy Preston had feared, naval funding was under attack because of the mail steamship subsidies. "The war and naval establishments are two principal sources of unnecessary and extravagant expenditures," proclaimed Democratic Congressman George W. Jones during an acrimonious exchange in February over Graham's call for increased subsidies for existing mail lines and the House Naval Committee's backing of a Philadelphia businessman's request for a five-million-dollar loan to build ten new mail steamers, six of which would run between San Francisco and China. They demonstrated, said Jones, that the "Whig Party is true to its instincts, extravagance and profligacy in squandering the public money."[38] Jones chose to ignore the fact that Graham had called for a reduced appropriation for the navy. The Democrats controlled both houses of Congress, and in this situation any proposal for increased expenditures was fair game in the attempt to brand the Whigs as the party of big spenders.

Graham's indecisive support for the navy left Perry confused about the administration's commitment to the Japan expedition. A week after Congress adjourned, he wrote Delano that he was afraid the reduced appropriation would mean that it was impossible to spare the ships needed for the expedition. Further, he could not even, as he put it, have "a definitive conversation" with Secretary Graham because Graham was at home with a cold. A further aggravation was Perry's inability to get Mercator Cooper's account of his trip to Japan published in the Washington newspapers because they were so crowded with reports about the end of the congressional session.

Nevertheless, Perry remained hopeful about the expedition.

He was pleased that his proposal had been brought before the government through Webster's good offices and trusted "that those who have taken interest in the project will not relax their efforts to bring about the measure."[39] In March, Perry was ordered back to New York to inspect a new mail steamer. Back at work, he wrote Delano that he had found a favorable disposition in Washington toward the expedition, although he was still worried about the naval appropriation and "the peculiar political character" of the expedition. He also returned Mercator Cooper's report, having given up his effort to get it published, since he now preferred to keep the expedition a secret until it became clear whether the government backed it or not.[40]

After Perry left Washington, momentum continued to build slowly for a Japan expedition but with less involvement of Perry and on a much smaller scale than he had proposed. Perry knew that there had been a discussion at the Cabinet level about an expedition, but he appears not to have known that Webster had sent a request to the Dutch for maps of Japanese waters and later made an inquiry about Japanese policy toward foreigners. At the end of April, the Dutch ambassador replied, explaining that foreign ships were excluded from Japan, but that in 1842 the Japanese had decided to provide supplies for shipwrecked vessels or ships that came into their ports asking for provisions. At the same time the Japanese had asked the Dutch to "inform the other powers that the above mentioned resolution does not infringe upon, or otherwise imply any modification whatever of the system of separation and exclusion which was adopted more than two centuries ago by the Japanese government."[41]

The Dutch report explained why the *Morrison* had been fired upon in 1837, while Commodore Biddle and Mercator Cooper had not. Webster also received a communication from China at about the same time reporting that three more American whalemen had been taken from Nagasaki to Batavia aboard a Dutch ship. It was reported that the sailors were treated well by the Japanese, but that one of them had fallen overboard on a voyage in Japan and drowned. His body was preserved in salt and taken to the Dutch graveyard in Nagasaki for burial.[42]

Perry's efforts had stirred enough interest in the Fillmore

administration that when another opportunity presented itself, Webster seized upon it immediately. Again shipwrecked sailors were to be the unwitting diplomatic couriers. Another group of Japanese sailors had been picked up and taken to San Francisco by an American vessel. In early May, Captain J. H. Aulick, who was about to depart for China to become commander of the East India Squadron, suggested that he could return the sailors to Japan and use the opportunity to press the Japanese to open commercial relations.[43]

Webster moved quickly. Within a month he instructed Aulick to go to Edo to negotiate a treaty of amity and commerce with the Japanese. "The moment is near," Webster wrote in his instructions to Aulick, tapping a ready supply of fulsome rhetoric, "when the last link in the chain of oceanic steam navigation is to be formed." It was the president's opinion, he went on, that steps should be taken to establish a steamship line from San Francisco to China. For this reason, the United States wanted to buy, "not the manufactures of his [the Emperor's] artisans, or the results of the toil of his husbandmen, but a gift of Providence, deposited, by the Creator of all things, in the depths of the Japanese islands for the benefit of the human family." In short, American merchants— Webster's friends, the Whig merchants—wanted to buy coal, Japan's gift from God. No less than "the interests of commerce, and even those of humanity" demanded that the Japanese sell coal to the Americans. One of the eastern ports of Japan would be the best place to procure this heavenly gift, but if the Japanese were resistant, they could arrange to ship it to an offshore island. Despite his protestations earlier in the same instructions that the United States was only interested in coal, Webster ordered Aulick to seek a commercial treaty as well as an agreement that would protect shipwrecked American sailors.[44]

Aulick was further armed with a letter from President Fillmore, another remarkable diplomatic document, addressed to "HIS IMPERIAL MAJESTY THE EMPEROR OF JAPAN, Great and Good Friend." Aulick, Fillmore explained, was not a missionary. He was being sent to promote friendship and commerce. The United States now stretched from sea to sea. And from California and Oregon, which were rich in gold, silver, and precious stones (a striking invention), "our steamers can reach the shores of your happy land in less than twenty days." More and more ships every year would be passing Japan on their way to China. These ships needed coal and a harbor where they could purchase it. "Let us consider well what new interests arise from these recent events which have brought our two countries so near together," Fillmore concluded, "and what purposes of friendship, amity, and intercourse, they ought to inspire in the breasts of those who govern both countries."[45]

On June 8, 1851, Aulick departed in the new steam frigate *Susquehanna* with orders to proceed to China to pick up the ship-wrecked Japanese sailors. In his wake, Aulick left Commander Glynn, the rescuer of Ranald MacDonald and the men from the *Lagoda*, still promoting himself as a candidate for commander of the Japan expedition. Glynn wrote to President Fillmore just two days after Aulick's departure, indicating that he had spoken personally with the president about an expedition. His letter once again presented what were becoming the standard arguments for seeking a treaty with the Japanese.

Although Aulick made it to China by the fall of 1851, he had less luck than the hapless Glynn. Aulick had been in East Asian waters only a short time before he was ordered to hand over temporary command of his squadron to Captain Franklin Buchanan. Aulick, to his amazement, was being charged with a number of irregularities: to wit, he had taken his son aboard his ship as a passenger without permission and he had fraudulently claimed to have taken a Brazilian diplomat to Rio de Janeiro at his own (Aulick's) expense. Aulick, it turned out later, was the target of a vicious campaign of gossip. But for now, despondent and in ill health, he was ordered to remain in Macao to await his successor.[46]

While Aulick was on his way to China, Perry continued to shuttle back and forth between New York and Washington in connection with his job supervising the construction of mail steamers. His mind, however, was on the future. Though he was still involved in planning a Japan expedition and often wrote of it in proprietary terms, his real desire was to command the Mediterranean Squadron. William Sinclair, a longtime friend, served as Perry's eyes and ears in the Navy Department. Perry could count on him to report on the department's inner workings and perhaps even to put in a good word for him from time to time. Perry wanted to command the Mediterranean Squadron, he explained to Sinclair in May, so that he could be near his family. His son-in-law August Belmont was planning to lead a large family outing to Europe the next winter. Perry was hoping to be stationed nearby so that he could spend time with them. If his family was not going to be in Europe, he confided in Sinclair, he would prefer not to go to sea again "under the present state of discipline in the Navy." Flogging had been abolished in 1850, and many an old line officer, like Perry, had opposed this reform as a threat to discipline aboard ships.[47]

Perry received nothing more than a polite acknowledgment from Secretary Graham that he would give "attention and respectful consideration" to his application. In October Perry again wrote to Sinclair, this time with a sense of urgency about the Mediterranean Squadron. Belmont's plans to go to Europe were "now so far advanced as to make it desirable for me to make some arrangements as to my whereabouts during the ensuing winter." Sinclair's response was discouraging. Perry was not even being considered for command of the Mediterranean Squadron.[48]

Instead Perry was in for a rude awakening. On November eighteenth, the same day that Graham sent out the order relieving Aulick of his command, the secretary ordered Perry to Washington. Perry was to be the new leader of the Japan expedition. Perry hurried to the capital by train, going directly on the evening of his arrival to Graham's house on H Street. But to Perry's annoyance Graham was so preoccupied with preparing his annual report for the opening of Congress that he had little time to discuss Perry's new assignment with him. Perry did manage to extract a promise from Graham. If the department did not plan to increase the size of the squadron, Graham would send Perry to the Mediterranean. When he returned to his home in North Tarrytown, he wrote Graham to remind him of his promise. His new assignment was "a serious disappointment, and cause of personal inconvenience," Perry wrote. He had been led to believe, he said not entirely accurately, since Sinclair had warned him that he would not get the appointment, that he would get the Mediterranean command. For this reason he had made unspecified arrangements (probably to meet his family in Europe). Against his wishes, Perry had returned to the Japan expedition.

Perry now turned his "strong disinclination to go out as the mere relief or successor to Commodore Aulick" into a carefully worded effort to rearrange his new command to his liking. The problem with merely succeeding Aulick, he explained to Graham, was in not being charged with "some more important service" and provided with "a force competent to [carry out] a possible successful issue [of] the expectations of the government." He would prefer the Mediterranean Squadron. His rank and command experience meant that he merited it—unless "the sphere of action of the East India Squadron and its force be so much enlarged as to hold out a well-grounded hope of its conferring distinction upon its commander."

With his letter, Perry sent some new notes on the expedition. He also referred Graham to the private letter he had written eleven months earlier, the letter in which he described his Ireland-England strategy of seizing Ezo (Hokkaido) to force Japan to open diplomatic relations. The times were propitious, his notes read. It would be a matter of direct expediency for the United States to take the lead in bringing Japan "into friendly and reciprocal intercourse with the nations of the world, and to anticipate, a result inevitable in itself and consequent upon the extraordinary progress of the times." The expedition would certainly be an experiment. But Perry was confident, whether it succeeded or not, that "it would have the good wishes of the entire community, and especially would be advocated and sustained as I have good reason to know by the commercial classes."

The expedition should be strictly naval and should include at least three first-class steamers of war, one or two sloops of war, and one fast-sailing and well-armed supply ship. The least that could be expected as a result was to open one or two ports for supplies and repairs and as a stopover on the way to Shanghai. He reminded Graham that the squadron would "render essential service" to the whaling fleet by an exhibition of force near what had become "the favourite and most profitable resort of our whaling ships." Finally he suggested that "any direct proposition according to established rules of diplomacy would be a failure." Instead he preferred to follow a course that the Japanese would not be prepared for, one that employed kindness and forbearance but disregarded "many of their absurd marine and municipal distinctions."[49]

Once reconciled to his new assignment, Perry wasted no time in getting in touch with Joseph Delano. Perry began feeding information that Delano was collecting about whaling to Secretary Graham, including reports of more American whalemen shipwrecked in Japan.[50] Webster might have trumpeted the goal of a Japan expedition as a step in establishing a steamship line between San Francisco and China, but Perry was sticking to whaling for his public explanation.

Ordered to Washington in January 1852, Perry threw himself with enthusiasm into organizing the expedition. In Washington, Graham made an effort to provide Perry with the number of ships he wanted. He also allowed Perry to choose his officers, spend a reasonable amount of money, and basically control the destiny of the expedition. Perry continued to insist on secrecy. So Graham said nothing about the expedition in his annual report to Congress submitted in November 1851. He only mentioned that dispatching the brand-new war steamer *Susquehanna* to East Asia under Aulick earlier in the year was an effort to create "a favourable impression for our interests and commerce . . . in the peculiar countries of the East."[51] As Perry contacted more and more officers about his plans, word began to leak out that something major was afoot in relation to East Asia. Why else was such a large squadron being assembled? Besides worrying about a political backlash, there was the problem of rival diplomatic missions. England, France, and Russia were rumored to be dispatching squadrons to Japan. Hence Perry's urgency to get under way and reach Japan first.

The expanded East Asia squadron was being put together around the steamer *Mississippi*. One of the oldest steamers still in service, the *Mississippi* had served as Perry's flagship in Mexico and had the reputation of being one of the most dependable steamers ever built. The *Susquehanna*, another steamer, was already in East Asian waters. A third steamer, the *Princeton*, was initially assigned to the squadron, although it was still in the Boston Navy Yard being rebuilt. Later Graham promised Perry the newly commissioned steamer *Powhatan* and the rebuilt steamer *Alleghany*. For sailing ships, Perry at first was promised the sloops of war *Plymouth* and *Saratoga*, which were already on their way to the East Asian station. Later Graham added the ship of the line *Vermont*. All in all, it was shaping up to be the largest squadron ever assembled in peacetime.[52]

To command his vessels, Perry turned to the officers who served under him during the Mexican War, men he described as "the old Gulfers." He asked Captain S. S. McCluney to command the *Princeton* and Sidney S. Lee the *Mississippi*. Perry retained Captain Franklin Buchanan, the first superintendent of the U.S. Naval Academy, who was already serving in China as temporary head of the East Asia squadron since Aulick had been relieved, as commander of the *Susquehanna*. John Kelly commanded the *Plymouth* and W. S. Walker the *Saratoga*. He advised those officers who were still selecting their crews to recruit mostly landsmen and boys. Since flogging had been abolished, they would have to depend on "moral suasion," and he was worried about how the more experienced (and hardened) sailors would respond to less rigorous discipline.[53]

In January, Perry was anticipating that the squadron would depart sometime in March. But he was overly optimistic. For one thing, his own conception of the expedition was becoming increasingly ambitious. Perry's intellectual interests were wide ranging. Thus, it is little wonder that under his guidance the expedition began to develop into something considerably beyond his and numerous others' original conception of a purely diplomatic expedition. Perry wanted not only to open the ports of Japan but also to study all aspects of Japanese history, natural history, and geography and to record as much as he could about this strange country.

At first Perry attempted to get Congress to back a major scientific expedition, but when the funds were not forthcoming, Perry began hiring artists and scientists as acting master's mates at a pay of twenty-five dollars a month. For Perry, the stern disciplinarian, this arrangement had the added virtue of making them "amenable to Naval law."[54] It would also head off the possibility of conflicts

PRINCETON. VERMONT. ALLEGHANY. ST. MARY'S. MACEDON

A SUPERB VIEW OF THE UNITED STATES JAPANESE SQUADRON,

VANDALIA.   PLYMOUTH.   SARATOGA.   MISSISSIPPI, [FLAG SHIP.]   SUSQUEHANNA.   POWHATAN.
UNDER COMMAND OF COMMODORE PERRY, BOUND FOR THE EAST.

Naval ships promised to Commodore Perry

between naval officers and civilians, which had disrupted other expeditions. In this way Perry hired two artists: Peter Bernard Wilhelm Heine, a twenty-five-year-old German who had been in the United States for only three years, and Eliphalet Brown, Jr., a New York daguerreotyper and engraver. From the navy Perry selected the Reverend George Jones as his flag chaplain, probably because of Jones's additional expertise in geology and astronomy. Perry added a French chef for diplomatic banquets and an Italian bandmaster to handle musical affairs. The State Department contributed an agronomist, a young South Carolina physician named Dr. James Morrow, and sent him to Hong Kong without consulting Perry. Perry would fill out the ranks of shipboard intellectuals when the squadron reached China.

To prepare himself for the expedition, Perry turned to Mercator Cooper and the whaling captains introduced to Perry by Joseph Delano for firsthand information about the seas around Japan and the approach to Edo Bay. For some reason, Perry never got a look at the detailed chart of Edo Bay that Cooper recovered from the hulk of the junk from which he rescued eleven Japanese sailors. Instead Perry acquired a set of charts from Holland for thirty thousand dollars, including some brought from Japan by Philipp Franz von Siebold, the German naturalist and physician who was attached to the Dutch factory in Nagasaki in the 1820s. Von Siebold wanted to join the expedition, but Perry turned him down because he suspected he was a Russian spy. Von Siebold was a controversial figure in Japan, where he had illegally gotten hold of a map from a Japanese astronomer. Accused there also of being a Russian spy, von Siebold was imprisoned by the Japanese and later banished. As for the poor Japanese astronomer, after he died in prison, his body was pickled and sent to Edo, where his corpse was then decapitated.[55]

Besides reading von Siebold's massive work on Japan based on his stay at Deshima and a trip with a Dutch delegation to the shogun's court in Edo, Perry pored over the other available published works. A number of these were written by Europeans who had been to Nagasaki, but none of them was more current than von Siebold's thirty-year-old account. These included Engelbert Kaempfer's *The History of Japan*, written by another German physician who resided at the Dutch factory in the late seventeenth century and traveled to Edo with a Dutch delegation. He also read the Russian naval captain Vasilii Golownin's narrative of the three years he spent in captivity in Hokkaido early in the nineteenth century. Even astute observers like Kaempfer and von Siebold were limited in their knowledge of Japan by the reluctance of their Japanese sources at Nagasaki and their restricted view of the country, a view framed by the shuttered windows of their palanquins as they were carried along the highway to visit the shogun in Edo. Some of these accounts, bowdlerized and pirated, began to appear in English translation as rumors of an American expedition sparked a minor publishing boom and led to a spate of magazine and newspaper stories both in the United States and England.[56]

The accuracy and details of these accounts varied widely. Most agreed that Japan had two emperors, one religious, the other secular, that the country was feudal in makeup, dictatorial in practice, closed to foreigners, hostile to the practice of Christianity, and that the Japanese were superior to the frequently maligned Chinese. Beyond these basic facts, the accounts became increasingly fantastical.

Soon after the public first heard of the Japan expedition, in April 1852, Washington's Whig newspaper, the *National Intelligencer*, carried a letter from W. D. Porter describing the history of Japan in terms of an ongoing (and fictional) conflict between Dearios and Cubos that began in 1142. Presently Japan was ruled by the Dearios, a caste of military officers. Japan's largest city was Meaco on an island in a lake in the middle of Niphon. Meaco, with a population of 592,000, was graced by numerous universities, colleges, and temples. In Edo the emperor's castle was originally covered with gilt tiles. And in Nagasaki, a naval depot, naval vessels, for which the Japanese had not yet found a use, were stored away for emergencies. In the nursery the first thing children were taught was "the art and grace of suicide." As a result they played at stabbing themselves with their fingers and falling over dead. "The lover cuts out his intestines before his obdurate mistress," Porter went on, "and the latter pours out her heart's blood in the face of her faithless lover, the criminal executes himself; and, in fact, the whole nation, from early youth, revels in the luxury of suicide." In the interior of Japan, Porter explained, there was a large valley called the Valley of Upas filled with carbonic gas. "It is covered with the skeletons of numerous wild and tame beasts and birds. The Emperor, it is said, often sent criminals to the valley to bring away a precious gem of inestimable value, and the bones of men also whiten its deadly sides." The Japanese, Porter concluded, were "alive to commercial feeling." Direct trade, he estimated, would increase commerce by two hundred million dollars a year.[57]

As March 1852 approached, it became increasingly clear that Perry was nowhere near getting the expedition under way. The *Princeton* was still under construction in Boston. Once completed she had to be towed to Baltimore to be fitted with new engines. Meanwhile Perry continued with his preparations. He asked Delano about the possibility of getting whaling ships to haul coal for the steamers to Hawaii or another island near to Japan. He also asked Delano if he knew the whereabouts of a group of shipwrecked Japanese sailors that were reported living in Hawaii. He wanted to take them with him.[58]

With time on his hands, Perry traveled from Albany to Boston to New Bedford to Providence, collecting what he described to the Navy Department as "specimens of manufacturing and mechanical production, curious arms, statistical, and other documents." The department approved of Perry's actions, but Graham warned him that he was not to spend public moneys on this collection. Perry was determined to present the Japanese with "practical evidence of the wonderful development of this country, which will go far to convince them of the fact that sooner or later they must give away to the tide of circumstances and influences which has already begun to serve against the permanency of their absurd and exclusive institutions." Perry viewed the presentation of gifts as part of a larger commercial strategy. "Experience and the history of commerce has shown," he wrote, "that the introduction among uncivilized and half-civilized people of commodities (in quantities however small) whether of usefulness or ornament, has invariably begotten a desire to obtain larger supplies, and thus the consumption of American products in the East has increased in a very extraordinary degree."

To whet the appetites of the Japanese he procured a case of Colt arms, a daguerreotype camera, a telegraph, clocks, stoves, farm implements, two folios of James Audubon's *Birds of America* and *Quadrupeds of America*, and a quarter-size steam locomotive with tender, cars, and track. The government eventually agreed to pay for these gifts.[59]

With Perry traveling about the country talking with more and more people about the expedition, it was inevitable, no matter how much he insisted on secrecy, that word would get out about his plans. Information began to escape in bits in pieces. In early March there was a rerun of Congress's 1850 call for information about what was happening with Japan. Again the documents relating to Captain Glynn and the *Lagoda* incident were sent to the Senate, this time with a copy of Webster's order to Aulick for the aborted expedition of the year before—the God's gift of coal letter—and Fillmore's seriocomic letter to His Great and Good Friend The Emperor.[60]

The administration, however, made no mention of further plans for an expedition. That would come at the end of the month when Frank Stanton, chairman of the House Naval Affairs Committee, made a chance remark about the expedition on the House floor. In lieu of the abolition of flogging, he was urging his colleagues to pass a new code of discipline for the navy before the Japan expedition left for East Asia. Then the press got into the act. The *Morning Courier and New York Enquirer*, owned by Perry's friend and neighbor James Watson Webb, made some references to the expedition. Meanwhile in Boston, *Our Country*, a paper closely aligned with Daniel Webster, announced that the expedition was being "heralded to the world as a great national movement . . . one of the most important ever undertaken by our Government." In an article that accurately listed the ships assigned to the squadron, the paper went on to say that the expedition reflected great credit on its originators, "especially on the distinguished Secretary of State," who was known for his "sagacious measures of diplomacy."[61] It was Perry, of course, who had planted the idea of the expedition in Webster's fertile but well-pickled brain, but he knew the ways of politicians and said nothing about Webster's supporters' attempt to steal the limelight for him.

The day after Stanton's chance remark, Solon Borland, a Democrat from Arkansas, rose in the Senate to ask, "What expedition?" He offered a resolution calling on the president to inform the Senate about the object of the expedition. Borland, a frequent critic of the administration particularly over the issue of mail subsidies, was insistent, since he had understood Stanton to say that the expedition was either under way or about to leave. Little did anyone know about Perry's problems.[62]

There followed a week-long wrangle in the Senate during which Borland attempted to land a few body blows on the Whigs in general and Daniel Webster in particular. The more carefully he aimed his punches, the more Borland insisted that he did not object to the expedition. He did not suspect the administration of doing anything wrong. He wasn't attributing bad motives. But . . . wasn't the administration practicing a kind of secret diplomacy more suitable to the monarchs of Europe? Didn't the Senate have a right to know the particulars of an expedition for which they had to pay the bill? Just what was the size of the force that the administration was thinking of sending to Japan?

Ultimately Borland tried to tar the Whigs with the brush of interventionism. Borland was amazed that the party which had opposed the Mexican War and the recent filibustering campaign against Cuba in the name of nonintervention was now proposing to "interfere directly, by force and arms, if necessary, in the affairs of a nation with which we are not only at peace, and with which we know of no cause of quarrel, but with whom we have no relations at all." The Whigs, Borland charged, were willing to toy with the possibility of a war in Asia. And as for Webster, Borland was compelled to mention his presidential ambitions and that he had obviously prevailed upon his chosen instrument, *Our Country*, "to shadow forth, rather dimly to the public, to be sure, some great project to be undertaken." In short, Webster had leaked the plan to the press to bolster his chances for the Whig nomination later in the year.[63]

Other comments were in a lighter vein. The explanation for the expedition was quite simple, said John Hale, the New Hampshire Whig who had led the fight to abolish flogging and the grog ration: the country was burdened with a bloated naval officers corps that cost about $800,000 a month but had nothing to do. The expedition was "simply a means of employing some of the ships and some of the men, and of expending some of the millions [sic] that are appropriated daily for the Navy." Would the Japan expedition be like an earlier expedition to determine the border between the United States and Mexico, asked Senator Thomas Rusk of Texas, an expedition which he described as having sent "an immense amount of bugs and lizards, and animals of that sort, to be transported here at the expense of the Government, for which we have already been asked to pay $80,000."[64]

While other senators noted that they too knew nothing about the expedition, and some said they really did not care, a handful of Whigs and Democrats defended the administration's secrecy, warning that public notice—already given in the press, of course—might alert the country's commercial rivals, especially a certain European nation (undoubtedly England). Only New York's William Seward, a fellow Whig but a bitter rival of Fillmore's, tried to put the expedition in some kind of strategic context. Little wonder, since the red-haired, bandy-legged Seward was known for his close ties to Minturn and Grinnell, along with Howland and Aspinwall, the preeminent New York merchant firm with a stake in the China trade. For two hundred years, the European powers had employed commercial treaties, naval expeditions, and armed power to parcel out and control the commerce of Asia. Only Japan had escaped from their monopoly of trade. Now that the United States had reached the Pacific, the only appropriate question was, said Seward, "Why have not the United States before sent an expedition to the East?"[65]

In the end, the supporters of the expedition prevailed. Over Borland's objection, but with his consent, his resolution was laid aside. It was decided instead to request information from the administration in executive session.[66] The issue of the Japan expedition had been aired publicly, and rancorously, for the first and last time, and despite a few political shots directed at the Whigs, the Senate had expressed a general sense of support for the expedition as one of the most important ever undertaken.

Perry did not fare as well, however, when the mail subsidy issue was raised once again in Congress during a phenomenally complex debate that raged in both houses during the spring and early summer. When the Fillmore administration backed an increased subsidy for the New York to Liverpool line, there were charges of swindle, government support for a monopoly at the expense of private enterprise, and that the needs of the rest of the country were being ignored while Collins was involved in an effort to beat "John Bull in a boat race across the Atlantic." The issue of convertibility to war steamers was raised again. And Perry was dragged into the debate when the Senate's call for all information about the contracts produced a number of letters that Perry had written about the convertibility of the mail steamers. Perry had " 'ridden both sides of the sapling' at the same time," a critic of the subsidies charged while suggesting that Perry was not a credible witness on the issue. Finally, Anglophobia, the most effective argument in the arsenal of the supporters of mail subsidies, plus what one senator described as "the most powerful and determined outside pressure I have ever seen brought to bear upon any legislative body," prevailed. Texas Congressman W. H. Polk, the former president's brother, accused the critics of mail subsidies of anti-American pandering to British interests, of bowing to the power that had attacked Americans at Lexington and Bunker Hill, of begging the English, "Good mother, won't you carry our mails for us?"[67] The navy again had come under attack for participating in the mail scheme as had Perry, but the expedition remained unscathed.

Meanwhile behind the scenes, Fillmore, Graham, and Perry were working to cut Howland and Aspinwall in on the profits to be made in supplying the expedition with coal. Without a large supply of coal disbursed along the route of the expedition, the American steamers would never make it to Japan. In March, the department began to receive bids from suppliers offering coal for the expedition. The navy, however, had already appointed two agents, who received a five percent commission on coal bought for its steamers. On April 1, Fillmore sent a cryptic note to Graham asking for an interview before the navy entered into a contract for coal for the expedition. Five days later Howland and Aspinwall, proverbial recipients of government largesse in the mail steamship business, were appointed agents to provide coal at a ten (!) percent commission. Out of their ten percent they were to pay the navy's regular coal agents five percent. Perry had conferred with William Aspinwall about the expedition, and, according to one of Secretary Graham's informants, Perry's son Oliver arranged for the purchase of coal for Howland and Aspinwall in England. In the first shipment Howland and Aspinwall arranged for the delivery of 10,000 tons worth about $149,000, paying a commission of $14,900. In the next two years of the expedition Howland and Aspinwall estimated that they would ship another 24,000 tons.[68]

As the weeks slipped by, Perry was growing increasingly impatient over the delays in fitting out the *Princeton* with new engines. He had been to Baltimore and found the delays "unpardonable and altogether unnecessary." In desperation he wrote Sinclair to see what kind of penalties could be imposed on the contractors because of their "barefaced deception." He was doubly concerned, Perry wrote, because the chances were three to one that "the work will prove defective."[69]

By early summer all appeared to be ready with the exception of the *Princeton*. The storeship *Supply* had departed for China in May. But then two events occurred that further delayed Perry's departure. In June Graham was nominated as Winfield Scott's vice presidential candidate at the Whig Convention in Baltimore. Thereafter Graham paid little attention to the Japan expedition. In July reports reached Washington that a British naval squadron had been sent to Canada to deal with depredations committed by American fishermen. American fishermen were banned by an 1818 convention from fishing within three miles of the coast of Nova Scotia, New Brunswick, and Prince Edward Island. The Americans had chosen to ignore this agreement. Instead they fished where they liked and on occasion took whatever supplies they needed from the locals. "For God's sake send a man-of-war here," begged one Canadian, "for the Americans are masters of the place—one hundred sail are now lying in the harbor. They have stolen my firewood and burnt it on the beach." There were reports that at least seven American fishing boats had been seized by British cruisers attempting to police the unruly Americans. The fisheries dispute and the resulting boarding and seizure of American fishing schooners was just the kind of incident that stirred American jingoism to a feverish pitch, evoking memories of British arrogance on the high seas prior to the War of 1812.[70]

At the end of July, Perry was dispatched from New York aboard the *Mississippi* with instructions to look for an amicable solution to the fisheries dispute. The voyage turned out to be more of a summer pleasure cruise than a tense diplomatic mission. The *Mississippi* stopped frequently off the Canadian coast to talk with the American fishermen and to warn them to adhere to the 1818 protocol. Ashore Perry was wined and dined by the British consul in Eastport, Maine, while a ball was organized in honor of the American officers at St. John's in Newfoundland. Perry's talks with the vice admiral in command of the British squadron were amicable. Perry even put in a request for the most up-to-date charts and sailing instructions for East Asian waters. All in all, the fisheries conflict was greatly exaggerated, Perry reported when he returned to New York on September first to accolades in the press.[71]

Soon after his return from Canadian waters, Perry met with Webster to get his instructions for the expedition. Webster was fading fast. John Pendleton Kennedy, the new secretary of the navy, had reported after an August Cabinet meeting that Webster, though sunburned from fishing, was losing his "alacrity of mind and body."[72] Webster, despite his earlier attempt to waylay credit for the expedition, was most generous with Perry. Perry, he said, had originated the idea for the expedition; he should write his own instructions. By October twenty-fourth, Webster was dead, and Perry had decided that rather than wait for all of his ships to assemble, he would depart for China and rendezvous with the rest of the squadron there.

Perry's instruction appeared over the signature of C. M. Conrad, the acting secretary of state. They stated the objects of the expedition as:

1. To effect some permanent arrangement for the protection of American seamen and property wrecked on these Islands, or driven into their ports by stress of weather.

2. Permission to American vessels to enter one or more of their ports in order to obtain supplies of provisions, water, fuel, &c, or, in case of disasters, to refit so as to enable them to prosecute their voyage.

It is very desirable to have permission to establish a depot for coal, if not on one of the principal islands, at least on some small uninhabited one, of which, it is said, there are several in their vicinity.

3. The permission to our vessels to enter one or more of their ports for the purpose of disposing of their cargoes by sale or barter.

It is important, the instructions went on, for Perry to back up his arguments "with some imposing manifestation of power." Thus, he should proceed with his entire force to the coast of Japan at some point he thought advisable and attempt to open communications with the government and, if possible, to see the emperor in person. Perry was to emphasize that the president of the United States entertained "the most friendly feelings towards Japan," but was surprised to know that Americans who came to Japan, specifically on the *Morrison, Lagoda,* and *Lawrence,* were "treated as if they were his [the emperor's] worst enemies." Perry was to explain to the Japanese that his government "does not interfere with the religion of its own people, much less with that of other nations."

Perry was to recognize that the Japanese "are very excited against the English, of whose conquests in the east, and recent invasion of China, they have probably heard." For this reason, he was to explain that the Americans, though they speak the same language as the English, are "connected with no government in Europe." Instead he was to emphasize that the United States was directly across the ocean where large cities lay within twenty days by steamer from Japan. American commerce in the Pacific was increasing daily. "That part of the ocean will soon be covered with our vessels," and Japan and the United States were "becoming every day nearer and nearer."

If Perry's expressions of the president's desire to live in peace and friendship failed to produce a relaxation in the system of exclusion or promises of humane treatment for American sailors, he was to "change his tone and inform them in the most unequivocal terms that it is the determination of this government to insist" on humane treatment. For further acts of cruelty, Perry was to tell the Japanese, "they will be severely chastised." Conrad went on to remind Perry that the president did not have the power to declare war. Thus the expedition was to be pacific in character unless he needed to resort to force in self-defense or in retaliation for an act of personal violence against himself or one of his officers. Perry was to be courteous and conciliatory, to submit with patience and forbearance to acts of discourtesy without compromising his own or his nation's dignity. In the main, he was to "do everything to impress them [the Japanese] with a just sense of the power and greatness of this country." The instructions noted that Perry was invested with large discretionary powers and that any departure from usage or error of judgment would be viewed with indulgence. Finally Perry was directed to call at Macao and Hong Kong to give additional weight to the American commissioner's demands for reparations from the Chinese government. He was to stay in China as long as he deemed advisable if he could do so "without serious delay or inconvenience."

Another letter from Fillmore to his Great and Good Friend, the Emperor of Japan, was sent with Perry. For the most part it repeated the content of the letter sent the year before with Aulick. But it went into greater detail about the ways in which a commercial treaty could be arranged. This Fillmore letter suggested suspending Japan's ban on commercial relations for a trial period of five or ten years or the negotiation of a treaty limited to a few years with the possibility of renewal.[73]

On October twenty-fourth, Perry, increasingly eager to get under way, sailed in the *Mississippi* from New York for Annapolis. He had wanted to move the *Mississippi* for some time. She had been loaded with all the supplies available in New York and was over-crowded, with 383 men aboard, 130 over her normal complement. Besides she was anchored partially obstructing the passage in the East River, and Perry was afraid of "an explosion of public opinion."[74] Perry planned to meet the *Princeton*, which was now scheduled to be finished on November 1, at Annapolis. But November 1 came and went and still no *Princeton*. With nothing to do but wait, Perry held a farewell reception for the president and a large party aboard the *Mississippi* on November 8. Winfield Scott, the Whig candidate for president, and his running mate, the former Secretary of the Navy William Graham, had been roundly defeated by Franklin Pierce six days earlier. Fillmore, now a lame duck but the man who had backed an expedition to Japan, was greeted with a 21-gun salute, the yards were manned by sailors in dress blues, and the band struck up a lively tune. The president was accompanied by his daughter, and William Sinclair, Perry's friend at the Navy Department, was part of the crowd that thronged the deck of the *Mississippi*.[75]

Ten days later the *Princeton* finally pulled into view at four o'clock in the afternoon, only to run on a mudbank near the mouth of the Severn River. The *Mississippi* went to her rescue, but the *Princeton* managed to back off under her own power. Perry ordered the ill-fated steamer to head for Norfolk where the two ships were to load their final supplies. But within a half an hour the ship signaled that she could not keep up enough steam to make headway. Eventually the *Princeton* limped into Norfolk only to be declared unfit for service after a survey of her new boilers. Perry was furious. He had set the odds at three to one against her ever making the voyage to Japan, and he had been right.[76]

From Norfolk Perry rushed back to Washington to seek a replacement for the *Princeton*. He was told he could have the steamer *Powhatan* when she returned from Cuba. There was one last gathering for Perry at a men's social club on G Street attended by three members of Fillmore's Cabinet, including Kennedy, Edward Everett, soon to be secretary of state, and a number of other politicians and Washington luminaries. Then Perry rushed back to Norfolk. Here the *Mississippi* was getting her coal bunkers filled and her final supplies. Stevedores swarmed over the ship loading barrels of pork, preserved vegetables, flour, self-rising flour (an experiment), rice, whiskey, beans, sugar, butter, molasses, pickled beef, and raisins, boxes of cheese, mattresses and mattress covers (for the officers' bunks), tarpaulins, canvas, lumber, charcoal, awnings, lamp oil, paint, and one complete set of submarine armor.

At 1:30 P.M. on November 24, 1852, the anchor was hauled, the engines were started ahead fast, and the *Mississippi*, less the large squadron promised by the Navy Department, steamed alone in a light breeze from the north-northeast toward the Chesapeake Bay and the open sea. In a parting shot, the *Baltimore Sun* two days before his departure had predicted that Perry "would sail about the same time with Rufus Porter's aerial ship." Now that Perry was under way, the *Baltimore Sun* suggested "abandoning this humbug, for it has become a *matter of ridicule abroad and at home.*"

4

MIST OVER CHINA, FROST OVER JAPAN

It may be said that my anticipations are too sanguine. Perhaps they are, but I feel a strong confidence of success. Indeed, success may be commanded by our government, and it should be, under whatever circumstances, accomplished. The honor of the nation calls for it, and the interest of commerce demands it.[1]
> —MATTHEW CALBRAITH PERRY to Secretary of the Navy John Pendleton Kennedy, Madeira, December 15, 1852

I do not pretend to justify the prosecution of the opium trade in a moral and philanthropic point of view, but as a merchant I insist that it has been a fair, honorable, and legitimate trade.[2]
> —WARREN DELANO

There is nothing to be hoped for in Japan equal to the advantages now actually enjoyed in China.[3]
> —HUMPHREY MARSHALL, U.S. Commissioner in China, to Commodore Matthew Calbraith Perry, May 13, 1853

Seen from our viewpoint, how can we know whether the mist gathering over China will not come down as frost on Japan.[4]
> —SHIONOYA TOIN, 1847

AT SEA AT LAST AND ALONE, the *Mississippi* steamed eastward across the Atlantic toward the island of Madeira off the western coast of Africa, her giant paddle wheels dipping rhythmically into the water with hypnotic regularity. The old steamer, riding low in the water, rolled along at a steady seven knots, a plume of black smoke trailing off to leeward. With extra copper on her bottom and her coal bunkers expanded to hold 600 rather than the usual 450 tons, the ship drew three additional feet of water, and her bow dipped easily into the oncoming waves. After ten days, the wind shifted from the south to the north-northeast, and then blew hard from the west. Now the steamer strained and labored, wallowing

U.S. steam frigate *Mississippi* off Madeira;
Narrative of the Expedition

along in a heavy, uncomfortable sea. Several days out the *Mississippi* crossed the Gulf Stream, and the weather changed dramatically. Gray skies gave way to sunshine, the stoves used to warm the interior of the ship were stored away, and the black-hulled ship with its broad white stripe cut through a sea flecked by iridescent whitecaps and bordered by great billowy clouds that heralded the beginning of the tropics.

Seventeen days out of Norfolk, the *Mississippi* reached Madeira, which looked in the haze like a great humped serpent reposing in the sea. Anchoring in Funchal Bay in the shadow of the old Portuguese fort that stood on a pinnacle above the harbor, Perry sent ashore for coal. The *Mississippi* had been consuming 26 tons a day. So while the officers entertained themselves ashore, the crew went about the grimy two-day task of loading 440 tons into the bunkers. Then after the ship had taken on ten thousand gallons of fresh water and six bullocks and the commodore had stored away fifteen quarter kegs of the best Madeira wine for his friends in New York, the *Mississippi* weighed anchor and headed south for the Canary Islands. Skirting the Canaries to the westward, Commander Sidney S. Lee ordered the paddle boards removed from the great wheels. The water was blown from the boilers. The tall stack was lowered to its chocks on the deck. And the sails were set in hopes of saving coal by heading for the Cape of Good Hope pushed along by the northeast trade winds.

Perry's voyage to Madeira and his three-day stopover allowed him time to reflect further on the purposes of the expedition. Before departing southward, he left at Madeira a letter for the secretary of the navy to be carried home by the first ship heading to the States. He acknowledged that he still felt some doubts about the immediate success of the expedition, and he continued to emphasize that his first goal was to secure one or more ports of refuge and supply for whaling and other ships. If he could not get the Japanese to agree to open ports on the mainland without recourse to bloodshed, he planned to secure these ports at islands south of Japan. Specifically he was contemplating the occupation of the principal ports of the Ryukyu Islands—"a measure justified not only by the strictest rules of moral law, but which is also to be considered, by the laws of stern necessity." A further argument for their occupation was "the amelioration of the condition of the natives," although he did acknowledge that "the vices attendant upon civilization may be entailed upon them."

To bolster his plans, Perry reminded the secretary that the Ryukyus were under the sway of the "Prince of Satsuma," the man whose troops had fired upon the *Morrison* in Kagoshima Bay in 1837. Besides, Perry explained, in his previous role as subjugator of numerous towns during his commands in Africa and Mexico, "I have found no difficulty in conciliating the good will and confidence of the conquered people, by administering the unrestricted power I held rather to their comfort and protection than to their annoyance." In short, Perry claimed that the navy departed from these scenes of subjugation sped on its way by the humble gratitude of the conquered.

At the ports of refuge he planned to occupy, Perry wanted to encourage the natives to grow foodstuffs to supply American vessels. For this purpose he had brought a quantity of garden seeds, but he now wanted a collection of common agricultural implements. Perry also requested a small printing press with which he planned to print publications that would describe "the true condition of the various governments of the world, and especially to set forth the extraordinary prosperity of the United States under their genial laws." This task was particularly important to "counteract the discreditable machinations of the Dutch," whom Perry seemed to imagine were spending much of their time with the Japanese maligning Americans in general and his expedition in particular.

Most important, Perry in his letter to the secretary for the first time placed the expedition in a global strategic context, particularly in relation to the United States' chief rival, Great Britain. Great Britain, Perry explained, was now in possession of the most important fortified points in the East India and China seas, especially in the latter. Singapore covered the southwestern entrance to the China Sea, Hong Kong the northeastern. Borneo, to which the British had sent an expedition in 1846, represented an intermediate point. From these fortified positions England was on the verge of "shutting up at will and controlling the enormous trade of those seas, amounting, it is said, in value to 300,000 tons of shipping, carrying cargoes certainly not under £15,000,000 sterling." To prevent the British from monopolizing the China trade, the Americans had to act quickly. Fortunately there were many islands in the western Pacific, including Japan, left untouched by this "annexing government," and these islands lay along the steamer route from California, "which is destined to become of great importance to the United States." Now that Perry was free of Washington and the controversy surrounding steamship lines, he could state his objectives clearly: ports of refuge for whalers might be the ostensible reason for the Japan expedition, but the United States' global rivalry with England and the need to secure ports on a Pacific steamship line were its real raisons d'être.[5]

As the *Mississippi* breezed along in the trades toward the Cape of Good Hope, life aboard settled into a monotonous routine exacerbated by the crowded conditions. The crew was piped to quarters morning and evening for inspection. Once a week they were beat to general quarters, simulating going into battle. The powder magazines were opened, the guns cast loose and worked, the marines sent to their stations beside the pikemen, who were lined up to repel boarders. At other times there were fire drills, signaled by the ringing of the ship's bell and the stationing of crew members at the falls for the lifeboats. Then there were all the manifold forms of polishing, scrubbing, scraping, painting, and repairing that kept the crew occupied (and out of trouble) and left a navy vessel "shipshape and Bristol fashion."

Right after Christmas, Perry began to put his own mark on the expedition with two general orders. The first stated that all notes and drawings made by any member of the expedition were to be turned over to him. They would become the property of the government, from whence they might not be returned. Perry especially warned against informing any newspaper about movements of the squadron, its regulations, or matters of discipline. Perry and his family had fought enough battles in the prints, and he had no intention of doing so during this command.

His second order showed another side of Perry's character. He had objected, Perry explained, to pressure put on him before the expedition departed to employ civilian scientists on the voyage. Instead he invited all the officers of the squadron—and ordered his commanders to assist them—to use their spare time to contribute to the general knowledge accumulated by the expedition. With this in mind, Perry appended a list of subjects that might be pursued including hydrography, meteorology, military affairs, geology, religion, diseases and sanitary laws, and fourteen other subjects. Always a believer in the integration of education into shipboard life, Perry now urged his officers to take on this important though secondary task of the expedition.[6]

When Perry's order sequestering all notes and drawings was read from the quarterdeck, it caused the first shipboard grumbling, particularly from the handful of civilians who were experiencing naval discipline for the first time. It was unjust, complained Commander Sidney S. Lee's clerk, J. W. Spalding, one of the best of the unofficial chroniclers of the expedition, "being based upon the ridiculous premise that because a government may have claim upon your thews and sinews, or your mental aptitude in the line of your profession, that it likewise has property in the product of your brain."[7]

The men of the Japan expedition were dealing with an older and more difficult Perry, a man who was aware of the historical significance of his acts, a significance that he guarded jealously and promoted judiciously. His chronic rheumatism undoubtedly contributed to his testiness. He had been afflicted with recurring pain in his joints for years, ever since he was drenched fighting a fire along the Smyrna waterfront on a Mediterranean cruise in the 1820s. Now fifty-eight, Perry had gained weight and sported a comfortable paunch. His face was fleshier, the corners of his mouth drawn down in a perpetual scowl, but his auburn hair remained free of gray, curling abundantly around his ears. He could still be counted on to be straightforward, if intimidating, with his men, and he retained the magnetism of command that had surrounded him for years. When Perry was in command, his men agreed, events of great importance were likely to transpire.

As the year wound down and the *Mississippi* steamed southward to the Cape of Good Hope, finback whales visited the ship for hours at a time. The crew was treated to a spectacular display of zodiacal lights and was served an extra round of grog on Christmas. There were minor accidents. A man fell overboard at night, but was found in the water. Perry, claimed Spalding, was more concerned about the delay and possible damage to the paint job when a boat was lowered than about the man himself. From then on, the sailor appeared deranged by the fall. Another man had his head caught in some machinery. He recovered, although his head was badly cut and somewhat flattened.[8]

As the trades diminished, the *Mississippi* was forced to resume steaming, and Perry decided to put into Jamestown on the island of Saint Helena to secure more coal. At Saint Helena, where Napoleon had died a British captive, the squadron had reached the first outpost of the British Empire, which stretched eastward from Capetown to Ceylon, Singapore, and Hong Kong. Madeira was

Portrait of Matthew Calbraith Perry, 1856;
daguerreotype by Beckers and Ward

Portuguese territory, but it was slowly being taken over as a health spa by wealthy Britishers. Saint Helena, after being discovered by the Portuguese in 1502, had passed back and forth between the British and the Dutch, but was now firmly in British hands. Both islands were monuments to the decline of the great empires of Portugal and Holland, the European countries which had opened the markets of the East more than three hundred years earlier but no longer played a major role in that part of the world. The British Empire was ascendant in the world Perry was entering, and it weighed heavily on his mind that he was now at the mercy of the British for coal wherever Howland and Aspinwall's ships were absent. The *Mississippi* was cruising along one of England's important steamship lines, one that tied the mother country to its colonies in Africa and the East. Exasperated with the United States' lack of coaling facilities, Perry complained in his journal, "Every nation in the world having war steamers and every private steam navigation company are ahead of our navy in all that belongs to improvements in ocean steamers." The *Mississippi*, Perry lamented, was regarded when it was launched as the most advanced war steamer in the world. Since those days, the navy had built steamers like the *Princeton*, and the United States had done nothing but regress in the competition for naval ascendancy.[9]

Thirteen days sailing from Saint Helena the *Mississippi* dropped anchor in Table Bay, South Africa. Capetown with its brick and stone buildings was a recapitulation of a small British city, but here the subject peoples of the East—Chinese, Malays, Bengalis—rubbed shoulders with the local retainers of the British Empire. In the interior, the British were still fighting a vicious war against the native population. Tribal raiders continued to keep the British off balance with lightning strikes against isolated farms, and the northern frontier was ablaze with violence. Meanwhile, near Capetown, a visit to see Soyola, the captured warrior chief who lived in a small country jail with his two wives, was a must for all visitors to South Africa, an excursion that Perry did not miss.

Perry found Capetown "a dull and stupid place," confined as he was to his hotel when he went ashore because of the dust storms and heat. The natives, or what remained of them, were worse. They were, Perry confided in his journal, "of the most savage and beastly

character, utterly disgusting in their persons and habits." But he
went on to say that Americans had no right to rail against the way
the British treated natives since the Americans were not far behind
when it came to "the frauds and cruelties committed upon our native
tribes." It was just that the British, Perry found, excused their acts
with "disgusting hypocrisy."[10] At Capetown Perry effected his first
rendezvous with one of Howland and Aspinwall's coal steamers,
but still had to purchase coal from the British. Then, after a week,
the *Mississippi*—less the deranged seaman, who was sent home, and
seven deserters, who had probably jumped ship to head for Australia's gold fields—was on its way, its decks cluttered with twelve
bullocks and eighteen sheep.

Sailing under clear skies once around the Cape of Good Hope,
the *Mississippi* made it to Mauritius, the former French sugar-
planting colony now under British sway, in fifteen days, arriving
on February eighteenth. Along the way, as a cautionary measure
against scurvy, the crew was served a potent brew made up of five
gallons of whiskey, fifteen of water, and two of lime juice plus
twenty pounds of sugar. For Spalding, the cruise now took on an
idyllic cast. The ocean was calm, the days cloudless, the nights
balmy, and the sea at sunset "a sight most beautiful to look upon,
its whole bosom bathed in fiery floods, and way above, tower above
tower, rose in radiance and glory illuminated clouds."[11] From
Mauritius, after a rendezvous with another Howland and Aspinwall
coal ship, the *Mississippi* steamed north and then east in a circuitous
route designed to keep the ship away from the violent hurricanes
that swept the Indian Ocean at that time of year.

The *Mississippi*'s next stop was Point de Galle in Ceylon, the
principal rendezvous for British mail steamers that served the
routes connecting England with India, Ceylon, Burma, Singapore,
and China via the Isthmus of Suez and the Red Sea as well as the
Cape of Good Hope. The ship was greeted by a swarm of native
canoes bearing Sinhalese, Indians, and Arabs, dressed in all manner
of bright colors, some in skirts, others in vests, some with their hair
done up on the back of their heads with a comb, others with shaved
heads. Those who were not asking to do the sailors' washing offered
enticing handfuls of sapphires, rubies, and cat's-eyes, stones that
usually turned out to be nothing more than colored glass.

Coal for the British steamers was piled high along the water-front outside the stone walls of the old Portuguese city. Despite the abundant supply, officials from the British-owned Pacific and Orient Steamship Company were under orders not to sell any to the Americans. Perry instead had to buy some from the British government and then wood, a poor substitute, when he could not

Point de Galle, Ceylon; *Narrative of the Expedition*

buy enough. To Perry's further embarrassment, he arrived to find that the American consul was confined to his quarters for failure to pay a debt. For Perry, Point de Galle was just another reminder of the makeshift nature of the United States' budding commercial empire.[12]

Five days steaming across the Bay of Bengal brought the *Mississippi* to the entrance to the Strait of Malacca. To navigate this often tricky passage, a pilot was usually brought aboard. But Perry was eager to press on. The *Mississippi* had been at sea for more than three months and still had 2,500 miles to go before arriving at Hong Kong. Perry had spent more than enough time steaming from coal depot to coal depot.

Having passed through the strait, a pilot finally came aboard on the afternoon of March twenty-fifth, bringing the first mail of the voyage, and then guided the steamer through the final group of islands into the bustling port of Singapore. Singapore was the great crossroads of seaborne Asian trade, and the *Mississippi* anchored among a polyglot collection of the ships of all nations: bulky British mail steamers, sleek American clipper ships, lateen-rigged Malay *prahus* with their long, curving bows and elegant lines, numerous ungainly-looking Chinese junks with their high sterns and low wedge-shaped bows, an eye painted on either side. Since Sir Stamford Raffles bought the island of Singapore from the Rajah of Johore and Singapore in 1819, the British had converted this former pirate haven into a modern city. Massive warehouses lined the quay. Some of the merchants owned commodious houses fronting the bay while others lived in spacious bungalows in the suburbs. Despite the mix of nationalities, the Americans found that the town had a predominantly Chinese flavor. The Chinese, with the exception of a few wealthy merchants, were crowded into poorly ventilated and filthy quarters near the waterfront while the Malays lived in cagelike bamboo huts built on stilts above marshy ground with a single plank serving as an entranceway.

In Singapore Perry hustled around trying to scare up more coal. But there was none available. The British steamship company had already contracted for every ton that came from local mines. In time Perry struck a deal with the company. Their supplies were short in Hong Kong. In exchange for coal advanced in Singapore, Perry promised to provide the British with coal in Hong Kong from that being brought by Howland and Aspinwall's supply ships. Perry, in his spare time, did some quick shopping, adding to his shell collection and buying a model of a Malayan *prahu* for the New York Yacht Club. Three days later, Perry and the *Mississippi* were away again, on the last leg of their voyage to China. In departing Perry noted that with sufficient naval force England could command this entrance to the South China Sea.[13]

Crossing the South China Sea was the most perilous piece of

navigation faced by the *Mississippi*. These waters were a maze of shifting shoals, reefs, banks, and islands crisscrossed by inexplicable tides. Many of the more than one hundred reefs were marked "imperfectly known" on the chart. And the passage was rendered the more dangerous, Perry wrote in his journal, because of "the rapidity with which those little architects, the coral zoophytes, build up these foundations of future islands, that the work of a few years may materially change the character and depth of the soundings."[14] The crossing was all the more onerous because of the oppressive heat. The sails, which were draped from the rigging so as to direct a breeze down into the steamy interior of the ship, proved ineffective, and a number of firemen stoking the coal furnaces in a boiler room that was already intolerably overheated passed out on the job.

Within a week the weather had changed—to blanket weather, Spalding wrote—and the *Mississippi*, having crossed the South China Sea without mishap, was churning through waters crowded with hundreds of fishing boats working in couples, each with a net astern. These were the outriders of the fabled Middle Kingdom of China. Because of the fog that night, the *Mississippi* anchored under the Ladrone Islands at the mouth of the western channel that led into the estuary of the Pearl River. On the morning of April seventh, the *Mississippi* entered Chinese waters, steaming for Macao, the city built by the Portuguese during their days of colonial splendor. As the crew crowded along the rail, they were not particularly impressed: the islands they passed were barren and unspectacular, the water brown and turbid. Somehow the scenery lacked the exotic overtones of the mysterious Orient so long anticipated. But after four months they had reached their interim destination, the staging ground for the Japan expedition.

The *Mississippi* paused briefly at Macao, just long enough for Perry to confer with the Portuguese authorities, to pick up a pilot, and for Mr. DeSilver, the naval storekeeper, to come aboard and receive his orders for resupplying the ships that would congregate in Hong Kong for the voyage to Japan. From Macao the *Mississippi* steamed across Lintin Bay to Hong Kong, England's new colonial outpost in China. Seized by the British in 1841, Hong Kong was one of the spoils of the Opium War. In ten short years a burgeoning

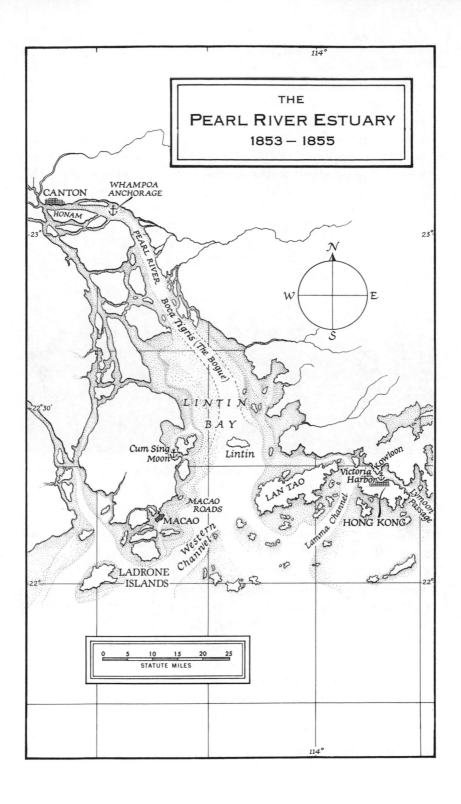

THE

PEARL RIVER ESTUARY

1853 — 1855

young town had sprung up along a narrow bench hewn from the foot of 1,800-foot Mount Victoria and had grown into a symbol of the abundant and precisely mannered life of the British colonies. Hong Kong was the military and administrative headquarters for the British Empire in the Far East. At one end of Victoria Road, the paved main street which paralleled the waterfront, stood the solid brick buildings on granite foundations that housed govern-

City of Victoria, Hong Kong, 1854;
painting by an unknown artist

ment offices and the military barracks. The waterfront itself was lined with piers and brick godowns, or warehouses. Ships from around the world rode at anchor or crowded the piers while a large part of the Chinese population lived aboard hundreds of junks that jammed the waterfront. Ranging up the steep sides of Mount Victoria were scattered the substantial homes of government officials and local merchants—built in what one commentator described as "an Anglo-something style, with verandahs"—and an Anglican church with the bishop's mansion attached.[15]

Despite the limited success of Hong Kong as a commercial center—it had taken some business away from Singapore, but had given it up to Shanghai—there was an opulent, flourishing air about the town, according to the well-known American travel writer Bayard Taylor, who would soon join the Japan expedition. Taylor noted with admiration the local men's club, library, the racetrack, yacht regattas, reading and billiard rooms, and bowling alley, a particular favorite of the Americans. "I doubt if there be another class of men, who live in a more luxurious state than the foreign residents of China," Taylor concluded. "Their households are conducted on a princely scale." Their homes abundantly furnished, they served the finest food and were attended by "a retinue of well-drilled servants, whose only business it is to study their habits, anticipate all their wants."[16]

For many of the Americans, the British residents of Hong Kong provided an interesting study in the mores of the mother country. "The people are very stiff," wrote a young junior officer, "and all seem afraid of compromising themselves by accidentally speaking or associating with some body of lower caste, it seems [sic] a regular village coterie with the governor & folks at the head of it whilst the shopkeeper's wife turns up her snout at the tailor's lady &c &c."[17]

Arriving in Hong Kong, the *Mississippi* exchanged salutes with the American sloops of war *Plymouth* and *Saratoga*. The store ship *Supply* was anchored nearby along with a number of British and French warships, but to Perry's amazement the *Susquehanna*, the steamer which was to serve as his flagship, was nowhere in sight. Soon the decks of the *Mississippi* were crowded with officers from the other American ships. In a joyful reunion, mail from home, a most precious commodity, was handed out, old acquaintances were renewed, and new ones were formed. The next day there was an even more ostentatious display of ceremonial firepower as Perry paid his respects aboard French and British warships and visited British officials ashore. Perry was saluted and responded in kind with a series of thundering cannonades that rumbled back from the heights of Mount Victoria. "From the rising to the setting of the sun nearly," wrote Spalding, who counted 179 shots fired, "it was powder burning."[18]

The commodore, however, was left fuming. He had departed from home without the fleet promised him by the Navy Department and had arrived in China to find his flagship missing. The *Susquehanna*, it turned out, had gone to Shanghai commandeered by the new American commissioner, Colonel Humphrey Marshall of

Kentucky. Perry had met Marshall in New York while he was planning the expedition and had issued orders for his commanders to obey Marshall. Marshall had arrived in January with instructions to seek enforcement of the Treaty of Wanghia, which had been signed by the Americans and the Chinese in 1844. Unable to deal with the Chinese in Canton, Marshall had ordered the *Susquehanna* to Shanghai so that he could gather firsthand information about the massive rebellion that was sweeping the southern half of China. Perry had unwittingly given up his flagship while sailing into a political maelstrom.[19]

The American treaty, which Marshall was to enforce, was a by-product of British firepower, one of the results of the Opium War. When the commissioner dispatched by the imperial court to halt the illegal opium trade closed the port of Canton in 1839, the British, who dominated the trade, had responded by sending an expeditionary force of ten thousand men aboard twenty-five warships and fourteen steamers. After almost three years of fighting, marked by the wholesale defection of imperial troops, the British forced the Chinese to sign the humiliating treaty of Nanking. Besides ceding Hong Kong, the treaty called for opening four ports in addition to Canton to foreign trade, the payment of a $21 million indemnity to cover the opium destroyed and the cost of the war, the establishment of a separate foreign-controlled legal system for foreigners (extraterritoriality), an end to the monopoly of foreign trade enjoyed by a handful of Chinese merchants (the Cohong system), and the reduction of import duties to a level acceptable to the British.[20]

In the wake of the British invasion, the Americans, bolstered by the threat of three meager warships grandly called the East Asia Squadron, extracted basically the same concessions from the Chinese in the 1844 Treaty of Wanghia. But by the time that Marshall arrived in China, the Chinese were still resisting the implementation of both treaties. Marshall soon after his arrival reported to Washington that he was appalled by "the indifference, if not contempt, with which the Chinese officials treat the functionaries of foreign powers." Violations of the United States–Chinese treaty had "piled up": foreigners, though they were allowed to trade there, were excluded from entering within the city walls of Canton and

Foochow; a number of claims (very minor ones, as it turned out, amounting to a few thousand dollars) had not been settled; some Americans were being prevented from building on property they had purchased in Foochow; and in a final insult the Chinese official to whom Marshall was to present his credentials and his complaints had scheduled a meeting and then had blithely departed for Peking *the day before.*[21]

In early 1853, as Marshall quickly found out, there were even more ominous clouds darkening the horizon. A rebellion of staggering proportions, one that would prove to be the greatest uprising of the nineteenth century, was sweeping southern China. The rebellion, moreover, was led by a young man who claimed to have been converted to Christianity by a foreign missionary. Bedeviled by strange visions, Hung Hsiu-ch'uan,* the son of a poor farmer from a village of Hakka outcasts near Canton, fused his own version of messianic Christianity with utopian beliefs and raised a people's army among the poor, the oppressed, and the outlawed. Hung rallied his followers, who now numbered in the tens of thousands, at Chin-t'ien. Here they lived communally, sharing money, food, and clothing. After Hung proclaimed the Taiping T'ien-kuo, or Heavenly Kingdom of Great Peace, in early 1851 with himself as the Heavenly King, the Taiping rebels, now a phalanx of thirty-seven thousand fighting men and women accompanied by a ragtag bevy of camp followers, broke out of Kwangsi province, marching and fighting toward central China. Along the way, the Taipings grew in strength and began to present themselves as Chinese rebels fighting against the hated foreign dynasty that had been imposed on China by the descendants of northern Manchu tribesmen in the early seventeenth century.[22]

When Marshall arrived in China, the rebels were moving eastward by foot and by water along the Yangtze valley toward Nanking. On March nineteenth, the rebels, now half a million strong, took Nanking after tunneling under and mining the city walls. In

---

* I have spelled Chinese names in the traditional manner for the sake of consistency and to avoid confusion regarding quotations from nineteenth-century documents. I have followed Chinese usage in writing Chinese personal names, i.e., family name followed by given name.

a frightful massacre an estimated twenty to forty thousand Manchu soldiers, officials, and their families were put to the sword, their bodies thrown into the Yangtze. When the rebels took Yangchow and Chinkiang by the end of the month, they now sat astride the Grand Canal, the main transportation and communication system that linked northern and southern China as well as Shanghai and the interior. Business at Shanghai, the most important port in the foreign trade, ground to a halt, and rumors began to spread that the rebels would soon be coming to Shanghai.[23]

It took Humphrey Marshall fewer than three weeks after his arrival in January to become impatient with the prevarications of the Chinese officials in Canton. Other than having an acute mind, Marshall, who was a cousin of Supreme Court Justice John Marshall, lacked most of the requisites of a diplomat. A West Point graduate, minor hero in the Mexican War, lawyer, Kentucky congressman, and loyal Whig, he was appointed commissioner to China only after a number of other men had turned down Secretary of State Daniel Webster's offer. Marshall was an egotist with an exalted view of his position, a tireless complainer who was easily irritated by the complications of a difficult foreign post, and quick to discover a personal insult when differences of opinion arose. He was destined to knock heads with the thin-skinned new commodore of the East India Squadron.

When the imperial commissioner left him cooling his heels in Canton and the governor of the province refused to see him because he was too busy in the imperial commissioner's absence, Marshall turned to Commodore Aulick for a naval vessel to take him to Nanking, where he hoped to present his credentials to a Chinese official. To Marshall's great annoyance, Aulick refused. Aulick was under orders to keep his ships near Hong Kong in anticipation of Perry's arrival. Aulick's refusal was a very gross discourtesy, Marshall reported in a dispatch, one that had embarrassed him in front of the Chinese because he could not command the use of his own government's vessel and subjected him to the ultimate insult of having to consider going north in a British ship. Marshall and Aulick exchanged increasingly nasty letters over questions of rank and civilian versus military prerogatives. It bothered Marshall little that the luckless Aulick was so sick in mind and body that he could barely communicate with his aides. Marshall was forced to bide his time in Canton until Aulick's departure, when he prevailed upon John Kelly, the acting squadron commander, to provide him with the steamer *Susquehanna* to go north.[24]

As time passed, Marshall had further reasons to travel north. The foreign community had been tracking the progress of the Taiping rebels since the inception of the rebellion, intrigued by the reports that Hung was a Christian of some sort. The rebels were thought to be in the neighborhood of Nanking. "China," Marshall reported on March nineteenth, the day Nanking fell, "is now in the midst of a bloody revolution—a war for the Empire."[25] Marshall wanted to be near the scene of the action to better assess the strength of the contending armies. Then if he could not present his credentials to a Manchu official at Nanking, he planned to sail farther north to the mouth of the Pei-ho River, which would put him closer to Peking, the imperial capital. There he hoped that he would be received by the emperor himself. Just how Marshall planned to prevail upon the Chinese to recognize his existence with one steamer when the British could not get a response to their demands with troops and a fleet, Marshall did not explain.

With Humphrey Marshall gone north to Shanghai or some other destination with his flagship, it was Perry's turn, when he arrived in Hong Kong a little more than two weeks after Marshall's departure, to be outraged. "This extraordinary and injudicious exercise of doubtful authority has greatly embarrassed me," Perry confided to his journal. "It presents a feature of questionable official conduct calculated to injure the harmony and consequent efficiency of the squadron."[26] Moreover, Marshall had taken Paul Forbes, the American consul at Canton, who was also head of Russell and Company, the largest American merchant house in China, and Dr. Peter Parker, the missionary-doctor who served as secretary of the legation, with him, depriving Perry of advice and information. And unfortunately for Commander Kelly, the perpetrator of the crime, he had to face the commodore's wrath and then sail off to find the flagship and order it to remain in Shanghai until Perry arrived with the rest of the fleet.

After a few days the *Mississippi* returned from Hong Kong to Macao for coal and supplies. Established as the seat of the Portuguese empire in China and Japan in the early sixteenth century, Macao was now a summer residence for the foreign merchants who were eager to escape the oppressive heat of the factories at Canton. While the more high-minded officers explored the churches, old mansions, and the other sights of the city, some of the sailors got their first taste of shore liberty since Capetown. When they returned, ten were confined for disorderly and outrageous conduct.

After four days at Macao, the *Mississippi* steamed toward the mouth of the Pearl River, headed for Whampoa, the anchorage for foreign ships trading at Canton. On its starboard the *Mississippi* passed Lintin Island, two and a half miles long with a thousand-foot-high brush-covered hill at its south end. Before the Opium War, the British, American, and Parsee opium dealers maintained heavily armed receiving ships—the warehouses of the opium trade—tied up in deep water at the northwest end of the island. Drug deals were struck at the factories in Canton, where the Chinese opium merchants promptly paid their bills in silver. At Lintin the British and Parsees off-loaded opium from ships bringing it from India.

Russell and Company, a well-established American firm in the China trade, also maintained its receiving ships at Lintin. Russell's and other American ships transported a small portion of the Indian opium while bringing their own supplies from Turkey. Russell and Company was the leading American participant in the drug trade. Once the opium had arrived, the receiving ships were visited by Chinese vessels known as "scrambling dragons" or "fast crabs," long, narrow crafts built of unpainted wood, bristling with weapons, and propelled at a fast clip by mat sails and long rows of oars. The Chinese had repeatedly barred the import of opium, but the crafty foreigners claimed that the trade took place in international waters, although Lintin was well within the Pearl River estuary. Besides it was a Chinese problem, the foreigners argued, since their merchants bought the drug and paid the bribes that allowed it to come ashore.[27]

"We were threatened and re-threatened with the direst penalties if we continued to sell *foreign mud* to the people, whereby they were ruined in health and plunged in inanition, while the precious metals oozed out of the country. Truly, forbearance could be no longer exercised," wrote William Hunter, a partner in Russell and Company, about pre-treaty days, "and we continued to sell the drug as usual." Warren Delano,* Russell's senior partner in China in the 1840s, wrote that he could not justify the trade from "a moral and philanthropic point of view, but as a merchant I insist that it has been a fair, honorable, and legitimate trade."[28]

The lists of imports kept by American consuls seem to indicate that the opium trade never represented more than ten percent of the Americans' overall trade with China. There was also a handful of merchants, such as D. W. C. Olyphant and his partner Charles W. King, who as religious men opposed the trade. The closing of Canton and the Opium War increased the American role in the trade, as the British moved their illegal cargoes to American ships. After the war and the restoration of the trade, the United States government made one feeble effort to end the drug traffic. Caleb Cushing, the first American commissioner, was instructed not to interfere by protecting smugglers from the Chinese enforcing their laws against illegal trading. He was also ordered to arrest Paul Forbes, the American consul, if his firm, Russell and Company, was found to be involved in the trade. In addition, the Treaty of Wanghia described opium as contraband. But the Americans, with the exception of a brief attempt by a U.S. naval vessel to put a halt to American participation in drug smuggling, never bothered to enforce the antismuggling provisions of the treaty.[29]

By the 1850s, the tea and coolie trade outweighed opium in importance for the Americans. The drug trade, however, continued to flourish; transactions now took place openly in a number of locations while American and British ships moved on up the coast to the new ports opened by the treaties, where they traded offshore with their Chinese customers. In 1852 it was reported that $82 million worth of the drug was stored in Hong Kong warehouses under the guns of Fort Murray, and it was said by some that opium was the trade item producing the greatest revenues in all of world commerce. Needless to say, Paul Forbes was never arrested. Russell

* Warren Delano was Franklin Delano Roosevelt's grandfather.

and Company's senior partner was the American consul in Canton when Perry arrived. Russell and Company still dominated America's China trade and was still selling opium. And Paul Forbes, if he had not gone to Shanghai, would have been Perry's host in Canton.

Past Lintin Island, the *Mississippi* entered The Bogue, the mouth of the Pearl River, a name derived from the Portuguese-cum-Latin *boca tigris*, or mouth of the tiger. She steamed past the Chinese forts with their long whitewashed walls, which had been shelled mercilessly by British warships and then attacked from the rear during the Opium War, then past the narrow place in the river where the Chinese had stretched a great chain across on rafts in a futile effort to keep the British out. Along the way two fast boats attached themselves to the *Mississippi*'s stern to protect themselves from the swarms of pirates that made their home among the numerous islands and mud flats of the river. When one of the boats, which was overloaded with salt being smuggled up the river, was dragged under, the *Mississippi* paused to help bail out and right the Chinese craft. The second boat, fearing a similar fate, cast loose. Proceeding to Whampoa unprotected, it was overtaken and plundered by pirates once it was out of sight of the *Mississippi*. "Of all the races they [the Chinese] are probably the most knavish," Perry, an instant expert on the Chinese character, concluded. "From the highest mandarin to the lowest boatman the art of deception and trickery is practised with consummate skill and audacity."[30]

At Whampoa, the *Mississippi* anchored below the first bar among the sleek American clippers, bulky East Indiamen, and ships from around the world. Here the Pearl River turned westward and shoaled up to a depth that kept deep-draft ships from proceeding any farther toward Canton, which was still twelve miles away. At Whampoa Perry was picked up by a boat owned by Russell and Company and taken to their residence near the city. Between Whampoa and Canton, the commodore traveled along a crowded waterway jammed with all kinds of craft—ferries that plied back and forth across the river, plain tea boats, great oceangoing junks with black eyes painted on their bows, richly decorated mandarin boats with double banks of oars, flying flags with the name of the mandarin and his district inscribed on them, and egg-shaped *tanka* or passenger boats with women at the helm in wide breeches, with plaited hair and braceleted wrists. Along the shore, clustered together and tied to poles thrust in the mud, innumerable houseboats formed a great floating metropolis whose population grew denser as one approached Canton. Here and there were more exotic craft, such as the flower boats, with painted glass windows and their

Chinese junks on the Canton River;
watercolor by Peter Bernard Wilhelm Heine

deckhouses intricately carved with birds and flowers, from which at night came the sounds of Chinese musical instruments and the laughter of young prostitutes.

Perry was disappointed with this river scene and by Canton when he reached it. Traveling from Whampoa to the factories, he wrote, was like passing through "two lines of receptacles of poverty and filth." Rather than "the sketches of imaginative boyhood," Perry found only "filth and noise, poverty and misery, lying and roguery."[31]

Before the Opium War, Canton was the heart of the China trade, the one city after 1759 where foreigners were legally permitted to buy and sell their wares. To the Chinese court, trade was little more than a favor granted to lowly barbarians, the *fan kwae*, or foreign devils, as the Chinese called those who came to Canton. China was the Middle Kingdom, literally the center of the world, the measure of all the great accomplishments of civilization. Her emperor was the Son of Heaven, the Lord of Ten Thousand Years. "Our Heavenly Court treats all within the Four Seas as one great family," Com-

View of Old China Street, Canton; *Narrative of the Expedition*

missioner Lin Tse-hsu, the man who provoked the Opium War, wrote to Queen Victoria; "the goodness of our great Emperor is like Heaven, that covers all things."[32] In the Chinese scheme of things, other nations came to honor China, bringing tribute to Peking as the barbarians along its interior borders had done for centuries.

Before the Opium War, an intricate commercial system evolved at Canton around the sixteen foreign factories that stood on fifteen acres alongside the river. Foreign trade was monopolized by the Cohong, a small group of very wealthy Chinese merchants who purchased the privilege at the imperial court for an extravagant price. The trade was carefully regulated—for the collection of duties, fees, and bribes—by corrupt officials. Other regulations—for example, barring weapons from the factories, prohibiting foreigners from learning Chinese or rowing on the river, restricting visits outside the factory area, banning smuggling and the opium trade— were blithely ignored as often as possible. "And so in numerous ways," William Hunter, the Russell partner, recalled, "everything worked smoothly and harmoniously by acting in direct opposition to what we were ordered to do. We pursued the evil tenor of our ways with supreme indifference, took care of our business, pulled boats, walked, dined well, and so the years rolled by happily as possible."[33]

There were fortunes to be made in the China trade. At first, the ships were undersized, the crews small and very young (often all in their early twenties and younger), the investment highly speculative, and the journey long and perilous. But a successful voyage paid off handsomely. The first American ship to reach Canton, the *Empress of China*, turned a profit of $37,727 on an investment of $120,000. In short, the China trade was exactly the kind of undertaking that appealed to the dangerously adventurous and impulsive spirit of the young American male. By the time of Perry's arrival, the trade was consolidated under the control of a handful of New York– and Boston-based merchant houses: Russell and Company, Grinnell, Minturn and Company, Augustine Heard, A. A. Low and Brothers, Olyphant and Company, N. L. and G. Griswold, Howland and Aspinwall, and W. S. Wetmore. Despite the money to be made, the constant problem was what to import into China. Americans wanted silk, tea, rattan, nankeens, and porcelain. The Chinese said they were self-sufficient and stuck by their claims. After 1840, as fashions changed, tea and to a lesser extent coolies became the major exports from China. American merchants could not continue to export specie to China. Opium was a partial solution to the problem for a while, but into the 1850s there continued to be an uneven balance of trade with China.

When Perry arrived in Canton, the square in front of the factories was filled with gardens, and new factories had been built to replace those burned by mobs during the Opium War. Each factory was a narrow brick and stone building, actually a succession of buildings, grouped into four clusters separated by narrow alleys. Modest as they were, the factories stood out with their whitewashed walls and green awnings among the low, dingy, brown brick and stone buildings, with firewood and clotheslines on their roofs, that made up the surrounding western suburbs of Canton.

The American community in China, never more than a couple of hundred people, was a small but self-contained world, largely under the influence of its merchant leaders. The consular service was the creation of the merchant community, since it was customary for the State Department to accredit members of the leading firms in the China trade as consuls and vice consuls. Russell and Company provided a disproportionately large number of consuls and vice consuls. At the time of Perry's arrival, besides Paul Forbes, Russell's senior partner, who was consul, D. C. Spooner, another Russell partner, was the vice consul while Edward Cunningham, another partner, was consul in Shanghai.

In the period after the Opium War, as trade shifted to Shanghai and tea became the major export, the Americans, free of the restrictive Cohong system, participated in the China trade with a renewed sense of self-confidence. The Americans had one thing that worked continuously to their advantage—the superiority of their sea captains and their vessels. For the Yankees, the China trade had become the proving ground for new innovations in naval architecture, and it was the opium business that triggered an important early effort to build more speed into sailing vessels. In the 1840s the Forbes clan and Russell and Company sent a number of small clipper-built schooners out to China to work the opium trade. These sleek craft, with narrow hulls and tall raking masts modeled after the earlier Baltimore clippers, were more like yachts than merchant vessels, although they were heavily armed and carried large crews. Their great speed permitted them to make up time that would have otherwise been lost working against the strong tides and currents in the South China Sea and against the northeast monsoon. These schooners soon became the envy of the British.

At about the same time, the firm of Howland and Aspinwall, Perry's old acquaintances from the mail steamship business and the supplier of coal for the Japan expedition, bought a secondhand Baltimore clipper, the *Ann McKim*, which unlike the smaller schooners was a full-size ship. When the *Ann McKim* made a run from Canton to New York in a record ninety-six days, Howland and Aspinwall decided to risk building an even more radical clipper ship. The *Rainbow* was designed by John Wills Griffith, the first American shipbuilder to bring a scientific approach (tank testing of ship models, for example) to naval architecture. Griffith stood conventional assumptions about ship design on their head. Instead of the traditional "cod's head and mackerel tail"—that is, a rounded

The clipper ship *Rainbow*; painting by Fred S. Cozzens

bow to push the waves aside and a thin stern to reduce drag—he sharpened and extended the bow, flaring it outward near the deck. He rounded off the stern and shaped the hull so that it was narrower than on any other ship of its size. Finally he added extremely tall masts and a rigging design that would carry a superabundance of sail.

Because of Griffith's radical innovations, the *Rainbow* came to be known along the East River waterfront as Aspinwall's folly. The old salts claimed that if it was dismasted, it would dive to the bottom with its sharp bow. Sure enough, the *Rainbow* lost its masts on its maiden voyage in a winter gale four days out of New York, but did not sink. However, during one day the *Rainbow* logged an incredible fourteen knots, and on her second voyage, she went out to Hong Kong in ninety-nine days and returned in eighty-four.[34]

With their fast clipper ships, the Americans now posed a threat to the British in the carrying trade. America's global aspirations always seemed to be stated in disproportionately bombastic terms for such an underdeveloped nation. "The word *world* is in great use with us Americans, when we assert our superiority and discourage competition," Philip Hone noted in his diary in 1850. "The best in the world, the handsomest in the world, the fastest in the world, unmatchable; there is no use in the world for the world to try to equal us."[35] In the case of the shipping business, the Americans had something to brag about—and even more so when the British repealed the Navigation Act in 1849, opening the carrying trade between China and England to their American competitors. The Americans rushed in with their clipper ships and quickly took over the trade. When A. A. Low's clipper the *Oriental* arrived in London with the first load of tea, huge crowds went to the West India Docks to see her. And she was a sweet sight: long and slim, 185 feet by 36, a black hull with tall raking masts. In the wake of this visit, the British began to buy their ships in America. While Perry was supervising the construction of mail steamships at shipyards along the East River in the early 1850s, the same yards were turning from building steamers to building clipper ships for the British. With the largest merchant marine in the world, the Americans were challenging the British for domination in the global carrying trade. The British still held a monopoly on steamship service to the Orient; it was the Yankees who got the tea to the London market in the shortest time.[36]

From his headquarters at the Russell residence in Canton, Perry went about his business, hiring a Peruvian bark to be used as a dispatch vessel and forty Chinese laborers and servants who were taken aboard the *Mississippi*. Perry also went to talk with Samuel Wells Williams and Elijah Bridgman, two of the most respected and accomplished members of the American missionary community in China. Perry had written Williams from Hong Kong saying that he wanted to discuss the expedition with him and hire him as an interpreter. Now Perry explained that he had heard before he left the United States that Williams was eager to join the expedition. Williams, however, was hesitant to sign on. Perry had not gotten permission from the American Board of Commissioners for Foreign Missions for him to leave his work as head of the missionary press in Canton.

Perry persisted. He had turned down Philipp Franz von Siebold's offer to become the interpreter because he thought that Williams was eager to go. Moreover, he assured Williams that the expedition would be a peaceful one, unless they were attacked by the Japanese. The problem, Williams replied, was that whatever his reputation in the United States, he was not the Japanese linguist that Perry thought he was. Perry would have been better advised to take von Siebold, Williams felt. Williams had learned some Japanese from the shipwrecked sailors that he had accompanied to Japan aboard the *Morrison* sixteen years earlier, he explained. But he had not kept up with the language.[37]

Williams's wife, Sarah Walworth Williams, was even more resistant to the idea of her husband going to Japan. She was charmed by the naval officers who had made polite social calls at their home near the factories, but she took an instant dislike to Perry, perhaps only because he was trying to separate her husband from her and their three young children. In the end, Williams found a replacement at the press and went. But he set certain conditions. He could not leave until early May. He would not work on the Sabbath, and he wanted comfortable accommodations. Perry agreed, offering to pay Williams $300 a month and arranging for him to go aboard the *Saratoga* and sail from Hong Kong to the Ryukyu Islands while Perry sailed on to Shanghai to find his missing flagship.[38]

Through Williams and Bridgman, Perry had made contact with the other important element of the American community in China. Williams had arrived in China at the age of twenty-one, four years after the first American missionary. Born in Utica, New York, he was the son of a printer, publisher, and bookstore owner, brought up by a mother who believed that children should be either constantly employed or at worship. Williams grew up as a little adult, stiff and shy, devoted to books and so dedicated to hard work that he could not tolerate an idle hour in himself or anyone else. Strong-minded and opinionated, Williams had no close friends, according to his son, because of his disdain for "all manifestations of an unruly spirit."[39]

Williams graduated from the Rensselaer Institute (later Rensselaer Polytechnic Institute) aspiring to be a botanist. But that

Watercolor portrait of Samuel Wells Williams by an
unknown Japanese artist and photograph from
Life and Letters of Samuel Wells Williams

was not to be. His father had been asked by the American Board of Commissioners of Foreign Missions to find a printer for a press that was being sent to Canton by Olyphant's church in New York City. In Canton Williams edited the *Chinese Repository*, a monthly journal dedicated to reporting on current events and all aspects of Chinese life. Williams's first impression was that the Chinese were receptive to the preaching of the gospel. But his optimism did not last long. For the missionaries faced both the opposition of the Chinese and the hostility of the East India Company, which did not want the missionaries interfering with its lucrative relationship with the Cohong merchants. Constantly harassed, Williams found it easier to work in Macao, where the press was moved in 1835. In

Macao, Williams later recalled, the mission, despite the new free-doms permitted by the Treaty of Wanghia, did not make a convert until 1850. Before his departure, a discouraged Williams wrote to his father, "The torpor of mind in heathen countries is inconceivable to one who has all his life lived in a Christian land."[40]

A young man living under difficult circumstances, Williams had to wrestle as well with his own personality. He had mellowed somewhat, becoming more affable and outgoing, but under the pres-sures of working in China, he retreated into himself and his work, becoming as he confessed, "unhappy and cross as a man with a toothache in a smoky house on a cold and rainy day."[41]

Unable to reach more than a handful of Chinese, the mission-aries ended up preaching to the foreign community: the merchants, sailors, and clerks who gathered in Whampoa, Canton, and Macao. There were occasional efforts to hand out tracts at the examinations for entry to officialdom held in Canton and even fewer forays into the countryside, where the peasants sometimes treated them kindly. At other times they were set upon by mobs howling "*fan kwae, fan kwae*" and pelted with stones and bits of clay.[42]

As the years passed, the missionaries inevitably fell into a closer and closer relationship with the merchants, serving them and the various consular services as interpreters. When the issue of opium came to the fore, the missionaries found themselves in a delicate situation. Williams and his colleagues aired the issue in the *Chinese Repository*, where a variety of points of view were presented. Williams himself viewed the opium traffic as an evil and the Opium War as unjust. But a number of the most prominent American missionaries, led by Peter Parker and Bridgman, backed British intervention.[43]

In the end the missionaries allied themselves with the mer-chants in their efforts to open China to foreign trade. After all, both the merchants and the missionaries saw trade as part of a heavenly design for the establishment of civilization in China. "Free trade begets a free interchange of thought," Williams wrote after returning from Japan in 1837, "and with the goods, the civilization and Christianity of foreign nations will extend."[44]

In 1844 Williams returned home, married, and went back to China with a wife and infant son. Williams at first was pleased with the "new" post–Opium War China. Missionaries could now work openly, regular services were being held in Chinese, and the more adventurous missionaries could begin to explore the interior. What Williams had not counted on was the growing hostility of the Cantonese to foreigners, a hostility triggered by British soldiers raping and looting during the Opium War and exacerbated by British demands to enter the city walls. "Our preaching is listened to by few, laughed at by many, and disregarded by most," Williams wrote to his brother. There were other problems, too. Lack of interest in Chinese affairs among the new merchants led to the closing of the *Chinese Repository*. Petty rivalries among the various denominations hindered the work of missionaries. And for Williams, his Chinese employees stole his type, his books, and his tools. "It is much easier," a frustrated Williams wrote to a friend, "loving the souls of the heathen in the abstract in America than it is here in the concrete, encompassed as they are with such dirty bodies, speaking forth their foul language and vile natures, and exhibiting every evidence of depravity."[45]

For Williams and the other missionaries, there was one bright star in the firmament, the Taiping rebellion led by Hung Hsiuch'uan, who was thought to be a convert to some form of Christianity. Beginning in 1851, reports had filtered out from Kwangsi Province, where Hung was organizing his followers. But the full dimensions of this massive uprising were not comprehended until Hung and his followers burst from the confines of Kwangsi Province and marched toward Nanking, calling for the establishment of a new dynasty. The missionaries greeted these reports from the interior as a positive, even a heavenly sign. "God is moving this beehive of people," Williams wrote to his brother and sister-in-law, who were missionaries in the Middle East, "and they will soon make a stir in the old regime ousting the Manchus and bringing in civilization and progress."[46]

The merchants were less confident of the future and less enamored of the rebels. For them, the question was simple. What impact would the Taipings have on foreign trade? They had heard that the Taipings entertained none of the hostility toward foreigners that was common in Canton. But the uprising was threatening communications with the interior and gradually strangling trade at Shanghai.

In China Williams had retained his interest in Japan despite the deterioration of his language skills. Two of the shipwrecked Japanese sailors from the *Morrison* had converted to Christianity— "the first fruits of the church of Christ in Japan," Williams noted— and with their assistance he and another missionary had translated three books from the Bible. When he was in New York in 1846, he had a font of Japanese type struck, and he continued to write about Japan. Thus for Williams Perry's offer was an opportunity to pioneer new territory for the church.[47]

Finished with work and shopping in Canton, Perry moved to Russell and Company's elegant mansion in Macao. On April twenty-seventh after loading more coal at Macao and picking up water and a coastal pilot at Hong Kong, the *Mississippi* sailed for Shanghai to search for the missing flagship, leaving the *Saratoga* to wait for Wells Williams. The journey along the coast was a treacherous one, as the steamer was beset by fogs, irregular tides, and tricky currents. After five days the *Mississippi* entered the mouth of the Yangtze River, a passage feared and hated by foreigners. The river entrance was guarded by long shoals, the North and South Sands, that extended on both sides beyond the sight of land. Though the channel was two miles wide, there were neither lighthouses nor navigational marks to assist the pilot. The *Susquehanna* and the *Plymouth* had both run aground at the entrance, but the *Mississippi* was more fortunate. At one point she did stray from the channel into nineteen feet of water, one foot less than she drew, but the power of her engines pushed her through the fluid, yellowish mud.

Shanghai stood on the banks of the Whangpoo River, a tributary of the Yangtze that joined the main river at Woosung, the city's opium smuggling depot. Along the Whangpoo, flat, monotonous fields broken by sluggish streams and irrigation ditches extended in both directions away from the diked river banks. Single houses and villages surrounded by green-budded fruit trees, bamboo, and willows broke the monotony. These habitations were con-

nected by narrow paths that ran along raised dikes through the
fields. Here and there ancestral burying grounds poked up from
the fields, where the unburied coffins of the poor were simply left
on the ground and covered with canvas. Reclaimed from marshes
that were drained in the tenth century, every available piece of
land, including the sides of the dikes, was cultivated, giving the

The American Consulate, Shanghai; *Narrative of the Expedition*

impression of a land jammed with rice and wheat fields interspersed
with vegetable gardens.[48]

As the *Mississippi* rounded the final bend before Shanghai, a
mile-long forest of masts could be seen across the intervening fields,
as if floating on the land. Then the city came in sight, first the
handsome mansions of the foreign settlement, some built in Pal-
ladian style, surrounded by sumptuous gardens, next a neat Gothic
church, and finally the three-storied American consulate, which
was the headquarters of Russell and Company and one of the handsomest buildings along the waterfront. Twenty foreign ships and
innumerable junks were anchored in front of the foreign settlement.

Among them were the missing *Susquehanna* and the *Plymouth*, as well as two British war steamers and one French.

The Chinese city lay farther to the south along the river and was separated from the foreign compounds by a creek and surrounded by a semicircular wall thirty feet high and five miles in circumference. Shanghai—literally "above the sea," as in raised from the sea by the draining of the surrounding marshes—had been a major trading center for two thousand years, ever since the river channel was first dredged. From here in days gone by, Chinese merchants sent porcelain, silk, and textiles to offshore islands where they were traded for, among other things, Japanese copper- and lacquerware. Within the ten-foot-thick wall, built originally to rebuff Japanese pirates, lived an estimated 300,000 people. The poorer classes were jammed into two-story wooden houses built along narrow, winding stone-paved streets and dark alleys. The streets were lined with ditches filled with black, foul-smelling slime. Public toilets stood open at intersections, and men carrying human offal hustled down the streets. The ground floors of many of the buildings were given over to shops, while the residents lived in the back or on the second floor. The fancier stores were located near the center of the city, their bright red signs with golden lettering hanging from the eaves. Better-off families lived in low stone buildings with tile roofs and open verandahs decorated with boxes of white and crimson peonies and an orchid with a yellowish green flower. The foreigners stayed away from the Chinese city as much as possible. They had their own lavish social life at the settlements, which thrived and sparkled because of the presence of so many warships and their gallant officers.[49]

Since the Opium War, Shanghai had become the center of foreign trade with China because of its greater proximity to the tea- and silk-producing areas of Fukien, Kiangsu, and Chekiang. Many of the Chinese merchants associated with foreign trade in Canton had followed the trade to Shanghai, where their Cantonese dialect labeled them as outsiders. Intendant Wu Chien-chang, the official who ruled over the city and the surrounding countryside, was actually a silent partner of Russell and Company. The intendant, a Cantonese, had been a member of the Cohong in that city, and under his rule, Shanghai had thrived as a smugglers' paradise. In Shanghai there was measurably less hostility to foreigners, although the relentless pressure of the foreign merchants for additional concessions had begun to stir resentments.[50]

In the weeks after the arrival of the *Susquehanna*, while Perry was still in the south, Shanghai had been convulsed with rumors about the plans of the Taiping rebels, and trade ground to a halt except for some exchange of tea for opium. "Each hour brought a new rumor," recalled Taylor, "and each day led to conclusions and conjectures which the morrow proved to be unfounded." The rebels had captured Nanking, it was reported, which was true enough. But then it was said that Shanghai was their next objective. Twenty thousand had been slain in Nanking, and the streets were jammed with piles of corpses. The rebels had quartered the body of one of Nanking's most powerful officials, and the pieces were nailed to the city's gates. His daughter was stripped naked in public, bound to a cross, and her heart cut out. One day there were reports of gun fire at Woosung. The rebels were said to be spreading the word that the foreigners were not human. No, the British said, the rebels were in touch with supporters in Shanghai to reassure the foreigners that they would not be attacked if Shanghai was taken. Meanwhile bodies floated down the river, and anxiety grew apace. As the hysteria grew, fed by wild speculation, the wealthy Chinese began to abandon the city, taking their families and their possessions with them while shopkeepers bundled up their goods and headed for the countryside.[51]

The British had already begun to prepare for the defense of the foreign settlements. In the middle of March, two British war steamers had arrived at Shanghai. Troops were landed to patrol the streets of the foreign settlement. The merchants formed defense committees and began military drills. To protect the settlement, the British dug a shallow ditch through the racetrack—hardly deep enough to stop a European cavalry charge, Taylor sniffed. When this led to conflict with Chinese whose family graves were being disturbed, the British threatened to fire on the protesters. The intendant alternately ordered and begged the foreigners to send warships to support the imperial forces at Nanking. Finally he chartered an opium-receiving ship from Russell and Company and sent it, manned by foreign mercenaries recruited from the sailor riffraff that lived along the waterfront, up the Yangtze. It promptly ran aground.[52]

The British, French, and Americans all proclaimed their neutrality in the war between the imperials (or imps, as the foreigners

Photograph of Colonel Humphrey Marshall,
American commissioner in China

called them) and the rebels. The British, however, insisted on their own proclamation, while the British and Americans formed separate defense committees. Social relations between the British and the Americans were amiable enough. But there was mutual suspicion when it came to diplomatic initiatives. Each nation was wary lest the other take advantage of the chaotic situation to build new ties to either the rebels or the Manchu dynasty.

"The Commissioner, Marshall," Sir George Bonham, the British plenipotentiary, superintendent of trade, and governor of Hong Kong, wrote home, "is a big, coarse, headstrong man, has never been out of Kentucky before he came here, and will I fear give us annoyance and embarrass our proceedings—he already wants to have a squabble with me but I will not afford him the opportunity if I

can possibly avoid it."[53] Slowly more reliable reports began to reach
Shanghai, and the panic subsided. A British missionary disguised
as a Chinese reached Soochow, only seventy miles away, and reported back that the city was quiet and still in the hands of imperial
troops.

Upon his arrival on May fourth, Perry moved into Russell and
Company's palatial residence on the Bund. Said to have cost
$50,000, it was furnished with floor-length silk drapes and expensive
inlaid furniture made by Chinese craftsmen. From the front entrance a huge cannon pointed out toward the street.[54] Humphrey
Marshall was here as well as Perry's son Oliver H. Perry II, who
had gone out to China ahead of his father and had been acting as
Marshall's secretary. Marshall had much to report, not all of which
reflected favorably upon his diplomatic endeavors. Marshall had
tried to go up the Yangtze to Nanking in the *Susquehanna* to gather
information about the rebels, even though he had been told repeatedly that the *Susquehanna* drew too much water to manage it.
Marshall persisted, and the *Susquehanna* ran aground thirty miles
upriver. The Americans turned on the principal Chinese pilot, but
he assumed an attitude of haughty indifference until beaten to his
knees by a Chinese employee of Cunningham's. When the bumboat,
a type of Chinese craft that was routinely hired to accompany
foreign ships for the purpose of running errands, was sent to fetch
more pilots, it took off, not even hesitating when fired upon by the
Susquehanna. During the night the *Susquehanna* worked its way
off the shoal. But the steamer had become separated in the darkness
from its fleet of scouting junks and ran aground several more times
before coming to rest in the middle of some fishing weirs. The next
day the *Susquehanna* returned to Shanghai with all aboard in a
chastened mood. Marshall's first diplomatic initiative had turned
out to be a bad joke.[55]

There is no record of Perry's first encounter with Marshall,
but it must have been an unpleasant one. Marshall had not only
commandeered Perry's flagship, he had run it aground in the
Yangtze, seriously risking damage to a ship that Perry considered
indispensable to the success of the Japan expedition. The next day
the two went to introduce Perry to Sir George Bonham. Bonham
had just returned from a visit to Nanking aboard the British war

steamer *Hermes*, a shallow-draft vessel that made it up the Yangtze. Bonham was not impressed with the long-haired rebels, perhaps because the rebels had asked him to curtail the opium trade. They were a disorganized and undisciplined lot whose number was greatly exaggerated. In fact, they would eventually be forced to abandon Nanking and retreat to the south. Bonham's emissaries had reported that the rebels were eager for friendly relations with the British and had spoken of the fact that they were all children of the same God. The rebels also made it clear that they had no intention of attacking Shanghai. Perry noted that others who had accompanied Bonham did not share his negative evaluation of the rebels, and Marshall left the meeting more suspicious than ever of British intentions.

Soon after Perry was visited by the intendant, who asked him to send his squadron to back the imperial forces against the rebels. This was impossible, Perry reponded. He had no authority to intervene in the conflict. American intentions toward China, he assured the intendant, were friendly. But the American commissioner still had not been accredited by the government at Peking. That was a necessary first step toward the establishment of cordial relations.[56]

So far, but no further, Perry was in tune with Marshall's intentions. Both the British and the Americans were disposed to use the insurrection as a fulcrum for attaining leverage with the government in Peking. Marshall, however, wanted to go one step farther. He had to do something, anything, to exploit the situation and keep up with the maneuvers of the British. For one thing, Marshall still wanted an American warship to convey him to the mouth of the Pei-ho River, where he hoped to present his credentials to a representative of the imperial government. For another, he was appalled that Perry intended to sail off to Japan taking his squadron with him at a time when he judged that American merchants required the protection of American warships.[57]

Meanwhile Perry had moved his quarters to the *Susquehanna* and immersed himself in the social life of the foreign settlement. There was a grand ball for the officers of the foreign warships followed by nightly dinners and receptions, an exchange of visits with the intendant, a theatrical performed by the sailors of one of the British warships, and the spring meeting at the racetrack. Perry was impressed by the sumptuous lives of the well-to-do merchants. Everything was to his liking, right down to his favorite soda water, from the Congress spring at Saratoga, New York. But Perry as always was conscious that, as a naval officer, he was enjoying other people's wealth, not his own. "But alas for us officers and crew of the Navy," he lamented in his journal, "visiting, as we do, all climes for the protection of the interests of these very merchants—we spend our lives in hard service to die in comparative penury."[58]

While Perry enjoyed himself, Marshall was busy. First he made a personal request that Perry leave him a ship or ships. When Perry declined, Marshall pulled his trump card. On May eleventh he forwarded a letter to Perry from the American merchants at Shanghai asking him if the rumors were true that he intended to withdraw the American warships from Shanghai. Marshall in his covering letter contended that American property (valued by the merchants at more than $1 million) would be at risk if the American ships withdrew. Moreover, the rebels' occupation of the countryside around Nanking meant, Marshall claimed, that hostile armies could be at Shanghai in thirty-six hours.[59] Perry was incensed. Marshall had turned Perry's own supporters, or at least their employees in China, against an expedition that was clearly being carried out in the interests of the China trade and Shanghai in particular.

Perry's reply was prompt and curt. He had made every effort to acquaint himself with the situation in China and "so long as I command the United States naval forces in these seas, I shall be mindful to watch over the American interests in China."[60] He said nothing of his plans for the squadron, however. Rebuffed, Marshall changed his tune. He no longer insisted on the protection of American interests in Shanghai. But he had to get to the mouth of the Pei-ho. He reminded Perry that he had sent a letter to Peking at the time of the fall of Nanking indicating that he wanted to present his credentials to the imperial court. There had been no reply, but the Shanghai intendant had told him that it might take two or three months to hear from Peking. With the country in the midst of a revolution, there was no better time to press his demand for recognition.

Marshall acknowledged that the reason for the Japan expedition was "the idea of future progress in peaceful and profitable intercourse with China." But perhaps the United States would prefer to modify its plans with regard to Japan until its relations with China were more fully developed. "There is nothing to be hoped for in Japan equal to the advantages now actually enjoyed in China," Marshall wrote to Perry, "and it appears to me no effort should be spared to preserve the beneficial and prosperous commerce already open with this great, extensive, and productive country." The Japan expedition, Marshall concluded, was only of secondary importance. China was the most pressing issue.[61]

Nothing that Marshall could have said could have been more offensive to the commodore. The Japan expedition of *secondary* importance! It was the China trade and the interests of the American merchants in China that had brought Perry to the gates of the Japanese empire. With his sophisticated grasp of the geopolitics of East Asia and the need to establish a trans-Pacific communication system that would undermine British hegemony in the region, Perry had a broader grasp of the relationship of Japan to American interests in China. He had no intention of sacrificing three years of preparation because of the demands of a political appointee. He had not asked for this command. Indeed he had sacrificed a comfortable station in the Mediterranean with his family nearby for this arduous undertaking, and now an impetuous and self-important diplomatic amateur was trying to tell him how to handle his affairs.

Perry was angry, but he was also cautious in his dealings with Marshall. He had been in similar conflicts over the demands of civilian diplomats and the prerogatives of naval command. He knew that he would probably hear more about this controversy. So Perry was careful to give in a little and then fill the public record with enough documentation to justify his departure for Japan. He would leave a ship in Shanghai for a time. But he had no intention of allowing Marshall to take one of his ships to the mouth of the Pei-ho. To protect his flank, he got Commander John Kelly—the very one who had gotten him into this mess—to send him (Perry) a letter saying that he had examined the charts for the entrance to the Pei-ho River and found that it was extremely hazardous for a vessel with the draft of the *Plymouth* to enter the river. Finally he ordered Kelly to remain at Shanghai with the *Plymouth* for the protection of the American settlement.[62]

After this exchange, Perry and Marshall were no longer speaking to each other. In a parting shot, Perry wrote to Marshall explaining his reasons for leaving the *Plymouth* at Shanghai while barring it from traveling to the mouth of the Pei-ho. Such a move, Perry asserted, "would doubtless produce unfriendly relations between the United States and China, and retard, rather than advance, the object so much desired, of establishing an American embassy at Pekin." Of course, Perry concluded, as his squadron prepared to get under way, his decision could be referred to his superiors at home *without inconvenience*, and he would follow their instructions.[63]

Marshall had been finessed, left fuming on the beach at Shanghai. Both he and Perry knew that it would take at least half a year to refer their dispute to Washington and get new instructions. But Perry had no intention of waiting, and Marshall was left behind to write another letter to the secretary of state cataloguing his complaints. Perry had "inflicted deep injury upon the United States in their relations with China." His actions were "grossly unjust and injurious" to Marshall. And in a final insult, Perry had left without telling Marshall how to get in touch with him, since the location of the rendezvous for his squadron was a secret.[64]

Perry had no more time for Marshall. Instead he was preoccupied with making final preparations and planning the dangerous passage down the Yangtze. Things were already off to a bad start, an ominous portent for normally superstitious sailors. The *Supply* in coming in from Hong Kong had run aground on the North Sands at the mouth of the Yangtze and was in danger of pounding to pieces on the shoal. Perry dispatched the *Mississippi* to assist the *Supply*. A day later, on a calm, warm, sunny morning, Perry departed on the *Susquehanna*. It was a festive occasion as the entire foreign population gathered along the Bund to watch the commodore's ship—its band playing and black smoke billowing from its stack—thread its way through the dense river shipping.

The next day, however, the weather changed dramatically, and a gale lashed the steamer as it approached the mouth of the river towing a junk laden with coal. At the mouth, the *Mississippi* rendezvoused with the *Susquehanna* and the *Supply*, now free of the bar. But then the coal junk drifted into the *Mississippi* and had to be cast off. Whereupon the junk went up on the same bar. The coal was unloaded, the steamers' bunkers crammed full, but the junk was a total loss. For three days the squadron lay at anchor in the shelter of some islands at the mouth of the Yangtze awaiting the arrival of the *Caprice*, the bark hired in Canton as a dispatch and supply vessel. When the *Caprice* failed to arrive, Perry signaled for the squadron to get under way, only to meet the *Caprice* standing into the river mouth. "Shortly after passing the islands," Taylor wrote, "a streak of dazzling emerald appeared on the horizon, heralding our release from the treacherous waters of the Yang-tse-Kiang."[65]

5

THE OUTER DOOR
OF THE HERMETIC
EMPIRE

The number of all sorts of vessels sailing in the Japanese seas will be greater than ever before, and how easily might a quarrel occur between the crews of those vessels and the inhabitants of Your Majesty's dominion![1] —KING WILLIAM II of Holland to the the shogun of Japan, February 15, 1844

We felt as if we had arrived at the outer door of the hermetic empire.[2] —J. W. SPALDING, Captain's Clerk, *Mississippi*

It was part of the Commodore's deliberately formed plan, in all his intercourse with these orientals, to consider carefully before he announced his resolution to do any act, but, having announced it, he soon taught them to know that he would do precisely what he had said he would.[3] —COMMODORE MATTHEW CALBRAITH PERRY, *Narrative of the Expedition*

FREE OF THE YANGTZE SANDBARS, the American squadron headed in a southeasterly direction for the Ryukyu Islands. The China coast was familiar territory to American merchantmen and lately the navy, but Perry was now entering waters that were well-known only to wandering whalemen. The *Susquehanna* forged steadily ahead followed by the *Mississippi* with the *Supply* in tow, both steamers carrying topsails to reduce their coal consumption. The western tip of Japan lay some six hundred miles due east of Shanghai, but Perry hoped to establish a foothold and perhaps a coal depot at Okinawa in the Ryukyu Islands and then to use the island as a forward base for the final approach to Edo. It was the principle, J. W. Spalding wrote, "of reaching the old hen by first going at the chickens."[4]

Before leaving Shanghai, Perry had added a professional writer to the expedition's intellectual cadre. Bayard Taylor had at first been rebuffed by Perry because of Perry's opposition to taking anyone but naval personnel on the voyage. Finding Taylor gentlemanly and unassuming, Perry finally gave in, making him a master's mate with the pay of three hundred dollars a year plus six dollars a month for rations. Taylor's joining the expedition was in fact a notable coup. The twenty-eight-year-old Taylor was one of the most popular American travel writers of the day, and his account of the expedition would undoubtedly add the musings of a professional to the amateur efforts of those shipboard diarists who still continued to write after Perry laid claim to their output in the name of the government.

The bearded Taylor, with his long, wavy, brown hair and expressive brown eyes, was the epitome of the romantic literary figure. At the age of nineteen, he had wandered from his home in Pennsylvania to Europe and then had returned to write *Views Afoot or Europe Seen with Knapsack and Staff*. The book won him instant renown, going through six editions in its first year. After failing as a newspaper publisher, Taylor went to work for Horace Greeley, writing a series of ballads about California for the New York *Tribune*. Taylor had never been to the West, so his ballads were presented as translations of the writings of a Spanish gentleman in Saint Louis. Later when gold was discovered, Taylor did visit California, writing both newspaper articles and a book on his travels via Panama and Mexico. Upon his return, he married his tubercular fiancée, who died within two months. Feeling "the old impatience and longing for motion and change"—that quintessential American restlessness—Taylor eventually took off for Africa, the Middle East, and the Orient. Along the way, he heard from the *Tribune* about the Japan expedition. When the newspaper offered to pay his expenses and a higher fee than originally offered for his articles, he pushed on to China to meet up with the Japan expedition.

With a uniform made from French cloth by a Chinese tailor in Shanghai and fitted with buttons borrowed from some officers, Taylor joined the artist and interpreter's mess aboard the *Susquehanna*, welcomed no doubt by the artist Wilhelm Heine, who was an old friend from New York. Given the ship's crowded living conditions, Taylor ended up berthing on the orlop deck next to the

Portrait of Bayard Taylor

hatch that covered the powder magazine, a dark and overheated recess deep within the bowels of the steamer. His mess, however, dined in the cockpit and was waited upon by a cadaverous Chinese man and cooked for by someone whom Taylor described as "an incorrigible black deck-hand."

The *Susquehanna* was somewhat less crowded because it had lost all but one of its complement of shipwrecked Japanese sailors. Almost a year before his departure, Perry had been informed that a group of sixteen shipwrecked sailors had reached California. They had been picked up near Hawaii from the hulk of a coastal trading junk that had been blown off the coast of Japan in a storm. Perry had hoped to take these orphans of the sea with him to Japan as a friendly gesture designed to counter the expected intransigence of the Japanese officials. Accordingly, the Japanese had been shipped to Hong Kong to await Perry's arrival aboard the *Susquehanna*. While in the States, the Japanese had been treated with great kindness, so much so that they had often speculated about the reasons for it. One of them suggested that they were being fattened up for a future meal. But their captain concluded that the Americans were "simply good and charitable people," who understood that they had lost everything at sea.

Aboard the *Susquehanna* in Hong Kong, however, their treatment took a decided turn for the worse. Here the Japanese sailors became targets of abuse. This change in attitude, the Japanese thought, was because of the fact that the *Susquehanna* had been on the China station for so long a time that the officers and men had become accustomed to abusing the Chinese in the manner of other westerners. Finally, the Japanese became outraged, and eight of them decided to abandon the *Susquehanna* after being beaten and abused by an officer because they came topside to escape the heat below.

At the first opportunity, eight of the sailors jumped ship and started for Nanking, using the passport of a Chinese priest. The very same night the eight sailors returned to the *Susquehanna*, stripped of everything but their shirts and drawers. They had traveled only a dozen miles inland before wandering into a nest of pirates and robbers, who relieved them of their possessions. After this futile attempt to escape, all of the party, except one who returned to the United States, went on to Shanghai aboard the *Susquehanna*, where they continued to wait for Perry. In Shanghai all but one of the sailors abandoned the *Susquehanna*, hoping to make their way to the Chinese port that traded with Nagasaki. Sam Patch, as he was known, remained aboard the *Susquehanna* as it traveled toward his homeland.[5]

The passage from the mouth of the Yangtze to the Ryukyu Islands proved uneventful except for the increased vigilance on the part of the Americans. The warm days were spent preparing for whatever eventuality greeted the squadron in potentially hostile waters. The crew was drummed to general quarters on a daily basis. The gunners practiced firing the great swivel guns on the decks of the steamers. The ships' boats were armed and equipped with spare

masts, sails, battle axes, muskets, pistols, cutlasses, bandages, laud-
anum, and an array of other items that would allow them to serve
as landing craft or to survive alone on the open sea. For his own
use ashore, Perry had an octagonal marquee made out of red, white,
and blue canvas. He also issued new orders. Lookouts were to be
posted in port as well as at sea, and they were to report all movements of boats and ships to the officer of the deck. Sentinels with
loaded muskets and six rounds of cartridges were to be stationed
on the decks.

They were about to encounter, Perry explained, "a singular
people," who had refused all contact with foreigners for more than
two centuries. His intention was to approach these people in a
friendly and conciliatory manner. For this reason everyone who
had contact with the Japanese was to behave with the greatest
prudence, forbearance, and discretion. The Americans would only
resort to extreme measures when all other means were exhausted.
After two days, the first outlying islands of the Ryukyu group came
into sight. On the third day in heavy thundershowers, the squadron,
joined by the *Saratoga*, just arriving from Hong Kong, passed
between two coral reefs and entered Naha harbor. "We felt," Spalding wrote, "as if we had arrived at the outer door of the hermetic
empire."[6]

The *Saratoga*'s crossing had also been uneventful. But for
Wells Williams it had been an extremely unpleasant trip. Life
aboard a naval ship was a rude shock for this rigid Puritan. The
first night he was treated to the profane roaring and singing of a
drunken seaman who had been locked in the brig after bringing
liquor aboard and then breaking into the spirit closet. The next
morning the man was found dead in his cell sitting in a chair. "So
he died, this James Welsh, as a fool dieth," Williams confided to
his journal, "for no 'drunkard can inherit the kingdom of heaven.' "

Once the *Saratoga* got under way, the situation hardly improved. Williams found the strangeness of his new life disconcert-
ing. There were too many people crammed into too little space, and
when the wind came up strong from the north, the pitching of the
ship made him seasick. His second day at sea was the Sabbath, but
there was no service of a public nature, and this, Williams judged,
was a bad arrangement. Then too his thoughts turned to Japan and

the consequences of a successful expedition. He pondered the possibility that the merchants in China would try to sell opium along the coast of Japan as soon as the country was opened. Williams could think of no way to avoid this development. "This view would be saddening," he concluded, "if one did not remember that the mixture of good and evil in this world is necessary for the development of the probationary plan on which this world is governed."[7]

When the squadron entered Naha harbor on the island of Great Lew Chew (Okinawa) on May twenty-sixth, the Americans were greeted by the British flag being run up a flagpole that stood in front of a house perched on a coral outcrop north of town. Before dark torrents of rain obscured their view, the Americans found themselves gazing upon an appealing scene. Gently undulating hills rose from the water's edge toward wooded highlands broken by rocks and crags. The deeply green hillsides were cultivated and dotted here and there with white shapes, which the Americans took to be houses, but were actually horseshoe-shaped tombs fashioned from blocks of lava faced with limestone. Naha itself appeared to be several blocks of neat wooden houses with red tile roofs surrounded by walls made from coral blocks. Through a glass the Americans could see an inner harbor where a number of Chinese and Japanese junks were tied up. People carrying white umbrellas were leaving the town and moving toward the seashore. In contrast to China, Okinawa, according to Bayard Taylor, "charmed us like a glimpse of paradise."[8]

Two hours after their arrival, a crude flat-bottomed boat was paddled up to the *Susquehanna*, and two officials with several attendants came aboard. Bowing repeatedly they presented a yard-long red greeting card. The two men were dressed in fine grass-cloth robes, one salmon, the other blue, tied at the waist with blue sashes. On their head they wore oblong yellow caps, on their feet white sandals. Their beards were long and black but sparse, and they looked more Japanese than Chinese. "Everything about them gave evidence of a care and neatness which I have never seen surpassed," Taylor reported. In the absence of an interpreter, it was hard to determine what they wanted. But then one of Perry's Chinese servants came forward and explained that they were there to greet the Americans. Perry, meanwhile, remained out of sight.

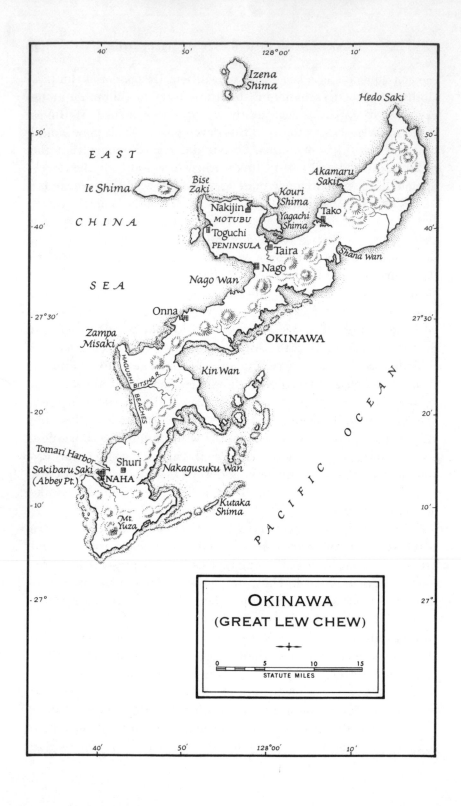

40'　　　　　50'　　　　128°00'　　　　10'

Izena
Shima

Hedo Saki

50'　　　　　　　　　　　　　　　　　　　　　　　　　　50'

E A S T

Ie Shima

Bise
Zaki

Akamaru
Saki

C H I N A

Kouri
Shima

40'　　　　　Nakijin　　　*Yagachi*　Tako　　　40'
　　　　　　MOTUBU　　*Shima*
　　　　Toguchi
　　　　PENINSULA　Taira

Shana Wan

S E A

Nago

Nago Wan

OKINAWA

27°30'　　Onna　　　　　　　　　　　　27°30'

Zampa
Misaki

Kin Wan

P
A
C
I
F
I
C

O
C
E
A
N

20'　　　　　　　　　　　　　　　　　　　　　　20'

Tomari Harbor
Sakibaru Saki　Shuri
(*Abbey Pt.*)　NAHA

Nakagusuku Wan

10'　　　　　　　　　　　　　　　　　　　　　　10'

Mt.
Yuza

Kutaka
Shima

27°　　　　　　　　　　　　　　　　　　　　27°

OKINAWA
(GREAT LEW CHEW)

0　　　5　　　10　　　15
STATUTE MILES

40'　　　　　50'　　　　128°00'　　　　10'

It was his decision not to meet with anyone whose rank was not equal to his own. "It was not meet," the official narrative of the expedition explained, "that he should be made too common to the eyes of the vulgar."[9] Instead the two Okinawans were shown around the ship, exclaiming over its size as they went. With little to do in the absence of Perry, the officials soon left.

As soon as the Okinawans had departed, a small boat came bobbing toward the *Susquehanna* out of the warm driving rain. It made its way to the flagship, and a thin, nervous man with an Eastern European accent clambered aboard. The new arrival was Bernard John Bettelheim, a British missionary. Bettelheim, who was a well-known figure to those who studied the reports of Western ships that had called at the island over the years, was shown to Perry's cabin, where he and the commodore conversed for three hours. Bettelheim's story was a remarkable one. He had been living on the island since 1846, and over seven years had been a source of unremitting trouble for the Okinawans. To their great pleasure, at the very moment they spotted the squadron entering the harbor, Bettelheim had been discussing his departure with two local officials.[10] Because the Ryukyus were a dependency of the Satsuma domain in Japan's western island of Kyushu, Bettelheim in fact had penetrated the invisible barrier thrown up by the Tokugawa shoguns in the seventeenth century to keep Christianity out of the Land of the Gods. Unknowingly, this eccentric missionary had played a major role in forcing the shogun to admit the inevitability of dealing with foreigners. Bettelheim, Williams wrote without understanding the full meaning of his words, was "the entering wedge of more extended operations of others."[11]

Portrait of
Bernard John Bettelheim

Bettelheim had come to Okinawa with his wife, daughter, a governess (who refused to go ashore), and a Chinese assistant as the representative of the London Naval Mission—to "delight my soul in the results of Protestantism on a virgin soil." Instead he found himself among a hapless people, who, because of the location of their island kingdom at a strategic ocean crossroads, were forced to appease two mighty overlords, the Chinese and the daimyo of Satsuma. The Ryukyuans were the offspring of a triple migration, coming over the centuries from islands to the south, the Asian mainland, and Japan. The people were a Chinese-Melanesian-Japanese hybrid with an early tradition of female rule. Chinese Taoists before and after the birth of Christ had spoken of magic islands to the east where the inhabitants had learned the secret of immortality and of the transformation of base metals into gold. The first Chinese expedition to seek the magic islands is thought to have reached Okinawa in the seventh century, at about the same time that scholars in Japan took notice of an island people to their south.[12]

The first Okinawan king, born according to tradition in 1166, was the son of an Okinawan woman and a Japanese adventurer. Two centuries later Okinawa fractured into three separate kingdoms. Chuzan, the central kingdom, became a tributary state to China's Ming dynasty and ultimately united all of the Ryukyus under its rule. Although the people spoke a language related to Japanese, Chinese administrative forms and codes became predominant in the Ryukyus, and Chinese became the language of the mandarin class. In time the Okinawans joined the great China-centered trade network that extended from Japan to India and probably as far as Africa and the Americas. Though they had only foodstuffs and building materials to offer, the Okinawans prospered immensely as middlemen between Japan and China, and Okinawan traders were familiar figures in the ports of Southeast Asia and the Philippines.[13]

The great period of prosperity and Chinese influence came to an end with the consolidation in Japan of the rule of the Tokugawa shoguns in the early seventeenth century. During the preceding century Japanese pirates and the equally piratical Europeans led by the Portuguese had disrupted established trade routes in East Asia. Marco Polo had written of "a great island to the East" called Cipango, where gold was abundant, and the Portuguese had heard stories of the use of gold bars and gold dust in the Okinawan trade and were eager to get their hands upon them. But it was Japan, and specifically the Shimazu family, that seized control of the Ryukyus. First the Shimazus, feudal lords and skillful traders of the extensive Satsuma domain, which at that time embraced all of Kyushu, insinuated themselves into the trade between Japan and China, acting as the agent of earlier shoguns. Then when trade between Japan and China came to an end, Satsuma turned to Okinawa as a place to acquire the Chinese goods it could no longer get in direct trade. During the bloody wars that preceded the consolidation of the Tokugawa shogunate, the Okinawans had refused requests to send men and supplies to the mainland, asserting their independence from the rival lords who had plunged Japan into chaos.[14]

When Tokugawa Ieyasu won a decisive victory over his opponents at the battle of Sekigahara in 1600 and then proclaimed himself the first Tokugawa shogun, Okinawa became a pawn in the establishment of peaceful relations between Ieyasu and the Shimazu clan, which had fought against Ieyasu at Sekigahara. To punish the Shimazus, Ieyasu reduced the size of their domain to its two original provinces. To placate Ieyasu, the Shimazus asked permission to punish the Okinawans for their display of independence. In 1609 the Shimazus, after contriving an excuse for an invasion, conquered the Ryukyus and then, after looting the royal palace on Okinawa, carried off the king to present to Ieyasu as a token of submission. The Okinawan king was forced to acknowledge that the Ryukyus had been a dependency of Satsuma "since ancient times" and to swear an oath of eternal allegiance. The king also signed and accepted new laws that gave the Shimazus monopoly control over Okinawa's trade with China, as well as extensive control over all other aspects of Ryukyuan society.[15]

The problem for the crafty Shimazus was that the Ryukyus had long been a tribute-bearing dependency of China. After the conquest of the island, the Okinawans were ordered not to reveal to anyone the nature of their new ties to Satsuma. Their tribute ships continued to sail to China, but for a time they went only every ten years, carrying with them Satsuma men disguised as Ryukyuans. In time Chinese influence declined, but the Okinawans were ordered not to speak Japanese in the presence of foreigners, since it might provide a clue as to which of their two masters they really served. Meanwhile the Shimazu clan was busily extending its influence in the islands. A liaison office for the Ryukyus was established at Kagoshima, where the Shimazus had their main castle, and a Satsuma official, the *zaiban bugyo*, was stationed in Naha. Supported by a police force, really a phalanx of spies known as *metsuke*, the Shimazus kept the Okinawans under constant surveillance. Inevitably Europeans ships called at Okinawa, but soon after Satsuma took control, they were barred from the islands.[16]

When foreigners reached Japan, as Commander Glynn did aboard the *Preble* looking for the missing American whalers in 1849, they were invariably told that Japan's restrictions on foreign trade were part of the ancient laws of their land. But the fact was that Ieyasu, the first Tokugawa shogun, had aggressively sought foreign trade during the initial years of the Tokugawa shogunate. When his successors barred foreign trade, the Tokugawa family retained personal control over the single trade outlet at Nagasaki. And in permitting Satsuma to control the Ryukyus, they permitted, or at least looked the other way, while one domain set up its own trade link with China.

At first, trade with China through Okinawa proved very lucrative for the Shimazus. The Okinawans were compared to the cormorants in the Nagara River in Japan; they were allowed to catch fish but were prevented by a ring around their neck from swallowing them. But in time the Shimazus squeezed too much tribute out of the Okinawans. The far-ranging Okinawan traders were forced to become farmers and on some islands became almost slave laborers, providing food and sugar cane for Satsuma. The island's economy declined, plagued in addition by famine, typhoon, drought, and epidemics. Ironically the Okinawans in the years before Perry's arrival had to turn to the wealthy merchants of Kagoshima for loans to maintain their tribute relationship with China. Although trade declined, Okinawa remained the center of Satsuma's trade with China, a trade that remained technically illegal according to the laws of the Tokugawa shoguns.[17]

At the end of the eighteenth century, Westerners rediscovered Okinawa. The British, the first to explore the Ryukyus, established the myth that the Okinawans were Asia's equivalent to Rousseau's natural man. The Okinawans were polite, friendly, even hospitable. There were no weapons in sight, no indications of crime, and when the British explorers sailed away the islanders gathered in canoes around their ships and along the shore by the thousands to bid them farewell. The myth of the gentle islanders even survived the killing of a British sailor who was part of a group of sailors attacked by villagers when British sailors came ashore to steal cattle.

When reports of this incident, filtered through Kagoshima, reached Edo, the Bakufu, the shogun's government, issued a new expulsion edict in 1825. The Ryukyuans were enjoined to drive all foreigners away. "Should any foreigners land anywhere," the edict stated, "they must be arrested or killed, and if the ship approaches the shore it must be destroyed." British ships, however, continued to visit the islands, seeking trade and an entrée to Japan. The Ryukyuans reluctantly received the foreigners when they forced themselves upon them but turned aside their offers of trade, insisting on their poverty, a claim that was dismissed by Westerners as typical Asian duplicity.[18]

After the Opium War, the British began to survey the waters and islands around Okinawa. But it was the French who made the first move to establish a foothold on Okinawa. In 1844 a French warship, the *Alcmène*, visited the island and offered to establish a protectorate. The French explained to the Okinawans that the British had designs on their island, and they, the French, were there to protect them. The Okinawans turned down the offer, and the French sailed off leaving a Catholic missionary and promises that they would return with a naval squadron in the future. Indeed, the French were back two years later with a four-ship squadron commanded by an admiral. This time the French were more insistent. They were arrogant and abusive, near violent in their insistence on a trade treaty. The Okinawans, however, resisted French demands, and again they sailed away, leaving a second missionary.[19]

If the Okinawans were baffled by the strange behavior of the foreigners, the Shimazus and the Bakufu were definitely threatened by the arrival of the French. Both the Shimazus and the Bakufu had become concerned about the ocean frontier to the south when European trade with China and Southeast Asia began to increase at the end of the eighteenth century. Scholars in Edo turned their attention to the Ryukyus as the first line of defense against Western intrusion. The Japanese spoke of *sakoku*, chaining off the land, and the Ryukyus were definitely a weak link. In Satsuma a debate developed between those who favored closing the islands to foreigners and establishing a military outpost there and those who favored opening a trade depot for Westerners at Okinawa. The debate was intensified by the British victory in the Opium War.[20]

To add to the Bakufu's consternation, in 1844, the year that the *Alcmène* delivered the first French missionary to Okinawa, King William II of Holland had sent a letter to the shogun offering him the friendly advice that it was time to "ameliorate the laws against foreigners, lest happy Japan be destroyed by war." King William reviewed, in particular, the events of the Opium War, pointing out that "the mighty Emperor of China after a long and fruitless resistance, was finally compelled to succumb to the superior power of European military tactics. . . . The number of all sorts of vessels sailing the Japanese seas will be greater than ever before," the king warned, "and how easily might a quarrel occur between the crews of those vessels and the inhabitants of Your Majesty's dominion!"[21]

After the departure of the French squadron, Shimazu Narioki, the daimyo of Satsuma, turned to Abe Masahiro, the youthful head of the Roju, the governing council of the shogun's government, for advice while the Ryukyuans sent a delegation to China to appeal to the Ch'ing (or Manchu) dynasty to intervene with the French. Narioki's appeal to Abe was itself an admission of the seriousness of the situation, since the Ryukyus were Satsuma's private domain and the center of its illegal smuggling operations. The Shimazus, moreover, were hereditary enemies of the Bakufu. As *tozama*, or outside daimyo, they were excluded from the councils of the government. In his report on the French visit, Narioki made a startling proposal: Satsuma should be allowed to trade with France. Abe, who was essentially Japan's prime minister, turned to Narioki's son, Nariakira, for advice.[22]

The thirty-seven-year-old Nariakira was a remarkably accomplished man from one of the wealthiest houses in Japan. His grandfather, Shigehide, had expended lavish sums supporting the so-called Dutch scholars who had congregated around Nagasaki gleaning information about the West from the Dutch traders at Deshima Island in Nagasaki. Nariakira had met and been inspired by Philipp Franz von Siebold as a young man. He spoke Dutch, collected books from the West on a wide range of topics, and was a careful student of western technology, shipbuilding, and armaments manufacturing. For a time he even kept a diary, writing out Japanese words in the western-style alphabet. Among his many accomplishments, he took the first photograph in Japan and built the first reverberatory furnace, enhancing his domain's cannon casting capabilities. Nariakira also had a solid grasp, as solid as one could have in the isolation of Japan, of world affairs. He was among those who looked beyond his domain and argued that Japan could not continue to live in isolation. Japan, he believed, should build up its military defenses and open its doors to trade. In his mind the two were connected: trade would bring the technology that was needed to build up enough military power to rebuff Western advances.[23]

At the time of the arrival of the French warships at Okinawa, Nariakira and Abe Masahiro were just beginning to bridge the traditional barriers that kept the Shimazus outside the councils of the Bakufu. They found common ground in their having come of age during a time of increasing pressure from the West. Despite his father's designation as a *tozama* daimyo, Nariakira also had his own ties to the shogun Ieyoshi—his sister was the shogun's wife.[24]

Nariakira explained to Abe that the Ryukyus had a *yang* relationship with China and a *yin* relationship with Japan. That is, they were openly a tribute state of the weakened Manchu emperor but secretly a dependency of Satsuma. He proposed that the Ryukyus be permitted to trade with France and France alone, either at Fukien in China or at an island under Chinese control. Permitting Satsuma to trade with France was a way to respond to European pressures on Japan to open trade by accepting limited trade *outside* of Japan. Christianity, however, would be barred from the islands, and Satsuma would build up its defenses.

Abe took Nariakira's proposal to the shogun. And in a rare interview with the Shimazus, the shogun instructed them to handle the situation in the Ryukyus according to their own judgment. Thus, at the urging of his senior councilor, Abe Masahiro, the shogun declined to take a stand, agreeing in effect to permit the Shimazus to open trade with a Western nation. The Shimazus and Abe had laid the grounds for reversing one of the fundamental postulates of the Tokugawa shogunate, the restriction of trade to annual Dutch and Chinese trading ships at Nagasaki. The one condition was that Satsuma was to keep the matter a secret from the other daimyo. In anticipation of renewed pressures from barbarian warships, Nariakira hurried off to Satsuma to help bolster domain defenses. Once there, he sent a message by express ship to the *zaiban bugyo* in Naha: the Okinawans were to permit trade only when there was no other choice.[25]

In 1846 the French returned again with a four-ship squadron and a proposal for a trade treaty. When the Okinawans insisted that they were too poor to trade with foreigners, the French resorted to violence. Horrified, the Okinawans agreed to sign a treaty. At this point the French left, saying they would return in six months to conclude the negotiations. But when they did return the next year, they stopped only long enough to remove one of the Catholic missionaries from the island. (He was soon replaced by a second French missionary.) Not knowing that the Shimazus were ready to concede to their pressure to open trade—or probably that there even was a clan called Shimazu—the French sailed away, missing the opportunity to open trade with Japan.[26] The Shimazus now turned their full attention to the eccentric Bettelheim, and this forlorn character became the center of a prolonged struggle over Japan's exclusion policy.

Bettelheim was a strange character on a stranger mission. He was a Hungarian Jew, a convert to Christianity who had failed in his efforts to win converts among England's Jews. Bettelheim was both an accomplished linguist who spoke ten or twelve languages and a medical doctor who had served in the Egytian Navy and the Turkish Army. To his surprise, Bettelheim was less than welcome in Okinawa. The authorities immediately turned down his vaguely philanthropic request to come ashore to work as a doctor. Bettelheim, not easily denied, hired a native boat and got ashore with his wife and family. After hours of argument, the Okinawan officials gave in, allowing Bettelheim and his family to spend one night in a Buddhist temple. Once ashore, the Bettelheims could not be dislodged, the ship that brought them having sailed away.

The Okinawans had no choice but to move the Bettelheims into the annex of another Buddhist temple that stood apart from the city of Naha near the seashore. The *zaiban bugyo*, as Satsuma's local eyes and ears, immediately reported to Kagoshima in minute detail on the Bettelheims' invasion of the island, even carefully listing their possessions (a mirror, a quilt, six chairs, a mosquito net, twenty-four white boxes, an iron bathtub, one umbrella, etc.). Bettelheim was probably a Christian missionary, the *zaiban bugyo* reported, although he had not said so. To the islanders, the Bettelheims were at first objects of intense interest. The Okinawans particularly wanted to see Mrs. Bettelheim, since they had never seen a Western woman. They were also fascinated by Bettelheim's spectacles and his two large dogs. To the natives, Bettelheim became *nanmin-nu-gancho* (bespectacled man) or *inu-gancho* (bespectacled doggy man).[27]

Bettelheim and his family were placed under close surveillance. Guards were posted at the gates to the temple compound. Interpreters and cooks who doubled as spies were assigned to his household and then rotated to keep them free of the taint of Christianity. A retinue of interpreters followed the missionary when he left his quarters while the *metsuke* went before him, ordering the Okinawans to bar their doors and close their windows. The Okinawan officials at the urging of the *zaiban bugyo* made a special effort to keep Bettelheim from learning Japanese or finding out about the Ryukyu's subordination to Satsuma. These restrictions did little more than whet Bettelheim's appetite. Within six months, he had mastered enough of the native language to attempt preaching in public. At other times he went from house to house, often throwing tracts into open doors or windows.

When Bettelheim began to draw crowds, the police drove the Okinawans away with bamboo staffs and sticks. The confrontations between Bettelheim and the Okinawan authorities became increasingly bitter. Bettelheim, frustrated with the passive resistance of his translators, grew impatient and abusive, throwing their possessions about but never actually striking them. Events took an ugly turn when Bettelheim attended the funeral of the king, who died on October 27, 1847. He, his wife, and the French missionaries were threatened by an angry mob, and Bettelheim was struck on the hand. Thereafter the authorities were more determined than ever to restrict Bettelheim's activities. Additional guardhouses were built right next to his residence and along the lanes leading from it. Teams were organized in each neighborhood to keep him from entering people's houses. The authorities even managed to buy off Bettelheim's Chinese assistant, turning him into a new source of information about the missionary's activities.

Under this kind of pressure Bettelheim became increasingly eccentric in his behavior. He threw stones at houses that barred their doors, he snuck into others by climbing through holes in the surrounding walls, he lurked in the bushes, calling to passersby, he attacked a guardhouse with a knife, and evaded his guards by sneaking out the back of his residence at odd hours.[28]

In frustration, the Okinawans decided to appeal to China to intervene with England and France to get rid of the three missionaries. The British, however, were preoccupied with enforcing their treaty with China, and there was little enthusiasm for a new diplomatic initiative in the direction of Japan. The British did dispatch a ship to Naha in 1849 with a letter from the British minister for foreign affairs proposing to open trade and supporting the presence of Bettelheim. The captain of the British ship returned to report that the only danger faced by Bettelheim was his own lack of discretion and that he was incapable of advancing "the interests of commerce or to propagate the Christian Religion in any way whatever."[29] The Okinawans for their part greeted every ship that called at Naha, including Commander Glynn aboard the *Preble*, with a request to remove Bettelheim and his family from the island.

Meanwhile Shimazu Nariakira was enmeshed in a bitter and ultimately bloody succession struggle within his own domain. He continued to follow events in the Ryukyus, however. He was well aware that the Ryukyuans' appeal to the Chinese authorities to do something about Bettelheim could cause problems for Satsuma's special relationship with the islands. Nariakira was concerned that unless something was done to placate the Ryukyuans, who were saddled with the unhappy task of dealing with the obstinate missionary, there might be an uprising in Okinawa itself. Or worse, an incident involving Bettelheim might lead to the British using force on the island. With Abe Masahiro's support, Nariakira called upon a number of other feudal lords to put pressure on his father to resign. In 1851 Narioki gave in, and Nariakira became the new lord of Satsuma. Japan's western frontier, the one facing the troubled lands of China, was now ruled by an enlightened daimyo who believed in limited trade with the west and a strong defense against foreign incursions.[30]

While the Satsuma succession struggle unfolded in Kagoshima and Edo, the Okinawan officials increased the pressure on the Bettelheims. Both he and his wife were manhandled. Their servants were assaulted. The merchants who supplied him with food—he and his wife were not permitted to shop on their own—were selling him barely edible produce, which kept him and his family near starvation. One daughter was shoeless, and he suspected that someone was introducing poisonous snakes into the pens with his chickens and goats and was attempting to poison his family.[31]

In this situation, Bettelheim was reduced to begging in the streets for food. In his complaints to the Okinawan officials, Bettelheim had constantly threatened them with the British Navy. Unknown to Bettelheim, the Foreign Office had responded to his request for protection with the suggestion that he be removed from the island. Finally, in 1850, the Foreign Office dispatched a ship to Naha, and the Okinawans were informed that if they did not stop persecuting Bettelheim, the British would resort to force. The British steamer's visit had the desired effect. Bettelheim appeared to be able to summon a warship and a military escort of fifty marines. In the future the Bettelheims were treated much more circumspectly.[32]

Bettelheim, in fact, began to make inroads among the Okinawans. His guards and a number of officials had visited him even in his darkest hours for medical advice. Now he was asked to help inoculate the islanders against smallpox, made a number of converts, and exchanged banquets with the Okinawan officials. The Okinawans, though, were still hostile to his missionary work. When he converted one of his own guards, the officials persuaded the convert's family that he was crazy and should be confined. At first he was locked in a filthy cage in his family's yard where his legs were confined in a device something like the stocks; he was finally taken to another part of the island, where he died.[33]

Once Shimazu Nariakira had become the new daimyo of Satsuma, he became directly involved in l'affaire Bettelheim. At his succession audience with the shogun, the shogun had ordered Nariakira to remove Bettelheim from the island. Nariakira had agreed to prevent the introduction of Christianity into the Ryukyus, but Bettelheim had been trying to convert the Okinawans for five years. Nariakira, with the connivance of Abe Masahiro, proposed a different approach. Satsuma would instruct the Ryukyuans to ask the Chinese to help them a second time to prevail upon the British to remove Bettelheim. If that did not work, the Ryukyuans would offer to begin trade with England at Naha, again as a way to keep the barbarians at arm's length. Like the French, the British viewed missionary activities on Okinawa of little importance and decided not to push for trade after the British steamer's visit in 1850. In 1851 a British warship made another perfunctory call. This time the commander insisted upon marching under armed guard to the royal palace at Shuri, an event that the Okinawans took as a new and extreme form of humiliation. The British commander left with the usual negative impression of Bettelheim and without mentioning trade, which Shimazu Nariakira was prepared to offer to the British if they pressed the question.[34]

The Okinawans, urged on by the *zaiban bugyo*, now made one last effort to get rid of Bettelheim. This time the method was exorcism. When Bettelheim came down with influenza, the *zaiban bugyo* prescribed a rite of extermination. Bettelheim's portrait was painted, and a Buddhist priest prayed for his death in front of the portrait day and night. Bettelheim, however, quickly recovered and returned to his missionary work with renewed enthusiasm. Despite his recovery, Bettelheim had paid a price during his seven-year guerrilla war with the Okinawan authorities. He had become an insomniac, he was deathly pale, with hands that seemed like birds' claws, his eyes were infected, his mannerisms nervous and agitated.[35]

Commodore Perry formed his first impressions of the Okinawans during his three-hour conversation with Bettelheim. Neither Perry nor Bettelheim, however, knew anything about the changes that Bettelheim's presence in Okinawa—and the visits of French and British warships—had brought about in Edo and Kagoshima. As far as both of them were concerned they faced implacable intransigence from the Okinawan officials. Bettelheim did allow that his treatment had changed in recent months. But it took little effort for Bettelheim to convince Perry that for chicanery and diplomatic treachery the Okinawans were unsurpassed.

After his talk with Perry, Bettelheim was wildly enthusiastic about the commodore. Bettelheim wrote in his diary that Perry was very communicative, many sided, and gifted with an abundance of talent. His frankness contrasted marvelously "with the morose taciturnity of our English Envoys." It did not bother Bettelheim that Perry was set against introducing the question of religion into his talks with the Japanese. After all, Bettelheim concluded, "the religious aspect of the question is purely political." Whatever its minor shortcomings, the American squadron was all that Bettelheim had prayed for, and so Bettelheim had offered to serve Perry as a son served his father. As for Perry, he had misgivings about Bettelheim's character, but he wrote in his journal, "he will be useful to us, however, and we must make the best of our means." Perry, for his part, planned "to interpose a little Yankee diplomacy" to offset the Okinawans' Asian duplicity.[36]

Perry's first opportunity came on the very next day, May twenty-seventh, at seven in the morning when four boats carrying a bullock, several pigs, a goat, some fowl, vegetables, and eggs made their way to the flagship. From the splendid isolation of his cabin, Perry sent out the order that the gifts should be refused and the Okinawans barred from coming aboard. After waiting around for a short time, the four boats headed back to Naha. Meanwhile a number of junks cleared the inner harbor and appeared to be headed north toward Japan.

After the Okinawans left, Perry sent for Bettelheim to join him for breakfast, where they were when Wells Williams came aboard the flagship. During breakfast, Perry laid out his plans to explore the island. One party led by the Reverend George Jones, the *Susquehanna*'s chaplain, would go ashore while two other parties would survey the waters along the eastern and western shores of the island. Perry wanted the shore party to collect samples of all minerals, animals, and vegetables they found. Perry also made it known that he wanted to procure a building ashore where Eliphalet Brown, the daguerreotyper, was to set up his camera and start taking pictures.

Portrait of the chief magistrate of Naha;
Narrative of the Expedition

While Bayard Taylor took a boat to explore the reefs at the entrance of the harbor and collect samples of coral, Williams, Bettelheim, and Lieutenant John Contee went ashore in search of some officials to whom they could explain Perry's demands. Bettelheim took them to his residence and introduced the two Americans to his wife and three children (two of whom were born on the island), and then the three walked on into town, where they had been summoned to meet with Naha's chief magistrate. They found the magistrate, a sixty-two-year-old man dressed in yellow robes and surrounded by a large group of well-dressed officials, at an open-

sided meeting hall. Taking a seat, Williams informed the old gentleman through a Chinese interpreter that Perry's intentions were
friendly. He had refused the gifts because it was against American
law to accept them. Instead they wanted to purchase supplies, and
Perry would like to invite the regent—whom Bettelheim had explained ruled on behalf of the eleven-year-old prince and his queen
mother—aboard the *Susquehanna*. Williams also mentioned that
the Americans would like to procure a building ashore to be used
as a hospital. The magistrate was polite and responsive as he conversed with the Americans over tea, pipes, and refreshments. He
did not respond directly to the invitation to the regent, but did
say that he would pass on Perry's request. After forty-five minutes,
the Americans left, returning to the flagship.[37]

The next day, May twenty-eighth, Perry received a four-page
letter from Bettelheim—"the oddest mélange I ever read," concluded Williams when he saw it—advising Perry not to let the
Okinawans near the ship.[38] Perry, accordingly, sent for the missionary, who came aboard and in his usual rapid-fire delivery was
at the point of convincing Perry and Williams to call off the visit
when the regent's boat was seen approaching the flagship. The
regent, whose name was Shang Ta-mo, was a feeble old man with
a long white beard. Helped up the flagship's ladder by two of his
subordinates, he was met at the gangway by Captains Franklin
Buchanan and Henry Adams, who as captain of the fleet was Perry's
chief of staff. A party of marines was hastily drawn up on the deck
in dress uniform and a 3-gun salute was fired, with a blast that
sent several of the regent's party to their knees. While Perry waited
in his cabin, the regent and his escorts were shown about the ship.
The Okinawans maintained an air of dignified gravity until they
were shown the engines. When the great pistons rose and fell with
a hiss, a sigh, and a monumental clanking of machinery, a number
of the party bolted up the ladder and headed for the boats.

After the tour, the regent, who now appeared to be near exhaustion, was taken to meet the commodore. Perry chose to make
a dramatic entrance. With the band playing, he strode forth from
his cabin to greet the regent, who tried as best he could to maintain
his placid demeanor. Seated in his cabin, Perry had the interpreters
again explain that his intentions were amicable, that he had come

Portrait of Shang Ta-mo, regent of the Ryukyu Islands;
Narrative of the Expedition

to open relations with the Okinawans. He spoke of the nearness of the two countries across the Pacific and the growth of California during the gold rush. The Okinawans listened patiently, the old regent appearing half-stupefied, Williams thought. Perry went on to say that he felt compelled to return the regent's visit by going to the castle at Shuri on June sixth. This last proposal caused a visible look of dismay from the Okinawans. After talking among themselves, they responded that the queen mother was sick and that the few presents they had brought aboard with them and which Perry had accepted were so inconsequential that they did not deserve a response. Would not Perry prefer to come to a banquet with the regent at another location on June second? But Perry, being Perry, would not take no for an answer. He would be there on the sixth, and he expected a reception worthy of his rank and his role as a diplomatic representative of the United States. To complete their tour, the Okinawans were shown a few objects that the Americans thought would interest them, including a barometer and a revolver. But the regent now appeared so tired and his attendants so despondent that after a glass of wine with Captain Buchanan, they were escorted to the gangway, the band playing all the while, where they climbed into their boats and left.[39]

As soon as the regent left, Perry gave permission for groups of officers from the three ships to go ashore. Spalding's group walked toward Naha through winding lanes, past an occasional house surrounded by coral walls on which cactus and flowering vines grew. Even the poorest houses were neat in appearance, and most of them were surrounded by gardens growing tobacco, corn, and sweet potatoes. To enter Naha they climbed over a low rise on carefully cut steps and entered a street that, like most of the streets in the city, was paved with stones of all shapes and lined with the same well-built coral walls. Occasionally a crowd gathered to watch them pass. But as soon as the Americans tried to speak with anyone, the Okinawans fell back at the urging of a group of men who seemed to be assigned to escort the foreigners.

Naha itself was shut down, the shops shuttered, and the stalls of street vendors so recently abandoned that their goods still sat in the open. When the Americans came to the marketplace, it too was all but deserted. The people Spalding and the other officers did encounter, mostly men and children and an occasional old woman, but no younger women, were distinguished by their dress. The commoners wore a single brown garment while the better classes wore robes and fixed their long hair on the tops of their head with silver pins. The children ran about naked. The Americans walked on, noting the paved road that led toward Shuri Castle and a number of carefully constructed stone bridges.[40]

While his officers were exploring Naha and its environs, Perry was discussing his next moves with Bettelheim and Wells Williams

Street in Naha; *Narrative of the Expedition*

over dinner in his cabin. Perry wanted Williams and Bettelheim to go ashore the next day and press the authorities for a building. In addition, he asked Bettelheim to act as an intermediary in purchasing supplies for the squadron, a job that Bettelheim found difficult because of the immense amount of paperwork in both English and Chinese. Bettelheim, however, was eager to please "father" Perry, hoping to insinuate himself into the expedition on a more permanent basis. He already had understood Perry to say, whether Perry did or not, that he was to act as a translator along with Williams. Bettelheim saw an opening because of what he perceived as Williams's linguistic shortcomings. An accomplished linguist,

Bettelheim noted that Williams spoke more Cantonese than Mandarin, which was the dialect employed by the Okinawan officials, and that Williams's teacher spoke the Ningpo dialect.

Things between the two translators were off to a bad start. Williams was put off by Bettelheim's odd mannerisms and his way of interjecting himself into matters that Williams thought were his responsibility. Bettelheim found Williams so pallid in appearance, probably from his uncomfortable voyage, that he asked if he was sick and was taken aback by what he described as Williams's "frozenness of behaviour." Bettelheim further antagonized him when he refused to accommodate Williams's ailing Chinese teacher at his home. Having determined that the teacher was an opium smoker (Williams thought he had given it up), Bettelheim would not let him stay. Bettelheim in time came to like Williams; Williams could not say the same.[41]

After a day of heavy rains, the exploring party was put ashore on May thirtieth to undertake a walking tour of the island, which Perry thought would take five or six days. The commodore instructed them to take particularly careful note of the geology of the island in hopes of finding coal. Meanwhile Bettelheim went to the *Saratoga* to get Williams to accompany him ashore to see about renting a building. Williams, Bettelheim, three officers, and some Chinese servants walked to the nearby village of Tomari, where Bettelheim pointed out a building that served as a public reception hall. While one of them climbed the coral wall and opened the gate, a messenger was dispatched to find Naha's chief magistrate. Instead of the magistrate, Itarashiki Satonushi, the chief interpreter for the royal family, arrived at the hall after an hour's delay. Itarashiki, a handsome man with a dark beard and skin swarthier than most of the Okinawans, was well known to Bettelheim. They had jousted for years over many issues in Bettelheim's long combat with the authorities. But in recent times, after Bettelheim treated him for an infected boil on the back of his head, Itarashiki had softened toward the missionary.[42]

Over the customary tea and pipes, the Americans explained that they needed to rent a building to use in supplying their ships. This was impossible, Itarashiki replied through his Chinese interpreter. But as to supplies, the Americans need only present them

with a list, and they would provide them. The British had once
used a house ashore, why couldn't Americans? No, no, this was
impossible! Could two or three Americans spend the night there?
Again the answer was no. And then to Williams's surprise, Itarashiki, who had been growing increasingly impatient, got up and
walked over to them, saying in broken English, "Gentlemen, Doo
Choo [Ryukyu] man very small, American man not very small. I

Portrait of Itarashiki Satonushi,
interpreter for the regent;
Narrative of the Expedition

have read of America in books of Washington—very good man,
good man. Doo Choo good friend of American. Doo Choo give America all provision he wants. American no can have house on shore."

Still the Americans insisted that they were going to leave some
people at the building to spend the night. With that, Itarashiki left,
saying that he had to consult with the magistrate. Williams returned to the *Susquehanna* to pick up some food and bedding and
report to the commodore. Perry was not pleased with this less than
satisfactory outcome to his first initiative, but he was not prepared

to do more than accept it. Back at the reception hall, Williams and
the other Americans waited for Itarashiki's return. Because he was
gone so long, they were sure that he had gone to Shuri Castle to
talk with the regent. Or had he gone to consult with the *zaiban
bugyo*, the invisible representative of the Satsuma domain?

When Itarashiki returned, he still insisted that the Americans
could not stay. But to no avail. Williams and another officer accompanied by three Chinese servants bedded down for an unpleasant night of fighting off fleas and mosquitoes. Williams confessed
that he was ashamed of their tactics. "It was a struggle between
weakness and right and power and wrong," he concluded with considerable exaggeration, "for a more high-handed piece of aggression
has not been committed by anyone." He had finished his first day
in Okinawa as "an unwilling agent" of violence and wrong.[43]

Itarashiki and all the Okinawan officials had indeed been consulting closely with the *zaiban bugyo*, Kawakami Shikibu, keeping
the hidden official informed about the activities of this new group
of barbarian intruders and listening attentively to his suggestions
about how to deal with them. The *zaiban bugyo*'s office in turn
reported on events in Okinawa to the Ryukyu office in Satsuma.
The *zaiban bugyo* was, in fact, orchestrating the Okinawans' dealings with the Americans. It was he, for example, who had ordered
the Okinawans to take the bullock, pigs, and other supplies out to
the *Susquehanna* on the morning after Perry's arrival. The
Okinawans had taken some Chinese translators with them, the Okinawan officials explained in their report to the *zaiban bugyo*, men
from the Chinese village established near Naha centuries ago.
Turned away at the flagship, they had gone to another ship, where
the interpreters had talked briefly with some of the Chinese deckhands—until they were waved away by an officer. Leaning over
the rail, the deckhands told them that the ships were American
from Shanghai but that they had no important business to conduct
at Okinawa. As to their ultimate destination, the Chinese interpreters could not find out.

A little later, the officials' report continued, Itarashiki had
gone to Bettelheim's house to see what he would say about the
Americans. Bettelheim explained that the Americans had come to
open trade with Japan, Korea, and the Ryukyus. But when the

regent went aboard the flagship, he understood Perry to say that his ships were going to California, that he planned to stay in Naha until all of his ships had gathered there (seven in number with seven thousand men), and that he wanted to establish friendly relations between the Ryukyus and the United States.

In their report the Okinawan officials assured the Satsuma officials that they had explained to the Americans that the Ryukyus were too small and too poor to open relations with a foreign power. They had asked the Americans not to stay long and had been told that the Americans would pay for their supplies. The Okinawan officials did not bother to go into the details of what was transpiring on the island. Reports of Perry's insistence on visiting Shuri Castle and renting buildings, Williams's decampment at the meeting hall, and the landing of an exploring party would undoubtedly not go down well with the Satsuma officials. Instead, the Okinawans explained, the Americans had come ashore to walk on the beach under their watchful guard.[44]

On the morning of May thirty-first, Williams was replaced at the meeting hall by a sick officer and a Chinese servant. Itarashiki showed up to object to the occupation of what was, in fact, Tomari's town hall while the Okinawans brought the sick man gifts of fruits and vegetables. After receiving a written protest from Itarashiki, the Americans settled into a long conversation with him about events in Europe, China, and America. Though the Americans attributed Itarashiki's knowledge to Bettelheim's influence, Itarashiki had, in fact, been educated in Peking and had learned English from an Okinawan who had learned it from the Irish naval officer who founded Bettelheim's mission.[45]

The next day the Okinawans responded to Perry's peremptory tactics. They refused to deal with the question of supplies at the Tomari town hall, insisting instead that their purveyors would deal directly with Bettelheim. Williams was impressed with the "degree of quiet resistance an organized government like this can offer to violence, without an overt act of violence."[46]

A week after his arrival, Perry had yet to visit the shore. Instead he was spending his time aboard the flagship exchanging elaborate diplomatic missives with the Okinawan authorities concerning the rental of a building and his visit to Shuri Castle. To

沖縄縣琉球首里舊城之圖
甲午初夏陽日
螢山畫并

Scroll painting of Shuri Castle

Williams's surprise, when he went ashore on June second, he found the regent at the Tomari town hall and an elaborate banquet laid out on five tables. Hundreds of people were gathered nearby waiting to get a glimpse of the American commodore. Williams was left with the embarrassing task of explaining that Perry would not be coming. Undaunted, Itarashiki ordered some attendants to gather up the food, which they brought out to the *Susquehanna* and laid on the deck, dividing it up among the men and officers. The Okinawans then were shown to their boats with a marked lack of courtesy. Perry made no appearance. The banquet, he later explained, was an effort to entrap him and prevent him from going to Shuri. And since he had only been given a verbal invitation—the written invitation finally turned up among some other papers two days later—he considered his negative response when the regent had visited the flagship five days earlier satisfactory.[47]

Unable to meet the American commodore face-to-face, the Okinawans' next move was to send Perry a petition begging him not to come to Shuri. It was true that a British officer had visited the castle, but he had forced his way in. Ever since then the queen dowager had been dangerously sick. In their petition, the Okinawan officials beseeched Perry to demonstrate his humanity and benevolence by not further endangering her. If he insisted on making a return visit, he could be received at the prince's residence. And with regard to the rental of a building, they had found a temple that would be suitable for the squadron's purposes. Perry was pleased with this new response, although he doubted that there was any such person as the eleven-year-old prince to whom he was asked to direct his visit. Perry was determined not to depart for Japan until he had reached an accommodation with the local authorities, and this was the first indication that they were bending to his will.[48]

Williams spent most of June fourth preparing the presents for the trip to Shuri. Under the watchful eye of the *zaiban bugyo*, the Okinawans were also busy selecting presents for Perry. Finished with the presents, Williams turned to working on Perry's response to the Okinawans' petition. Perry again emphasized that his intentions were peaceful, but it was his duty to go to the castle "where high functionaries are usually received, and where an officer of the Queen of England recently had an audience." Perry hoped that their ship's band might amuse the queen and that their doctors might treat her if she was indeed sick.

Just as Williams was about to leave the flagship with the petition, the regent suddenly came alongside with Bettelheim in tow carrying another petition pleading again with Perry not to go to Shuri. It was for him a matter of life and death, the regent insisted. Buchanan steered the Okinawans away from Perry to his own cabin and with a certain amount of impatience offered them some brandy that was so strong that they could not drink it. After a time, they left. "It was a childish visit," Williams noted in his journal, his sympathy for the Okinawans having fled as fast as it had appeared, "and one hardly knows how to act toward such children, who must be in a manner coerced for their own good. To talk about the principles of international law being applicable to such people is almost nonsensical; they must be taught humanity and self-respect."[49]

While Williams and Buchanan were dealing with the regent, the exploring party returned. After five days of walking, they were tired but charmed by the striking beauty of the island and delighted with their treatment at the hands of the Okinawans. It was all quite spectacular, the Americans agreed, a lush intermingling of the pastoral English countryside and the exotic tropics. On the first day they had ambled past the royal city, which curved around the southwestern slopes of the low mountains north of Naha and was surrounded by ancient trees with twisted trunks, deep woods, and shaded lanes, all in a parklike setting. As they headed over the mountain ridge toward the eastern shore, passing thatched huts, streams lined with ferns and banana trees, and terraced fields full of rice, sorghum, sweet potatoes, beans, sugar cane, and corn, their guides ran before them warning the people to pull down their shutters and stay in their houses. The explorers spent the first night in their tents on a rise overlooking a broad bay. The second day they explored a large number of whitewashed limestone tombs and then the ruins of a great fortress sitting on the summit of one of the ridge spurs. From time to time, Taylor poked into a hut or two, trying to catch the residents at home, but invariably they had been warned and were either hiding within or had left altogether. The few people that they did encounter bowed reverently, a pained look on their faces, which the Americans attributed to the oppressiveness of a government that sent runners ahead to order the people about.[50]

On the second night, their guides insisted that they avail themselves of a government guest house. From then on the Americans were pleased to sleep on thick mats surrounded by fires that kept the pesky mosquitoes at bay. At night the darkened compound was an eerie sight as the light from the campfires and numerous torches flickered off the building and the overhanging trees, reflecting off

American explorers at a government guest house, Okinawa;
Narrative of the Expedition

dozens of faces that peered over the surrounding wall trying to catch a glimpse of these strange foreigners. The next day the Americans continued up the eastern shore of the island, spending that night in an elegant private residence surrounded by a garden. By this time Chang-yuen, the bearded leader of their escort, a man their Chinese coolies referred to as the Japanese consul, had written a record of their travels on a scroll that had reached several yards in length.

On the fourth day the Americans continued north, crossed the island, passing through a dense forest, and spent the night on the western shore in a large village set on a high promontory surrounded by palm trees, pines, and banyans. Their accommodations were becoming more lavish, and the meals a delight: fresh fish, eggplant, sweet potatoes, pumpkin, cucumbers. After a forced march of 27 miles and another stay in a guest house, they returned to Bettelheim's house after a long walk in the rain, having traveled 108 miles and explored the southern half of the island. The Reverend Jones, however, had found no signs of coal, although he had examined the geology of the island carefully.

All along the way, the Americans had been treated with kindness and hospitality, although their guides insisted on keeping the public away from them whenever they could. Their Okinawan bearers were eager workers, carrying their loads with an easy good humor, laughing when they fell on the slippery trails. Chang-yuen, their chief escort, "exhibited so much patience and kindly feeling," according to Taylor, that the Americans "all felt a cordial friendship towards him."[51] The Okinawans never winced, for instance, when the Americans trod upon the fine matting at the guest houses in their muddy boots. Remarkably, nowhere had they seen any signs of weaponry, and though they heard that there were Japanese soldiers stationed on the island, they never encountered them.

"We were surrounded with a secret power," Taylor concluded, "the tokens of which were invisible, yet which we could not move a step without feeling. We tried every means to elude it, but in vain." Villages that they visited were invariably deserted, and when the party split up and took off quickly in different directions to elude their escorts, they found almost no one. They could see people at work in the fields, but they kept their distance. The Americans had undoubtedly encountered the systematic neighborhood-by-neighborhood, village-by-village organizational system that the Japanese had put in place to rebuff the efforts of Bettelheim.[52]

Perry cared little about the niceties of the Okinawans' treatment of the wandering Americans. He was convinced that the Japanese, hidden though they were, were behind "this pertinacious system of crooked diplomacy." His visit to Shuri would send them a clear and forceful message about American intentions while demonstrating that those intentions were, as he described them, friendly. With Naha under the cannons of Perry's ships and the marines ashore drilling regularly, the Okinawans had no recourse

but to acquiesce in Perry's plan to make a courtesy call at Shuri
Castle.

June sixth was a breezy morning with a hint of showers hanging over the hills. Despite the repeated pleas of the regent, Perry
prepared to come ashore at Tomari. Create an "imposing spectacle"
was the order of the day. Accordingly at nine o'clock a signal flag
fluttered aloft on the flagship, and all the boats from the three ships,
each mounted with a cannon in the bow, made for the shore. Behind
them came Perry in his barge. He strode ashore, was greeted by
Chang-yuen, the so-called Japanese consul, and then passed in review before two companies of marines drawn up in formation.
Nearby a crowd of several hundred Okinawans watched.[53]

Precisely at ten o'clock, the Americans formed a line of march
with two field pieces at the front drawn by forty-eight sailors in
blue jackets and white trousers. They were followed by Williams
and Bettelheim, the band from the *Mississippi*, and a company of
marines. Next came the commodore himself. To impress the Okinawans he had had a palanquin built by the carpenters aboard the
flagship, evoking many a derisive comment from the crew. Painted
red and blue and draped with red and blue awnings, it was borne
by alternate groups of four Chinese coolies. Marine guards stood
to each side and "a handsome boy," attended by another Chinese
servant, walked alongside as a page. Perry was followed by more
coolies bearing gifts for the royal family, a party of forty officers,
the bands from the *Susquehanna*, and the *Mississippi*, and a second
company of marines. With the bands playing alternately, the party
struck out for Shuri, led by two Okinawan officials in long robes
and yellow caps, ensigns flying behind them. The bright sunlight
had by now broken through the clouds, sending sparkles of light
off the officers' swords and the troop's bayonets. Along the route
Okinawans gathered in ranks, those in the front kneeling so that
those behind could see while others ran through the fields to keep
up with the procession.

At the gates of Shuri, a tripartite portal with a tiled upward
turning roof, the Americans were met by the regent, Itarashiki,
and a large group of officials. The regent had come to plead with
Perry to visit his residence rather than that of the royal family.
Bettelheim immediately interjected himself into the conversation,

but Williams called him aside, and the procession entered the city, Perry waving to the frustrated regent as he passed. Inside the city, the Americans marched along a street lined with high walls. When they reached the palace gates, which were closed, another official begged Williams not to bring the marines into the palace. The marines were drawn up outside while an attendant rushed inside to open the gates. The portly Perry descended from his palanquin, and with the bands playing "Hail Columbia" walked into the palace.

Perry at the gates of Shuri Castle;
Narrative of the Expedition

Perry was led through a second gate and into a central courtyard, an eighty-foot-square area paved with alternating patterns of gravel and stone and surrounded by plain wooden one-storied buildings. Perry was seated on a lacquered camp stool in one of the buildings with his officers seated on either side of him. Facing the Americans now sat the regent, his three councilors, and a double rank of officials. On the wall hung a large red tablet with the words "the elevated enclosure of fragrant festivities" written on it in Chinese characters. After the two parties greeted each other, tables and smoking boxes were brought in, and tea and a kind of tough twisted gingerbread were served.

After a long silence, Perry spoke, inviting the regent and his councilors to visit him aboard the flagship and saying that he intended to leave within a day or two. They could visit him before he left or when he returned, which he intended to do. Perry also inquired after the health of the queen and offered the assistance of the ships' doctors. The regent then produced several large red greeting cards, and with his three councilors stepped toward Perry and bowed. Perry and his officers responded in kind. After another awkward exchange of bows, the Okinawans sat nervously, eyeing their uninvited guests and making no effort to prolong the conversation. Perry too had little to say. So after an hour Perry ordered the presents left in the reception hall and accepted the regent's invitation to visit him at his residence.

In the spacious, dark, red pillared central hall of the regent's residence, a sumptuous meal was laid out on the tables. Chopsticks, bowls, spoons, and earthen pots of sake surrounded by small cups were arranged at each place. On each table there were at least twenty different dishes, "the exact basis of some of which no American knoweth to this day," reported the official account of the meeting. The Americans did recognize sliced boiled eggs dyed crimson, fish rolls boiled in fat, cold baked fish, slices of hog's liver, sugar candy, cucumbers, salted raddish tops, and bits of lean fried pork. The first four courses of the meal were soups, followed by gingerbread, a salad of bean sprouts and onions, dough covering sugary pulp that looked like a bright red fruit, and a particularly appealing mixture of beaten eggs and aromatic white root. The Americans attacked the food with gusto. Rising frequently to toast their guests, sake was consumed freely while the Okinawans seemed to visibly relax.

After twelve courses, the Americans at a signal from Perry, who was bored with the proceedings and sufficiently stuffed, rose to leave, although the Okinawans, who were both surprised and relieved by Perry's abrupt preparations to depart, assured them that there were twelve more courses yet to come. Once again the procession formed, with Chang-yuen in the lead. In the rear as the Americans marched back to the shore, a number of young officers took turns riding four frisky ponies that were provided by the

Okinawans. By 2:30 P.M. the Americans, still tipsy from the drinking, were back on their ships.

Perry was pleased with his visit to Shuri Castle. "It was part
of the Commodore's deliberately formed plan, in all his intercourse
with these orientals, to consider carefully before he announced his
resolution to do any act," explained the official narrative; "but,
having announced it, he soon taught them to know that he would
do precisely what he had said he would." Perry remarked in his
journal on "the suavity of manner and apparent sincerity of their
[his hosts'] hospitality, giving them credit at least of being good
actors if they were not sincere." He was impressed by the beauty
of the countryside, the well-paved roads, and the utter cleanliness
of every place they visited. It was such a striking contrast, he
thought, to the filthiness of Canton and Shanghai.[54]

Having exerted his "moral influence," Perry began to wind up
the squadron's affairs in Okinawa. He had to complete negotiations
for use of a building to replace the Tomari town hall, make arrangements to pay for supplies acquired from the Okinawans, finish
a survey of the tides, and get the daguerreotypers to complete their
project. The Americans were provided with the use of part of the
abandoned temple complex that included the Bettelheim's residence. The Okinawans did make one last effort to avoid accepting
payment for the supplies they had provided. In the end they lined
up at a table manned by the flagship's purser at Bettelheim's house
and walked off with $150 in Chinese coins.[55]

The Americans found their final dealings with the Okinawan
officials to be easy and amicable. But then Perry faced the problem
of what to do about his own interpreters. Williams's Chinese teacher
was so sick from opium use that he could no longer function as an
interpreter, while Bettelheim had made a bid to join the expedition.
It had taken very little time, however, for Bettelheim to alienate
the commodore. He had offered preposterous suggestions for keeping the regent off the flagship, such as hanging scaffolding over the
side with men painting as a reason for not allowing him aboard.
He had written long fawning letters speaking of Perry's "glorious
mission," calling his flagship a "throne" and Perry an "autocrat."
Unasked, he had interjected himself into the discussions with the

regent about the visit to Shuri Castle and had accompanied the regent on his unannounced mission to the flagship.

Williams, who had Perry's ear, was particularly hostile to the rival linguist. Williams had his own problems with the commodore. He found him to be "a sort of autocrat, who rules all as much as he can, even down to very small matters." He also found the atmosphere of the flagship "adverse to piety" and for this he blamed Perry. Williams could not complain, however. He reported to his wife, who continued to write him letters denouncing Perry, that Perry treated him well and seemed to be generally liked.

Williams was particularly vitriolic when it came to Bettelheim. Referring to his remittance of funds to Hong Kong aboard the *Caprice*, Williams wrote in his diary that Bettelheim, a fellow missionary who had endured abuse and poverty for his beliefs, was "not at all backward in sending, or begging for things, while, he, Jew-like, puts his money in the bank."[56]

Then too, Bettelheim objected when the Okinawans gave Perry permission to leave some stock in a yard near Bettelheim's house, and Perry became so angry that he threatened to force Bettelheim to remove his flagpole from which he had flown the British flag. Despite his impatience, Perry had tried to be generous with Bettelheim, providing him with supplies from the squadron, having shoes made for his children and the ships' carpenters repair his house and fit his study with windows. He had also taken time to visit his wife and family. For his part, Bettelheim reported that Perry kissed his daughters but told his son that he did not kiss boys.[57] In the end, though, Perry turned down the missionary's offer, condemning him to remain on the island for a while longer.

During the more than two weeks that the Americans had been at Naha, Perry had probed the outer defenses of the Japanese empire, and in doing so had found that Okinawa was definitely a weak spot. Beyond that, he knew little about Japan and its complicated relations with the outer islands or about the Shimazus' as yet unfulfilled plan to open trade there. He knew that the Japanese were somewhere in the background and suspected that Satsuma played some kind of role in this relationship. But he never found out about the *zaiban bugyo* or Satsuma's central role in Ryukyuan affairs.

On the morning of June ninth, the *Susquehanna* got under way, taking the *Saratoga* in tow. The *Mississippi* and the *Supply* were left at anchor. Eliphalet Brown, Jr., and William B. Draper, the two daguerreotypers, had been settled in a house in the village of Tomari. Two sailors were living in a tent near the beach to make regular measurements of the tide. A sick sailor was still occupying the building wrested from the Okinawan officials. Captain Sidney S. Lee of the *Mississippi* was left in command with strict warnings from the commodore to allow none but the best behaved sailors ashore. With that Perry sailed off for the Bonin Islands.

6

TO THE
BONIN ISLANDS AND
BACK TO NAHA

*We have acquired in the East generally a character for encroachment,
and if the French and Americans should for once be willing to share
this with us, the participation is calculated to do us no harm.*[1]
—J. F. DAVIS, British Plenipotentiary and Superintendant of Trade,
to Lord Aberdeen, August 6, 1846

*In the accomplishment of a friendly intercourse with Japan, which of
course must be a work of time, the possession of Lew Chew and the
Bonin Islands will be all important. So far as it rests with me, I will
continue to hold a controlling influence over them. With respect to
Lew Chew, I can conceive of no greater act of humanity than to protect
these miserable people against the oppressions of their tyrannical
rulers.*[2]   —COMMODORE MATTHEW CALBRAITH PERRY,
Journal, June 23 to July 2, 1853

*To me they appear like school boys who need some threatenings and
coercion for their own good to show them that nations have mutual
claims. But what can weakness and might, such as are here in contact,
do? We are our own expounders of what we wish them to consider
right; but they are not able to see the matter from the same
position.*[3]   —S. WELLS WILLIAMS, *Journal*, July 1, 1853

HAVING MET WITH INITIAL SUCCESS AT NAHA, Commodore Perry
was eager to explore the Bonin Islands, located some eight hundred miles to the east of Naha, and perhaps lay claim to them. For

the time being, Perry had accomplished all that he could at Okinawa. He had forced his way into Shuri Castle, despite official opposition, and had compelled the hapless Okinawans to abandon their age-old practice of providing supplies to passing ships without compensation. On trips ashore to look around Naha, he had seen no signs of the Japanese presence other than the Japanese sailors who manned the junks in the harbor. He had talked briefly with a number of them, but they had said little. Still he was confident that the message of his intent would be quickly relayed to Japan. For their part, the overpowered Okinawans had done little to resist the foreign onslaught, with the exception of keeping Perry from meeting face-to-face with the queen mother and the young prince.

Before strong winds from the southwest monsoon, the *Susquehanna* towed the *Saratoga*, both ships with sails set and three boilers at work on the flagship, at a steady pace of nine and a half knots. A day and more out from Naha, Williams's Chinese teacher died a horrible death from opium addiction. He had first become ill on the passage from China, but Williams had thought it was seasickness, his teacher having convinced him that he had sworn off opium. Soon, though, he could not leave his hammock, where he suffered from constipation and occasional delusions. After Bettelheim refused to allow him to convalesce at his house, the teacher had begun treating himself with pills that contained opium, hartshorn, and mercury. At first Williams took them away from him, but he was so miserable that Williams eventually returned them. The teacher had brought along his pipe as well, but Williams would not permit him to smoke. For three days before he died, he mumbled incoherently, his hands and feet shook when he slept, and when awake, he moaned, and his eyes, glassy and vacant, rolled up into his head while his face turned a ghastly yellow. When he died, he was little more than a skeleton. Wrapped in his hammock with a cannonball, his opium pipe in his hand, he was consigned to the deep.

It was the first death from opium addiction that Williams had ever seen. He was shocked by this awful spectacle and concerned that his teacher "was never touched with a sense of sinfulness." It was "a doleful mistake" to bring him along, Williams wrote his wife, instructing her to cut off the monthly allowance of twelve dollars

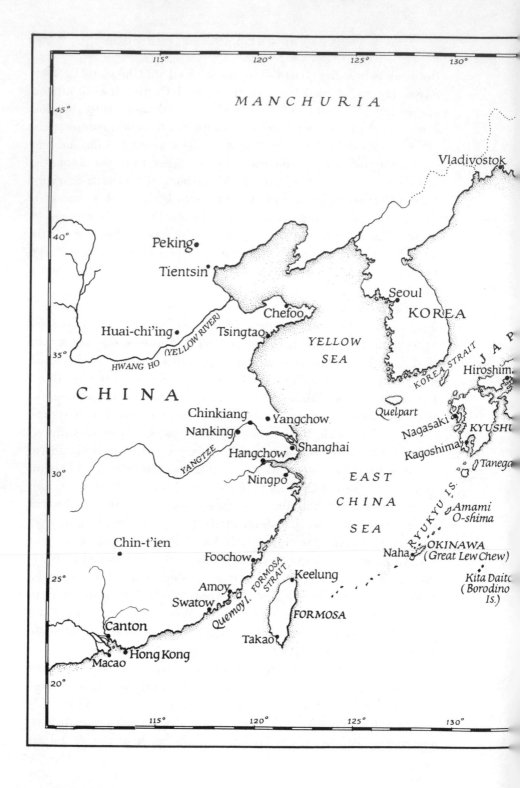

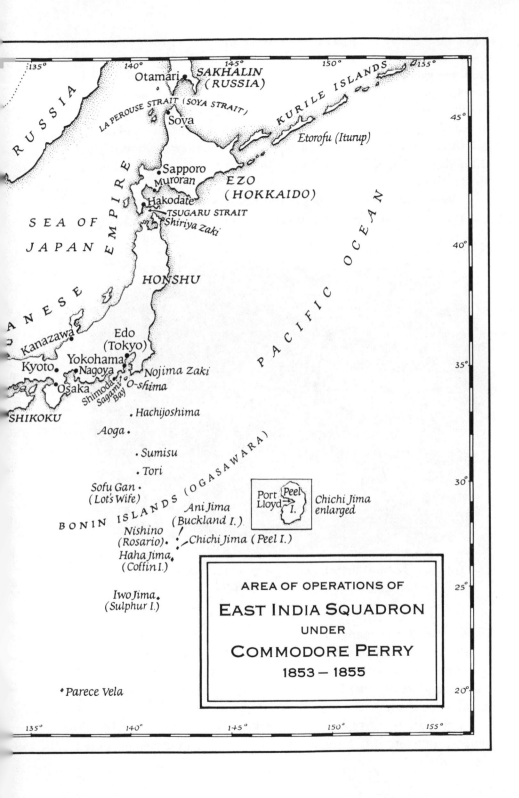

RUSSIA

135° 140° 145° SAKHALIN 150° 155°
Otamari (RUSSIA)

LA PEROUSE STRAIT (SOYA STRAIT) KURILE ISLANDS

Soya 45°

Etorofu (Iturup)

Sapporo
Muroran EZO
Hakodate (HOKKAIDO)

SEA OF TSUGARU STRAIT
Shiriya Zaki

JAPAN 40°

HONSHU

PACIFIC OCEAN

Kanazawa
Edo
(Tokyo) 35°
Yokohama
Kyoto Nagoya Nojima Zaki
Osaka Shimoda O-shima
Sagami Bay
SHIKOKU Hachijoshima

Aoga

Sumisu

Tori

Sofu Gan
(Lot's Wife)

BONIN ISLANDS (OGASAWARA)

Ani Jima
(Buckland I.) Port Peel Chichi Jima
Lloyd I. enlarged

Nishino
(Rosario) Chichi Jima (Peel I.)

Haha Jima
(Coffin I.)

Iwo Jima
(Sulphur I.)

AREA OF OPERATIONS OF

EAST INDIA SQUADRON

UNDER

COMMODORE PERRY

1853 – 1855

Parece Vela

135° 140° 145° 150° 155°

30°

25°

20°

that she was paying the teacher's family. Williams figured he had already paid out eighty-six dollars, and he admitted he was not feeling very charitable, since his teacher had lied to him so often about his opium habit. Two weeks later Williams softened and asked his wife to keep giving the teacher's widow money because it was difficult for a widow to survive in China without a married son to support her.

Aside from this, Williams found his new quarters on the *Susquehanna* pleasant. He lived in a small hurricane house of three

Natural tunnel, Port Lloyd, Bonin Islands;
Narrative of the Expedition

rooms—two for sleeping, one for work—that was built especially for the artists against the taffrail on the stern of the flagship. The one drawback was the constant swearing of the officers and men. "Awful and swift must be the fate of most of them if they do not mend and repent," he wrote to his wife.[4]

After an easy five-day cruise broken only by regular calls to general quarters, the *Susquehanna* and the *Saratoga* made Peel

Island, the six-mile-long main island in the Bonin group, on the morning of June fourteenth. The islands were in fact three clusters of islands, one of which was visited and surveyed by a British naval explorer in 1827. The southern cluster, the Coffin Islands, was named after a whaling captain thought to be from Nantucket because of his name, who reported their position for the first time in 1823. The year after the British visit, the Russians laid claim to the islands, and Perry was eager to assert an American claim, since the Bonin Islands could serve as a coal depot for the projected San Francisco to Shanghai steamship line. Peel Island, with its small harbor at Port Lloyd, rose 1,600 feet abruptly from the sea to form two bright green pinnacles, known as the Paps. The island was a huge volcanic formation, and along the coast lava outcrops formed fantastic shapes that appeared to be so many castles, towers, and strange beasts.

The islands were a popular port of call for whalers, who collected the giant turtles, which lived in the surrounding waters, and bought supplies from the polyglot community of seaborne wanderers that lived on Peel Island. The community was founded at the urging of the British consul in Hawaii by two Americans, a Britisher, a Dane, and an Italian, who led a party of Hawaiian men and women to the island in 1830. Thirteen years later, only one of the nonnative "founders" of the little colony, Nathaniel Savory, of Massachusetts, still lived on the island.

As the American ships approached Peel Island, they spotted two whaleships, one British and one American, sailing among the islands. At the entrance to Port Lloyd, the flagship fired a gun to call a pilot, and a colorful-looking shoe-less character in a tattered straw hat, blue cotton jacket, and pantaloons came aboard. He appeared to be half Portuguese and half Hawaiian. He directed the ships to anchor in twenty-one fathoms of water in a tight little harbor surrounded on three sides by land.

Taylor and a party of officers went ashore, where they found an Englishman and two Hawaiians sitting near two turtles that were turned over on their backs. Nearby were several empty shells that gave off a foul odor. The Englishman showed them to a neat little cabin surrounded by gardens full of melons, sweet potatoes, and sugar. Here they met Nathaniel Savory. Savory was a taciturn

soul who said little except to respond to questions. He lived with
a Guamanian woman and their children and made a living selling
sweet potatoes at two dollars a barrel and other vegetables and
fruit to passing whalers. Savory also ran a still for the manufacture
of rum from sugar cane. Nearby lived an Englishman with sun-
bleached hair and a deep red sunburned complexion who appeared
to be fifty years old. His companion was a great fat Hawaiian
woman who helped him raise watermelons and laughed uproari-
ously when the Americans devoured the fruit with a vengeance. In
all there were thirty-nine people living on the island, many of them
runaway whalers with their islander wives and a number of
children.

The next day Perry dispatched two exploring parties, one under Taylor to survey the southern half of the island while another
party under an assistant surgeon went to the north. Taylor's party
was directed to a steep path that led into the jungle by an islander
who turned down their request that he accompany them as a guide.
He said that the path would take them to the main settlement on
the other side of the island. The path led into a dense thicket of
palms, tamarinds, and vines that became so thick they obscured
the sunlight. Moisture dripped from the vegetation, streams ran
everywhere, and numerous land crabs scrambled away from their
feet. As they approached the summit of the mountain the under-
growth became so tangled that the explorers had to descend by
swinging from tree to tree.

They soon came to a valley where two thatched huts were
surrounded by numerous plots of sweet potatoes, taro, tobacco,
sugar cane, pumpkin, and Indian gooseberries. The huts, however,
were uninhabited. After guns were fired to signal their arrival, an
islander with blue tattoos all over his face emerged from the jungle.
He introduced himself as Judge, a native of Nukuhiva in the Mar-
quesas Islands, the very island where Melville had "lived among
the cannibals." A friendly soul, Judge recruited a Tahitian companion, and the two undertook to guide the explorers. After climbing up the side of a steep ravine, they started a wild boar and shot
it. When they went to descend the other side, however, they found
themselves at the edge of a steep precipice. After inching along the

edge, they descended again by sliding down the vegetation, careful to brake their fall by grasping at roots.

After another treacherous ascent and descent, they reached the beach where, exhausted from the heat and the climb, they built a fire and cooked the boar's liver and kidneys. After a rest the party was faced with the arduous task of retracing their steps back to Judge's valley and through the jungle to Port Lloyd. One of the men by this time was so incapacitated that their Tahitian guide agreed to take him back to the ships by canoe. The rest of the party, after another difficult climb and several false starts into the impenetrable jungle, straggled onto the heights above Port Lloyd after dark. They fired a volley to signal their return, and were finally returned to the flagship at 10 P.M. The second party had already returned to report that the northern half of the island was very much like the southern, thick with vegetation, abundant cultivatable areas, and plentiful supplies of water.

The next day it was Perry's turn to do some exploring. He set out with a party of officers for Buckland Island to picnic and fish. With them they took a number of sheep and cattle purchased in Shanghai. Perry, as was customary among sea captains, hoped to populate the islands with stock that would serve as a source of food in the future. At Buckland Island, Perry was particularly amused by the land crabs, which he described as "helmeted little animals marching about in all directions in search of food." Perry and his officers dined on the wild boar shot the day before and then watched as the bones seemed to walk off under their own locomotion, carried away in fact by the land crabs.

Perry was charmed by these bounteous islands with their rich soil, timber supplies, and ready supply of fish, but he had business to finish in Okinawa before leaving for Edo Bay. Before departing, he gathered together some of the islanders and counseled them to adopt laws for a municipal government. Distributing seeds, he said that he hoped to return in the future with farm implements and more livestock. He also made Savory a U.S. naval supply agent and acquired title to a piece of land with a thousand yards of waterfront, which would be suitable space for offices and wharves.[5]

Perry left the Bonins with the sense of having accomplished

one of the major objectives of the expedition, undoubtedly a source of satisfaction this early in his voyages. He had been instructed to locate ports of refuge and sources of supplies for ships sailing the surrounding seas. This he had done at Naha and Port Lloyd. More important, he had found "suitable stopping places, for a line of mail steamers, which I trust may soon be established between some one of our Pacific ports and China." This accomplishment, reported Perry, who was never shy about singing his own praise, "will be distinguished, even in the history of these remarkable times, as of the highest importance to the commerce of the United States, and the world." To travel from Shanghai to San Francisco via the Bonin and Hawaii islands, Perry pointed out, would take thirty days. In contrast, mail sent from England to Shanghai via the fastest route currently took fifty-two to fifty-five days. Along a Pacific route, Port Lloyd would make an admirable coal depot and stopover for steamers. Its climate was perfect, the harbor commodious and safe. With additional labor, the soil could be made to produce much more food. Williams, in fact, suggested bringing coolie labor from China to build port facilities and cultivate the fields.

There was one problem, however, and that was England. Perry had taken a step in the direction of denying England strategic control of the China Sea, but England was still "the most prominent claimant" to the island. Perry noted nervously that the islanders occasionally flew the British flag, although he assured the secretary of the navy in the report on his visit that "the inhabitants practically disown the paternity of the English sovereign." Moreover, the copper plate that the British had nailed to a tree in 1827 had disappeared. Perry was sure—he had read it in translations of the early Dutch writings on Japan—that the Japanese had been the first to claim the islands. (The Japanese, in fact, had used the islands as a penal colony in the sixteenth century.) Considering this situation, he suggested that the United States seek an agreement with England to make Port Lloyd a free port, "a place of resort to vessels of all nations, and especially a stopping place for mail steamers under such regulations as may be agreed upon." The other alternative was for Perry to take possession of the islands for the United States, a bolder move that he was prepared to undertake, of course, with instructions.[6]

Perry knew nothing of England's own fascination with the Bonin Islands and their role in that country's muted aspirations to open trade with Japan. Even though he had an imperfect understanding of exactly where the Bonin Islands lay, the British consul in Hawaii had encouraged the settlers who went there in 1830 to settle the islands, hoping that Chinese junks bound from Canton to Nagasaki could be persuaded to trade with the British. But it would be a trip taking the junks hundreds of miles off course. The next year the venerable British East India Company discussed the possibility of securing the islands as a base for opening trade with Japan. The Foreign Office, however, paid little attention to these schemes. When Bonin's new settlers themselves asked for British protection, the colonial office turned them down. Further British plans for opening trade with Japan, some of them involving the Bonin Islands, were hatched by British diplomats and merchants after the Opium War. Indeed, a secret expedition was at the point of departure in 1846 when the British dispersed its naval support to other missions considered more important. In general British diplomats and merchants were more preoccupied with the problems of expanding trade with China. "We have acquired in the East generally a character for encroachment," British diplomat Sir J. F. Davis wrote to London in 1846 withdrawing his plans for a Japan expedition, "and if the French and Americans should for once be willing to share this with us, the participation is calculated to do us no harm."[7]

This British attitude explains the benign nature of their response to the Perry expedition, which attracted quite a bit of attention in the London press during the year before Perry's departure. "Her Majesty's government," Lord Malmesbury, foreign secretary during this period, wrote to Sir George Bonham, the highest-ranking British diplomat in China, "would be glad to see the trade with Japan open; but they think it better to leave it to the Government of the United States to make the experiment; and if that experiment is successful, Her Majesty's Government can take advantage of its success."[8] The British continued to keep in touch with the expedition even after it had left Shanghai. When Perry returned to Naha after the voyage to the Bonin Islands, Wells Williams received a letter from Sir John Bowring, whose post Bonham had held while Bowring was on leave, reporting that Bowring's reports indicated that Japan would take a hard line about opening their ports to trade.[9]

On June eighteenth, the two American ships departed for Okinawa, leaving one deserter from the *Saratoga* on Peel Island to join the colony of modern day Robinson Crusoes. Perry might have been charmed by the islands, but his officers had found the price of food and laundry high while the quality of the laundering, they felt, left much to be desired.

When Perry arrived in Naha on June twenty-third, he found that Commander Kelly and the *Plymouth* had joined the squadron, arriving at Naha ten days earlier. Kelly reported that trade had resumed at Shanghai and stores were open, stocked with goods. Humphrey Marshall and the Shanghai merchants were now without a warship to protect Americans interests, and Marshall had again rallied the Shanghai merchants to try to prevail upon Kelly to keep the *Plymouth* there. This time, the merchants raised the ante, saying that they would look to the government for "full remuneration" if any property was lost because of the absence of the *Plymouth*. At no time since the signing of the Treaty of Wanghia, they told Kelly, had it been so necessary to have a man-of-war at the treaty ports.[10]

Perry quickly alerted the secretary of the navy that there might be some "dissatisfaction" among the American merchants. However, it was impossible to please everyone "as each party conceives that their particular interests should be cared for, irrespective of the claims of other." He did plan, Perry reported, to send a ship to Shanghai and another to the other treaty ports as soon as he had visited Edo. Moreover, Perry had been privately assured by Paul Forbes and Marshall himself that there was no immediate need to keep the *Plymouth* in Shanghai.[11] Perry was clearly reinforcing his line of defense in the event that this controversy greeted him upon his return to the United States.

As soon as the *Susquehanna* anchored in the Naha roads, Bettelheim hurried out to visit the commodore, finding him in a friendly mood and looking remarkably healthy. The *Plymouth* had brought a new supply of livestock, and Perry was eager to present some to the Okinawans as a gift in hopes of improving the breed of cattle on the island and enhancing future supplies of meat attainable there. Kelly, for his part, was ready to relieve his ship of the smell.

Meanwhile Williams was busily at work preparing invitations in Chinese for the regent, Naha's chief magistrate, and a number of other officials for a banquet to be held aboard the *Susquehanna*. But when he took them to the chief magistrate's office, he was told that he must readdress the invitation to the regent, who had been replaced. A rumor immediately began to circulate around the squadron that the regent had offended "the spies" and had been forced to commit suicide—ripped himself up, as the Americans liked to say. The regent, in fact, had been retired by the ruling council in favor of Shang Hung-hsun, another member of his family. The reason, the Okinawan officials explained in a secret message to the Ryukyu office in Satsuma, was that Shang Ta-mo had not been able to prevent the Americans from entering Shuri Castle. He had tried "at the risk of his life," the officials reported with considerable exaggeration, and now his presence could only make their ordeal of negotiating with the Americans more difficult. The officials concluded their report by saying that they did not plan to make the regent's retirement known to the public until some later date. As for the Americans, they could only conjecture that the removal of the regent had something to do with their presence. The regent had warned the Americans that his fate lay in their hands, and now he had gone to a well-deserved exile, concluded Williams, who described him as an "imbecile," a "child," and a "nonentity." When Bettelheim gloated over the demise of his longtime opponent, Williams—no slave to consistency—criticized Bettelheim roundly for his conduct.[12]

In the days before the banquet, a number of Okinawan officials pressed members of the expedition for information: where had Perry been in his absence, when were they leaving, and what was their destination? Williams took the opportunity to point out the location of the Bonin Islands and to press upon the Okinawans the idea that many ships would be calling at their island in the future. No one offered any information about when they would depart or their destination. More coal arrived from Shanghai aboard the *Caprice*, and the crews of the steamers went about loading their

ペルリ

嗣子

Portrait of Lieutenant Oliver H. Perry;
watercolor by an unknown Japanese artist

bunkers in preparation for departure. Besides mail, the *Caprice* brought more Chinese laborers to replace the crewmen who had sickened and died because of the tropical climate. Among them were a new Chinese teacher and a servant for Williams.

Perry took time to write to his wife. He noted that he had received four letters from home. So he considered himself "tolerably fortunate." But other officers had received four times as many, Buchanan getting four from his wife alone. He was glad to hear that his daughter Caroline Belmont had safely delivered a boy, though he would have preferred a girl. He warned his wife, whom he assumed had gone to Europe with the Belmont family, that she had to keep an eye on their nineteen-year-old daughter Isabella ("Bell"), "especially in her intercourse with whiskered foreigners" since "one half the travellers you now meet in Europe are either swindlers, pickpockets, or coxcombs, and Bell is a little volatile." He was awaiting the arrival of a ship from Shanghai (with more coal) before going to Edo. "What my success will be there is very problematical," he wrote. "I do not anticipate much this summer." He was disturbed—"nothing can be more disgusting to me"—by the Navy Department's refusal to dispatch the ships that they had promised him. As for his son Oliver, he was "well and as lazy as ever. He is my secretary but seems to suffer if he has a letter to write or to copy. He will never succeed in this part of the world and I doubt whether he will ever be successful in anything. He has no bad habits, but is imbued with a listless laziness that seems inconquerable. He is not the least use to me and, in fact, is only occupying the place of a person that might assist me greatly in my laborious duties."[13]

On the day appointed for the feast, Perry began to fidget nervously. It was raining steadily and he didn't know whether the officials would show up or not. So Perry dispatched Bettelheim and Williams in boats in the rain to look for the officials. They met them on their way out to the flagship. But Bettelheim became agitated because the regent's boat would arrive at the flagship ahead of him. He hollered loudly for the Okinawans to wait for him, but they paid no attention and rowed on. Williams tried to keep his disgust to himself. The festivities appeared to be off to a bad start.

The eighteen officials led by the new regent were a colorful sight as they climbed aboard the *Susquehanna*. The regent, a swarthy man of about forty-five, wore a violet robe with a Chinese silk sash and a crimson hat on his head. The chief magistrate wore white with a crimson hat, the others wore yellow. Each man had his hair pinned up with massive gold pins. The guests were shown about the flagship. But it was a hurried tour in the rain and oppressive heat. Perry in his impatience was eager to get his guests to the table, which was set up in his cabin. Heine and A. L. C. Portman, the Dutch interpreter who doubled as a daguerreotyper, sat nearby to capture the group's portrait on paper and metal plate. A lavish feast of turtle soup, goose, kid curry, and numerous other delicacies was served with French and German wines, Scotch and bourbon, madeira, sherry, and Holland gin. The band played away outside the cabin, featuring its soloists on flageolet, hautboy, clarinet, and cornet.

Soon the whole company was in a convivial mood with the exception of the new regent, who showed a strong family resemblance to his predecessor and was equally reserved, speaking only when addressed. "The tide of wine and wassail was fast gaining on the dry land of sober judgment," recounted the official narrative. "All reserve was now fully thawed out. The quiet repose of a calm contentment sat enthroned on the shining face of the jolly old mayor of Napha [sic]. The wrinkled visages of the two withered old treasurers flushed and expanded into rubicund fullness. The regent alone preserved his silent, anxious demeanor, and all he drank was neutralized in its effects by his excessive dignity."[14]

Bettelheim showed the strongest effects of the copious imbibing. He was up and down like a puppet on a string, all the while gesticulating in his erratic manner. Gifts were exchanged, and the Ryukyuans thanked Perry for his gift of livestock. After a time, the Ryukyuans rose to leave, but Perry would not let them depart. They had to have another round, and he had to tell them of his planned trip to Japan and his hopes for friendly relations with the Japanese. When the Ryukyuans were finally released, the rain was beating down so hard that they had to wait in Buchanan's cabin until it subsided. Perry judged the day a triumph of diplomacy while Bettelheim retired to settle accounts with the ship's purser and was soon in a row accusing him of cheating him.

*

Every day that Perry remained at Naha was another day that the eight additional ships promised him by his government might arrive in time for his trip to Japan. The lack of ships and lateness of the season had convinced him that he would accomplish little more in Japan than reconnoiter Edo Bay and "ascertain the temper of the Japanese government." Now he planned to make his "principal demonstration" the next spring. For these reasons, Perry was anxious to get underway. There was little more for him to accomplish at Naha. "Every day," he wrote in his journal, "points out the importance and positive necessity of bringing the government of Japan to some sort of reason, and the least objectionable course will be to establish an influence which they cannot prevent, here at the very door of the empire." He was determined to "hold a controlling influence" over the Ryukyuans and thought that he had made a good beginning. He was also convinced that reports of his actions were reaching Japan.

Perry had cast himself as the liberator of the people of Loo-Choo (or Lew Chew), as the Americans called the islands. "I can conceive of no greater act of humanity than to protect these miserable people against the oppressions of their tyrannical rulers," he wrote.[15]

Williams, on the other hand, was satisfied with the role of stern schoolmaster whose task was restrained by a touch of magnanimity. "To me," he wrote, "they appear like school boys who need some threatenings and coercion for their own good to show them that nations have mutual claims. But what can weakness and might, such as are here in contact, do? We are our own expounders of what we wish them to consider right; but they are not able to see the matter from the same position." Williams, too, was touched by the little things, such as a bucket of water that was left in his path by an unseen islander on one of his walking tours. Before his departure he found the islanders more friendly than ever, although still careful and reticent. He had encountered one group whose members put their fingers in their ears and laughed as "a new device to hinder intercourse."[16]

The weather was a further irritant. The stifling humidity of July had driven the temperature inside the *Susquehanna* to eighty-eight degrees, making life aboard the ship, despite the shade provided by deck awnings, almost unbearable. Finally, early on the morning of July second, the squadron got underway with the *Susquehanna* towing the *Saratoga* and the *Mississippi* towing the *Plymouth*. The *Supply* was left at Naha while the *Caprice* returned to Shanghai for more coal. As they left the anchorage, the steamers, deeply laden with fresh supplies of coal, wallowed under the bright sun. A strong wind was blowing from the east, and with the sailing ships in tow, the steamers were pushed steadily to the leeward ever closer to the shore. To clear the northern end of Okinawa, the squadron stood well to the eastward before heading north and east for Edo.

PART
II

PROLOGUE

AT THE TIME OF PERRY'S VOYAGE TO JAPAN, Japan was indeed, as Westerners said, a singular nation. Having been fenced off from the outside world by the second and third Tokugawa shoguns more than two hundred years earlier, the more enlightened leaders and scholars of Japan peered outward from their self-imposed isolation to see great forces beyond their control pressing in upon them. The nations of the West, led by England, had China in their grasp and were busily humiliating an Asian country that was regarded with great reverence by many Japanese. It only seemed a matter of time before Japan shared China's fate. Within the constricted confines of the Tokugawa world, events too seemed to spin out of control. Corruption was rife, famine and rebellion had recently stalked the land, the samurai were alternately self-indulgent and restless, and the prestige of the Bakufu, the shogun's government, was at an all-time low. It was as Tokugawa Nariaki, a member of the shogun's family and the foremost exponent of keeping the outer barbarians at bay, had written, a time of *naiyu-gaikan*, "of troubles at home and dangers from abroad."[1]

7

NAIYU-GAIKAN:
TROUBLES AT HOME
AND DANGERS
FROM ABROAD

We shall begin with an island that is called Cipango. Cipango is an island far out at sea to the eastward, some 1,500 miles from the mainland. It is a very big island. The people are fair-complexioned, good-looking, and well-mannered. They are idolaters, wholly independent and exercising no authority over any nation but themselves. They have gold in great abundance, because it is found there in measurable quantities.[2] —MARCO POLO, *The Travels of Marco Polo*

And I am most pleased to accede to your wishes concerning the encouraging of communication between our countries and the provision of facilities for maritime trade. Though separated by myriads of miles of sea and sky, we may in this way well be said to become like near neighbours.[3] —TOKUGAWA IEYASU to the King of England, October 8, 1613

This realm is a land of Divine Valour clearly manifest, but in letters we are inferior to foreigners.[4] —TOKUGAWA IEYASU

Ours is a splendid and blessed country, the Land of the Gods beyond doubt, and we down to the most humble man and woman are the descendants of gods . . . Japanese differ completely from and are superior to the peoples of China, India, Russia, Holland, Siam, Cambodia, and all other countries in the world, and for us to have called our country the Land of the Gods was not mere vain-glory.[5] —HIRATA ATSUTANE, 1811

As the American squadron steamed toward Japan, a thick
fog of unreality, thicker than the fogs that muffled the shores of
the northern islands, hung over the Bakufu, the senescent and
highly bureaucratized military dictatorship of the Tokugawa
shoguns. It was not that the Japanese had not been warned that
the Americans were coming to the Land of the Gods. The first
reports about an American expedition had reached Edo, the shogun's capital, in 1852 by way of the Dutch factor (or business agent)
at Nagasaki. The Dutch report, inspired as it was by Secretary of
State Daniel Webster, was remarkably accurate: the Americans
would be seeking trade and a coal depot, Matthew Calbraith Perry
had replaced J. H. Aulick as commander of the expedition, and the
American squadron would be made up of two steamships and two
other ships.[6]

True, it had taken a while for the Dutch report to pass through
the convoluted ranks of officialdom and reach the actual leaders of
the government. The ever-cautious governor of Nagasaki, after some
hesitation, had forwarded the Dutch report to the censors in Edo.
In Edo, the *metsuke*, the official censors who served as the Bakufu's
secret eyes and ears, had at first held up the report. The Dutch
king, eight years earlier, in 1844, had had the effrontery to write
directly to the emperor to warn him about the disasters that faced
Japan if it did not heed the bloody lessons of the Opium War and
open its doors to trade. The Bakufu had thanked the Dutch king
for this "evidence of hearty good will" but insisted that Japan would
adhere strictly to its "ancestral laws" and bar trade with all countries except Holland, China, Korea, and the Ryukyu Islands. Then,
however, the Dutch king was directed to "cease correspondence";
there would be no response to future letters.[7] Now the censors were
faced with the weighty problem of determining whether this latest
communication from the Dutch, which also included a request to
open trade, fell within the purview of this ban on further communication or whether it was merely the Hollanders' annual report
to the shogunate, which was the Bakufu's sole official source of
information about the outside world.

The censors turned the problem this way and that. After

lengthy debate and a solemn exercise of their bureaucratic prerogatives, they forwarded the report to the Roju, the supreme council
that ruled in the name of the shogun. Finally the Dutch report was
brought to Abe Masahiro, who as Roju Shuseki, or senior councilor
in the Roju, ran the government on behalf of Shogun Tokugawa
Ieyoshi. Abe showed the letter to the four daimyo charged with the
defense of Edo Bay and warned them to be ready for whatever
eventuality the American arrival would bring. He then cautioned
all those who knew of the Dutch letter to keep it a secret.

But rumors, as they will, trickled down through the many
layers of officialdom until one of the two governors of Uraga, where
the customs house at the entrance to Edo Bay was located, wrote
to Abe to find out if there was any truth to these alarming reports
of a squadron headed for Japan. Abe's response was to belittle the
report: the Dutch factor was by nature a profit-seeking fellow, and
this fascinating piece of intelligence was little more than a ploy to
squeeze some trade concessions out of the Japanese and expand the
Dutch role in Japan's limited overseas trade.[8]

Once before, in 1838, the Dutch had sent such a message, saying
that the British were sending a ship to Japan. This earlier message
had caused an uproar in the Bakufu, but no ship had ever materialized. Abe wished to prevent any recurrence of panic, and besides
it was the traditional approach of the Bakufu's high officials to try
to keep all their actions secret. But Abe Masahiro faced a more
serious problem: many officials and even members of the Roju chose
to dismiss the possibility of an American expedition altogether.[9]
Japan had enjoyed its seclusion for so long that they simply refused
to believe that any foreign power was a threat to this Land of the
Gods.

When the American ships reached the Ryukyus, the Okinawan
officials sent their carefully edited reports about American movements to the *zaiban bugyo* in Naha, and the *zaiban bugyo* in turn
reported by express boat to the Ryukyu office at Kagoshima. But
all of this took time. Meanwhile Lord Abe was having his own
problems grasping just what the Americans planned to do, despite
the clarity of the Dutch report. On June twelfth, while Perry was
exploring the Bonin Islands, Abe wrote to Matsudaira Echizen, a
powerful daimyo who was a member of a collateral branch of the

Tokugawa family and one of his closest advisors, that the Americans would go to Nagasaki this year and to Uraga the next. "We must be well-prepared for this," he concluded.[10]

It was not until July fifth, three days after the Americans had set sail for Edo—and almost six weeks after the Americans arrived off Naha—that Shimazu Nariakira, who as the daimyo of Satsuma served as the overlord of the Ryukyu Islands, sat down to write Abe Masahiro about what had transpired on Okinawa. Nariakira was on his way from Edo to Satsuma, and although he reported that the Americans were planning to sail to Edo to discuss a commercial treaty, his letter reflected a curiously detached attitude toward this alarming turn of events. The *zaiban bugyo* had reported that the Americans would stay about a month before departing for Edo. If this was true, the Americans were already on their way, which indeed they were. "We may not have to worry very much," Nariakira wrote nonchalantly, "for they seemed very honest and we especially told them not to stay for a long time."[11]

Besides, it was not the Americans that the Japanese were concerned about. First they had feared the Russians, their aggressive neighbors to the north, and then for years, even before the Opium War, the Japanese had watched for British incursions along their poorly defended coastline. The Dutch report of 1838 about the impending visit of a British warship had sent ripples through the bureaucracy that continued on into the intelligentsia, setting off a back current that shook the Bakufu. A minor official showed a group of scholars known as the Old Men's Club a document saying that the Roju had decided the British ship should be driven away with force, and if anyone tried to land, the ship should be destroyed and all the crew killed. The scholars were advocates of *rangakusha*, or Dutch learning, the careful study of Dutch and other European books in pursuit of foreign knowledge about everything from medicine to military tactics. One of this group, a poor, masterless samurai known as Takano Choei, who often supported himself by working as a hairdresser, wrote a pamphlet about the British warship titled "A Dream." Takano's pamphlet became an overnight sensation.[12]

"It was late one winter night," Takano wrote. "The voices of men were stilled and the echo of their footsteps was rarely heard.

The door of my room creaked in the wind. With my mind engrossed in thought, it was not easy to sleep, and I was leaning upon my desk trying to read a book by the light of an oil lamp. At length my eyes were weary and I began to doze away. I seemed to enter a large room where some scores of scholars were gathered, talking upon various subjects." In his dream, Takano overheard a long exchange between two scholars who were discussing the report that "one Morrison, an Englishman, is about to enter the Bay of Yedo [Edo] to propose that the country be opened for trade; but under pretence of bringing back to Japan castaways."

One of the scholars described England as a country about the size of Japan with a smaller population. Her people were industrious, well versed in the arts and military affairs, and considered it their duty to make their country rich and strong. With skillful navigators and aggressive merchants, there was no other country like England. England, he went on, controlled dominions with a population and land mass more than four times her own. These included North America (described as lying to the west of South America), East India, southern and western Africa, New Holland, and South America (described as near Brazil and California). To control her dominions England possessed a navy of 25,860 warships with a complement of 178,620 high officers, 406,000 lower officers, and a million sailors!

As for Morrison, he was a professor and Chinese scholar who was in command of all British warships in the South Seas. His objective in returning the castaways was to open trade with Japan. The Bakufu, however, was planning to drive Morrison away. "Such treatment has never been found anywhere else in the world," the scholars lamented. And if this is the Bakufu's response, Japan will no longer be known as a Righteous Country. The proper response, the scholars suggested, was to welcome the British at Nagasaki and reward them handsomely for their kind treatment of the Japanese sailors. Then, perhaps from the British, Japan could learn something about the world of trade.

Takano had confused Robert Morrison the missionary, who had died in 1834, with the ship *Morrison*, which under the command of the American merchant-missionary Charles King, accompanied by Wells Williams, had been driven away by cannon fire in 1837.

It was not until the year after the *Morrison*'s departure that the Bakufu found out the name of the ship from the Dutch. Takano had seen a report that discussed the arrival of the *Morrison* and the prospects for another visit.[13]

Whatever the circumstances, Takano's pamphlet was widely read, even by the shogun, one source reported. For his efforts, Takano was arrested, his books and papers were confiscated, and he was imprisoned for life. The Confucian scholars who functioned as house intellectuals for the Bakufu considered Dutch learning subversive. By suggesting opening the country to the British, Takano had thereby undermined one of the legal pillars of the shogun's rule. Four years later, Takano was released for a time and went into hiding before he was returned to prison. From then on he led a furtive existence, wandering from place to place, teaching and writing while making a living translating Dutch books about military science for various daimyo. Despite his friendship with powerful daimyo such as Shimazu Nariakira, Takano was pursued relentlessly by his enemies in the Bakufu. Finally, in 1850, a former prisoner betrayed Takano to gain his own freedom, and Takano's house in Aoyama was surrounded by the police. At first Takano fought back, wounding two of the policeman, but then he calmly ended his life by cutting his own throat.[14]

The outcome of the Opium War only served to increase the Bakufu's apprehensions about the British, fueled as they had been earlier by Takano's dramatic exaggeration of British naval power. Information about China brought by Dutch and Chinese merchants flowed in through Nagasaki, and a steady flow of pamphlets about the Bakufu's exclusion policy—some saying it should be modified, others that it should be strictly enforced—emerged from Japan's intellectuals. "Once they have finished off the business in China," wrote Sakuma Shozan, an acquaintance of Takano's and a student of foreign military science, "they will send warships to Nagasaki, Satsuma, and Yedo."[15]

The immediate result of the Opium War—and not coincidentally Takano's pamphlet—was the modification in 1843 of the 1825 law that called for either the expulsion of foreign ships or their destruction. Foreigners were now to be offered water and supplies and *then* told to leave. This fear of the British inspired Bakufu

officials at Nagasaki to treat officers from a British ship that called
there in 1845 with particular courtesy and contributed to Shimazu
Nariakira's plan to open trade with first France and then England
through the Ryukyus.

The Japanese were less clear about how the Americans fit into
the world of foreign powers that was slowly closing in on them. It
is evident that they knew something of the flowery-flagged devils,
a name they picked up from the Chinese. How else would Itarashiki
Satonushi, the Ryukyuan interpreter, have known of George Washington? One of the first Japanese books about America had been
published in Kyoto in 1708, a time when the Tokugawas had been
in power for 105 years and America was still a small cluster of
colonies scattered along the Atlantic seaboard. Its author, a Nagasaki merchant, reported that America was a continent that lay
to the east of Japan and was peopled by men and women who wore
"birds' feathers and the skins of tigers and leopards" and that the
upper classes wore "gold and silver ornaments." In the eastern part
of the continent lived people who loved to fight, ate human flesh,
liked strong drink, and worshiped the devil. To the south of this
continent lay islands covered with poisonous trees and grasses and
inhabited by large birds whose wings gave off light when they flew
at night and by demons who raised great waves to frighten passing
ships.[16]

The first reports of the formation of the United States appear
to have reached Japan in 1809, and by 1848 the Dutch were providing the Bakufu with fairly detailed annual reports of the important developments in this new country. Thus, the Dutch
informed the Bakufu of the war between the United States and
Mexico, the expansion of U.S. territories to the Pacific, the gold
rush, Taylor's death, and Fillmore's ascendancy. At the same time,
Japanese writings about the United States became increasingly
accurate. An atlas published in 1847 sketched, with only minor
errors, the country's history, provided biographical information
about George Washington, and described the evolution of the country from "provinces" to states, commenting, "There are no kings,
or lesser rulers, however; in every state, a number of wise men are
chosen as government functionaries, instead." The atlas described
the U.S. Navy of 1829 less accurately. It was not the navy that

Perry had lived with and lamented. The U.S. Navy was reported to be made up of forty-seven frigates, with new ships being built every year. Most of the fleet, the atlas concluded, was anchored in the Great Lakes. The first Japanese book devoted solely to the United States was published in the year that Perry reached Japan. "In the New Country, there is no distinction of ruler and subject; only the difference between noble and base, high and low." They lived, however, in very similar houses. Office holders were treated by the masses with "respectful fear," but only for a period of four years. The book was illustrated with prints of Christopher Columbus ("Koronbus"), the Battle of Saratoga, with Washington (sic) on horseback, and an American family at the dinner table, the men wearing hats and the tablecloth reaching to the floor, draped over the knees of the diners.[17]

Even if Abe Masahiro had known the exact date of the arrival of the American ships, there was little that he could have done. Even before he had assumed the post of senior counselor, in 1845, he had supported the calls for rearmament that had originated with a number of the country's most influential intellectuals backed by a handful of great lords. But he knew that the halfhearted buildup in coastal defenses, indicated by the new batteries that lined the shores of the Uraga Channel, could do little to stop a modern naval squadron. Sakuma Shozan had visited these batteries before Perry's arrival and reported that "the arrangement of them made no sense and none of them could be depended on as a defense fortification. Upon discovering this, I unconsciously looked up to Heaven and sighed deeply; I struck my chest and wept for a long time."[18] What could Japan's pitifully antiquated cannons do against steamers armed with high-powered swivel guns? Abe could do nothing more than await the arrival of the Americans. Meanwhile the customs house officials at Uraga had their instructions: tell foreigners to go to Nagasaki. Nagasaki was the only port where foreigners could be received.

Since 1603 the Tokugawa clan, from its castle in Edo, had ruled Japan peacefully in the name of the emperor. And that was just the problem. Tokugawa Ieyasu (1542–1616), the founder of the dynasty, had been a great warrior chief, ruthless strategist, careful student of government, and a man more comfortable in a military camp than in the elegant surroundings of some of the castle towns. But the sixty-year-old Ieyoshi (1793–1853), the twelfth Tokugawa shogun, was a docile man of few opinions who lived within Edo castle isolated from the realities of Japan. Surrounded—some would say manipulated—by the women of the inner court, or *ooku*, he was content to let the Roju rule on his behalf. In short, the

Tokugawa Ieyasu, the first Tokugawa shogun;
painting by Kano Yasunobu

Bakufu, now a vast and complicated bureaucracy, had gone soft at the very moment when it faced its greatest challenges from both without and within.

Tokugawa Ieyasu was born in 1542 a member of the Matsudaira clan and the heir to the small Mikawa domain, which sat astride the great highway known as the Tokaido and was centered on the castle town of Okazaki. It was an era of bloody internecine warfare, a time of shifting alliances that pitted domain against domain, family against family, and often lord against liege and father against son as the fiercely independent daimyo fought to extend their lands at the expense of their neighbors. It was also a time of alliances that were sealed by the exchange of hostages, executions, and forced suicides that could snuff out an entire family. Through plots and counterplots, marches and countermarches, one lord after another attempted to unify and pacify a Japan that had staggered through decades of civil war.

At the age of five Ieyasu was turned over by his father to the neighboring and more powerful Imagawa clan as a hostage. On his way to his place of confinement, Ieyasu was kidnapped by another daimyo, who at first threatened to kill him, but then traded him back to the Imagawa in exchange for a hostage son. As a young man, Ieyasu was instructed in the civil and martial arts by a Zen monk who was well known for his grasp of military tactics and his understanding of the relationship between military strategy and political governance. At the age of ten Ieyasu took on his first military responsibilities as commander of the Mikawa family's martial guard. At fifteen, he successfully led his men into battle, destroying a minor fort controlled by Oda Nobunaga (1533–1582), the most powerful daimyo then attempting to gain control of the domains that surrounded Kyoto, the home of the imperial family and the equally weak Ashikaga shoguns.

It was Oda Nobunaga's father who had kidnapped and threatened the five-year-old Ieyasu. But this presented few problems for Ieyasu, who quickly realized that Oda Nobunaga possessed the skills and the blood lust, if not the military force, that would make him the dominant power in at least one third of Japan. So Ieyasu became his follower, ultimately proving his loyalty by ordering his first son to commit suicide after he was accused, unjustly as it turned out, of plotting against Nobunaga.[19]

When Nobunaga was killed by an assassin, Ieyasu allied himself with his most powerful general, Toyotomi Hideyoshi (1537–1598). By 1590 this man of humble origins held most of Japan under his sway. Ieyasu had avoided fighting in most of Nobunaga's and Hideyoshi's wars, including two invasions of Korea, because he was busy extending his own domain along the Tokaido. But in the final campaign during Hideyoshi's consolidation of power, Hideyoshi and Ieyasu overran their mutual enemies to the east. As a reward for his support, Hideyoshi offered Ieyasu the eight provinces of the Kanto Plain, which were centered on the shabby castle town of Edo. In a celebrated moment in Japanese history, the two conquerors sealed the arrangement by standing side by side and urinating. Hideyoshi's offer was, of course, a shrewd one. By accepting the rich prize of the Kanto provinces, Ieyasu relinquished his strategic position astride the Tokaido while Hideyoshi, mindful of the instability of all alliances in Japan, had put greater distance and the Hakone Mountains between himself and his most likely rival. Thus it was said that Ieyasu retreated into leadership of the empire.

Before his death, Hideyoshi appointed his five most prominent allies to be regents to guarantee his son Hideyori's accession as shogun. Ieyasu was regarded as the most powerful of these lords. But when he and some of his allies undertook a military campaign against an independent daimyo in the Kanto provinces, one of his rivals put together an alliance of western daimyo bent on the destruction of Ieyasu and his followers. The two armies met at Sekigahara in one of the great battles of Japanese history. Without a preponderance of military force, Ieyasu still was the victor because of his aggressive tactics, the fragmented leadership of his opponents, and his skillful prebattle negotiations with a number of opponents who abandoned the alliance and came over to his side during the battle.

Even before the decisive battle of Sekigahara, Ieyasu had begun to build a system of governance that would eventually evolve into the Tokugawa Bakufu, literally, tent government. Ieyasu's disposition of rewards and punishments after the battle has traditionally been regarded as the basis for his military system of government. After viewing the severed heads of his opponents and then displaying them on the Sanjo Bridge in Kyoto as an object lesson, Ieyasu began to rearrange control of the domains. He confiscated the lands of some ninety smaller lords and gave them to his vassals, those who had been his loyalest supporters. They came to be known as the *fudai*, or inside lords. Their new domains were placed strategically so as to command the major roads that approached the Kanto Plain or adjacent to the lands of Ieyasu's most prominent former enemies. Thus the Ii clan, among Ieyasu's oldest and most loyal vassals, was given the Hikone domain astride the

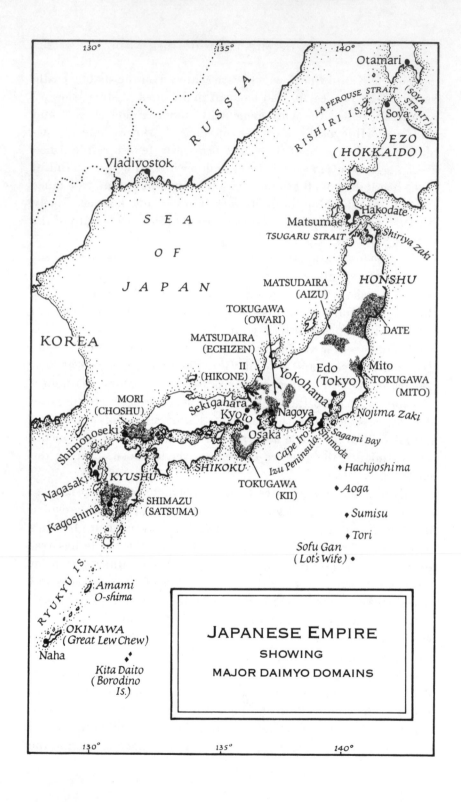

130°　135°　140°

Otamari

RUSSIA

LA PEROUSE STRAIT (SOYA STRAIT)

RISHIRI IS.

Soya

EZO
(HOKKAIDO)

Vladivostok

SEA

OF

JAPAN

Hakodate

Matsumae

TSUGARU STRAIT

Shiriya Zaki

HONSHU

MATSUDAIRA
(AIZU)

TOKUGAWA
(OWARI)

KOREA

MATSUDAIRA
(ECHIZEN)

DATE

II
(HIKONE)

Edo
(Tokyo)

Mito

Yokohama

TOKUGAWA
(MITO)

MORI
(CHOSHU)

Sekigahara

Kyoto

Nagoya

Nojima Zaki

Osaka

Cape Iro

Sagami Bay

Shimonoseki

Shimoda

SHIKOKU

Izu Peninsula

Hachijoshima

Nagasaki

KYUSHU

TOKUGAWA
(KII)

Aoga

Kagoshima

SHIMAZU
(SATSUMA)

Sumisu

Tori

Sofu Gan
(Lot's Wife)

RYUKYU IS.

Amami
O-shima

OKINAWA
(Great Lew Chew)

Naha

Kita Daito
(Borodino
Is.)

JAPANESE EMPIRE

SHOWING

MAJOR DAIMYO DOMAINS

130°　135°　140°

Tokaido near Lake Biwa from which the Ii could keep a watchful eye on events in Kyoto, the home of the emperor.

Ieyasu disposed of lands to members of his own Matsudaira clan in a similar fashion. Thus two branches of the Tokugawa family (the Tokugawa of Mito and the Matsudaira of Aizu) guarded Edo to the northeast and east while two other members of the family (the Tokugawa of Owari and the Matsudaira of Echizen) were ranged in a band across the waist of Honshu, just east of the Ii's Hikone domain. The Tokugawa-Matsudaira family houses became known as the *shimpan* daimyo. Their role became largely cere- monial, and they were excluded, except in cases where there was no heir from the main branch of the Tokugawa family, from pro- viding successors to the shogun. The three closest family houses, the Tokugawa of Kii, Mito, and Owari, known as the *gosanke*, or three families, were considered the most prestigious members of the collateral families, but their role as advisors or meddlers in Bakufu affairs, depending on one's perspective, did not evolve until the eighteenth century. In many ways Ieyasu considered the *fudai* dai- myo more reliable followers than the collateral branches of his own family, and in time the *fudai* houses would control the bureaucratic ranks of the Bakufu. Ieyasu well knew that in an era of internecine warfare, it was the members of one's own family that one had to watch most closely.

Finally, Ieyasu dealt with his enemies. Some of them lost their lands altogether. Some had their holdings reduced. But others, like the Shimazu of Satsuma, were treated with leniency. Ieyasu, after all, meant to rule the whole country, and he was astute enough to recognize that there was no need to create the basis for future challenges to his family's rule. His former enemies became known as the *tozama*, or outside lords, and they were barred from playing a role in the governance of the Bakufu. For his immediate family, Ieyasu kept about one fourth of the total land area of Japan, in- cluding the key ports of Nagasaki and Osaka. Most of the Tokugawa lands were concentrated on the Kanto Plain, but there were also vast holdings as well as gold and silver mines spread across the country.[20]

Having survived years of bloodshed and anarchy, Ieyasu, in rearranging the disposition of domains, necessarily thought in mil-

itary terms. His was a military dictatorship that emphasized strategic deployment and control of his family and vassals as well as
of his former enemies and was founded on the forthright exploi-
tation of the peasantry. Although the daimyo were given latitude
to rule their own domains, the Bakufu kept them in check by supervising marriages, preventing unauthorized contact between daimyo, and dispatching *metsuke* to pry into every corner of domain
affairs. There was also strict supervision of castle building and
repair and movement along the major highways and by sea. The
centerpiece of Ieyasu's control system for the daimyo was *sankin
kotai*, the requirement that the daimyo leave his wife and children
in Edo as hostages and live there himself during alternate years.
In the code of behavior for military families, Ieyasu enjoined the
daimyo to pursue both war and the arts ("on the left hand learning,
on the right the use of weapons"), to live frugal lives, to avoid
drunkenness and licentiousness, and to choose capable advisors. The
dynasty that Ieyasu founded attempted to balance the needs of the
central government (the shogun's immediate family and retainers)
against the autonomy of the daimyo. When this system worked, as
it did for most of its 265 years, daimyo and Bakufu resonated
harmonically. When it did not, there was always the threat of a
return to the violent conflicts of the sixteenth century.

Soon after Ieyasu had established himself as the third great
unifier of Japan, the emperor notified him, in 1603, that he was
prepared to confer upon him the title of *sei-i taishogun*, literally,
barbarian-expelling generalissimo. Ieyasu, who now claimed descent through the Minamoto shoguns (who ruled in Kamakura from
1192 to 1338) from Hachiman, the god of war, only held the office
of shogun for two years. It was absolutely essential for the Old
Badger, as he was called, to confer the title of shogun upon his son
and companion in arms, Hidetada (1579–1632), while he was still
alive so that Ieyasu could employ the threat of his formidable
military might to assure that his branch of the Tokugawa family
would retain control of the office through generations.

Ever since the rise of the first shogun, in 1192, the emperor
had been little more than a figurehead whose destiny was determined by the vagaries of those who held the real power in the land.

In the century and a half before the rise of Ieyasu, the fortunes of
the imperial family had reached their lowest ebb. As the earlier
Ashikaga shogunate (1338–1573) disintegrated, the emperors were
reduced to pauperdom. Ieyasu, however, did everything that he
could to ingratiate himself with the royal family. He lavished land
and money upon them. But he also carefully mapped Kyoto so that
he would know where all the members of the royal family, its entourage, and the court nobility lived. In fact, Kyoto was occupied
militarily by the Bakufu, with the emperor being "guarded" by
Tokugawa troops under the command of a Bakufu official known
as the *shoshidai*. Ieyasu further bound the imperial family to his
own by presenting the Emperor Go Mizuno with one of Hidetada's
daughters as a consort. It was her son who became the next emperor.

Ieyasu's instructions to both the court nobles and the emperor
were simple: apply yourselves to your studies, read the first article
of both the code for court nobles and the emperor. The unspoken
corollary was even more pointed: stay out of politics. In short, the
emperor and the aristocratic families were prisoners of the shogun
consigned to a life of artistic triviality under the strict supervision
of the shogun's troops. "Court nobles are gold and silver," Ieyasu
is reputed to have said, "while the military houses are like iron and
copper. Gold and silver are certainly precious, but they are not as
useful as iron and copper."[21]

Even with the subjugation of the imperial court and investiture
of Ieyasu's son as shogun, there remained one threat to the future
of Tokugawa rule: Toyotomi Hideyori (1593–1615), the young
son of Hideyoshi, the man whose destiny Ieyasu had usurped by
becoming the sole ruler of Japan. After the death of his father,
Hideyori remained virtually a prisoner under the watchful eye of
Ieyasu within the walls of the Toyotomis' huge castle in Osaka.
Though married to one of Hidetada's daughters, Hideyori lived in
constant fear of his wife's grandfather. Finally, in 1614, Ieyasu
found a pretense for attacking Osaka castle. After a long and costly
campaign that included a massive bombardment of the castle—
leveling its outer walls and filling its moats—Hideyori and his
remaining followers retreated to the inner keep, where he and his
mother committed suicide. A slaughter followed that claimed the

life of Hideyori's eight-year-old son and heir. In a gruesome finale, the road from Fushimi to Kyoto was lined with the heads of the defeated, ranged in sixteen rows.

A restless intellectual who was largely self-taught, Ieyasu showed tremendous interest in the world beyond Japan. During Ieyasu's time, Japan reached the outer bounds of its worldly travels. There were Japanese communities throughout Southeast Asia, as well as in Taiwan and China. A Japanese delegation visited the pope in Rome, while one enterprising Kyoto merchant sailed to Mexico in search of trade. Japanese pirates raided the coast of Korea and China, and Japanese bodyguards served the kings of Burma, Siam, and Cambodia.[22] At the moment of its greatest internal turmoil, during the sixteenth century when Ieyasu was still a young man, Japan had attracted the interest of the European powers, particularly Portugal. Marco Polo had written of Cipango as "a very big island" with "gold in great abundance," and Christopher Columbus had set out across the Atlantic with Cipango as an objective. The Portuguese explorer Vasco da Gama had rounded the Cape of Good Hope in 1497, and the first Portuguese reached Japan in 1542. They were received in a friendly manner by the Japanese, who were particularly fascinated by their firearms.

The Japanese had historically been receptive to foreign cultures. Buddhism, Confucianism, classical poetry, new systems of governance, all the great achievements of the Asian mainland— most of them associated with China—had been welcomed in the islands of Japan, contributing to the Japanese voracious curiosity about things foreign. It was said that Japanese scholars and statesmen were happy if they could commune with Chinese poets in their dreams.

Besides firearms, which were coveted in these times of violent conflict, the Portuguese brought foreign goods, a more advanced knowledge of navigation, and Christianity, a religion that was being pressed upon the peoples of Asia in one of the greatest missionary efforts in history. Seven years after the arrival of the first Portuguese, Francis Xavier came to Kagoshima in 1549. In time, three daimyo converted to Christianity. One of them, Omura Sumitada, established the port of Nagasaki, and Nagasaki under Jesuit administration became the principal center of Portuguese trade with Japan. By 1582 there were an estimated 150,000 Christian converts in Japan.

Oda Nobunaga, the first of the three great unifiers of Japan, supported Christianity while waging a ruthless war of extermination against the armed Buddhist sects. Hideyoshi spoke of conquering Korea and China and converting them to Christianity. But in a sudden about-face he issued an edict in 1587 condemning the teaching of Christianity and calling for the expulsion of all missionaries within twenty days. The reason for Hideyoshi's attack on Christianity has never been fully explained. Some thought it was because the Christian settlement at Nagasaki was protected by cannon supplied by the Portuguese; others that he opposed the growing ties between the church leaders and certain daimyo. Whatever the reason, it is clear that Hideyoshi became alarmed about the growth of Christian influence at a time when his own control of the country was far from secure.[23]

Conversions continued, however, and severe persecution of Christians and enforcement of the expulsion order did not come for another forty years. Ieyasu was initially tolerant of Christianity but more interested in the profits from foreign trade. He particularly hoped to build up Edo as a port rivaling the other ports of Japan. Probably to weaken Portuguese domination of Japan's foreign trade, Ieyasu personally received envoys from the Dutch and Spanish and befriended the English pilot Will Adams, who built ships for him and became his confidant and advisor about affairs European.

In time, though, Ieyasu too became wary of Christians. He was disgusted by the bribery and subterfuge employed by a number of Christian daimyo and concerned that they were plotting with the support of foreigners to overthrow the Bakufu. Ieyasu had come to power at the head of an alliance of eastern daimyos by conquering a largely western alliance. Christianity had had a greater impact in western Japan; western Japan was the center of foreign trade; and it was through the ports of western Japan, such as Nagasaki and Hirado, that new ideas and military supplies, both threats to Tokugawa hegemony, were coming. In 1614 Ieyasu ordered all missionaries expelled from Japan, and Christianity was banned. The decrees, however, were never strictly enforced, and Ieyasu continued to hope for increased foreign trade.

Ieyasu's successors, Hidetada and particularly the sadistic Iemitsu (1604–1654), the third shogun, finally and irrevocably turned on the foreigners. In a series of increasingly restrictive orders promulgated in 1633, 1635, and 1639, Iemitsu attempted to seal off the country from foreign influence. Japanese and Japanese ships were forbidden to go abroad. Those Japanese found secretly doing so were to be put to death. Foreign commerce was monopolized by the shogun and barred except at Nagasaki, and all nations except the Dutch and the Chinese were barred from trade. Any Portuguese ship that entered a Japanese port was to be attacked and destroyed. The Dutch were confined on Deshima Island, in Nagasaki harbor, and their families were ordered out of the country. The practice of Christianity was strictly forbidden.

To make his point, Iemitsu ordered the extermination of more than thirty thousand Christian peasants who rebelled against the regime in the Shimabara Revolt. When the Portuguese sent a ship to test the new exclusion order, fifty-seven members of the crew were decapitated after refusing to renounce their faith. Their ship was burned, and the survivors were sent back to Macao as a grim warning. Finally, Iemitsu set up a board of inquiry to pursue the eradication of Christianity. Trampling on a Christian symbol, the peculiar rite that Ranald MacDonald underwent in Nagasaki in 1847, was introduced as proof that one was not a Christian, and Buddhist monasteries and temples were ordered to register all persons residing in the vicinity.[24]

Unwittingly, Iemitsu had accomplished a remarkable feat of long-lasting significance. He forged the final link in the chain of Japan's isolation from the great imperialist wars and rivalries that would sweep Europe and then North America and the Middle East for the next two centuries. While the Land of the Gods slumbered in isolation, its feudal system immune from the external pressures of emerging capitalism and its global trading system, empires rose (England, France, Holland) and fell (Portugal and Spain), and a new republic, the United States of America, launched the first anticolonial revolt and emerged on the world scene with global ambitions of its own.

Ieyasu built Edo, the capital of the Tokugawa shogunate, from a small village centered around a dilapidated castle surrounded by swampy lowlands into the principal city in Japan. He ordered the marshes drained. Two rivers were shaped into deep moats that

Edo Castle; photograph by Felice Beato

provided a ten-mile defense perimeter for the first castle town. The soil excavated from the moats was used to reclaim the swampy areas. Three thousand ships were requisitioned to transport massive hewn stones to face the sides of the moats. The gray-black, carefully fitted boulders gave the walls of the shogun's castle a forbidding look as they rose in a gentle curve from the deep moats. The first castle—there were subsequent additions and reconstructions—was surrounded by 1,400 yards of stone ramparts from seventy to eighty feet high. The castle itself, built of wood except for a large stone keep, grew to a mile in diameter with a four-mile perimeter. Its white stuccoed towers with their tile roofs rising gracefully out of groves of cedar trees, the castle and its grounds dominated the center of the new city. According to the descriptions of foreigners who visited Edo in the time of Ieyasu and his son Hidetada, the castle was surrounded by a complicated arrangement of three moats that were almost impossible to decipher. One entered the grounds through a series of huge well-guarded gates that were set in massive stone walls and made of wood banded with iron. The grounds inside included not only residences, but woods, gardens, ponds, and recreational areas.

The daimyo built their mansions at first inside and then outside of the moat, their location determined by their relationship to the shogun. Thus the mansions of the collateral Matsudaira families of Aizu and Echizen stood right next to the front gate of the castle. The mansion of the Shimazu of Satsuma was located well to the south of the castle, adjacent to the Zozoji, the elaborate temple of the Buddhist sect favored by Ieyasu. The original mansions, at least those of the wealthier daimyo who owned two or more, were quite spectacular. One of the Ii clan's two mansions was approached through a two-storied gate sixty feet long ornamented with gilded rhinoceros and small horses. The tiles of the surrounding barracks had gilded bellflower crests that were said to shine in the dark.

Within the walls of a typical residence, there was a spacious compound complete with barracks for troops, housing for retainers, and gardens surrounding a sprawling wooden mansion with a tile roof and typically Chinese upturned gables. The walls of the interior were lavishly decorated with paintings and painted screens and the ceilings too were painted, the beams being joined by elaborate bronze and gilt fittings. Numerous alcoves featured highly valued incense burners, nested food boxes, writing implements, and tea ceremony utensils usually imported from China. Many of the original mansions were subsequently destroyed in the recurring fires that plagued Edo's wooden buildings. They were usually rebuilt in a simpler style.[25]

Mercator Cooper, the errant whaling captain from Sag Harbor,

was the first American to catch a glimpse of Edo when he visited
Edo Bay in 1845. But it was springtime, and he saw nothing but
a wooded city, probably the eaves of a temple or daimyo's mansion,
and above the treeline the distinctive fire towers, with legs and
crisscross bracing.[26] Westerners, undoubtedly influenced by the
tales of Marco Polo, imagined Edo to be a golden city, a Japanese
version of the Seven Cities of Cibola that had lured Coronado into
the deserts of the American Southwest. But Ieyasu had depleted

Mansion of the daimyo of Satsuma; photograph by Felice Beato

Japan's gold mines before his death, and the city was considerably
less colorful: less colorful, for instance, than the bright polychro-
matic wood block prints found in the famed artist Hiroshige's *One
Hundred Views of Edo* (published in 1856).

Much of the city in Perry's day looked drab from the browns
and grays of the unpainted wooden siding used in many of the
buildings. The daimyo and their retainers occupied about seventy
percent of the city, and the rest was given over to the shops and
homes of the thousands and thousands of people who had come to

the city to serve the needs of the daimyo families. Many of them were jammed into poor tenement housing in dingier parts of the city, particularly in the neighborhoods between the shogun's castle and the Edo waterfront. The beauty of the city came from interspersing cultivated parklike areas among the residences, despite the city's large population. Temple grounds, gardens, artificial lakes, man-made hills designed for viewing Mount Fuji, and undeveloped land overgrown with trees and shrubbery gave the city a very pleasing appearance.

The increasingly luxurious life of the daimyo, their samurai retainers, and the wealthy merchants, along with the abundance of well-stocked shops, the theatre district, and the numerous entertainment quarters of the so-called *ukiyoe*, or "floating world," gave the city its color, and here one may view the city through Hiroshige's eyes. One might see the procession as a daimyo's wife is being carried in a red-roofed palanquin, banners in front and back, and led by her ladies in waiting, attired in brightly colored kimonos and *obe* followed by two-sworded samurai. Or a group of *daikagura* dancers from the Ise Shrine, the great mother shrine of Shintoism, performing a lion dance, sushi makers delivering their wares in boxes stacked on their shoulders, youths flying kites, or others carrying goods on shoulder poles or in carefully wrapped bundles on their backs. Aligned to provide a perfect view of Fuji, there was the street known as Suruga-cho, with its cotton goods shops, including that of a prominent merchant family named Mitsui, announced by bright blue awnings with white characters covering the exterior walls. One of the original theatre districts was destroyed in a fire in 1841. After Mizuno Tadakuni, head of the Roju during one of the periodic but ineffectual attempts in the early 1840s to reform the morals of the Edo population, banned the theatre, a new district was built adjacent to the famous Yoshiwara pleasure district. The new district was really a street three hundred yards long sealed off by a gate at one end and lined with kabuki and puppet theatres and teahouses.[27]

Edo in time became a city of a resplendent decadence that ebbed and flowed according to the trend set by the shogun himself. When the shogun surrounded himself with concubines and insisted

Suruga-cho; woodblock print by Hiroshige Utagawa,
from *One Hundred Views of Edo*

on a life of luxury, all Edo, or at least that part that could afford it, followed eagerly in his footsteps. Daimyo and merchant vied with one another to see who could give the most extravagant parties. During the late eighteenth century, a period known for its excesses, a samurai gave a famous party that was attended by a number of daimyo. Entertainment was provided by geisha, and in time the entire company was so drunk that they began pelting one another with the food. Eventually they wrecked the samurai's home and then moved on to the Yoshiwara pleasure quarter to finish off the night. There were at least forty officially licensed pleasure quarters, but Yoshiwara was the most famous of these outposts of the floating world. The word *ukiyoe* was a pun on the Buddhist concept of the suffering world, and it came to symbolize the excesses of Bakufu life. Prostitution was legalized and controlled, as all else was under the shogun. And life in the pleasure quarter had its own elaborate rituals and hierarchies, as did life in the shogun's castle.[28]

What a contrast to Washington, the half-finished frontier town, with its neo-classical pretensions and its global ambitions! Edo was the capital of an empire that had turned in upon itself at a time when seclusion, at least in that part of Asia coveted by the Western powers, was no longer a viable way of life.

Edo flourished as the seat of Tokugawa rule. The Bakufu evolved from a personalized form of government that was largely military in its outlook into a sprawling civil bureaucracy, one of the most highly organized and sophisticated civil governments in the world. By the time of Perry's arrival, when Edo's population stood at about one million, it was the largest city in the world, and it has been estimated that 17,000 men occupied 250 different positions in the government. In the Tokugawa scheme of things members of the *tozama, shimpan*, and *gosanke* houses were barred from Bakufu office. Thus virtually all the officials came from the *fudai* houses, which had established their loyalty to the shogun and were considered less likely to cause dissension in the ranks of the Bakufu.

Ieyasu and his son Hidetada ruled through the assistance of the vassal lords with whom they had formed close personal rela-

PRINCIPAL BAKUFU OFFICIALS
(After Conrad Totman)

SHOGUN

GREAT COUNCILLOR
(Tairo)

SENIOR COUNCILLORS
(Roju)

KYOTO DEPUTY
(Kyoto shoshidai)

SUPERINTENDENT
OF TEMPLES AND
SHRINES
(Jisha bugyo)

GRAND CHAMBERLAIN
(Sobayonin)

KEEPER OF OSAKA
CASTLE
(Osaka jodai)

JUNIOR COUNCILLORS
(Wakadoshiyori)

Edo City Magistrates
(Edo machi bugyo)

Superintendent of Finance
(Kanjo bugyo)

Finance Personnel
(Kanjo shu)

Intendants
(Daikan)

Comptrollers
(Kano gimmiyaku)

Inspectors General
(Ometsuke)

*Major Officials in Other
Cities*
(Ongoku bugyo)

Office of Foreign Affairs
(Kaibogakari)

*Chiefs of the Pages and
Attendants*
(Kosho todori; konando
todori)

Inspectors (Censors)
(Metsuke)

*Captains of the Bodyguard,
Inner Guard, New Guard*
(Shoiban gashira;
koshogumi ban gashira;
shimban gashira)

tionships largely on the battlefield. With Iemitsu's ascendancy
(from 1623 to 1654), civil institutions were beginning to emerge
staffed by members of the *fudai* families, and the shogun for a time
ruled through the agency of his personal household, usually led by
a grand chamberlain. By the nineteenth century the Roju (the
senior council) and Wakadoshiyori (junior council) had emerged
to rule the Bakufu. Over time, the shoguns, as the emperors had
before them, became mere figureheads isolated from the centers of
power that were located at various levels of the bureaucracy. The
shogun retreated into the vast maze of 350 rooms that made up the
Middle Interior of Edo Castle. Here he lived in isolation with his
guards and personal attendants while nearby in the Great Interior
(*ooku*) with its 400 rooms lived the women of the court with their
own elaborate ranking, beginning with the shogun's wife in the
senior position. Increasingly the women of the Great Interior came
to play an important if not decisive role in the life of the shogun.
By the time of the placid Ieyoshi (from 1837 to 1853), the women
of the *ooku* had gained control of important lines of communication
between the shogun's sequestered world and his senior officials.[29]

The leading Bakufu officials were stationed throughout the
castle according to rank and the effective power of their offices.
And by Perry's time, the bureaucracy had spilled out of the castle
into a number of adjacent buildings. Although the Roju and to a
lesser extent the Wakadoshiyori effectively ran the Bakufu, middle-
level officials exercised disproportionate influence. They controlled
key instruments of rule, such as the budget and the office of the
metsuke, or censors, the shogun's feared and influential spies. By
custom it was difficult for a higher official to meddle in the affairs
of an office like that of the *kanjo bugyo* (budget officials) or even
to meet them face-to-face. This made decision making a challenging
undertaking, particularly when dealing with a situation such as
the arrival of the Americans, because there was no clear consensus
about what to do. Influential daimyo, each with his own relation
to the shogun, had to be consulted, and then the various centers of
bureaucratic control had to be propitiated. Finally the shogun had
to be approached, usually through his chamberlain or an influential
consort, to get his agreement or at least ex post facto approval of

a course of action. All this led to an unwieldy form of government that lurched along, hoping to avoid crisis.*

Isolated from pressures from the outside world, the Bakufu after one hundred and more years of peace began to feel in the middle of the eighteenth century the pressures of its own internal contradictions. The Bakufu sat atop a rigid and finely graded hierarchical structure that rested heavily upon the backs of the peasantry. Confucianism taught that there was a class structure that put the samurai at the top followed by the peasant, artisan, and finally, in the most contemptuous position, the merchant. Though second in this hierarchy and accorded a measure of literary respect, the peasants were cruelly exploited to produce tribute in the form of rice and other goods that supported the Bakufu, the daimyo, and all the other members of the samurai class. Estimated to be seven to ten percent of the population, the samurai, unless driven by necessity, would not deign to be gainfully employed.

The peasants were, with certain exceptions, bound to the land, their lives closely regulated. According to one of Ieyasu's closest advisors, the peasants were to be encouraged to produce enough to live on and to provide seed for the next year, but no more. A decree of 1649 that was sent to all villages in Japan listed tasks to be carried out both day and night, barred the purchase of tea and sake, ordered the peasants to eat millet, vegetables, and other coarse foods rather than rice, which was to be saved for the payment of taxes, and prescribed the proper material for clothing (cotton or

* The historian E. H. Norman wrote: "The list of officials in charge of justice, religion, finance, town and city administration was extremely elaborate, so that the whole administration of the Bakufu might be compared to a labyrinth with dark winding passages, some blocked or walled up, some tracing concentric curves, others running parallel and never meeting, others again fantastically interwoven and crisscrossed; it would be a bold Theseus who could thoroughly explore this maze with its weird crepuscule and hollow echoes. The Tokugawa passion for keeping the left hand of its administration in ignorance of the right hand's activity, while it succeeded in playing off one group of high officials against another, resulted at times of crisis, when quick decisions were necessary, in the most bewildering confusion."[30]

hemp, but no silk). In addition, the peasants were expected to donate their labor for other projects organized by their lords and masters, such as transportation and road building.[31]

Treated by some daimyo and the samurai class in general as little better than animals, the poorer peasants found life at best grim. "Common people," read the code of the Tokugawa house, "who behave unbecomingly to members of the military class, or who show want of respect to direct or indirect vassals may be cut down on

Execution ground; photograph by Felice Beato

the spot." In line with the dominant neo-Confucian ideology, the peasants were urged to regard their village and district heads and local officials as their real parents and to revere their provincial lords as the sun and moon while treating higher officials as tutelary deities. The consequences of incorrect behavior were extreme. Arrest and imprisonment was invariably accompanied by torture, and prison conditions were such, as demonstrated by the experience of the mutinous crew of the *Lagoda*, that a long sentence often meant death. Execution was by decapitation or crucifixion, often after prolonged agonies.

Faced with a legacy of civil war and a resistant population, the Bakufu was a thoroughly dictatorial regime that practiced an eerily modern form of totalitarianism. Through the *gonin-gumi* system (association or group of five), the populace was organized and controlled down to the house-to-house level. The five-man group, backed by informers, was ordered to keep an eye out for tax evaders and to mobilize the people for periodic tramplings on the cross to prevent the revival of Christianity. As an additional form of control, the peasants were ordered to register at their local Buddhist temple or Shinto shrine. A spy system, which also reached down into the village, was centralized in the office of the *ometsuke* in the shogun's castle in Edo. The *metsuke*, trained in the arts of disguise, shadowing, and surreptitious entry of homes, were charged with a wide range of responsibilities, including reporting on the activities of the Bakufu officials themselves. While the literacy level was high and literary traditions continued among the peasantry, the Bakufu attempted to limit both the content and extent of knowledge. "It is enough to follow the books of old," read a "reform" edict issued in the late eighteenth century, "there is no need to write new ones." The populace, wrote one statesman about the late Bakufu years, was enjoined to "be stupid, be stupid."[32]

The central problem of the Bakufu and each daimyo was supporting a nonproductive class, the samurai, who lived on a stipend and for the most part in urban centers and whose demands continually threatened to outstrip the peasants' ability to produce. *Sankin kotai*, the enforced residence of the daimyo and his family and retainers in Edo on alternate years, swelled the population of the city and encouraged the daimyo and their retainers to live a life of ease and luxury, which became increasingly difficult to sustain. At the same time, Bushido, the code of the samurai, taught the need for a balance between *bu* and *bun*, military training and scholarly pursuits. Making money and selling goods or engaging in any type of productive activity other than what was required when holding an official position with either the domain or Bakufu government was supposedly beneath the dignity of the samurai, but the administration of the ever more complex political economy of Japan was beyond the capabilities of most of the country's rulers.

With no wars to fight, the samurai became bureaucrats or scholars while those without recourse to those positions struggled on the margins of the growing market economy. "On looking at the condition of the present day military classes," Sugita Gempaku (1733–1817), physician and Dutch scholar, wrote, "I observe that its members have grown up in a most fortunate age of prosperity which has continued for nearly three hundred years. For five or six generations they have had not the slightest battlefield experience. The martial arts have steadily deteriorated. Were an emergency to occur, among the Bannermen and Housemen [the shogun's military forces] who must come to the shogun's support, seven or eight out of ten would be as weak as women and their morale as mean as merchants'. True martial spirit has disappeared completely."[33]

Katsu Kokichi, a samurai who lived in Edo and died there in 1850, has left a fascinating memoir of the life of a marginal samurai in the years before Perry's arrival. Kokichi was a low-ranking retainer of a daimyo but could not or would not find employment as an official. Instead he divided his time between brawling in the streets, hanging around fencing studios and the pleasure quarter, and earning his livelihood, which was buying and selling swords. He was an open-handed and generous soul, a self-confessed thief and a clever con artist, quick to lend his friends what little money he had and equally quick to take offense and respond with violence. In short, he was a typical resident of the Edo demimonde. As such, he and his ilk were a constant worry to those Bakufu officials who feared for the future stability of the government.[34]

Not to be ignored were the other aspects of the samurai's lack of a productive role in the Japanese economy. Idleness supplemented by a tradition of scholarly pursuits sponsored with various degrees of largesse by the daimyo led to a charged intellectual atmosphere. In this context, the samurai intellectuals studied the Chinese classics, revived an interest in Japanese history, debated the proper relationship between Japan and the West after the Russians began to make their appearance in the late eighteenth century, and examined Western technology and science. Every daimyo had his scholarly advisors, as did the Bakufu. Despite official strictures (including torture and execution) against "heterodox schools of thought," the debates grew increasingly intense, pitting Dutch scholars against the conservative Confucianists supported by the

Bakufu and the more radical antiforeignists, who decried the softness of the government. As the Western powers drew nearer, these debates, such as the one inspired by Takano Choei's "Dream," were informed by a sense that the practical solutions that emerged from these discussions would determine whether Tokugawa rule could meet the challenges of the contemporary world.

Before the Opium War, however, the problems of internal instability, not foreign pressures, were what plagued the Bakufu. Beginning some time after 1765, famine and rebellion began to haunt the countryside. For one thing, the daimyo were eager to extract greater tribute from the peasants. At the same time the commercialization of the economy led to growing polarization in the village itself, with the poorer peasants additionally victimized by a wealthy class of peasant landowners and financial middlemen. The daimyo, increasingly dependent on Edo and Osaka merchants, who turned the tribute crop into cash, squeezed the merchants, and the merchants in turn squeezed those below them until as much as possible was extracted from the peasants. Famine further aggravated the situation. During one of the worst periods of suffering, in the late 1770s, drought was followed by frightful storms that leveled much of Edo, and then came an epidemic that is estimated to have killed 190,000 people in that city alone.

When the peasants began to resist, the Bakufu responded with greater police surveillance through, among other things, the establishment of a network of informers. The problem, according to a Bakufu order sent to a local official, was that "the people are of violent and stubborn temper and disorderly elements come out of them." The peasants responded with everything from illegal petitions to uprisings, house smashings, and desertion of their villages in a series of outbursts that crested in the Tenmei uprising of 1786 and 1787 and culminated in simultaneous riots in Edo and Osaka. In Edo alone 980 rice shops and dozens of other establishments were demolished in an orgy of destruction.[35]

There followed a period of retrenchment, the Kansei reforms, that led to relative quiescence until the 1830s, when another period of drought and famine ensued, leading to 455 recorded peasant uprisings, 103 urban riots (which often featured the smashing of wealthy merchants' houses), and 465 other village disturbances. The unrest peaked in the great Osaka uprising of 1837, which Wells Williams and the other passengers aboard the *Morrison* were told about when they arrived in Kagoshima Bay after being driven away from Uraga. The Osaka uprising, during which fires set by the rebels burned about one fifth of the city, confirmed the Bakufu's worst nightmares: it was an uprising that brought together disaffected samurai and wealthy peasants in defense of the poor. It did not, however, spark a general rebellion against the Bakufu, but it was greeted with widespread sympathy, and understandably sent shock waves through the Bakufu.[36] It added to the general feeling of malaise, and when coupled with the growing foreign impingement, it is not surprising that many commentators spoke of *naiyu-gaikan*, a Japanese adaptation of a Chinese phrase that meant "troubles at home and dangers from abroad."

8

THE BAKUFU
CONFRONTS THE
OUTER BARBARIANS

Today, the alien barbarians of the West, the lowly organs of the legs and feet of the world, are dashing about across the seas, trampling other countries underfoot, and daring, with their squinting eyes and limping feet, to override the noble nations. What manner of arrogance is this![1]
—AIZAWA SEISHISAI, *Shinron*, 1825

Although foreign trade is against our national law, now the situation has come to a point where we cannot reject trade. We should allow only Ryukyu to trade so that we will be able to prevent a foreign invasion of our mainland.[2]
—SHIMAZU NARIOKI to Abe Masahiro, 1845

We should build warships and consolidate coastal defenses. Then if barbarians come to our sea, we should shoot every single one of them to death thereby stirring up military prowess so as to maintain Tokugawa rule throughout the ages.[3]
—TOKUGAWA NARIAKI to Lady Anegakoji, Autumn 1846

Certainly [the foreign encroachment] justifies reissuing this uchi harai *[repel and destroy] law, but at present one can scarcely say that our coastal defense preparations are fully completed. There would be occasions when enforcing the law would invite conflict, and in the event we reissued the* uchi harai *order and the foreigners retaliated, it would be a hopeless contest, and it would be a worse disgrace for Japan.*[4]
—ABE MASAHIRO to Tokugawa Nariaki, August 1846

ABE MASAHIRO, the young lord of Fukuyama, came of age and entered the Bakufu during these years of growing turmoil. Born in 1819, Abe came from a distinguished clan whose long service to the Tokugawas epitomized the loyalty of the great *fudai* families, whose members served in the top ranks of the Bakufu. The Abe family had stood beside the Tokugawas from the very beginning. Abe Shigetsugu had served in the Roju under Iemitsu, the third shogun, and had been one of thirteen retainers who committed ritual suicide (*junshi*) upon the death of their lord, a practice that was later outlawed. When Abe entered the Roju in 1843, he was the fourth member of his family to do so, members of his family having served in the Roju for close to half the years of the Tokugawa Bakufu.[5]

Even as a child Abe was brilliant, dignified, and well mannered, seemingly conscious of his destiny. His father was a scholar, painter, and disciplined martial artist who divided his day between work in the morning and reading in the latter part of the day, often keeping at his studies until midnight. Many scholars were brought to his mansions to teach his retainers and his children. He especially wanted them to learn the knowledge that could be gained from Dutch books. At a young age, Abe took after his father and became known for his considerate treatment of those who served him. He studied archery, the use of the spear and sword, riding, history, and the works of Confucius. Later in his life he took to poetry and painting, painting both in a Western style (a rarity at that time) and according to Japanese tradition.[6]

As the sixth son, Abe was not expected to become the next daimyo of Fukuyama. Instead he was to be adopted by another family that needed an heir. But when the last of his brothers died, he became the lord of Fukuyama at the age of nineteen. He was immediately faced with the great famine of the 1830s. His grandfather, Abe Masatomo, had faced a similar crisis in the 1780s and had not fared well. The Abe family was known for its heavy-handed taxation policies. As early as 1717, hundreds of peasants had marched on the Abe castle, ultimately winning many of their demands. A later rebellion was less successful; its leaders were exe-

Portrait of Abe Masahiro

cuted. A fourth rebellion was triggered in 1786 by attempts to extract higher taxes and the ruthless activities of the local official who masterminded this effort. As heavy rains and flooding drove the price of rice skyward in 1786, the Abe family decided to increase their levies in selected villages.

According to a local account, on the night of a full moon in the year of the horse (December 1786), "the entire population rose up like a disturbed nest of bees," crying out, "Let's get Endo [the Abe factotum] to satisfy ourselves." Abe Masatomo at first dismissed the peasants' demands as "merely a selfish request." Twelve hundred samurai were mobilized but retreated before a much larger contingent of rock-throwing peasants. Ultimately Abe Masatomo gave in to the peasants' demands, fired his official, and released seventy peasants who had been arrested. For successfully ending a rebellion in a major *fudai* domain, Abe Masatomo was awarded with a position on the Roju.[7]

When Abe Masahiro faced a similar crisis, he benefited from the reforms that had followed the Tenmei uprising of 1786–1787. In addition to extending domain control over each village and further regulating the dress and consumption of the peasants, grain warehouses had been set up to provide for famine relief. It was said that not a person died from starvation in Fukuyama and that Abe's neighbors envied the way he handled the crisis.

At twenty Abe was assigned to a ceremonial job in the shogun's castle in Edo. From there he moved on to the office of the *jisha bugyo*, who was in charge of temples and shrines. Abe finally attracted the attention of Shogun Ieyoshi when he accompanied him on a visit to Toshogu shrine in Ueno. When the shogun asked about the height of the pillars in the shrine, Abe was the only one with a quick enough mind to make the calculations on the spot. From then on the shogun paid close attention to Abe's career.[8]

Abe was the best of the small handful of leaders that was coming to power at both Edo Castle and in some of the leading domains. Energetic and astute, Abe quickly developed a sophisticated understanding of the complexities of bureaucratic rule and a sound grasp of the twin threats, foreign and domestic, faced by the Bakufu. He received his first education during the unsuccessful reform efforts of the Roju chief Mizuno Tadakuni. Influenced by the powerful Tokugawa Nariaki, the daimyo of Mito and leading member of the *gosanke*, or Three Houses, Mizuno had tried to check the power of the Osaka merchants while directly challenging the drift toward decadence in Edo itself. Beginning in 1841 Mizuno issued a number of regulations (known as the Tenpo reforms) that all but shut down the merchant guilds. He also took on the high-living Edo populace by closing theatres, teahouses, archery and story-telling booths, demolishing the homes of a number of wealthy

Portrait of Tokugawa Ieyoshi

citizens, and banning them from the city. He barred women from studying the *samisen* (a stringed instrument) or learning *joruri* (a form of poetry), lifted the licenses of professional hairdressers, specified what kind of materials could be used for clothing, banned certain kinds of combs and hairpins, outlawed novels, and prohibited the use of decorated signboards.

Mizuno's most prominent opponents were the women of the shogun's *ooku*. It was reported that the shogun could no longer get ginger sprouts for his favorite dish of stewed fish. When he asked why, his consorts told him it was because of Mizuno's reforms, which he vaguely remembered discussing with Mizuno. Rising prices,

shortages, and the attack on the gaiety of city life broadened the
base of Mizuno's opposition. Finally, he even fell out with his friend
and mentor, Tokugawa Nariaki. In 1843 Mizuno was removed from
the Roju, and Abe Masahiro became a member.[9]

Abe, though only twenty-four, could have become head of the
Roju. But the next year the shogun's castle went up in flames, the

Women of the *ooku*

shogun barely escaping alive. Not so with his consorts, many of
whom burned to death. The Roju was faced with the thankless task
of raising new funds to rebuild the castle at the same time that it
was called upon to respond to the letter from the Dutch king about
the results of the Opium War. Abe, perhaps acknowledging his
inexperience or too cautious to risk his future in these difficult
days, preferred to push for Mizuno's recall to handle these challenges.

As a Roju member Abe was immediately put in charge of
foreign affairs along with Makino Tadamasa, a docile man who
deferred to Abe. Abe began as a staunch supporter of the seclusion

policy and as an advocate of building up the Bakufu's military power, particularly its coastal defenses. When news of the disastrous Chinese defeat in the Opium War reached Japan, Mizuno, under pressure from Shogun Ieyoshi and a member of the Roju, decided to relax the seclusion policy. Mizuno particularly feared that actions such as the shelling of the *Morrison* in 1837 would lead to an incident that would provide an excuse for a British invasion of Japan. In 1843 Mizuno ordered that foreign ships coming for supplies be provided with food, firewood, and water, asked to leave, and instructed never to return. Abe Masahiro, however, opposed weakening the Bakufu's seclusion policy.[10]

Mizuno's decision to relax the seclusion policy drew the fire of his friend, Tokugawa Nariaki, the most articulate and forceful spokesman for antiforeign sentiment. Then while Mizuno was out of office, Tokugawa Nariaki's enemies in his own domain moved against him. In 1844 he was charged with seven crimes against the Bakufu. Among them were his too insistent advocacy of respect for the emperor, his repeated calls for building up national defenses, and his attacks on Buddhism in favor of Shinto. His attacks on Buddhism in particular provided the pretext for moving against him. Buddhist priests in the Mito domain were outraged when Nariaki ordered the seizure of temple bells, which were then melted down into cannon. The Buddhists took their case to Edo, and Abe Masahiro lent them a sympathetic ear. Nariaki was removed as daimyo of Mito and confined to his hunting lodge at Komagome, two miles north of the shogun's castle. His councilors were also removed from office, and many of them were jailed.[11]

Mizuno's efforts to reform the Bakufu had proved to be a dismal failure. Now the Roju was moving against the most influential advocate of military preparedness at a time when the threat from the outside world seemed greater than ever before. As usual in the confused world of Edo, the initiatives of the Bakufu made little sense. Moreover, Nariaki was more than an advocate of a strong defense. He was a Tokugawa, a member of a *gosanke* house whose reforms in his own domain had won him support throughout Japan. It was Nariaki's very success that seemed to threaten the Bakufu. His efforts threatened not only the bureaucratic prerogatives of the *fudai* houses who ran the Bakufu, but they also introduced a further element of instability into the delicately balanced system of Tokugawa rule.

The irascible and articulate Nariaki ruled a domain some seventy-five miles northeast of Edo. As a direct descendant of the eleventh son of the founder of the Tokugawa shogunate, the forty-four-year-old Nariaki, a handsome man with a sparse goatee and mustache, was known by tradition as the vice shogun (*tenka no fuku shogun*), one of the shogun's principal advisors. Also by tradition, the daimyo of Mito was permitted to ignore the practice of alternate attendance in Edo and to live full-time in the city.

The Mito domain was one of the great centers of Japanese learning, associated as it was with the writing of an official history of Japan that had been begun in 1657, and Nariaki epitomized the samurai fusion of statecraft, military skills, and the arts. In Mito he built the Korakuen, Japan's first public garden, centered around a plum orchard, and in a corner of the garden he built an austere but decorous pavilion known as the Kobuntei—a simple wooden structure dedicated to the pursuit of the arts. Above the gate leading into the Kobuntei were written lines from a classic Chinese poem: "When we love literature, the flowers open. When we stop, the flowers close." Nariaki himself wrote in at least two styles of calligraphy, crafted his own No masks, and showed skills as a painter. He was also a careful student of military matters. Using the crude blast furnaces available at the time, he built numerous cannons embossed with his signature, which he offered to the Bakufu.

After Nariaki became daimyo in 1829, Mito was associated with a decidedly activist style of intellectual discourse. Tokugawa Nariaki and his disciples, the Mito intellectuals, were exponents of *sonno joi*, a doctrine that called for revering the emperor and expelling the barbarians. They were also at the forefront of a movement that called for thoroughgoing domestic reform in an attempt to arrest what the Mito intellectuals perceived as the disastrous decline of the shogunate. Employing slogans with widespread appeal such as "Shinto and Confucianism are one," "Literary and military [training] are not incompatible," and "Loyalty to sovereign and loyalty to parents are one in essence," the Mito thinkers attracted numerous followers, among other daimyo and their restless samurai intellectuals.[12]

The founding creed of the modern-day Mito school was written in 1825 by Aizawa Seishisai, a Mito scholar. Aizawa's essay, the

Portrait of Tokugawa Nariaki

Shinron, was a laudatory response to the new "repel and destroy" decree directed against foreigners, particularly those who were beginning to call at the Ryukyu Islands. In 1824 Mito itself had been visited by British whalers, who put twelve men ashore to search for supplies. Aizawa had made direct contact with the foreigners, questioning a group of Englishmen who were held for a time in a house near the coast.[13] Seizing upon what he saw as "one chance in a thousand years" to make it clear that foreigners were the enemy, Aizawa penned the *Shinron*.

Our Divine Land is where the sun rises and where the primordial energy originates. The heirs of the Great Sun occupied the Imperial Throne from generation to generation without change from time immemorial. Japan's position at the vertex of the earth makes it the standard for the nations of the world. Indeed, it casts light over the world, and the distance which the resplendent imperial influence reaches knows no limit. Today, the alien barbarians of the West, the lowly organs of the legs and feet of the world, are dashing about across the seas, trampling other countries underfoot, and daring, with their squinting eyes and limping feet, to override the noble nations. What manner of arrogance is this!

Aizawa went on to argue that although the earth appears to be round, Japan, the Divine Land, was actually located at the top of the earth. America, in contrast, "occupies the hindmost region of the earth; thus, its people are stupid and simple, and incapable of doing good things." Aizawa called on all great men to "rally to the assistance of Heaven" lest "the whole natural order will fall victim to the predatory barbarians." Quoting Sun Tzu's *Art of War*, he urged the Japanese "not to rely on their not coming upon you; rely on your own preparedness for their coming. Do not depend on their not invading your land; rely on your own defense to forestall their invasion."[14]

Aizawa saw a direct connection between the state of nationalist rivalries in the Western world and Western expansion into Asia. "So when there is trouble in the West," he wrote, "the East generally enjoys peace. But when the trouble has quieted down, they go out to ravage other lands in all directions and then the East becomes a sufferer." Commerce followed by Christianity was the means the barbarians used to subjugate other countries. "When those barbarians plan to subdue a country not their own, they start by opening commerce and watch for a sign of weakness. If an opportunity is presented they will preach their alien religion to captivate the people's hearts. Once the people's allegiance has been shifted, they can be manipulated and nothing can be done to stop it."[15]

Aizawa had sharp words for the Dutch scholars. "There is nothing harmful about it," he said of *rangakusha*. "However, these students who make a living by passing on whatever they hear have

been taken in by the vaunted memories of the Western foreigners
. . . and the weakness of some for novel gadgets and rare medicines,
which delight the eye and enthrall the heart, have led many to
admire foreign ways." Then in a prescient mood, he warned, "If
someday the treacherous foreigner should take advantage of this
situation and lure ignorant people to his ways, our people will adopt
such practices as eating dogs and sheep and wearing woolen clothing. And no one will be able to stop it. . . . It is like nurturing
barbarians within our own country."

There was only one way for the Bakufu to resist these awful
possibilities, Aizawa argued. "If . . . the Shogunate issues orders to
the entire nation in unmistakable terms to smash the barbarians
whenever they come into sight and to treat them openly as our
nation's foes, then within one day after the order is issued, everyone
high and low will push forward to enforce the order."[16]

More than a call to arms, Aizawa's *Shinron*, which was circulated widely but not actually published until after Perry's departure, was a dramatic challenge to the Japanese people to
rediscover and renew their native traditions. Mito intellectuals, like
Aizawa, regarded the founding myths of the sacred Yamato state
as nothing less than history itself. These legends, as recounted in
the *Kojiki* (*The Record of Ancient Matters*) and *Nihongi* (*Chronicles of Japan*), the great Japanese classics written in Chinese in
the eighth century, recreated the history of the early Japanese
dynasties, tying the origins of the emperor system directly to the
gods themselves.

According to these wondrous tales, two gods, Izanagi no Mikoto
and Izanami no Mikoto, the Man who Invites and the Female who
Invites, were ordered to create a new world where the gods could
live. With a jeweled spear they stood on the floating bridge of
heaven and dipped the end of the spear into the waters of the ocean
that covered the earth. When they raised the spear from the water,
the droplets that fell from its tip formed Kyushu, the first island
of Japan. After the two gods built a splendid palace, they were
told the secret of lovemaking by a pair of magpies. Their offspring
included a leech who was set adrift in a reed boat, a small island
called Foam, or Awaji, that died soon after birth, and Shikoku, one
of the four main Japanese islands. Next to be born were more islands

and then the rivers, mountains, herbs, and trees. Their last child, Fire, killed his mother Izanami, who went to the Land of Darkness. In search of his beloved wife-sister, Izanagi followed her. But his wife, now a spectral figure already in a state of decay, sent the thunder gods and a host of thunder warriors after him. When Izanagi, having escaped from the thunder gods, stopped to bathe in a river to wash himself after his trip to the underworld, numerous other gods were born from his discarded clothes and his skin. Finally three gods that greatly pleased Izanagi were born: one Amaterasu, the sun goddess, from his left eye; the moon god from his right eye; and the ocean god from his nose. To these gods Izanagi turned over the entire universe, giving Amaterasu the Plain of High Heaven, the moon god power over the night, and the ocean god power over the seas.

In time special envoys sent from heaven pacified the Central Land of Reed Plains on Honshu, Japan's main island, and Ninigi, the grandson of Amaterasu, was sent to rule this land. To Ninigi, Amaterasu gave a necklace, a jeweled mirror, and a sword made from the tail of a dragon, the three sacred regalia of the Shinto religion. Ninigi had three sons, and one of those who ruled over Kyushu for 580 years had a grandson, Jimmu Tenno, the Divinely Brave Heavenly King. Jimmu Tenno became the first emperor of Japan. Komei, the emperor of Japan when Perry arrived in 1853, was the 119th emperor from the 67th generation of the family, which traced its ancestry to Amaterasu, the sun goddess.[17] Hence, according to Aizawa, there was "an intimate communion between gods and men. . . . Religion and government being one," he wrote, "all the Heavenly functions which the sovereign undertakes and all the works that he performs as the representative of Heaven are means of serving the Heavenly forebears."[18]

This potent combination of religion and patriotism appealed to the poetic souls of many Japanese samurai, and Aizawa's *Shinron* would have a profound impact on the growing debate over Japan's seclusion policy. In addition the reform program designed by Nariaki and his followers for the Mito domain became a model for other domains across the nation and ultimately an inspiration to the ill-fated Mizuno Tadakuni. Nariaki began a massive land reform designed to return the samurai to his original status as a farmer-warrior. "Today's warriors live only in the castle towns," Aizawa wrote in the *Shinron*. "All they talk about is women, eating and drinking, actors and dramatic productions, gardening and floral arrangements, bird-catching and fishing. Their fencing practice and lance work are only for personal vendettas; their study of archery and gunnery are solely for show; their riding just for ceremonies."

In a further effort to reduce domain expenditures and promote a close relationship between samurai and the land, Nariaki reduced the size of the domain office in Edo. Through his own style of dress and behavior he tried to exemplify simplicity and encouraged the development of the martial arts and the construction of coastal defense systems. Finally he built the Kodokan, a sprawling educational complex headed by Aizawa and Fujita Toko and dedicated it to spreading the fusion of Shinto and Confucianism, preaching military preparedness, and studying Japanese history. In short, Nariaki and his disciples tried to remake Mito after an image of the past.[19]

The year after Abe Masahiro signed Nariaki's arrest warrant, Mizuno Tadakuni was sent into his final retirement, and Abe became the head of the Roju. Abe was faced not only with the problem of responding to the Dutch king's letter about the dangers of Western encroachment in light of the Opium War, but also with the arrival of British and French ships in the Ryukyus. More than anything, Abe had to quickly devise a consistent policy with regard to the growing number of visits by foreign ships. But consistency was not an easy virtue in these very difficult times. Abe was a cautious man, though by necessity an indefatigable intriguer, whose concerns centered on maintaining the shogun's rule. To do this, he had to mollify the various factions that coalesced around other influential Bakufu officials and around the more vocal daimyos, such as the trade-oriented Shimazus and Tokugawa Nariaki, the most forceful exponent of a hard-line approach toward foreigners. So Abe reversed himself and set out to placate Nariaki by intervening to get Nariaki released from house arrest. After his release, Nariaki was still barred from political activity in his own domain and from involvement in the politics of the Bakufu, but this was a start.[20]

Meanwhile, the Roju, after allowing the Dutch delegation that brought their king's letter to wait for three months, ordered the Dutch to leave, saying that they would respond to the king's letter at some future date. At first the Roju kept its dealings with the Dutch a secret. Soon, however, the Roju was forced to issue a proclamation acknowledging that the Dutch had asked to open trade after rumors swept Edo that the Japanese would soon go to war. More than nine months later, in July 1845, the Roju replied to the Dutch: there would be no trade and no further correspondence.[21]

In the same year, when the French returned to the Ryukyus again pressing for trade, Abe had to respond to the Shimazus' request that the Ryukyus be allowed to trade with France either through Fukien, in China, or through one of the Chinese islands. Abe was taken aback by the Shimazus' proposal. He was being asked to take a step beyond Mizuno Tadakuni's 1843 decree, which called for the provision of water and firewood before ordering foreigners away, by opening trade albeit secretly with a foreign power. For assistance, Abe called in Tsutsui Masanori, a specialist in foreign affairs who held the powerful post of *ometsuke*, or chief inspector. Tsutsui, in turn, met secretly with Narioki's son, Shimazu Nariakira, to solicit his views on the matter. This was a bold move given the fact that the Shimazus were a *tozama* house and by custom not privy to the affairs of the Bakufu. Initially Abe was wary of the Shimazus. After all, they were hereditary enemies of the Tokugawa. But Matsudaira Yoshinaga, one of his principal advisors, encouraged Abe to become friends with the young Shimazu. He was loyal to the Bakufu and a supporter of coastal defense, Yoshinaga explained.[22]

In the end, Abe accepted—and got the shogun to bless—the Shimazus' idea of permitting the Ryukyuans to trade with France. Abe hoped that an open presentation of the Shimazus' views at Edo Castle would lead to a discussion of whether it was appropriate to deal with foreigners in this manner. The Shimazus decided, however, against broadcasting their views about opening trade. It was too controversial a stand. In addition they were reluctant to draw attention to their smuggling activities. A Shimazu retainer did meet with *metsuke* Tsutsui Masanori, getting the support of this important part of the bureaucracy. But there was opposition in other parts of the bureaucracy. It was not that they objected to trade per se; they were worried that the Ryukyu's trade with the French would interfere with the Bakufu's profitable trade at Nagasaki. Fearing that refusing to trade with the French might lead to war, Abe, however, was determined to go ahead, despite opposition. Abe acknowledged that opening trade in the Ryukyus might lead to trade elsewhere. But his retainers noted that the Ryukyus did not produce much and thus were incapable of extensive trade with foreign nations.[23]

Abe was beginning to move, albeit cautiously, in two directions at once. He had originally been a supporter of Nariaki's antiforeign line. Now he was working with the Shimazus to devise a strategy that anticipated the necessity of opening negotiations at arm's length with one or more European powers at Naha. He also approved the return of the shipwrecked Japanese sailors in August 1845, brought by Mercator Cooper—just this once—despite opposition. At the same time, though, he was insisting on improvements in Japan's coastal defense, a seemingly hard-line approach that was designed to appeal to the Bakufu's most influential critic, Tokugawa Nariaki. In fact, Abe was still grasping for a consistent policy and in doing so had decided to contravene Bakufu tradition by working with strong daimyo such as Nariaki and Shimazu Narioki, regardless of the strictures on their involvement in the Bakufu because they were members of a *gosanke* and a *tozama* house.

Soon after responding to the Dutch, Abe made another gesture in the direction of Nariaki. He asked for a report on coastal defenses, increased the number of Bakufu officials in charge of coastal defense, and ordered the construction of new batteries on Mount Hirane at Uraga. Abe also showed the correspondence with the Dutch to the daimyo from the *shimpan* houses, the twenty-three collateral houses of the Tokugawa family. "I have never heard of an exchange of letters with a foreign country," Nariaki wrote indignantly to Abe about the Dutch king's letter in February 1846. He warned that the *shimpan* houses should not be on good terms with foreigners, since they might ask to open trade and for permission to preach Christianity. Besides, the foreigners were only interested in selling "useless toys" to the Japanese. Abe responded, reassuring Nariaki that he had only showed the letter to the heads of the *shimpan* houses at the urging of the shogun. Nariaki wrote back warning that the *komo* (red hairs) were very shrewd. "They know that with sweet words and communications they will be able to deceive us although it is impossible for them to defeat Japan in a war." He advocated adhering to the expulsion decree and suggested that it might even be advisable to sever trade relations with Holland and China.[24]

Nariaki might be excluded from the affairs of the castle, but he had his own sources of information and soon got word of the arrangement that Abe and the shogun had made with the Shimazus for opening trade with the French. He immediately wrote to Abe. The Ryukyus, as he had predicted, had come under foreign pressure. The policy of allowing Satsuma to trade secretly with France through the Ryukyus would lead to the foreign barbarians wanting to trade, open communications, and propagate Christianity in the Ryukyus. If the foreigners were permitted to do one of these, they would ask for the other two. The result would be the gradual invasion of islands closer to the Japanese coast. Nariaki hoped that foreign demands would not be accepted. He added that he had heard reports from Satsuma that the Ryukyus had in effect already been given to the French and the British. The Shimazus must resist the foreigners. "It is superficial," he rebuked Abe, "to advocate that peace is necessary to protect national interests. It is inevitable that the foreigners are prepared to go to Uraga and so on."[25]

Abe's response was a slippery one. Without mentioning the Shimazus' proposal to open trade with the French in China, he denied that Japan would permit trade with the French *in the Ryukyus*. Satsuma was in charge of dealing with the matter, he explained to Nariaki, but the Shimazus would do nothing to threaten national prestige. He tried to reassure Nariaki by invoking Nariaki's own defense strategy. The coastal areas of Uraga, Nagasaki, Matsumae, and Satsuma would now be allowed to build warships, and the Bakufu was discussing whether they should build a ship themselves.[26]

A graver danger soon loomed dangerously close to Edo itself. In July 1846, the American Commodore James Biddle suddenly appeared off Uraga with two warships. One of them, the *Columbus*, was a mighty ship of the line sporting ninety-two guns. Biddle, despite being knocked down by a Japanese soldier, only pressed his proposal for an opening of trade halfheartedly and then went away. But Abe took careful note of the size and strength of these two formidable warships, which had all but violated the shogun's inner sanctum. He now had a firsthand understanding of the weakness of the empire's coastal defenses. Accordingly, he convened the *san bugyo* and the *kaibogakari* (office of coastal defense) to discuss a proposal to restore the 1825 decree, which had called for the expulsion of foreign ships. He also proposed that daimyo with coastal domains be ordered to build up their defenses, that peasants be organized into military units, that the defenses of Edo Bay be built up, and that the Bakufu begin construction of warships.[27]

It took the *kaibogakari* almost seven weeks to prepare its response to Abe's proposals. But when the coastal defense officials finally did respond, they replied that they disagreed strongly with Abe's proposals. The 1825 decree might be the best policy, but things had changed since those days. The Western powers were no longer fighting among themselves. Instead they were ready to invade and loot other countries. Restoring the "repel and destroy" decree would only invite retaliation. If the foreigners had no way to rescue their shipwrecked sailors, for example, it was "not entirely unlikely" that they would jointly invade Japan and force an agreement upon the Bakufu. Look at what happened to the Ch'ing dynasty! They did not understand the foreign bandits. As a result they were defeated and forced to make concessions. The best policy, the defense officials concluded, was to abandon the 1825 law and stick with Mizuno Tadakuni's conciliatory decree of 1843.[28]

Although Abe in his proposals was now sounding very much like Tokugawa Nariaki, Nariaki remained suspicious. Abe, for one thing, had kept his correspondence with Biddle a secret. He also had not been able to sway key parts of the bureaucracy. After Biddle's departure, Abe wrote to Nariaki at his mansion in Komagome, "Certainly [the foreign encroachment] justifies reissuing this *uchi harai* law [the repel and destroy decree of 1825], but at present one can scarcely say that our coastal defense preparations are fully completed. There would be occasions when enforcing the law would invite conflict, and in the event we reissued the *uchi harai* order and the foreigners retaliated, it would be a hopeless contest, and it would be a worse disgrace for Japan."[29]

Nariaki's response to Abe's inability to mobilize the Bakufu was to begin to seek new allies for the expulsion policy in the private quarters of the shogun and the imperial court. To get to the shogun, Nariaki decided to go through the *ooku*. Perhaps the most influential of the women around Ieyoshi was his favorite consort, Lady Anegakoji. Her real name was Hashimoto Ioyoko, and she was the younger sister of the chief counselor to the emperor and a member of a noble family in Kyoto. Anegakoji was a *jōrō*, an aide to the shogun's wife. Her rank was such that in her presence even a member of the Roju had to sit in a lower position. She was well known for her energy and brilliance. Among those who stood in awe of her were Mizuno Tadakuni. He after all had clashed with members of the *ooku* over his Tenpo reforms and was now in exile. Anegakoji was reputed to have tremendous influence over the shogun's family. She also had ties with the emperor's family, especially Emperor Komei's younger sister, who was her niece. Deserved or not, Anegakoji also had a reputation for accepting bribes from those who solicited her assistance to intervene with the shogun. Abe had recognized Anegakoji's influence and tried to court her support. Abe was liked by the shogun because of his magnanimity and his lack of impetuosity in dealing with the problems of the Bakufu, and Abe found it useful to go through the *ooku* to win the support of the shogun. "Anegakoji conspires with Abe often," a Mito official wrote in 1846. "It is said that whatever the shogun says is originally from her, and she secretly discusses matters with Abe."[30]

After Biddle's departure, Nariaki wrote to Anegakoji, warning that if Abe permitted the discussion of Japan's northern and southern defense perimeters to drag on indefinitely, the Japanese would start losing territory to the foreigners. "You may think that Japan is a major country," he warned, undoubtedly with the intention of alarming the shogun, "but the foreign barbarians consider her merely as a small island. Since we are in such a dangerous situation, I hope that the Shogun will issue orders to take proper measures."

Anegakoji wrote back saying that Nariaki's message had reached the shogun. "He found it quite true, and therefore ordered that an inquiry and preparations to expel the foreign ships be immediately carried out." Before giving orders to expel foreign ships, Nariaki responded, "we should build warships and consolidate [our] coastal defenses. Then if barbarians come to our sea, we should shoot every single one of them to death thereby stirring up military prowess so as to maintain Tokugawa rule throughout the ages." Anegakoji forwarded Nariaki's advice to the shogun.[31]

Two months later Nariaki wrote Anegakoji again. "Rumor has it that in the sixth month when Shimazu returned to Satsuma, Ise no kami [Abe] gave him an instruction. If he approved of Ryukyu trade it will lead to grave disaster later. Therefore I hope that the shogun will inquire of Ise no kami and others about their policy hereafter." Anegakoji replied that she would find an opportunity to the present Nariaki's message to the shogun. "We are very, very afraid of the foreign ships," she wrote. "We have no idea of what to do about them." Nariaki might have sources inside the castle, but they apparently had not told him about the shogun's role in permitting the Shimazus to revise the trade policy in the Ryukyus.[32]

There are also indications, though not decisive proof, that Nariaki was using his influence in Kyoto to get the emperor to take an active part in the discussion of how to deal with the foreigners. Nariaki after all had extensive relations with the court. He was the regent for the fifteen-year-old emperor Komei, and his younger sister was the wife of an important court official, Takatsukasa Masamichi, with whom Nariaki carried on a secret correspondence. Nariaki's adopted younger sister was the wife of Konoe Chushi, the *udaijin*, or minister of the right. Soon an unprecedented event transpired. A letter that bore all the marks of Nariaki's meddling emerged from the imperial household, was handed to the *shoshidai*, the shogun's representative in Kyoto, and sent on to the shogun.

"We were under the impression," the letter read, "that the government was capably led, that military affairs were in good order, and, in particular, that maritime defenses were strong. Nevertheless, there have been numerous foreign encroachments. We are, therefore, filled with anxiety and desire that henceforth our warriors, one and all, so conduct themselves that they may be prepared for more serious challenges. They should, accordingly, perfect military strategy and devote themselves to their duty so that the danger to the Land of the Gods will come to an end and, little by little, the Imperial Mind will be put at ease." In the future, the emperor wanted to be informed about the arrival of foreign ships.[33] The imperial court, which had remained snugly wrapped in the aesthetic cocoon of Kyoto for more than two hundred years, was beginning to stir and take notice of the outside world.

There was little that the emperor could do, cut off as he was from the political life of his empire. He did send an emissary with an imperial edict to a special ceremony held at the Iwashimizu Hachiman-gu, the Shinto shrine dedicated to the war god Hachiman, from whom Tokugawa Ieyasu had traced his lineage. In asking for divine protection, the edict noted that barbarian ships had come to Japan and that the emperor was constantly concerned, "waking and sleeping," about how to respond.[34]

Abe had little choice but to comply with the request of the emperor. No matter how much a prisoner of the Bakufu, the operative historical fiction was that the shogun ruled on behalf of the revered Son of Heaven. For a time Abe reported to Kyoto on the arrival of foreign ships, urging the emperor not to worry. But after the crisis of 1845–1846 subsided, Abe's reports became sporadic and the court lapsed, until Perry's arrival, into its usual somnambulism.

The unprecedented number of arrivals of foreign ships since the end of the Opium War, including two visits from American ships to Edo Bay, had produced a state of crisis in the Bakufu and had led to Abe and the Shimazus' plan to open trade through the Ryukyus. But 1846, the year of frenzied maneuvering, had come and gone, and nothing had really happened. There were no foreign attacks, no trade or treaties forced upon the unwilling Okinawans or the Bakufu. The lack of conclusive events lulled many in the Bakufu into complacency. But for Abe it renewed his sense of the need to push for greater preparedness. The past three years could well be, he knew, the dress rehearsal for greater, more cataclysmic events that were sure to come.

Thus Abe turned once again to Tokugawa Nariaki. Nariaki was a man of overweening ambition, and one of his ambitions that Abe supported, perhaps even more than Nariaki did, was for his son Keiki to become next in line for the office of shogun. Abe knew the

Bakufu from the inside. Having stood closer than any other leader to the ineffectual Ieyoshi, he recognized the need for a strong shogun. The alternative was not promising. Ieyoshi's twenty-two-year-old son Iesada was mentally incompetent, a young man who preferred to play with his kittens rather than hear about the problems of the outside world. Between Keiki and the shogunate stood the pathetic Iesada's mother, another of the shogun's favorite consorts. She wanted her son to be the shogun, and she and the powerful chamberlain Hongo Yasukata, a man with influence beyond the shogun's private quarters, had ready access to Ieyoshi. In 1841 Ieyoshi had named Iesada his heir. But he may have recognized that this was not a permanent solution to the succession problem, for he remained well disposed toward Nariaki's son.[35]

The problem was how to put Keiki in a position where he could move into the line of succession, since as a member of a *gosanke* house he was barred from that position. In 1847 Abe paid Nariaki a personal visit at his hunting lodge in Komagome to tell him that his son had been adopted into another branch of the Tokugawa-Matsudaira clan and would now become the daimyo of Hitotsubashi. Ieyoshi's father had been the lord of Hitotsubashi before he became shogun, and thus Keiki, who would henceforth be known as Yoshinobu, could eventually become shogun.[36]

This arrangement appeared to further strengthen Nariaki's ties with Abe, but Nariaki was still restive over the way in which Abe and the Shimazus planned to handle the issue of trade in the Ryukyus. He wrote to Shimazu Nariakira that the foreigners appeared to know that Satsuma traded through the Ryukyus and that it would be difficult to prevent them from coming to the Uraga or other places on the mainland. Now aware of the shogun's role in condoning Satsuma's initiative, Nariaki noted that when Ieyoshi had accepted the arrangement, he had instructed the Shimazus to be both vehement and generous in their dealings with the foreigners. To date they had only been generous. Nariaki hoped that the Roju would take a more decisive stand on the issue of trade through the Ryukyus.[37]

With Abe, Nariaki was less patient. The concessions offered to the West through the Ryukyus were more than he could bear, and he continued to memorialize Abe on the issue. Abe tried to put him

at his ease after one such letter by assuring him that he shared his
concern and would make an inquiry into the matter. "It is doubtful
you are worried about this matter," Nariaki shot back in an extraordinary letter, given the power of Abe's office and the usual
respect for hierarchy. "If you were worried, it would have been
unreasonable that two years ago when Nariakira returned to Satsuma you told him that although trade could not be permitted by
the Bakufu since it was banned, it would be proper to trade without
official permission. The Western barbarians are more thoughtful
than a child. They might have withdrawn since they thought that
if they took away the Ch'ing [Manchu] dynasty, the Ryukyus would
effortlessly fall into their hands and therefore they would not have
to vainly open war against such a small country as the Ryukyus."[38]

Meanwhile Abe was also strengthening his ties to Shimazu
Nariakira. Nariakira had spent all but eight months of his life in
Edo. So when he began to play an active role in domain affairs,
pushing for a buildup of coastal defenses, he was treated as a meddlesome outsider. Ultimately his right to succeed his father was
challenged by a half-brother. To undermine his opponents, Nariakira revealed to Abe the extent of Satsuma's illegal trade with the
Ryukyus, and Abe in turn confronted one of Nariakira's principal
opponents with the fact of Satsuma's smuggling. The official committed suicide, triggering a period of turmoil. In 1851 Nariakira,
with the support of Abe, succeeded in pushing his father aside to
become daimyo.[39] Japan's westernmost domain, one of its wealthiest
and the one with a history of contact with the outside world, was
now ruled by a dynamic lord who believed in a strong defense and
limited trade with the West.

Abe was less successful with his own bureaucracy. In 1848 he was
able to work out an agreement for the defense of Edo Bay with the
fudai houses charged with military responsibilities in the Edo area.
He then turned again to the bureaucracy with his proposal to
restore the 1825 edict. This time he attacked head-on the *kaibogakari*'s argument that the restoration of the 1825 decree would
lead to "the decline of the country." On the contrary, not to build
up Japan's defenses would force the daimyo to exhaust themselves

"running around" trying to protect Japan from the superior military force of the Western powers. Moreover, Abe argued, with little regard for consistency, the Western powers seemed more interested in trade than war. They seemed willing to "become gradually intimate" with Japan and were less likely to "commit lawless acts." To minimize the expense of coastal defenses, Abe again proposed that the peasantry be mobilized for military service. To this suggestion, he added that *bushi* (members of the samurai class) should be sent back to the domains to take up arms.[40]

If anything, the *kaibogakari* was more hostile than ever to Abe's defense proposals. Four months later the defense officials, with little sense of urgency, replied that they were "entirely opposed" to Abe's proposals. With their superior weaponry the Westerners could not be stopped by merely reiterating the expulsion decree. But if the coastal defenses were built up and the samurai were sent home, the expenditures would impoverish the domains, set the daimyo against the Bakufu, and ultimately lead to political instability. There was little to do, the defense officials argued, but deal with the arrival of each ship on a case-by-case basis.[41]

In disgust Abe withdrew his proposal. Moreover, his attempts to build up Japan's coastal defenses had finally undermined his own position in the Roju. In one sense, the *kaibogakari* was right: his efforts to mobilize the country were leading to instability, and he, ironically, was becoming one of the targets of the restive daimyo. A faction was forming around Aoyama Tadagana, the daimyo who held the third seat in the Roju. Aoyama was the spokesman for those Bakufu officials who resented Abe's efforts to restore Tokugawa Nariaki to influence. To make things worse, the powerful Ii family was objecting to its assignment to provide forces to defend Edo Bay. The Ii were arguing that it was more important to defend Kyoto and the imperial presence than it was to defend Edo. And if the Ii pulled out of the arrangement to defend Edo Bay, the whole structure of defense around the shogun's castle city was threatened with collapse. With the support of key daimyo, Abe moved quickly to rid himself of Aoyama. Aoyama was prevailed upon to submit his resignation, which, according to custom, was at first turned down and then finally accepted.[42]

Moving on shakier ground, Abe nonetheless continued his campaign to restore Tokugawa Nariaki to political influence and to take incremental steps to build up coastal defenses. In 1849 Abe had asked the Roju, with Aoyama gone, to approve a meeting between the shogun and Nariaki at his mansion. The reason given was that Ieyoshi wished to see his sister, who was the widow of Nariaki's brother. But it clearly sent a signal that Nariaki was returning to favor at Edo Castle.[43]

At about the same time, work was begun on batteries at Kannonsaki, the narrow neck of land north of Uraga that was regarded as the throat of Edo Bay. To prevent these minimal efforts toward a defense buildup from becoming an economic burden on the daimyo, Abe continued to arrange loans for daimyo who were charged with defense responsibilities while the Bakufu took over public works projects in some of the domains. At the same time Shimazu Nariakira pressed ahead with plans to build a western-style steamship. He had had some of his Dutch scholars translate a six-volume Dutch work on steamships, and then after receiving permission to build twelve ships, three of them to be steamships, he had a model completed in Kagoshima in 1852.[44]

In the same year Nariaki was finally returned to his full privileges as daimyo of Mito and as a member of the *gosanke*. He was summoned to the castle by the shogun himself to discuss the marriage of Nariaki's son Yoshiatsu, the daimyo of Mito, to a member of an aristocratic family from Kyoto. Nariaki now returned to his privileged place alongside the other two lords of the Three Houses in the Upper Room of the Great Corridor. He had vanquished the clique of lesser daimyos who were advising his son Yoshiatsu in Mito, and his followers had been released from prison and allowed to participate once again in politics. The night of Nariaki's meeting with the shogun, Nariaki's return to influence was celebrated with a wild party at his mansion in Komagome. Songs were sung, and food and sake consumed in abundance while the dancing and poetry recitations went on until the small hours of the morning.[45]

There was little to celebrate, however, in relation to Abe, Nariakira, and Nariaki's effort to build up Japan's military defenses. Abe had pushed steadily for greater preparedness, starting with his exchange of letters with Nariaki in 1846. True, there was more training, more cannon were cast, and some coastal batteries had been constructed. But other measures suggested by Nariaki and later Nariakira, such as the construction of warships, were only in the initial stages. And all sensible advocates of a strong defense knew that the Bakufu and domain leaders' antiquated artillery, foot soldiers equipped with pikes and archaic muskets, and earthwork forts were no match for Western weaponry. Positioned to guard the entrance to Edo Bay were only 124 cannons capable of throwing more than a three-pound shot. And now there was a new problem. A fire in the summer of 1852 had destroyed much of the *nishimaru*, the western compound of Edo Castle where Iesada, the shogun's heir, lived. Abe ordered the reconstruction of the *nishimaru*. But this effort absorbed the entire cash budget of the Bakufu for one year, and Abe did not dare put the usual pressure on the daimyo to contribute to the effort.[46] In short, the Bakufu was bankrupt and close to defenseless in an ever-threatening world. Under these circumstances, no matter how bellicose the pronouncements coming from leaders like Nariaki, it was quickly becoming apparent to Abe Masahiro and many other influential Bakufu and domain leaders that Japan at some point would have to forego its historical policy of isolation.

To add to Abe's worries in 1852, the Dutch at Nagasaki notified the Bakufu that the Americans were sending a four-ship squadron including two steamships to Uraga to demand trade with the Bakufu. It was a new threat from an unexpected quarter, and the Abe Masahiro who moved to deal with this latest unfortunate turn of events was very much a chastened leader. He had given up trying to prevail upon the bureaucracy to support a call for a national defense effort. The *kaibogakari*, and especially their budget office, had warned him that it was too expensive, too potentially disruptive of the precious stability of the Tokugawa system. Instead they urged him to deal with each intrusion as it occurred. Some of them had even suggested opening trade with the West. Abe knew about the firepower of the American ships from Biddle's visit. The pitiful batteries that protected the entrance to Edo Bay could hardly withstand an attack from a modern warship. But he did not know how to react when the inevitable incursion came.[47]

9

THE COMING OF THE UNIVERSAL YANKEE NATION: THE FIRST VISIT

The attack upon Japan is more than an expedition, it is an adventure.[1]   —J. W. SPALDING, clerk to the commander
of the *Mississippi*

I am sure that the Japanese policy of seclusion is not according to God's plan of bringing the nations of the earth to a knowledge of his truth.[2]   —S. WELLS WILLIAMS, journal entry, July 4, 1853

I was well aware that the more exclusive I should make myself and the more exacting I might be, the more respect these people of forms and ceremonies would be disposed to award me, hence my object, and the sequel will show the correctness of these conclusions.[3]
                    —MATTHEW CALBRAITH PERRY, July 1853

ON JULY 2, 1853, the American squadron, four ships, sixty-one guns, 967 men, headed finally for Edo Bay, eased into the northeast current, the one that the Ryukyuans described, perhaps with ominous overtones, as the current that always goes to Japan but never comes back. In these unknown waters Commodore Matthew Calbraith Perry turned to von Siebold's chart, which he found remarkably accurate, to guide his ships toward the coast of Japan.

With Japan a few days' distance, Perry pressed ahead with his preparations for any eventuality. Beyond defending the squadron against an attack by the Japanese, Perry was also readying his men for the possibility that they would have to make a landing and deliver the president's letter by force. There were daily musters at general quarters—twice on July seventh—and frequent target practice with both the big guns and small arms. The one break from shipboard routine came on July fourth, when the order came to "splice the main brace," and the crew was treated to an extra ration of grog as the ships' guns thundered a salute across the empty ocean. The salute, Wells Williams wrote in his journal, announced "the coming of the universal Yankee nation to disturb [Japan's] apathy and long ignorance."[4]

By sunset on July seventh the chart indicated that the squadron was within forty miles of Cape Iro at the southern end of the Izu peninsula. The Americans were about to enter Sagami Bay, the great semicircular body of water some forty miles across from which the Uraga Channel stretched into the more protected Edo Bay. Accordingly, the ships were headed out to sea for the night. At four in the morning the two steamers with the sloops of war in tow churned on once again for the entrance to Edo Bay, and soon, despite the haze, they could see the precipitous Izu Peninsula and an occasional junk headed seaward. When they first spotted land, a surge of excitement ran through the crews of the four vessels. "It was like the impact of liquor on someone who had never drank before," wrote one young assistant engineer aboard the *Mississippi* in a letter to his girlfriend.[5] As they passed more and more junks, the Americans could see the Japanese sailors standing and gesturing, evidently amazed by the sight of four black ships moving effortlessly over the water at eight or nine knots without a sail set, thick, black smoke pouring from the two lead ships. The hapless crew of one junk, finding themselves in the path of the squadron, dropped their sails in great alarm and sculled quickly out of the way. Two or three junks were seen to come about and head for land, perhaps to alert the authorities about the arrival of the American ships. Perry had expected to approach a fog-shrouded coast. But as the squadron crossed Sagami Bay, the summer sun burned through the haze, revealing the steep, green-forested and scarred mountains of the Izu Peninsula and in the distance, towering over this strange land, the awe-inspiring volcanic cone of Mount Fuji. From the squadron an occasional shot rang out as some of the guns were scaled (fired to dislodge rust and burned powder that adhered inside the barrels) in preparation for their arrival in Edo Bay.

In the early afternoon the squadron rounded Cape Sagami at the entrance to the Uraga Channel. At a signal from the commodore, the ships hove to, and the commanders gathered aboard the flagship for last-minute instructions. Perry reviewed his plans for dealing with the Japanese. To Perry's way of thinking, Commodore James Biddle, when he entered Edo Bay in 1846, had made the fundamental mistake of allowing his ships to be surrounded by guardboats while unlimited numbers of Japanese were permitted to swarm over their ships. Perry, in contrast, was intent upon making a very strong impression from the start. No Japanese was to be allowed to communicate with any ship except the flagship. Then no more than three Japanese were to be allowed aboard at a time. "I determined," Perry reported to the Navy Department, "to practice upon them a little of their own diplomacy, by forbidding the admission of a single individual aboard any of the ships, excepting those officers who might have business with me." He would "confer personally with no one but a functionary of the highest rank in the empire. . . . I was well aware that the more exclusive I should make myself and the more exacting I might be, the more respect these people of forms and ceremonies would be disposed to award me." He was prepared to fire on the Japanese guardboats to prevent them from surrounding the ships. Finally, whether he would land troops by force would "be decided by the development of succeeding events."[6]

When the commanders returned to their ships, the decks were cleared for action. Sections of the forward rail on the steamers were removed to provide a clear shot for their bow guns. Ports were lowered, guns were run into place and loaded, ammunition was organized, muskets, cutlasses, and boarding pikes were laid out for use, and the men were called to general quarters. Among the men, elation gave way to anxious excitement. Did they face combat or at least a shelling once they came within range of the shore? Once in the Uraga Channel, the steamers moved more cautiously,

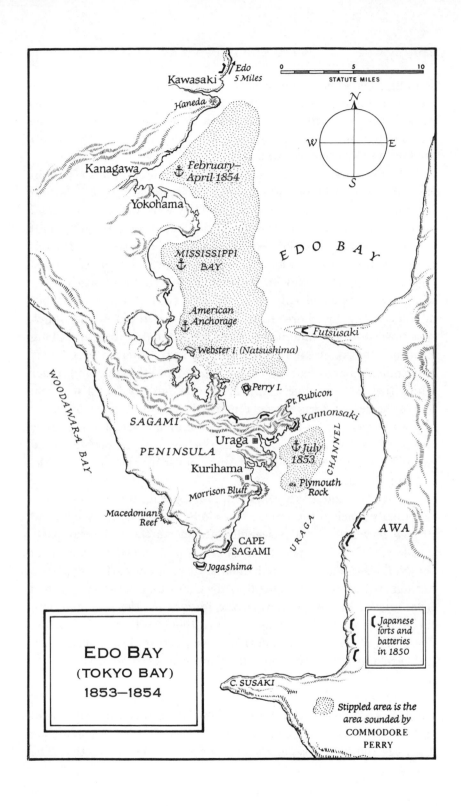

Kawasaki

Edo
5 Miles

Haneda

Kanagawa

February–
April 1854

Yokohama

MISSISSIPPI
BAY

American
Anchorage

Webster I. (Natsushima)

Perry I.

Pt. Rubicon

Kannonsaki

SAGAMI

PENINSULA

Uraga

Kurihama

July
1853

Morrison Bluff

Plymouth
Rock

Macedonian
Reef

CAPE
SAGAMI

Jogashima

WOODAWARA BAY

URAGA   CHANNEL

AWA

Futsusaki

E D O   B A Y

0   5   10
STATUTE MILES

N

W   E

S

C. SUSAKI

Japanese
forts and
batteries
in 1850

Stippled area is the
area sounded by
COMMODORE
PERRY

EDO BAY
(TOKYO BAY)
1853–1854

sounding spars extending from their bows, and the leadsmen in the chains frequently casting their lead for the bottom. As the ships drew within two miles of the cape, a dozen boats sporting large banners put out from the shore, but in little or no time were left bobbing in the steamers' wakes.

At about five o'clock, the four ships anchored in a line so that their guns could be brought to bear on Uraga and two forts that lay along the peninsula to the north. They were within a thousand yards of the entrance to the Uraga bight and a mile and a half south of Kannonsaki, the last promontory that protected the entrance to Edo Bay. It was now clear enough to see the shore distinctly. The squadron lay opposite steep cliffs that rose into heavily wooded heights cut deeply by ravines that ran down to a number of inlets along the shore. In numerous places the uplands, which rose toward higher mountains, were heavily cultivated, and along the shore, the Americans could see a number of villages. The Americans quickly noted that both Cape Sagami and the headland under which they were anchored appeared to be heavily fortified. From one of the nearby forts a rocket, marked by a burst of smoke in the air, was fired just as the ships dropped anchor and then another was fired as the ships swung into the wind, their bows pointed toward the southwest and their guns covering the forts and the town of Uraga.

After two and a half years of planning and preparation, Perry had finally reached the Land of the Gods. Wells Williams, who had prayed fervently for a peaceable outcome to the visit, was back, just north of the very spot where he, as a member of the crew of the *Morrison*, had been fired upon sixteen years earlier. The two nations had come to a moment of decision. As guardboats rushed from several directions toward the four ships, the Japanese and the Americans faced one another down the barrels of their cannon. They shared for a brief time the opportunity to begin their inevitable relationship either on a friendly or a warlike basis.

On July sixth, while the American squadron was still well out of sight of the coast of Japan, Kayama Eizaemon went to Kurihama, a village south of Uraga, to take part in gunnery practice. The

Japanese, clad in broad samurai pants and open tunics, wrestled with their antiquated fieldpieces, which looked more like the cannon used by the Portuguese in the fifteenth century than those aboard the American ships. On July eighth, the third day of practice, Kayama was relaxing after lunch, enjoying a brief respite from the heat with some men from the coastal defense forces. During the hour of the ram, about 2 P.M., three fishermen from Jogashima Island just off the southern tip of the Sagami Peninsula rushed into the practice area in a state of great excitement. That morning from their boat they had seen four foreign ships, two of them afire with smoke pouring out of them, heading into the Uraga Channel. Kayama left immediately, hurrying along the less than two miles of road back to the *bugyo*'s residence in Uraga. Kayama was a *yoriki*, a police magistrate and an aide to one of the two *bugyos*, or governors, of Uraga; the arrival of the foreigners meant that he had work to do.[7]

For years Uraga had been the principal customs house for junks in the coastal trade entering Edo Bay. Here the customs officials inspected the papers of inward-bound junks and checked to see if each member of the crew was listed in the manifest. The customs officials were particularly vigilant in their search for women, who were not allowed to travel freely. The Japanese sailors aboard the *Morrison* told Williams that captains caught transporting women into Edo Bay were decapitated. Once the arriving junks were checked over, they were given a passport to enter Shinagawa, the great port serving Edo. Uraga was one of the numerous checkpoints employed by the Tokugawa shogunate to maintain its rigid control over the populace. More recently, because of the greater number of foreign ships being seen off the coast, officials who specialized in foreign affairs had been assigned to Uraga. In normal times, all foreign affairs were conducted through the port of Nagasaki, the normal posting for officials knowledgeable in the ways of foreigners. But these, as Kayama knew, were not normal times, and he and a number of *yoriki* were assigned to Uraga for just such an eventuality as had now come to pass.

Kayama, though jovial and respectful of his superiors, was annoyed at the news of the arrival of the foreign ships. He for one was not surprised at this turn of events. Kayama, in fact, had been prepared for some time for this very event, despite official denials emanating from the highest levels of the shogun's government. In the autumn of the year before, he had heard rumors of the coming of American warships seeking a lease for a coal depot. He had asked one of the former governors of Uraga about these tales. The governor had written to the second governor of Uraga, who always resided in Edo, asking about the rumors, and he in turn had referred the matter privately to no less a personage than Abe Masahiro, the head of the Roju. Lord Abe confirmed that the head of the Dutch factory in Nagasaki had reported that the Americans would send warships to Japan. This was the report that Abe had belittled and had insisted, though he knew differently, that any information about an American expedition was completely unfounded.

However, the former governor of Uraga had shown Kayama the Dutch report in confidence. After a careful study of its contents, Kayama could only be skeptical of Abe's conclusions. For this reason, at the governor's urging, Kayama worked out what he later described as his "humble but well-considered strategy." There was not a lot to Kayama's "strategy," which really amounted to nothing more than a reiteration of the standard refrain that had been repeated to the crew of the *Morrison*, Captain Mercator Cooper, and Commodore Biddle. Kayama planned to tell the Americans, if they should arrive, that Edo Bay was not the proper place according to Japanese law to conduct foreign affairs. Go to Nagasaki.

By early spring Kayama began to doubt that the Americans would ever arrive. Maybe Abe Masahiro was right, and he was just overanxious. Kayama did recall, however, that Karaiton (John Clayton), the American Sutaatsu-Sekeretaarisu (secretary of state in the curious melange of English, Dutch, and Japanese that had infiltrated the language of those who tried to follow events in the outside world), had talked once of opening trade with Japan. This thought kept the need to be ready for the Americans foremost in Kayama's mind.[8]

At Uraga Kayama could see the four huge American ships, their black hulls looming out of the haze, moving slowly toward their anchorage less than a mile off the beach. He clambered aboard Guardboat Number Four, the long sleek craft at his command. With a black tassel at its bow and a flag with three horizontal black and white stripes amidship, the craft was propelled by near-naked oarsmen who shouted in unison as they deftly skulled Kayama through the fleet of guardboats that was converging on the ships from all directions. He could see that some of the boats had already reached one of the ships—it was the *Saratoga*—and were attempting to tie themselves alongside. To no avail: the American sailors simply cut

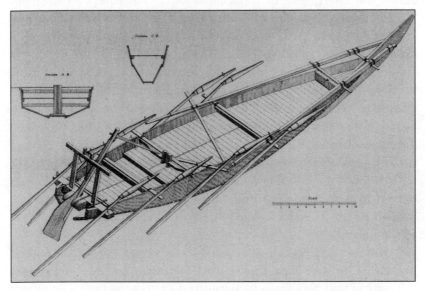

Japanese guardboat; *Narrative of the Expedition*

their lines and pushed them away. When some of the men then swung themselves up the chains, they were greeted with pikes, cutlasses, and drawn pistols. Another craft approached the *Mississippi* before she even dropped her anchor, and a two-sworded official attempted to climb over the port bow. He found himself looking down the barrel of a loaded musket. Turning white with anger, his crew hollering in his ear, he tried again, where the rail was lower, but was again repulsed by crewmen with pikes. Drifting toward the turning paddle wheel, he pushed off and gestured at the Americans not to anchor while he pulled his sword in and out of its scabbard and held aloft a letter that he seemed to want to deliver.

Nakajima Saburonosuke, Kayama's fellow *yoriki* who was in command of Guardboat Number One, approached the flagship *Susquehanna*'s gangway, holding up a banner with "Depart immediately and dare not anchor" inscribed on it in French in large letters. From the gangway, Williams called out to Nakajima in his rudimentary Japanese that they wanted to see a high official who could deliver a letter to the emperor. After a confused exchange in Japanese, the interpreter in Nakajima's boat yelled back in English, "I can speak Dutch," since this proved to be the extent of his English. Thereupon A. L. C. Portman, the Dutch interpreter, came forward to hear in well-spoken Dutch a series of rapid-fire questions about the squadron's country of origin, its armaments, and its intentions now that it had entered Japanese waters. None of the questions were answered. The Japanese interpreter in Nakajima's boat insisted that the Americans should allow him and the other Japanese officials, which now included Kayama in his craft, aboard the *Susquehanna*. The Americans said that they would only talk with a high official. Where was the governor of Uraga? He was barred by law from boarding ships in the channel, the Japanese replied as their boats bobbed up and down alongside the *Susquehanna*.

Kayama and Nakajima ordered their boats together and talked over what to do. Then they called out again to the Americans, suggesting that Nakajima be permitted to negotiate with an officer of comparable rank. Somehow Williams and Portman, by guile or misunderstanding, were led to believe that Nakajima was the "vice governor" of Uraga. When asked what to do, Perry ordered them to wait for a time and then allow Nakajima aboard.[9]

While this confused palaver over minute hierarchical gradations was carried on near the gangway, Perry remained in his cabin, his son Oliver scurrying back and forth with reports about each exchange in the discussion. Having settled these ponderous matters of rank, the gangway ladder was lowered, and Nakajima and his interpreter were escorted to Commander Franklin Buchanan's cabin, where they conferred with John Contee, Perry's flag lieutenant. In Buchanan's cabin, the Americans were confronted with a highly agitated Japanese official standing before them in a black cloak thrown over a shorter undergarment gathered at the waist where two swords, one short and one long, were tucked into his waistband. On his feet he wore sandals over white socks with a separate section for his big toe. For headgear Nakajima wore a red lacquered helmet made of bamboo that was shaped like a shallow inverted basin. His helmet covered a head that was shaved on the crown, leaving a fringe of hair that was drawn up in the back and pinned so that it projected forward over his bald pate. The front

Nakajima Saburonosuke
meets Commander Franklin Buchanan;
Narrative of the Expedition

of his helmet as well as the sleeves and back of his cloak bore the Tokugawa coat of arms, three golden hollyhock leaves pointing inward from a circular border.

Contee got quickly to the point. They had brought a letter from their president that they wanted to deliver to the emperor. For this purpose they wanted a high official to be sent aboard the flagship so that they could deliver a copy of the letter and arrange a day for the commodore to deliver the original. Nakajima, who by now had calmed down and was seated with his swords at his side, replied that Nagasaki was the only place that this kind of negotiation could take place. No, they would not go to Nagasaki, Contee replied. They expected the commodore to be properly received near where they were anchored.

Their intentions were friendly, Contee went on, but they would not permit the guardboats to surround the ships. The Americans had noted that a number of the guardboats were equipped with food, water, and sleeping mats, as if ready for a long stay. In other guardboats they could see artists sketching the American ships. If the guardboats were not removed immediately, the commodore intended to use force to remove them, Contee told Nakajima.

Nakajima rose abruptly, went to the gangway, and shouted out an order. With that, most of the boats turned toward the shore while a number of them remained at a respectful distance. But some hovered tentatively, only dispersing when an American launch with a light gun mounted on the bow approached them. Nakajima came back to say that he had no authority to make any arrangements regarding the president's letter. He asked for paper, and having written down what had transpired, showed it to Portman, thrust it into the front of his garments, and prepared to leave. Before leaving, Nakajima indicated that the next day an official of higher rank would come from Edo, an official who might know better what to do.

While Nakajima conferred with Contee, Kayama waited in his boat. A Chinese interpreter attached to his command noticed a Chinese man standing by the rail. He tried to strike up a conversation with the Chinese man, but his efforts were frustrated when an American officer came up and pushed the man aside. Kayama was duly impressed by the rigorous discipline aboard the flagship.

Nakajima and Kayama returned promptly to Uraga to confer with the governor. About 6 P.M. Nakajima returned to the flagship in another effort to find out the reason for the American visit, the extent of their armaments, and the number of men aboard the ships. He was again rebuffed, as was his second effort to persuade the Americans to go to Nagasaki. The Americans, Contee explained, had been ordered to deliver the letter in Edo, and if a high official did not come for a copy of the letter, they would be compelled to deliver the letter themselves. Would Nakajima like to take responsibility for refusing to accept the letter, Contee asked. Having thought quickly about this unpleasant eventuality, Nakajima turned to leave. But first he made a respectful visit to the huge Paixhan pivot gun mounted aft. Noting carefully how the powerful weapon commanded the town of Uraga, he checked the guns near the gangway and climbed down into his boat. Darkness was falling and there was little else he could do until the next day.[10]

While Nakajima was making his visits to the American flagship, the governor's (*bugyo*'s) office, located in an unpretentious wooden building tucked against a steep, wooded hillside just south of the Uraga inlet, became the pivot of frenzied activity. Toda Izu, the governor of Uraga in residence, dispatched messengers to the four daimyo who were in charge of coastal defense, alerting them to the arrival of the Americans and warning them not to approach the American ships. These messengers ran into other messengers hurrying in from the various command posts along the coast, bringing their own reports on the sighting of the American vessels. After Nakajima returned from his second visit to the American flagship, a fast boat pulled out of Uraga and sculled up the coast, its oarsmen working at a ferocious pace, bearing reports from Toda Izu and Nakajima addressed to the Roju and the *ometsuke*'s office.

It was dark before the reports reached the office of Ido Iwami, the Uraga *bugyo* in Edo, and were taken on to the Roju's office at Edo Castle. Toda estimated the number of guns on two of the ships at sixty, speculating that one of the ships was ironclad. (None of them were.) He reported that one of the ships "moves freely without sculls. It goes so rapidly that our men sent to receive them cannot catch up with it." The Americans, Toda continued, were "self-possessed" in their manner when they told Nakajima that they would not negotiate with anyone but a high official from Edo. Finally, the Americans had warned that more ships were on the way. Toda concluded his report saying that given the strength of the American squadron, he could not predict what would happen at Uraga.[11]

Meanwhile, the story of the fearsome black ships jumped from village to village as word filtered up from the coastal towns into the interior. In no time, the populace was in a state of panic. Soldiers moving toward the coast from their encampments led by great drums mounted on wheels and hauling their cannon with them

Toda Izu, governor of Uraga;
Narrative of the Expedition

along the crowded roads pushed past the first fear-stricken villagers who were headed in the opposite direction with their possessions on their backs. In Edo, isolated as it was from the realities of the surrounding countryside, there was little panic at first, although the daimyo, who were in charge of the defense of Edo Bay, like Ii Naosuke, the great *fudai* lord of Hikone, rushed off to join their troops. The Bakufu, however, took immediate precautions, declaring a state of emergency and mobilizing its troops around Edo Castle. It was possible that the Americans would move beyond their present anchorage and even attempt to reach Edo itself.[12]

As dusk gathered, the Americans could see the tall cone of Mount Fuji bathed in pink and violet hues. An occasional rocket arched aloft from the east shore of the Uraga Channel while signal fires were lit along the beach and on many of the higher peaks. The Japanese were alarmed by the sound of a sunset gun from the squadron, but when all appeared quiet around the ships, there was little to do but maintain the tense watch over the four dark forms that lay off the shore. Otherwise things appeared peaceful, the silence only broken by the doleful tolling of a temple bell, the striking of the ships' bells, and the calls of the American sailors as they changed watch. In the distance the Americans could see immense numbers of boats tied up along the shore near Uraga, each one lit with a lantern, "making one long necklace of light," as one diarist wrote. Despite the apparent calm, the Americans remained on their guard during the night. Steam was kept up on the *Mississippi* and *Susquehanna* while armed watches were ordered to keep an eye out for fire ships that might be sent down upon the American vessels. Commodore Perry, having slept for a time, rose as was his custom after midnight to dictate a journal entry to his clerk. Referring to the dispersal of the guardboats, Perry ordered his scribe to write, "The first important point is gained."[13]

At midnight, highlighting the eerie specter of the four great ships anchored off the dark shore, a spectacular comet—a blue fireball with a red wedge-shaped tail—lit up the sky. Like a fiery rocket trailing bright sparks, it bathed the American ships in a strange blue light as the glow played along their decks and spars. From just above the horizon in the southwest it moved in a straight line toward the northeast, where it finally disappeared just before dawn.

"The ancients," an officer wrote, "would have construed this remarkable appearance of the heavens as an omen promising a favorable issue to an enterprise undertaken by them, and we may pray God that our present attempt to bring a singular and half-barbarous people into the family of civilized nations, may succeed without resort to bloodshed."[14]

Soon after sunrise the next day, July ninth, the fog burned off, and the Americans went to work. Boats were lowered to begin a systematic survey of the waters south of Kannonsaki. In the morning light, the Americans could see the shoreline more clearly. Along the beach north and south of Uraga were a number of villages, and farther to the south, perhaps two miles, the bluffs seemed less abrupt and cultivated lands reached back from a pebbly beach. The Americans quickly trained their glasses on the shoreline, looking for signs of troop deployments and fortifications. The nearest fortifications, two sets of earthworks on the southern side of Kannonsaki about a mile and a half away, were only half-finished. Many of the embrasures lacked guns, and those that stood in place seemed only of light caliber. In front and behind the earthworks and at a number of places along the shore, the Americans noted lengths of black and white striped cloth stretched between poles. They did not know what to make of these "dungaree forts," supposing them to be set up to hide soldiers. It became readily apparent that the Japanese were not very well armed.

The first Japanese boats approached the American ships just after dawn. But they turned out to be only artists intent on sketching the American ships. Japan had a lively popular press, known as the *kawaraban*, one-sheet affairs that employed illustrations, poetry, and satire to keep the people abreast of the latest developments. And these were undoubtedly artists whose drawings would soon grace their pages. At 7 A.M. two more boats approached the *Susquehanna*, bearing Kayama Eizaemon and two translators. The three were halted at the gangway while the Americans inquired about their intentions and rank. Then they were shown to Commander Buchanan's cabin, where they talked with him, Contee, and Captain Henry Adams, Perry again remaining in splendid isolation.

Kayama presented a colorful picture as he shuffled across the deck in his sandals. Taylor described him as dressed in an elaborate overgarment made of silk and embroidered with gold and silver in a pattern resembling peacock feathers. The Americans took Kayama to say that he was the governor of Uraga. Whether this was duplicity on Kayama's part or the result of translating from Japanese to Dutch to English and back it is impossible to say. This was the moment for which Kayama had waited ever since he had first heard that the Americans were coming to Uraga. He asked about the commodore's intentions and was told that he was there to deliver a letter from their president to a high official in Edo. After delivering a short discourse on Japan's ancient laws, Kayama explained that his government could not receive the American president's letter at Edo. It would have to be taken to Nagasaki, and even if it were delivered here, the reply would be sent to Nagasaki.[15]

The commodore had no intention of going to Nagasaki, the Americans replied. They had written to the Japanese government the year before, laying out their plans, and if the Japanese now refused to receive the letter, they would go ashore with sufficient force and deliver it themselves. They showed Kayama and his interpreters Fillmore's letter and a copy of Perry's letter of credence. Why, asked Kayama, did they require four ships to deliver such a small letter? "Out of respect for the emperor," the Americans rejoined to a doubtful Kayama.

Kayama now suggested that he would go ashore to receive further orders; the Americans should not expect to hear from him for four days. It took only one *hour* to steam to Edo, the Americans responded after Perry's son had been sent off to consult with the commodore. They could not wait four days. They would expect a reply by July twelfth—three days.

What were the American boats doing, Kayama then asked. Surveying was the reply. This was illegal according to Japanese law, Kayama insisted. The Americans were operating according to American law, the Americans responded. All the while Kayama and his aides had been furiously taking notes. Now that the con-

versation appeared to reach an end, he offered water and supplies
for the squadron, but was told that the squadron needed no supplies.
After receiving final instructions to describe the American president in the same terms as the emperor, Kayama and his two aides
departed for Uraga.

The Americans were impressed by the dignified bearing and
quiet self-assurance of the Japanese officials. They even seemed
congenial despite their unpleasant task. While Kayama was answering questions at the gangway before coming aboard, one of the
Japanese turned to Williams and asked if he was an American,
perhaps to test his Japanese. When Williams said in his broken
Japanese that he was, the interpreter laughed in a friendly manner.
Williams, despite his title of official interpreter, had been relegated
to the role of observer and advisor, although Perry rarely acknowledged that anyone but himself devised the plans for how to deal
with the Japanese. Williams's Japanese, as he had tried to explain
to Perry in Canton, was inadequate, and the Japanese to Dutch to
English translation involving Portman seemed to be working, despite the time that it took to get anything done and the occasional
misunderstandings.

As for Perry, he was carefully keeping score in the stuffy heat
of his cabin. He was heartened by the reports from the first survey.
The Japanese defenses, Taylor wrote, "appeared laughable after all
the extravagant stories we had heard." The boats had counted only
fourteen mounted guns, the largest a nine-pounder. The battery
south of Uraga inlet was a fake. That night Perry judged his officers'
insistence that the American survey was being conducted in Japanese waters according to American law "a second and most important point gained."[16]

For his part Kayama concluded from the attitude of the American officers that "they intended, whatever the cost, to carry out
their mission." He too had seen how the great guns were trained
on Uraga and the pathetic coastal batteries. Having practiced with
the Japanese guns, he knew all too well that the Japanese would
have little chance against the Americans' sophisticated weaponry.
Convinced that it would be a great embarrassment to the Bakufu
to be forced to receive the letter under the threat of an American
attack, he tried to assure the Americans that his government did

not intend to disregard the letter from the American president. Patience, he counseled them, having quickly decided that the Bakufu had no other choice but to receive the letter as the Americans demanded.[17]

At 2 P.M. Kayama left Uraga by fast boat for the capital. He was bearing dispatches from Toda Izu that made basically the same recommendation he had made to Toda when he came back from the American flagship in the morning: to preserve their dignity the Japanese must not be forced to accept the American president's letter under the threat of attack. The Americans appeared prepared for any emergency, and there was no way that the forces gathered around Uraga, although they outnumbered the Americans, could resist them. They wanted a response in three days, by July twelfth. The Japanese had no choice but to deal with the foreigners peacefully.

By five o'clock Kayama had reached the office of Ido Iwami. But as he turned the morning's encounter over in his mind, Kayama was annoyed. After delivering a verbal report to Ido, he got to what he considered the heart of the matter. Hadn't Abe Masahiro himself denied that there was any validity to the reports of an American expedition? In the light of the past two days, Ido was forced to acknowledge what Kayama had suspected since the year before. A respected official from a prominent *fudai* family, Ido had had earlier dealings with Americans. He was the governor of Nagasaki before whom Ranald MacDonald and the crew of the *Lagoda* had been brought for questioning. Abe had known all along that the Americans were coming to Edo. Kayama was crestfallen. "I could not keep my tears from falling for a long while," he wrote in his account of the events, "deploring the policy of our highest authorities who had maintained complete secrecy about this matter." Ido and Kayama talked late into the night, Ido trying to console the distraught Kayama. The result of the Roju's penchant for secrecy, Kayama felt, was that the Bakufu had already suffered a setback, and the negotiations were not yet underway. Finally Ido asked Kayama to stay. The Roju was meeting in the morning, and Kayama should await the outcome of the meeting before returning to Uraga.[18]

During the night of July eighth word slowly filtered into Edo

that an American squadron was anchored off Uraga making demands of the Bakufu. The first reports, passed by word of mouth,
were of dubious accuracy. Californians, according to one of Edo's
purveyors of fact and fancy, had brought a letter from the "King
of Washington" in the United States, which they wished to deliver
to the governor of Uraga. The Japanese had been told not to surround the ships with guardboats, but some officials were permitted
to go aboard the flagship. When Japanese boats approached other
American ships, they were fired on with carbines. The Americans,
this diarist concluded, were acting "in an unusually high-handed
manner" and were "extremely impolite."[19]

An unknown court physician who ran a school of Dutch learning and kept a running account of these tumultuous times, was
aroused at dawn on July ninth by the loud voices of his students
who were discussing the arrival of the black ships. Since a number
of them were students of the military sciences, they were eager to
go to Uraga and see the American ships. The doctor gave his permission and instructed his students to carefully observe what was
happening. When the doctor went to visit one of his patients, Endo
Tsunenori, the daimyo of Mikami and a member of the Wakadoshiyori, or junior council, Endo complained that he was being summoned to the castle for a meeting the next day. Endo had little
intention of going, he told the doctor; he could not summon the
energy in the summer heat. Anyhow, the arrival of the Americans
did not seem to be a particularly pressing matter. Later as the
doctor made the rounds of his patients, he found that only those
who had a special interest in the affairs of the Western world or
were officials in the Bakufu knew about the arrival of the American
ships.[20]

The next morning, Sunday, July tenth, the grim-faced members of the Roju assembled in their meeting room at Edo Castle.
They were finally forced to confront a situation that Abe had anticipated for years, an event that many Bakufu officials had refused
to acknowledge would ever happen and even then refused to view
as particularly alarming. A well-armed naval squadron was anchored within twenty-eight miles of the capital, threatening to dispatch troops to the very heart of the Bakufu. Abe and Makino
Bizen, the daimyo of Nagaoka and the Roju member in charge of

national defense, quickly assembled the officials of the all-important second tier of the bureaucracy—the three *bugyos* and *ometsuke* and *metsuke*—and asked for their opinions. Makino himself was for accepting the American president's letter at or near Uraga, but ultimately the discussions, despite the urgency of the situation, were inconclusive.[21]

With the bureaucracy in its usual muddle, Abe had no other choice but to stall for time. Thus at 3 P.M. Kayama was sent back to Uraga with orders for Toda Izu. For now, the Roju was empowering *him* to deal with the Americans. He should make every effort to persuade them to *leave peacefully* and take the letter to Nagasaki. The Roju hoped to reach a decision by the next day. At the same time, to get a better sense of the disposition of forces at Uraga, Abe sent one of his trusted retainers to Uraga. Abe was not yet ready to make an initial concession that might set the tenor for all further deliberations with the foreigners. He had three days to reach an agreement about how to proceed. So for now he was content to buy time, a decision that hardly made it any easier for poor Kayama, who spent the entire night returning to Uraga by the coastal road. Meanwhile the Bakufu continued its preparations for the eventuality that the Americans would sail past Kannonsaki and land near Edo. Makino Bizen ordered six more daimyo to mobilize their troops and keep them in readiness to guard the shores of Edo Bay.[22]

That night Abe sat down to write to Tokugawa Nariaki. He enclosed Toda Izu's report about what had transpired at Uraga with Toda's recommendation to accept the American letter. After some perfunctory remarks about the summer heat, he explained that the Roju was still debating their response. He was hoping for Nariaki's advice and wanted to meet with him the next day when he came to the castle.[23]

Nariaki dashed off a quick response, sending the letter at 2 A.M. on the morning of July eleventh. He too had been kept in the dark about the Dutch letter spelling out American intentions and was caught off guard by the sudden appearance of the Americans. Of course, he was worried about the foreign ships. But as Abe knew, he had presented his views in the past, and they had been ignored. Now he did not know what to do. Frankly, he was confused about the proper response. It would be wrong to try to drive the ships away, which would only lead to a war. And even though the Bakufu might win the war, the Americans would end up occupying islands along the coast. On the other hand if they received the letter, it would create problems. It would plant the seeds of conflict and lead to further concessions—like communications, trade, and the renting of land—and eventually to the seizure of all of Japan. If the ships stayed for three or four months, there could be disturbances within the country and even chaos in Edo. "All we can do," concluded Nariaki, the feared advocate of expelling the barbarians, "is leave it to the discussions of many people and make a decision."[24] For Abe, Nariaki's response confirmed two things: that Nariaki was as confused as the Bakufu officials about how to respond, and perhaps more important, he was not promoting an aggressive military initiative that could lead to disaster.

Tokugawa Nariaki was disturbed by the indecisiveness of his letter to Abe. Though he had been up most of the night, he rose early the next morning and dashed off another note to the head of the Roju. He was eager to meet with Abe and hear his plans in addition to presenting his own "foolish views." For if they did not have a policy from the start, it would be difficult to figure one out later on. While solicitous of Abe, Nariaki was petulant in a letter to Matsudaira Echizen. The Roju was treating him shabbily. He was like the general of a defeated army. The Roju had already missed an opportunity to expel the Americans. Therefore he did not feel that he was in a position to discuss the foreign ships.[25]

Meanwhile the Americans had spent a quiet day on Sunday, July tenth. Aboard the ships the capstans were draped with cloth to serve as makeshift altars, and church services were held. Because of the Sabbath, the survey was discontinued. But there was still plenty of traffic in the Uraga Channel. Small fishing smacks had returned to their trolling, larger junks could be seen coming up the channel to check in at Uraga, and numerous boats, bringing the curious, came out and circled the ships. During the day a boat approached the *Susquehanna* from Uraga bearing some new officials, but the Americans refused to permit them aboard. They noted their courtly manner, wondering who they were. Perhaps it was the emissary sent by Abe Masahiro or one of the growing number of people who were rushing to Uraga to get a look at the American ships. The Americans saw new signs of military preparation on the shore—forts being constructed, troops rushing about, cannon being test-fired—but at night there were fewer beacon fires. Wells Williams, watching from the deck of the *Susquehanna*, found all this activity unsettling, since it distracted one "from the seriousness of the day." "I think to lead a life of godliness on board a man-of-war," he wrote in his journal, "must require a large measure of the Spirit."[26]

With one day left until the expiration of the ultimatum to the Japanese to respond to the American request, Perry, on Monday morning July eleventh, again dispatched the survey boats, this time in the direction of Edo under the protection of the *Mississippi*. Perry hoped that movement of the heavily armed steamer in the wake of the survey boats would sound alarm bells in Uraga and ultimately Edo. Sure enough, a boat with a *yoriki* aboard was soon seen emerging from the Uraga bight headed for the flagship. The Americans, having told the Japanese on July tenth that they wanted no more visits until there was a response to their request to deliver the letter, refused to allow the official aboard.

Toda Izu next ordered Kayama to the flagship while he dispatched Nakajima up the coast to try to stop the survey boats. Kayama was to demand the recall of the steamer. Exhausted from his overnight ride from Edo, Kayama nevertheless hustled aboard his guardboat and was sculled out to the flagship, where he was allowed aboard. Although Kayama claimed in his diary that he asked the Americans to recall the *Mississippi* after delivering a lecture on the laws of Japan, the Americans understood him to say that he had only come to tell them that their letter would probably be received the next day and forwarded to Edo. Oh, and incidentally, Kayama appeared to add as an afterthought, what was the steamer doing headed toward Edo? Perry's ploy had worked. Perry lost no time sending a message from his cabin that Kayama should tell the governor that unless there was a satisfactory response to his request to deliver the letter at Edo, he would have to return

the next spring with a larger fleet. If this was going to be the
outcome of their visit, he had to conduct the survey to find a more
favorable anchorage near Edo.[27]

Kayama, tired as he was, appeared to be in a genial mood. He
stayed for a drink, took a glass of wine, and seemed pleased by the
offer of a tour of the ship when he came with the message from Edo
the next day. When Kayama departed, the Americans with a certain
amount of trepidation turned to watch the *Mississippi* and the
survey boats, knowing that they were being used as decoys and
might well fall into a trap. Lieutenant Silas Bent, who commanded
the boats, had been ordered to stay within signal distance of the
squadron and to avoid any confrontations. As a precaution, the
Susquehanna's cable was hauled in far enough to allow the ship to
slip its anchor chain at a moment's notice. Steam was kept up. Soon,
however, the *Mississippi* and the boats disappeared past Kannonsaki, and as the boats worked along the shore, they began to pull
ahead of the *Mississippi* itself. From the anchorage the men on the
flagship could see troops with banners flying moving rapidly along
the sandbar known as Futsusaki that extended from the eastern
shore of the Uraga Channel. The soldiers climbed aboard boats and
headed in the direction that the American boats were headed when
last seen. Something was clearly happening around the point.

Once around Kannonsaki, the survey boats were approached
by a number of guardboats that waved them back toward the American anchorage. Other boats cut in front of them trying to block
their passage. But Bent pressed on. The two lead boats were armed
with brass howitzers loaded with grape and cannister shot, but the
Americans saw no evidence that the Japanese were armed. At last
Bent found himself head-to-head with a line of about thirty-five
boats that were approaching him in such a way as to bar any farther
movement up the bay. Bent ordered his men to rest on their oars
and to afix their bayonets to their muskets. The Japanese boats
kept coming. Bent now ordered the boats to change course and sent
one of the boats to find the *Mississippi*, which could no longer be
seen behind them. For a time the Japanese and the Americans sat
silently in the water staring coolly at one another, both sides under
orders not to make the first move. Then suddenly the *Mississippi*
loomed up behind the American boats. Bent now decided that the

Americans had gone far enough. They had found what appeared to be the channel that ran up to Edo, and in the distance they seemed to see the hazy outlines of the city.

With that the survey boats passed lines to the steamer and were towed back down the bay, where they were greeted warmly by an anxious squadron. On the way one of the boats was approached by a Japanese guardboat. The samurai in the bow called out in English, "Are you going back?" and then tried to make fast

Confrontation between U.S. survey boat and Japanese guardboats, July 11, 1853; *Narrative of the Expedition*

to the American boat, much to the amusement of the Americans who cast him loose. The Americans, Kayama wrote in his diary, had finally responded to *his order* to recall the flagship.[28]

Reports that an American steamer had passed Kannonsaki and was headed toward the shogun's capital only aggravated what was turning out to be an ugly scene in Edo. Despite the orders of the Bakufu to the people not to discuss the foreign ships and to remain at work, panic was beginning to spread. The day before, on what had been a peaceful Sabbath aboard the American ships, rumors began to run wild in Edo. The foreigners were coming to demand an audience with the shogun. No, they were coming to demand the lease of one of the islands in the Izu archipelago. The Americans were going to anchor off Shinagawa and bombard the city. The soldiers of the Aizu domain—they were guarding the east side of the bay—had requested permission to fire on the Americans. Anyhow, the Americans were coming, a fact that seemed to be confirmed by the Bakufu's order that a fire bell should be rung near the waterfront if the Americans attacked.

By nightfall on July tenth guarded whispers gave way to animated conversations, as people began to ignore the official notices that warned against discussing the foreign ships. On July eleventh, with the Bakufu mobilizing troops inside the city to protect the daimyos' mansions in the southern part of the city and along the Shinagawa waterfront, it appeared that the Americans would have to fight their way into Edo. Messengers mounted on sweating horses came and went from the batteries and military outposts along the coast. Troops rushed through the heat and dust to their new positions. There was a run on secondhand weapon stores. The price of weapons and rice soared, and soon there were few weapons left. Soldiers hustled through the streets wheeling handcarts filled with old weapons. Blacksmiths worked overtime fashioning new weapons to meet the growing demand. It was impossible to buy gunpowder anywhere. Those daimyo who mobilized first had bought it all: no further supplies were available. The daimyo who lived along the bay began to evacuate their families. The evacuees pushed along through the crowded streets where many people seemed to be wandering aimlessly in confusion. City officials began to plan for the general evacuation of the populace.[29]

To placate the gods, the Bakufu sent a messenger to the Toshogu shrine in Ueno with a gift of one hundred plates of silver. The messenger was to ask the priests to pray for peace. Nariaki in a letter to Matsudaira Echizen sneered at this desperate recourse to religion. "Since this is an unusual world," he wrote, "the wind of Buddha may blow [the American ships out of the bay]. However, I have never heard of it yet. Even a small amount of money could be used for gunpowder and bullets."[30]

Even Lord Gendo, the blasé member of the Wakadoshiyori, was upset. When his diarist-doctor made his morning call on July eleventh, Gendo pressed him with questions about the foreign ships and their country of origin. When the doctor told him something of the American ships, he could only say with dismay that the

situation was "very annoying." Later in the day, the doctor visited
the offices of the *kanjo bugyo* and the *kaibogakari*. These officials
usually greeted his questions with claims of ignorance. Today things
were different. The officials plied him with questions about the
United States, her military strength, population, the character of
her people, etc.[31]

In the evening word reached Edo Castle that the *Mississippi*
had passed Kannonsaki, penetrating the inner bay. The Roju could
no longer stall for time. Stalling had worked in the past. They had
put the Dutch off for months in 1844 and 1845. But no country
had ever approached Edo with a squadron of warships. For one,
Abe Masahiro had to tell the shogun about the Americans' arrival.
When he informed the shogun, Ieyoshi reacted with complete shock,
and it seemed to his retainers that from that moment the shogun's
health began to decline.

It was midnight of July eleventh before Abe could assemble
the Roju, the Wakadoshiyori, and the other officials who were attending meetings at the castle. They had to come up with a response
that night in time to send a reply to the Americans on July twelfth,
the next day. A consensus had developed among most of the key
officials, particularly those in the three *bugyos* offices and the *kaibogakari*. They had no choice but to expel the Americans, since
they had disobeyed the order to go to Nagasaki. But . . . just this
one time, since they were improperly armed, they should accept
the American letter but tell them that they would respond at Nagasaki. Moreover, there was a precedent. They had received a communication from the American Commodore Biddle at Uraga in
1846. The *metsuke* and the *ometsuke* were more inclined to adhere
to their earlier instructions. Tell the Americans to go to Nagasaki
to deliver the letter, they recommended. They too, however, were
opposed to any attempt to expel the American ships.[32]

As for Abe, he played his hand closely, never revealing too
much of what he held. His close friend and advisor Matsudaira
Echizen was clearly for accepting the American letter, and his views
more than likely reflected Abe's own. But Abe was too astute to
place himself too far ahead of his associates. Abe had not fashioned
a complete consensus among the Bakufu officials, but it was as close
as he could get with the little time that he had. Even Nariaki, the

spokesman for antiforeign sentiment, had suggested that a majority decision was the best that they could do.

It was well past midnight, and now that the decision had been made, there was little left to do. Makino Bizen summoned Ido Iwami and handed him the order for Toda Izu. "Accept the letter," it read. "Deal with the matter, bearing in mind the details we mentioned to you orally, and both of you [Ido Iwami and Toda Izu] should consider it thoroughly. Cope with the matter properly so that our national honor will not be lost and no trouble will arise in the future." The two governors had been instructed to tell the Americans that they would receive the letter near Uraga but would reply at Nagasaki. Toda hurried off to his own office, where he turned the order over to a messenger, who immediately departed for Uraga and the first substantive exchange with the Americans.[33]

Perry had sent the *Mississippi* across the imaginary line between Kannonsaki and Futsusaki, passing what the Japanese referred to as the throat of Edo Bay and the Bakufu considered to be a strategic line of defense for Edo itself. In this way the Americans had hoped to cast fuel upon the fire in Edo, but little did they know how far and how fast it had burned. The next morning, July twelfth, at 9:30 A.M. three boats, this time larger than the usual guardboats, with finer lines, and rowed not sculled, emerged from the mist that hung along the shore. They pulled up to the *Susquehanna* bringing Kayama and two interpreters. Kayama had just received his new orders from Edo. He and his interpreters were shown into Buchanan's cabin, where they told Buchanan and Adams that the Japanese were prepared to accept the letter in the near future in the vicinity of Uraga, but they would reply at Nagasaki, either through the Dutch or the Chinese. Perry responded with a written memo that he had no intention of going to Nagasaki to receive the reply and in no way would allow either the Dutch or the Chinese to act as intermediaries. Further, if the Japanese did not receive the American president's letter and respond to it, he would take their actions as an insult "and will not hold himself accountable for the consequences."

The Japanese officials were also presented with a letter from

Perry addressed to the emperor saying he wanted to discuss the preparations for the delivery of the American letter with "one of the highest officers of the Empire of Japan." In short, Perry was fed up with the discussions with officials such as Kayama. He wanted to talk to someone with authority to act. Perry, however, had written his letter before the arrival of Kayama, anticipating that there would be further delays before he could reach an agreement about delivering the president's letter. But here was Kayama with a response, perhaps not the right response, but nevertheless a response. In short, Perry's letter was moot, but being Perry he insisted that a copy of his and the president's letter be delivered to the emperor.

Kayama was taken aback. He had heard nothing about copies of letters. The discussions, which suddenly seemed to be progressing, broke down just as quickly, and both parties spent the rest of the day quibbling over what Kayama described as "unessentials" (letters, copies of letters, credentials, who had misled whom) as Kayama rowed back and forth to Uraga. Finally Williams, having had enough of this petty contention, intervened, suggesting that the Japanese could meet Perry's demand to be received by a high official because Ido Iwami was in fact "the prince of Sagami," whose domain included Uraga. The air was cleared, and the discussions moved on. The reception, it was decided, would take place on the morning of July fourteenth. Perry wanted the reception to take place near the ships. Kayama suggested an unidentified location farther to the south. More space was needed to conduct the appropriate ceremonies. It was decided to reach a decision the next day.[34]

In the early evening after long and arduous but not unfriendly discussions, the various points of agreement were committed to paper, and Kayama and the two interpreters were taken on a tour of the ship. They marveled at the size and complexity of the ship's engines and looked carefully at the guns and muskets, quickly identifying the Paixhan gun by name. They found a copy of a daguerreotype fascinating. They had heard of photography, but never actually seen a picture. They particularly enjoyed the brandy and whiskey mixed with sugar offered to them. Kayama drained his glass and smacked his lips with sheer delight.

The Americans were warming to their visitors, particularly the affable Kayama. They were impressed by "a certain gentlemanly aplomb, . . . that self-contained manner which bespeaks high breeding," and their studied politeness, which seemed to be habitual among the Japanese rather than reserved for ceremonial occasions. When shown a globe, their visitors picked out New York and Washington. They asked about railroad tunnels, a canal across the Isthmus of Panama, and if the ship's engines were similar to those used in railroad trains.

While the officials toured the ship, a number of officers took the opportunity to inspect their swords, which they had left aside. They found them to be made of good, well-tempered steel with solid-gold mountings and scabbards made of sharkskin. All the while Williams was practicing his Japanese, trying to extract some information from the three visitors. "They were rather skittish," he found, and even pleaded ignorance of the names of towns along the bay. In time though one of them volunteered the names of the emperor and his two predecessors, and Williams concluded that the emperor was neither a very powerful nor influential figure in the government. They also acknowledged that Japan had an abundant supply of coal, thereby giving the lie to the denials of the men who had visited the *Preble* in Nagasaki several years before.[35]

Meanwhile in Edo Abe Masahiro was meeting with his advisors to further define the Bakufu's response to the Americans. The meeting took place at the urging of Ido Iwami. He had already left for Uraga but was not satisfied with the Roju's tendency to postpone decisions and then provide him and Toda Izu with less than complete instructions. Such a maneuver could result in forcing the two governors to accept all responsibility for reversing one of the central policies of the Bakufu. Accordingly, Abe and his advisors drafted a new statement that now acknowledged that it was Bakufu policy to negotiate with the Americans. "We are extremely sorry," it read, "to go against the principle since the Kanei era [in the reign of Tokugawa Iemitsu, 1623–1651] and abandon a policy of our nation. However, it is not the best decision for our Empire to initiate a war with them [the Americans]. We should be patient and make compromises with them in order to make them leave soon and to reach a better solution later on."[36]

During the day the Bakufu continued to deploy its troops in and around a panic-stricken Edo. Soldiers now lined nearly every inch of the waterfront. The guard at the gates of Edo Castle was doubled, defense officials were dispatched to inspect coastal defense installations, orders were given to ring the fire bells in the event that the Americans tried to land at Shinagawa, and preparations were made in the event that Abe Masahiro himself chose to go into battle. A notice was circulated that when Makino Bizen, the Roju member in charge of defense, sounded the fire bells, all those assigned to defense of the city were to don fire-fighting gear (a heavy but ineffectual leather cloak and hood) and report to their posts. Plans were put into place for the evacuation of the populace along the shoreline. People already were fleeing from the Shiba neighborhood south of the center of the city, taking what they could carry with them. South of Edo the roads were crowded with gun carriages, carts carrying arms and provisions, and packhorses being led by porters. The price of rice continued to go up as did armor. No fish had been available for three days. "It is quite as if the whole town was to be burnt to ashes at this very moment," the court doctor wrote.[37]

On the night of July twelfth, Abe Masahiro finally found the time to visit Tokugawa Nariaki at his residence at Komagome. Even though he was ordered to meet with Nariaki by the shogun himself, Abe still took the precaution of meeting secretly with Nariaki. Nariaki after all had no official standing in the Bakufu and thus was technically not a party to formulating a response to the Americans. He was already upset about the delay in meeting with Abe, who had originally wanted to meet the night before but had been prevented by the emergency meeting of the Roju. He supposed, Nariaki wrote to Matsudaira Echizen before meeting Abe, that this was because Abe did not need to ask the views of "a foolish old man."

Nevertheless he greeted Abe graciously when he arrived at about 7 P.M. and took him to an inner building of his compound where he served sweets, tea, soup, and rice. Abe showed Nariaki the shogun's order, which read "Come to the castle and participate in consultations on coastal defense." Nariaki bowed reverently before it. Abe must have been shocked, however, when Nariaki, in a

complete about-face from his earlier letters, now proposed that the
Roju order the seizure of the American ships, a stratagem that he
borrowed from a fifty-year-old treatise on national defense. They
talked well into the night, but in the end Abe made it clear that
he had no intention of undertaking such a harebrained scheme. He
had heard from his own retainer about the strength of the American
ships, and there was no way that they could be attacked and seized.
Abe, however, invited Nariaki to come to the castle on a daily basis
to consult about the Americans. Nariaki was so elated he quickly
composed and chanted a line of verse: "Cloud and fog are gone, I
look up at the pure and clear light of the moon." About midnight
Abe rose to leave. Before his departure, Nariaki presented him with
the breastplate from one of his own suits of armor and one hundred
cannons for the Bakufu.[38]

July thirteenth was hot and hazy, the temperature soaring to 87
degrees. But the sea breeze kept the heat down while the awnings
stretched over the decks of the American ships provided some shade.
Aboard the flagship, Perry and his officers waited patiently for a
visit from Kayama. They roamed the deck, climbing to the top of
the paddle boxes to watch the shore, where they could see that more
troops were arriving from the east side of the channel and finally
a large junk from Edo. Great, black-winged hawks rode the gentle
updrafts along the cliffs near Uraga and Kannonsaki. Gulls gathered around the American ships, picking over the refuse thrown
overboard. The survey boats, now unopposed, worked along the
shore off Kurihama, sounding to see if there was enough water for
the ships to approach the shore and provide cover in the event that
this was to be the place where the commodore landed.

About four o'clock Kayama made his appearance, offering numerous apologies for the delay. After Ido Iwami's arrival from Edo,
Ido, Kayama, and Toda had conferred about the details of the
reception. Toda was particularly amused by his recent promotion
to daimyo. In order to impress the Americans with his status as a
high official, he was now ranked, at least in the letter, as one of the
lords of the land. Aboard the flagship Kayama produced the Bakufu's letter instructing Toda Izu to receive the letter from the

American president plus a letter from himself assuring the Americans that Toda was an official of "very high rank equal to that of the Lord Admiral."*

The Bakufu's letter was wrapped in velvet and placed in a sandalwood box. However, when Williams asked to take a closer look, Kayama refused to let him touch it. Kayama knew that the letter would not bear close inspection. Of course, it had not been written by the actual emperor, as the Americans thought. For Emperor Komei knew nothing of what was transpiring at Uraga. As for the shogun, whom the Americans usually described as the emperor, he was ill and not a party to the deliberations about dealing with, the foreigners anyhow. Therefore the Roju had written the letter, which was then presented as the desired letter "from the emperor."

Kayama emphasized that Toda was only empowered to receive the American president's letter, not to enter into any kind of discussions. Therefore he would remain silent during the reception. The two sides then turned to the final details of the meeting, particularly the question of location. Perry had to prepare for the eventuality that the Bakufu had chosen the location for military purposes, that is, as a suitable place for attacking the American troops once they were ashore. His mind was eased by one thing: by the time of Kayama's arrival, Bent had reported the results of the survey of the waters near Kurihama. There was sufficient water off the shore to bring the American ships in close enough to bring the beach within range of their guns. So Kurihama was agreed upon, as was the time (the next morning between eight and nine o'clock to avoid the heat) and the number of Americans to attend.

Kayama pursued every detail down to the minutest arrangement, even apologizing for not being able to provide chairs like the one he was sitting in and wine and brandy and inquiring whether Perry planned to put the letter into the actual hand of Toda Izu. After two and a half hours, both parties appeared satisfied. They

---

* The Japanese referred to Perry as an admiral. There were no admirals in the American navy at the time, one of the outcomes of the efforts to prevent the formation of a naval aristocracy. The Japanese, however, assumed that the highest-ranking naval officer was an admiral.

continued to talk well into the evening, one of the interpreters asking Williams if American women were white and asking him how he learned Japanese. Williams also produced a map of Edo, and for the first time, Kayama offered some information about the city. The map, he said, appeared to be seventy years old. The city had changed much, but he could recognize some of the places indicated on the map. After this congenial conversation, Kayama and the two interpreters rose to leave, and one of the interpreters blurted out in English, "Want go home."[39]

After Kayama's departure, Perry called his commanders together to go over plans for the next day. He was still trying to fathom the Bakufu's reason for choosing this particular site. There had been quite a lot of troop movement ashore during the day, and Perry remained suspicious of "the well known duplicity of the people with whom I had to deal."[40] He ordered the commanders to position their ships early in the morning along a line from their anchorage to Kurihama. Meanwhile in the gathering dusk, the Americans could still see signs of preparation ashore, and even after dark they could hear carpenters working on the reception hall, a racket that continued until almost dawn.

The Bakufu too was preparing for any eventuality. Troops from the Hikone and Kawagoe domains were moved to Kurihama while troops from Aizu were readied to go aboard boats if necessary. A commander, who had been at Uraga on maneuvers with newly trained troops when the Americans arrived, was assigned the job of guarding the reception area. At the same time the Roju ordered renewed vigilance in and around Edo in the event that the American squadron entered Edo Bay. The leaders of troops armed with muskets were ordered to patrol the city streets while more *metsuke* were sent to keep watch along the shoreline.

On the appointed morning the Americans rose early, the boilers were fired on the steamers, three of the ships weighed anchor, and the steamers began to head south toward Kurihama. Delayed by the lack of wind, the *Saratoga* finally moved to its position between Uraga and Kurihama. The *Plymouth* remained opposite the forts on Kannonsaki. Aboard all the ships, the crews were beat to general quarters. Their decks were cleared for action, and their guns run out. The boats that were not going ashore were lowered and equipped with weapons in the event that those who were to go ashore were attacked and needed reinforcements. The two hundred fifty men who were to go ashore, selected the night before by lottery, rushed here and there collecting their weapons, the officers polishing their swords, strapping on their Colt revolvers, and putting on full dress uniforms while the sailors and marines wore clean blue pants and white frock shirts. Percussion caps were distributed for the muskets, and each sailor and marine was issued twenty rounds of ball cartridges.

As the mist burned off, the Americans could see the results of the noisy night's work. It was a spectacular sight. The batteries at Kannonsaki had been expanded and were now decorated with ornamental cloth screens. Two pavilions stood in the woods near the batteries. Rounding the point north of Kurihama, they could see a simple reception hall—what appeared to be three, freshly constructed pyramid-shaped buildings—bedecked with colorful flags and banners that stood out in the bright morning sun. Cloth screens hung with blue tassels stretched at intervals all the way from the point north of the beach to the other side of the reception hall, which had an entranceway made of similar panels. Banners and flags were everywhere, emblazoned in bright colors with the crests of Hikone and Kawagoe and the hollyhock crest of the Tokugawa. In the center of the screens stood nine tall standards with broad scarlet pennons hanging all the way to the ground. In front of the screens stood throngs of soldiers in loose formation armed with spears, bows, muskets, and matchlocks, fuses for their weapons coiled on their right arms. Some were dressed in lacquered hats, short skirts, and dark colored sleeveless frocks tied at the waist with sashes; others wore dirty white baggy breeches with tight stockings; still others resembled Chinese troops. To the rear could be seen more soldiers and mounted cavalry. Nearby sat their officers on stools, recognizable by their two swords, their richly caparisoned horses standing farther off. A few women could be seen peeking from behind the screens near the reception hall, and on a slope near the village itself a throng of people had gathered to witness this momentous event. What Williams described as a few miserable fieldpieces were lined up in front of the troops. Along the beach a line of some fifty guardboats, each decorated with a red flag, were drawn up. In all there appeared to be more than the five thousand troops promised by Kayama, as soldiers could be seen from one end of the beach to the other and back into the woods behind the beach. It made one think, wrote the young Spalding, "that he had come to be a spectator of some joust or tourney."[41]

When the *Susquehanna* and the *Mississippi* dropped anchor off Kurihama at eight-thirty, their spring lines set to bring their guns to bear on the beach, Kayama, Nakajima, and two interpreters came aboard. The Japanese were dressed in fine, brocaded silk over garments trimmed with yellow velvet and covered with figures embroidered in gold thread. The Americans were most taken with Nakajima, whose dark skin offset his colorful outfit, which included black socks and wide, short trousers which reached just below his knees and did not quite cover his hairy legs. He looked to the Americans like "an unusually brilliant knave of trumps." The somber Williams, who had to borrow a coat and a sword to create at least the semblance of military formality, found the colorful outfits of the Japanese officials "singularly grotesque and piebald" though "the effect was not unpleasant."[42] Kayama and his companions were in an jolly mood. Unperturbed by the delay aboard the flagship, they enjoyed themselves, watching the Americans rush here and there as they got ready.

Finally at ten o'clock, a flag was run up on the *Susquehanna*, fifteen boats gathered alongside the flagship, were loaded, and then pulled toward the shore, flanked by two Japanese boats carrying Kayama and company. With the boats halfway ashore, a great thundering salute of thirteen guns rolled out from the sides of the flagship, and Perry stepped into his white barge. Kayama directed the American boats toward a temporary pier made of bags filled with sand and straw. Captain Buchanan was the first American to step ashore in Japan in an official capacity. He was followed by a sailor and marine escort, which formed two lines on the beach. The boats were pulled back some fifty yards and anchored with their small bow guns trained on the beach. When Perry stepped ashore to the roll of drums, the officers formed a double line and he strode between them. Marine Major Jacob Zeilin led the procession with sword drawn, and Perry fell in line between two huge black stewards who, armed to the teeth, served as his bodyguards and carried

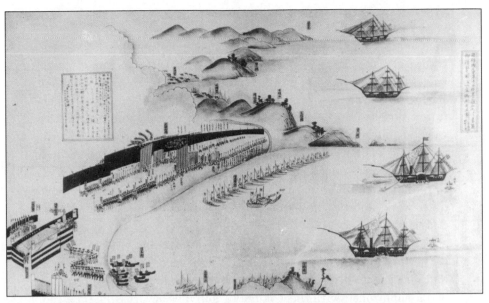

Japanese view of the American landing at Kurihama, July 14, 1853

The American landing at Kurihama, July 14, 1853;
Narrative of the Expedition

his pennant. They were followed by two cabin boys carrying two rosewood boxes wrapped in scarlet cloth with the various letters enclosed. With a band playing "Hail Columbia," which echoed from the nearby hills, the procession followed Kayama and the other interpreters up the beach toward the reception hall. The Americans were visibly excited, aware of the historical significance of their reception. Taylor noted "the regular, compact files of our men, and their vigorous, muscular figures, and the straggling ranks of the mild, effeminate-featured Japanese." The Japanese, for their part, were suitably impressed by the precision marching of the Americans.

At the reception hall, the commodore and his officers passed between two groups of guards armed with ancient flintlock muskets and entered a white canvas outer room about forty feet square, its walls emblazoned with the Tokugawa hollyhocks. Crossing on a red felt pathway, they stepped up into a raised inner room with carpeted floors. The entranceway to this room was hung with fine purple cloth, again with the Tokugawa crest, the ceiling was thatch, and the walls were covered with gauze curtains decorated with paintings of shrubbery and cranes wheeling in flight. On the left in front of a number of officials Toda Izu, stern but dignified, sat on a camp stool in a maroon silk robe with an overgarment of red offset by blue socks. Ido Iwami sat beside him. Both wore the extended shoulder wings of court dress. Toda seemed to the Americans to be about fifty, with a friendly, intelligent face. Ido Iwami appeared younger, though his face was more wrinkled.

The two governors rose and exchanged slight bows with Perry as he entered the room and was shown to an armchair, which the Japanese evidently had been able to procure. After a long silence during which neither party moved, Kayama, now kneeling between the two parties with another interpreter, introduced the two governors by name. Then the second interpreter, Tatnosuke Hori, asked Portman in Dutch if the commodore was ready to deliver the letters. Tatnosuke, once a companion of Ranald MacDonald's, conveyed Perry's reply to the two governors while bowing his head to the floor. Perry beckoned to the cabin boys, and they stepped forward, bearing the two rosewood boxes with gold hinges. The black stewards then opened the foot-long boxes and took out the letters, displaying their seals, which were encased in six-inch-by-three-inch solid gold boxes. The rosewood boxes along with translations in Dutch and Chinese were placed within a large scarlet lacquered box provided by the Japanese. Portman described the various documents to Tatnosuke, who relayed the information to Kayama, who

Commodore Perry escorted by a steward;
watercolor by an unknown Japanese artist

with appropriate bows repeated the information to the two governors. Finally Kayama presented Portman with a document, which he explained was a receipt.

Again an awkward silence settled over the gathering, broken after a time by Perry when he asked Portman to explain that he was leaving for the Ryukyus and Canton in two or three days and would be glad to deliver any messages or dispatches. He planned, he went on, to return in April or May of the next year. Somewhat confused by the translation, Tatnosuke asked Perry to repeat his

statement about when he would return. Next he asked if Perry
planned to come with the same number of ships. "All of them,"
Perry responded, "and probably more, as these are only a portion
of the squadron." Perry went on to say that there was a revolution
in China led by insurgents who had seized Amoy and Nanking and
wished to introduce a new religion. Tatnosuke had one more question: what was the cause of the revolution in China? "It was on
account of the government," Perry replied. But his response, undoubtedly deemed offensive by Tatnosuke, went untranslated.[43]

Delivery of the president's letter, July 14, 1853;
Narrative of the Expedition

Kayama and Tatnosuke rose, closed the lacquered box, and
told Portman that the reception was concluded. The whole affair
had taken less than half an hour. As Perry rose, the two governors,
who had maintained their sphinxlike demeanor during the proceedings, also stood, bowing again only slightly as Perry left the
room. Outside Perry waited for a time near the entrance while the
boats were brought back to the landing. An American who caught
sight of Toda and Ido after Perry departed reported that they
appeared to relax. In fact, a relaxed air settled over the whole

spectacular gathering. Williams chatted with some of the onlookers, answering questions about American women and how to learn about military strategy. He invited two people to visit the ship to see the engines and a revolver. Meanwhile a number of Japanese soldiers moved down the beach to get a closer look at the Americans. Some American officers compared swords with their Japanese counterparts while sailors and marines strolled along the beach, picking up shells and stones as souvenirs of this historic encounter. Others encountered hostile stares or studied indifference, and as the Americans marched back to their boats, some of the sailors called out to the Japanese soldiers asking "for a chaw" or making other remarks. Finally the Americans departed to the strains of "Hail Columbia" and "Yankee Doodle."

Two boatloads of Japanese officials, including the military commander from Uraga, followed the commodore back to the flagship and were invited aboard for the trip back to the ship's anchorage. The Japanese quickly busied themselves measuring the ship's guns and studying the workings of its engines. Nakajima, who had annoyed the Americans over the past few days by his insistence on sticking his nose into everything (he was "bold and pushing"), grabbed a musket from the gun rack and went through a mock-serious imitation of the manual of arms. The Japanese officials were particularly curious about the Chinese deckhands, asking about them, according to Taylor, the shipboard specialist in racial matters, with faces "expressive of great contempt and disgust."[44] Portman responded that they were hired in Shanghai as servants. At Uraga the visitors were sent ashore after seeing a pistol fired and being shown engravings of commercial steamships and a number of American cities.

Once the visitors were over the side, disappointed as they seemed by the shortness of their visit, Perry quickly ordered the the two steamers under way. He had read the translation of the receipt and was not pleased with the hortatory tone of its last sentence which said, "The letter being received, you will leave here." Perry was not aware, though Williams noted a difference between the original and the translation, that the Japanese version of the letter of receipt was much sterner in its tone, saying, in effect, that receiving the president's letter at Kurihama was a violation of Japanese law and that the Americans should understand this and depart. All the same, Perry, whatever the Japanese phrasing, was intent on making it clear to them that he could not be ordered away. Rather, he would do just the opposite, hoping that moving even closer to Edo "would produce a decided influence upon the pride and conceit of the government, and cause a more favorable consideration of the President's letter."[45]

So the steamers, sounding all the way, rounded Kannonsaki, finally anchoring in the bay where the *Mississippi* had turned

Japanese view of a tearful Perry pleading with a samurai

around after accompanying the survey boats during their confrontation with the Japanese guardboat three days earlier. The survey boats were again dispatched toward Edo, and soon enough Kayama hurried up the ladder, a sour look on his face, to inquire why the Americans had rounded Kannonsaki. During a petulant exchange that seemed to drag on and on, the Americans tried to reassure Kayama that they had nothing but friendly feelings for Japanese and were simply looking for a more protected anchorage for when they returned the next year. Kayama insisted that entering the inner bay was against the law, but after a time he gave up, fearing that he might jeopardize the warm feelings generated during the reception and his last visit to the flagship. Exhausted, he returned to Uraga reporting to Ido and Toda at midnight.[46]

By four in the afternoon word reached Edo Castle that the reception of the American letters had come off without a hitch. But the rest of the news was alarming. Despite the expectation that the Americans would leave immediately, they in fact had moved closer to Edo, anchoring some ten miles north of Kannonsaki. The Roju had hoped that with the reception of the letters the crisis would pass and some semblance of order could be restored in Edo. But such was not the case. Rumors spread that the Americans had landed at Kanagawa and were marching around unchallenged. During the night more troops were mobilized and sent to a hilltop overlooking Shinagawa. Edo spent another restless night. This was clearly not the time to discuss the content of the American president's letter.

The next day, July fifteenth, Perry persisted in his efforts to unsettle the Bakufu. At an early hour he dispatched the survey boats. Three of them worked their way into an inlet and up a small river where they were greeted by crowds of Japanese, who had gathered all along the shore to see the American steamers. Under the approving eyes of the officials commanding the nearby guard-boats, the people on the shore offered the Americans water and fresh peaches while the Americans pulled up to the riverbank, where they shared tobacco with the Japanese. Finally, a stern-faced official ordered the curious Japanese away. The American sailors returned to the flagship enchanted by the civility of the Japanese—despite an occasional person who made the sign of cutting one's throat—and enraptured by the beauty of the countryside with its neat thatch-roofed villages, extensive cultivation, and intensely green groves of trees. In the afternoon Perry had his flag transferred to the *Mississippi*, which steamed another ten miles north, bringing the Americans within seven miles of Edo. Perry could now see a forest of masts, junks anchored, he thought, at Shinagawa, and farther on numerous low buildings, which he took to be Edo itself. This close to Edo, Perry decided it was time to turn back.

He was becoming "apprehensive of causing too much alarm, and thus throwing some obstacle in the way of a favourable reception at court of the President's letter."[47]

During Perry's absence, Kayama, noting a different configuration of signal flags, returned to the *Susquehanna*, bringing a number of gifts for the commodore. In Perry's absence, he was not allowed aboard. He sat instead in his boat alongside the flagship, brooding over the impact of Perry's latest move upon the populace of Edo. The hours passed, darkness fell, and still no sign of the commodore. Kayama had little choice but to send a message back to Uraga that Perry had gone toward Edo and the two sailing ships had joined the steamers at their anchorage. He was forced to spend an uncomfortable and unhappy night aboard his guardboat under the lee of Natsushima Island.

"All my subordinates fell sound asleep from the fatigue of the day," Kayama wrote in his diary, "but however I might try I could get no sleep tossed about in the small boat, my mind tormented with the thoughts of how I should argue them [the Americans] into returning to the former anchorage making them thus obey my remonstrances." In Edo the Bakufu remained in a state of hypertension that only intensified during the day. That night, with four ships anchored within seven miles of the city, the Roju, Wakadoshiyori, and *san bugyo* were called to the castle, where they met attired in fire gear and ready to go into battle.[48]

At daylight on July sixteenth, Perry ordered the squadron back to a protected anchorage just north of Kannonsaki. The sleepless Kayama pulled alongside even before the anchor hit bottom. Unsure of Perry's intentions, he again reassured the Americans that the Bakufu would receive the president's letter favorably, suggesting that it might work to the Americans' disadvantage to be cruising about the inner bay. Kayama had brought a number of presents, including some lacquer ware, five rolls of silk brocade, pipes, and fans with what Taylor described as "hideously distorted and lackadaisical pictures of Japanese ladies," perhaps samples of the ever popular erotica. The Americans judged the other gifts "interesting specimens of Japanese manufacture, and though not very valuable . . . creditable evidences of mechanical skill."[49] They refused, however, to accept them unless Kayama would receive their presents in exchange. This he could not do, Kayama insisted, since it was a violation of Japanese law and might cost him his life. Finally he gave in, and the Americans brought out gifts that they estimated were of greater value than Kayama's, including some tea, three engravings, three histories of the United States, coarse cotton, loaf sugar, three swords, a case of champagne, and a jug of whiskey. Kayama insisted that these goods were too valuable. But when the swords were removed, he agreed to accept them.

In the afternoon Kayama returned again, this time in an expansive mood, bringing further gifts of eggs and fowl in cages. Kayama and Tatnosuke were soon enjoying the food and liquor offered by the Americans, and in no time had become openly convivial, talking of their affection for their new American friends. Kayama pantomimed that he would be driven to tears by their departure. Tatnosuke leaned forward during the repast to report in a low whisper that there was a good chance that the Bakufu would give a satisfactory answer to the president's letter and that Kayama would be promoted to *bugyo* of Uraga. When Captain Buchanan remarked that the Americans planned to leave the next day, the mood suddenly changed. Perhaps a little tipsy, Kayama and Tatnosuke were nonetheless on official business. Would Buchanan care to put that in writing, Tatnosuke asked. Certainly not, Buchanan answered coldly. When it came time to depart, Kayama and Tatnosuke warmly took the hands of the American officers, bowing from one to the other and then with final bows hurried over the side. In their boat, Kayama broke open the case of champagne, knocked the neck off a bottle on the gunwale, and raised the bottle in a toast to his new friends.

At daybreak on July seventeenth the squadron got under way, the steamers taking the two sailing vessels in tow. They passed the Kannonsaki forts with banners still flying, soldiers clearly visible on the parapets, and then the reception hall still sitting behind the beach at Kurihama. All along the shore, people could be seen gathered to watch the parade of ships. Off Cape Sagami at least a thousand boats, each with a full complement, crowded up to the steamers to bid the Americans a final farewell.

10

WAR AT HOME, PEACE ABROAD: JAPAN BETWEEN PERRY'S VISITS

Things are often out of my control because, in the last analysis, I am not good enough to be the leader of the government.[1]
— ABE MASAHIRO, July 1853

In these feeble days men tend to cling to peace; they are not fond of defending their country by war. They slander those of us who are determined to fight, calling us lovers of war, men who enjoy conflict. If matters become desperate they might, in their enormous folly, try to overthrow those of us who are determined to fight, offering excuses to the enemy and concluding a peace agreement with him. They would thus in the end bring total destruction upon us.[2]
— TOKUGAWA NARIAKI to the Bakufu, August 14, 1853

There is a saying that when one is besieged in a castle, to raise the drawbridge is to imprison oneself and make it impossible to hold out indefinitely; and again, that when opposing forces face each other across a river, victory is obtained by the force which crosses the river and attacks. It seems clear throughout history that he who takes action is in a position to advance, while he who remains inactive must retreat. Even though the Shogun's ancestors set up seclusion laws, they left the Dutch and Chinese to act as a bridge [to the outside world]. Might this bridge not now be of advantage to us in handling foreign affairs, providing us with the means whereby we may for a time avert the outbreak of hostilities and then, after some time has elapsed, gain a complete victory?[3]
— II NAOSUKE to the Bakufu, October 1, 1853

WITH THE AMERICAN SQUADRON GONE, Edo, at least on the surface, returned to normal. People went back to work, shops opened, and the troops were ordered to stand down. But Japan could never be the same. In a brash act of defiance, the American gifts were burned on the beach at Uraga, but this futile gesture was in reality a confession of the underlying impotency of the Bakufu, an admission that even though the leaders of the Bakufu had known of Perry's plans, they had not been able to prepare a response in advance. It was only because of Perry's deft tactics, particularly his decision to move his ships gradually into Edo Bay, that the Roju, with Edo on the verge of pandemonium, finally took the bit in its teeth and came to a decision to accept the American president's letter.

Abe Masahiro was despondent over the Bakufu's inept performance, as well he should have been. He had shown great skill in consulting and placating the various factions, from the hard-line supporters of Tokugawa Nariaki to the foot-dragging bureaucrats in the *kaibogakari*. He had gone beyond the confines of the *fudai*-dominated enclaves of Edo Castle to build a consensus. But in the end he had failed in his attempts to fashion and implement an effective policy for dealing with the feared foreigners.

In a long rambling discussion with an old retainer at his mansion on a hot summer night soon after Perry's departure, he confessed that affairs were often out of his control. He simply was not skillful or knowledgeable enough to be the leader of the government. He had tried, but when he wanted to discuss the threat of foreign ships with the other leaders of the Bakufu and the influential daimyo, many of them accused him of fronting for the Dutch. When he solicited Tokugawa Nariaki's advice about coastal defenses, they told him he was an eccentric for listening to that meddlesome old man. He had not neglected coastal defenses. It was just that their construction had been delayed by one thing or another. In this situation, he did not want to remain as the head of the Roju. But he had no choice. There was no other person who was ready to take his place.[4]

Also, Abe and his fellow officials were in a difficult position because the confrontation between the Americans and the Bakufu had been played out before the startled Japanese people. Many had ignored the authorities and rushed to the seacoast to catch a glimpse of the mighty black ships. The Bakufu could no longer hide behind its customary veil of secrecy. Word quickly spread along the inevitable rumor trails about what Kayama Eizaemon had suspected all along: the Bakufu had known that the Americans were coming and had decided not to warn the people. Critical words formed on every tongue, and Abe Masahiro and the Bakufu were the targets of many a new convert to reform.

"Nowadays nothing but the bitterest complaints are heard around me," wrote the court doctor in his diary describing the Bakufu's "extravagant negligence." He, for one, was pleased that the Americans had come. "In my humble opinion this first visit of a foreign fleet was indeed good medicine for the entire Japanese nation," he went on. "In government circles they for the first time have realized the formidable might of the foreign powers."

A junior councilor had told him, moreover, that the Americans were different from the British: they seemed sincere and honest, their military discipline was strict, and they knew the rules of politeness. However positive an impression the Americans had made, the predominant mood, many noted, was one of growing hostility toward foreigners. The Bakufu was committed to expelling the barbarians, to keeping the Land of the Gods inviolate, but it had accepted the humiliation of allowing foreign troops upon sacred soil. It was time to return to the ancient laws of the House of Tokugawa and punish the barbarians for their insolence.[5]

More creative citizens found other imaginative ways to vent their anger. Among a poetic people, streetcorner wags took to composing short squibs, known as *rakushu*, that played on the double meaning of certain words. "Do they think Japan is sweet?" read one such effort. "The American ships are sticking to the Uraga offing." Or another: "Barbarians used to be shocked by the wind of Ise [the central shrine of the Shinto religion]. But now Ise [Abe's honorific title was Ise no kami] is shocked. It's upside down [literally *abekobe*]." And a third: "Although America came, Japan is *tsutsuganai* [safe and sound or without guns]."[6] Whatever the case, Abe in particular came in for a large measure of the criticism, since few knew of his futile efforts over almost a decade to prepare the nation for foreign encroachments.

There were other threats to the stability of the Bakufu. "The lower orders," as Nariaki described them, were again feeling rebellious. At the very moment that Perry was approaching Japan, thousands of peasants in the Nanbu domain in northern Honshu were carrying out a well-organized revolt against the local authorities. The uprising, which culminated in a mass exodus from Nanbu, must have added to Abe's sense of the precariousness of the moment.[7]

Abe, however, had little time for doleful self-flagellation. The Americans had said they would return, and he had no reason to doubt their word. He had the two letters that Perry had handed over at Kurihama, President Millard Fillmore's and Perry's own, plus the very bellicose letter that Perry had given to Kayama Eizaemon to explain the meaning of a white flag.[8] So he now knew what the Americans wanted. Emphasizing Japan's and America's status as Pacific neighbors and his friendly intentions, Fillmore asked for friendship and a commercial experiment, specifically either commercial relations for a trial period of five or ten years or the negotiation of a treaty that could be renewed or suspended after a number of years.[9]

One of Perry's letters followed the more detailed instructions that he had drafted for himself under the cachet of the State Department before leaving Washington. He repeated Fillmore's statement that his intentions were friendly but went on to say that he "was surprised and grieved to learn that when any of the people of the United States go, of their own accord, or are thrown by the perils of the sea, within the dominions of your imperial majesty, they are treated as if they were your worst enemies." In light of the incidents involving the *Morrison*, *Lagoda*, and *Lawrence*, Perry could not desist from reading the emperor a stern lecture on the behavior of Christian nations where "it is considered a sacred duty to receive with kindness, and to succor and protect all, of whatever nation, who may be cast upon their shores." He wanted "some positive assurance" from the emperor that in the future Americans would be treated "with humanity."

Perry went on to emphasize with considerable exaggeration that it was now possible to reach Japan from the "large cities" of the West Coast—San Francisco was a burgeoning boom town but hardly a large city—in eighteen or twenty days, and that the Japanese seas "will soon be covered with our vessels." Japan and the United States were day by day coming nearer and nearer, but friendship could not exist between the two nations unless the Japanese ceased treating Americans like enemies. Perry concluded by saying that he "hourly expected" the arrival of the rest of his squadron, but as evidence of his friendly intentions, he had only brought four of the smallest ships to Japan. He intended, however, to return the next spring with a much larger force.[10]

Then there was "the white flag letter" with its angry, self-righteous words accusing the Bakufu of "sin against divine principles" and its promise of military defeat if the Bakufu did not accept the Americans' demands. Was Perry really for peace, or was he looking for an excuse to attack? Interestingly, there was no mention, either in Fillmore's or Perry's letters, of coal or a coal depot. Perry had already acquired two locations for a coal depot, in the Bonin Islands and Naha, and the subject of coal supplies— about which the Bakufu had been informed by the Dutch—was to be left to future negotiations.

Abe immediately turned to Tokugawa Nariaki, apparently for advice, but as it turned out, his intentions were much more subtle. The very day of the departure of the American squadron, Abe, knowing full well that Nariaki had proposed attacking the Americans, wrote to Nariaki emphasizing the urgency of preparing for the next visit and asking him to present "your enlightened strategy and novel policy."[11] The next day Abe sent Tsutsui Masanori, his favorite intermediary from the *kaibogakari*, and Kawaji Toshiakira with copies of Fillmore's and Perry's letters to meet with Nariaki. Kawaji had become a *kanjo bugyo* (finance official) the year before and, now a member of the *kaibogakari*, he was an ally of Abe's in those bureaucratic warrens where opposition to Abe's plans was concentrated.

The message that two officials were waiting for him at Komagome reached Nariaki at the Sugi riding grounds. He hurried home, changed his clothes, and invited them into an inner room.

The two officials found Nariaki in a genial mood, undoubtedly pleased with his new role as a party to the Roju's discussions about how to deal with the Americans. Kawaji and Tsutsui first showed Nariaki a letter from Abe in which he asked Nariaki to discuss his views openly with the two officials. Next they showed him Fillmore's and Perry's letters. He appeared surprised at the range of the Americans' demands. There was a possible strategy, the two officials explained. The Bakufu could offer the Americans half the Dutch trade with Japan, which amounted to a paltry one ship a year.

Where would the trade take place, Nariaki asked. That had not been decided yet, the officials responded. Nariaki immediately objected. The supply of silver to pay for Dutch goods was already declining. If they gave the Americans half the Dutch trade, it would reduce the amount of specie available to pay the Dutch. Anyhow, the Americans, even if they agreed at first, would soon object to the small amount of trade. In the end, even if they began trade at Nagasaki, they would come to Edo, and a war would break out. Nariaki was adamant; he did not even want the question of opening trade brought to him for discussion, since it was against national law.

Kawaji and Tsutsui were ready with a second possibility: they could prolong the negotiations, perhaps for five or ten years, without giving a definitive answer. This strategy of "keep them hanging on" (*burakashi seisaku*) would give the Bakufu time to restore its military power. Nariaki found this suggestion a little more to his liking. If Abe could assure him that it could be carried out without disagreement, it would reduce the likelihood of domestic disturbances. He noted the Bakufu's tendency to raise a fuss when a foreign ship arrived but to do nothing once it had departed. Keeping the Americans hanging on was a good strategy for the time being, but only because there was no other choice. Kawaji and Tsutsui must have known in advance that Nariaki would react negatively to suggestions of opening trade with the West. But by impressing Nariaki with the idea that Abe was considering a policy that was repugnant to the Lord of Mito, they had gotten him to commit to the lesser of two evils, the strategy of "keep them hanging on."[12]

Abe's intentions were now clearer: he needed Nariaki's prestige to give substance to his efforts to build up the Bakufu's defenses. But he also wanted Nariaki committed to his notions of diplomacy, preposterous though they were, given Perry's steely determination. Kawaji pursued the tactic of tying Nariaki to the "keep them hanging on" strategy by writing Fujita Toko, one of the most respected intellectuals from the Mito school, the man who had run the Kodokan (Nariaki's school) with Aizawa Seishisai and had drafted many of Nariaki's memorials on national defense. Kawaji emphasized that Abe and Nariaki's objectives were the same: to reestablish the military prestige of the Bakufu, expel the barbarians, and revere the imperial household. However, Abe wanted Fujita to show Nariaki the enclosed report on the financial condition of the Bakufu. Nariaki would be surprised, but the Bakufu could not finance a war with the foreigners even if it lasted less than a year. If Fujita could prevail upon Nariaki to say that he agreed it was difficult to go to war with the American barbarians, it would have a calming effect on those who respected Nariaki's views. In ten years the situation would be different, Kawaji tried to reassure Fujita. Then the Bakufu would be in a position to expel the barbarians.[13]

Once he was over his initial despondency, Abe began laying plans for a massive buildup of Japanese defense capabilities. On July twenty-third he sent a delegation of officials including Kawaji to survey the coastal areas around Edo Bay to decide where eleven new batteries should be built. Rather than bolstering the fortifications that controlled the narrows between Kannonsaki and Futsusaki, the officials proposed building a series of batteries on landfill off the port of Shinagawa, just south of Edo. Simultaneously, Shimazu Nariakira began work on the gunships—for which the Bakufu had given him permission earlier in the year—to be used to protect Satsuma's trade with the Ryukyus. What had been put off for ten years, however, could not be made right overnight. Actual construction would not begin on the Shinagawa batteries until September, and no one had solved the problem of how to pay the Dutch for the millions of dollars' worth of weapons that Abe had ordered.[14]

On July twenty-eighth Abe faced a new and potentially more debilitating crisis: Tokugawa Ieyoshi, the sixty-year-old shogun

and nominal ruler of Japan for seventeen years, died. Informed of
Perry's arrival while attending a No play, he had fallen ill, many
thought from the shock of hearing that a foreign naval squadron
was at his doorstep. He never recovered. His successor was the
twenty-nine-year-old Iesada, the half-wit who liked to cook beans
for his retainers, play with his kittens, and chase his retainers, with
a gun fitted with a bayonet; he was a man who could neither produce
an heir nor fully understand the implications of his position. The
death of the shogun inevitably introduced a new element of instability into the already shaken Bakufu. New lines of communication
had to be established between the Roju and the Middle Interior in
Edo Castle, where the shogun lived in isolation, lines that ran
through the *ooku*. Here Abe was on firmer ground. He had long
enjoyed a close relationship with Hongo Yasukata, Ieyoshi's trusted
chamberlain whose close friend was Iesada's mother. Abe responded
quickly, deciding to keep the shogun's death a secret for the time
being.[15]

The very next day Abe began to disseminate the two American
letters, first to Bakufu officials and then to the daimyo of the collateral branches of the Tokugawa house. Then he went to see Tokugawa Nariaki. Ieyoshi had left a will written when he recognized
that he was not likely to recover. "Do not deal with the matter of
the foreign country halfway," Ieyoshi had written. He went on to
urge that Abe make Nariaki an advisor. Accordingly Abe offered
Nariaki an official position as defense advisor, a move that was
supported by both Shimazu Nariakira and Matsudaira Echizen.
Nariaki, as etiquette demanded, turned him down repeatedly. Finally Abe prevailed upon him, explaining that the dying shogun
had called him to his bedside to make this request and that it was
also the desire of the new shogun.[16] Both men knew the unfortunate
Iesada and the unlikelihood that he was taking a forceful stance
on behalf of Nariaki, but a wish that was spoken in his name was
sufficient. Nariaki agreed to take a position in the Bakufu.

A week later on, August fifth, numerous palanquins led and followed by pikemen and retainers streamed under banners that slack-
ened in the summer heat toward the main gate of the castle. The

daimyo were on their way to the castle for their regular monthly audience. Dressed formally and kneeling by rank, they gathered in a large meeting hall that looked out on one of the castle's inner gardens. This was more than a ceremonial gathering, however, as Abe had copies of the American president's letter handed around to those who had not seen it before. "The arrival of the Americans' ships is a grave incident for our nation," Abe told the assembled daimyo. "Therefore read the letter very carefully and if you have opinions do not hesitate to tell us. It will not matter even if your opinion may give offense to the authorities. We accepted this letter at Uraga as an expedient measure. Hence do not adhere to old precedents." Indeed, Abe's asking the daimyos' opinion was an unprecedented event, unprecedented not only in the history of the Tokugawa Bakufu but also in the whole history of Japan. Abe was consulting not just the various centers of power but the entire aristocracy of Tokugawa Japan.[17]

For the next three months responses were brought to the Roju's offices at the castle. The responses were about equally divided over the question of how to respond to the American president's letter. Many daimyo and Bakufu officials rejected the American demands out of hand. Opening ports to foreign trade had long been a topic of intellectual debate. Now it came out that there was a powerful faction, led by the wealthy *fudai* daimyo Ii Naosuke and Hotta Masayoshi, who were willing to advocate this radical departure. But it was Tokugawa Nariaki who was among the first to respond, and he submitted a number of memorials that called for the rejection of the American demands. "If we accept their forceful demands, we will damage our national prestige," he argued in a letter titled "Maritime Defense: My Foolish Opinion." "If we open diplomatic relations with them, it will bring back the evil religion, Christianity. If we trade with them, we will import unnecessary goods which will inflict a great loss on us."

Nariaki's most important memorial listed ten reasons why, in choosing between war and peace, "we must never choose the policy of peace." Among them he noted that Japan's military prowess had been clearly demonstrated by a number of events, including the conquest of Korea; none of these, however, had taken place within the last two hundred years. The Americans were arrogant and discourteous. Their entering Edo Bay, firing salutes, and surveying without permission were an outrage, "the greatest disgrace we have suffered since the dawn of history." Thus to fail to expel the Americans or to reach an agreement with them would make it impossible to maintain national dignity. Trade would lead to Christianity and then further demands, all of which would mean repeating the blunders that China committed in the Opium War.

Rather then trade with America, Nariaki urged, the Bakufu should stop trading with the Dutch. It was not a case, as the Dutch scholars claimed, of Japan being the only nation in the world that practiced seclusion; rather it was the importance of completing military preparations so that Japan could *go out* into the world of the great powers and "spread abroad our fame and prestige." It was important to expel the Americans because the defense effort was exhausting the daimyo who were in charge of defending Edo Bay, and permitting the Americans to deliver a letter at Uraga was "allowing the foreigners to enter by the back door," thereby rendering the guarding of Nagasaki futile. There was also the threat that "the lower orders may fail to understand its [the Bakufu's] ideas and hence opposition might arise from evil men who had lost their respect for the Bakufu authority. It might even be that Bakufu control of the great lords would itself be endangered."

Finally, Nariaki addressed the argument that Kawaji and Tsutsui had made on their visit to his mansion. There were those who argued, Nariaki wrote, that "the Bakufu should show itself compliant at this time and should placate the foreigners, meanwhile exerting all its efforts in military preparations, so that when these preparations are completed it can more strictly enforce the ancient laws." Nariaki acknowledged that this seemed reasonable enough. But the problem was that the Bakufu was "temporizing and half-hearted" when it came to military preparations. There was not the slightest chance that the daimyo would complete preparations unless the Bakufu set an example in military matters. "But if the Bakufu, now and henceforward, shows itself resolute for expulsion, the immediate effect will be to increase ten-fold the morale of the country and to bring about the completion of military preparations without even the necessity of issuing orders." Kawaji and Tsutsui's secret visit to Komagome had paid off. Nariaki had spoken of pre-

paring for war, and though he had not exactly embraced the idea
of keeping them hanging on, noting that this strategy was in the
hands of a weak-kneed Bakufu, he would accept it for the time
being.[18]

Shimazu Nariakira also supported the rejection of the Americans demands. He was adamantly opposed to beginning trade with
the West and alarmed because reports from Okinawa indicated that
Bettelheim, the British missionary, had said that the Americans
were determined to go to war. His response, however, was more
cautious than Nariaki's: he did not believe that the Bakufu could
expel the Americans. Even if it could, the ships which the Americans had recently based in China and the Bonin Islands would
interrupt Japan's sea communications. He accepted the idea of
negotiating as a way to gain time; three years should be enough
time to complete rearmament. The preparation of coastal defenses
should be concentrated at Uraga, and Tokugawa Nariaki should be
put in charge. Shimazu Nariakira made this last recommendation—
which he had been suggesting in his private correspondence ever
since the Americans departed—with tremendous reservations, for
he knew that as a *tozama* daimyo he had no status in the deliberations of the Bakufu.[19]

A number of officials from the *san bugyo* offered their own
analysis of the situation. It was clear to them that the Americans
and the Dutch were "in collusion in a cunning plot to betray us."
The Dutch factory chief was due to meet with the shogun the next
year, and the Americans would probably pick this time to return
to Edo. What the Americans did at that time would be determined
by how the Bakufu responded. The wrong response could lead to
violence and the destruction of the capital city. Thus, the officials
suggested, it would be best to tell the Americans that their demands
were "not unreasonable," but could not be accepted. They should
"depart at once, never to return again hereafter." If, however, the
Americans pressed their demands, the Bakufu should offer to open
trade with the Americans, but only if the Americans got the other
foreign powers to agree that the United States alone would be
permitted to become a trade partner. Though it was unlikely that
the Americans would accept this arrangement, the negotiations
would serve the all-important purpose of buying time. Beyond sup-

porting the call for greater efforts to build up coastal defenses, the various *bugyo* called for the construction of modern warships because, even with better coastal defenses, it was not likely that they could stop a foreign squadron.[20]

With Ii Naosuke's response and that of a number of other important daimyo the idea of opening trade with foreigners finally

Portrait of Ii Naosuke, daimyo of Hikone

surfaced as a policy alternative. Accepting Abe's injunction to be blunt even if it offended the authorities, Ii noted that before Shogun Iemitsu, Japan had traded with the outside world. It was time to return to that early practice. He advocated the licensing of trading ships, which could be supported in part by the investments of wealthy merchants from the larger ports and sent to the Dutch East Indian port of Batavia to trade. If the Americans wanted coal, they could purchase it at Nagasaki after Japanese needs were filled. Beyond that, the Bakufu could allocate some of its trade goods to the United States, Russia, and so on. Most important, the Bakufu should build steamships and powerful warships. The emphasis at first should be on the development of a merchant marine, but its secret raison d'être should be the establishment of a modern navy.

But even Ii could only go so far. The purpose of all this, he explained, was to permit the Bakufu to *return* to the policy of seclusion at a later date. It was necessary, of course, to explain to the spirits of their ancestors that trade was a universal practice. Beyond this, the Bakufu should notify the imperial court so that the court could send messengers to the great shrines to explain to the gods that foreign trade was in the interest of "tranquility at home and security for the country."[21]

If Abe had hoped for unanimity, the responses to his appeal must have sorely disappointed him. Many of the *fudai* lords who dominated the government were for a cautious approach even if it involved trade. Nariaki, wedded to a mystical notion of the Japanese martial spirit, thought preparation for war was the only true policy. A powerful member of the Tokugawa family, he was supported by some of the most forceful *tozama* lords. Even Shimazu Nariakira, the man who had suggested opening trade with both the French and the English, had turned away from this possibility. In the end Abe's search for a consensus turned out to be more a test of the political climate in the bureaucracy and among the major daimyo than the means for forging a new policy for dealing with foreigners.

Hoping that the Roju could speak with a unified voice, Abe heard only cacophony, but Abe and his advisors could not wait for the emergence of a consensus. Abe had to move ahead quickly, and his first task was to get the Roju to approve Nariaki's appointment as defense advisor. This was no easy task. At least two members of the Roju were opposed to the appointment, as was the shogun's official foreign policy advisor, Hayashi Daigaku, head of the Bakufu's official university. Nariaki may have been a Tokugawa, but his taking an official role in the Bakufu was a threat to *fudai* control of the bureaucracy. As for Neo-Confucian scholars like Hayashi, they feared the encroachment of Nariaki and his renegade intellectuals upon their intellectual preserve.

Dismayed, Abe considered resigning as head of the Roju. But his close retainers prevailed upon him to stay. "If you resign," one of them told him bluntly, "it would look as if you wanted to escape the difficulties so that you could feel at ease. The Bakufu would end up taking a time-serving stance and end up in the gutter." Abe pressed on, and a little more than a week after his meeting with Nariaki he prevailed upon the Roju to accept his appointment.[22]

Thus Abe committed himself, at least at this point, to yet another effort to build up coastal defenses. Nariaki, meanwhile, began to flesh out in secret communications to Abe what he meant by preparation for war. The first steps should be reinstatement of the exclusion order of 1825 and the publication of a Great Proclamation calling on all classes to mobilize for war. At the same time, he advocated keeping the word *peace* "in the heart of the *kaibogakari*." In other words those dealing with foreign policy and coastal defense rather than domestic policy should be searching for a peaceful solution. Because Nariaki's policy was deliberately contradictory, it is difficult to find the point where realistic concerns overcame his preoccupation with the mythic past. Nariaki only made the situation worse by suggesting to Abe, undoubtedly in one of his more fanciful moods, that in a land engagement the Japanese could defeat the foreigners with sword and spear, and that during negotiations a small group of men could stab the captains of the American ships to death and kill all the crew.[23]

In private, Nariaki was thinking very different thoughts, according to Matsudaira Echizen. In a letter to Echizen in which he explained what he meant by "war at home, peace abroad" (*naisen gaiwa*), he acknowledged that it was "impossible to swim against the trend of the times." Friendship with foreign nations was inevitable, and since it was difficult to expel the barbarians, the Bakufu should "open a road for trade and friendship with them." He urged Echizen to carry out this policy when the time came. For himself, Nariaki had lived as the ringleader of the antiforeign elements, and he was determined not to change that appearance until he died.[24]

Having embraced Nariaki, Abe now had to contend with continuing opposition, centered in the offices of the various *bugyo*, to his views. At the center of Nariaki's strategy was the idea of mobilizing the populace to prepare for war. Nariaki with the assistance of Fujita Toko drew up a proclamation that was an exact replica of one of the memorials he submitted to Abe earlier. Before presenting the draft to the Roju, Abe rewrote it, toning it down considerably, but even then almost all of those who were party to the discussion of the proclamation opposed publishing it. Without sufficient arms, what was the point of making bellicose statements, they asked. Would not that only endanger the country? Kawaji and the officials of the *kaibogakari*, the bureaucratic home of the peaceful approach, noted that Nariaki was committed to peace abroad. Wouldn't calling for war convince the people that the Bakufu was two-faced? Nariaki confessed that this appeared to be double-talk, but it was not a question of the Bakufu granting trading rights to the Americans; it was more a question of refraining from denying them. It was most important to communicate to the people that once they were prepared militarily, they would expel the Americans.[25] Nariaki's first initiative as Abe's principal advisor had failed for lack of support.

Meanwhile the Bakufu faced another serious threat, this time from a quarter where they had long expected danger. A Russian squadron of four ships had arrived at Nagasaki on August twenty-first. The Russian admiral, Evfimii Vasil'evich Putiatin, brought a letter from his government asking for a delineation of the northern boundary between Japan and Russia and for the opening of trade at one or two ports. With the exception of the Dutch, the Russians had had more contact with the Japanese than any other major power. Cossack adventurers had arrived on the shores of the Pacific in the early years of the Tokugawa shogunate (1649) as the result of a violent scramble to establish a fur trade with China. During the reign of Peter the Great (from 1682 to 1725), the Russians began a more systematic attempt to explore and reach Japan via the stepping stones of the Kuril Islands. The northern barriers of the shogunate proved to be porous when it came to trade with the Russians. During the eighteenth century the Russians fought and traded with the Ainus and through the Ainus traded with the Japanese people of the Matsumae domain, including Ezo, as the island of Hokkaido was then called. The Russians mounted a number of expeditions to establish an official trade link with the Edo government, but were rebuffed. One of these expeditions, led by

Professor Adam Laxman, even spent the winter of 1792–1793 ashore in Ezo. After lengthy negotiations with officials from Edo, Laxman was given a permit to enter Nagasaki. Laxman, however, did not return to Nagasaki. Laxman arrived at a time when powerful forces in the Bakufu were pushing for expanded foreign trade, and to this day it is not known whether the Japanese meant to open trade with the Russians.[26] Edo scholars took note of Russia's advances, producing a body of literature that called for the bolstering of coastal defenses and colonization of northern Ezo as a defense against these red-haired barbarians.[27]

By the turn of the nineteenth century the Russians, through the United American Company, had pushed their outposts along the eastern side of the Pacific as far south as California. Trade with Japan was seen as part of an overall strategy to make the north Pacific a Russian lake. In their renewed contacts with the Japanese, the Russians confirmed the Bakufu's opinion that they were dangerous interlopers to be feared for their aggressiveness. After the Rezanov expedition failed to persuade the Japanese to open trade during a visit to Nagasaki during the winter of 1804–1805, the Russians raided Japanese communities on Sakhalin and Etorofu (one of the Kuriles) to send a clear message to Edo about the consequences of not opening trade. But from then until the Opium War, the Russians lost interest in the Kuril Islands and Japan. The czar instead was preoccupied with suppressing liberalism at home and maintaining Russian influence with the decaying Ottoman Empire in the Middle East.[28]

Putiatin began to push for an expedition to Japan in the wake of 'the Opium War, hoping to take advantage of the West's new commercial relations with China. He finally gained support when the Russians became concerned that the British, as the leading power in China, might be working to exclude Russia from its share of influence in the northern Pacific. While Putiatin was in Nagasaki, Russians had gone ashore on Sakhalin Island to set up a military outpost on its southern tip, just across the Soya Strait from Ezo. While the Russians and the Japanese exchanged threats of massacre and retaliation on Sakhalin, Putiatin, who did not approve of the occupation of Sakhalin, took a different approach from Perry's. He opened his ships to visits from the Japanese and spoke of his respect for the ancestral laws of Japan. That was why he had come to Nagasaki instead of Uraga. Putiatin was treated with great courtesy, and after the usual insistence that the laws of the land prevented the Bakufu from receiving letters, the Japanese, following the Roju's instruction to accept the letters, finally gave in.

The Russian letters were rushed to the Roju, and after more delay, Tsutsui and Kawaji were dispatched to Nagasaki to tell the Russians that the death of the shogun had left the Bakufu so busy with the investiture of his successor that it did not have time to address the question of the northern boundary of Japan. In four or five years they would probably be able to settle the question. As for the opening of ports, this was against the ancestral law, etc. Putiatin finally became impatient, noting that Russia had no need to deal with the Bakufu with the assistance of the Dutch at Nagasaki. Russia had plenty of warships of its own, and he would go to Edo if he did not get a satisfactory answer soon. When Putiatin suddenly departed empty-handed on November twenty-third, the Japanese feared that he had gone to Uraga. But in fact Putiatin had heard about rumors of a Russian war with England and France over the Eastern Question (the division of European territory still controlled by the tottering Ottoman Empire) and had decided to return to China for supplies and further information.[29]

In Nagasaki Kawaji and Tsutsui had applied the strategy of "keep them hanging on" to the Russians, and it had produced some results, though it was hard to decipher just what they were, since the Bakufu knew only that the Russians had not appeared at Uraga. The added presence of the Russians undoubtedly increased the sense of urgency in the Roju's discussions about how to deal with the Americans. In the coming year they faced the prospect of two foreign naval squadrons visiting their ports, while the Russians seemed poised on Sakhalin for some unknown misadventure. But in Edo, the Roju was in the midst of one of those prolonged periods of wrangling that epitomized the paralysis of the Bakufu. Abe had committed himself to Nariaki's defense strategy, a political strategy aimed at instilling a fighting spirit among the Japanese people. But members of the *bugyo* and the *kaibogakari* were wary of Nariaki's militancy, fearing that anything even suggesting the possibility of a confrontation with the Americans could lead to war. The debates continued on into the fall, hampered by Bakufu etiquette, which dictated that Nariaki could not meet face-to-face with his opponents in the various *bugyos'* offices.

For a time during the fall, Nariaki and the advocates of a strong defense appeared to be gaining ground. In September, Abe turned to the Dutch, ordering a steam corvette, fifty-six sailing corvettes, two steamships, a bronze carronade, and three thousand percussion-cap rifles. On October seventeenth, the law forbidding the construction of warships was repealed.[30]

Support for Nariaki's Great Proclamation was another matter. When the proclamation was discussed by the Roju in early November, there was almost total opposition. Incensed, Nariaki offered his resignation, and the Roju was confronted with yet another crisis of its own making. If Nariaki withdrew from the castle, word would surely leak out, to the instant discredit of the Roju and the Bakufu among those who wanted to attack the Americans when they returned. To avoid violence, the Roju believed it had no choice but to accept Abe's watered-down version of Nariaki's proclamation.[31]

Finally in December Abe, having won the Roju's approval, read the Great Proclamation to all the daimyo at a gathering at Edo Castle. It was the shogun's opinion that the daimyos' proposals boiled down to two words, *peace* or *war*. The Roju had agreed unanimously that defense measures in coastal and other areas were not sufficient. Therefore it was important to take a peaceful attitude toward the Americans when they returned. It had also been decided not to give a definite answer to Fillmore's letter proposing the opening of trade, Abe's instructions went on. If the Americans chose to attack and the response was inadequate, it would bring disgrace upon the country. For this reason, the Roju urged the lords to make military preparations and encouraged the daimyo to take measures to curtail their nonmilitary expenses. "Endure your loyal indignation," the proclamation concluded. "Conserve your dutiful courage. Observe their movements very carefully. If they start a war, all of you (high and low) must exert yourselves and serve faithfully so that we will never defile our national polity."[32]

Abe's instructions were hardly reassuring. He had clearly
ruled out a confrontation at least of Japanese making and was
hoping to put off indefinitely negotiating with the Americans. It
was a perfect consensus document, watering down the views of
Nariaki and blending them with the views of the advocates of a
peaceful response, such as Kawaji Toshiakira. But it was unlikely
to please anyone and, more than anything, was a public admission
of the weakness and muddle-headedness of the Roju under Abe's
leadership.

During the fall work finally began on a coastal defense system for
Edo Bay. Egawa Tarozaemon, the *daikan*, or governor, of Nirayama, a careful student of Western military techniques, was put
in charge. He was assisted by Takashima Shuhan, an expert on
Western gunnery who had been imprisoned during the repressive
regime of Mizuno Tadakuni for his efforts to experiment with Western weapons and now was suddenly released to work with Egawa.
After surveying the area, Egawa pointed out to the Roju that the
establishment of a static coastal defense system was hardly a satisfactory way to protect Japan.* Japan needed warships, needed
to send men abroad to study foreign military techniques, and
needed a manufacturing capability to make modern weapons.

Egawa's proposals were excellent, the Roju responded, but they
could not be carried out in less than five years. The Roju wanted
gun batteries to protect Edo right now. In July Egawa had proposed eleven batteries on both sides of the Izu Peninsula. With an
eye to its limited funds—landfill alone would cost seventy-one thousand gold ryo—the Bakufu suggested that Egawa begin with three
batteries to be built on landfill off Shinagawa.†

Thousands of laborers were mobilized to move the landfill from

---

* It is unfortunate that Egawa never met Perry. Perry could have told him
how he had spent his entire naval career fighting against the Jeffersonian
notion of coastal defense as a way to protect the interests of a seagoing commercial nation.

† The ryo weighed 11.2 grams and was 56.7 percent gold and 43.3 percent
silver. When Perry first purchased Japanese goods, each ryo was valued at
$4.00.

the sides of Mount Goten, from the hills where a number of daimyo's mansions stood, and from the grounds of the Sengoku temple while hundreds of stonecutters were recruited from all around the country. Logs were cut and moved to the shore while massive blocks of stone were brought from the Sagami and Izu peninsulas. Since Egawa and his men lacked the skills to manufacture large weapons from iron and steel, the guns were cast in bronze at primitive reverberatory furnaces set up outside of Edo. At the beginning of 1854 three more batteries were begun in the same area. When completed the six batteries cost ten times more than the original eleven proposed by Egawa.[33]

A number of the daimyo, inspired by the fecklessness of the Roju and its inability to come to grips with reality, promulgated their own plans for defense. Shimazu Nariakira finally received permission to build a model steamship in addition to the sailing ships that he was building to protect the trade expected through the Ryukyus. The steamship was to be sixty-five feet long powered by a fifteen-horsepower engine. The Saga domain had mastered the making of pig iron and requested a hundred thousand ryo to construct batteries armed with eighty-pound cannons for the protection of Nagasaki. Without funds, Egawa had to turn down Saga's request. Saga decided instead to manufacture eight-pound cannons. In some instances, plans were drawn up by hired scholars who knew little about military matters and less about the outside world. Instead they borrowed ideas freely from outdated treatises on military matters. One scholar suggested surrounding the American ships with fishing boats while soldiers were sent alongside to attack them, another that the ships should be burned, while a third merely stated that it was the shogun's job—the pathetic Iesada's—to expel the barbarians.

The construction at Shinagawa caused a new sense of alarm in Edo. Many people had begun to forget about the threat of the black ships, and now, it seemed, the Bakufu was preparing for a new confrontation at the city's doorstep. As people watched the coolies and stonecutters at work, they noted that if the Americans shelled the batteries, the populace along the shore behind the batteries would be in the line of fire.

The imperial court was also anxious about what would happen

when Perry returned. At the end of the year Abe received a letter from Takatsukasa Masamichi, Nariaki's close associate in Kyoto. He was writing *five months* after the emperor had been informed about the arrival of the American ships. The delivery of the letters at Uraga was a shocking incident, Takatsukasa wrote. "The Emperor is very worried, praying that we will not bring disgrace upon our country and suffer from disaster in the future." The emperor had written a poem: "Though the white waves are clamorous, what could they do? The kamikaze will blow in our country."

Abe wrote back acknowledging that the Roju was having "some difficulties" in dealing with the problem. The preeminent problem was national defense. "Although we have never neglected them [coastal defenses] until now," Abe wrote with studied ambiguity, "we have not yet completed them." He went on in this vein, twisting fact and logic to reassure the emperor that the shogun was "determined, with all his heart, to relieve the Emperor of his anxiety."[34]

Thus when the year ended, the Roju was as prepared as it would ever be. Abe's strategy—"keep them hanging on"—was not likely to appease the adamant commodore, and he had the beginnings of a coastal defense system that in no way could withstand a shelling from the American ships. The populace had not been mobilized to repel an invasion if there was one, and no one knew what to expect when Perry arrived. The future looked grim for the shaken Bakufu.

11

CHINA OR JAPAN: MASTERLY INACTIVITY AND THE NECESSITY OF ANNEXATION

As a mouse in the talons of an eagle, they [the Okinawans] promised everything.[1]
   —J. W. SPALDING, on the Okinawans during Perry's third visit

I received no communication from Commodore Perry, and know nothing of his designs. The peaceful and quiet anchorage he enjoys at Napa [Naha] was not more easily procured than will be his anchorage in any of the ports of Japan. I am persuaded that Japan has adopted the policy of "non-resistance, but non-intercourse." *Should that prove true, it would seem to terminate the expedition to Japan, unless it may be deemed good policy under that title to station the fleet so far from China to prosecute the collection of natural curiosities and of daguerrean sketches, or to exhibit to the natives the locomotive and other specimens of mechanical art with which* "the expedition" *is charged.*[2]   —HUMPHREY MARSHALL to Secretary of State
                              William Marcy, June 8, 1853

If we remain quiet, our relations with the Tartar [Chinese] government, should it triumph [over the Taiping rebels], cannot in the least be affected; and should the revolutionary party succeed, we shall be greatly the gainers. Therefore, for the present, the exercise of "masterly inactivity" *is our best policy, whilst all of our energies should be turned*

*to the bringing within the family of commercial, or at least trading
nations, the empire of Japan and its dependencies.*[3]

—MATTHEW CALBRAITH PERRY to James C. Dobbin,
Secretary of the Navy, August 31, 1853

*I shall in no way allow of any infringement upon our national rights
[in the Bonin Islands]; on the contrary, I believe that this is the
moment to assume a position in the east which will make the power
and influence of the United States felt in such a way as to give greater
importance to those rights which, among eastern nations, are generally
estimated by the extent of military force exhibited.... It is self-evident
that the course of coming events will ere long make it necessary for
the United States to extend its territorial jurisdiction beyond the limits
of the western continent, and I assume the responsibility of urging the
expediency of establishing a foothold in this quarter of the globe, as a
measure of positive necessity to the sustainment of our maritime rights
in the east.*[4]   —MATTHEW CALBRAITH PERRY to James C. Dobbin,
Secretary of the Navy, December 24, 1853

HAVING LEFT THE LAND OF THE GODS in a state of human turmoil,
the American squadron sailed back toward Okinawa only to encounter its first typhoon or at least its outer edge. On the second
day out, the wind blew up into a fierce gale forcing the two steamers
to cut loose the *Saratoga* and the *Plymouth*. The *Saratoga* was
dispatched to Shanghai to fulfill Perry's promise to protect the
American merchants from the threat of the Taiping rebels while
the *Plymouth* was ordered to survey the western shores of Amami-
Oshima, a large island in the Ryukyu chain. On the second day of
the storm, with the wind blowing more than fifty knots, steam was
reduced on the *Susquehanna* and the *Mississippi*, the guns were
lashed down, and the two ships were hove to as men scrambled aloft
to send down the yards and the top-gallant masts. For two days
the steamers thrashed and wallowed in the heavy seas, waves breaking over their decks and water washing in through their closed gun
ports. In the end little damage was done: the bowsprit came loose
on the *Susquehanna*, two boats were swept off the *Mississippi*, and

both steamers lost their forward-sounding spars and a jib boom or two.

Late on the day of July twenty-fourth, a week after departing Edo Bay, the two steamers approached Okinawa in a fog so thick that it was necessary to stand offshore until the next morning. In the harbor, rolling like a great log in the heavy sea, Perry found the *Supply*, which had remained at Naha during the squadron's visit to Japan, but not the *Powhatan,* which Perry hoped had finally arrived from the United States. The commander of the *Supply* reported that the Okinawans had continued to treat the Americans with reserved kindness during the squadron's absence. They had provided supplies through Bernard Bettelheim, the missionary, but pleading scarcity, they had provided fewer supplies than requested. They also continued to carefully monitor the Americans' activities with the usual number of "spies." Perry, flushed from his first taste of success in Japan, was now determined to extract further concessions as quickly as possible from the hapless Okinawans, since his ships were beginning to show the wear and tear of a long cruise and needed time in port to be refitted. He immediately sent a message ashore demanding an interview with the regent.

A day being set, Williams and Captain Adams went ashore to lay Perry's demands before Naha's chief magistrate. The commodore wanted the following: a rental agreement for a house for a year, a coal depot with sufficient room to store six hundred tons of coal, an end to the system of surveillance, and a free market, where the Americans could come ashore and purchase what they wanted. "Let the mayor clearly understand," Perry told Williams and Adams, "that the port is to be one of rendezvous, probably for years; and the authorities had better come to an understanding at once." In Perry's absence, a new chief magistrate had been appointed, and he listened with studied indifference to Williams and Adams's explanation of Perry's new demands. With the interpreter Itarashiki Satonushi, Williams was more pointed: the officers might carry pistols and hurt someone if the Okinawans persisted in following them.[5]

After drawing up what Williams described as "a threatening expostulation" to be presented to the regent, Perry and a group of his officers came ashore on the afternoon of July twenty-eighth. The chief magistrate met Perry outside the gate to the official building where the meeting was to take place, and once inside Shang Hung-hsun, the regent, took his arm and showed him to his seat at one of a number of tables that were laid out for a banquet. The Okinawans might be solicitous, but Perry was in no mood to be trifled with. Tea was served, and with Williams translating into Chinese, Perry got quickly to the point. His demands were reasonable, and he expected them to be met before he departed for China in a few days. The regent, more rigidly impassive than during their last encounter, suggested that they eat before the presentation of his letter. He preferred business before refreshment, Perry told the regent brusquely, but he gave in, sitting impatiently while the banquet was served.

During the meal, the regent asked what had transpired in Japan, and Perry offered a brief description of his landing on Japanese soil and the delivery of Fillmore's letter. After six or seven courses, Perry, no longer able to wait, asked to see the regent's letter. In his reply, Shang emphasized that Okinawa was a small and poor island, and Bettelheim's presence had already caused them many problems. Besides, many of their needs could only be met by imports from Japan and China. If they built a coal depot, their difficulties would be greatly increased. As for the purchase of goods in the markets, that was a matter that could only be decided by the shopkeepers. If they preferred to keep their shops shuttered, there was little that he could do about it. The men who followed them were not spies, but rather guides to help the Americans and keep them from being annoyed by the islanders. If these guides bothered the Americans, they would be withdrawn.

Perry listened to Williams's translation of the regent's letter with a slight deepening of his perpetual frown. He was fed up with Shang, the temporizing policy of his government, and his "thousand crooked arguments." When Williams finished, Perry ordered the letter returned: it was unsatisfactory and could not be accepted. The Americans had explored the island and knew that the soil was rich and food abundant. There had been some problems with the commodore's demands, Shang replied, and they had only responded

Construction of the Naha coal depot

after careful deliberation. Once again he tried to press the letter upon Perry, but Perry quickly rose, and before stalking from the meeting, informed Shang that if his demands were not met by noon the next day, he was prepared to land two hundred men, march to Shuri Castle, and occupy it until the matter was settled.[6]

The next morning Itarashiki and the chief magistrate came to the flagship, and the quibbling over Perry's demands resumed. If they built a coal depot, typhoons would destroy it, the Okinawans insisted, and if they simply left coal ashore, people would steal it. In time, though, the Okinawans, at the urging of the Satsuma officials stationed on the island, began to weaken, and soon they were discussing plans for the coal depot and for a bazaar to be held at the meeting hall in Naha on August first, the date set for the squadron's departure. That same afternoon Williams went ashore to see to the clearing of a site for the coal depot, and work commenced immediately.

At six o'clock on the morning of August first, while preparations for departure were under way aboard the ships, Perry and a group of officers went ashore to visit the bazaar. Itarashiki, attended by a flock of lesser officials, presided as chief bargainer over an odd assortment of lacquered cups, plates, and boxes, straw sandals, silver and brass hair pins, fans, silk and cotton sashes, pipes, and large supplies of tobacco. Trade was brisk, and as the Americans became excited and more impatient and insistent in their purchases, prices rose steadily. One hundred dollars in sales hardly approached the multi-million-dollar China trade, but it was a start, and for Perry, the principle of trade was the important thing.

Upon his departure, Perry left Captain Kelly and the *Plymouth* behind to look after American interests in Naha. After the typhoon season, sometime around October first, Kelly was to sail to the Bonin Islands and check on the fledgling community that Perry had encouraged to organize during his visit. Then Kelly was to sail south to a group of islands—the Coffin Islands to Perry, the Bailey Islands to the British—which Perry saw as the basis for an American claim to the Bonins. Kelly was to explore the islands thoroughly, looking for good ports and another location for a coal depot. To strengthen the American claim to these uninhabited islands, Perry provided Kelly with two engraved plates, one of which he was to nail to a tree; the other he was to bury at a certain distance and direction from the tree.

As always, Perry's strategic vision reached well beyond Japan, and with the limited number of ships at his disposal, he was doing all that he could to extend American interests in East Asia. To placate the American merchant community in China and circumvent further conflict with the irascible Humphrey Marshall, Perry dispatched the storeship *Supply*, which had been shuttling back and forth between China and Okinawa, to Amoy to check on the American community there.

It was not until six weeks after Perry's departure that Shimazu Nariakira reported to the Roju about what had transpired in Naha during the Americans' latest visit, and even then, if he was receiving accurate reports from Naha, he presented the events in a very different light. It all sounded very innocuous. Some Americans had gone ashore to draw pictures of the mountains, he wrote to Roju member Makino Bizen. They had unloaded a large supply of coal, met with Bettelheim, and walked around at various times. Beyond that, "there has not been any other incident yet," Nariakira wrote. Just in case, he had ordered strict surveillance of the Americans. There was no mention of a coal depot, the rental of buildings, the promise to *reduce* official surveillance, or the hastily organized bazaar.[7] In his dealings with a dependency of a Japanese daimyo, Perry had driven home an entering wedge, thereby further undermining the shogun's seclusion policy, but the Roju and Nariakira could do little about matters in distant Naha; they had more pressing matters to worry about closer to home.

Perry was well pleased with this first leg of the expedition. Before leaving Okinawa for Japan in early July, he had written to his wife that he had expected little from his first visit to Japan. But now in August, he had already managed to set one coal depot and acquire land for another, which could be used by steamers plying the Pacific between California and Shanghai; browbeaten the Okinawans into accepting the beginnings of trade and a permanent American presence on their soil; and established an American claim to the Bonin Islands. Moreover, in Japan he had successfully mas-

queraded as an American version of an Asian potentate and forced
the Japanese to accept Fillmore's letter. The Japanese and the
Dutch, Perry wrote on August 3, 1853, to James C. Dobbin, Franklin Pierce's new secretary of the navy, had expected the squadron
to go to Nagasaki, where they planned to receive the Americans
with cordiality, but "with a fixed design to throw obstacles and
delays in the way of any favourable issue to my visit." Eventually,
when he had run out of supplies, the delays would have forced his
withdrawal. Besides, Perry had no confidence in the Dutch with
"their servile submission to the capricious tyranny of the Japanese."[8] At Edo, he had demonstrated that the Japanese authorities
had no excuse for unreasonable delays. Perry had accomplished in
ten days in Japan, Bayard Taylor wrote, "more than any other
nation had been able to effect for the last two centuries. The universal feeling on board was one of honest pride and exultation."[9]

Headed for Hong Kong and a much-needed rest, the squadron
encountered the 127-foot, 22-gun sloop of war *Vandalia* south of
Taiwan, its guns flashing in the gathering gloom as it saluted the
approaching flagship. The *Vandalia* had left Philadelphia in early
March and had braved a long and stormy passage around the Cape
of Good Hope during which most of its men had come down with
scurvy. Commander John Pope came aboard the flagship to report
that the steam frigate *Powhatan* had also arrived in Hong Kong
and was on its way to Okinawa. Perry ordered the *Vandalia* back
to Hong Kong and hurried on. He hoped to catch the *Powhatan*
before she left in an attempt to catch up with the squadron, thereby
saving the coal that would be burned on a needless voyage to Okinawa and back. Perry's squadron now numbered six ships, almost
half the number promised him before his departure. How many
more would arrive during his stay in China was hard to determine.
On August seventh, after an absence of three months and eleven
days, the two steamers arrived in Hong Kong only to find that the
Powhatan had indeed departed, a disappointment to both Perry
and his men, who were looking forward to mail from home.

The China that Perry returned to was if anything in a more
chaotic state than when he left. The Taiping rebels seemed ascendant over the faltering Manchu dynasty, and their establishment
of the Heavenly Kingdom of Peace in Nanking had sparked nu-

merous revolts here and there along the coast and in the interior. In the Pearl River Delta law and order was on the wane, and piracy on the rise. Daylight robberies and kidnappings were commonplace. The Triads, secret societies that drew their strength from the desperate and the indigent, were on the move. Within days of Perry's departure from Macao to Shanghai in April, Triad members had posted placards in Canton attacking the local officials of the Manchu dynasty. By June there had been a number of uprisings in villages around the delta.[10]

Northward along the coast the same chaotic conditions prevailed. In May a rebel force captured the citadel at Amoy, one of the treaty ports. At the same time in Fukien province, the Small Knife Society declared itself in rebellion against the hated Manchu dynasty. In June a rumor spread that fifty thousand rebels were organizing to march on Canton. Although the insurgencies in the coastal cities were led by the secret societies, the foreign community saw the hand of the Taiping rebels everywhere. The Taipings had, in fact, dispatched an army westward *away* from the coastal cities. Their legions were circling through the valley of the Hwang Ho (Yellow River) recruiting new forces—many of them members of secret societies—preparatory to a drive upon Peking, a drive that their leaders hoped would topple the Manchu dynasty. When Perry reached Hong Kong, the Taiping were tied down by the siege of Huai-ch'ing, a city north of the Hwang Ho, halfway on their march from Nanking to Peking. Though there were contacts between the various secret societies that led the uprisings along the coast, they were hardly revolts under the control of a single organization.[11]

Despite the turbulence that seethed all around them, the foreigners remained remarkably immune in their comfortable enclaves. True, three British officers were killed with spears in a naval skirmish with pirates at Amoy. After visiting Amoy for four days at the end of July, the commander of the *Supply* reported that though there had been no trade for three months, "the persons and property of all foreigners have been most scrupulously respected, and not one act of violence or indignity has been offered to any individual, nor do they fear anything of the sort will occur." Of course, there were only three Americans in Amoy, all missionaries.[12]

Soon after his arrival, Perry moved into a large mansion in

the old Portuguese city of Macao. The leading Canton merchants wrote Perry that "the whole country about Canton is swarming with thieves and desperate fellows, who are lying in wait for an opportunity to attack and plunder the foreign residences." But this simply was not true. The downfall of the Manchu dynasty was the main objective of the various rebel factions that had sprung up

Macao; *Narrative of the Expedition*

across southern and central China, and their leaders were too astute to risk fighting a two-front war by simultaneously taking on the foreigners.[13]

Despite the complexity of the situation, Marshall, who continued to live in the American consulate at the Russell mansion in Shanghai, was deeply frustrated by his lack of naval support. He was convinced that the Taiping rebels had struck the death knell of the Manchu dynasty. The revolution was hurrying forward at an unanticipated pace, he reported to William Marcy, Franklin Pierce's new secretary of state. The Manchu dynasty was likely to lose control of China south of the Whangpoo by the end of the summer, and China was on the brink of total collapse. In twelve months he would not be surprised to see a reenactment in Shanghai itself of the worst scenes from the French Revolution.

"The citizens of the United States in China *are crying from all quarters for protection*," Marshall wrote to Marcy, "*and being already left defenceless, will be compelled, in case of any sudden emergency, to appeal to Great Britain, France, or Portugal to protect them.*" Where was the American Navy? This was Marshall's constant refrain in dispatch after dispatch, as he took every opportunity to remind Marcy that Perry had usurped civilian control of the military and decamped for Japan "to prosecute the collection of natural curiosities and of daguerrean sketches, or to exhibit to the natives the locomotive and other specimens of mechanical art with which 'the expedition' is charged."

Then there were the British; they were playing a double game, Marshall reported. Sir George Bonham, the British plenipotentiary, had personally told Marshall that he considered the Taiping revolt insignificant. But his interpreter, Thomas Meadows, had visited Nanking a number of times, and Marshall feared that the British, through their dealings with the rebels, might gain access to an inland port and thereby connect India to China by means of an overland route that would run from the Irrawaddy River to the Yangtze.[14] Marshall, like most Westerners, knew almost nothing about the interior of China, and it was not until several years later that Westerners discovered that more than a thousand miles separated the watershed of the Irrawaddy from the Yangtze.

Marshall was faced with a doubly complicated situation in his studied efforts to maintain American neutrality. American sailors were deserting to take jobs as mercenaries with the imperial army while a number of missionaries were infatuated by Hung Hsiuch'uan, the Heavenly King of the Taiping rebels, and his Sinocized version of Christianity. The missionaries were strong believers in what Marshall called "the theology of a renovated Asia."[15] One had traveled to Chinkiang where he had met with a rebel general and presented him with a pistol and a spyglass, an act that Marshall judged not only a violation of the Treaty of Wanghia but a capital offense as well. Issachar Roberts, the missionary who had first instructed Hung in matters of faith, was being asked to come to Nanking by Hung himself. Even Dr. Peter Parker, Marshall's own secretary and interpreter, was unduly sympathetic to the rebels, a fact that irked Marshall and contributed to a running feud between the two men.

Marshall had other, less petty matters to report, however, auspicious developments that he considered major advances in Sino-American relations. After numerous efforts to communicate with Peking through the imperial commissioner in Canton, Marshall had been invited, through the good offices of the Shanghai intendant and erstwhile Russell and Company partner, to present his credentials to I-liang, governor general of Liang-Kiang province. In an unintended parody of the Perry expedition, Marshall journeyed in early July—at the very moment that Perry was approaching the coast of Japan—in seven small boats and by sedan chair draped with the American flag to Kunshan, a small city forty miles west of Shanghai. During a pleasant exchange of views, both I-liang and Marshall agreed that it would be best for him to continue to reside at Shanghai and not to press the question of moving his quarters to Peking. Marshall noted that the emperor could court the favor of the Western powers by liberalizing trade, granting freedom of conscience, and opening the country to foreigners, all promises made by the rebels at Nanking. Having achieved little of substance, Marshall wrote a self-congratulatory dispatch to Marcy listing his major accomplishments: he was the first to carry the American flag into the interior; he could now communicate with Peking through I-liang as well as the imperial commissioner at Canton (who generally ignored his letters); and the people of the interior had seen a citizen of the United States for the first time in national costume.[16]

Under separate cover, Marshall wrote a confidential dispatch, which got more quickly to the point. The imperial government was impotent, ignorant, and conceited; all its officials were superlatively corrupt. The rebels were struggling merely for power and had no idea how to govern. As for the people, they were indifferent, insensible to popular rights, and incapable of declaring or maintaining them. The emperor had turned to the Western powers for assistance. True, he had only done this indirectly when the Shanghai intendant tried to hire some Western vessels to send up the Yangtze against the rebels. However, the British were in communication with Peking on some unknown matter, wrote Marshall, implying that it was on the question of providing support against the rebels.

Still, it was not the British but the Russians that the United States had to be worried about, Marshall declared. The Russians maintained a sizeable body of troops along the Chinese border, and there was a fleet in Hong Kong, which was ostensibly keeping an eye on Perry's activities but could be sent into action in support of the Chinese emperor. The Russians could readily suppress the rebellion. If they did, they would end up in control of central China, acquiring "a power on the Pacific which would not only nullify the projects of the United States in the future, but materially annoy us in the present." Almost any sacrifice should be made to keep Russia from expanding into China. Thus Marshall called for the United States to *intervene* "to quiet and tranquilize China." It would be a mission of humanity and charity, he argued, unlike England's ruthless conquest of India. It would in fact be intervention with no other object than "to preserve the nationality of China."[17]

One grand or not so grand diplomatic encounter, and Marshall, the righteous exponent of neutrality and critic of British imperialism, was newly converted to intervention. Further, he now had his own ideas about the relationship between intervention, steamships, and progress. If the Americans intervened, the rebellion would "fade away as a dream," and steamships, American steamships to be sure, would bring commerce and prosperity to the Yangtze basin. Moreover, steam would lead to the development of a Chinese navy capable of ending the smuggling of opium by both the British and the Americans. Marshall had more than once warned *these people*—the American opium merchants, the very merchants whose business Marshall was so eager to protect—against using the American flag to cover their activities. But they had always answered him with the argument that it was the Chinese responsibility to enforce the laws against opium, an argument that they offered while delivering opium over the sides of their ships into the hands of the Chinese customs officials. If the opium trade could be stopped—a trade that Marshall estimated to be worth $30 million—England's dominant position in the trade of the East would soon come to an end. This would be a great benefit to the United States because the opium trade was the major obstacle to the establishment of a steamship line between California and China.[18]

Marshall could spin his diplomatic fantasies for the State Department, but he was destined to remain a spectator during these momentous times, a spectator who was almost entirely ignored by a State Department that ranked China among the least of its priorities. Marshall had little choice but to adhere to a policy of strict neutrality, which he did in his usual lawyerly manner. The kind of sustained intervention that Marshall was talking about was a dream. Not even the British during the Opium War, with twenty-five warships, fourteen steamers, and ten thousand men, contemplated the kind of massive intervention that a reordering of the Manchu dynasty would have necessitated. And to the State Department, China was a distant commercial outpost, in effect a private diplomatic zone of the merchants of New York and Boston, not a candidate for military intervention.

During the summer it became apparent to Marshall that the situation was beginning to change uncomfortably close to home. In late August Marshall reported that Shanghai itself was "the theatre of action for a strongly organized band of men, who nightly commit robberies and murders in the midst of the city or in the suburbs, and who openly defy the public authorities."[19] On September seventh, while city officials were at a Confucian temple honoring the great philosopher on his birthday, the Small Knife Society seized the municipal buildings and homes of key officials. The city magistrate was killed during an attack on his mansion, and intendant Wu Chien-chang, the secret Russell partner, surrendered to the rebels. By 7 P.M. the leader of the Small Knife Society, himself a former employee of a foreign firm in Canton, was at the American consulate, where he assured Marshall that he would release Wu and prevent any confrontation between his followers and members of the foreign community.[20]

While Marshall was caught up in the Small Knife Society's seizure of Shanghai, Perry was working closely with the American merchants in Canton. As soon as he arrived from Okinawa, they applied directly to him for protection. Perry quickly sent the *Mississippi* up the river, moving the ship within striking distance of the city. When the *Supply* arrived from Amoy, he stationed that ship with 150 men directly off the factories and also offered to send marines with fieldpieces from the *Mississippi* to the factories.

As for the rest of the squadron, the *Vandalia*, the *Macedonian*, the *Susquehanna*, and the *Powhatan*, after her return from the unnecessary trip to Okinawa, were sent to Cum Sing Moon. Marshall could not resist reporting to Washington that this snug harbor was celebrated as being a squalid resort for opium smugglers. Both the *Susquehanna* and *Powhatan* needed extensive work done on their engines. The *Powhatan* was a floating disaster. On the voyage out, she had leaked so badly that she was often unseaworthy. At times water covered the fire room floor. The ship had caught fire twice because of improper fitting of a hatch and combing around a smokestack, and there had been numerous problems with the engines, including a breakdown that necessitated her staying in Okinawa for a week. The *Saratoga* had been dispatched to Shanghai, as Perry had promised Marshall before he left for Japan. But to Marshall's annoyance, the *Saratoga* was undergoing a thorough overhaul that involved the removal of its guns.

Perry too, as might be expected, had strong views on the Taiping rebellion, but they were closer to the ideas of those whom Marshall called the believers in "the theology of a renovated Asia." According to Perry, there were elements "at work in China which, at no distant period, will bring about a change of dynasty, and a state of things more consonant with the enlightenment of the present age." He agreed with Marshall that Peking would soon fall into rebel hands and that years would elapse before a new government could gain control of the country. Unaware, however, of Marshall's secret call for intervention, Perry pushed for his own form of neutrality. The true policy of England and the United States, he argued, should be "the exercise of 'masterly inactivity.'" Above all, Perry believed in Perry and the Japan expedition, and he intended to direct all his energies toward bringing Japan into the family of trading nations. As for China, nothing should be done that would jeopardize future relations with either side in the rebellion. It was for this reason, Perry explained to the secretary of the navy, that he had taken the *Susquehanna* away from Marshall and declined to cooperate in his attempt to reach the mouth of the Pei-ho.

He was hoping, Perry wrote, for something to happen that would calm the minds of the Canton merchants before it was necessary for him to depart for Japan. The ultimate success of the expedition, he argued, depended on "keeping up the moral influence upon the government of Japan, which my first visit imposed." This could be accomplished by "working upon the fears of the rulers," and this could be done only by taking with him "the most imposing force I can collect, not so much for actual coercive purposes, as for an object strictly diplomatic." He had already been notified that the steamer *Alleghany* and the 74-gun ship of the line *Vermont* had been withdrawn from the squadron, and he was hoping that there would be no other change of instructions.[21]

Meanwhile Marshall had finally heard from the State Department. In a dispatch dated June tenth, Marcy had instructed Marshall to work for an end to Chinese restrictions on foreign trade, to be vigilant in the protection of American rights and property, and to maintain cordial relations with the British. As for the naval forces in the area, they were to be devoted to the protection of American interests.[22] Armed with this dispatch, Marshall made one more attempt to gain control of the East India Squadron. He sent the acting consul in Canton to see Perry to ask for whatever ships the acting consul thought necessary to protect American lives and property. He next requested Perry to send a ship to Amoy and a steamer to Shanghai to be ready to protect the American residents of Ningpo, if that became necessary.[23]

Perry's response was icily correct. It would give him the greatest pleasure to cooperate most cordially with Marshall in the protection of American lives and property, as the steps he had already taken, which he outlined in his letter, would attest. He would give due attention to the suggestions of the acting consul at Canton, but beyond that, they would have no influence on the movement of the ships under his command. As for Amoy and Ningpo, he did not know of any American property in these cities that needed protection, except perhaps for that of the missionaries, and he could not believe that they were exposed to the slightest annoyance. The fact of the matter was that there was a larger force now protecting the American citizens in Canton and Shanghai "than has ever before composed the entire strength of the East India squadron." For this reason he had no intention of sending a steamer to Shanghai. Only the *Mississippi, his* flagship, was available, and he had no intention of using any coal, which he had accumulated at great cost and difficulty, to send her to the north. And finally, despite the exaggerated accounts of dangers to foreigners, Perry had not heard of one instance since he had arrived in China where an American or any other foreign citizen or his property had been molested.[24]

Even as he wrote to Perry, Marshall had suspected that his days in China were numbered, having read in a Washington newspaper, which must have been more than three months old, that he was going to be replaced. He wrote the State Department that he would undertake no new diplomatic initiatives that he himself could not complete or that might place his successor in an embarrassing situation.[25] He had quarreled with Perry and with Peter Parker, his own secretary, had alienated the British, and also turned the American merchants in Shanghai against him when he opposed their plans to support the English, who were using the seizure of Shanghai by the Small Knife Society as an excuse to turn Shanghai into a free port in violation of the treaties signed a decade earlier. Isolated, unhappy, and all but ignored, Marshall was finally willing to confess his impotence. But could he desist while events still swirled around him?

At his offices in his mansion in Macao, Perry turned to the tedious task of refitting his ships and preparing for the next phase of the expedition. He was immersed in a complicated and time-consuming job—all paperwork, details, and orders, with an occasional break to partake of the elaborate social rituals of the merchant-diplomatic community. The climate had taken a terrible toll on both the ships and his men. The moisture ate at the sails, cordage, and other furnishings, necessitating frequent replacements. There was also the perennial problem of coal supplies. Ever since his visit to Shanghai, Perry had been urging the navy to send all supplies to Macao and Hong Kong. He had also written Howland and Aspinwall, urging them to send coal to Hong Kong. He hoped they would continue to supply his squadron, he continued, since any one else would merely look to their profit.[26] Perry also set aside space for Wilhelm Heine and the other artists to work on their sketches and drawings and to process their daguerreotypes, while in another part of the building John Williams, Wells's hard-drinking brother, assembled and tested the telegraphic equipment that was to be a gift to the Japanese.

Equally pressing were problems with the officers and crew. It was an unusually hot summer and early autumn, and dysentery, typhus, and malaria spread rapidly among the men of the expedition. Many were afflicted in the heat by painful boils and other sores, some undoubtedly caused by scabies. Captain Joel Abbot of the newly arrived *Macedonian* reported 33 men sick out of 380. But this was fewer than other ships, who had 50 or 60 on the sick list. John Contee, Perry's trusted flag lieutenant and a participant in and recorder of much of the negotiations with the Japanese, insisted on resigning and returning to the United States. Contee was fed up after twenty-one years in the service. His health, he wrote Perry, would not stand the climate, and there were no prospects for promotion for a man of his age and rank. Two other lieutenants were sent home because of their health, and a midshipman was sent home to prepare for his examinations. Another lieutenant, J. H. Adams of the *Powhatan*, died from exposure to the heat. Perry also lost the bandmaster from the *Mississippi* and more than a dozen sailors.[27]

Perry too was affected by the climate. He returned from Japan exhausted by his responsibilities and succumbed to a bad cold in September. When the summer heat abated, he was laid up again by a return of his painful arthritis. "This cruise will use me pretty well up," Perry, who was now fifty-nine years old, wrote plaintively to his wife, "for my duties are very trying to my health." Perry wrote to the Navy Department begging for more lieutenants and passed midshipmen. The *Vandalia*, he noted, had sailed from home without a single midshipman. At one time all her lieutenants and her master were sick, and the deck had to be left in charge of a master's mate. When the secretary's reply finally arrived, the answer was that there were no men available to fill the gaps in Perry's beleaguered officers corps.[28]

There were further losses as a result of disciplinary measures. With the abolition of flogging, Perry had known that the expedition would be a test of "how the philanthropic principle of moral suasion answers." Early in the cruise Perry had complained that "the want of legal means for punishing men for the thousand faults they are daily committing has weakened the authority of the officers." Congress, he concluded, would have to seek a new remedy or "the Navy as an institution will go to the devil."

The navy survived, but there were plenty of discipline problems, though not an unusual number, in a squadron that would soon number ten ships and more than two thousand men. Perry apparently chose the layover at Cum Sing Moon to settle disciplinary accounts. The captain's steward from the *Vandalia* was tried and acquitted of murder. Two other sailors were tried for mutinous language, convicted, and forfeited pay. Three others were slapped in irons for unrecorded offenses, and there were a handful of other courts-martial. A number of men were read out of the service for their offenses, and at one point Perry, desperate for sailors, attempted to recruit four men who were convicted of mutiny aboard a clipper ship to replace them. The former mutineers were sent to the *Mississippi* in lieu of punishment, but refused to serve and ultimately were sent home.[29]

The only member of the expedition that Perry was eager to see depart was Bayard Taylor. He sailed for the States by clipper ship in early September with permission from Perry to violate Perry's own orders about communicating with the press. Taylor was to write a story for the *New York Herald* describing the first leg of the expedition, a story that would undoubtedly place the expedition in a favorable light.

Taylor also wrote of the problem with discipline in the new navy, but Captain Abbot of the newly arrived *Macedonian* reported a very different situation aboard his ship. On his passage out there was an "unusual degree of harmony and good will among the men and officers." The atmosphere aboard the *Macedonian* may have been the officers' and men's way of showing respect for the grieving

Abbot, who lost a son on the voyage. The sixty-one-year-old Abbot, unlike Perry, was a man of few political or family connections in Washington. In fact, he had antagonized the navy as a young officer by attacking corruption at the Boston Navy Yard. Thus Abbot, in an era when there were more senior officers than ships to command, spent much of his career on inactive duty. He did serve under Perry in the Mexican War, but from then until activated to bring the *Macedonian* to Japan, he spent only two years on active duty. A devout father of eleven children, nine of whom survived, Abbot spent his years at home in Warren, Rhode Island, shepherding his small investments and taking care of his children. Abbot, according to one of his officers, was "a plain common sense New England man, making no pretensions of show or humbug."[30]

Abbot's own lack of success as a naval officer did not keep him from doggedly pursuing a new command for himself and naval appointments for three of his sons. Perry at one point came forward to recommend one son for a midshipman's appointment while Abbot, very much in the exploratory spirit of the age, wrote to Daniel Webster that he was available to lead an expedition to Africa. When Abbot received a last-minute command for the Japan expedition, he arranged to have two of his sons assigned to his ship. With a third he failed.[31]

For one son, Nathan, a sixteen-year-old Brown University student with tuberculosis, the cruise, the family doctor hoped, would provide a change in climate and a cure for the disease. At first, young Abbot's health improved, but he was soon coughing and spitting blood. As the end approached, Nathan told his father that he was ready and willing to die, the sooner the better. He cried for a time. He wanted to see his mother again, but then he rallied and sent personal messages to his family, apologizing for any behavior that had offended. On the morning of his death, his brother gave him a little soup and then some wine and coffee. But his breathing grew more labored, and finally he put his hand by his head, turned on his side as if going to sleep, and died with a pleasant look on his face. His father had his body encased in lead and buried at Prince's Island, off Western Africa, leaving instructions for another son who was aboard a naval ship to retrieve his remains and return them to Rhode Island.[32]

Deaths from disease, accidents, and dissipation were also thinning the ranks of officers and men in China. Those men who were not aboard the ships guarding Canton and its approaches or aboard the *Saratoga* at Shanghai were condemned to wait for the next cruise at Cum Sing Moon. Their idleness was enhanced by the ready supply of cheap Chinese labor available for much of the refitting work. Five opium-receiving ships were anchored in the harbor, four under the British flag and one under the American, which was hauled down until the naval squadron left. It was "a paradise for sailors who love rum and women [not to mention those who wished to experiment with opium, as Bayard Taylor had] but a curse to everyone else, and even to them would they realize it," Lieutenant George Henry Preble of the *Macedonian* wrote to his wife. The day before, a drunken sailor jumped off the *Susquehanna* and drowned. Two boys from the *Macedonian*, tempted by the promise of rum if they could get ashore, jumped overboard and attempted to swim. They were picked up by a boat a mile away. At Macao a sailor from the *Vandalia* died after being jabbed in the eye with an umbrella by the captain's steward during liberty.[33]

To relieve the monotony and the grim threat of illness and death, there was, at least for Perry and his officers, a constant round of social gatherings. There were dinners with the French minister, the Portuguese governor of Macao, and the leading merchants, and there was the regatta ball at the Victoria Regatta Club in Hong Kong. The American merchants, particularly those who participated in the opium trade, were a wealthy lot and eager to entertain their naval protectors. Lieutenant Preble was told by Samuel Endicott of Salem, one of the leading opium dealers and a host to Perry and his officers, that he had just sold three hundred chests of opium at five hundred dollars a chest. He sold ten chests alone while Preble was talking with him. Preble reported that Endicott was reputed to have made two or three hundred thousand dollars in the trade, which was probably a modest estimate.[34]

Perry reciprocated the hospitality by making his bands available for performances in Macao and Hong Kong, indoors and out, and for regular dances. Perry, however, may have overestimated the cultural proclivities of the foreign community. A correspondent for the *China Mail* reported that a brilliant audience crowded into the Macao Philharmonic Hall to hear the band from the *Susquehanna*. He found, though, that popular airs rather than "a symphony or composition of high art" would have been received with far greater enthusiasm.[35]

The most popular events were the dramatic performances put on by the sailors and marines from the American squadron. The *Friend of China* reported an evening of entertainment aboard the *Susquehanna*. The deck awnings were raised to create a ceiling, and flags and banners were hung to decorate actual sets, which had been built and painted by the ship's carpenters. This hastily constructed theatre was as good "as some of the minor places of performance in England," sniffed the otherwise enthusiastic correspondent. The choice seats were the boxes, which were arranged along the catwalk that connected the two huge paddle wheels. First came the dramatic play *Rob Roy*, which was performed in appropriate Scottish brogue and in tartans sewn for the occasion by Chinese tailors. The clear favorite, however, were the Ethiopian Minstrels, who sang "I've Been to California" and other tunes and then featured "Mr. Buck's recitation (in Nigger character) and 'Walk your chalks Ginger blue' in first-rate style." The audience was particularly taken by Mr. Buck's dancing. The performance was followed by a splendid repast served from tables loaded with food.[36]

Perry had told the Japanese that he would return the next spring, but within six weeks of settling in Macao for the winter, Perry began to think in terms of an early return to Japan. Perry was informed by friends in the merchant community that the French were purchasing supplies for their squadron that was anchored at Hong Kong in preparation for a major voyage to an unknown destination. He had heard that they too were headed for Japan, "and yet I hardly believe it to be true, as it would be unfair to intermeddle at this time," Perry wrote to the secretary of the navy on September twenty-sixth. He was also concerned about Russian intentions. Admiral Evfimii Vasil'evich Putiatin had called at Canton in June after Perry's departure. He had told the American consul that he was headed for Japan to find Perry to cooperate with him in opening up the country. As of the end of September, Perry had not heard anything more about the Russians. He thought that Putiatin, unable to find him, had sailed on to Kamchatka.[37]

Perry was wrong. At that very moment (September twenty-sixth), Putiatin was anchored at Nagasaki, puzzling over what to do about the dilatory tactics of the Japanese and rumors of an outbreak of hostilities between England, France, and Turkey on one side and Russia on the other (in what was to become the Crimean War). By October Perry's sources in the merchant community had provided him with fairly accurate information on the move-

Minstrel show aboard ship; watercolor by an unknown Japanese artist

ments of the Russian squadron, and he was furious. The Russian ambassador to Washington had arrived in Shanghai from San Francisco with dispatches for Putiatin and while there had arranged with Edward Cunningham, the American consul, and J. S. Amory, the naval storekeeper, to borrow twenty tons of coal. At first blush, this was not a surprising development, since Cunningham also served as a consular agent for the Russians. Perry, however, had spent considerable energy collecting and hoarding coal for the next leg of the expedition. His intentions were twofold: to supply his own steamers with coal and to keep it away from the Russians and the French. Against his express orders, Amory and Cunningham had agreed to loan the Russians twenty tons. Perry wrote to the secretary of the navy asking that Amory be fired and expressing fear that Cunningham, who was also a consular agent of the French government, would make a similar arrangement with France. He also recommended placing the naval depot under the control of a merchant house with no connections to a foreign power, since the practice of allowing American consuls to represent foreign powers was "fraught with much evil."[38]

By early December Putiatin had arrived in Shanghai. Leaving his ships hidden in the lee of the Saddle Islands at the mouth of the Yangtze for fear of the French and British, he and his officers cautiously made their way to the foreign settlement, where they were questioned by Cunningham about what had transpired in Nagasaki. Putiatin reported that the shogun had died and that the Japanese said there would be no further negotiations for a year. From Shanghai he wrote to Perry asking for eighty tons of coal and expressing his hopes that "by mutual cooperation [they could] attain more easily the end that both our governments have in common." Perry, when he heard Putiatin's report, thought that the Japanese claiming the shogun had died was probably a trick to get rid of the Russian admiral; he expected to hear the same thing when he returned to Edo Bay. Perry, of course, had no intention of cooperating with the Russians. Nor would he lend them any more coal.[39]

The movements of the French and Russian squadrons lent a new air of urgency to Perry's plans to depart.[40] It was risky to undertake a winter voyage to Edo. Among whalemen, the waters off Japan in the winter were known for heavy fogs and violent storms. What was worse, Perry spent most of the holiday season in bed as a result of his arthritis. But Perry felt that he had little choice. He had gotten this far at tremendous expense in men and materials, and now he was faced by two powers who were threatening to capitalize on his accomplishments. By December the only reason for delay was the absence of the supply ship *Lexington*, which was bringing another printing press and more presents for the Japanese. As the holiday season with its frenetic round of party going approached, Perry, sick as he was, rushed to complete last-minute details. He had to find paper for the printing press. He ordered seeds to take to Japan, chartered a small, rickety steamer from the British for $500 a month to be armed and stationed off the Canton factories, preferred charges against the naval store-keeper at Macao for collusion with his brother, a local merchant, to profit at the expense of the navy, moved the naval depot from Macao to Hong Kong, worked out a schedule for the departure of the ships that would return to the United States after the expedition, prevailed upon eighty men whose terms of service had expired to stay on until the return from Japan, and sent a request to Washington that he be allowed to go home as soon as he returned from Japan without having to wait for his replacement.

During all this frenzied activity, Perry was surprised to hear from Sir George Bonham, the British superintendent of trade. Bonham wanted to discuss Perry's activities the previous summer in the Bonin Islands. He showed Perry a letter from a former British consul reporting that Perry had bought land at Peel Island for a coaling station and enclosing a pamphlet that claimed that the islands were discovered by the British and then settled by a group of men under the protection of the British consul in the Hawaiian Islands.

Perry begged to differ with Bonham. The pamphleteer had failed to name all the white men who had founded the colony at Peel Island. Among the original founders, Americans outnumbered the British two to one, and one of them was Nathaniel Savory of Massachusetts, the only one of the original group still on the island—and now an employee of the U.S. Navy, Perry did not add. Perry also felt compelled to dispute the British claim to sovereignty of the islands. The American whaler, Captain Coffin, had been there three years before the British naval officer who claimed to have discovered them. The question of sovereignty, Perry went on, was one to be settled by their two governments. His purchase of land was a private transaction meant to establish a port of refuge for whalers and a coal depot for a steamship line that would run from California to Shanghai. In the long run, Perry suggested to Bonham, occupancy and protection of the islands by any nation would be too expensive and of little importance. The real need was the establishment of a free port.[41]

While Perry downplayed the question of sovereignty with Bonham, he was much more belligerent in insisting upon American claims in the Bonins and elsewhere in a letter to Secretary Dobbin sent two days after his meeting with Bonham. There was only one difficulty with investing American capital in the Bonins, he wrote, and that was uncertainty about sovereignty. He had no intention of permitting "any infringement upon our national rights" in the Bonins. On the contrary, Perry believed that "this is the moment to assume a position in the east which will make the power and influence of the United States felt in such a way as to give greater importance to those rights which, among eastern nations, are generally estimated by the extent of military force exhibited." Perry acknowledged that he was acting on his own in this matter, and he asked to be instructed about U.S. policy with regard to the Bonins and "the influence which I have already acquired over the authorities and people of the beautiful island of Lew Chew [Okinawa]." Perry, like all Americans, had tremendous disdain for the "annexing policies" of the grasping British, but he too had tasted from the cup of imperial ambition in the Bonins, the Ryukyus, and Japan and was ambitious for a deeper draught. "It is self-evident," Perry assured Dobbin, who did not think it self-evident at all, "that the course of coming events will ere long make it necessary for the United States to extend its territorial jurisdiction beyond the limits of the western continent, and I assume the responsibility of urging the expediency of establishing a foothold in this quarter of the globe, as a measure of positive necessity to the sustainment of our maritime rights in the east."[42]

Perry had already invested fourteen lives in his claim to the Bonin Islands, for the *Plymouth*'s voyage to survey and establish a second claim to the islands had turned out tragically. A sudden typhoon had come up when the *Plymouth* was at Port Lloyd while one of her cutters was off on an excursion to fish and hunt for birds. The cutter and thirteen men disappeared without a trace. The storm was so violent that the *Plymouth* dragged four anchors across the harbor at Port Lloyd, and a whaler and a British schooner had been thrown up on the beach.

If Perry could free himself from his entanglement in Chinese affairs, he was ready to depart for Japan. The persistent commissioner Marshall was determined, however, to make one more effort to get a ship or ships away from Perry. In early November Marshall showed up in Macao and made his way to Canton. Perry provided a steamer to move Marshall from Macao to Canton, but there is no record of any encounter between these two antagonistic egos until Marshall, undoubtedly aware of Perry's impending departure, requested a steamer to take him back to Shanghai. Peking, Marshall claimed, was about to fall. At any moment, he expected news about the flight of the emperor on the steamer from the north. Marshall planned to return to Shanghai and proceed to Nanking to find out the state of the rebellion and to let the Taiping rebels know that he was ready to recognize "the Christian emperor" at an opportune time.[43] Marshall had forgotten his promise to the State Department that he would not undertake any new initiative. On the strength of inaccurate rumors about the impending fall of Peking—the Taiping army, lacking cavalry and munitions, was actually bogged down outside of the city—Marshall was ready to open diplomatic relations with the rebels.

Unfortunately, Perry responded tartly, he could not afford the number of naval vessels that Marshall's plans for intervention would require. Perry's plans for the coming season were already perfected and under execution. In fact, the *Macedonian* and the *Supply* had already left for Okinawa a week earlier, and the *Plymouth* and the *Saratoga* were under orders to sail from Shanghai to the same destination. Perry asserted that he had nothing to do with the diplomatic relations of the United States with China, and he had no intention of "using the force at my disposal in intermeddling in a civil war between a despotic government, struggling for its very existence, and without the power of enforcing its own laws, or of sustaining its treaty engagements, and an organized revolutionary army gallantly fighting for a more liberal and enlightened religious and political position." Marshall, of course, was offended by Perry's response, and he fumed away, penning a long reply to Perry, which Perry studiously ignored.[44]

Perry had had enough of Marshall and the China imbroglio, but he was not to escape unscathed. Within days of his planned departure on January fourteenth, Perry received two important communications. One, from the governor of the Dutch East Indies,

Perry had been expecting. The governor had been asked by the Japanese government to inform Perry that the emperor had died (really the shogun) and that his death and the succession of a new emperor, the period of mourning, the subsequent postponement of deliberations about the American president's letter, and the need for each governor to visit Edo in succession all would take "much time." Therefore the Japanese government was requesting that Perry not return to Edo Bay when he said he would.[45]

The second letter was much more disheartening. In it the secretary of the navy informed Perry that the president had appointed Robert McLane to replace Humphrey Marshall. Marshall had inspired a flood of antagonistic letters in the American press, and the Pierce administration, after consulting with R. B. Forbes, a Russell partner who had served as American consul in Canton, judged him too anti-British—or was it in reality too anti–opium trading and too anti–violations of the Treaty of Wanghia?—in his endeavors in China. McLane was instructed to seek a new, more liberal treaty and a fisheries agreement with the Chinese. Perry was to provide him with a steamer. There was more bad news: the steamers *Princeton, San Jacinto*, and *Alleghany* had turned out to be miserable failures, and the secretary was not going to dispatch any more ships for Perry's squadron.[46]

In Dobbin's letter and elsewhere Perry received fulsome praise from Washington. Marcy in his instructions to McLane referred to Perry as "that excellent officer."[47] Dobbin informed Perry that his mission had "attracted much admiration, and excited much expectation," and he complimented him for his resistance to Marshall's demands, thereby indirectly endorsing Perry's nonpolicy of "masterly inactivity." The department, Dobbin wrote, was gratified to learn that Perry had "avoided involving our government in the disturbances which agitate the people of China."

Still, Perry was sorely disappointed. Not only had his squadron been reduced from thirteen to ten, but he barely had enough men to sail those ships he had. And as for the steamers assigned, two of them, the *Susquehanna* and the *Powhatan*, were little better than "miserable abortions" in Perry's opinion. Perry, however, was characteristically uncowed even when it came to instructions from the State Department and orders from the secretary of the navy, which he described in his journal as "unexpected and annoying." Perry wrote a complaining letter to Dobbin, but he waited to send it until he had reached Naha on the way to Japan. He had decided to take all the steamers with him, including the *Susquehanna*, the steamer assigned to McLane, and then send her back to China for McLane's use when he arrived in the spring. After all, he had promised the Japanese that he would return with a larger force, and he could not back down on that promise. Further, for the first time, he called attention to his diplomatic status in the Far East. He was not just a naval officer in command of a squadron, and he hoped that his instructions put him on an equal footing with McLane. The date of his appointment gave him priority over McLane, and McLane, after all, was much younger and "far less experienced in the routine of public intercourse with foreign nations."[48]

A less determined man than Perry would have given in to the orders of his superiors, but not Perry. On January fourteenth, he gathered the three steamers and two supply ships at Hong Kong, and at half past ten the signal was set to get under way. The *Susquehanna* took the lead, followed by the *Powhatan* and the *Mississippi*, both towing supply ships. The line of smoke-belching steamers passed along the waterfront toward the Lymoon Passage. From the British warship *Winchester* a salute thundered up the sides of Mount Victoria, followed by the cheers of British sailors who had manned the yards. Perry and the squadron were under way, headed back to Okinawa and Japan.

12

TO
OUT-HEROD HEROD:
THE SECOND VISIT
TO JAPAN

This is really like opening the door and receiving robbers.[1]
—From the diary of KOGA KINICHIRO MASARU, Confucian scholar
who negotiated with the Russians at Nagasaki in January 1854

*Indeed, in conducting all my business with these very sagacious and
deceitful people, I have found it profitable to bring to my aid the
experience gained in former and by no means limited intercourse with
the inhabitants of strange lands—civilized and barbarian—and this
experience has admonished me that with people of forms it is necessary
either to set all ceremony aside, or to out-Herod Herod in assumed
personal consequence and ostentation.*[2]
—MATTHEW CALBRAITH PERRY in his *Journal*

*There will be no choice but to start trade with them.... The Americans
are short-tempered and violent, so although we are trying to reason
with them, they do not understand the ethics of humanity, justice,
loyalty, and filial piety.*[3]
—Report of the Japanese Negotiators to the Roju, February 24, 1854

*While Nagasaki has mattered only to merchants, this time they [the
Americans] have come to seize Japan. Therefore if we don't drive them
away now, the other foreign powers will follow. It is much more difficult
to defend against those foreigners than the one country which we are
dealing with now. In this respect now is the best time to drive away*

*[the Americans] because this will maintain the authority of the sei-i
[sei-i taishogun]. The other foreign powers will be frightened and will
decide not to come.*[4]   —TOKUGAWA NARIAKI, a memorandum

WELLS WILLIAMS, like Perry, had also been struck down by disease—"a low nervous fever which reduced me very much"—during the East India Squadron's layover in the Pearl River Delta. After two weeks in bed, Williams rallied, for which he blessed God, since he planned to return to Japan; that was where duty called him. His wife, Sarah, was ambivalent over Williams's departure. She thought that a change in climate would do wonders for his health, but she was not looking forward to a winter in Canton alone. "Things seem to be getting worse and worse," she wrote to her mother-in-law. When the imperial forces recaptured Amoy in November amid scenes of general slaughter, one of the missionary's houses was riddled with cannon shot while the missionary's wife was in labor.[5]

On January 14, 1854, Williams, equipped with crullers and a mince pie from Sarah, departed aboard the *Susquehanna* while his brother John embarked on the *Powhatan* as a telegraph operator. Williams was in a confident mood: "the time of God's working has come," he wrote to his missionary brother in the Middle East; "the utmost East can no longer be secluded, and seclude herself as she has done." Two centuries had passed since Japan closed itself off to "the devastating effects of Romanism and unscrupulous avarice. Now the signs indicate a breaking up of the indurated customs and seclusion of these suspicious races and the infusion of higher aims, purposes, knowledge and hopes, with perhaps dreadful revolution and bloodshed in their train."[6]

Williams took with him a new Chinese teacher, Luo Shen, who was a younger man than the poor addict who had died so dreadfully during the first voyage. Luo Shen, who was not an opium smoker, was also writing an account of the voyage, and he too felt that the portents were good for a successful expedition. On the second day out, he prayed for help and instruction and then looked up from the steamer's deck. In the clouds great cosmic forces swirled and turned, revealing themselves to the young Chinese teacher. "In the south," he wrote, "they assumed the form of a winged lion, springing up to the zenith, while those in the north were low and broken, like a slaughtered army. A few cloudlets seemed to have floated away from them towards the south, till they were arrested by the lion's breath, whose figure, moreover, continued to dilate, while the clouds in the north gradually disappeared altogether. After looking at these appearances, I said to my friend, 'the heavens prognosticate that our expedition will finally be successful, but difficulties will have to be overcome in the first.' 'Your words,' he said, 'are strange; let us wait for the event.' "[7]

Despite strong northerlies on the last days of the voyage, the six-day passage to Naha was uneventful. Arriving on January twenty-first, Perry found the *Vandalia, Macedonian,* and *Supply* in the harbor. Bernard Bettelheim soon was aboard to report that the Ryukyuan authorities appeared to be reconciled to Perry's demands and the presence of the American squadron. A delegation of officials sent by the Naha magistrate followed Bettelheim. They repaired to Captain Franklin Buchanan's cabin where, much to his annoyance, they remained for quite a while, reporting that the old regent was infirm but still living at Shuri Castle, that the new regent and chief magistrate were still in office, and that junks from Satsuma would begin arriving in March. Despite several days of gale force winds that hampered communications with the shore, Perry soon made his latest intentions known to the Okinawans. He sent Williams and a lieutenant ashore to inform the officials that he planned to undertake a three-day excursion around the island: they should prepare a cortege of coolies, chair bearers, and guides plus eight or ten horses. Along the way, Perry would visit Shuri Castle to see the regent.

Perry at first thought that there had been a marked change since his last visit to Okinawa. The spies had disappeared, the people appeared friendlier, and the women stayed at their stalls in the marketplace. The sailors from the ships that had been at Naha for weeks and even months off and on had made their accommodations with the shore. The islanders visited the ships almost every evening in their canoes to peddle their goods, and a ready supply of sake suddenly materialized aboard the ships, a fact testified to by the number of sailors clapped in irons for the offense of smuggling liquor aboard. Ashore small boys displayed their skill at counting in English and greeted the sailors with, "American, how do you do?"

Soon, however, Perry and the officials were at it again: quarreling over this and that as the Okinawans used what little resources they had in the way of passive resistance to obstruct the commodore's objectives. The Okinawans balked at the idea of a three-day excursion; they stalled when asked to prepare a bill for construction of the coal shed; they refused to supply samples of Japanese coins; and perhaps worst of all, the fishermen who worked the reefs ran away when Perry sent someone ashore to get some fresh fish for his breakfast. Luo Shen endorsed the American view of the Okinawans, according to Williams. They were crooked, nonsensical liars. Cane them, Luo Shen suggested. In his diary Luo Shen, without the need to please his employer, expressed a very different view of the Okinawans. "Their manners resemble those of the golden age in high antiquity," he wrote. Meanwhile Perry fussed and fumed, writing threatening letters to the regent.[8]

It was the marines who inadvertently stampeded the Okinawan officials into accepting Perry's demand. They went ashore one day to drill and were marching toward Shuri Castle accompanied by a throng of spectators when a very scared regent came running out to see what all the commotion was about. Williams quickly took advantage of the situation to inform Shang Hung-hsun that Perry would go to Shuri, objections or no, in two days. The Okinawans had little choice but to accept this latest affront, but they steadfastly refused to let Perry meet with the queen and the prince.

On February third, the Americans repeated the rituals of the summer before. A military parade, less elaborate but nonetheless featuring the portly commodore in his sedan chair carried by eight men, marched to Shuri Castle, where the commodore and his suite of officers were again entertained at a banquet at the regent's house. Perry really had little more that he wanted from the Okinawans. His real objective, he confided in his journal, was to accustom the Okinawans to the presence of Americans inside the castle walls.[9] There was little to quibble about except the matter of a set of Japanese coins. So the Americans sat back, relaxed, and enjoyed the repast and, on the way back, the panoramic view from the castle's hilltop.

While at Naha, Perry took time to answer the letter from the governor of the Dutch East Indies, relaying the Bakufu's request that Perry postpone his visit because of the death of the shogun. Perry's response was brusque. He thanked the governor for relaying the Bakufu's message but went on to say that the Japanese authorities understood the intentions of the American president well enough not to want to "throw any serious obstacles in the way of a friendly understanding between the two nations."[10]

By February seventh Perry was ready to depart. A week earlier he had sent the four sailing ships, *Lexington, Macedonian, Southampton*, and *Vandalia*, off to Edo. Coaling had been completed. The Okinawans had been presented with a barrel of whiskey, some flour, and a large supply of garden tools. In return, the Okinawans had provided more food than ever before. A young Okinawan, hoping for passage to America, smuggled himself aboard one of the ships and was sent ashore twice, since Perry preferred not to jeopardize his new relations with the Okinawans for the sake of a stowaway.

For Perry it only remained to settle the matter of the Japanese coins, for which he had given the Okinawans $49.24 in American coins. The Okinawan officials insisted that they could not meet Perry's demand since there were few Japanese coins on the island. Instead they returned the set of American coins. Perry, however, refused to accept them or even to meet the officials face-to-face. Wells Williams was incensed. He had spent less than a month with the commodore and was already growing impatient with his tactics. Perry, he wrote in his diary, was acting like "a disappointed child" over the coins. Perry, of course, had the final word. He steamed away, placing Okinawa, with two master's mates and fifteen sailors holding down the coal depot, under the surveillance of the American flag, pending the outcome of the negotiations in Japan—or instructions to the contrary from the Navy Department.[11]

The three American steamers departed Naha on February seventh. Perry had originally rushed the departure of the American squadron from Hong Kong because of his anxiety about the activities of the Russian fleet. As it turned out, his fears were well founded. Rebuffed by Perry in his efforts to organize a joint expedition, Admiral Putiatin had arrived in Nagasaki on January third, even before Perry left China. He departed a month later with little more than empty promises. After the usual squabbling over who would meet with whom and where, Putiatin finally met with Abe Masahiro's close advisors, Tsutsui Masanori and Kawaji Toshiakira, and two other officials. After several days of deliberations, interrupted by frequent and friendly banqueting, the Japanese promised that if trade was opened with any other foreign country, Japan would offer Russia the same concessions. Kawaji noted vaguely that since Russia was a neighbor, the Japanese considered Russia a defense against other countries. Putiatin, for his part, indicated that Russia was ready to come to Japan's assistance in the event of violent disturbances brought on by trading with the Western powers. And that was it: no treaty, no trade, no delineation of the boundary between Japan and Russia, and no agenda for future meetings. With Putiatin unwilling or unable—because of the impending war in the Crimea—to push as hard or as close to Edo as Perry, it was a fortuitous outcome for the strategy of "keep them hanging on."[12]

While Putiatin negotiated with Kawaji and company, Moryama Einosuke, the interpreter who had met with Commander James Glynn and befriended Ranald MacDonald while learning English from him, queried Ivan Goncharov, the Russian writer who was chronicling the expedition, as to Perry's whereabouts. Where had the Russians been? he asked Goncharov in English.

"In China," I said.—"What did you see?"—"A great deal . . ." "And what else?"—"Else . . . ?" I knew what he was after, and wanted to tease him.—"We saw Americans," I said.—"Whom did you see?" he eagerly interrupted.—"Commodore Perry . . ."—"Commodore Perry," he repeated even more anxiously.—"We didn't see him, but the captain of the American corvette *Saratog*! [sic]"—"*Saratoga*!" . . . "And where is Perry now? In the United States?" he asked, pushing his nose against my nose.—"No, not in the United States, but in Amoy." "In Amoy?"— "Or Ningpo."—"In Ningpo?"—"Or perhaps in Hong Kong," I remarked.[13]

Moryama learned little. Soon he, Kawaji, and Tsutsui were rushing back to Edo to ready themselves to deal with the elusive Perry.

For the four sailing ships under temporary command of Joel Abbot aboard the *Macedonian*, the passage to Edo Bay began as a lark. Although ordered to stay together, Abbot and Commander John Pope of the *Vandalia* were determined to test each other's mettle in a good old-fashioned sailing contest. They went at it in fits and starts, some days cautiously adding more sail during the day, then pouring it on under cover of darkness to the point where dawn often discovered one or the other sneaking off with all canvas billowing. At other times Abbot boldly challenged the *Vandalia*, luffing defiantly across her bow and signaling to make all possible sail. The *Vandalia*, though, was no match for the fleet-footed *Macedonian*. "She will wear [change tack by steering away from the wind] almost in the space of her length," Abbot wrote to his wife about the finest sailing ship in the U.S. Navy, "tack under almost any sailscud with ease and safety in furious gales and frightful seas— lay to like a duck—carries her heavy and powerful battery without complaining and as though her guns were only so many quills."[14] After hours of racing, the two leaders would have to trim back to allow the plodding *Lexington* and *Southampton* to catch up.

As the sailing ships approached the coast of Honshu, Japan's main island, cold, clammy fog lowered around them, and gale force head winds and sudden rain squalls interspersed with snow and sleet forced the ships to beat back and forth, slamming through one tack after another, just to gain a few miles. For a time the weather cleared, and the ships drifted with the tides under the lee of the land in a deep bay surrounded by high mountains, probably Suruga Bay to the west of the Izu Peninsula. Here the tides bore the *Macedonian* alarmingly close to the shore; her boat crews, singing a sea chanty, towed her out to sea again. Rounding the tip of the Izu Peninsula, the ships pounded on, often tacking every half hour as the squalls blew colder and colder, pelting the men with sleet and snow. In the clear patches they could see Mount Fuji mantled in snow standing above the clouds to the east and to the west the snow-capped volcano that formed the island of O-shima, smoke curling from its crater by day and fire glowing from the peak by night.

On February eleventh, Abbot judged the ships close enough to the entrance to the Uraga Channel to have the men summoned to battle stations and the guns shotted and run out for action. Soon, however, Abbot found that he was not sure where he was. The open body of water that he had taken to be the Uraga Channel was

The *Macedonian* aground in Odawara Bay; *Narrative of the Expedition*

turning into a closed bay. The chart Perry had given him, one that was drawn from a chart worked up by von Siebold, had put the sailing squadron twenty miles west of where they wanted to be. So Abbot ordered the helmsman to run off to the southwest. Suddenly with a sickening crunch, the *Macedonian* ran on a rock. Abbot quickly ordered the boats over the side to sound for deep water and then had an anchor and two kedges thrown over in an effort to winch the ship off the bottom. This failing, the crew began to horse the guns around the deck hoping to float her. Next sand, shot, coal, spare spars, anything that would lighten ship, were thrown over the side. All the while Abbot and his men worked in a cold sweat; it was a squally day, the barometer was falling, and at any moment the wind could blow up and smash his beautiful ship to kindling wood. Night fell and the men aboard the *Macedonian* worked on loading as much as they could into the boats and then preparing to heave the big guns over the side.

"O God," Abbot scrawled in his diary, "grant this favour I beseech thee for Christ sake and worthiness in his name. O God I ask it beseechingly!" Twice for a few moments the ship was afloat, but her stern continued to hang up on a rock as she thumped ominously on the bottom. In the morning a number of Japanese boats came alongside. Two officials clambered aboard, and one of them reported that the *Lexington* was already at anchor in Edo Bay. At two in the afternoon, the three steamers suddenly pulled into view. They had caught up with the sailing ships after riding out the worst part of the latest storm under the lee of O-shima. In no time two hawsers were run over from the *Mississippi*, and the *Macedonian* was pulled free of the rocks.[15]

The believers among the Japanese had claimed when the American squadron first appeared off Uraga the summer before that it would never enter Edo Bay because the gods would throw up a mighty sandbar between Kannonsaki and Futsusaki to barricade the way. Now, here was one of the American ships hard on the rocks off Kamakura, another anchored helplessly nearby. And times appeared propitious. It was the end of one era, Kaei, or Everlasting Happiness, and the beginning of another, Ansei, or Peaceful Politics. More than a week before the Americans' arrival the people of Japan had celebrated the beginning of the year of the tiger.

But this year, with talk of the return of the Americans rife and rumors that the Bakufu intended to deal with them peacefully, the celebrations had been hopeful, although nervously subdued. No one could say what the New Year would bring. Houses had been cleaned and decorated with pine branches and bamboo stalks. A sacred rope of straw woven with white pieces of paper hung over every doorway to ward off evil spirits and indicate that each house was the temporary abode of Toshigami, the god of the incoming year. On the eve of the last day of the year, people thronged the Buddhist temples at midnight to witness the 108 tollings of the temple bells, each sonorous ring dispelling another earthly desire for the year to come. In the remote and ethereal world of the imperial palace at Kyoto, the emperor rose at dawn on the first day of the year, the day of the new moon, to bow in the directions of the important Shinto shrines and the tombs of his ancestors and to offer prayers for the well-being of the nation. Throughout the Land of the Gods, New Year's Day was spent in quiet family gatherings where special noodles, rice cakes, and other delectables were eaten.

Despite the celebration, the new year brought little in the way of solace to the Bakufu officials in Edo beside the grounding of the *Macedonian*. For an era of Everlasting Happiness, the six years of Kaei had been a singularly unhappy period as foreign ship after foreign ship brought new demands upon the Bakufu, and the Bakufu could do little more than grope through contention and confusion for a way to meet these threats from abroad. Both Abe Masahiro and his close advisor Tokugawa Nariaki, after unprecedented consultation with all the lords of the land and leaders of the bureaucracy, were committed to Peaceful Politics for the new era, at least for now and at least as far as the foreigners were concerned.

Nariaki called his policy War at Home, Peace Abroad, and he was still committed to mobilizing the populace so that in the event that the naïve tactic of perpetual negotiations ("keep them hanging on") did not work, the people could be rallied to take back at some future date by force of arms what had to be given up for now at the bargaining table. Nariaki, however, was in a black mood. For twenty years he had been urging the Bakufu to prepare for this eventuality, he wrote to his youthful supporter, the twenty-six-year-old daimyo and clansman Matsudaira Echizen. They would not listen, and now it was too late. He was very regretful, but there was nothing they could do but try to delay the Americans.[16]

The first reports of the American ships had arrived in the cold and drafty offices of the Roju at Edo Castle on February eighth, eleven days after the celebration of the new year. They were brought by messengers who had gleaned their information from the few fishermen who were bold enough to brave the winter seas. The Bakufu officials knew full well that Perry would return to Uraga,

but they had not expected him so soon. Suddenly they were being
called upon to deal once again with the demands of the foreigners.
On February eleventh messengers reported that two sailing ships
were anchored north of Kannonsaki and inside Edo Bay while a
third was aground off Kamakura and a fourth was anchored nearby.
By the thirteenth, Perry had assembled his ships in the Uraga
Channel for a more decorous arrival. On a cool clear morning, the
three steamers, each towing a sailing ship, came surging up the
channel. The Americans were back, and as Perry had promised,
there were more ships than before, and they did not even bother to
stop at Uraga. Instead they steamed on into Edo Bay, pursued by
the guardboats from Uraga, and dropped anchor alongside the *Lexington* and the *Southampton* well north of Kannonsaki. Here was
Perry twenty-six miles south of the capital with seven ships, three of
them steamers, all of them powerfully armed, and 1,600 men.

There was no sense of panic as there had been the summer
before. The people near the coast were used to the sight of foreign
steamers and sailing vessels working their way up and down the
bay. Nevertheless troops again were mobilized, moving quickly to
their posts along the shore. At Uraga, Toda Izu, the resident governor, posted signs warning people that the penalty for approaching
the foreign ships was immediate arrest. He mobilized the local fire-
fighting units but urged the populace not to panic. Some overly
energetic firemen requested instructions about what to do in the
event of rioting. There were too many restless youth these days,
they explained. Would it be appropriate to kill them if they took
to the streets? To prevent the economic disruptions caused by the
Americans' first visit, signs were also posted barring shopkeepers
from arbitrarily raising prices.[17]

As soon as the American ships anchored, two guardboats
sculled rapidly up to the commodore's flagship. Perry, however,
had returned to his policy of self-isolation. He had little choice,
since he was again suffering from a painful attack of arthritis and
was confined to his cabin. So the boats were waved off and sent to
the *Powhatan*, where Captain Henry Adams allowed a heretofore
unfamiliar official named Kurokawa Kahei, two interpreters, and
three other officials to come aboard. After numerous polite inquiries
about Perry and the names of the various ships, the discussion

returned to the old path well worn the summer before. The Japanese officials insisted that the Americans should return to the anchorage off Uraga. Two officials appointed by the Bakufu to negotiate with Perry were stationed there and ready to meet with him. That was fine, Adams replied, but they intended to stay here. It was a safer anchorage, and they would be glad to meet the officials on the shore near their ships. If that was not acceptable to the Japanese, then they would simply move farther up the bay. Stuck in this familiar rut, the discussions ended.[18]

The Japanese, though, were in a friendly mood, particularly when offered their favorite beverage, sweetened whiskey. One even hinted that the negotiations would go to the Americans' liking. Where was the popular Kayama Eizaemon, the Americans asked over refreshments. He was ill, the Japanese responded, but would soon make an appearance. Toda Izu may have warned the populace about approaching the American ships, but in the days to come a shifting delegation of Japanese officials visited the *Powhatan* day after day seemingly for the sheer pleasure of coming aboard, often staying until they were escorted to the gangway. The pesky and intrusive interpreter Nakajima Saburonosuke returned and occupied himself making detailed drawings of the *Powhatan*'s great guns. Williams was greeted warmly by the Japanese interpreters, who had not expected to see him return to Edo Bay. One acquaintance showed him an illustrated book on weaponry, which appeared to have been put together on the basis of visits to the American ships the year before. Swords were compared, the engines and guns repeatedly inspected, autographs and name cards exchanged. The Japanese, however, only responded with laughter when it was suggested that they bring their wives aboard. Numerous gifts of food were brought for Perry as well as a collection of erotic woodcuts, no doubt for the commodore's personal edification. It was another proof of the lewdness of this exclusive people, Lieutenant George Preble of the *Macedonian* wrote to his wife. Preble had already been shocked by a woman who had raised her kimono and exposed herself to his boat crew when they were conducting a survey near the beach.[19]

The next day (February fourteenth) the Japanese delegation, led by Kurokawa Kahei, returned again. Kurokawa, Williams thought, was a higher-ranking official than Kayama, a fact denoted by his being attended by a young man who stood next to him at all times, holding Kurokawa's sword bolt upright. He was in fact a team leader from the Uraga *bugyo*'s office. The discussion again circled around the question of where the negotiations should take place. The Japanese suggested Kamakura, the ancient capital city of the Minamoto shoguns located on the western side of the Sagami Peninsula. Young Oliver Perry was dispatched to the *Susquehanna* to get his father's reply. Perry answered that he had no intention of moving, but that Adams could go ashore to discuss the matter with the high officials from Edo.

For a time the Japanese seemed alarmed. Had the Americans changed their attitude toward the Japanese? Adams reassured them that there had been no change in the commodore's attitude, but that it was customary to carry out diplomatic negotiations in the capital city. For this reason Perry should go to Edo to meet with the Japanese delegation. Perry could not be received in Edo, the Japanese replied. Furthermore, they hoped that Perry would not permit any further surveying of the bay nor allow anyone ashore. The survey boats were already out, but Adams said he would relay the Japanese request to Perry.

The tedious discussions about where to conduct the negotiations were complicated by Perry's confinement to his cabin aboard the *Susquehanna*. All the preparations had been carried out for transferring his pennant to the *Powhatan*, but Perry himself was too sick to move until February eighteenth. Meanwhile the daily talks went on without resolution until February twenty-first. Perry had seen Kamakura when the *Mississippi* went to the rescue of the *Macedonian*. It was no place to anchor his squadron. Moreover, he was concerned that the Japanese had some deceitful object in mind. It was important, he wrote in his journal, not to give in on any small matter lest he have to on a major issue. "Therefore it seemed to be the true policy to hold out at all hazards," he dictated in his journal, "and rather to establish for myself a character of unreasonable obstinacy than that of a yielding disposition." All of his previous diplomatic experiences, whether with barbarians or civilized people, had taught him that "with people of forms it is necessary either to set all ceremony aside, or to out-Herod Herod in

Kurokawa Kahei, interpreter; *Narrative of the Expedition*

assumed personal consequence and ostentation." He knew that he would be charged with arrogance, Perry wrote to Secretary of the Navy Dobbin, but he was "simply adhering to a course of policy determined on after mature reflection, and which had hitherto worked so well."[20]

On February twenty-first, Adams invited the Japanese officials to accompany him to Uraga aboard the *Vandalia* to meet the high official from Edo. Soon after getting under way, however, a strong gale blew up from the southwest, and the *Vandalia* was forced to anchor for the night under the lee of Kannonsaki. On the twenty-second, after the squadron had fired a deafening 21-gun salute in honor of Washington's birthday, Adams went ashore at Uraga with a delegation of fourteen officers and interpreters and was shown into a newly constructed wooden pavilion where he was met by a delegation of Japanese officials.

While the Japanese officials were making the long unpleasant winter run by boat back and forth from Uraga to the squadron's anchorage in an effort to get Perry to return to his original anchorage off the customs house, the Roju was making preparations for serious negotiations with the foreigners. To pursue the dilatory negotiating strategy agreed upon by Abe, Nariaki, and the Roju, the Roju on the very day that word of Perry's return reached Edo Castle appointed Hayashi Daigaku, the lord rector of the Bakufu's official university, to lead the delegation that would meet with Perry. Until the arrival of Perry, the Hayashis had been fierce adherents to the doctrine of expelling the foreigners. But Hayashi Daigaku had helped prepare a report for Abe that argued for permitting the Ryukyus to open trade with France through China, and Hayashi had clashed with Tokugawa Nariaki over the steps that should be taken when the Americans returned.

There was little love lost between Hayashi and Nariaki as it was. As the patron of the activist Mito school and the head of a family that had sponsored a rival history of the Bakufu, Nariaki was the Hayashis' foremost intellectual rival, a man whose ideas, the Hayashis felt, bordered on sedition. As for Nariaki, the worst that he could say was to call Hayashi "that old Buddhist," a term resonant with opprobrium when used by the dharma-hating Nariaki. Hayashi had opposed Nariaki's proposal to send a letter requesting Perry to postpone his return because of the shogun's death. Any attempt to discourage Perry, he argued (accurately, as it turned out), would simply goad him on.[21]

On February sixteenth, Hayashi and the three other members of his negotiating team were dispatched to Uraga. The team of commissioners included Ido Tsushima, one of the Uraga *bugyo*; Udono Minbu Shoyu, a *metsuke* (or censor) attached to the *kaibogakari*; and Izawa Mimasaka. Izawa, once the *bugyo* of Nagasaki, had only recently returned to favor with Abe Masahiro. He had led the attack on Takashima Shuhan, the noted weapons expert who languished in jail for years until released to work on the Shinagawa batteries, and had been removed from office when Abe came to power. Abe enjoined the commissioners to follow the proclamation read to the daimyo the year before, to act cautiously, and to make every effort not to disgrace the nation's honor. Abe's

Hayashi Daigaku, head of the negotiating commission; drawing by an unknown Japanese artist

instructions were vague, providing little in the way of useful guidelines for Hayashi. Tokugawa Nariaki could not resist a final barb as his archrival Hayashi prepared to leave. "What kind of magic do you have to negotiate with when we haven't decided how to carry out the discussions yet?" Nariaki asked.[22]

By this time Abe must have realized the fundamental inadequacies of a strategy that insisted on negotiating with no objective in mind, particularly when confronted with an opponent as determined as the American commodore. The very next day he and Nariaki met to discuss what directions the negotiations might take. Abe, as it turned out, was ready, even before the talks began, to make dramatic concessions. He would be willing to guarantee good treatment of shipwrecked sailors and to provide the Americans with a coaling station. The negotiators, he suggested, could offer the Ogasawara Islands (the very Bonin Islands where Perry had already acquired land for a coaling station). If the Americans would not accept that, he suggested Hachijoshima, an island prison colony 160 miles south of Edo. Nariaki was adamantly opposed to Abe's suggestion. If the negotiators refused all the Americans' demands, he insisted, the Americans would have no choice but to leave. Abe persisted, however, continuing to pressure Nariaki to accept the idea of meeting at least some of the American demands.[23]

Abe, too, seems not to have had all that much confidence in Hayashi's ability to resist the demands of the Americans. On February twentieth, the day before Hayashi was to meet with Adams, Abe ordered Egawa Tarozaemon, the respected *daikan*, or governor, of Nirayama who was supervising the construction of the coastal batteries at Shinagawa, to go to Uraga to persuade the Americans to depart. Abe suggested that he take Manjiro Nakajima with him as an advisor and translator. In the United States Manjiro was the best known of all Japanese and probably the only living Japanese that any Americans had ever heard of. A poor fisherman, he was blown out to sea during a storm in 1841 and picked up by an American whaling captain who took him to New Bedford. Here he became John Mung, the adopted son of a whaling captain and something of a celebrity. In 1851 he risked his life by returning to Japan via Okinawa. A ready and intelligent source of information about the affairs of the outside word and the United States in particular, he was found to be too valuable to imprison or execute; instead he soon developed friends and patrons in high places. Tokugawa Nariaki, however, was not one of them. He was suspicious of Manjiro and worried by Abe's orders to Egawa. Manjiro had been too close to the Americans and could not be relied upon in a tense situation. So Nariaki wrote to Egawa, countermanding Abe's order. Manjiro was not to meet the Americans or know anything about the Bakufu's negotiating strategy.[24]

On February twenty-second, the day appointed for Adams to go ashore at Uraga, three of the commissioners were waiting for him in the newly constructed pavilion. Hayashi decided not to attend, since Perry would not be there. To the amusement of the Japanese, the Americans seemed somewhat nervous in their presence, perhaps because the Japanese had surrounded the pavilion with a sturdy fence. At one point Izawa, who was an affable and friendly man and something of a clown, snapped his fan shut, and the Americans jumped back, putting their hands on their pistols. Despite this, the meeting was a pleasant one, but Perry had no intention of giving in to the Japanese request to meet at Uraga. Even the sudden reappearance of the affable and courteous Kayama on February twenty-third to make a personal appeal to Perry did

The American landing at Uraga, February 22, 1854;
Narrative of the Expedition

little to persuade the Americans. At least Kayama had not disemboweled himself, the usual American explanation for the absence of officials they had met in the past.

Perry's response to the impasse over the location of the talks was swift and predictable. On February twenty-fourth the squadron weighed anchor and moved up the bay, coming to rest off Kanagawa. The ships now lay halfway up the bay, and only fifteen miles south of Edo Castle. The survey boats, moreover, had been within four miles of Edo and had found six fathoms of water, which indicated that the squadron could easily approach the capital.

At Kanagawa, the American squadron was greeted by hordes of Japanese who, despite the threat of arrest, had come out in small boats to see the ships. An ugly scene quickly developed as the guardboats began driving the sightseers away. Perry was irate and was just about to send an order to the guardboats to stop or he would disperse them when the sightseers meekly withdrew.

Events were quickly spinning out of control. Both the commissioners and the Roju were on the verge of hysteria. The Roju knew full well that Perry was sounding the channel to Edo. Unsure of what to do next, the commissioners urged concessions. "There will be no choice left but to start trade with them," they reported to the Roju. The commissioners hoped to postpone the inevitable for as long as possible, but the Americans were short-tempered and violent. "Although we are trying to reason with them, they do not understand the ethics of humanity, justice, loyalty, and filial piety at all. They try to have their way by all means and seem to overwhelm us by force."[25]

Recognizing that the negotiations had been turned over to his enemies and that Abe Masahiro was leaning in the direction of concessions, Nariaki made a desperate bid to rally support at Edo Castle. Cut off from backing within the Roju and the most powerful niches of the bureaucracy, he turned to his allies in the *tomarizume*, a lesser chamber where the vassal daimyo with the longest ties to the Tokugawas held forth, most of them with little real influence. He begged them repeatedly to support his call for military action in the event that the Americans attempted to land at Shinagawa. "I insisted that if we drive them away, the other foreign powers would not come at all," Nariaki wrote later. "Yet Ii [Naosuke] argued that we would not be able to defeat them now. And all the *tomarizume* except Matsudaira Higo, who looked interested in my idea, tried to beg me not to implement my policy by touching their foreheads to the *totami* and this made Abe Masahiro decide to agree with them."[26]

Nariaki was opposed by the powerful and wealthy Ii Naosuke, who strongly supported the opening of trade. "If war broke out," Ii told Nariaki, "though you may be ready, we will not be able to send troops." Negotiations were yet to begin, and Nariaki was in danger of being isolated from the debate over how they would develop.[27]

While Nariaki fumed at his hunting lodge at Komagome, the

commissioners quickly sent a conciliatory letter to Perry. He was right in insisting on going up to Edo to be received according to the custom in Europe and Asia. But according to Japanese custom a reception hall had to be built and commissioners designated to treat with foreigners.[28] Kayama was dispatched to the flagship with a new ploy: offering supplies that could only be provided at Uraga. When Adams refused, Kayama turned to him suddenly and said, "Can you go ashore here this afternoon and pick out a suitable place?"

Surprised by this turn of events, Adams, Williams, and Captain Franklin Buchanan of the *Susquehanna* quickly went ashore with Kayama and picked a site for the new pavilion. It was a wheat field covered with winter stubble that lay near the beach on a flat expanse of land where the Tama River river emptied into the bay. Nearby was the small fishing village of Yokohama, made up of numerous thatch and mud and board houses, redolent with the smell of fresh night soil that was collected in large open vats that lined the waysides. When Kayama and the foreigners approached, the villagers fell to their knees, and Kayama brusquely indicated which houses would have to be demolished to accommodate the new reception hall. Kayama was so pleased that this matter had been settled that he presented Adams with his own collection of erotic woodcuts.

Perry's movement of the squadron had determined not only the location but also the direction of the negotiations. Two days after Kayama and Adams settled on a sight, the Roju sent a secret message to Hayashi and the commissioners. The negotiations should be conducted peacefully and the Americans' demands should be accepted. "Don't ask the Roju about the negotiations one by one [that is, as they proceed]," the message continued. "If you do, the Roju will have to consult the ex-chunagon [i.e., Nariaki]. Then peaceful negotiations will not be able to be carried out. . . . If you are accused of this [giving in to the Americans] later, the Roju will take responsibility for it."[29]

As there were no secrets in the Bakufu, at least within the walls of Edo Castle, Nariaki quickly found out about the covert instructions to the commissioners. Incensed, he demanded that the Roju recall Hayashi and Ido Iwami. In a sudden turnabout he then wrote to Abe Masahiro proposing to abandon the strategy of "keep them hanging on" in favor of a new strategy which he called "failing to catch both a fly and a bee." Instead of offering to lease a coal depot in the Bonin Islands or at Hachijoshima, the Bakufu should offer the Americans coal at Nagasaki, which they could obtain in three years. As for trade, the Bakufu should explain that in three years it was planning to conduct foreign trade in its own steamship. If the Americans did not accept the first offer, they might find the second acceptable. If they rejected both offers, they would fail to catch both a fly and a bee.[30]

Nariaki was playing a complicated game. Since Perry's first visit, he had believed that trade was inevitable, but, as he told Matsudaira Echizen, he had lived as the leader of the antiforeign element and planned to die as such. Having gotten nowhere even with his own supporters with his call to arms when Perry moved his squadron up the bay, Nariaki was now suggesting a conciliatory negotiating strategy in private correspondence with Abe. If Japan was forced to trade, he was arguing, she should control the trade herself.

At dawn on March second, Hayashi and Ido Tsushima returned to Edo for a meeting with Abe and the Roju. Hayashi explained that they faced an extremely difficult situation. The Americans were insisting on trade, and it was impossible to keep them waiting for three or four years without giving a specific answer. In addition, the Americans continued to say that they would go to Edo for talks. Once they did, even if the leaders of the government met with them but refused to open trade, they would resort to force. Disgusted, Nariaki wrote in his diary that the commissioners acted as if they had met with a group of tigers.[31]

With Hayashi back in Edo, pressure was building for concessions on the issue of trade. Nariaki's response was to feign a cold and retire to his hunting lodge. Dismayed, the Roju wavered. They were now looking for ways to appease the petulant Nariaki. On March third the Roju decided to hold the line on trade while offering to protect shipwrecked sailors and provide coal and water for foreign ships. Meanwhile Abe wrote Nariaki a conciliatory letter and dispatched an emissary to Nariaki's most influential advisor, Fujita Toko, to get him to persuade Nariaki to come back to Edo Castle.

The next day Nariaki returned to hear the Roju instruct the commissioners not to bend on the issue of trade.[32]

Having appeased Nariaki by a public display of support for his rejection of trade, Abe, at the request of Hayashi, wrote new, secret instructions for the commissioners. If pressed, they were to propose that trade begin in five years. If the Americans opposed this concession, they were to offer to begin trade in three years. The commissioners were also to offer to open Shimoda, an isolated port southeast of Edo on the Izu Peninsula, to trade if Perry found Nagasaki inconvenient. As for coal, the Americans could acquire supplies at Nagasaki for the next five years. They would decide on a coal depot after the alternatives were discussed. Finally, Japan would supply food, water, and firewood for American ships.[33]

Momentum in the negotiations now shifted to Yokohama where the nine American ships, including the recently arrived *Saratoga*, were anchored in a line, their guns covering the beach. While Japanese carpenters built a spacious reception hall and four other buildings out of rough pine boards, Kayama began to fish for an understanding of what Perry would ask for in the way of a treaty. He asked Adams how much coal would be needed by American steamers and what kind of supplies would be required by the squadron. Japan had a ready supply of coal, Kayama explained, but it was available only in Kyushu. Kayama was soon joined by Moryama Einosuke. Moryama had hurried back from Nagasaki and the negotiations with the Russians. He came aboard the flagship asking after Ranald MacDonald and James Glynn, the captain of the *Preble*.

With the negotiations about to begin, tensions mounted. Perry for one was still making threatening noises. The very day before negotiations began, Kayama and Moryama reported to the Roju that Perry had said he was ready to go to war if his proposals were rejected. In the event of war, he could call on fifty ships in nearby waters and fifty more in California to attack the Japanese.[34]

Abe Masahiro was also under pressure from a number of military commanders. During their surveys a number of Americans had gone ashore, and a number of Japanese commanders had requested permission to warn the Americans that they would be attacked. In a gloomy mood Abe restrained his commanders but

warned the daimyo in charge of defense and other defense officials
to be prepared for an American attack in the event of an impasse
at Yokohama. At the very least the negotiations could go on for
quite a while, and they could face a number of problems, including
the exhaustion of their troops and the need for farmers in coastal
areas to begin the planting season. Patrols along the shore should
be maintained day and night, but the commanders should find ways
to rest their men. In the event of an attack by the Americans, the
Roju was planning a quick assault with small ships.[35]

While the Japanese interpreters seemed to spend most of their
time visiting the flagship in search of liquid refreshment, Perry
and his staff worked on the draft of a treaty and an accompanying
letter. Williams found the letter to be "a specimen of diplomatic
special pleading and foreshortening quite refreshing to a beginner,
though what is said is well enough, the points which are untouched
being the completion of the whole subject." For the most part,
though, Williams was increasingly exasperated with Perry and his
officers. "I do not at all like the way in which this nation is spoken
of by the commodore and most of his officers," he wrote in his diary,
"calling them savages, liars, a pack of fools, poor devils; cursing
them and then denying practically all of it by supposing them worth
making a treaty with. Truly, what sort of instruments does God
work with!"[36]

While working on the draft of a treaty, Perry also found time
to attend to the problem of the near-loss of the *Macedonian*. He
wanted Abbot to delete all references in his report that might be
understood to implicate Perry because he had supplied Abbot with
inaccurate charts. Abbot did the best he could without rewriting
history. In his diary he made only one comment: "Selfish man!"[37]
It was at this time too that Perry had his officers introduce Sam
Patch (whose Japanese name was Sentaro), the sole remaining
member of the group of shipwrecked Japanese who had made their
way to China, to Kayama. It was a terrifying experience for Patch.
A peasant and a violator of the shogun's law, he fell to the deck
before the samurai and could not bring himself to look at or speak
to Kayama. Kayama played his part well, barely deigning to look
at the poor Patch.

*

March eighth, the day appointed for Perry to meet the commissioners, dawned bright and clear. Perry awoke to find that the
Japanese had curtained off the pathway from the beach to the
reception hall. Annoyed, Perry sent Adams and Williams ashore
to have the curtains removed. "Perry wants honor to be given in
his own style or not at all," Williams concluded.[38] Ashore Williams
found Nakajima flying about in a nervous state, barking orders in
a loud voice as he supervised last-minute preparations. He oblig-

The American landing at Yokohama, March 8, 1854;
Narrative of the Expedition

ingly had the curtains pulled down, providing a better view for
the large crowd of onlookers who had gathered to witness the spectacle. By previous agreement, at the reception hall the Japanese
mounted only a token guard armed with pikes, bows, and matchlocks, and these stood near the gaily bannered entrance. Perry
planned to go ashore with an escort of five hundred fully armed
men, including sailors and marines and three bands.

    At 11:30 A.M. the escort embarked in twenty-seven boats and
pulled up in two lines parallel to the beach. When the boats were
in position, the Commodore climbed into in his barge under a 17-

gun salute from the *Macedonian*. As Perry went ashore, the bands struck up "The Star-Spangled Banner," and Perry, followed by his officers and six black stewards at the rear, marched toward the reception hall between two lines of marines and soldiers. As Perry entered the reception hall, the boats, which had pulled back from the beach, fired a 21-gun salute in honor of the emperor and then a 17-gun salute in honor of Hayashi while a flag with the Tokugawa crest was run up the masthead of the *Powhatan*.

Hayashi and the commissioners, whose number had grown to five, had been waiting inside from an early hour. The reception hall, because of the chilly weather, was warmed by charcoal braziers and hung with paintings on cloth representing scenes from nature prominently featuring the crane, a symbol of peace. Hayashi and Perry exchanged greetings, and Perry explained that the cannon fire was a salute to the emperor and Hayashi. Moryama, who now assumed the role of principal interpreter as Kayama lingered around the edges of the discussions, introduced the commissioners. While refreshments were being served the commissioners left the room, as a way of insisting on their superiority by not eating with their uninvited guests.

After refreshments, Perry, his son, Adams, Williams, and A. L. C. Portman, the Dutch interpreter, moved to comfortable divans in an inner room where the commissioners sat on identical red divans facing them, Moryama kneeling at their feet. As soon as Perry and his suite were seated, Hayashi, a gravely dignified man, had Moryama hand over a scroll on which was written the reply to President Fillmore's letter. Perry perused the letter. It was impossible to respond at once to all the proposals made by the Americans, the letter signed by Moryama read, since "it is most positively forbidden by the laws of our imperial ancestors; but for us to continue attached to the ancient laws, seems to misunderstand the spirit of the age; however, we are governed now by imperative necessity."

Because of the death of the shogun and the accession of his son, there had been no time to settle other business thoroughly. The new shogun, however, had promised to observe the ancient laws, and for this reason, he could not change them. The Russian ambassador, the letter went on, had recently been at Nagasaki, but he had left without any answer to his requests. The Bakufu, however, understood the urgency of the American president's proposals. Therefore they were willing to save shipwrecked sailors and their vessels and to provide coal, wood, water, and provisions. They were also ready to prepare a harbor designated by the Americans for this purpose in five years. Meanwhile coal could be acquired at Nagasaki as of February 1855, if Perry would provide them with an estimate of American needs. The commissioners were also ready to provide whatever supplies they could for the squadron, the prices to be fixed by Moryama and Kurokawa Kahei. Having settled these points at this session, the letter concluded, they could sign a treaty at the next.[39]

In response Perry, who must have been stunned at the speed with which the commissioners got to the point, emphasized that the United States was seeking a treaty similar to the Treaty of Wanghia, which had opened four Chinese ports to trade with the Americans. With that, Perry handed over some notes on the importance of treaties in diplomatic relations and a letter to Hayashi that insisted on the friendliness of the United States' attitude toward Japan. Perry had withdrawn the summer before to permit sufficient time for the Japanese to consider the president's proposals. Now the president had sent three war steamers from the thousands that existed in the United States to Japan as proof of his friendly disposition as well as numerous "specimens of the most useful inventions of our country." It would be strange if Japan did not seize this opportunity to begin friendly intercourse with a people anxious to avoid future misunderstanding. Perry pointed out that China had profited enormously from its trade in tea and silk with the United States and that nearly thirty thousand Chinese had visited his country "where they have been kindly received, and permitted by the American laws to engage in whatever occupation best suited them." He did not dare return to the United States, Perry concluded, without a satisfactory response to all his proposals, "and I must remain until such are placed in my possession."[40]

An order had already been issued regarding fuel, water, and provisions for vessels in distress, Hayashi responded. They were also ready to provide coal, and there were laws already in existence that provided for the proper care of shipwrecked sailors, which

they were prepared to respect in the future. "We will assent, therefore, to two of these proposals," Hayashi concluded, "but the others,
regarding trade and so on, we cannot accept."[41]

Rather than respond, Perry turned quickly and unexpectedly
to another matter. Robert Williams, a marine aboard the *Mississippi*, had died two days earlier, and the Americans wished to bury
him. While on liberty Williams had been struck in the head by a
stone thrown by a Chinese man at Cum Sing Moon and had never
recovered. Perry wanted to purchase some land as a burial plot for
Williams and any others who might die during their stay. Caught
off guard, the commissioners withdrew to discuss Perry's proposal.
More refreshments were served. When the Americans protested that
it was customary in the United States for people to eat together as
a sign of friendship, two commissioners returned to join them. In
time Hayashi returned with a written response to Perry's request;
there was a temple set aside in Nagasaki for the burial of foreigners.
It would be best to take the body to Uraga. From there a Japanese
junk would take the body to Nagasaki during the appropriate
season.

But Perry persisted, proposing Natsushima Island, which the
Americans called Webster Island, since it was uninhabited. At that
very moment, in fact, a number of American sailors were ashore
on Natsushima looking for a possible burial site. The commissioners
in turn suggested a location at the foot of the Uraga lighthouse.
Uraga also would not do, said Perry. He was prepared to stay at
the reception house "for a year or two," however long it took to
settle the matter. Nettled, the commissioners gave in. They would
assign some ground in a temple yard near Yokohama for a burial
site. Perry expressed his gratitude profusely, to the point, thought
one Japanese in attendance, that he seemed on the verge of tears.[42]

While Perry and the commissioners talked, the sound of the
bands playing to entertain the onlookers filtered into the room.
Outside, the commodore's guard mingled with the crowd. Local
artists drew the Americans' portraits, paying particular attention
to their weapons while Wilhelm Heine and Eliphalet Brown worked
on their own renderings of the scene. "The only thing necessary to
make a good American portrait," Spalding wrote in his account of
the day, "was to draw a large nose, and sketch the balance of the

features around it."[43] Some of the friendlier villagers presented sprigs of japonica to the officers.

As Perry turned to the subject of shipwrecked sailors, his mood changed dramatically. In the United States, he explained, shipwrecked persons were rescued and treated with kindness. "I perceive," he went on, "no sign, however, that human life is counted in your country to be of great importance." The Japanese repelled foreigners with guns and treated shipwrecked sailors like slaves. "You thus seem to have no regard even for your own countrymen and to be exceedingly inhumane." He had reached this conclusion, he explained, because the Japanese refused to receive their own shipwrecked sailors when they wanted to return home.

Perry went on to say that his country had become "one of the great powers . . . our California faces Japan, the two being divided not by another country but by the Pacific Ocean." For this reason, the number of ships in Japanese waters was due to increase rapidly, and if the Japanese persisted in their harsh practices, the Americans would not overlook them. They were ready, in fact, to "exhaust our resources if necessary to wage war." They had recently gone to war in Mexico and had succeeded in capturing Mexico's capital city. "Circumstances," he warned, "may lead your country into a similar plight."

The discussions, despite Perry's protestations of friendliness and the Japanese willingness to accommodate Perry's demand for a burial site, were taking an unfriendly turn. If forced by circumstance, Hayashi responded, eyeing the dour-looking Commodore, the Japanese would also go to war. As for Perry's statements about Japan, they were simply not true since "many of your ideas have been created by mistaken reports." This was the natural result of the fact that Japan had no relations with other countries, Hayashi acknowledged. Japan, however, excelled "any country in the importance attached to human life." Japanese law prevented the construction of ships that could rescue vessels on the high seas, but foreign vessels in distress were provided with fuel and supplies.

As for the statement that shipwrecked persons were treated like slaves, that too was false. According to Japanese law, shipwrecked persons are to be treated kindly and sent to Nagasaki to be delivered to the Dutch captain to be returned to their homeland.

As for men like the crew of the *Lagoda,* which Hayashi knew Perry was about to come to, they are "not of good character: they violate our laws and do as they please. Such we are obliged to detain temporarily before sending them to Nagasaki; but it is the unlawful behaviour of persons of this character which alone brings such treatment."

Perry insisted that American ships had frequently met with refusals to supply them with fuel and provisions and for this reason he desired a decree that would describe the method of acquiring fuel, water, and provisions. He came next to the question of why the Japanese did not permit commerce. Commerce, he emphasized, was an exchange of what a country had for what it lacked and that it brought great profit and great wealth.

Japan had found that what it produced was sufficient for its own needs, Hayashi responded. If the commodore had come to Japan to have greater value placed on human life and to seek assistance for ships, Hayashi went on, "You have attained your purpose. Now, commerce has to do with profits, but has it anything to do with human life?"

Stymied by the clever Hayashi, Perry thought for some time and then replied, "You are right. As you say, I came because I valued human life, and the important thing is that you will give our vessels help. Commerce brings profit to a country, but it does not concern human life. I shall not insist upon it."

Hayashi, with great adroitness, had drawn a line in the sand that Perry chose not to cross. He accepted Hayashi's argument about the difference between profit and human life. After all, Perry was a naval officer, not a New York merchant. Moreover, he was more interested in steamship lines and strategic gains than in commercial profit. The opening of trade, however, was spelled out in the official orders for the expedition, and it was central to Perry's mission, at least in terms of how it was conceived by the foremost political advocates of American commercial interests, such as the late Daniel Webster. So in one more attempt to press the point, Perry fumbled in his pocket and then, after a moment of indecision, handed over a copy of the Treaty of Wanghia to Moryama, explaining what it was and expressing the hope that the commissioners would look it over. Still, Perry concluded, he would not continue in the pursuit of commerce.[44]

As the talks progressed, the shadows lengthened in the room. Three enervating hours had passed as the conversation flowed awkwardly through the two translators from Japanese to Dutch to English and back. With the discussions at an end for the day, Perry asked the commissioners to visit the flagship for a banquet once the weather improved. Then Hayashi withdrew so that, according to a Japanese account of the discussions, he could "indicate that his rank is higher than that of Perry and also to enable him, in the interests of the country, to maintain an attitude of reserve."[45] Perry went outside. After inspecting the sheds attached to the reception hall, he strode down the beach with the bands playing.

It had been seven months since Perry first came to Japan. Having finally met with those who had the power to discuss his demands, Perry found them "prepared to concede much more than was anticipated." As a result, he wrote in his journal, he planned to hold out for additional concessions in hope that "something still more advantageous might be gained." The Japanese, in fact, were almost too conciliatory for Perry. He had fixed on Natsushima Island as a burial site for the dead marine because, he confessed in his journal, he was "anxious for special reasons to acquire an interest in this island to subserve some ulterior objects." Perry never explained what those "ulterior objects" were, and the question of Natsushima never came up again during the negotiations. Had Perry picked on Natsushima as a site for a coal depot or other commercial installation within easy distance of Edo?[46]

The next day the funeral for the marine was held at a small temple near Yokohama. The proceedings were striking for the novelty of the scene. Crowds gathered to witness the procession, which passed to the beat of a muffled drum, through the village on its way to the temple on a wooded hillside. Among the stone idols and carved gravestones of the temple yard, Williams was laid to rest with the Reverend George Jones reading the service of the Episcopal church. Nearby on a mat sat a Buddhist priest, robed in saffron, his head shaved, an altar, burning incense, a gong, and some sake placed before him. When the marines fired a volley, the numerous people gathered around the temple exclaimed in pleasure. As the Americans withdrew, the priest solemnified the burial with his own quiet chanting.

Meanwhile, the Japanese and the Americans translated and then began a careful examination of the documents that they had ex-

Robert Williams's funeral procession;
drawing by an unknown Japanese artist

changed. At the same time Kurokawa and Moryama visited the flagship to settle a number of important points. After thanking Moryama personally for his work during the previous day's deliberations, Perry sent the Japanese officials over to the *Mississippi* to confer with Captain Adams. Arrangements were made for the delivery of provisions to the squadron. A day was set for Perry to respond to Hayashi's letter (March twelfth) and another for the presentation of the presents (March thirteenth). Adams used the opportunity to press Moryama and Kurokawa for information about the tenor of the discussions among the commissioners. He showed Moryama a map of Japan and asked him to indicate what ports might be opened. Perry, Adams explained, would never accept an arrangement like the one by which the Dutch were confined to Deshima Island in Nagasaki harbor. Neither official would respond, saying only that those were the questions being deliberated and that the Americans had to show patience with the Japanese who were faced with a very novel situation.

On March tenth, Williams began drafting Perry's reply to the Japanese. Williams was shocked to find that Perry was now ready to exceed the demand for the opening of one port that was contained in President Fillmore's letter. Perry wanted five ports opened and was proposing to threaten the Japanese with a larger force if they did not comply.

"Yet what an inconsistency is here exhibited," Williams wrote in his journal, "and what conclusion can they draw from it except that we have come on a predatory excursion? . . . Perry cares no more for right, for consistency, for his country, than will advance his own aggrandizement and fame, and makes his ambition the test of all his conduct towards the Japanese."

Williams acknowledged that great good would result if the Japanese, whether from fear, policy, or inclination to learn, accepted Perry's new demand. "Yet I despise such papers as this drawn up this day," he wrote, "and it may defeat its own object; it certainly has lowered the opinion I had of its author."

For Williams, the experience of working with Perry was increasingly upsetting. "I have had the chief management of their preparation," he wrote about the translation of the reply to the commissioners, "and the vexatious manner in which Perry can annoy those under him without himself caring for the perplexity he occasions makes me glad that I never was disciplined to the navy, where undistinguishing obedience is required." There was never any praise for a job well done, Williams complained, just plentiful scolding, which annulled all desires to please one's superior.[47]

Ashore at their headquarters in the Kanagawa post house, the commissioners sent a report to the Roju describing their talks with Perry. They said little about their exchange with the commodore concerning the value of human life and commercial profit. As for permitting an American to be buried on Japanese soil, Perry was so insistent that they had no choice but to give in.[48] Nor did the commissioners say anything about Captain Adams's visit to the shore on March eleventh. Adams brought a message from Perry saying that he was pleased that the Japanese government had decided to change its policies, but that the concessions offered were not enough. Adams went on to say that Perry was hoping for a quick conclusion to the negotiations and that he was planning to send a ship to the United States to report on the progress in the negotiations and to request more ships. The Japanese replied that they were not yet ready to respond to Perry's demands, but that they had no objection to Perry and the other officers visiting the shore. They did not want any sailors or marines to come ashore, however. The Japanese appeared uneasy. They were undoubtedly confused about where they stood since Perry had changed his demands and indicated that he was sending for more ships. They pressed Adams to know if the Americans were still friendly and were reassured that they were.[49]

In Edo pressure was mounting on Abe Masahiro to hold the line on the issue of trade. After rallying a number of antiforeign daimyos, Matsudaira Echizen, an ally of Nariaki's, visited Abe to suggest that he call a conference of daimyo to reject trade. The foreign ships, he told Abe, had neglected and insulted Japan's ancestral laws. For this reason he was in agony, grinding his teeth with indignation. Though the Americans were now peaceful, it was hard to know what they might do, since the Americans had already gone ashore in several places and fired blank shots. Soon they would be inside Shinagawa with their survey. Abe reassured the young Matsudaira that he would never permit trade. They had denied the Russian request; therefore they could not afford to give in to the Americans. In time Matsudaira, who was being secretly informed by Nariaki about the negotiations, figured out the details of what was going on. After this Abe Masahiro studiously avoided meeting with him.[50]

On March thirteenth, the day that had been chosen for the Americans to present their gifts, the weather became stormy, raining off and on in squalls. It was a good day, the Japanese told the embarrassed Americans, to lie with the women. Despite the rain a group of marines and sailors under Abbot's supervision quickly assembled the presents in the sheds attached to the reception hall. Though the commissioners themselves evinced little interest in the foreign-made goods, Abe Masahiro paid careful attention to his personal gifts. Among them were two illustrated accounts of the American defeat of Mexico, which detailed Perry's role as the com-

Delivery of the American presents; *Narrative of the Expedition*

mander of the American naval squadron and the seizure of vast amounts of Mexican territory.[51]

Simultaneously the Japanese began to provide much needed supplies for the squadron: eggs, fowl, fish, grains, some vegetables, and sweet potatoes. The crews of the ships were delighted to receive the new supplies not only for the change in diet but also for the diversion of regular contacts with the Japanese. Food had been rationed on all the ships for two weeks, and the men had been reduced to a diet of salt meats, a source of chronic indigestion. "We were undergoing all the annoyances of a state of siege, without any of its excitements," wrote young Spalding. The Americans found the Japanese to be a curious tribe, particularly interested in guns, their clothing, and above all their buttons. Buttons soon became a gift of great value. The Japanese asked the English name for every object in sight, Preble reported, "and so pick up a vocabulary of our language. They generally give us the Japanese name, but it sounds so barbarous to our ears, we are not at much trouble to remember it." The Americans, however, encountered one problem. It was almost impossible to find out anything about Japan, its people, customs, politics, as their visitors were forbidden to speak of these subjects.[52]

The first excursions ashore by American officers caused some additional problems. On the day that the presents were sent ashore, a very alarmed Japanese official came to the Americans and reported that an American had been discovered walking toward Edo. Perry immediately ordered the recall gun fired and sent written instructions that all men were to return to their ships. The rumor soon swept the squadron that negotiations were broken off and there would be a war to the knife. After a time a shamefaced E. C. Bittinger, the chaplain on the *Susquehanna*, returned to his ship and the unhappy prospect of facing the wrath of the commodore and the rest of the officers for threatening their new privileges.

March sixteenth proved to be too stormy for a renewal of the talks. The next day the commissioners sent a letter in Dutch requesting a day's delay. Again they emphasized that they were prepared to protect shipwrecked sailors and provide coal and supplies, but that there would be no trade similar to the United States' trade with China. If there was to be trade, they went on, it would have to begin in Nagasaki on a trial basis in a year. Then after five years a second port could be opened.[53]

On March seventeenth the commissioners came from Kanagawa in a splendid double-decked barge flying the American flag, a gesture that must have pleased Perry immensely. Ashore, after an exchange of pleasantries, Hayashi asked Perry if he was satisfied with the Japanese response to his proposals. Perry replied with a question of his own: were the Japanese ready to supply American ships that merely wanted to buy provisions as well as those that were in distress? No, Hayashi answered quickly, noting Perry's circuitous approach to the question of trade. They would supply ships in distress, but they would not *sell* supplies to American ships. Perry said that the Americans intended to pay for supplies, since that was the custom in any country. Hayashi replied that the gift of supplies required no reimbursement.

Perry then tried another tack: what if the Americans gave gifts in return for the supplies? If they were gifts, that would be acceptable, Hayashi responded. Perry had found the code for talking about trade without talking about trade. Would the Japanese,

Imperial barge at Yokohama; *Narrative of the Expedition*

he asked, prefer that the "gifts" be goods produced in the United States or gold and silver? Hayashi's response was that if they gave goods, it would resemble commerce. For this reason, the Americans could use gold and silver. Perry and Hayashi had now agreed that the gift of supplies would be reimbursed with gifts of money. In this game of semantics, Hayashi had gone as far as he could to keep trade from being part of the final agreement.

Perry next moved to his expanded agenda. Instead of supplying goods at Nagasaki, why not provide them at Yokohama and at five or six additional ports? Perry specifically suggested Uraga or Kagoshima, Matsumae on the northern island of Ezo (now known as Hokkaido), and Naha. In addition, American ships should be permitted to enter any harbor to procure supplies.

So *this* is what Perry meant by additional concessions! The Americans must not come to Yokohama, Hayashi replied. Naha was in a very distant country. Matsumae also was too distant and belonged to a daimyo over whom the government had limited control. Why not Nagasaki? Nagasaki, of course, was a red flag for Perry. It was "a most inconvenient place," a place where the inhabitants were so used to the servile behavior of the Dutch that they would demand similar behavior from the Americans. Serious consequences might follow.

When Hayashi suggested that it would take time to answer Perry's new request, even a return to Edo for consultation, Perry began to lose his patience. The designation of one port did not require time. As plenipotentiary, he (Perry) had the power to make these kinds of decisions at his own discretion; he could not believe that Hayashi did not have the same powers. "Please give me an answer at once," Perry insisted.

Hayashi too was becoming impatient. Perry was most unreasonable in his statements. If he had desired a particular port, he should have mentioned it. The president's letter had only mentioned a port in the South, and they had designated Nagasaki, thinking that would settle the matter. Hayashi demanded an explanation of Perry's haste in light of the fact that he had not mentioned the port in earlier letters. Perry, confronted by the fact that it was he who had changed the terms of the negotiations, backed down; the question of additional ports need not be answered immediately.

With Perry taking a somewhat more conciliatory tack, the commissioners suggested that Shimoda might be the appropriate port. It was agreed that if the Roju accepted this proposal after the commissioners had consulted with their superiors in Edo, Perry would send one or two ships there immediately and that they would be met by Japanese officials. They also agreed that since Shimoda did not meet the American demands for more than one port, another port would be designated, probably in the southern part of Japan. Then it was agreed that a final decision on the ports would be reached on March twenty-third after the commissioners had had time to consult with their superiors in Edo.

The other issues discussed caused somewhat less contention. After a discussion of shipwrecked sailors that grew heated when the question of repatriation at Nagasaki came up, it was agreed that they would be repatriated at whichever ports were open. It was also agreed that the question of products to be traded and other arrangements would be settled after a second port was opened.[54]

The change in Perry's demands and the commissioners' willingness to suggest that Shimoda should be one of the ports complicated the delicate relations between Abe Masahiro and Tokugawa Nariaki. The commissioners now had to face the wrath of Nariaki, who, thinking that Christians did not normally hold funeral services, was already upset by the burial of an American marine on sacred soil.[55] Two days after the meeting with Perry (March nineteenth), the commissioners left for Edo at dawn. They went directly to the castle, where they first reported to Abe Masahiro and then met the next day with Abe and Nariaki.

Before the meeting, Abe faced the unpleasant task of preparing Nariaki for the shocking news that the commissioners had made concessions that Abe had authorized behind Nariaki's back. Thus he showed him one of the commissioner's, Ido Iwami's, private appraisal of the talks. Surprisingly, Nariaki, who was usually well informed by his supporters about the inner workings of the Bakufu, had not heard about the secret instructions to the commissioners suggesting that they concede the opening of Shimoda and even trade if necessary. The commissioners, Ido wrote, had tried to delay a decision but had been forced to concede Shimoda.

There was one consolation, Ido reported: they would not have to decide on the matter of trade during this visit. They would, however, have to meet again with the Americans to finalize the agreement on the ports. The commissioners had little choice, Ido explained, for the Americans would have resorted to violence if they had not been answered immediately. The commissioners were extremely bitter about the concessions, he concluded, but if they had not taken resolute steps things would have turned out less peacefully.[56]

When the commissioners met with Abe and Nariaki on March

twentieth, Nariaki's mood veered dramatically: he was furious that the commissioners, apparently on their own initiative, had suggested opening the port of Shimoda. Unaware of Abe's role, Nariaki blamed Ido Iwami. It must have been a slip of the tongue or perhaps an unauthorized arbitrary proposal. Nariaki insisted that Ido be removed as a commissioner and replaced with Kawaji Toshiakira, Abe's trusted aide. But Abe and Hayashi worked on Nariaki, finally thinking they had convinced him that both Shimoda and Hakodate, a port on the northern island of Ezo, should be opened. Lied to, isolated, and outflanked, Nariaki appeared to accept the fait accompli handed to him by Abe and the commissioners.[57]

Further debate on the issue of the opening of at least Shimoda was immaterial. It was all but an accomplished fact, for on the very day that Nariaki was remonstrating with Hayashi and Ido, the *Vandalia* and the *Southampton* sailed down the bay on their way to Shimoda to look over the port.

Spring and warmth had come while Perry and the commissioners moved quickly toward an agreement. The winter stoves were taken down on the *Macedonian*. In his amblings around Yokohama Williams found wheat in abundance pushing up through the rich black soil, camellias and peach blossoms, and here and there violets making their first appearance. He was often followed by large crowds, and when he had a chance, he spoke of the Resurrection. He found that the numerous towns around Yokohama seemed to be poor: slightly built houses, with almost no domestic animals, and few utensils. But the people, though invariably dressed in blue cotton, some of their clothes quite ragged, seemed healthy and well fed. On the bay the squadron turned to boat racing as a way of keeping the men from chafing at the monotony of scraping, painting, and repairing and their enforced captivity aboard the ships.

Perry could only be pleased with the concessions that he had extracted from the Japanese. When Kayama came out to the flagship to inform him that Hakodate was the second port that would be opened, he now had, with Shimoda and his de facto occupation of Naha, "three very convenient places of resort and refreshment for our ships, nearly equidistant from each other and belonging to an empire from which our flag has hitherto been by law excluded. Peel Island, one of the Bonin Group, would make the fourth." Although Perry knew nothing about the topography of Japan or about its internal communications system, he concluded that Shimoda "could not be more desirable" as a stopping-off place for American ships plying between California and China and for the American whalers that cruised off the shores of Japan.[58] He had been told by the commissioners that it was a safe and accessible port convenient for obtaining supplies from the interior, and this pleased him as well. Hakodate was particularly convenient for American whalers that passed through the Tsugaru Strait from the Pacific to the Sea of Japan. Perry and his officers and interpreters had spent months smoothing the way for the final negotiations, particularly through the good offices of Kayama Eizaemon and Moryama Einosuke. But most of the details had been agreed on in two sessions that lasted less than ten hours.

The commissioners too had reasons to be pleased. They had been authorized to permit the beginning of trade, which they had done, in the limited sense of permitting the Americans to pay for supplies that would be acquired at the open ports. The commissioners acknowledged that they had taken "the desperate measure" of agreeing to sell necessities to the Americans "to avoid using the word trade."[59] But they had resisted pressure to sign a trade treaty that would permit the flow of foreign goods into their ports and Japanese goods out. Japan, so far, had escaped the fate of China and the humiliating treaties that followed the Opium War. Above all, she had avoided a war. There was another small victory involved in opening the port of Shimoda, which Perry was yet to see. But the commissioners were not pleased. They had been forced to cast aside the "ancestral laws" of exclusion. This was no light matter, and for this they apologized profusely to the Roju. Despite the almost universally friendly encounters the Americans experienced with Japanese of all classes, antiforeign sentiment was still rife, particularly among the group of powerful daimyo and intellectuals who looked to Nariaki as their leader and spokesman. Furthermore, these powerful figures felt deeply humiliated by the concessions to the barbarians, which Abe, with great deceit, had maneuvered Nariaki into accepting.

In the increasingly unstable world of Bakufu politics, it was best not to take too much credit for an agreement that would protect the empire for now from foreign attack but might in the future cost its supporters either their careers or their lives. In fact, Nariaki had already written secretly to Abe Masahiro suggesting that Hayashi and Ido Iwami be ordered to commit seppuku to demonstrate to the Americans that the Bakufu would not tolerate "careless" negotiating.[60]

After the last negotiating session, tension between the Americans and the Japanese declined appreciably, and relations entered a celebratory stage. Perry dispatched the *Susquehanna* to China to be used by the American commissioner, Robert McLane, and soon after Abe Masahiro ordered the daimyo who were guarding the coast, with the exception of those in charge of the defense of the Yokohama area, either to withdraw their troops or greatly reduce them. Crowds of officials came from Edo to see the presents. They were particularly fascinated by the telegraph and the small train with its fully finished interior including miniature benches and curtains. The Japanese rode the train sitting on top of the cars,

and it was quite a sight to see a two-sworded samurai, his robes flying behind him, an excited look in his eye, going around the circular track.

On March twenty-fourth, Perry was invited ashore so that the commissioners could present their gifts. The reception hall, decorated with pots of japonica in full flower, overflowed with goods. They were carefully arranged according to the rank of the recipient, wrapped, and stacked on the floor, tables, and even on the divans. The presents included silks, brocades, samples of lacquer ware, some adorned with gold, boxes, pipes, fans, writing tables, and porcelain, including pieces of remarkable lightness and transparency. After the presents were displayed, Perry and his suite were treated to an exhibition of sumo wrestling, the first wrestler coming forward so that Perry could punch him in the paunch. Then the sumo wrestlers put on a display of strength by carrying sacks of rice, some hoisting two over their heads, others holding them in their teeth, on their backs, and at arm's length. Two hundred sacks of rice were eventually presented to Perry. In return Perry had the marines perform a close order drill, and the commissioners spent time using the telegraph and admiring the train.

"It was a curious, barbaric spectacle, reminding one of the old

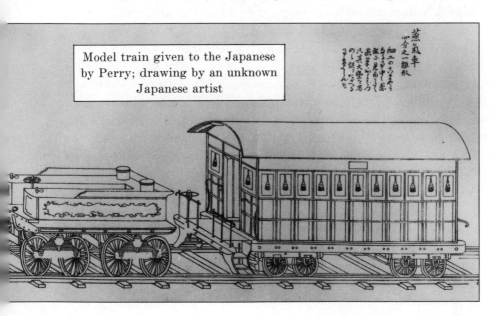

Model train given to the Japanese by Perry; drawing by an unknown Japanese artist

gladiators," Williams wrote in his diary about the lumbering and shouting sumo wrestling. "Indeed, there was a curious mélange today here, a function of east and west, railroads and telegraph, boxers and educated athlete, epaulettes and uniforms, shaven pates and night-gowns, soldiers with muskets and drilling in close array, soldiers with petticoats, sandals, two swords, and all in disorder, like a crowd—all these things, and many other things, exhibiting the difference between our civilization and usages and those of this secluded, pagan people." The American gifts showed "the success of science and enterprise" of "a higher civilization"; the Japanese entertainment was a "disgusting display" of "brute animal force" put on by a "partially enlightened people." As for the gifts, a number of Americans commented on their meagerness.[61]

Three days later, it was Perry's turn to entertain. On a rough day, the commissioners went first to the *Macedonian* to see the pride of the old sailing navy and then to the flagship. The five commissioners were dined in the commodore's cabin while a party of sixty ate at long tables on the deck. Toast after toast was drunk, the Japanese shouting out theirs at the top of their voices. Nakajima was at his most obstreperous, trying on an officer's cap and then inspecting himself in the mirror, calling out in a loud voice for the English names of various objects, and finally pouring himself a large glass of salad oil and drinking it down like wine. The commissioners were most impressed with four large cakes that bore their coats of arms. Whatever food was left over was carefully wrapped and stowed inside their kimonos. After dinner, the minstrels performed. As he prepared to leave, one of the commissioners, in a jovial mood after consuming whiskey punch, madeira, and champagne, threw his arm around Perry's shoulder and leaned his head affectionately on his epaulette, repeating again and again, "Nippon and America, all the same heart." "Oh, if he will only sign the treaty," Perry responded, "he may kiss me."

As the day of the treaty signing approached, there were still a number of points of conflict: the exact date of the opening of the ports, whether the Japanese would accept consuls, whether the Americans would be allowed ashore, and if so, where they could go. The Japanese were particularly resistant to the idea of any kind of permanent residence on Japanese soil. They also appeared apprehensive about Perry visiting Hakodate before they had had an opportunity to notify the local daimyo. Perry as usual insisted that he would go as soon as possible.[62]

After two long sessions to work out these details, Perry went ashore on March thirty-first, bringing copies of the treaty in Dutch, Chinese, and English. The commissioners brought copies in Dutch, Chinese, and Japanese. Both parties compared respective versions in Dutch and Chinese. Then a problem arose over whether to date

Dinner given for Japanese commissioners aboard the *Powhatan*;
Narrative of the Expedition

them according to the Western or Japanese calendar. Finally the signing began, but the commissioners balked once more when they saw the words "in the year of our Lord Jesus Christ." After the offending words were struck out of all but the English version, Perry and the commissioners signed the treaty.

Perry was in a gracious mood. He had not understood how strict the laws were in Japan before he came, he explained. He went on to apologize for any problems that he may have caused and to offer guns and warships if the Japanese should have to go to war. Dinner followed—a splendid repast of raw oysters, mushroom soup, boiled pears, eggs boiled, pressed, and cut in strips, seaweed cooked with sugar, boiled bream, crawfish, shrimp, greens, yams, fish soup, taro, boiled chestnuts, raw ginger, walnuts, mushrooms, and sponge cake, all washed down with tea and sake. After dinner, Perry brought up the possibility of visiting Edo. Hayashi asked him not to, as a personal favor, but Perry replied that he must. The Bakufu was determined, Hayashi explained, never to open the port of Edo or the bay to foreign shipping. With that the commissioners and Perry and his suite exchanged farewells.[63]

The treaty was an accord of peace and friendship. (See Appendix 1.) Shimoda was opened for the purchase of supplies as of the signing of the treaty. Hakodate was to be opened a year after the signing. No other ports were to be entered except by ships in distress. Shipwrecked sailors were not to be confined in Japan and were to be taken to either of the ports for repatriation. Supplies were to be procured only through the agency of Japanese officials. An American consul could be appointed to reside at Shimoda within eighteen months after the signing of the treaty. Finally, a most favored nation clause, providing that any rights granted to other nations would be granted to the United States, was added at Williams's suggestion.

On April fourth, the *Saratoga* sailed for home with the treaty, which was bound for Washington and the Senate. The bands played "Home Sweet Home" and many a sailor wept, reported Williams. It was time for farewells. Kayama and Nakajima were already gone, having returned to their posts at Uraga. One of the interpreters wrote a poignant note to Williams. "In the vast expanse of the world's extent, are not all the tender children of the Heavenly Ruler? Among them, courtesy, good faith, kindness, and justice ought to rule as they do among brothers; but if, covetous of gain, things are carried to an extreme, all ought to be ashamed of it and not speak thereof; yet to discourse of warlike affairs and the necessary modes of commotion, slaughter and battle is not unworthy of continual talk and research." It was a hint, Williams thought, that at the negotiations the Americans were "rather quiddling."[64]

Perry, however, was determined to visit Edo. Hayashi had begged him not to, saying that he would be embarrassed before his government. For his own part, Perry responded that he would be embarrassed before his own government if he did not. He finally agreed that viewing the city from the deck of his ship would suffice.[65] On April tenth Moryama and a group of officials, seeing that the flagship was getting under way, came aboard. Finding that Perry was planning to sail toward Edo, they again pleaded with him not to. Perry urged them not to be concerned; they could come with him and see that he would only approach the city and then turn around. When the ships passed Kanagawa, no salutes were fired,

Japanese view of the American squadron at Yokohama

to the relief of the Japanese, lessening the likelihood of panic in Edo. Moryama had decided that if the guns were loaded, he would place himself in front of one of them. One of the interpreters was so nervous that he was on the verge of becoming physically sick when Perry called to Moryama and asked him if the lighthouse he could see was in Edo. It was, Moryama replied, and the masts ahead were boats in the harbor. "How clearly Edo can be seen!" Perry exclaimed, scanning the outlines of the city, including Edo Castle, and pointing it out to his officers. With that Perry turned the ships about and headed back down the bay.

Telling Moryama that he and the Japanese officials could now leave, Perry explained that he had been forced to make this last trip because he had been ordered to do so by his government and was accompanied by a number of officers who did not agree with him. For that reason he had no choice but to go to Edo.[66] Having seen the city, Perry was privately convinced that if he had had to, he could have destroyed it with his cannon fire. Perry then said good-bye to the interpreters, thanking them profusely with great politeness and sending his regards to Hayashi and the other commissioners. "As one of the officers said," Wells Williams wrote in disgust, "it should have been on the First of April instead of the Tenth, to make such a humbug appropriate. I have upheld and approved the Commodore's acts in most cases, where others have sharply ridiculed them, but this day's work was small enough. I have now been three times bound for Yedo, approaching nearer each time, and perhaps the fourth trial will land me there or at least near enough to see it."[67]

In ones and twos the remaining American ships began to take their departure, with the *Macedonian* leaving on April eleventh and the flagship on the fourteenth. "It is often said and written by me," Perry concluded, "that this force was quite sufficient for all purposes of defense, and for the chastisement of insult, but not large enough to make any great moral impression, especially after the ostentatious display at home of the intentions of the government with respect to the Japan expedition. I claim the greater credit, however, in effecting more than the government anticipated, with the reduced means placed at my disposal, and under all the discouraging circumstances under which I labored."[68]

In their final report to the Roju, the commissioners noted that Perry had presented them with the draft of a treaty urging them to accept it in toto, but that they had "succeeded in modifying this and reducing it." In a number of ways, they insisted, they had acted to maintain national honor. They had kept Perry from going to Edo. They had forced him to agree not to survey Edo Bay. Further, the treaty was signed by the four commissioners and was not an official document from the Roju, and thus they had refused to seal their copy of the treaty jointly with Perry.[69]

It was true that the commissioners had held the line on trade. It was also true that Perry had not gone to Edo, but he had been surveying Edo Bay without interference and in full view of numerous Japanese ever since his arrival. As for the other triumphs claimed by the commissioners, they were little more than trivial. They had signed a treaty with a foreign power, and this was just the beginning of a new and turbulent era in the Land of the Gods.

13

TESTING THE
TREATY

*With regard to women and sake, as you know, they [Americans] are
ill-mannered foreigners. In this place, there are women who look like
despicable, illegal prostitutes and many other women. Although we
may be able to restrain them, when the foreigners walk by they may
come out to see them unscrupulously. If a large number of [the for-
eigners] come ashore, we may hardly be able to watch them. In that
case it will not be unlikely that some inconvenient things may happen.*[1]

—KUROKAWA KAHEI'S instruction to his guards
at Shimoda, June 1854

*If there is anything which has rendered the expedition to Japan pleas-
ant to me, it is the walks in search of flowers and the greater freedom
of intercourse with the people thereby obtained.*[2]

—S. WELLS WILLIAMS, *Journal*, June 22, 1854

*So the following compact was agreed to, very much on the part of the
effeminate islanders, like the compact of the poor chicken with the
horse in the stable: that if he [the horse] didn't tread on [the chicken's]
toes, [the chicken] wouldn't tread on his . . .*[3]

—J. W. SPALDING on the United States–Ryukyus Treaty

AS RECRIMINATIONS OVER THE TREATY grew in Edo, Perry set out
for Shimoda to test its limits. Shimoda was a major port of refuge
for Japanese coastal traders moving between the rice port of Osaka
and the warehouses of Edo. It had once been a boom town, first
during a gold strike, then when Tokugawa Ieyasu opened quarries
in the nearby mountains to carve out the immense stones that went

into building the moat for Edo Castle. Among other things, Shimoda was known for its inns and its women of easy virtue. There was a song:

> In Shimoda of Izu
> You need no anchor:
> The samisen of the geisha
> Can tie up your ship.[4]

Shimoda lay at the head of a narrow, mushroom-shaped bay in the shadow of Mount Buzan with double peaks known as "the breasts." It was a tight little harbor nestled along the mountainous coast of the Izu Peninsula and sheltered from all directions save the southwest. The craggy Izu Peninsula was only thinly populated, and it was a walk of four to five days from Edo to Shimoda, often over trails that were little more than stairs cut in the mountainsides.

With the opening of Shimoda, the commissioners had achieved a minor coup. They had succeeded in confining foreign ships to a small harbor that appeared to be close to but was well cut off from Edo. In fact, there had been a debate over Shimoda's isolation before the port was suggested. Some Bakufu officials advocated opening a port closer to the capital city, such as Yokohama, so that the foreigners could be kept under close surveillance. The idea of Shimoda seems to have originated with Egawa Tarozaemon. As governor of Nirayama, Shimoda was within his jurisdiction. Some, such as Sakuma Shozan, his former pupil, suggested that Egawa's motives were less than noble. It was an attempt by Egawa, Sakuma wrote later, to monopolize access to the learning and technology of the West. "This is nothing but a vicious private scheme," he went on. "It is deplorable that by and large in those days scholars of Dutch studies, though they were to pass their new knowledge on to the people, tended to call even trifling things their secrets so as to boast about their own schools."[5]

Whatever the case, Kurokawa Kahei and Moryama Einosuke hurried over the mountain trails while Izawa Mimasaka, the former *bugyo* of Nagasaki, who had served on the commission, was dispatched with another official to reopen the *bugyo*'s office in Shimoda. Kurokawa issued orders that the doors to people's houses were to be kept closed, spectators were to be kept back, and women, sake, and cows were to be kept hidden from the carnivorous, thirsty, and undoubtedly sex-starved Americans.[6]

For the American steamers it was a short voyage on a hazy spring day, April eighteenth, from Yokohama to Shimoda, where they were greeted by large crowds lining the bluffs of the headlands as they entered the harbor. Williams noted the remarkable terracing of the rice paddies along the eastern shore of the Izu Peninsula, ranging up fifty tiers in one place. He found the harbor, which was about half a mile wide and almost one mile deep, quite picturesque: well protected by high bluffs, palm trees, and bamboo groves along the shoreline with its white beaches, dramatic cone-shaped peaks behind the village, then higher crags running up to the rocky spine of the Amagi Mountains. Shimoda and the smaller village of Kakisaki lay at the head of the harbor, Shimoda at the convergence of two well-cultivated valleys. It was a village of about a thousand houses laid out in neat, half-paved, half-macadamized streets with gates at either end. Many of its houses were faced with a distinctive blue-black tile, banded with white laths in a diamond pattern. Shimoda showed an advanced state of civilization, Perry concluded, "much beyond our own boasted progress in the attention of its constructors to the cleanliness and healthfulness of the place. There are not only gutters, but sewers, which drain the refuse water and filth directly into the sea or the small stream which divides the town."[7] Perry had sent the sailing ships ahead one at a time to permit a thorough survey of the harbor and its approaches. This proved to be a wise decision, for the *Southampton* found a large rock covered by only twelve feet of water at low tide right in the middle of the channel.

Perry's first order of business after being greeted by the officials from Edo was to send Williams and Portman ashore with a long list of provisions needed by the squadron. Most of these items could not be supplied at an out-of-the-way place like Shimoda. Two days later Perry went ashore and was entertained at the Ryosenji Temple, where he was waited on by three well-known geisha, one of whom called herself Cow, another Horse.[8] Soon after, Perry issued an order permitting all the officers to go ashore.

Williams and Dr. James Morrow, the expedition's agronomist,

set off to explore the countryside and look for wild flowers. They were followed by a single officer, but in other parts of the town groups of armed men followed the American officers, pushing back crowds and forcing shopkeepers to close their doors. It was a replay of their reception on Okinawa, and Perry was not pleased.

But before Perry could confront Kurokawa and Moryama about the surveillance, he was presented with quite another problem. During the night of April twenty-fourth, a cry of "Merikan, Merikan" was heard from the water alongside the *Mississippi*. The cry came from two Japanese men in a small boat trying to hand a letter up the gangway. The Japanese were waved off and directed toward the flagship, where they floundered up the ladder bedraggled and half-naked. The Americans were confronted with two young men, Yoshida Shoin and Kaneko Shigenosuke. The two men, sometime students of the Dutch scholar Sakuma Shozan, were determined to broaden their knowledge of the world by returning with Perry to America. Yoshida was by far the more interesting of the two. Born to a low-ranking samurai, he was adopted into a scholarly family in Choshu. Precocious, untidy, and awkward, he was lecturing his daimyo on the writings of the great Chinese military theorist Sun Tzu at the age of eleven. He went to Nagasaki for a while to study Dutch and observe the foreigners, but then made his way to Edo to join the throngs of earnest young intellectuals who were debating the impact of the black ships on the future of their country. He studied for a while under Sakuma and then traveled some more, this time without a passport, which led to the loss of his samurai rank and stipend, something which Yoshida regarded as a mark of distinction rather than a source of shame.[9]

When Perry came to Yokohama, Yoshida like many of his peers was drawn to the site of the negotiations. He had hoped to get aboard the Americans ships there, but he could not. Thus he and his friend walked to Shimoda, where they thrust a letter into young J. W. Spalding's jacket when he was ashore. They then stole a boat, and after one abortive attempt ended up on the flagship's deck at three o'clock in the morning. They were scholars, their note read, ashamed to come before distinguished persons; ignorant of arms and their use in battle, the rules of strategy and discipline, they knew nothing. They wished to travel the five continents, but they were prevented from doing so by the laws of their country. They had seen the American ships "come riding on the high winds and careering over the waves with lightning speed, coasting along the five continents" and hoped that Perry, since they faced the "extremest penalty," would consent to hide them and take them away with him.[10]

Perry was impressed with the sincerity of the two young men. But he had just signed a treaty with the Japanese and could not take them with him without violating at least the spirit of that document. Perry promised, however, that he would say nothing about their request. He ordered them put ashore well away from the two villages and instructed the boat crew to try to find their boat, which had gotten away when they boarded the flagship. The next day a Japanese guardboat found the stolen boat drifting in the harbor; aboard were the two fugitives' clothes, swords, and a farewell poem Yoshida had addressed to Sakuma Shozan. Having recovered the boat, Moryama went out to the flagship where he made repeated and pointed inquiries, but was told nothing about what had transpired.

Meanwhile, Yoshida and Shigenosuke, dispirited by the failure of their plans and aware that the stolen boat would be found, turned themselves over to the authorities. Several days later, some American officers saw them confined in a cage behind barracks in the back of town. Perry pleaded for their lenient treatment. But the two men were quickly sent back to Edo, where Sakuma Shozan had already been arrested, and from there to their respective domains. Prison was a brutal affair, and Shigenosuke died after only three months of captivity. Yoshida, after a time, was removed from prison to house arrest and then was freed altogether. He established a village school but turned eventually to plotting against the Bakufu. A man of many contradictions, he burned with a desire to assassinate the official who had gone to Kyoto to persuade the imperial court to accept a commercial treaty with the United States. His indiscretions and inept bungling, however, cost him his life. He was beheaded at Edo in 1859 but soon became a national hero for his efforts in breaking through the barriers established by the Bakufu to human knowledge.[11]

As there was little that Perry could do about Yoshida Shoin

and Shigenosuke Kaneko, he turned instead to applying some well-placed threats to the problem of surveillance ashore. He would take armed men ashore and seize those who followed him and then sail back to Edo, he told Kurokawa, if the practice was not ended. Kurokawa's response was exactly what Perry did not want to hear: the Dutch at Nagasaki were always followed by Japanese soldiers. That might be the case, Perry replied, but the Americans had just signed a treaty with the Japanese that guaranteed free intercourse, and he would not tolerate this kind of treatment. Kurokawa apologized, saying that he had left Yokohama before the treaty was signed. For now, he would permit houses to be opened, and the guards would be withdrawn. But he would have to refer the matter to Edo before making a final decision.[12]

Perry had other demands too. He needed a place for his use when he was ashore. He was not satisfied with the exchange rate which the Japanese officials used to determine the value of American money, and though the treaty stipulated that the Americans could buy supplies from the Japanese officials, Perry wanted his officers to be able to purchase goods from local shopkeepers.[13] Trade was in the wings, ready to make its appearance in a new costume.

The Japanese officials appeared flexible. They assigned the guest house at the tree-shaded Ryosenji Temple in a quiet corner of the village for Perry's use. For actual trade, they substituted an awkward arrangement whereby the American officers could designate items that they wished to purchase, and the interpreters would supervise the exchange of money and their delivery to the ships. It was hardly a satisfactory arrangement, however, since Americans calculated that they were paying prices inflated by 200 to 300 percent. When twenty-one-year-old G. W. Parish fell to his death from the topsail yard, the Japanese arranged for a new burial site at the Gyokusenji Temple in Kakisaki. "Here surrounded by Japanese," Williams wrote in his diary, "lies the body of poor Parish who had run away from his parents in Hebron, Connecticut, and had given them no notice of his course since, an instructive commentary on the rashness of disobedience to parents." Robert Williams, the young marine buried in Yokohama, was soon moved to a grave alongside Parish's.[14]

As for the surveillance, it subsided only temporarily. In a short time, the officers again noted that they were being followed and watched carefully. Inevitably there was an incident that brought the issue to a head a second time. Three officers, after spending a day shooting birds, decided to spend the night at one of the nine Buddhist temples that surrounded the village. They informed one of the translators, Tatnosuke Hori, so that he would not become alarmed. He offered no objections at first, but when the men were bedding down for the night, Tatnosuke, a little tipsy from drinking, burst in with a group of armed men and ordered the three Americans back to the ships. When the Americans indicated that they had little intention of leaving, Tatnosuke left, eventually arriving at the flagship some time after midnight to demand that Perry call the men back to the ship. Meanwhile the remaining Japanese soldiers became belligerent, finally pulling on the Americans' feet to get them to get up and leave. With that the Americans kicked over their lanterns, pulled their pistols, and cocked them. The Japanese quickly left.

The next day, Perry, undoubtedly in a foul mood after being awakened in the middle of the night, resurrected the marines yet again, telling Kurokawa that if he did not apologize, he was going to send a troop ashore to arrest the Japanese soldiers. After a long palaver touching upon interpretations of the treaty and the need to consult the commissioners, Kurokawa backed down, disavowing the actions of his subordinates.[15]

There were other matters less susceptible to open diplomacy. Shimoda was a sailors' town, offering all the amenities so desired by sailors who had been away for a long time at sea. Kurokawa had anticipated what might happen when the Americans came ashore. "With regard to women and sake, as you know, they are ill-mannered foreigners," he warned his men. "In this place, there are women who look like despicable, illegal prostitutes and many other women. Although we may be able to restrain them, when the foreigners walk by they may come out to see them unscrupulously. If a large number of [the foreigners] come ashore, we may hardly be able to watch them. In that case it will not be unlikely that some inconvenient things may happen."[16]

Naturally curious and mostly young and exuberant, the American officers had an eye for "inconvenient things." One principal form of entertainment was visiting the public baths where men, women, and children congregated freely and quite naked. The bathers greeted the prurient Americans warmly, laughing and pointing, according to Preble, at that which "every other human I have ever heard of, savage or civilized, seeks to conceal." Having witnessed this spectacle, Williams, the anxious Puritan, judged Japan the most lewd of all the heathen nations. Women thought nothing of exposing both their knees and their breasts while both men and women were on occasion seen naked on the streets.[17]

Japanese woman at Shimoda;
Narrative of the Expedition

William Speiden, the son of the purser on the *Mississippi*, and his friends were interested in more than watching naked bathers. They wanted to meet the women of Shimoda. They followed a pretty young woman, who turned to see if they were coming, down a side street. She led them to a house where there were five other women. Expecting the women to flee, they were surprised when they were instead invited in. Fumbling for some means of communication, they took out their watches to show to the women. One of the men, who was fond of jewelry, removed his breast pin and a number of rings and tried them on one of the women. She was evidently pleased. After a time, they parted, bowing and shaking hands.[18]

Not all the encounters between the officers and the women of Shimoda were quite so innocent, at least according to an anonymous haiku poet who lived in Shimoda. The Americans, he claimed, submitted a petition to the authorities asking to patronize the local houses of prostitution. The authorities granted them permission and notified the brothel keepers, who were delighted. But the prostitutes, once they heard about their new customers, pleaded with their masters, "We are, to be sure, ill fated, engaged thus in an ignoble profession. Nevertheless, we have never made any contract saying we should go so far as to sleep with foreigners!" The brothel keepers were forced to report the prostitutes' response to the Americans. The Americans, the poet wrote, were like men "returning empty handed from a mountain loaded with treasure." One American came up with a suggestion: they did not have to sleep with the women. They only wanted to drink with them. The prostitutes accepted this arrangement, but one of the Americans continued to press his suit, giving one of the women a bolt of fine purple cloth. The prostitute was pleased, treating the American with special kindness. That night it occurred to her that if she received such a fine present for just serving drinks, what might she get for giving the American her body? So one night she seduced the American. He was delighted, says the poet, for his strategy had worked. From then on he gave her presents every night, "gradually depleting the ship of its supplies" until a senior officer found out and put an end to his scheme.[19]

Shore leave was a privilege reserved only for the officers, and they enjoyed their relative freedom of movement immensely. Williams, however, was not sure that their souls or their intellects had benefited from their stay at Shimoda. "It is sad to see," he wrote in his diary, "how few are the sources of enjoyment, occupation, or instruction which those around me have or find for themselves in such a spot as this, where the ordinary amusements and company found in seaports are wanting. They [the officers] scold the Japanese, the Commodore, the ship, the Expedition, but their own evil tempers are never blamed; truly, it is sad to see such perversity and waste of time."[20]

As for the men, they went ashore only as part of boat crews or to serve on other work details such as the seining of fish. Two of the first sailors to reach the beach took French leave and were tried and punished for desertion. The fleshpots and grog shops of Cum Sing Moon were but a distant memory; the men had been confined to the ships for three to four months. Naturally enough, morale deteriorated along with their diet. In a small isolated port, such as Shimoda, the Japanese were capable of supplying only a small part of the squadron's needs. On a regular basis, their guard-boats brought fresh supplies of chicken, fish, sweet potatoes, and greens. The chicken, fish, and sweet potatoes were reserved for the officers. The men were fed the greens (turnip and radish tops) along with hard tack, salt beef, beans, and rice.

Aboard the *Vandalia* the cooks for the sailors' messes refused to even touch the greens. Instead, some sailors complained to an officer that they were being deprived of their rightful rations. They would eat what they were given, the officer replied. The crew continued to refuse to eat the greens, but the stalemate was partially broken when the *Macedonian* returned from the Bonin Islands with a load of sea turtles and fresh fish. The men, however, continued to refuse to eat the greens. In retaliation, Commander John Pope cut their rations of beans and pickles. The affair of the greens ended when the remaining supply was found to be rotten.[21]

In early May, having tested the treaty in Shimoda, Perry sent the *Macedonian, Vandalia,* and *Southampton* ahead to Hakodate and set out with the steamers *Powhatan* and *Mississippi* for a prearranged rendezvous with officials representing the commissioners. Perry had spent twenty-five days at Shimoda, most of it haggling over petty matters with the local officers. He was satisfied that he had "impressed the people with a just idea of the friendly relations he wished to establish with them, and taught the authorities that no infringement, in the slightest degree, of the stipulations of the treaty of Yokohama [Kanagawa] would be allowed to pass with impunity." This was the message he planned to convey to the commissioners, who had arranged before Perry left Yokohama to meet him in Shimoda when he returned from Hakodate to review the provisions of the treaty.[22]

The two steamers headed north along the coast of Honshu, accompanied by occasional pods of whales and schools of porpoises. During the day they stayed within five or six miles of the land, stopping on occasion to throw the deep sea lead and inspect samples brought up from the bottom. Three days steaming brought the ships to the entrance to the Tsugaru Strait, then known to the Americans as the Straits of Sangar, the main entrance to the munificent whaling grounds of the Sea of Japan and the Sea of Okhotsk. Here a great flow of tide and current issued forth at the rate of six knots, which kept the steamers from making Hakodate until the next day.

On the morning of May seventeenth, the steamers anchored alongside the three sailing ships in Hakodate's inner harbor, a body of water sheltered by a low neck of land and the mountainous peninsula on which the town itself stood. The Americans found themselves in the eastern crook of a magnificent, spacious bay with room enough, as Perry put it, to moor a hundred sail. It was, all agreed, a kind of northern Gibraltar. Having left Shimoda in the warmth of spring, the Americans were now back in a wintry climate where the hills were bare and sere and snow clung to the low rock peaks behind the village. With a population of about six thousand, Hakodate was larger and seemed to be more prosperous than Shimoda, its wealth derived almost entirely from a vigorous trade in fish and seaweed with the rest of Japan.

Hakodate was within the domain of Matsumae Izu, a minor lord holding sway from his castle town of Matsumae over a remote but vital part of the empire far from center of things in Edo. The Matsumae were exempt from the usual controls directed from Edo, and the Matsumae, regarded as one of Japan's most independent feudal families, preferred it that way. In this way they could trade freely with the Ainus and, through the Ainus, with the Russians and the Chinese. The Matsumae domain, however, constituted the northern border of Japan, where for a century there had been not only trade but also recurring tensions with the Russians. Pressure from the Russians, in fact, was one of the factors behind the subjugation of the Ainu population and the colonization of the southern part of the island. Fearing the Russians, the Bakufu placed Matsumae under direct control of a local *bugyo* from 1802 to 1821. During this time the first systematic attempts to explore and map Ezo and the northern islands were carried out. Even before the ascendancy of Abe Masahiro, Tokugawa Nariaki, wary of the marauding Russians, had identified Matsumae as "the back door to Japan." He at first proposed that the Bakufu resume direct control of the domain and later that the domain be placed under his direct suzerainty. Both proposals were ignored, and by the time of Perry's arrival there were only the most rudimentary signs of any efforts that had been made to defend the entrance to Hakodate harbor.[23]

The officials sent by the commissioners to meet Perry in Hakodate had not arrived by the time the first American ships dropped anchor off the town. Panic set in immediately, and for days the Americans, watching from the decks of their ships, noted long lines of people, many with their goods on horseback, streaming out of the city. The flowery-flagged devils, it was rumored, had come to exact revenge for the imprisonment of Ranald MacDonald and the mutinous crewmen from the *Lagoda*. Before Perry arrived, the local officials refused to meet with Captain Abbot. But upon Perry's arrival four very terrified officials came aboard the flagship and were relieved, though visibly surprised, when Williams and Lieutenant Silas Bent explained that they were there as a result of the Treaty of Kanagawa.

The next day Williams, Portman, Luo Shen, and the young Perry went ashore and explained to the *bugyo* through the good offices of Luo Shen that they wanted to make arrangements similar to those worked out at Shimoda: the purchase of supplies, allowance of some trade, the right to walk within seven *ri* [1 *ri* = 2.43 miles, thus about 17 miles] of the village, and the use of some buildings ashore. Having no idea how to respond, the officials asked for time to consult their daimyo, whose castle was in Matsumae some eighty miles away. Perry gave them until nine o'clock the next morning. After the interview Williams and the other Americans walked around the town. The villagers, almost entirely men since the women and children had fled, fell to their knees before them. They noted the large gabled houses with porches facing the street, a fire bucket and broom perched upon each ridgepole, roofs strewn with cobblestones, and the large population of scruffy dogs.

Matsumae Kageyu soon appeared to represent the interests of his kinsman, the daimyo Matsumae Izu, and he and the local officials readily gave in to Perry's demands except for his request to visit their overlord at his castle in Matsumae. This was rejected in no

Street in Hakodate; *Narrative of the Expedition*

uncertain terms. While Matsumae Kageyu insisted that he had all the necessary authority to deal with the commodore, he also insisted on referring the question of how far the Americans could go in their visits ashore back to Edo. After the numerous confrontations at Shimoda, the Americans found the officials of Hakodate to be in general quite friendly and personable. "It is more agreeable, too," Williams wrote, "to see a well dressed crowd than such almost nude men and loosely attired women as S[h]imoda presents."[24]

The people of Hakodate, on the other hand, were a bit overwhelmed by their new guests. The local officials soon presented Perry with a list of complaints about the activities of his officers ashore: gambling in the temples, climbing over walls to get into houses and yards, removing goods from shops without paying for them, and purchasing swords. Perry responded quickly, confining the officers to their ships for a day and carrying out an investigation that netted a number of swords and purloined goods.[25]

With little to do in the absence of the emissaries from Edo, Perry wrote his first report to the secretary of the navy since leaving Edo Bay. Shimoda and Hakodate could not be surpassed in terms of convenience and size. How they could have surpassed Yokohama and the tabooed Nagasaki, Perry did not make clear. In Shimoda, the authorities had been kind and attentive, furnishing as much in the way of supplies as the country could provide. The officers and crew members who had gone ashore had traveled freely about the town and country "without the slightest hindrance or molestation," with the exception of the one incident at Shimoda. Perry chose not to mention the endless haggling in Shimoda over surveillance of his men ashore.[26]

The rest of the time Perry, like the other officers, entertained himself with shopping and occasional trips ashore to see the few points of interest, mainly the four large Buddhist temples and three Shinto shrines. As the ranking officer in the squadron, Perry made sure that he got first pick of the goods offered by the Japanese. On one occasion, Williams was ashore to arrange for a selection of goods to be laid out for his inspection. Meanwhile a group of officers stood around waiting for Perry, who was late, to arrive. Once Perry had picked over the goods and departed, a near riot ensued as the officers rushed forward to grab what was left over. Williams, of course, was appalled.[27]

The local officials reported to Matsumae Izu that Perry seemed to suspect that the emissaries sent by the treaty commissioners from Edo were hiding out nearby. In fact one of them, Hirayama Kenjiro, was just across the straits staying at an inn in Miumaya; the second, Namura Gohachiro, was in Matsumae. Hirayama and Namura were on a double assignment. Besides dealing with Perry, they were to go to Sakhalin Island to assay Russian intentions. The Bakufu had become deeply concerned about Russian activities on Sakhalin after the Russians built a fort on the southern tip of the island over-looking the straits between Sakhalin and Ezo in October 1853. At first the Japanese, fearing a Russian attack, had abandoned the nearby villages, but slowly during the winter and spring of 1854, the Japanese had returned, followed by an increasing number of officials. In another trip to Nagasaki, in April, Putiatin had spoken of continuing his negotiations at Sakhalin. But instead he had

dispatched two ships to the Russian outpost. They had arrived a
week before Perry's arrival at Hakodate. Putiatin, as it turned out,
had always been opposed to the occupation of Sakhalin; it was a
hindrance to settling the northern boundary dispute and opening
trade with Japan. Besides, the outbreak of the Crimean War made
it risky to maintain a weak outpost within range of the British fleet
in China. In June, the Russians, under orders from Putiatin, abandoned their Sakhalin outpost.

The two Japanese officials on their way to Sakhalin were apparently planning to depart for the island, bypassing a meeting
with Perry altogether. But after repeated pleas from Matsumae
Izu, who feared that Perry would march on his castle, Hirayama
decided to go to Hakodate to meet with the commodore.[28]

On May twenty-seventh, Perry sent Williams ashore to complain to the local officials. The continued absence of women and
children from Hakodate was a mark of unfriendliness. Further, the
commodore was annoyed by the delay in the arrival of the emissaries. If they did not show up in six days he was going to return
to Shimoda. Four days later Perry dispatched the *Vandalia* to
Shanghai to replace the *Southampton* and sent the *Macedonian*
back to Shimoda. That very morning Perry received a message
saying that two of the emissaries had decided to delay their trip
to Sakhalin in order to meet with Perry.

But when Flag Lieutenant Bent went ashore in a boat to bring
the officials to the flagship, they studiously ignored him, preferring
instead to remain at the customs house sipping tea and smoking
their pipes. Perry, not to be trifled with any longer, was preparing
to send a hundred marines with two fieldpieces to occupy Hakodate
when the two emissaries suddenly appeared at the gangway. They
were delayed, Hirayama explained apologetically, because they
were waiting for some presents for the commodore. Perry accepted
this explanation but repeated his complaint about the unfriendly
absence of women and children. Hirayama's explanation for why
women and children had fled was a novel one, which must have
amused Perry: it was true that they were terrified of foreigners,
but they also fled from Japanese officials. During the talks, Perry
attempted to get Hirayama and his delegation to reach an agree-

Matsumae Kageyu and officials; *Narrative of the Expedition*

ment over how far the Americans could travel in their walks ashore. But Hirayama deferred the question to the treaty commissioners, saying that he did not have the authority to reach a decision.[29]

A reception and military parade was planned ashore for the next day. But thick fog blanketed the harbor, and Perry decided to send his gifts ashore without going himself. After many days of waiting, the arrival of the emissaries was decidedly anticlimactic if not somewhat bizarre. After the talks Hirayama reported that the Americans were surprisingly easy to deal with. They seemed friendly and had no plans to march on Matsumae.[30]

As for Perry, he was eager to get under way for Shimoda, where he had arranged to meet the commissioners. On the morning of June second, the two steamers, during a break in the fog, eased their way out of the harbor and headed south. Two American sailors remained behind buried in yet another new graveyard. Their mates wrote their epitaphs, which were inscribed on each headstone by a Japanese stonecarver:

> Sleeping on a foreign shore,
> Rest, sailor, rest! thy trial o'er;
> Thy shipmates leave this token here,
> That some, perchance, may drop a tear
> For one that braved so long the blast
> And served his country to the last.

One hundred hours later, the steamers were back in Shimoda under the warm sunny skies of approaching summer. In Perry's absence, the commissioners, their number now increased to seven, had arrived in Shimoda, taking over all the principal temples for their residences while every available room in the inns and public buildings was packed with their retainers. Before leaving Edo, the commissioners had reviewed the reports sent them by Kurokawa Kahei and had gotten Abe Masahiro's approval on a long memorandum outlining how they should handle Perry upon his return from Hakodate. Perry was not dealing with the obsequious and powerless Okinawans, and it is clear that Perry was misled when he concluded after his first visit to Shimoda that the local authorities "seemed anxious to facilitate the views of the Commodore."[31]

The commissioners, for one, planned to continue sending guards to accompany the Americans when they came ashore. If Perry complained, they would moderate their stance, since he and his officers were part of a treaty delegation. "It is true," the commissioners wrote, "that from their viewpoint the escort was as unpleasant as flies in May." Nevertheless when Perry was gone, surveillance of American visitors would be strict. They also planned

Exercise of troops for imperial commissioners at Ryosenji,
June 8, 1854; *Narrative of the Expedition*

to continue the arrangement whereby sales of goods would be handled through government officials, and they hoped to keep the Americans from bringing guns ashore to shoot birds. The other matters were less significant—no sales of cows and mirrors, no visits to the volcanic island of O-shima, only one fire bell to be sold, only "harmless" books on Confucian morality to be available for purchase, and so on.[32]

The very next day Perry went ashore with a large escort to begin a series of almost daily meetings with the commissioners at the Ryosenji Temple. Hayashi, resplendent in scarlet trousers, explained that the Bakufu had declared Shimoda an imperial city and the two additional commissioners were its new governors. Hayashi went on to propose the construction of watch stations, which the Americans were not to pass without permission, at a distance of seven *ri* from Shimoda. Moreover, he wanted Perry to remove the navigational buoys he had placed in the harbor and a large box that the Americans had placed on the shore as a mark to facilitate finding the entrance into the harbor.

Perry was anxious to finish his discussions with the commissioners. He knew that they would go on longer than expected. But it took almost two weeks of tedious and painfully convoluted negotiations to arrive at a series of additional regulations that governed the implementation of the Treaty of Kanagawa. The commissioners were determined to debate each matter in the minutest detail while Perry was not ready to give an inch. The talks ebbed and flowed, and there was the usual posturing on both sides. For a time, Perry refused to allow his officers and interpreters to go ashore to continue the discussions. At one crucial juncture both Perry and Hayashi boycotted the most elaborate banquet yet prepared for the Americans, a development that cast a pall over the gathering.

The talks were interrupted from time to time by efforts to keep the few sailors allowed ashore in line. On one occasion, Perry's barge crew and some of the band became drunk to the point of immobility while the commodore was busy at the Ryosenji Temple with the commissioners. On another, two sailors burst into a shop, pulled the spigot out of a sake barrel, filled a large basin, and tossed off the contents. When the shopkeeper tried to stop them, one of the sailors drew a knife and wounded him in the hand. "Such is one of the precursors of the trade with Christian America," Williams concluded, "though I hope the Japanese have discrimination enough to perceive and make a difference between the sailors who behave and those who act like fiends."[33]

The discussions also returned to the question of Sam Patch (Sentaro), the Japanese sailor who had shipped aboard the flagship. Moryama Einosuke insisted that he remain in Japan. Perry responded that it was up to Patch, but that if he remained the commissioners had to guarantee his safety. Patch was brought on the deck where he fell to his knees before Moryama until Bent, in disgust, ordered him to stand up. In the end Patch, despite his ill treatment at the hands of the officers of the *Susquehanna* in China, preferred the life of an American sailor and his close friendship with a marine named Goble over the fate of being a subject of the shogun.

The additional regulations finally agreed to by Perry and the commissioners covered all the points raised by Perry, though there was one major disappointment. (See Appendix 2.) The Japanese could put up watch stations anywhere they pleased, but the Americans could go through them as long as they did not go more than seven *ri* from Shimoda. At Hakodate the Americans could travel only five *ri* from the town. Any foreigner caught passing these limits could be arrested and returned to his ship. The Ryosenji Temple in Shimoda and the Gyokusenji Temple in Kakisaki were set aside as resting places for the Americans when they were ashore, and an official burial ground was established at the Gyokusenji. A harbor master and three pilots were appointed. The peculiar form of quasi-trade was permitted to continue. The shooting of birds was strictly prohibited. An exchange rate of 1,600 copper cash [4,000 cash equals 1 ryo] to the dollar was established, an arrangement which the Americans continued to feel benefited the Japanese significantly.

Coal was the one disappointment. During the negotiations the Japanese hauled in several tons of it. When the engineers examined it, however, it was found to be of inferior quality. In the end Perry agreed to convey the message to his government that the Japanese could not provide coal supplies at Shimoda.

As the days grew longer and hotter, the Americans began to prepare for their departure. Final banquets and gifts were exchanged, the commissioners' banquet marred only by the departure of some of Perry's officers to pursue two boatmen who had disappeared in search of liquor. As parting gifts the commissioners presented Perry with a large block of granite for the Washington Monument and three small spaniels, highly valued pets in Japan. The bands played for the general public in the temple yard of Ryosenji, the people responding by presenting the band members with pieces of fresh fruit. A minstrel show attended by an estimated three hundred Japanese was performed aboard the flagship. A final bazaar was organized. Perry, of course, made the first purchases after complaining about the high prices. The rest of the officers were disappointed by the few goods offered. Williams and his doctor friend Morrow made their last excursion into the countryside where the freshly transplanted rice seedlings lent a bright green hue to the narrow valleys and terraced hillsides.

There was one delicate matter that remained unsettled. The day before Perry's departure for Hakodate a month earlier, A. L. C. Portman, the Dutch translator, had written to Moryama. The people of Shimoda acted warmly toward the foreigners, but there was one problem, Portman felt: the women were hiding themselves. "I do not think that it would be disastrous if I made friends with Japanese women. I find it very unreasonable that the [Japanese] officials have bought up all the women and own them." It was reported, in fact, that Kurokawa, the officials under him, and the interpreters were all keeping women at their quarters. And Portman undoubtedly knew about the customs that had evolved during the Dutch's more than two centuries of confinement on the island of Deshima in Nagasaki Harbor. There, women were allowed to come and go freely. Some of the occupants, including von Siebold, had fathered children by these women, and there were stories of a graveyard where the unwanted children of these mixed arrangements were buried. In light of this situation, Portman appealed to Moryama on the basis of his Dutch nationality. He was not any foreigner; he was a citizen of a country whose government had enjoyed a long and friendly relationship with the Japanese.

In response to Portman's request, one of the officials invited him to his office and tried to console him by giving him a small piece of a kimono. The official reported his encounter with Portman to the two new *bugyos*. They in turn proposed to the Roju that prostitutes be used to entertain the Americans. A lively debate ensued, but there was no time to settle the question before the Americans departed.[34]

On June twenty-third, Perry, having transferred his broad pennant to the *Mississippi*, ordered all communication with the shore cut and the steamers moved down to the entrance of the harbor in preparation for an early start the next morning. In the afternoon

Moryama and another interpreter came aboard for a last visit and to settle the accounts for the supplies provided. Perry entertained the two with cake and wine in his cabin. Finding Moryama in an expansive mood, Perry questioned him about the raid against the Dutch carried out at Nagasaki by the British ship *Phaeton* in 1808. The governor and eleven others had committed suicide, Moryama replied. The captain of the *Phaeton*, Perry told the startled Moryama, was now a British admiral at Hong Kong and would likely be in Japan the next year. Befriend him and drink his champagne, Perry advised. The conversation turned from suicide to forms of capital punishment. Moryama explained that crucifixion was reserved for regicides, but decapitation, not hanging as in the West, was the common form of capital punishment.[35] On this grim note, Perry ended his last official contact with the Japanese.

Perry was ready to depart on June twenty-fifth, but the weather was so rainy and the sea so rough that he postponed the squadron's departure for a day. The commissioners, however, were in a greater hurry than the commodore. From the decks of their ships, the Americans could see a long line of palanquins attended by soldiers, their banners drooping in the rain, winding along the beach toward Kakisaki on their way back to Edo. The next day the squadron once more prepared to get under way. The *Macedonian* and the *Supply* quickly found themselves making little headway against a southerly wind. The Japanese sent out some towboats, but they too made little progress. Finally Perry, worried that the heavy seas and contrary winds would push the two ships on the rocks, ordered them to anchor until conditions were more favorable for their departure. With that, the steamers, taking the *Southampton* in tow, turned their bows toward Okinawa.

In Perry's absence, murder and riot had come to the sleepy island paradise of Okinawa. During the spring and early summer minor incidents involving the American sailor-occupants had escalated into a major confrontation. First some children had either stoned one of the master's mates left in charge of the coal depot or had thrown some rocks which landed near him, depending on whose account of the events one believed. Next there was an incident in the market involving either the purchase or theft of some meat in which a sailor either threatened a butcher or an official with a knife. Again the accounts varied, but all agreed that someone beat the sailor severely with a club. Finally, two sailors were found lying drunk in the street while their companion, a sailor named William Board, was found in the bottom of a boat, frothing at the mouth and all but dead. The Okinawans claimed that they found him drowning in the water and had placed him in the boat. But an examination of Board's body revealed that his skull had been fractured.

Perry immediately demanded an investigation. The badly frightened Okinawans at first stuck to their story of the sailor's accidental drowning. Perry issued an ultimatum: explain Board's death and produce the culprits involved or he would seize the forts at the mouth of the junk harbor and prevent any ships from sailing. The next day Williams and Bent were invited to an official hearing during which one of the alleged assailants was beaten on the soles of his feet in order to extract a confession. After the hearing, Itarashiki Satonushi, the interpreter, offered a new version of how the sailor died. Board and two companions had broken into a house and stolen some liquor. Board, after his companions had passed out, broke into another house and was in the act of raping a woman when her cries attracted neighbors. They drove the sailor from the woman's house and stoned him as he fled back toward the beach. At the beach they left him in the water to drown. To Williams, this account seemed far more credible. In response, Williams delivered a stern lecture on the shortcomings of their original investigation, warning them that "the life of an American was too serious a matter to be trifled with, however great the provocation." With that, he and Bent departed, leaving behind the draft of a treaty that Perry wished to conclude with the regent.[36]

Despite their new account of the death of the American sailor, the Okinawans had not yet produced any suspects. So Perry sent a detachment of twenty marines ashore to occupy the forts at the entrance of the junk harbor and to suffer the relentless nightime attacks of the mosquitoes. It was, young Spalding wrote disapprovingly, like "bullying a fly."[37] A day later, the Okinawans brought aboard Perry's flagship the man who they claimed was the

chief culprit, his arms trussed to his side. He was one of six im-
plicated in the crime, Itarashiki explained; he had been sentenced
to be banished to a remote island for life. The five others were to
be banished for eight years while the mayor of Naha was to continue
in office without pay and four officials were to lose their jobs for
writing a false report.[38]

Perry was well satisfied with this outcome, and he turned instead to the matter of the treaty, giving the Okinawans three days
to prepare for negotiations. After the drubbing they had taken in
the affair of the drunken rapist, the Okinawans had little stamina
left to resist Perry's proposal for a treaty, particularly after they
heard of the new treaty with Japan. There was only one matter in
the draft that bothered them. Perry had referred to the Ryukyus
as an independent nation, but this would undoubtedly offend the
Chinese emperor with whom they enjoyed a tributary relationship.
About Japan and their subjugation by the Shimazu clan, they
would say nothing. The new treaty was a straightforward document
calling for courteous treatment of American citizens, the right to
purchase supplies and other goods, the right to go ashore and move
about without hindrance, the continuance of the graveyard, and
the appointment of pilots. The treaty, Spalding concluded, was like
the agreement between the chicken and the horse who lived in the
same stable. The chicken agreed not to tread on the horse's toes if
the horse would not tread on his.[39]

The treaty was signed on July eleventh at an elaborate banquet, which pleased the Americans since they much preferred Okinawan cuisine to Japanese. More gifts were proffered, including
fifteen pieces of cotton for the woman assaulted by Board. The bands
played and marched along with the marines through Naha to the
delight of the local people. Perry once again entertained the regent
and a group of officials aboard the flagship, and he again refused
to take home with him a Japanese man who had swum out to the
flagship.

Having arranged with the local officials to maintain the coal
depot, there was only one more matter to settle: Perry prevailed
upon the Okinawans to donate a temple bell and a block of stone,
both to be placed in the Washington Monument. Williams wondered
whether the bell, about which Perry seemed quite obsessed, would

be a monument to his folly or his glory. Perry had already given Bernard Bettelheim permission to move aboard the *Powhatan*. His replacement, the Reverend E. H. Moreton, had arrived some months earlier with his family, and the two missionaries, forced to live together until Perry's return, were not getting along. Nor was Bettelheim with Williams, as they continued to vie for the role of chief translator. Grateful to Perry, Bettelheim undertook a final effort to ingratiate himself with the commodore by preaching a sermon comparing Perry to Jesus Christ and drawing a parallel between Perry's mission to Japan and Jesus' upon earth. Bettelheim, who had worked himself to the point of physical collapse, had already pronounced his final benediction on the Okinawans: "They are all liars—not a word of truth in them." As for the Okinawans, they wrote a long letter to Perry, pleading with him to take the Moretons back to China.[40]

On July 17, 1854, Perry dispatched the *Powhatan* to Ningpo and Amoy to check on the fate of the small missionary settlements in those two cities while the *Mississippi* set its course for Hong Kong. The last of the Ryukyus, the outer reaches of the Land of the Gods, soon fell below the horizon.

14

FILIBUSTERING TOWARD HEAVEN BY THE GREAT WESTERN ROUTE

The truth is every incident connected with the Japanese expedition is looked upon with great interest and there is one universal demonstration of applause of every event which has occurred. . . .[1]
—MATTHEW CALBRAITH PERRY to S. Wells Williams,
March 13, 1855

It may be safely predicted that many years will not elapse before this magnificent country will be numbered amongst the most important of the eastern nations, with which a profitable trade will be established by the interchange of many of our manufactured articles for the products of a country already possessed of great resources.[2]
—MATTHEW CALBRAITH PERRY, *Narrative of the Expedition*

The whole enterprise of this nation, which is not an upward, but a westward one, toward Oregon, California, Japan, etc., is totally devoid of interest to me, whether performed on foot, or by a Pacific railroad. . . . It is perfectly heathenish,—a filibustering toward *heaven by the great western route. . . . What end do they propose to themselves beyond Japan? What aims more lofty have they than the prairie dogs?*[3]
—HENRY DAVID THOREAU to Harrison Blake, February 27, 1853

From the day of Perry's arrival for more than ten years our country was in a state of indescribable confusion. The government was weak and irresolute, without power of decision.[4]   —KATSU AWA

I am therefore convinced that our policy should be to stake everything on the present opportunity, to conclude friendly alliances, to send ships to foreign countries everywhere and conduct trade, to copy the foreigners where they are at their best and so repair our own shortcomings, to foster our national strength and complete our armaments, and so gradually subject the foreigners to our influence until in the end all the countries of the world know the blessings of perfect tranquillity and our hegemony is acknowledged throughout the globe.[5]

—HOTTA MASAYOSHI, 1857

UPON ARRIVING IN HONG KONG in late July, Perry—as he had written to his wife before the second voyage to Japan—was just about used up. He had been at sea for more than seven months, and his earlier sickness, recurring arthritis, and the stress of commanding the squadron and completing negotiations with the Japanese and Ryukyuans at four different locations had left him more than eager to return home. It had been a trying voyage, and even a younger man like thirty-eight-year-old Lieutenant George Preble of the *Macedonian* noted that his own hair was turning gray and a new bald spot like a silver dollar was clearly visible. The treaty had left Japan aboard the *Saratoga* in April, arriving in Washington almost simultaneously with Perry's return to China. Perry was anxious to find out how the treaty had fared in the Senate and how the news of his successes had been greeted in the United States.

Even before leaving for Japan on his second visit, Perry had put in a request for orders relieving him of command of the East India Squadron as soon as he reached China, a request which he repeated a second time. When he arrived in Hong Kong, his orders were there. He was to turn command of the East India Squadron over to Joel Abbot and return home either aboard the *Mississippi* or by commercial steamship.[6] There was also another letter waiting for him from James C. Dobbin, Franklin Pierce's Secretary of the Navy, which hinted that the results of the expedition were not greeted with universal approval.

The department approved his actions in securing a coal depot in the Bonin Islands, Dobbin wrote. "At some future and no distant day, I have no doubt, from its geographical position, it will be found convenient and important for a line of steamers to Shanghai or Hong Kong, from the Sandwich Islands or San Francisco, to China." Dobbin also approved of the way in which Perry had handled the British when they questioned his intentions in the Bonins. But, he continued, Perry's plan to hold the Ryukyus as a way to pressure the Japanese into opening a port of refuge or as the basis for claims growing out of the treatment of American sailors was "more embarrassing." The subject had been laid before the president. He appreciated Perry's patriotic motives, but was "disinclined without the authority of Congress to take and retain possession of an island in that distant country, particularly unless more urgent and potent reasons demanded it than now exist." In addition, if resistance developed, "it would also be rather mortifying to the island, if once seized, and rather inconvenient and expensive to maintain a force there to retain it." As Perry was to find out, from Washington the Ryukyus and Japan appeared of little consequence, and his plans for quasi-colonies, protectorates over a number of Asian nations, and a strong regional presence to counter the threat of a "British monopoly" of East Asia were neither understood, nor if they were, welcomed.[7]

The China to which Perry returned was lurching faster than ever toward anarchy: the anarchy of shifting alliances of opportunity and random acts of rebellion. While Perry was in Japan during the winter and early spring, the northern expeditionary forces of the Taiping rebels had abandoned their march on Peking. Now the beddraggled Taiping troops were either scattered to the west or retreating southward along the Grand Canal toward Nanking. In Nanking, the rebel capital, factionalism was on the rise among the rebel leaders, a deadly factionalism that a year later would turn rebel against rebel and result in horrendous massacres. The Small Knife Society still held the walled city of Shanghai, but the imperial troops were tightening the noose.

In April, marines and sailors from the *Plymouth*, under Captain John Kelly, which had been left in Shanghai by Perry, had, in fact, been drawn into a brief firefight with the imperial troops, the seriocomic Battle of Muddy Flat. Having charged the imperial troops with harassing foreigners, a joint force of British and Americans joined by a few Small Knife soldiers ousted the imperial troops from one of their camps and burned it. It was a poorly executed maneuver during which a number of British and Americans managed to kill one another in a crossfire. When Wells Williams reached Ningpo aboard the *Powhatan*, he found a Portuguese corvette attacking some Chinese war junks with little regard for the fact that their shells fell among the houses of the missionary settlement. Piracy was worse than ever around the Pearl River Delta, and there had been rebel attacks around Canton.[8]

China no longer appeared on the break of a glorious morn. "The hopes entertained of the good the Taiping rebels would do are rapidly fading into disappointment at their fanaticism and disorders," Williams was forced to conclude. There was one encouraging development. For the first time since his arrival in 1833, Williams at Ningpo had actually entered a walled Chinese city.[9]

Commissioner Robert McLane had arrived in Hong Kong on March 13, 1854. He was the first American commissioner to receive instructions from Washington that went beyond vague orders to watch out for American interests. McLane's instructions were to work with the British to negotiate new commercial treaties that would extend the concessions extracted by the foreigners after the Opium War. McLane had visited Shanghai aboard the *Susquehanna* and then had gone on up the Yangtze to Nanking in hopes of meeting with the Taiping leaders. Insulted by his treatment at the hands of the rebels, McLane wrote them off as too ignorant and peculiar to be recognized as de facto rulers of part of China. McLane instead opened negotiations with the imperial government. At the time of Perry's arrival he was working on an agreement with the British plenipotentiary for them to sail in tandem to the mouth of the Pei-ho to begin negotiations with representatives of the imperial government.[10]

With McLane pursuing a consistent policy and the *Susquehanna* at the commissioner's disposal, Perry no longer needed to compete with the civilian representative of the U.S. government for control of either his fleet or his country's China policy. Instead he turned his attention to preparing for his departure. First, however, he had to settle a ticklish question that had arisen with regard to another American naval expedition. The North Pacific Expedition had been the pet project of John Pendleton Kennedy, Fillmore's secretary of the navy when Perry had left the United States. Kennedy had conceived the idea of the expedition with Lieutenant Cadwallader Ringgold, a close friend. It was to be a scientific expedition charged with surveying the waters of the North Pacific and the Arctic, again in relation to the important whaling grounds in the area. But Ringgold had not been able to get beyond Hong Kong. Instead he had been sidetracked into committing ships to chase pirates in the Pearl River Delta and to assist the imperial forces in fighting off rebel attacks near Canton. Then Ringgold began to act very strangely, repeatedly overhauling his ships and going nowhere. Ringgold contracted a fever, delirium set in, and rumors spread that it was more than malaria; it was alcohol or even drugs. When Perry arrived in Hong Kong, he convened a court of medical inquiry and had Ringgold removed from his command and sent home. In his place, he put Lieutenant John Rodgers. Rodgers was the son of Perry's old mentor, Commodore John Rodgers, and his eldest daughter's brother-in-law. The Perry-Rodgers-Slidell clan was at it again.[11]

There was little left to do beyond receiving the accolades of the American merchant community in China. In a letter twenty-three representatives of the merchant houses, including Russell and Company, Augustine Heard, and Wetmore and Company noted that "the name of *Perry*, which has so long adorned the naval profession, will henceforth be enrolled with the highest in Diplomacy:—Columbus, Da Gama, Cook, La Pérouse, Magellan—these inscribed their names in History, by striving with the obstacles of Nature, you have conquered the obstinate will of man, and by overturning the cherished policy of an Empire, have brought an estranged but cultivated people into the family of Nations;—You have done this without violence; and the World has looked on with admiration to see the barriers of prejudice fall before the Flag of our Country without firing a Shot." Moreover, the merchants did not neglect to mention that Perry had attended to their interests too, providing the "protection so much required by the important interests at stake in this country."[12]

Perhaps more touching was a farewell message of "humble

tribute" from a group of crew members aboard the *Mississippi.*
Noting their great sense of respect and esteem, they remarked upon
their good fortune to have served under him during "the high and
important negotations which you have accomplished with a numerous and powerful people." They wished him well in the future
and thanked him "for the uniform regard which you have ever
evinced for our comfort."[13] Perry had been a difficult, but ultimately
fair taskmaster, many of the men felt, and his very presence cast
an aura of destiny about his flagship.

On the morning of September eleventh, Perry went aboard the
Pacific & Orient steamer *Hindostan* with his flag lieutenant, Silas
Bent. It was a festive occasion, the docks lined with Chinese and
foreigners alike. The *Mississippi* and the *Macedonian* fired a final
13-gun salute, and the crusty old commodore, those around him
noted, stood at the rail with tears in his eyes. In his wake he left
his secretary-son Oliver to assume the post of U.S. consul at Canton,
the first Canton consul in recent memory who was not a member
of the merchant firm of Russell and Company.

Perry's first stop after a long journey via the Isthmus of Suez,
Trieste, Vienna, and Berlin was The Hague in Holland. His son-
in-law August Belmont, the monied Democrat or "the Austrian-
born Jew banker," as the New York newspapers liked to call him,
had been appointed chargé d'affaires and then minister to the court
of King William III. Belmont was instructed to put pressure on
the Dutch government to open additional ports to American shipping in the East Indies, but he spent most of his time plotting to
force Spain to sell Cuba to the United States, using his hired spies
to float threats of an invasion.[14] Perry's wife and his twenty-one-
year-old daughter, Isabella, were staying with the Belmonts at The
Hague, and the family reunion, the first in two years, was a happy
one. Perry reacquainted himself with his grandchildren and told
many a tale of his travels. The family favorite was his story about
being offered one of an imprisoned African chieftain's five wives.
Perry's children loved to tease their mother about what she would
have done if Perry had accepted the offer.

In The Hague Perry undoubtedly heard that the Treaty of
Kanagawa was received in the United States with deafening silence.
Commander Henry Adams had delivered the treaty to President

Pierce in July. Pierce had submitted it to the Senate, which went into a brief executive session on July thirteenth for the first reading of the treaty. Two days later the treaty was read again in executive session and then ratified by unanimous consent. The treaty with Okinawa was ratified the next day.

By the time Pierce signed the treaty on August seventh, Adams had already left for Japan to exchange ratifications with the shogun's government. The New York and Washington newspapers briefly noted the arrival of the treaty with almost no commentary. There were no comparisons of Perry, as there had been in China, to Columbus, Magellan, and da Gama. Only the *Morning Courier and New York Enquirer*, owned and edited by Perry's friend and Tarrytown neighbor, James Watson Webb, offered any congratulatory remarks. The treaty and the expedition, Webb wrote in his sparse and ultimately inaccurate commentary, "constitute an era of our Commercial history. By means of them twenty million people are brought into immediate intercourse with us, and are made tributary to our prosperity."[15]

The silence was odd. American interest in Japan had continued during Perry's absence. In 1853 when the Crystal Palace opened in a spectacular steel and glass building near Fifth Avenue, there was a Japan collection on exhibit and daguerreotypes of Perry and his officers. In November, Bayard Taylor's accounts of the expedition had appeared in five editions of the *New York Daily Tribune*. James Gordon Bennett, the acerbic scion of the scandal-mongering penny press, had followed the expedition in the *New York Herald* closely. Bennett had also written florid paeans to the future of the China trade and had warned of the dangers of Russian influence in China and the Pacific, but he also predicted that Perry's second visit would be a failure and advised the Pierce administration to prepare to use force.[16] Perry had proved Bennett and all his earlier newspaper critics wrong, but when the treaty arrived, Bennett chose not to comment—as yet.

What had happened? The truth was that Perry was about to return to a very different country from the one he had left in December 1852. The Golden Age of the early fifties was drawing to a close. The United States, despite the notable achievements of Secretary of State William L. Marcy—he signed twenty-four treaties, the most ever negotiated during one presidency—was slowly turning in upon itself, reopening the scabbed-over but still festering wound of slavery. The Kansas-Nebraska Act, permitting the residents of the two territories to determine whether they would accept slavery, was signed by Pierce six weeks before the Treaty of Kanagawa arrived in Washington. It was an open invitation to fight a guerrilla war over the future of the Kansas Territory. Some would say that the horrible events in "bleeding" Kansas constituted the first act or at least the prologue to the Civil War. The United States, which in less than a decade had vanquished Mexico, doubled its size, become a continental power, taken the China trade from England, projected its naval power into the Pacific, and proclaimed the superiority of its democratic way of life, was suddenly caught up in an inevitable conflict over the very undemocratic practice of slavery.

Pierce at his inauguration had boldly proclaimed that "the policy of my administration will not be controlled by any timid forebodings of evil from expansion" and that "the acquisition of certain possessions" was "essential for the preservation of the rights of commerce and the peace of the world." Despite Pierce's embrace of territorial expansionism, American's vision of the future as it surveyed the globe was becoming clouded. Cuba, Central America, and even Hawaii still remained in view and even within grasp. But Pierce and Marcy had rejected Perry's suggestion that the Ryukyu Islands should be included among the possessions that the United States should seize as its own. Distant places like China and Japan, which were so clearly apparent on the horizon when Perry left New York in 1852, were dissolving in the particulate mists.

Before leaving The Hague for England, Perry wrote an extraordinary letter to his friend Webb confessing his "bitter feelings which are engendered by the conduct of our government." "The adage that no man can be a prophet in his own country may well apply," he noted. In Europe he had been received with "marked attention from the very highest classes who have striven to award me praise for my recent public acts." As soon as he had arrived in Trieste, he had been invited to dine *en famille* with Archduke Charles, the brother of Franz Joseph, emperor of Austria. In Holland, he and Bent had been received by the king, queen, and prime minister. (The Dutch too had predicted that Perry would fail because of the small size of his squadron. But they were gracious in receiving Perry, who had vilified them often and roundly as toadies to the ways of the Japanese.) He mentioned these events, Perry explained to Webb, because it showed that "foreigners can appreciate the services of American Naval officers though their own countrymen look upon such with indifference. And judging from former experience I can expect nothing from my fellow citizens at home especially the mercantile community for whose interests I have devoted a whole life saying nothing of the opening of the Ports of Japan and Lew Chew and the establishment of ports of refuge in the Pacific and China Seas." True, army and navy officers were often awarded with a public dinner. But this was not a compliment; it was a "painful obligation imposed upon the guest of making a bad and sometimes unintelligible speech."

If the government was not going to recognize his achievements, then Perry would himself. In a sense, he had already begun his own press campaign by permitting Bayard Taylor to ignore his order sequestering all written accounts of the expedition. All the written material on the expedition including the various journals and diaries that Perry had requisitioned from its members and the various charts, drawings, paintings, and daguerreotypes (six hundred in total) were on their way to New York aboard the *Mississippi*. Perry asked Webb if he would publish the letters he had exchanged with the New York and Boston merchants in China to "show that there are merchants abroad who can bear witness to the services of a naval man." They would also, of course, give Perry's side of his quarrel with Marshall in the event that Marshall had been intriguing against him in Washington. Webb was to treat Perry's remarks with "*strict confidence*." Perry was forced to turn to Webb because "the truth is [that] the only reward an officer can receive is the applause of his friends and fellow citizens for being much abroad and keeping aloof from politics—he actually commands less influence with the reigning powers of the government than the lowest and dirtiest pot house politician."

He was planning to seek an appropriation from Congress, Perry explained to Webb, to publish his journal along with some of the illustrated material and "the most complete vocabulary of the Japanese word ever yet published." If the appropriation was large enough, he planned to turn editorial duties over to another person because, unlike some in the navy, he did not "have the vanity to suppose myself capable of writing this work myself."[17]

Despite his bitterness, Perry was not about to abandon his work on behalf of "the mercantile community." From The Hague Perry went on to England, leaving his family just before Christmas. Congress had appropriated funds for six more mail steamers, and he wanted to examine some large new screw-propelled steamers built by the English. "Judging by the miserable abortions put afloat of late, one might reasonably suppose that information was wanted somewhere," he wrote to Webb. Perry had one other purpose for visiting England. He wanted to talk with Nathaniel Hawthorne, who was serving as American consul in Liverpool, about the possibility of writing an account of the expedition. Hawthorne was a fellow Democrat and had written a campaign biography of his fellow Bowdoin College graduate Franklin Pierce. Hawthorne, however, turned Perry down, saying that his public duties barred him from taking on the job. Instead he suggested Herman Melville. Perry "did not grasp very cordially at any name that I could think of," Hawthorne wrote in his diary. Little wonder, since Perry was hardly likely to be receptive to the idea of turning the job over to a writer whose first works had established him as the advocate of the common sailor and harsh critic of the naval autocracy.

Hawthorne found Perry "a brisk, gentlemanly, off-hand (but not rough) unaffected, and sensible man, looking not so elderly as he ought, on account of a very well-made wig. . . . I seldom meet with a man who puts himself more immediately on conversible terms than the Commodore." Hawthorne was impressed by the topic: "It would be a desirable labor for a young literary man, or, for that matter, an old one; for the world can scarcely have in reserve a less hacknied theme than Japan." He was wrong about Perry's wig, however. Perry still sported a full head of red-brown hair untouched by gray.[18]

On January eleventh Perry arrived in New York aboard the *Baltic*, one of the mail steamers whose construction he had overseen. Again the press did little more than note his arrival. More ink was spilled over a recent robbery that netted $10,000 from the safe at

Commodore Perry after his return from Japan;
photograph by Mathew Brady

August Belmont's New York offices. Five days later the round of congratulatory events, which Perry so longed for, began. The New York Chamber of Commerce convened a special meeting at the Merchants Bank to decide on an appropriate way to honor Perry. The meeting was attended by the cream of the community, which Perry had criticized only two months earlier for their failure to recognize his work on their behalf. John Aspinwall of Howland and Aspinwall was there as were A. A. Low and George Griswold, both leading figures in the China trade. Moses Grinnell, one of the handful of men who was recognized as a leader of the New York merchant community, read a resolution that said in part that Perry's "whole course has been one most acceptable to the whole American people; and it must in the end add greatly to the commercial interests in this country."

George W. Blunt, a publisher of nautical books and maps and an old friend of Perry's, noted that Perry had "completely reversed the ordinary course of diplomacy. He has been abroad in an entirely peaceful spirit of conquest, and broken down the barriers of the most exclusive port in the world. He had done what never was done by any other expedition. He made no concessions, but stood up as a right-minded sailor, and broke down all the barriers that have heretofore existed." Another member waxed even more enthusiastic. "Having opened a great highway for commerce, civilization and Christianity will surely follow after," he claimed. "This is perfectly certain." In recognition of his achievements, the Chamber eventually presented Perry with a massive silver service of some 381 pieces.[19]

The Chamber of Commerce meeting was just the beginning of a round of celebratory events that in the end featured enough fulsome (and often inaccurate) oratory to placate even Perry. There was a dinner at the mayor's mansion attended by an illustrious crowd, which included General Winfield Scott, Martin Van Buren, Washington Irving, and George Bancroft. There was a reception at Newport, Rhode Island, his birthplace, with the governor and General Assembly in attendance. The merchants of Boston struck a gold medal with his likeness on one side and a message of thanks on the other. Perry's name even surfaced briefly as a possible presidential candidate.

Perry was satisfied with the acclaim. With considerable exaggeration, he wrote to Wells Williams that "every incident connected with the Japanese expedition is looked upon with great interest and there is one universal demonstration of applause."[20]

The Pierce administration never organized an event that paid homage to Perry. The administration did give in to his pleas for special compensation as a diplomatic envoy. The State Department, Perry explained in a letter to Marcy, had given him funds for incidental expenses incurred during the negotiations. But he had chosen not to use them, relying instead on the government to compensate him when he returned. Congress obliged by voting him $20,000.[21]

Perry never heard further about his running controversy with Humphrey Marshall. Marshall saw to it that his correspondence with Perry was printed in full by the House of Representatives. But Marshall was his own worst enemy. "Mr. Marshall, though an excellent and amiable gentleman," wrote the *New York Daily Times*, "seems to have had a remarkable facility for falling out with everybody that he had to deal with."[22]

Perry did have to contend with a major attack on the expedition and minor attacks on his character. In Europe Philipp Franz von Siebold, the German naturalist whom Perry barred from the expedition because he had suspected him of being a Russian spy, wrote a pamphlet in which he assigned the prize of opening Japan to Russia. Von Siebold had accompanied Putiatin to Nagasaki, and he insisted that Japanese officials there had told the Russians that they would soon open the country to trade. Putiatin signed a treaty with the Bakufu in Shimoda in February 1855, but it did not provide for the beginning of trade.[23]

At home, the Washington press raised the question of what Perry was going to do with the dogs given to him by the Japanese. Perry gave one to President Pierce, and his own two were still on their way from Japan aboard the *Mississippi*. They resembled the kings of Spain, Perry wrote to Webb in a humorous vein. And it is supposed that they were descendants of dogs acquired when a Japanese embassy visited Europe in the reign of Charles II. Perry never received his dogs; they died en route off Chile. Young William Speiden, son of the *Mississippi*'s purser, wrote their elegy:

Happy dogs to die
Upon the broad blue sea,
For there your bones will lie,
Buried and forever be.[24]

Back in New York Perry settled into a new house at 38 West Thirty-second Street, which he bought with a $20,000 loan from Belmont and decorated with the numerous bric-a-brac acquired in his travels. The commodore had made some money in China by investing his salary so as to take advantage of the inflated price that Chinese merchants in Hong Kong were willing to pay for Mexican silver dollars. But it was not until he received his additional pay from Congress that he was able to pay back his son-in-law. On Belmont's behalf, Perry stopped by his New York offices regularly to keep an eye on his business. In turn Belmont tried to get Perry interested in forming a syndicate to buy real estate in Central Park.[25]

With his naval duties reduced to serving on the board charged with thinning the ranks of aging, incompetent, and just plain drunken senior officers, Perry rented two rooms in the offices of the American Bible Society in Astor Place to work on his account of the expedition. He hired the Reverend Francis L. Hawks, rector of Calvary Church, as the author-editor, and Hawks hired Dr. Robert Tomes, a physician and author of popular biographies, as his assistant. Hawks was a popular sermonizer and lecturer on historical topics as well as the author of a number of histories and biographies and the editor of a biographical dictionary.

Perry and Hawks had a wealth of written and illustrative material to draw on: the diaries and/or notes of Perry, his son, Captain Adams, lieutenants Contee and Bent, Bayard Taylor, Chaplain George Jones, official letters and reports, the numerous charts and maps that resulted from the surveys, and other reports and letters as well as Eliphalet Brown's daguerreotypes and Wilhelm Heine's drawings and paintings. He could not, however, get Wells Williams to contribute, no matter how much he pleaded, flattered, and even threatened. In addition to a vocabulary, he asked Williams to write a brief sketch of Japanese history, "which would reflect high credit on yourself." Perry even intervened to get Williams appointed secretary to the American legation in China replacing Dr. Peter Parker. In a letter to Williams, Perry described how he had personally recommended him to Marcy and how Marcy had repeated the recommendation when President Pierce walked into the room. Williams took the job, but his attitude toward Perry had hardened. Perry, Williams wrote to a friend, "evidently wishes to make a grand performance out of other people's lives, much as he has of his own."[26] Perhaps Williams hesitated to send his journal because it chronicled his disagreements with Perry.

Perry's work on the narrative triggered a rush to publish other books about Japan. D. W. C. Olyphant, the missionary merchant, tried to interest Williams in writing an introduction to a new, cheaply bound edition of the accounts of the voyage of the *Morrison*, which Williams had first written for the *Chinese Repository* in 1837. Boston historian Richard Hildreth rushed into print with *Japan As It Was and Is*. Much to Perry's annoyance, it was becoming clear that others besides Williams had violated his order to turn over their journals. Taylor, although he could not retrieve his journal from the Navy Department, went ahead anyhow, publishing a book on his travels titled *A Visit to India, China, and Japan in the Year of 1853*. J. W. Spalding, the purser's assistant aboard the *Mississippi*, soon came out with *The Japan Expedition: Japan and Around the World, An Account of Three Visits to the Japanese Empire*.

Perry kept Williams abreast of these developments in a letter in which he asked Williams once again to send his journal since "it was well understood that all information collected by anyone on the Squadron during the cruises to Japan was to belong to the Government." Perry was not sure if Taylor's book violated this "well-understood compact," but he was sure that Spalding had. Perry had not seen Spalding's account yet; it was still in production. But he was confident "from the shallowness of his mind" that the book would not be "remarkably profound."[27]

Between visits to Saratoga Springs to relieve his arthritis and to Washington to plead for money to publish the narrative, Perry continued his work in New York. Congress promised $400,000 to publish 34,000 copies of what was to be a three-volume work, but the money was provided in dribs and drabs. The first volume, a narrative account of the expedition, came out in the spring of 1856. Perry then arranged with D. Appleton and Company to publish a less elaborate edition of this volume. Soon after the first volume appeared, Perry discovered that the contractor for public printing in Washington had used the plates from Volume I to print 1,500 additional copies to sell for his own (the contractor's) profit. Washington, Perry wrote to Belmont, had "far exceeded all previous history in open and barefaced Corruption." Perry soon ran out of funds to retain his staff. So he completed the work on the last two volumes alone, poring over the copy day after day to prepare it for the printer.[28] These two volumes were published in 1857.

Narrative of the Expedition of an American Squadron to the China Seas and Japan . . . under the Command of Commodore M. C. Perry, United States Navy was a classic of American exploration literature. Beautifully (and expensively) illustrated with a number of full-color plates and Heine's lithographs made from the daguerreotypes, which were unfortunately destroyed by a fire, the *Narrative* was at once a history of earlier voyages to Japan, a study of Japanese, Okinawan, and even Chinese society, and a compelling account of the expedition itself. Perry had carefully reviewed much of the literature on Japan either before his departure or during his voyages, and he drew extensively on his and others' observations about life on these isolated islands. The descriptions of Japanese and Ryukyuan society are fascinating, if often speculative, given the unwillingness of both the Ryukyuans and the Japanese to impart much information about their own countries.

From the start Perry had conceived of the expedition as a scientific as well as diplomatic endeavor. Hence the second volume was a collection of essays on the geology of Okinawa, Formosan coal, the botany of Okinawa, a survey of the west coast of Japan, the Black Current, cyclones, birds, and shells. The third volume was a study of zodiacal light, a phenomenon no longer of interest to navigators. Perry had realized a fascinating fusion of the practical and the literary. The reader could travel the rapidly expanding world without giving up the comfort of his parlor while the sea captain could use Perry's detailed descriptions of how to approach Shimoda, for example, to avoid piling his ship on the rocks.

Perry, as he had been throughout his career, was careful to

give credit to his officers for their numerous contributions to the expedition. But given Perry's well-developed ego and excessive sensitivity about his own and his family's claims upon history, the narrative took a few liberties. Perry's abrupt and rude behavior at Shuri Castle in June 1853 when he precipitously departed after sampling his meal was described as an invitation "politely declined."[29] Poor Abbot took the blame for grounding the *Macedonian* on the voyage to Edo in January 1854. It was now clear why Perry had pressured him to rewrite his report.[30] In the face of President Pierce's decision not to back his seizure of Okinawa, Perry's placing the island under the surveillance of the American flag became "merely a measure of precaution," a statement that was boldly contradicted in another volume of the *Narrative* in which Perry laid out his strategy for extending American influence in Asia.[31]

While Perry often gave credit in the *Narrative* to his officers, the common sailors received scant attention except when their deaths proved significant, as in the case of Board, the rapist, and Robert Williams, the marine buried near Yokohama, or when they were occasionally mentioned by last name only as members of this or that exploring party. There was one long passage, undoubtedly written by Hawks, in which the sailors were portrayed as a happy lot spinning yarns and dancing away their idle hours in the forecastle.[32] Time and again the expedition was described as one in which violence was eschewed and no lives were lost. There was little mention of and no tally of the dozens of men who lost their lives, whether to natural causes, drink, or accident, while toiling aboard the ships of the East India Squadron.

The *Narrative*, of course, reflected Perry's view and the popular view that his encounters with the Japanese were a confrontation between the representatives of a civilized nation and a semibarbaric people who were suspicious of foreigners, addicted to duplicity, excessively obeisant in the face of authority, often brutish (the sumo wrestlers, for example), and prone to lewd behavior. These were the characterizations that Williams finally grew tired of hearing from Perry and his officers, although Williams's own journal employed them freely. Perry, however, had more to say about the Japanese in the *Narrative*. They were inordinately curious with a strong pictorial sense evidenced by their eagerness to sketch all that they saw. Among his gifts was a drawing of a horse rendered by Hayashi Daigaku, the head of the treaty commission. "The Japanese," he concluded, "are, undoubtedly, like the Chinese, a very imitative, adaptive, and compliant people; and in these characteristics may be discovered a promise of the comparatively easy introduction of foreign customs and habits, if not of the nobler principles and better life of a higher civilization." In contrast to their curiosity, they were very uncommunicative about themselves. When asked about their life and customs, they invariably answered that it was against the law to divulge information to foreigners.[33] This proved to be a serious obstacle, Perry had to admit. And it would remain so until Americans of intelligence learned the language and were allowed to live in Japan.

The criticism most often leveled at Perry was that he failed to negotiate a commercial treaty with the Japanese. For this reason, James Gordon Bennett of the *New York Herald* described the expedition as "an expensive failure."[34] Even Perry's supporters, such as the members of the New York Chamber of Commerce, seemed confused about what he had and had not accomplished. They assumed, for example, that the Treaty of Kanagawa was basically a trade instrument. In his book J. W. Spalding fueled the controversy by mocking the outcome of the expedition and noting that the General Assembly and governor of Rhode Island did not understand the difference between a trade agreement and a diplomatic pact.[35]

In the *Narrative* Perry answered his critics while trying to enlighten his friends. Japan, when he arrived, was "in a state of voluntary, long-continued, and determined isolation." It was unlike other nations that engaged in trade; it was a nation that repudiated commerce as evil. For this reason it was necessary to "settle the great preliminary that commerce would be allowed at all." Perry presented the Japanese with a copy of the Treaty of Wanghia, which opened four ports in China to American vessels. The Japanese studied it carefully for a week and then replied that trade could not be begun *yet*. Perry was not surprised by the Japanese response, but he accepted it. (There was no description in the *Narrative* of the exchange between Perry and Hayashi in which Hayashi bested

Perry in a debate over the relative merits of human life and commercial profit.) The problem then became one of providing in the treaty for the establishment of a resident consul and the purchase of supplies in such a way that would lead to future trade. This, Perry felt, he had accomplished. In fact, from his first letter to

Drawing of a horse by Hayashi Daigaku,
the commissioner's present to Perry;
Narrative of the Expedition

Secretary of the Navy William Graham about the expedition, Perry had argued that this initial contact would not lead to a trade agreement.

The treaty showed that the Japanese, while recognizing that trade was inevitable, wanted to experiment with contact with foreigners before establishing trade. Thus, "all, and indeed, more than all, that, under the circumstances, could reasonably have been expected, has been accomplished." Perry knew, the *Narrative* explained, "that our success would be but the forerunner of that of other powers, and as he [Perry] believed that new relations of trade once commenced, not only with ourselves, but with England, France, Holland, and Russia, could not, in the progress of events, fail effectually and forever not only to break up the old restrictive policy, and open Japan to the world, but must also lead gradually to liberal commercial treaties." In the future, Perry argued, Japan promised to be "amongst the most important of eastern nations, with which a profitable trade will be established."[36]

Perry, however, was interested in more than the problem of trade with Japan; he was dedicated from the start to the projection of American power in the western Pacific. In a short essay in Volume II, Perry returned to his earlier arguments on this subject. He offered a bold proposal, worthy of the strategic cast of his usual thinking but fraught with the contradictions of a democratic American trying to recut the cloth of traditional imperialism to fit a more equitable pattern. In his essay Perry called for the acquisition of Asian territory, the founding of American settlements in Asia, and the establishment of a number of protectorates, particularly in Southeast Asia. World commerce was on the increase, he argued, and there was a need to employ "the constantly accumulating capital" brought forth from the mines of California and Australia. In this situation it was important for the United States to open new avenues of trade in Asia. Many of the nations of Asia were under the sway of the European powers, but there were still countries that enjoyed "comparative independence." The United States had signed treaties with Japan, the Ryukyus, and Siam during an era when the government showed little interest in Asia. The day would soon come, however, "when political events, and the unanimous and urgent appeals of our commercial men, will make it obligatory on the United States to look with greater solicitude to our eastern commerce, and to extend the advantages of our national friendship and protection as well to Japan and Lew Chew as to other powers but little better known to western nations." Perry had in mind Siam (Thailand), Cambodia, Cochin China (Vietnam), parts of Borneo and Sumatra, and especially Formosa.[37]

Heretofore the trade potential of Asia had not been realized because in their negotiations with people like the Chinese, the European powers had treated their local counterparts as inferiors. The local people, knowing full well the "grasping propensities and love of encroachment" of the European powers, resisted their demands. It was incumbent upon the Western governments "to set the example of national probity before undertaking to coerce those of the East."[38]

In reexamining the Opium War, Perry argued that its causes could not be commended, but its results were beneficial to the Chinese. The English, however, had made the mistake of *being too cautious.* Instead they should have seized the opportunity "to establish throughout the empire a more liberal form of government." Moreover, the situation in China still necessitated the intervention of the United States and the Western powers to bring about a revolution, both civil and military. "The end would therefore unquestionably justify the means," Perry concluded; "and if ever an armed insurrection of one or more nations with the political condition of another could be fully justified, it would be, as I have stated, in bringing by force, if such result were necessary, the empires of China and Japan into the family of nations, upon the basis of equal international *duties* as well as rights."

The wheel had come full circle. Perry, who had preached "masterly inactivity" to Humphrey Marshall in China in order to protect the mission of the East India Squadron, was now calling for international intervention in order to "more thoroughly Europeanize" China.

But there was more. "The duty of protecting our vast and rapidly growing commerce will make it not only a measure of wisdom, but of positive necessity, to provide by timely preparation for events which must, in the ordinary course of things, transpire in the east. In the developments of the future, the destinies of our nation must assume conspicuous attitudes; we cannot expect to be free from the ambitious longings for increased power, which are the natural concomitants of national success. The annexation of one country or province, whether by conquest or purchase, will only tend to increase the desire to add another and another, and we, as a nation, would have no right to claim exemption from this universal vice, and in this view we should be prepared to meet the inevitable consequences of our own ambitious tendencies."[39]

In short, the United States alone should take the initiative by beginning to build new settlements in Formosa so that in time the island could become a source of coal for American steamers and an entrepôt for American trade in the East. Here Perry returned to the dispatch he wrote to the secretary of the navy in December 1852, on his way to China. England was quickly monopolizing the trade of the Orient, and the United States had no choice but to take over Formosa so that it "would rival the great commercial marts of Hong Kong and Singapore."[40]

Perry knew full well the moral and historical aversion that some of his fellow Americans felt toward the idea of becoming a colonial power. Colonialism evoked the memories of two wars fought to free their country from the crushing embrace of the mother country. So Perry chose another word, *settlement*, but his design was still very much in the grand imperial mold. He was in the end a realist, whose ideas carried him beyond morality when he advocated the inevitable expansion of trade and the concomitant projection of power. In the fallen world of great power politics, Perry advised the United States to accept the vices of empire and get on with the work of expansion.

Perry was not advancing his ideas in a vacuum. He had sent Joel Abbot and the *Macedonian* to Formosa to survey the harbor of Keelung and look for coal on the way back from Japan in the summer of 1854. In 1855 Gideon Nye, Jr., a merchant friend of Perry's and another merchant-adventurer, had raised the American flag in Formosa after securing a monopoly on the camphor trade. In 1857 Dr. Peter Parker, who had finally risen to the post of commissioner in China, forwarded with approval Nye and his associate's proposal for the establishment of an independent government on Formosa. One reason for a government protected by the United States, Parker wrote in a dispatch to the State Department, was to gain control of Formosa's coal supplies for an American steamship line.

Simultaneously, Nye wrote to Perry asking him to use his influence with the president to back his plan. Marcy, however, ignored Parker's and Nye's plans—and Perry's bold vision of expansion—and when Parker asked for a naval expedition as large as the one sent to Japan to back up Nye's scheme, Marcy turned him down.[41]

In the *Narrative*, Perry also advanced in greater detail his plans for the establishment of a colony at Port Lloyd in the Bonin Islands. In speeches and letters he continued to argue that the

United States' claim to the islands predated the British. Lieutenant George Preble reported, after sailing from Edo to Port Lloyd aboard the *Macedonian* in April 1854 on a cruise that was designed to reassert the United States' claim to the islands, that Perry had purchased ten acres at Port Lloyd for Howland and Aspinwall.[42] But already by 1856 Perry's and Howland and Aspinwall's dream of a great American steamship line that crossed the Pacific from San Francisco to Shanghai, thereby reversing the flow of international commerce and turning it into American hands, which had been the original hidden agenda of the expedition, was fading, at least for the immediate future.

The momentum for a trans-Pacific steamship line had diminished. Perry did return to the subject in a speech to the American Geographical and Statistical Society in March 1856. Meanwhile Howland and Aspinwall had completed their railroad line across Panama, giving them monopoly control of that route and of steamship travel from Panama to San Francisco. Congress's attention was focused on new plans for a transcontinental railroad. It was not until 1867 that Howland and Aspinwall bid on and received a $500,000 subsidy to carry the mails across the Pacific.[43] When the American steamers sailed for the Orient, they followed Matthew Maury's great circle route, calling at Yokohama on the way to Shanghai.

Even Perry's harshest critics noted his accomplishments. "He has worked hard and is deserving of much credit," Joel Abbot wrote from Hong Kong to a fellow officer. "He is rather a hard and unpleasant horse to be associated with being very selfish and exacting and feeling but little disposition to benefit others any further than it has a direct bearing upon his own fame and interest or that of his family and connections. He therefore does not make many real warm-hearted friends. And I fear he would disparage and pull down any one for a small amount of imaginary bumcumbe [buncombe] and consideration for himself or family connections."[44] Abbot, of course, had tried himself to pull strings at the Navy Department with a modicum of success, placing two sons aboard the *Macedonian* and one in the Naval Academy. But he resented Perry's more influential ties and greater success. Upon departing for Japan, Abbot had written a touching letter to his wife saying that, at his age, "changes may be expected and we may never meet again on earth." They did not. Despite pleas to be relieved of command of the East India Squadron, Abbot died in Hong Kong, mourned by his officers and sailors as a kind and Christian man.[45]

Among other accounts of the expedition, Williams's journal remained unpublished until early in the next century. Williams was a constant critic of the commodore; insufficient attention to the Sabbath was his greatest sin. But Williams judged the appointment of a naval officer to head to the expedition a wise choice "as it secured unity of purpose in the diplomatic and executive chief, and Perry is probably the only man in our navy capable of holding both positions, which has been proved by the general prudence and decision of his proceedings since he anchored at Uraga last July." There was no officer under him, Williams went on, "whose judgment and knowledge entitled him to the least weight in his [Perry's] mind; all except Buchanan, spent their thoughts in criticizing what he did and wishing they were going home." In this situation, if the commodore and the envoy had been two different persons, the expedition might have been crippled and its intentions thwarted. "But a dilemma was avoided," Williams concluded, "and Perry regarded all under him as only means and agents to serve his purpose, perhaps too often disregarding wishes and opinions of a comparatively trifling nature. But that extreme is almost unavoidable in minds of strong fibre, and bred for years to command, as he has been, such power has habit."[46]

Williams was less confident about the results of the expedition. Time alone would disclose them. He referred instead to "a paper of a general character" that he had composed with Perry's permission for Commissioner Hayashi before leaving Shimoda the last time. In it he pointed out that "Japan could learn much which would be of enduring benefit to her by adopting the improvements of western lands, and allowing her people to visit them and see for themselves." The president, he explained, had sent out with the expedition this particular collection of gifts (the telegraph, model steam locomotive, farm tools, books, drawings, etc.), not because they were interesting curiosities but so that the Japanese could learn to make them or obtain the assistance of those who could. The history of the past two hundred years in the West showed that

Japan had nothing to fear from "a greater extension of liberty" and that "no one could wish them to do aught which would be injurious or hazardous."

In general, Williams felt that the impression made by the squadron was favorable, and he prayed that "the light of revealed truth be permitted to shine upon the benighted and polluted minds of this people. . . . Among a people so inquisitive and acute, it cannot be long before some will be able to break away from the trammels which now bind them to Japan, and see, for as long as they wish, what Christianity has done for other lands, and what it will do for their own." Williams, in the end, saw "a vast reward for the expenses of this Expedition, and a gain to the cause of humanity and goodness beyond calculation in paltry gold or silver or traffic."[47]

As his twilight years advanced and his mind turned to the problems of his estate, Perry, in the face of competing claims, came to believe that he had originated the idea for the Japan expedition. In the *Narrative*, Commander James Glynn's carefully thought-out letter to Howland and Aspinwall, which advanced the argument for an expedition to Japan to lay the groundwork for a steamship line, was reduced to a plea from Glynn to establish communications between the United States and Japan.[48] Ranald MacDonald is never mentioned. In 1857 Perry solicited a letter from James Watson Webb in which Webb wrote that when they were neighbors in Tarrytown, Perry had spoken often about plans for the expedition, showing him his notes as to how it should be conducted. "I need not add," Webb wrote, "that I not only considered you the originator of the expedition, but the man of all others in the United States who was the best qualified to bring it about."[49]

In February 1858, Perry, now almost sixty-four years old, came down with a cold, which, aggravated by his arthritis, persisted for a month. He developed a fear of climbing steps, but his family felt confident that he would recover. At two in the morning on March fifth, he died of what was described as "rheumatism of the heart." The funeral was a grand one, a military pageant with five hundred men from the Seventh Regiment, two hundred officers from the First Division of the New York State Militia, and most impressive, a uniformed contingent of men and officers who had served under him on the Japan expedition. On one of the coldest days of the winter, they marched along crowd-lined streets, down Fifth Avenue to Fourteenth Street, then across to Second Avenue to St. Mark's Church on Tenth Street, the minute guns booming from navy ships in the ice-jammed harbor, church bells tolling their solemn hymn.[50] In the end, the commodore was laid to rest in the family plot in a graveyard in Newport, Rhode Island.

"The sum of Commodore Perry's character is this," wrote James Watson Webb in his obituary, "he was a model of a Naval Officer, scrupulously exact in his discipline and thoroughly American in all his views. He had the valor of a hero and the capacity of a statesman, but both were outshown by a magnanimous heart which beat only to the measures of generosity and justice."[51]

And what of Japan in the wake of the departing American naval squadron? In January 1855, Captain Henry Adams returned to Shimoda, which had been leveled by an earthquake and tidal wave, to exchange copies of the ratified treaty with the Japanese. He was greeted by Izawa Mimasaka, the commissioner who had become *bugyo* of Shimoda, and his assistant, Kurokawa Kaḥei. Adams had come back too soon, the Japanese officials explained. The treaty called for an exchange of ratifications *after* eighteen months. Adams insisted that the English and Dutch versions of the treaty specified *within* eighteen months, and the discussions quickly fell into that maddening pattern of delay, obfuscation, and confusion that had plagued the original talks. The Japanese seemed genuinely confused by the meaning of the word *within*, but as to another of Adams's demands, that the emperor sign the ratification, they were more adamant. The head of the Roju was the sovereign power, not the emperor, by whom the Japanese meant the shogun. It took more than three weeks to settle these matters. In the end, the Japanese appeared to concede to Adams's demands. Ratifications were exchanged, and Adams was told that the shogun had signed the instrument along with Abe Masahiro and other members of the Roju. Adams went home satisfied, not knowing that only the signatures of Abe and members of the Roju appeared on the document.[52]

From the time of Perry's arrival until the opening of Yokohama in 1859, Shimoda continued to serve as a testing ground for relations with foreigners. A fortnight after Perry's departure from Shimoda in June 1854, an American clipper ship, the *Lady Pierce*, dropped anchor off Uraga. Her captain, seeking the distinction of being the first to trade with Japan under the new treaty, was received warmly but told that he could only go ashore at Shimoda or Hakodate. The *Lady Pierce* went on to Shimoda but found the Japanese unwilling to trade. On December 4, 1854, Admiral Putiatin arrived in Shimoda aboard the Russian ship *Diana* after being denied entrance to Osaka. Putiatin renewed his efforts to negotiate a treaty but was interrupted by a staggering earthquake that leveled Shimoda and Kakisaki and repeatedly flushed and filled the harbor like a giant toilet bowl, leaving the *Diana* first on the bottom and then whirling in one frightening maelstrom after another. The *Diana*, badly crippled, survived only to founder on a voyage along the coast. The Russians continued their negotiations during Adams's visit, finally signing a treaty modeled after the Treaty of Kanagawa on February 7, 1855.[53]

Soon after Adams's departure, another American ship, the *Caroline E. Foote*, arrived at Shimoda from Hawaii on her way to Hakodate with a load of supplies for whalers. The Japanese were in for a new surprise. The ship's company included three women and two children. The Americans were housed at the Gyokusenji Temple but told that there would be no trading. After a time the American captain chartered his ship to the Russians, who having lost the *Diana* needed a means of transport to Petropavlovsk. The Bakufu, it now became clear, was willing to allow foreign ships to call at Shimoda for supplies but remained hostile to trade and to permitting foreigners to live ashore.

The Bakufu also clarified one other important matter for local officials. After a lengthy exchange of opinions between various levels of the bureaucracy, Abe Masahiro ordered the Shimoda *bugyo*'s office not to employ prostitutes to entertain foreigners. The foreigners would be impressed by their generosity if they provided them with women, Abe argued, but they were under no obligation to do so. Further, if the foreigners became "addicted to Japanese women," those with high positions might enjoy their companionship

while those of lower rank might be denied these pleasures and turn
to the women of Shimoda instead. Prostitutes could be used to get
the foreigners to lessen their demands, but the eventual impact
could be disastrous, both on efforts to improve "the public morals
of obscene Shimoda" and on the effort to mobilize the country
against the foreigners.[54]

The conclusive test of the Treaty of Kanagawa came with the
arrival of Townsend Harris, the first American consul, in August
21, 1856. Harris had instructions to press for a commercial treaty
with the Bakufu. The Japanese, however, resisted the idea of accepting a consul, insisting that the treaty called for an exchange
of consuls only by mutual agreement. The Bakufu officials were
clearly misreading the treaty, where an exchange of consuls at the
insistence of either party was called for in Article XI. The Bakufu
kept Harris isolated in the Gyokusenji Temple in Kakisaki and
bogged down in frustrating negotiations for months. Meanwhile
they heard through the Dutch at Nagasaki that the British had
captured and bombarded Canton in the Arrow War because of
China's failure to live up to the treaty that ended the Opium
War. Harris, who if anything was more obstinate and idiosyn-
cratic than Perry (the evidence also indicates that he had serious problems with alcohol and perhaps opium), threatened and
cajoled.

Ultimately, it was the possibility that a British or joint British
and French squadron might be on its way to Japan to chastise the
reluctant Bakufu, a threat that Harris played on for all it was
worth, that led to a breakthrough in Harris's talks with the Bakufu
officials. In late 1857 Harris found himself in Edo at an audience
with the half-witted shogun, Iesada, who acted like a petulant child
but spoke briefly to Harris. Late in the afternoon of July 29, 1858,
Harris and the Bakufu negotiators signed a trade treaty aboard
the steamer *Powhatan*. The treaty called for the opening of Hakodate, Nagasaki, Niigata, Hyogo (near Osaka), and Kanagawa
(changed later to Yokohama) to trade. The American envoy was
permitted to live in Edo, and after January 1, 1862, the city of the
Tokugawa shoguns would be open to American residents.[55]

Commodore Perry had died more than four months earlier.
But he was vindicated by the new trade agreement. He had always

insisted that he had laid the groundwork for future trade and that a commercial agreement was inevitable.

In the three years between Perry's return from Japan and his death, his vision of the projection of American power into the Pacific was ignored in the face of increasingly bitter recriminations, then outright bloodshed, over the purely domestic issue of slavery. The United States was embarked on a course that would lead to civil war. Japan too was headed for chaos, civil war, and the downfall of the shogunate, which would come a decade after Perry's death. In Japan, however, international rather than domestic issues, specifically the arrival of the Western powers at the very gates of the shogun's castle in the person of Perry and his squadron, were the precipitating element that led to the final conflict.

In the years immediately after Perry's departure, the European powers' involvement in the Crimean War (England, France, and Austria allied with Turkey against Russia) and England and France's attack on China in the Arrow War offered the Bakufu a brief respite, time enough to try once again to mobilize against the threat of foreign intrusion. The debate over how to confront the barbarians raged on, pitting Nariaki's followers—the exponents of *joi*, or the expulsion of the foreigners, backed by the increasingly active outside daimyo—against the followers of Ii Naosuke's more conciliatory policy of opening trade with the West. In 1855 Abe Masahiro gave up his efforts to reconcile the contending factions and resigned from the Roju. He died two years later at the age of thirty-eight.[56]

With Abe's resignation, Tokugawa Nariaki lost whatever influence he had previously exerted within the Bakufu. Under the new head of the Roju, Hotta Masayoshi, the Bakufu signed trade agreements with Holland, Russia, the United States, England, and France. These treaties granted foreigners extraterritoriality and further undermined the sovereignty of the Bakufu by setting tariff rates. Thus the treaties were very much of the pattern of those forced upon China after the Opium War. What most Japanese had for so long dreaded had finally come about, without, of course, the invasion of the homeland.

In the course of negotiating the treaties, Hotta Masayoshi repeated Abe Masahiro's strategem of 1853: he circulated an account
of a discussion with Townsend Harris in which Harris talked of
why Japan had to open itself to the outside world. Hotta sent it to
all the feudal lords, various parts of the bureaucracy, and to the
emperor's court in Kyoto. To his surprise Hotta found that while
both pro and anti forces were critical of the proposed treaties, both
parties recognized the inevitability of trade. Tokugawa Nariaki,
always ready with a new initiative, proposed, for example, that the
Bakufu send him at the head of a group of *ronin* (masterless samurai), criminals, and younger sons of merchants and farmers to the
United States to set up a trading post![57]

To complicate matters further, the emperor's court emerged
as a new factor in the increasingly complex equation of power.
Many of the noble families had been greatly influenced by Nariaki's
ideas and by his sub rosa machinations among court officials during
the 1840s. Accordingly, they prevailed upon the emperor to reject
Hotta's appeal for support for the American treaty. Hotta's effort
to build a consensus, like Abe's before him, had backfired, and in
1858 he resigned in favor of Ii Naosuke. Under Ii, the Bakufu signed
the American treaty and then treaties with the other foreign powers
without the court's consent. These treaties opened Yokohama, Nagasaki, and Hakodate to foreign trade in 1859.[58]

Known as the unequal treaties, these new agreements further
undermined the already weakened Bakufu. The Bakufu was now
ranged against the court and a group of reforming lords, who like
Shimazu Nariakira hailed from the outside domains, the traditional
enemies of the Tokugawa. The Bakufu had disobeyed "the Imperial
command" and aroused the anger of the Gods, one chronicler of the
period wrote, over "the continual pollution of our country by the
visits of the outer barbarians." From many directions and in many
different voices came calls for the reform of the Bakufu while the
domains themselves—Mito, Satsuma, Choshu, and others—began
their own experiments with reform, the manufacture of weapons,
construction of ships, and attempts to start new industries. Many
of these reformers supported one thing in common: the designation
of Nariaki's son, Tokugawa Yoshinobu, the daimyo of Hitotsubashi,
as the successor to the dim-witted shogun, Tokugawa Iesada.

Ii Naosuke, as *tairo*, or regent, blocked Yoshinobu's succession. Tokugawa Iemochi, the head of one of the *gosanke* houses, became shogun upon Iesada's death, and Ii moved against Nariaki's supporters, instituting the Ansei purge. In August 1858, Nariaki was banished to Mito where he was to remain incommunicado for the last two years of his life while his supporters were subjected to torture, banishment, and death by "voluntary" suicide, decapitation, and immolation. Ii's purge turned many of those who had advocated the reform of the Bakufu into its bitterest enemies. It was at this time, for instance, that Yoshida Shoin, the young samurai who had asked Perry to smuggle him aboard his steamer to America, was executed for plotting against one of Ii's retainers. And a year later Ii himself was assassinated, cut down in the snow at the Sakurada Gate just outside Edo Castle by a band of samurai and Shinto priests, most of whom came from Mito.

With Ii gone from the scene, violence grew apace while a party led by Yoshinobu called for reform, "unity of the Court and the Bakufu," cancellation of the treaties, and perhaps even the expulsion of the barbarians. The Bakufu, however, had been fatally weakened, and in the growing climate of lawlessness, anonymous samurai sought to provoke a confrontation with the barbarians by attacking foreigners. Among those killed was Henry Heusken, a young Dutchman who served as Townsend Harris's interpreter. When Yoshinobu spoke of expelling the barbarians, by which he meant opening *negotiations* to persuade them to withdraw, the leaders of the Choshu domain upped the ante by firing on American, Dutch, and French merchant ships in the Strait of Shimonoseki in June 1863. The British were the first to respond. In retaliation for the killing of a British official in Yokohama, they bombarded Kagoshima on the Satsuma Peninsula, leveling much of the city, including the new factories set up by Shimazu Nariakira. A year later a joint force of American, Dutch, French, and British warships destroyed the coastal forts in Choshu, and British and French troops were stationed on Japanese soil.

After decades of rhetoric about expelling the barbarians, Choshu's precipitious attempt put an end to the idea forever. Two years later, in 1865, the court finally gave its approval to the unequal treaties while the Bakufu promised to seek their revision. The end for the Bakufu, however, was now in sight.

For one thing, the feudal order was in an advanced state of decay. Indeed, the very ground that it rested upon was subject to frightening tremors. A market economy dominated by the big city merchants, their village counterparts, and wealthier peasants was rapidly supplanting the remnants of the old Bakufu and daimyo-controlled economic order. This development was accelerated by the beginnings of foreign trade in 1860, after which parts of the economy, and particularly key urban centers, were increasingly linked to the vagaries of the world market. The results were inflation and growing poverty for the poorer peasants and new prosperity for the richer peasants and merchants, who produced and sold goods, particularly silk, for the foreign market. Class polarization increased in the countryside, followed by a new round of popular uprisings on an unprecedented scale.[59]

Simultaneously, the Bakufu, with one eye on "the lower orders," began its death struggle. First came a revolt in Kyoto staged by samurai from Choshu, which was put down by the Bakufu with the help of Satsuma. But when the Bakufu moved against Choshu with the intention of destroying the ruling Mori clan once and for all, Satsuma came to Choshu's defense. The Bakufu lacked the support to mount a successful offensive against its opponents. In August 1866 Iemochi died and Tokugawa Yoshinobu became the shogun. A year later he offered to resign but then made one last halfhearted attempt to resist the combined military forces of Satsuma and Choshu. When that failed, he retreated to Edo Castle, where he agreed to step down as shogun on May 3, 1868.

With Yoshinobu's resignation, 265 years of Tokugawa rule came to an end. Much of the maneuvering in the last two years before Yoshinobu's demise had involved the issue of who would ultimately gain control of the fifteen-year-old emperor, Mutsuhito. He was the Meiji emperor, and the young samurai reformers proclaimed a new government in his name. They stripped the Tokugawas of their lands and power, dismantled the Bakufu, and abolished the daimyo system. In the spirit of national unity, Japan set out on a new course to build unity and strength and revise the humiliating unequal treaties. *Fokoku-kyohei*, "enrich the country and strengthen the army," became the new operative slogan. Since the Opium War, Japan's leaders and intellectuals had studied the Western imperial powers carefully, first as they extracted concessions from the Ch'ing dynasty, then as Perry and his successors worked their aggressive stratagems against the Land of the Gods itself. As many foreigners had noted, the Japanese were careful students of the ways of the outer barbarians. Perry called them "a very imitative, adaptative, and compliant people." Now the Japanese were ready to assimilate the lessons that had been forced upon them and to begin their bid for parity with the great powers and ultimately for an empire of their own.

15

THE BLACK SHIP METAPHOR, THE SECOND OPENING OF JAPAN, AND GLOBAL HEGEMONY

The memory of those ships—known as the "black ships" because of both their color and their impact—is forever etched into Japan's psyche.[1]
—CLYDE V. PRESTOWITZ, JR., former U.S. trade negotiator, 1989

We stand in Tokyo today reminiscent of our countryman, Commodore Perry, ninety-two years ago. His purpose was to bring to Japan an era of enlightenment and progress, by lifting the veil of isolation to the friendship, trade, and commerce of the world. But alas the knowledge thereby gained of Western science was forged into an instrument of oppression and human enslavement.[2]
—GENERAL DOUGLAS MACARTHUR at the surrender ceremony aboard the U.S.S. *Missouri*, September 2, 1945

There was also a deeper issue, which I came to call the "black ship mentality." The Japanese press always casts its bureaucrats in the role of defending the sacred islands from invasion. Trade is seen both by the Japanese public and its officials as a zero-sum game; and while the necessity of keeping the U.S. market open imposes on them the need to use the free-trade rhetoric of the West, no Japanese bureaucrat who values his reputation can think of making a concession until he has demonstrated publicly that there is absolutely no alternative.[3]
—CLYDE V. PRESTOWITZ, JR., former U.S. trade negotiator, 1989

Perhaps we did not win the war, perhaps the Japanese, unknown even to themselves, were the winners.[4]
                    —THEODORE H. WHITE, *The New York Times,* July 28, 1985

Japan does not aspire to replace America as the world's leader; it will be content to stay number two. . . . The Japanese people have yet to find a new and exciting goal for their energies.[5]
                    —OKITA SABURO, former minister of foreign affairs, Summer 1989

We still do not have a clear idea of whether to depend on the U.S., or to do as much as we can ourselves. But I think that whenever we can, we are going our own way.[6]
                    —HAGI JIRO, chief of planning, Japanese Self-Defense Agency,
                    June 24, 1989

The American nuclear umbrella is just an illusion as far as the Japanese people are concerned. . . . The time has come to tell the United States that we do not need American protection. Japan will protect itself with its own power and wisdom.[7]
                    —ISHIHARA SHINTARO, former Liberal Democratic Party
                    cabinet minister, 1989

At a conspicuous public level, each side already engages in the ritual reenactment of patriotic anger.[8]   —JOHN DOWER, 1986

And let everyone realize his limitations. It is the biggest dew drop that falls first from the leaf.[9]   —TOKUGAWA IEYASU

SEPTEMBER 2, 1945, was a surprisingly cool day for late summer in Japan. Dull gray clouds hung low over Tokyo Bay. At 5 A.M. a delegation of officials from the imperial government led by the foreign minister and the army chief of staff left the flattened and burned-out remains of Tokyo. The delegation was driving to Yokohama to go aboard the U.S.S. *Missouri,* General Douglas MacArthur's flagship, to sign the instruments of unconditional surrender, which would bring World War II to an end. Along the highway the Japanese officials could see nothing but miles and miles of debris and destruction. It looked as if the gods themselves had descended to earth and burned and looted in random fury. "The ghastly sight of death and desolation was enough to freeze my heart," wrote Kase Toshiakazu, a member of the delegation. "These hollow ruins, however, were perhaps a fit prelude to the poignant drama in which we were about to take part for were we not sorrowing men come to seek a tomb for a fallen Empire?"

Sony buys Columbia Pictures; cartoon by M. G. Lord

Whether they thought of it or not, these nine men were traveling the same road that Hayashi Daigaku, Kayama Eizaemon, Toda Izu, and many other officials had trod as they shuttled back and forth between Edo, Uraga, and Yokohama in their difficult dealings with another formidable American naval force under Commodore Matthew Calbraith Perry. The destruction they witnessed was, of course, not the work of the gods, but of American B-29s, and it was the tragic result of the relationship that had begun ninety-two years earlier on the beach at Yokohama.

At Yokohama the military members of the delegation left their swords at the office of the prefectural governor and went aboard an American destroyer to be ferried to the flagship. Where the black ships of Perry's East India Squadron had once anchored, the horizon was filled with swarms of gray warships anchored in tight lines, their guns like those of Perry's fleet trained on the shore. Earlier the Eighth Army had landed at Yokohama, occupying what remained of the city and the surrounding countryside. The *Missouri* towered over them as the delegates approached in a small launch. Rows of sailors dressed in immaculate whites hung over the rail, straining to catch a glimpse of the defeated Japanese. The officials clambered aboard and faced MacArthur, who stood head and shoulders over the diminutive and sullen delegates. Draped over the rear turret was a tattered American flag bearing thirty-one stars. It was Perry's flag, the commodore's ensign that had flown from his flagship in these very same waters, brought to Tokyo especially for the occasion. Standing before the flag and the ranks of American officers, the Japanese officials felt, Kase wrote, "like penitent boys awaiting the dreaded schoolmaster."

MacArthur stepped to the microphone, and then after his brief remarks, the Japanese and allied representatives signed the surrender documents. At the very moment that MacArthur proclaimed the proceedings at an end, the clouds parted and the sun shone through as 400 B-29s and 1,500 fighter planes roared over the fleet. After the surrender ceremony, MacArthur addressed an American audience by radio.

We stand in Tokyo today reminiscent of our countryman, Commodore Perry, ninety-two years ago. His purpose was to bring to Japan an era of enlightenment and progress, by lifting the veil of isolation to the friendship, trade, and commerce of the world. But alas the knowledge thereby gained of Western science was forged into an instrument of oppression and human enslavement. Freedom of expression, freedom of action, even freedom of thought were denied through appeal to superstition, and through the application of force. We are committed by the Potsdam Declaration of principles to see that the Japanese people are liberated from this condition of slavery.[10]

It was not surprising that MacArthur turned to Perry at this pivotal moment in Japanese history. For both the Japanese and the Americans, Perry and his squadron of black ships was in 1945 and still is today the central metaphor that describes their long and convoluted relationship. Granted, this is more so for the Japanese because Perry's arrival marked their reentry into the outside world and their first entry into the world of global capitalism. For the more than two hundred and fifty years of the Tokugawa shogunate, the Japanese had viewed the world as if through the wrong end of a telescope, only to have the reality of Western expansion into Asia brought suddenly and sharply into focus by Perry's arrival off Uraga.

For most Americans the opening of Japan remains an obscure event, one of many instances of the United States' aggressive diplomacy throughout the world. Its significance is misunderstood by American historians and policymakers and confused on occasion by the lay public with Robert Peary's trek to the North Pole. At the cost of 100,000 American, 150,000 Okinawan, and 2.5 million Japanese lives, the United States fought a major war with Japan for control of the Pacific and then forged an often antagonistic alliance that today is not only our most important bilateral relationship but also one whose impact has major implications for the world economy. Thus it is startling how little Americans know about Perry and his endeavors.

In his own time Perry's peers, whether eager to praise or criticize him, misinterpreted the significance of what he had accomplished. So it is not surprising that such misunderstandings should have persisted or rather should have resurfaced in the Cold War era. It was thought in the 1850s, despite Perry's explanation in the official narrative of the expedition, that he had opened trade with Japan. Little was said about what he had actually accomplished through the signing of the Treaty of Kanagawa and less was understood about his real objectives in visiting Japan.

The first of the small handful of historians who researched and wrote about Perry viewed his accomplishments solely in the context of Japan. William Elliot Griffis, the missionary-scholar who wrote Perry's first biography, in 1887, saw Perry much as Perry would have liked to have been seen. For Griffis, writing in the early years of Japan's rapid industrialization under the leadership of the samurai reformers who had overthrown the shogun, "the object lesson in modern civilization, given by Perry on the sward at Yokohama, is now illustrated on a national scale."[11] Perry, as Perry had claimed, had brought civilization to half-civilized Japan.

It took a historian with a broader view of events in Asia—and a practical need to understand them—to first plumb the larger strategic significance of the Japan expedition. Tyler Dennett was doing background research for the Washington Naval Conference of 1921–1922, which would produce among other things the first and last successful agreement to limit Japanese naval power in the Pacific. In his research, Dennett worked his way systematically through documents at the U.S. State Department and Navy Department and put together the first accurate analysis of Perry's intentions.[12] Without discussing Perry's long-standing ties with New York's China merchants and his job supervising the construction of the government-subsidized mail steamers, Dennett identified coal supplies as a key reason for Perry's visit. Without discussing the numerous schemes for a steamship line that would connect San Francisco and Shanghai, Dennett suggested that Perry, in a sense, went to Japan for the sake of the United States' ties with China. More important than that, he described Perry's formulation of his intentions as "the first comprehensive statement of the basis of an American policy for the Pacific." Perry appeared to Dennett to be the first American official "to view the commercial but also the political problems of Asia and the Pacific as a unity."[13]

Before Perry, the United States' Asia policy, such as it was, was the private creation of a handful of powerful, politically connected merchants, largely from New York and Boston. For these merchant-capitalists, diplomatic relations might have been important but they were a subordinate part of their narrowly focused strategy of market penetration. Perry changed all that. He had commanded U.S. naval forces during the conquest of Mexico and was very much in tune with the increasingly interventionist tenor of U.S. foreign policy as it manifested itself in the Caribbean and Central America. Moreover, as a naval officer who had played a key role in the beginnings of a steam navy, he of necessity had to think in strategic terms. To serve the interests of his merchant friends, naval power needed to be projected great distances. To reach the new markets of China—again a necessity according to

Perry, given the expanding nature of American capitalism after the California gold rush—an aspiring power like the United States had no choice but to emulate the territorial ambitions of the British. Simply put, a steam navy and the new merchant steam fleet, which would inevitably replace even the fleet-footed clipper ships, needed coaling stations.

Beyond that, the United States had to deal with what Perry called the "monopolistic" intentions of the British. In the middle of the nineteenth century, England was *the* hegemonic imperial power, and Perry was a careful student of British imperialism in all its manifestations. He had witnessed the beginning of the end of the era of naval sail and followed the beginnings of England's steam navy, noting carefully the use of mail subsidies to build convertible steamships. He had traversed the route of the British-owned Peninsula and Oriental Steam Navigation Company on his way to China and had noted that, with Singapore, England controlled one entrance to the South China Sea. With Hong Kong, England also controlled both a major strategic island and a burgeoning entrepôt near the very heart of the China market. Perry knew of and challenged England's claim to the Bonin Islands, a claim that if sustained would give England control of an outpost sitting astride the eastern entrance to both the South and East China seas. In Perry's mind England was well on its way to securing what are called today the sea lanes of control (SLOCs) that led to the China market.

All of Perry's studies of the former mother country pointed to one conclusion: the United States, whatever its misgivings about territorial acquisition, must indulge in this "universal vice" and acquire its own territory in Asia. With coaling stations in Japan, Okinawa, and the Bonin Islands, the United States would control the northeasterly approach to China that followed Maury's great circle route across the North Pacific.

Perry's problem was that he voiced his imperial ambitions at a time when the United States was not yet ready to act upon them. First came the great turning inward during the Civil War, which was followed by a period of domestic expansion. The construction of the transcontinental railroad and the subjugation of the Indian population in the West were followed by a new overseas expansionary dynamic that culminated in the Spanish-American War and the United States' occupation of the Philippines. To justify the American seizure of the Philippines, President William McKinley used an argument remarkably similar to Perry's: if the United States did not hold on to the islands, some European power would.[14] A little over fifty years after his death, Perry's vision of the projection of American power into the Pacific was vindicated.

For the next half century and more, however, the United States remained an Atlantic-oriented power, and the problem of Japan, until the 1930s, hovered around the edges but was hardly central to the formulation of American foreign policy. Although the United States, England, and Japan quarreled incessantly over their interests in China, ultimately it was Japan's projection of its own power into Southeast Asia beginning in 1938 that led to Pearl Harbor. Japan, in the United States' view, was seeking hegemony in East Asia and threatening to undermine both American interests and those of the British empire.[15]

Thus before World War II, the United States began to define its Pacific interests not only in terms of the China market but also in terms of those countries to which Perry had suggested that the United States "extend the advantages of our national friendship and protection"—namely Thailand, Vietnam, Indonesia, and Taiwan. Among its would-be allies, England and France were influential powers in Southeast Asia. So in a sense the United States went to war with Japan not only to protect its own interests but also the interests of British and French imperialism.

In the aftermath of Hiroshima and Nagasaki, the United States, now the hegemonic power in the Pacific, assumed protective responsibility for the wreckage of Japan's Greater East Asia Co-prosperity Sphere. In the new era of national liberation struggles, the United States also inherited the burdens of decolonization in places such as China, Korea, Vietnam, and the Philippines. The results for the United States were the bloody and tragic wars in Korea and Vietnam.

In the postwar years, Perry began to be seen in the United States not in the context of U.S. strategy in the Pacific Basin but in terms of the larger global confrontation with Russia. According to Perry's only serious modern biographer, the official naval his-

torian Samuel Eliot Morison, Perry was a harbinger of the Cold
War. Perry, it was true, had believed in the inevitability of geography and that belief brought Russia to mind. Thus in his address
to the American Geographical and Statistical Society, Perry noted
that

it requires no sage to predict events so strongly foreshadowed to us
all; still "Westward" will "the course of empire take its way." But the
last act of the drama is yet to be unfolded. . . . to me it seems that the
people of America will, in some form or other, extend their dominion
and their power, until they shall have brought within their mighty
embrace the Islands of the great Pacific, and placed the Saxon race
upon the eastern shores of Asia. And I think too, that eastward and
southward will her great rival in future aggrandizement [Russia]
stretch forth her power to the coasts of China and Siam: and thus the
Saxon and the Cossack will meet once more, in strife or in friendship,
on another field. Will it be friendship: I fear not! The antagonistic
exponents of freedom and absolutism must meet at last, and then will
be fought that mighty battle on which the world will look with breath-
less interest; for on its issues will depend the freedom or the slavery
of the world.

Despite his study of naval history, Morison, who took on the
role of Perry's hagiographer, ignored both the importance of steamship lines and Perry's larger strategic vision. Instead he sought to
defend Perry against the "left wing" charge of being just another
imperialist. "It is therefore correct," Morison wrote, "to call Perry
an 'imperialist,' but he was an imperialist with a difference, es-
chewing forcible annexation, punitive expeditions, or forcing religion and trade on people who desired neither."[16] If this is the case,
it is difficult to understand in Morison's terms just what Perry, by
his own account, was doing in China, Okinawa, the Bonins, and
Japan.

Morison's description of Perry as a proto–Cold Warrior was
typical of the ideological obfuscation that masked the history of
the projection of American power into the Pacific Basin. According
to established ideology, Japan in the Cold War years became the
keystone of a *defensive* strategic arc that ran from Hokkaido in the
north to Thailand in the south. The arc, it was said, was a kind of

cordon sanitaire constructed to protect freedom and democracy from the spread of communism. To reach this conclusion, however, it was necessary to ignore history, Perry, and the nature of the dictatorial regimes in Korea, Taiwan, and Vietnam, which the United States nurtured and sustained. The United States had come to the shores of Asia as part of the *offensive projection of power* into the eastern Pacific on behalf of the masters of a political economy who judged the markets and resources of Asia to be crucial to its growth, and Perry was their harbinger.[17]

For Japan World War II resulted in what Tokugawa Nariaki had warned Abe Masahiro would happen to the Land of the Gods if the Roju did not expel the barbarians: its occupation by a foreign power. With all the moral fervency that Perry and his fellow expansionists had summoned with great righteousness, the United States during its occupation of Japan set out to recreate Japan in its own image. But this course was abandoned as early as 1949. In the interest of combating Russia's supposed threat to northern China, Korea, and Japan itself, Japan was resurrected as an ally, albeit a junior partner that continued to "host" the armed forces of its conqueror. Japan now became a bulwark against communism, a model of a successful capitalist democracy, the keystone of the Pacific, and by the 1980s—in the imagery of former Prime Minister Nakasone Yasuhiro—a giant aircraft carrier stationed off the coast of Russian Siberia.[18]

Ironically, the United States, in rebuilding Japan, accepted the argument of the Japanese warlords who had set out to conquer Asia in the 1930s. Japan, they had argued, was a small island with a limited population that needed the markets and resources of Asia to survive. In the postwar world the United States offered only one proviso: Japan was not to renew its ties with China, which was now under Communist control. Instead Japan, sheltered by the United States' strategic umbrella and with its conqueror as its sponsor, was to renew its economic penetration of Southeast Asia. As early as 1949 George Kennan spoke of Japan's need for an "empire to the south." During the Eisenhower administration it became axiomatic that the growing U.S. presence in Southeast Asia, which increasingly focused on Vietnam, was not only for the good of the United States but also for the good of its closest Asian ally.[19]

Perry would have understood and endorsed the United States forming a strategic arc that swept through Southeast Asia. He would have been pleased, if stunned, that in the wake of England's withdrawal from Singapore in 1965, the U.S. Navy was now responsible for control of the vital Strait of Malacca, the entrance to the South China Sea from the west. But Perry, no less than Abe Masahiro or Tokugawa Nariaki, would have been amazed at the twists and turns of modern diplomacy. Japan, having emulated Perry in its first military expedition to the Asian mainland in 1876, was being invited to build a new economic empire under the guns of the modern equivalent of the black ships.

For the United States, the era of the Pacific Basin dawned in the 1960s. With more than half the world's trade now running back and forth across the Pacific with the United States at the center of that trading system, Captain James Glynn's claim in his letter to Howland and Aspinwall that a Japan expedition would lead to redirecting trade with Asia into American hands had been substantiated. In this situation the black ship metaphor began to take on new and ominous meanings for the Japanese. Japanese historians, often influenced by Marxism and definitely influenced by Japan's subordinate role in the new American imperium, now saw Perry transfigured from a stern but beneficent figure, a precursor of MacArthur, who offered Japan the blessings of Western technology, into a menacing figure who had used the threat of a naval bombardment to force Japan to open its doors. More important, the black ships came to symbolize the growing confrontation between Japan and the United States over trade issues, which began over textiles in 1968. These clashes evoked not only the negotiations between Perry and Hayashi Daigaku on the beach at Yokohama; they were shadowed by other ghosts from Tokugawa Japan. The United States, in short, saw itself as demanding the second opening of Japan.

Even after 135 years of complex and often tragic relations, American understanding of Japan still reached barely beyond the shores of Tokyo Bay. This was at the heart of the growing conflict with Japan. The arrival of the black ships had triggered the downfall of the Bakufu in a peculiarly Japanese "revolution from above." The deeply conservative samurai reformers who carried out the Meiji restoration threw out many aspects of Tokugawa feudalism and concentrated political and economic power in the hands of a centralized state apparatus. After a careful study of foreign political, military, and economic systems, the Japanese framed a constitution with the assistance of a number of German advisors that provided for a stunted form of democracy within a system that increasingly emphasized hierarchy, militarism, loyalty, and unquestioned worship of the emperor as a living god—all values that were profoundly at odds with and in fact superseded the claims of nascent democracy. In this context it was the state and particularly the new bureaucratic fiefdoms that took the lead, pushing Japan through forced industrialization in order to catch up with the West and avoid the fate of China. Internationally, Japan, again playing a catch-up game, emulated the Western imperialist powers, particularly the British, in its efforts to build an empire.

In the 1930s Japan's democratic facade had crumbled, leaving an avowedly fascist clique of politicians, military figures, and bureaucrats, who were closely allied to Japan's four great *zaibatsu*, or commercial combines (Mitsui, Mitsubishi, Sumitomo, and Yasuda), in power. This clique, or rather shifting alliance of cliques, opted ultimately for military expansion on the Asian mainland and war with the United States.

In 1945 the black ships had returned, bearing occupation forces to a defeated Japan. MacArthur and a determined group of reformers within the Supreme Command of Allied Powers (SCAP), in a second revolution from above, set out to remake Japan in the image of a Western democracy with a competitive capitalist economy. Again, as in the early years of the Meiji regime, the reforms touched only certain aspects of Japanese society (the land system, for example). Buffeted by popular upheaval at home and the perceived threat of communism from abroad, both of which were linked in the Americans' eyes, the reform effort was called off.

Supremely adaptive and with no other choice, the Japanese at first went along with MacArthur. Then when the American reformers lost their momentum, Japan's leaders quietly began to reintroduce many elements of the prewar authoritarian system. It was a problem of how to be "a good loser," wrote Yoshida Shigeru, the three-time prime minister who worked closely with SCAP from 1945 to 1954 to refashion what historian John Dower called "the new conservative hegemony." Being a "good loser," according to Yoshida, "meant that I was going to say all that I felt needed saying but that I would co-operate at the same time with the Occupation Forces to the best of my power. Whatever harm was done through the Occupation Forces not listening to what I had to say could be remedied after we had regained our independence."[20]

SCAP signaled the end of the reform experiment with its own internal purge of Communist suspects in 1947 and 1948. Next, SCAP ordered the Japanese to purge the civil service of suspected Communists and fellow travelers. A series of events followed that set the new Japan well on the road to restoring many of the features of the old: the restoration of the *zaibatsu* (now known as *keiretsu*), the depurge of two hundred thousand former war criminals, tougher labor laws that weakened those introduced by SCAP's discredited New Dealers, and the beginning of Japanese rearmament.[21]

With the Korean War, the United States' remilitarization of the Western Pacific began to prime the economic pumps in Japan. At the same time the United States encouraged Japan to focus on building an export-oriented economy. Vietnam proved to be a further instance of American military Keynesianism; demand for war matériel again strengthened Japan's economy. By the end of the Vietnam era, Japan was experiencing rapid economic growth.

It was at this point—starting in 1968 with the issue of textile exports to the United States—that the United States first became alarmed about the economic stirrings of its willful pupil to the east. There had been complaints about Japanese barriers to the import of U.S. capital in the 1950s. But now Japan was threatening to undermine an important domestic industry with its cheap exports. Again the Japanese employed a tactic that it had learned from a past master of cutthroat capitalism. Following a practice developed by the great American trusts in the late nineteenth century, the Japanese engaged in predatory pricing: cutting prices below cost, driving local competitors into bankruptcy, and then taking over the market.[22]

Beginning with the textiles dispute, the black ships returned, this time loaded with oranges, beef, rice, and baseball bats—all commodities that American companies wanted to sell in Japan. The Japanese, however, had built a fleet of their own, which brought automobiles, steel, and consumer electronics to the shores of America. United States–Japan relations were wobbling into a ritualized pattern that Clyde V. Prestowitz, Jr., who served the U.S. Commerce Department as a trade negotiator from 1981 to 1986, argued began with Perry's arrival.[23] And each round of negotiations seemed to exacerbate feelings between the two powers, so that by 1986 John Dower could write, "At a conspicuous public level, each side already engages in the ritual enactment of patriotic anger." Politicians and commentators would wonder who had won World War II, and Howard Baker could conclude during his 1984 presidential campaign that there were two pertinent facts about United States–Japan relations: "First, we're still at war with Japan. Second, we're losing."[24] In economic terms the United States had experienced a major power inversion, and according to Clyde Prestowitz, what was at stake in these negotiations was no less than the global economic hegemony of the United States.[25]

From an American perspective the problem was acute myopia, an inability to bring the world of Japanese economic power into clear focus. It is a disability that can be traced directly to the illusions of racial superiority that inflamed the minds of the great missionary imperialists of the nineteenth century and persists today. The lesson they preached was a simple one: to succeed, Japan had to become civilized like the West. To recover in the postwar world, Japan had to become like the United States: democratic, capitalistic, and espousing free trade. Japan, ever adaptive, played along with the illusion. It was part of being a good loser.

What has been missing from the American analysis during the intensifying trade wars is the understanding that from the era of the great Tokugawa shoguns, the Japanese have been building their own type of nation state, one that puts a premium on the exercise of power through the bureaucracy. The foundation of the modern state was laid in the Meiji era when a nurturing alliance was formed between the great ministries, led in our day by the Ministry of International Trade and Industry, and the huge economic combines, such as Mitsubishi and Mitsui. Initiative, known today as "administrative guidance," was taken by the ministries. It was the ministries that led the forced industrialization in the post-Perry years, and again it was the ministries that provided the overall blueprint for rebuilding the economy after Hiroshima and Nagasaki.[26] For the ministries, American notions of competitive capitalism and free trade, to the extent that they are practiced in the United States, are among the few foreign ideas which will be adapted by Japan only when they are forced upon Japan by foreigners, particularly the United States.

Clyde Prestowitz's account of his experiences as a trade negotiator during the second opening of Japan provides a telling picture of the limitations of the American negotiating strategy and the impact of the economic power inversion on the United States. In a sense, this inversion has led to a dramatic role change at the negotiating table: the Japanese now come to the table as equals and at times, like Perry in 1853–1854, even have the upper hand. In contrast the United States, lacking a sense of power and purpose, is mired in bureaucratic infighting that has prevented the emergence of a realistic strategy for dealing with Japanese economic power. Moreover, as Prestowitz has pointed out, the Japanese, having mastered American lobbying skills, and playing upon American eagerness for Japanese investment, now conduct their strategy at both the state and national level. "The battle," according to Prestowitz, "always takes place on American ground."[27]

In the 1980s, there was no unanimity of purpose in Washington, Prestowitz argues, because different bureaucratic camps had different views of Japanese strategy. The State Department and the National Security Agency understandably viewed the problem of trade friction with Japan in light of Japan's strategic role in Asia. From their perspective, Japan should not be pushed too hard on trade issues because it might jeopardize Japan's overall strategic relationship with the United States. On the other hand, the Treasury Department, the Council of Economic Advisers, and the Office of Management and Budget were the bailiwicks of doctrinaire free traders who opposed any kind of trade agreement that was at variance with their principles. The free traders' sense of strategy was that the United States should press Japan to embrace their ideology with a sweeping commitment to a doctrine that is not even enforced in the highly subsidized American economy. This left Commerce to push for a strategy that was Japan-specific, that addressed the peculiarities of the Japanese political economy and went beyond hortatory appeals to the virtues of free trade. All of this eerily evoked Abe Masahiro's problems trying to formulate a strategy for dealing with the inevitable foreign incursion.[28]

During the Bush administration, the black ships returned to Japan, this time bearing a document known as the Structural Impediments Initiative. While earlier agreements focused on lowering the barriers to specific American commodities, this new agreement, signed in 1990, provides for systemic changes in the Japanese economy. It is very much in the spirit of Perry's and MacArthur's calls for Japan to become more like the United States. Hailed by both sides as a major breakthrough in United States–Japan relations, it remains to be seen exactly how the agreement will be implemented. Rather than undergoing a fundamental change in relations, the United States is likely to experience protracted negotiations over implementation of the agreement. The Japanese will continue to play the role of "good losers" as they stall through negotiations in an attempt to retain the initiative. They will continue to use the black ship metaphor to their own advantage while retaining certain key elements of Abe Masahiro's strategy of "keep them hanging on." The Japanese press, Prestowitz argues, portrays the ministries as protecting Japan from another invasion by the black ships. Meanwhile the ministries can use prolonged negotiations—in a modern equivalent of "keep them hanging on"—to achieve their goal of capturing the American market: the longer the negotiations, the farther along this road the Japanese will have traveled by the time the agreement is implemented. Finally, in the phenomenon known in Japan as *gaiatsu*, the Japanese will continue to use foreign pressure as a way to bring about necessary internal reforms.[29]

In this charged atmosphere, so redolent of the past, where are United States–Japan relations headed? One's view depends on an analysis of both American and Japanese intentions. The United States in the twilight years of the American empire, though increasingly anxious about the consequences, seems determined to continue building up Japan as a major world power. Japan is being encouraged to take on much of the foreign-aid burden that the United States shouldered after World War II. At the same time the United States continues to pressure Japan to rearm, regardless of the reservations of those Asian countries who remember the atrocities committed by the Japanese during World War II. With regard to the Japanese penetration of the American economy, the United States has yet to show signs of developing a response that both protects domestic industry while acknowledging the importance of Japanese capital. The danger is that any new initiative to challenge the Japanese is likely to evoke the kinds of racism and chauvinism that poisoned United States–Japanese relations in the past. For the time being, the United States is seduced by a nostalgic and unrealistic view of its global role, one that was appropriate to the years of American hegemony that stretched from 1945 to the Tet Offensive of 1968. According to this view, the Japanese will be content to follow the American lead.

As for the Japanese, there are signs that some of their leaders, at least, are playing Tokugawa Nariaki's game. In the way that Nariaki embraced a double message with the slogan War at Home, Peace Abroad (*naisen gaiwa*), one for domestic consumption, the other for overseas, Japanese leaders are sending out binary signals about their global ambitions. "Japan does not aspire to replace America as the world's leader," wrote Okita Saburo, Japan's foreign minister from 1979 to 1980, "it will be content to stay number two." At the same time, in a controversial book, *The Japan That Can Say "No,"* Ishihara Shintaro, a former Liberal Democratic Party cabinet minister, has suggested that Japan seriously consider and raise with the United States the possibility of going it alone in its quest for global influence.[30]

According to a number of popular commentators, such as Sony's Morita Akio and McKinsey consultant Ohmae Kenichi, Okita's thinking reflects the last gasp of Japan's occupation mentality. Japan, they argue, must emerge from its adolescence by standing up to its former master. To these commentators, who represent the dominant thinking in Japan's political and economic establishment, the United States–Japanese alliance is axiomatic. Some adjustments must be made to accommodate Japan's growing economic power and political power, to make a partnership of equals, but there is no alternative to the alliance itself.

Okita Saburo acknowledges that "the Japanese people have yet to find a new and exciting goal for their energies."[31] With the revival of Japanese nationalism and the Japanese new sense of their place in the world, some Japanese are discussing where to direct those energies, which raises questions about Japan's objectives. The United States has already prevailed upon Japan to build up sufficient military power, although Japan is barred by Article IX of its constitution from deploying forces for anything but self-defense, to project naval power a thousand miles from its shores. Japan, with the third largest military in the world, is being asked to help maintain the sea lanes of strategic control that entered into Perry's thinking about Asia. Apparently unconscious of the irony, Prime Minister Kaifu Toshiki announced recently that he would like to "begin studying the dispatching of the self-defense forces overseas [sic!] for the purposes of international cooperation, fulfilling the protection of Japanese overseas, and contributing to keeping peace." At about the same time, Hagi Jiro, chief of planning for the Japanese Self-Defense Agency, expressed reservations about Japanese acceptance of its place in the shade of the United States' strategic umbrella: "We still do not have a clear idea of whether to depend on the U.S., or to do as much as we can ourselves. But I think that whenever we can, we are going our own way."[32]

Ishihara Shintaro suggests an even more forceful way for Japan to readjust its role within the United States–Japan alliance. Calling the U.S. nuclear umbrella "an illusion," Ishihara suggests that "the time has come for Japan to tell the U.S. that we do not need American protection."[33] He admits that cancellation of the United States–Japan Security Treaty of 1960, the strategic mainstay of the alliance, is "not feasible." But his argument suggests that a number of Japanese leaders are thinking in terms of an independent projection of Japanese power on a regional if not a global basis. And that way of thinking, naturally enough, revives fears, particularly among Asian nations, of a return to the long period of Japanese expansionism that began with the fall of the shogun and culminated in World War II.

It is too early to determine if any of Japan's leaders aspire to the global hegemony that marked the late Pax Americana. Japan today is locked into a formalized trilateral relationship with the United States and the European Economic Community, and in the years to come there is very little indication that any one power will be able to take on the hegemonic role that England assumed in the nineteenth century and the United States in the late twentieth. At present the conditions do not exist—worldwide depression, domestic crisis, and a militarily expansionist leadership clique—that could tempt the Japanese to pursue the irrational politics of the 1930s. For now, both Americans and Japanese will have to contend with the inevitable tensions that accompany a relative shift of power away from the United States toward the other side of the Pacific Basin.

The people of Asia have paid a heavy price for both American and Japanese attempts to establish hegemony in the region. Empire, as Perry argued, is a universal vice, and the wages of sin have been fearful levels of death and destruction. Today the United States appears determined to demonstrate that it has not lost its staying power by invading nations, such as Grenada and Panama, that are small enough to be subjugated. At the same time the thrust of American expansionism remains very much as it was in Perry's era: through the Caribbean, across the Isthmus of Panama, and into the Pacific Basin. Panama and the Philippines are still outposts of the American empire while Nicaragua, as it was in Perry's time, is still a contested area. Despite the sobering lessons of Vietnam, the United States in many ways has not grown beyond the kind of self-righteous interventionism that was at the heart of Perry's approach to empire building in the Pacific. Japan meanwhile appears content to play a more benign role through the extension of its trading empire and its foreign-aid programs. It remains to be seen how either power or both together would respond to another major crisis in the region, such as a dramatic intensification of economic competition or a prolonged civil war in the Philippines or even China. What the future holds only time will tell.

APPENDIX 1

Treaty of Kanagawa, March 31, 1854

The United States of America and the empire of Japan, desiring to establish firm, lasting, and sincere friendship between the two nations, have resolved to fix, in a manner clear and positive, by means of a treaty or general convention of peace and amity, the rules which shall in future be mutually observed in the intercourse of their respective countries; for which most desirable object the President of the United States has conferred full powers on his commissioner, Matthew Calbraith Perry, special ambassador of the United States to Japan; and the august sovereign of Japan has given similar full powers to his commissioners, Hayashi-Daigaku-no-kami, Ido, Prince of Tsus-Sima; Izawa, Prince of Mimasaki; and Udono, member of the Board of Revenue.

And the said commissioners, after having exchanged their said full powers, and duly considered the premises, have agreed to the following articles:

ARTICLE I.—There shall be a perfect, permanent, and universal peace, and a sincere and cordial amity, between the United States of America on the one part, and between their people, respectfully, [respectively,] without exception of persons or places.

ARTICLE II.—The port of Simoda, in the principality of Idzu, and the port of Hakodadi, in the principality of Matsmai, are granted by the Japanese as ports for the reception of American ships, where they can be supplied with wood, water, provisions, and coal, and other articles their necessities may require, as far as the Japanese have them. The time for opening the first-named port is immediately on signing this treaty; the last-named port is to be opened immediately after the same day in the ensuing Japanese year.

NOTE.—A tariff of prices shall be given by the Japanese officers of the things which they can furnish, payment for which shall be made in gold and silver coin.

ARTICLE III.—Whenever ships of the United States are thrown or wrecked on the coast of Japan, the Japanese vessels will assist them, and carry their crews to Simoda or Hakodadi, and hand them over to their countrymen appointed to receive them. Whatever articles the shipwrecked men may have preserved shall likewise be restored, and the expenses incurred in the rescue and support of Americans and Japanese who may thus be thrown upon the shores of either nation are not to be refunded.

ARTICLE IV.—Those shipwrecked persons and other citizens of the United States shall be free as in other countries, and not subjected to confinement, but shall be amenable to just laws.

ARTICLE V.—Shipwrecked men, and other citizens of the United States, temporarily living at Simoda and Hakodadi, shall not be subject to such restrictions and confinement as the Dutch and Chinese are at Nangasaki; but shall be free at Simoda to go where they please within the limits of seven Japanese miles (or *ri*) from a small island in the harbor of Simoda, marked on the accompanying chart, hereto appended; and shall in like manner be free to go where they please at Hakodadi, within limits to be defined after the visit of the United States squadron to that place.

ARTICLE VI.—If there be any other sort of goods wanted, or any business which shall require to be arranged, there shall be careful deliberation between the parties in order to settle such matters.

ARTICLE VII.—It is agreed that ships of the United States resorting to the ports open to them, shall be permitted to exchange gold and silver coin and articles of goods for other articles of goods, under such regulations as shall be temporarily established by the Japanese government for that purpose. It is stipulated, however, that the ships of the United States shall be permitted to carry away whatever articles they are unwilling to exchange.

ARTICLE VIII.—Wood, water, provisions, coal, and goods required, shall only be procured through the agency of Japanese officers appointed for that purpose, and in no other manner.

ARTICLE IX.—It is agreed, that if, at any future day, the government of Japan shall grant to any other nation or nations privileges and advantages which are not herein granted to the United States and the citizens thereof, that these same privileges and advantages shall be granted likewise to the United States and to the citizens thereof without any consultation or delay.

ARTICLE X.—Ships of the United States shall be permitted to resort to no other ports in Japan but Simoda and Hakodadi, unless in distress or forced by stress of weather.

ARTICLE XI.—There shall be appointed by the government of the United States consuls or agents to reside in Simoda at any time after the expiration of eighteen months from the date of the signing of this treaty; provided that either of the two governments deem such arrangement necessary.

ARTICLE XII.—The present convention, having been concluded and duly signed, shall be obligatory, and faithfully observed by the United States of America and Japan, and by the citizens and subjects of each respective power; and it is to be ratified and approved by the President of the United States, by and with the advice and consent of the Senate thereof, and by the august Sovereign of Japan, and the ratification shall be exchanged within eighteen months from the date of the signature thereof, or sooner if practicable.

In faith whereof, we, the respective plenipotentiaries of the United States of America and the empire of Japan, aforesaid, have signed and sealed these presents.

Done at Kanagawa, this thirty-first day of March, in the year of our Lord Jesus Christ one thousand eight hundred and fifty-four, and of Kayei the seventh year, third month, and third day.

APPENDIX 2

Additional Regulations
Signed at Shimoda, June 17, 1854

ARTICLE I.—The imperial governors of Simoda will place watch stations wherever they deem best, to designate the limits of their jurisdiction; but Americans are at liberty to go through them, unrestricted, within the limits of seven Japanese ri, or miles; and those who are found transgressing Japanese laws may be apprehended by the police and taken on board their ships.

ARTICLE II.—Three landing-places shall be constructed for the boats of merchant ships and whale-ships resorting to this port; one at Simoda, one at Kakizaki, and the third at the brook lying southeast of Centre Island. The citizens of the United States will, of course, treat the Japanese officers with proper respect.

ARTICLE III.—Americans, when on shore, are not allowed access to military establishments or private houses without leave; but they can enter shops and visit temples as they please.

ARTICLE IV.—Two temples, the Rioshen at Simoda, and the Yokushen at Kakizaki, are assigned as resting-places for persons in their walks, until public houses and inns are erected for their convenience.

ARTICLE V.—Near the Temple Yokushen, at Kakizaki, a burial-ground has been set apart for Americans, where their graves and tombs shall not be molested.

ARTICLE VI.—It is stipulated in the treaty of Kanagawa, that coal will be furnished at Hakodadi; but as it is very difficult for the Japanese to supply it at that port, Commodore Perry promises to mention this to his government, in order that the Japanese government may be relieved from the obligation of making that port a coal depot.

ARTICLE VII.—It is agreed that henceforth the Chinese language shall not be employed in official communications between the two governments, except when there is no Dutch interpreter.

ARTICLE VIII.—A harbor-master and three skilful pilots have been appointed for the port of Simoda.

ARTICLE IX.—Whenever goods are selected in the shops, they shall be marked with the name of the purchaser and the price agreed upon, and then be sent to the Goyoshi, or government office, where the money is to be paid to Japanese officers, and the articles delivered by them.

ARTICLE X.—The shooting of birds and animals is generally forbidden in Japan, and this law is therefore to be observed by all Americans.

ARTICLE XI.—It is hereby agreed that five Japanese ri, or miles, be the limit allowed to Americans at Hakodade, and the requirements contained in Article I, of these Regulations, are hereby made also applicable to that port within that distance.

ARTICLE XII.—His Majesty the Emperor of Japan is at liberty to appoint whoever he pleases to receive the ratification of the treaty of Kanagawa, and give an acknowledgment on his part.

It is agreed that nothing herein contained shall in any way affect or modify the stipulations of the treaty of Kanagawa, should that be found to be contrary to these regulations.

In witness whereof, copies of these additional regulations have been signed and sealed in the English and Japanese languages by the respective parties, and a certified translation in the Dutch language, and exchanged by the commissioners of the United States and Japan.

SIMODA, JAPAN, *June* 17, 1854.

M. C. PERRY,

Commander-in chief of the U. S. Naval Forces East India,
China, and Japan Seas, and Special Envoy to Japan.

NOTES

Chapter 1
A GOOD CAUSE FOR A QUARREL

1. William S. Lewis and Murakami Naojiro, eds., *Ranald MacDonald: The Narrative of His Early Life* (Spokane: The Eastern Washington State Historical Society, 1923), p. 54.

2. Herman Melville, *Moby-Dick; or, The Whale* (New York: Hendricks House, 1952), p. 109.

3. Lewis and Murakami, *Ranald MacDonald*, pp. 128–29.

4. Ibid., p. 138.

5. Ibid., pp. 138–48.

6. Ibid., pp. 148–50.

7. Ibid., pp. 150–52.

8. Robert H. Ruby and John A. Brown, *The Chinook Indians: Traders of the Lower Columbia River* (Norman: University of Oklahoma Press, 1976), pp. 113–14, 130.

9. Samuel Eliot Morison, *The Maritime History of Massachusetts, 1783–1860* (Boston: Northeastern University Press, 1979), pp. 46–47.

10. Washington Irving, *Astoria* (New York: P. F. Collier & Son, 1864), p. 33.

11. Lewis and Murakami, *MacDonald*, p. 120.

12. Ibid., pp. 79–81.

13. *Astoria* is Washington Irving's account of the establishment of the famous fur post based on interviews with Astor and his associates and access to Astor's business papers. Peter C. Newman, *Caesars of the Wilderness* (Markham, Ontario: Penguin Books, 1987), pp. 103–4, 106–7, 207.

14. Lewis and Murakami, *Ranald MacDonald*, pp. 82, 89–92.

15. Ibid., pp. 121–23.

16. Ibid., p. 131. In an appendix to *Captain Bonneville: Tales of a Traveller* (New York: P. F. Collier & Son, 1864), Irving included a letter from Nathaniel

Wyeth about the arrival of the shipwrecked Japanese at Vancouver. He thought the letter interesting "as throwing light upon the question as to the manner in which America has been peopled" (p. 523).

17. Ibid., p. 28.

18. Ibid., p. 25.

19. Ibid., pp. 118–19.

20. Ibid., pp. 40, 133.

21. Ibid., pp. 152–54.

22. Ibid., pp. 154–58.

23. Ibid., pp. 159–61.

24. Ibid., pp. 163, 166, 167.

25. Ibid., pp. 171–73.

26. Ibid., pp. 177–80.

27. Ibid., pp. 182, 184–85, 187–88.

28. Ibid., pp. 191–92.

29. Ibid., pp. 194–95.

30. Ibid., pp. 211–21.

31. Ibid., pp. 223–25.

32. Ibid., pp. 209, 225–27, 232.

33. Ibid., pp. 238–39.

34. Ibid., pp. 234–37.

35. *Official Documents Relative to the Empire of Japan*, United States Senate, 32nd Congress, 1st Session, Executive Document 59, p. 8. There is a halfscale model of the *Lagoda* in the New Bedford Whaling Museum.

36. Ibid., pp. 10–11, 22.

37. Ibid., pp. 11–15.

38. Ibid., pp. 15–16, 19, 24.

39. Ibid., pp. 16–17; Lewis and Murakami, *Ranald MacDonald*, p. 247.

40. *Official Documents Relative to the Empire of Japan*, pp. 6–7.

41. Ibid., pp. 28–30, 32, 45–47.

42. Ibid., pp. 32, 48.

43. Ibid., pp. 33–37.

44. Ibid., p. 50.

45. Ibid., pp. 25–28; Lewis and Murakami, *Ranald MacDonald*, pp. 240–42.

46. *Official Documents Relative to the Empire of Japan*, p. 50.

47. Lewis and Murakami, *Ranald MacDonald*, p. 196, n. 217; Melville, *Moby-Dick*, pp. 107, 109, 478; Morison, *The Maritime History of Massachusetts*, p. 319. In his brilliant study of Melville, *Call Me Ishmael* (San Francisco: City Lights, 1947), Charles Olson concludes with a chapter on "Pacific Man." "The Pacific is, for an American," he writes, "a 20th century Great West. Melville understood the relation of the two geographies. . . . We must go over space, or we wither," p. 114.

48. Foster Rhea Dulles, *Yankees and Samurai* (New York: Harper & Row, 1965), pp. 1, 3–7; Sakamaki Shunzo, *Japan and the United States, 1790–1853*,

Transactions of the Asiatic Society of Japan, Second Series, XVIII (1939), pp. 4–11.

49. Allen B. Cole, "Captain David Porter's Proposed Expedition to the Pacific and Japan," *The Pacific Historical Review*, IX (March 1940), pp. 61–65; Tyler Dennett, *Americans in Eastern Asia* (New York: Octagon Books, 1979), pp. 128–34; *Official Documents Relative to the Empire of Japan*, p. 63.

50. S. Wells Williams, "Narrative of a Voyage of The Ship *Morrison*," *The Chinese Repository*, VI (September and December, 1837), p. 227. Charles King also wrote an account of the voyage, *The Claims of Japan and Malaysia upon Christendom*, 2 vols. (New York: E. French, 1839). The first volume is *Notes on the Voyage of the "Morrison" from Canton to Japan*.

51. Williams, "Narrative," p. 359.

52. Ibid., p. 376.

53. King, *The Claims of Japan*, I, pp. 174–86.

54. Dennett, *Americans in Eastern Asia*, pp. 249–50. The Log of the *Manhattan* is in the Old Dartmouth Historical Society, New Bedford, Massachusetts. See also, F. C. Winslow, "Captain Mercator Cooper's Voyage to Japan," *The Seamen's Friend*, Honolulu, February 2, 1846.

55. *Official Documents Relative to the Empire of Japan*, pp. 64–66.

56. Ibid., pp. 67–69. For a sailor's account of Biddle's visit to Japan, see Charles Nordhoff, *Man-of-War Life* (Annapolis: Naval Institute Press, 1985), pp. 177–89. See also David F. Long, *Sailor-Diplomat: A Biography of Commodore James Biddle* (Boston: Northeastern University Press, 1983).

57. *Official Documents Relative to the Empire of Japan*, p. 72.

Chapter 2
PERRY GROWS UP WITH THE NAVY

1. *Official Documents Relative to the Empire of Japan*, United States Senate, 32nd Congress, 1st Session, Executive Document 59, pp. 58, 62.

2. Herman Melville, *White-Jacket; or, The World in a Man-of-War* (New York: New American Library, 1979), pp. 22, 75.

3. A. S., "Thoughts on the Navy," *The Naval Magazine*, II (January 1837), p. 24.

4. Extract from the *New York Herald*, January 8, 1851, in *Official Documents Relative to the Empire of Japan*, pp. 82–86.

5. Robert Greenhalgh Albion, *The Rise of New York Port, 1815–1860* (Boston: Northeastern University Press, 1967), pp. 174, 201–2; Colonel Duncan S. Somerville, *The Aspinwall Empire* (Mystic, Conn.: Mystic Seaport Museum, 1983), pp. 16–30, 43–53.

6. *Official Documents Relative to the Empire of Japan*, pp. 57–62.

7. Hamilton DeRoulhac, ed., *The Papers of William A. Graham* (Raleigh: North Carolina Department of Archives and History, 1957), IV, pp. 16–22.

8. Calbraith Bourn Perry, *The Perrys of Rhode Island* (New York: Tobias A. Wright, 1913), pp. 7–8, 43, 45–47.

9. Ibid., pp. 53–57.

10. Harold Sprout and Margaret Sprout, *The Rise of American Naval Power, 1776–1918* (Princeton: Princeton University Press, 1939), pp. 13, 15. Edward L. Beach, *The United States Navy: 200 Years* (New York: Henry Holt and Company, 1986), and Dudley W. Knox, *A History of the United States Navy* (New York: G. P. Putnam's Sons, 1948), were also helpful.

11. Sprout and Sprout, *The Rise of American Naval Power*, p. 46.

12. Samuel Eliot Morison, *"Old Bruin": The Life of Commodore Matthew C. Perry, 1794–1858* (Boston: Little, Brown and Company, 1967), pp. 15–24.

13. Ibid., pp. 26–27, 31–32.

14. William Elliot Griffis, *Matthew Calbraith Perry: A Typical American Naval Officer* (Boston: Cupples and Hurd, 1887), pp. 39–40; Morison, *"Old Bruin,"* pp. 38–41.

15. K. Jack Bauer, "Naval Shipbuilding Programs," *Military Affairs*, XXIX (Spring 1965), p. 34; Sprout and Sprout, *The Rise of American Naval Power*, pp. 88–89.

16. For information on the Slidell family, see Morison, *"Old Bruin,"* p. 50, and Louis Martin Sears, *John Slidell* (Durham: Duke University Press, 1925).

17. See, for example, Perry to John Rodgers, June 27, 1819, New York–Historical Society, and Perry to Passed Midshipman John Rodgers, January 28, 1850, *Matthew Calbraith Perry Papers*, Beinecke Library, Yale University. See also Charles Oscar Paullin, *Commodore John Rodgers* (Cleveland: The Arthur H. Clark Company, 1910).

18. Morison, *"Old Bruin,"* pp. 64–69.

19. Ibid., pp. 77–83, 95–103. For an account of the U.S. Navy's campaign against pirates, see Gardner W. Allen, *Our Navy and the West Indian Pirates* (Salem: Essex Institute, 1929).

20. Perry to William Ballard Preston, July 4, 1850, *Perry Papers*, Beinecke Library.

21. For Perry's personality and relations with his fellow officers and subordinates, see Griffis, *Matthew Calbraith Perry*, pp. 397–401. Griffis interviewed a number of men who had known Perry, but I could not locate Griffis's research notes in his papers at Rutgers University.

22. Melville, *White-Jacket*, pp. 20, 22.

23. Griffis, *Matthew Calbraith Perry*, pp. 401, 403; Morison, *"Old Bruin,"* pp. 117–18, 132–35, 406–7.

24. Harold D. Langley, *Social Reform in the United States Navy* (Urbana: University of Illinois Press, 1967), p. 24.

25. Perry to John Rodgers, November 22, 1827; Perry to the secretary of the navy, February 4, 1828; Perry to John Rodgers, February 6, 1828, *Rodgers Family Naval Historical Foundation*, Library of Congress.

26. Sprout and Sprout, *The Rise of American Naval Power*, pp. 102, 105–7.

27. A.S., "Thoughts on the Navy," *The Naval Magazine*, II (January 1837), pp. 6, 18, 33.

28. Ibid., pp. 10, 14.

29. Beach, *The United States Navy*, pp. 148–49; David Budlong Tyler, *Steam Conquers the Atlantic* (New York: D. Appleton-Century Company, 1939), p. 138.

30. Morison, *"Old Bruin,"* pp. 127–30.

31. Perry to [illegible], July 8, 1838, *Matthew Calbraith Perry Papers*, Library of Congress.

32. Sprout and Sprout, *The Rise of American Naval Power*, pp. 113–14.

33. For an account of the naval reform movement, see Langley, *Social Reform in the United States Navy, 1798–1862*.

34. Vernon Louis Parrington, *Main Currents in American Thought* (New York: Harcourt, Brace and Company, 1930), II, p. 231.

35. Morison, *"Old Bruin,"* pp. 41–49.

36. James Fenimore Cooper, *Naval History of the United States* (Philadelphia: Lea and Blanchard, 1840), II, pp. 306–18.

37. James Fenimore Cooper, *The Battle of Lake Erie; or, Answers to Messrs. Burges, Duer, and MacKenzie* (Cooperstown: H. and E. Phinney, 1843), pp. iii–iv; Morison, *"Old Bruin,"* pp. 140–43.

38. For accounts of the *Somers* "mutiny" that reach diametrically opposed conclusions, see Beach, *The United States Navy*, pp. 177–95, and Morison, *"Old Bruin,"* pp. 144–62. Harrison Hayford, ed., *The Somers Mutiny Affair* (Englewood Cliffs: Prentice Hall, 1962) is a helpful collection of documents and newspaper clippings.

39. James Fenimore Cooper, *Proceedings of the Naval Court Martial in the Case of Alexander Slidell MacKenzie* (New York: Henry G. Langley, 1844), p. 197; Hayford, *The Somers Mutiny Affair*, p. 34.

40. Hayford, *The Somers Mutiny Affair*, p. 49.

41. Ibid., pp. 3–7, 10–16, 19; Morison, *"Old Bruin,"* p. 159.

42. Cooper, *Proceedings*, p. 331.

43. Ibid., pp. 264–65, 306; James Fenimore Cooper, ed., *Correspondence of James Fenimore Cooper* (New Haven: Yale University Press, 1922), II, pp. 487–88, 494–98.

44. Cooper, *Proceedings*, pp. 331–33.

45. Morison, *"Old Bruin,"* pp. 163–64.

46. Charles Nordhoff, *Man-of-War Life* (Annapolis: Naval Institute Press, 1985), p. 21.

47. Melville, *White-Jacket*, p. 75.

48. Langley, *Social Reform*, pp. 74–83.

49. Both Melville and Nordhoff witnessed floggings, while Melville claimed that he escaped flogging at the last minute aboard the *United States*. Morison (*"Old Bruin,"* p. 90) estimates that there were 163 floggings during the *United States'* fourteen-month cruise, mostly for drunkenness. Langley, *Social Reform*, p. 172; Melville, *White-Jacket*, pp. 135–39, 286–87; Nordhoff, *Man-of-War Life*, p. 121–23.

50. Melville, *White-Jacket*, pp. 35, 81, 83, 387.

51. Langley, *Social Reform*, pp. 210, 238, 265–66.

52. Melville, *White-Jacket*, p. 54; Nordhoff, *Man-of-War Life*, p. 34.

53. Morison, *"Old Bruin,"* p. 107.

54. Langley, *Social Reform*, p. 27.

55. Morison, *"Old Bruin,"* p. 164.

56. Ibid., p. 228.

57. Griffis, *Matthew Calbraith Perry*, pp. 401–2; Morison, *"Old Bruin,"* p. 253.

58. Perry, *Perrys of Rhode Island*, pp. 67–68.

59. For Belmont's career before he met Caroline Perry, see David Black, *The King of Fifth Avenue: The Fortunes of August Belmont* (New York: The Dial Press, 1981) and Irving Katz, *August Belmont: A Political Biography* (New York: Columbia University Press, 1968). Morison, *"Old Bruin,"* p. 254; *New York Herald*, November 7, 1849. Caroline Belmont's wedding gift is described in "Memorandum Executed by Jeremiah Larocque, August Belmont, John Hone, and Francis Griffin on October 29, 1849," *August Belmont Papers*, Houghton Library, Harvard University.

Chapter 3
THE COMMODORE IN THE CITY OF MAGNIFICENT INTENTIONS

1. Hamilton DeRoulhac, ed., *The Papers of William A. Graham* (Raleigh: North Carolina Department of Archives and History, 1957), IV, p. 16.

2. *Report to Accompany Bills Senate Numbers 457 and 458*, U.S. Senate, 32nd Congress, 1st Session, Committee Report 267, p. 5.

3. *Congressional Globe*, 32nd Congress, 1st Session, p. 945.

4. Ben Perley Poore, *Perley's Reminiscences of Sixty Years of the National Metropolis* (Philadelphia: Hubbard Brothers, 1886), I, p. 357.

5. Elizabeth Fries Ellett, *Court Circles of the Republic* (Hartford, Conn.: Hartford Publishing Company, 1870), pp. 433–44; Robert J. Rayback, *Millard Fillmore: Biography of a President* (Buffalo: Henry Stewart, 1959), pp. 92–93.

6. Constance McLaughlin Green, *Washington* (Princeton: Princeton University Press, 1962), I, pp. 209–12.

7. Charles Dickens, *American Notes* (New York: Trade Publishing Company, n.d.), pp. 108, 112.

8. See, for example, the *Journal of John Pendleton Kennedy*, who served as secretary of the navy in the Fillmore Cabinet, for a running account of the social life of a cabinet member. *John Pendleton Kennedy Papers*, Enoch Pratt Free Library, Baltimore, Maryland.

9. Aaron Haight Palmer, *Documents and Facts Illustrating the Origin of the Mission to Japan* (Washington: Henry Polkhorn, 1857).

10. DeRoulhac, ed., *Papers of William A. Graham*, IV, pp. 16–21.

11. Robert Greehalgh Albion, *The Rise of New York Port, 1815–1860* (Boston: Northeastern University Press, 1967), pp. 237, 239; Joseph Delano Hitch, Jr., "Captain Joseph C. Delano," typed ms. in Old Dartmouth Historical Society, New Bedford, Massachusetts; Geoffrey C. Ward, *Before the Trumpet: Young Franklin Roosevelt* (New York: Harper and Row, 1985), pp. 66–67; Francis B. Whitlock, *Two New Yorkers: Editor and Sea Captain, 1833* (New York: The Newcomen Society of England, 1945), pp. 17, 21–22.

12. Perry to Joseph Delano, January 16, 1851, Old Dartmouth Historical Society.

13. John R. Bockstoce, *Whales, Ice, and Men: The History of Whaling in the Western Arctic* (Seattle: University of Washington Press, 1986), pp. 27–29; Samuel Eliot Morison, *The Maritime History of Massachusetts, 1783–1860* (Boston: Northeastern University Press, 1979), pp. 314–18.

14. Mercator Cooper to Joseph C. Delano, February 8, 1851, Old Dartmouth Historical Society.

15. Perry to Delano, February 26, 1851, Old Dartmouth Historical Society.

16. Irving H. Bartlett, *Daniel Webster* (New York: W. W. Norton and Company, 1978), pp. 254–56, 276, 279, 285, 287; Claude M. Fuess, *Daniel Webster* (Boston: Little, Brown & Company, 1930), II, p. 249; *Kennedy Journal*, August 11, 1852.

17. Rayback, *Millard Fillmore*, pp. 300–17.

18. Fletcher Webster, ed., *The Private Correspondence of Daniel Webster* (Boston: Little, Brown and Company, 1875), II, p. 416.

19. Rayback, *Millard Fillmore*, pp. 305–8.

20. *Message from the President of the United States*, U.S. Senate, 32nd Congress, 1st Session, Executive Document 1, p. 5.

21. Perry to Delano, February 26, 1851, Old Dartmouth Historical Society.

22. Perry to John Young Mason, November 14, 1848, *Matthew Calbraith Perry Papers*, Library of Congress.

23. *Report of the Committee on the Post Office and Post Roads*, U.S. Senate, 31st Congress, 1st Session, Committee Report Number 202; *Report of the Postmaster General*, U.S. Senate, 31st Congress, 1st Session, Executive Document 77; *Steamers Between California and China: Report of the House Committee on Naval Affairs*, U.S. House of Representatives, 31st Congress, 2nd Session, Report 34.

24. David Budlong Tyler, *Steam Conquers the Atlantic* (New York: D. Appleton-Century Company, 1939), pp. 136–37, 142, 144, 145; *Report of the Secretary of the Navy: Information in Relation to Contracts . . . Steamships between New York and California*, U.S. Senate, 32nd Congress, 1st Session, Executive Document 50, p. 20.

25. Sprout and Sprout, *The Rise of American Naval Power*, pp. 116–17, 130–32. For two assessments of United States naval power in comparison with England's, see *Report of the Navy Department*, U.S. Senate, 29th Congress, 1st Session, Senate Document 187, and a letter from the Department's Bureau Chiefs published in *Niles Register*, LXX (March 14, 1846), p. 18.

26. Tyler, *Steam Conquers the Atlantic*, p. 144; Sprout and Sprout, *The Rise of American Naval Power*, pp. 133–35.

27. Tyler, *Steam Conquers the Atlantic*, p. 147.

28. *Steam Communication with China and the Sandwich Islands*, U.S. House of Representatives, 30th Congress, 1st Session, Committee Report 596, p. 15.

29. Ibid., pp. 16, 19–33.

30. *Report of the Secretary of the Navy: Information in Relation to Contracts . . . Steamships between New York and California*, pp. 16–17, 88–93, 125, 132–143.

31. Colonel Duncan S. Somerville, *The Aspinwall Empire* (Mystic: Mystic Seaport Museum, 1983), pp. 34–37.

32. Alexander Crosby Brown, *Women and Children Last: The Loss of the Steamship* Arctic (London: Frederic Muller Ltd., 1962), pp. 15, 17.

33. *Report of the Secretary of the Navy*, U.S. Senate, 31st Congress, 1st Session, Senate Executive Document 1, p. 432. The Sprouts in *The Rise of American Naval Power* describe the mail subsidy program as "a sordid scramble for spoils," p. 138.

34. Samuel Eliot Morison, *"Old Bruin": The Life of Commodore Matthew C. Perry, 1794–1858* (Boston: Little, Brown and Company, 1967), pp. 257–58; Perry to William Ballard Preston, January 25, 1850, *Matthew Calbraith Perry Papers*, Beinecke Library, Yale University; *Report of Mr. Rusk*, U.S. Senate, 31st Congress, 1st Session, Committee Report 202, pp. 4, 114–15; *Report of the Secretary of the Navy: Information in Relation to Contracts . . . Steamships between New York and California*, pp. 90, 125, 132–43.

35. John Haskell Kemble, *The Panama Route, 1848–1869* (Berkeley: University of California Press, 1943), pp. 44–45.

36. Tyler, *Steam Conquers the Atlantic*, p. 205.

37. *Report of the Secretary of the Navy*, U.S. Senate, 31st Congress, 2nd Session, Senate Document 1, pp. 199, 203, 205.

38. *Appendix to the Congressional Globe*, 31st Congress, 2nd Session, pp. 394–96.

39. Perry to Delano, March 12, 1851, Old Dartmouth Historical Society.

40. Perry to Delano, April 8, 1851, Old Dartmouth Historical Society.

41. Manfred C. Vernon, "The Dutch and the Opening of Japan by the United States," *Pacific Historical Review*, XXVIII (February 1959), p. 39; *Official Documents Relative to the Empire of Japan*, U.S. Senate, 32nd Congress, 1st Session, Executive Document 59, pp. 78–79.

42. *Official Documents . . . Empire of Japan*, ibid., pp. 73–74.

43. Robert Erwin Johnson, *Far China Station: The United States Navy in Asian Waters, 1800–1898* (Annapolis: Naval Institute Press, 1979), pp. 50–51.

44. Ibid., pp. 80–81.

45. Ibid., p. 82.

46. Ibid., pp. 51–53.

47. Perry to William Sinclair, May 26, 1851, June 6, 1851, June 15, 1851, *Matthew Calbraith Perry Papers*, U.S. Naval Academy Museum.

48. Perry to Sinclair, October 21, 1851, *Perry Papers*, U.S. Naval Academy Museum.

49. Perry to Graham, December 2, 1851, *Perry Papers*, Beinecke Library.

50. Perry to Delano, December 18, 1851, Old Dartmouth Historical Society.

51. *Report of the Secretary of the Navy*, U.S. Senate, 32nd Congress, 1st Session, Executive Document 1, p. 6.

52. Matthew Calbraith Perry, *The Japan Expedition, 1852–1854: The Personal Journal of Matthew C. Perry*, Roger Pineau, ed. (Washington: Smithsonian Institution Press, 1968), p. 87; Matthew Calbraith Perry, *Narrative of the Expedition of an American Squadron to the China Seas and Japan, performed in the years, 1852, 1853, and 1854, under the Command of Commodore M. C. Perry, United States Navy, by Order of the Government of the United States* (Washington: Beverley Tucker, Senate Printer, 1856), I, pp. 79–80.

53. Morison, *"Old Bruin,"* p. 275; Perry to Captain S. S. McCluney, January 23, 1852, copy in possession of Captain Roger Pineau, USNR Ret., original owned by William C. Huber, Jr.

54. Morison, *"Old Bruin,"* p. 278.

55. Donald Keene, *The Japanese Discovery of Europe, 1720–1830* (Stanford: Stanford University Press, 1969), pp. 150–52; Morison, *"Old Bruin,"* p. 275; Vernon, "The Dutch and the Opening of Japan," p. 41.

56. Iriye Akira, "Minds Across the Pacific: Japan in American Writing, 1853–1883," *Papers on Japan* (Cambridge: Harvard University East Asian Research Center, 1961), I, pp. 2–6; Morison, *"Old Bruin,"* pp. 276–77; Perry to S. Wells Williams, April 25, 1853, *Williams Family Papers*, Sterling Library, Yale University. For contemporary articles on Japan, see "Japan— The Expedition," *American Whig Review*, XC (June 1852), pp. 507–15; "Japan," *Democratic Review*, CLXV (April 1852), pp. 319–32; P. Vinton, "Japan," *Putnam's Monthly*, I (March 1853); *Harper's Monthly*, September 1852; *The Presbyterian Review*, December 1852.

57. *National Intelligencer*, April 14, 1852.

58. Perry to Delano, February 29, 1852, Old Dartmouth Historical Society.

59. Morison, *"Old Bruin,"* pp. 279–80; DeRoulhac, ed., *Papers of William A. Graham*, IV, pp. 278–79.

60. This led to the printing of *Official Documents Relative to the Empire of Japan*.

61. *Congressional Globe*, 32nd Congress, 1st Session, pp. 1005–6.

62. Ibid., pp. 928, 942, 1005.

63. Ibid., pp. 943, 1006.

64. Ibid., pp. 943–44.

65. Ibid., p. 945.

66. Ibid., p. 948.

67. Tyler, *Steam Conquers the Atlantic*, pp. 205, 210–11.

68. DeRoulhac, ed., *Graham Papers*, IV, pp. 279, 434–36; *Report of the*

Secretary of the Navy . . . in relation to the contract with Howland and Aspinwall . . . , U.S. Senate, Special Session (March 14, 1853), Executive Document 2.

69. Perry to Sinclair, May 3, 1852, U.S. Naval Academy Museum.

70. *Kennedy Journal*, July 24, 1852.

71. Morison, *"Old Bruin,"* pp. 280–82.

72. *Journal of John Pendleton Kennedy*, August 11, 1852.

73. Perry's instructions and Fillmore's letter appear in *A Report of the Secretary of the Navy . . . relative to the naval expedition to Japan*, U.S. Senate, 33rd Congress, 2nd Session, pp. 2–11.

74. Perry to Kennedy, October 5, 1852, *Kennedy Papers*.

75. *Kennedy Journal*, November 8, 1852. *Flag Journal: U.S. Naval Expedition to Japan, 1852–1854*, November 8, 1852, Rutgers University Library; Perry, *Journal*, p. 3.

76. *Flag Journal*, November 18, 1852.

Chapter 4
MIST OVER CHINA, FROST OVER JAPAN

1. *A Report of the Secretary of the Navy . . . relative to the naval expedition to Japan*, U.S. Senate, 33rd Congress, 2nd Session, p. 14.

2. Geoffrey Ward, *Before the Trumpet: Young Franklin Roosevelt* (New York: Harper and Row, 1985), p. 71.

3. *A Report of the Secretary of the Navy . . . relative to the naval expedition to Japan*, p. 25.

4. R. H. van Gulik, *"Kakkaron*, A Japanese Echo of the Opium War,"* *Monumenta Serica*, IV (1939–1940), p. 500.

5. *A Report of the Secretary of the Navy . . . relative to the naval expedition to Japan*, pp. 12–14.

6. Matthew Calbraith Perry, *The Japan Expedition, 1852–1854: The Personal Journal of Matthew C. Perry*, Roger Pineau, ed. (Washington: Smithsonian Institution Press, 1968), pp. 8–10.

7. J. W. Spalding, *The Japan Expedition: Japan and Around the World, An Account of Three Visits to the Japanese Empire* (New York: Redfield, 1855), p. 31.

8. Ibid., pp. 34–35.

9. Perry, *Journal*, p. 29.

10. Ibid., p. 24.

11. Spalding, *The Japan Expedition*, p. 55.

12. Perry, *Journal*, p. 43.

13. Ibid., p. 47.

14. Ibid., p. 52.

15. Jan Morris, *Hong Kong* (New York: Random House, 1988), p. 70.

16. Bayard Taylor, *A Visit to India, China, and Japan in the Year 1853* (London: Sampson Low, Son and Company, n.d.), p. 471.

17. Allan B. Cole, *With Perry in Japan: The Diary of Edward Yorke McCauley* (Princeton: Princeton University Press, 1942), p. 79.

18. Spalding, *The Japan Expedition*, p. 85.

19. Marshall's instructions are in U.S. Department of State, *China Instructions*, I, pp. 76–78, National Archives, Washington, D.C.; *Correspondence between the State Department and the late Commissioner to China*, U.S. House of Representatives, 33rd Congress, 1st Session, Executive Document 123, pp. 9–12; *A Report of the Secretary of the Navy . . . relative to the naval expedition to Japan*, p. 17.

20. Peter Ward Fay, *The Opium War, 1840–1843* (New York: W. W. Norton and Company, 1976), p. 362. For the Chinese perspective on the Opium War, see Arthur Waley, *The Opium War through Chinese Eyes* (Stanford: Stanford University Press, 1968).

21. Humphrey Marshall to Secretary of State, February 7, 1853, February 8, 1853, *Dispatches from U.S. Ministers to China; August 5, 1852–February 22, 1854*, VIII, National Archives.

22. For descriptions of Hung Hsui-ch'uan and the Taiping Rebellion, see Jean Chesneaux, et al., *China from the Opium Wars to the 1911 Revolution* (New York: Pantheon Books, 1976), pp. 89–101; Immanuel C. Y. Hsu, *The Rise of Modern China* (New York: Oxford University Press, 1983), pp. 226–32; and S. Y. Teng, *The Taiping Rebellion and the Western Powers* (London: Oxford University Press, 1971), p. 131.

23. Taylor, *A Visit to India, China, and Japan*, pp. 296, 310–11.

24. See, for example, Commodore J. H. Aulick to Marshall, February 5, 1853, and Marshall to Aulick, February 7, 1853, *Dispatches from U.S. Ministers to China*, VIII; S. Wells Williams to James Dwight Dana, February 23, 1853, *S. Wells Williams Correspondence, Williams Family Papers*, Sterling Library, Yale University.

25. Marshall to Edward Everett, March 19, 1853, *Dispatches from U.S. Ministers to China*, VIII.

26. Perry, *Journal*, p. 54.

27. For a description of the American role in the opium trade, see Jacques M. Downs, "American Merchants and Opium," *Business History Review*, XLII (Winter 1968), pp. 418–42; John King Fairbank, *Trade and Diplomacy on the China Coast: The Opening of the Treaty Ports, 1842–1854* (Stanford: Stanford University Press, 1969), p. 208; Fay, *The Opium War*, pp. 45, 48, 49, 61; Charles Clark Stelle, *Americans and the China Opium Trade in the Nineteenth Century* (New York: Arno Press, 1981).

28. Wiliam C. Hunter, *Bits of Old China* (London: Kegan Paul, Trench and Company, 1885), p. 1; Geoffrey Ward, *Before the Trumpet*, p. 71.

29. Stelle, *Opium Trade*, pp. 83–87, 93–95.

30. Perry, *Journal*, p. 55.

31. Ibid., p. 54.

32. Chesneaux, et al., *China*, p. 81.

33. Hunter, *Bits of Old China*, p. 2; Hsu, *The Rise of Modern China*, pp. 139–66. Hunter's *Bits of Old China* and *The Fan Kwae at Canton* (London:

Kegan Paul, Trench and Company, 1882), Robert B. Forbes, *Personal Reminiscences* (Boston: Little, Brown and Company, 1882), and Frederick Wells Williams, *The Life and Letters of Samuel Wells Williams, LL.D., Missionary, Diplomatist, Sinologue* (New York: G. P. Putnam's Sons, 1889), pp. 55–60, are among the best firsthand accounts of factory life in Canton.

34. Arthur H. Clark, *The Clipper Ship Era* (Riverside: 7 C's Press, 1970), pp. 57–72, 195–210. This is a reprint of an account of clipper ship days written by a clipper captain. Colonel Duncan S. Somerville, *The Aspinwall Empire* (Mystic: Mystic Seaport Museum, 1983), pp. 16–23; A. B. C. Whipple, *The Challenge* (New York: William Morrow, 1987), pp. 25–32.

35. Allen Nevins, ed., *Diary of Philip Hone* (New York: Kraus Reprint Company, 1969), p. 908.

36. *Report of the Secretary of the Navy*, U.S. Senate, 31st Congress, 2nd Session, Senate Document 1, p. 199; E. K. Haviland, "Early Steam Navigation to China," *American Neptune*, XXVI (1966); Whipple, *The Challenge*, pp. 37–38.

37. Perry to Williams, April 9, 1853, *Williams Correspondence*; Williams, "A Journal of the Perry Expedition to Japan, 1853–1854," *Transactions of the Asiatic Society of Japan*, XXXVII, Part 2 (1910), p. iv, 1–2.

38. Sarah Walworth Williams to Catherine Huntington Williams, April 20, 1853, *Williams Correspondence*.

39. F. W. Williams, *The Life and Letters of Samuel Wells Williams*, pp. 4, 8–9, 10, 16, 18, 19–20.

40. Ibid., pp. 39, 60, 64–65, 80.

41. Ibid., p. 67.

42. Ibid., p. 68.

43. Ibid., p. 122; Fay, *The Opium War*, pp. 241, 242.

44. S. Wells Williams, "Narrative of a Voyage of The Ship *Morrison*," *The Chinese Repository*, VI (September and December, 1837), p. 227.

45. F. W. Williams, *Life and Letters of Samuel Wells Williams*, pp. 144, 159, 165, 169, 172–73, 174. Williams was unduly pessimistic as recent studies of the impact of the missionaries now show. A number of early converts went on to serve their own government and the foreign community as translators and middlemen while others became successful missionaries and/or businessmen in their own right. See, for example, Carl T. Smith, *Chinese Christians: Elites, Middlemen, and the Church in Hong Kong* (Oxford and New York: Oxford University Press, 1985).

46. Williams to William Frederick and Sarah Pond Williams, April 16, 1853, *Williams Correspondence*.

47. F. W. Williams, *Life and Letters of Samuel Wells Williams*, p. 99.

48. Taylor, *A Visit to India, China, and Japan*, pp. 295–96.

49. Ibid., pp. 325–26, 329, 334, 335–36; Betty Peh-T'i Wei, *Shanghai: Crucible of Modern China* (Hong Kong: Oxford University Press, 1987), pp. 8, 10–11.

50. Fairbank, *Trade and Diplomacy*, pp. 159–60, 393–95.

51. Taylor, *A Visit to India, China, and Japan*, pp. 295, 296, 306, 308, 309, 310–11, 313–14, 318.

52. Ibid., pp. 315–16, 319; Chester A. Bain, "Commodore Matthew Perry, Humphrey Marshall, and the Taiping Rebellion," *The Far East Quarterly*, X (May 1951), p. 261.

53. Fairbank, *Trade and Diplomacy*, p. 415.

54. Ivan Goncharov, *The Frigate Pallada* (New York: St. Martin's Press, 1987), pp. 355–56. Goncharov went on to write the celebrated novel *Oblomov*.

55. Taylor, *A Visit to India, China, and Japan*, pp. 297–302.

56. *A Report of the Secretary of the Navy . . . relative to the naval expedition to Japan*, pp. 19–20.

57. Ibid., pp. 23–26.

58. Perry, *Journal*, p. 60.

59. *A Report of the Secretary of the Navy . . . relative to the naval expedition to Japan*, pp. 22–23.

60. Ibid., p. 23.

61. Ibid., pp. 23–26.

62. Ibid., pp. 27–28.

63. Ibid., p. 27.

64. *Correspondence between the State Department and the late Commissioner to China*, pp. 122–28.

65. Taylor, *A Visit to India, China, and Japan*, p. 365.

Chapter 5
THE OUTER DOOR OF THE HERMETIC EMPIRE

1. *Meiji Japan Through Contemporary Sources*, Vol. II: 1844–1882 (Tokyo: The Centre for East Asian Cultural Studies, 1970), p. 3.

2. J. W. Spalding, *The Japan Expedition: Japan and Around the World, An Account of Three Visits to the Japanese Empire* (New York: Redfield, 1855), p. 103.

3. Matthew Calbraith Perry, *Narrative of the Expedition of an American Squadron to the China Seas and Japan, performed in the years, 1852, 1853, and 1854, under the Command of Commodore M. C. Perry, United States Navy, by Order of the Government of the United States* (Washington: Beverley Tucker, Senate Printer, 1856), I, p. 193.

4. Spalding, *Japan Expedition*, p. 103.

5. Joseph Heco, *The Narrative of a Japanese* (Yokohama: Yokohama Printing and Publishing Company, n.d.), I, pp. 115–22.

6. Spalding, *Japan Expedition*, p. 103.

7. S. Wells Williams, "A Journal of the Perry Expedition to Japan (1853–1854)," *Transactions of the Asiatic Society of Japan*, Vol. XXXVII, Part 2 (1910), p. 5.

8. Bayard Taylor, *A Visit to India, China, and Japan in the Year 1853* (London: Sampson Low, Son & Company, n.d.), p. 367.

9. Perry, *Narrative*, I, p. 155.

10. Yoshihiko Teruya, *Bernard J. Bettelheim and Okinawa: A Study of the First Protestant Missionary to the Island Kingdom, 1846–1854*, Master's Thesis, University of Ryukyus, 1954, University of Colorado, 1958, p. 346.

11. Williams, "Journal," p. 7.

12. George H. Kerr, *Okinawa: The History of an Island People* (Rutland: Charles E. Tuttle Company, 1958), pp. 21–22, 29–31, 33–34, 39–43.

13. Ibid., pp. 43–44, 45–46, 77–78, 90–94.

14. Ibid., pp. 136, 139–43, 156.

15. Ibid., pp. 156–64.

16. Ibid., pp. 166–69, 180. Robert K. Sakai, "The Ryukyu (Liu-ch'iu) Islands as a Fief of Satsuma," in John K. Fairbank, ed., *The Chinese World Order* (Cambridge: Harvard University Press, 1968), p. 119–20.

17. Kerr, *Okinawa*, pp. 184, 241–43.

18. Ibid., p. 262.

19. Robert K. Sakai, "Shimazu Nariakira and the Emergence of National Leadership in Satsuma," in Albert M. Craig and Donald H. Shively, eds., *Personality in Japanese History* (Berkeley: University of California Press, 1970), pp. 211–13.

20. Kerr, *Okinawa*, p. 240.

21. *Meiji Japan*, II, p. 3.

22. Kerr, *Okinawa*, p. 78; Sakai, "Shimazu Nariakira," pp. 216–17.

23. Kanbashi, Norimasa, *Satsuma jin to Yoropa* (Kagoshima: Chosakusha, 1982), p. 90.

24. Ibid., p. 91.

25. Sakai, "Shimazu Nariakira," pp. 217–18; Watanabe Shujiro, *Abe Masahiro-jiseki* (Tokyo: Tokyo University Press, 1910), I, p. 92.

26. Sakai, "Shimazu Nariakira," p. 212.

27. Teruya, *Bettelheim*, pp. 15–17, 27–28, 36. William Leonard Schwartz, "Commodore Perry at Okinawa from the Unpublished Diary of a British Missionary," *American Historical Review*, LI (January, 1946), pp. 262–63.

28. Teruya, *Bettelheim*, pp. 37, 55, 58–59.

29. W. G. Beasley, *Great Britain and the Opening of Japan, 1834–1858* (London: Luzac and Company Ltd., 1951), p. 80.

30. Sakai, "Shimazu Nariakira," pp. 224–32.

31. Teruya, *Bettelheim*, pp. 217, 222–23, 228–35, 237.

32. Ibid., pp. 241–42, 245–51.

33. Ibid., pp. 262–64, 266, 269–73.

34. Ibid., pp. 288–290, 302–6, 308.

35. Ibid., p. 312. See Ivan Goncharov's description of Bettelheim in *The Frigate Pallada* (New York: St. Martin's Press, 1987), p. 442.

36. Schwartz, "Bettelheim Diary," pp. 264–65; Matthew Calbraith Perry, *The Japan Expedition, 1852–1854: The Personal Journal of Matthew C. Perry*, Roger Pineau, ed. (Washington: Smithsonian Institution Press, 1968), p. 61.

37. Williams, "Journal," pp. 7–9. Throughout the book conversations between Perry, his officers, and interpreters, and Okinawan and Japanese officials, are reconstructed from eyewitness accounts, such as the *Narrative*, Perry's *Journal*, Williams's *Journal*, and Bayard Taylor's account of the expedition.

38. Ibid., p. 9.

39. Perry, *Narrative*, I, pp. 155–56; Williams, "Journal," p. 9–11.

40. Spalding, *The Japan Expedition*, pp. 114–16.

41. Schwartz, "Bettelheim Diary," pp. 265–66.

42. Teruya, *Bettelheim*, p. 319.

43. Williams, "Journal," pp. 12–14.

44. For the role of the *zaiban bugyo*, see Tokutomi Soho, *Perry Raiko Oyobi Sono Toji*, in *Kinsei Nihon Kokuminshi* (Tokyo: Minyusha, 1929), XXXI, p. 26; Shimazu Nariakira Bunsho Kankokai, *Shimazu Nariakira Bunsho* (Tokyo: Yashikawa Kobunkan, 1969), III:1, p. 502.

45. Williams, "Journal," p. 14; Teruya, *Bettelheim*, p. 354.

46. Williams, "Journal," p. 14.

47. Ibid., pp. 16–17.

48. A translation of the petition and Perry's reply is in Perry, *Journal*, pp. 63–64.

49. Williams, "Journal," p. 19.

50. Accounts of the exploration of the island appear in Perry, *Narrative*, I, pp. 154–186; and Taylor, *A Visit*, pp. 371–76.

51. Taylor, *A Visit*, p. 373.

52. Ibid., pp. 374–75.

53. Perry, *Narrative*, I, pp. 188–94.

54. Ibid., p. 193; Perry, *Journal*, p. 68.

55. Williams, "Journal," p. 25.

56. Williams, "Journal," p. 17.

57. Schwartz, "Bettelheim Diary," pp. 268–69.

Chapter 6
TO THE BONIN ISLANDS AND BACK TO NAHA

1. W. G. Beasley, *Great Britain and the Opening of Japan* (London: Luzac and Company, 1951), p. 68.

2. Matthew Calbraith Perry, *The Japan Expedition, 1852–1854: The Personal Journal of Matthew C. Perry*, Roger Pineau, ed. (Washington: Smithsonian Institution Press), pp. 84–85.

3. S. Wells Williams, "A Journal of the Perry Expedition to Japan, 1853–1854," *Transactions of the Asiatic Society of Japan*, XXXVII, Part 2 (1910), p. 46.

4. Williams to Sarah Walworth Williams, June 8, 1853, and June 23, 1853, *Williams Correspondence, Williams Family Papers*, Sterling Library, Yale University, New Haven, Connecticut.

5. Matthew Calbraith Perry, *Narrative of the Expedition of an American Squadron to the China Seas and Japan, performed in the years, 1852, 1853, and 1854, under the Command of Commodore M. C. Perry, United States Navy, by Order of the Government of the United States* (Washington: Beverley Tucker, Senate Printer, 1856), I, p. 211.

6. *A Report of the Secretary of the Navy ... relative to the naval expedition to Japan*, U.S. Senate, 33rd Congress, 2nd Session, pp. 29–32; Williams, "Journal," p. 34.

7. Beasley, *Great Britain and the Opening of Japan*, pp. 10–11, 12, 17–18, 20, 60–71.

8. Ibid., p. 93.

9. Sir John Bowring to Williams, June 21, 1853, *Williams Correspondence*.

10. *A Report of the Secretary of the Navy ... relative to the naval expedition to Japan*, pp. 40–41, 42–43.

11. Ibid., pp. 39–40.

12. Williams, "Journal," pp. 37, 41.

13. Perry to Jane Slidell Perry, June 24, 1853, Columbia University Library, New York, New York.

14. Perry, *Narrative*, I, p. 218.

15. *A Report of the Secretary of the Navy ... relative to the naval expedition to Japan*, p. 32; Perry, *Journal*, p. 86.

16. Williams, *Journal*, pp. 44, 46.

Chapter 7
NAIYU-GAIKAN

1. The phrase *naiyu-gaikan* used here and as the title for Chapter 7 is found in W. G. Beasley, *The Meiji Restoration* (Stanford: Stanford University Press, 1972), p. 41.

2. Marco Polo, *The Travels of Marco Polo* (Harmondsworth: Penguin Books, 1958), pp. 215–16.

3. A. L. Sadler, *The Maker of Modern Japan: The Life of Shogun Tokugawa Ieyasu* (Rutland: Charles E. Tuttle Company, 1937), p. 261.

4. Ibid., p. 387.

5. Hirata Atsutane, *Summary of the Ancient Way (Kodo Taii)*, in William Theodore de Bary et al., eds., *Sources of Japanese Tradition* (New York: Columbia University Press, 1958), II, p. 39.

6. Sakamaki Shunzo, "Japan and the United States, 1790–1853," *Transactions of the Asiatic Society of Japan*, 2nd Series, XVIII (1939), pp. 127–28.

7. The Dutch king's letter and the shogun's reply are found in *Meiji Japan through Contemporary Sources*, Vol. II: 1844–1882 (Tokyo: The Centre for East Asian Cultural Studies, 1970), pp. 1–8.

8. Kayama Eizaemon, *Memorandum of Kayama Eizaemon, Yoriki in the*

Staff of the Uraga Governor (Typewritten translation by Muto Kiyoshi in possession of Captain Roger Pineau, USNR Ret.), pp. 2–3.

9. D. C. Greene, "Osada's Life of Takano Nagahide [Choei]," *Transactions of the Asiatic Society of Japan*, XLI (August 1913), p. 422; Bob Tadashi Wakabayashi, *Anti-foreignism and Western Learning in Early-Modern Japan: The New Theses of 1825* (Cambridge: Harvard University Press, 1986), p. 58.

10. Watanabe Shujiro, *Abe Masahiro jiseki* (Tokyo: Tokyo University Press, 1910), II, p. 688.

11. Shimazu Nariakira Bunsho Kankokai, *Shimazu Nariakira Bunsho* (Tokyo: Yashikawa Kobunkan, 1969), III:1, p. 484.

12. Takano Choei, "A Dream," trans. in Greene, "Osada's Life of Takano Nagahide [Choei]," pp. 423–30.

13. Ibid., p. 422.

14. Ibid., pp. 436, 440, 453, 455, 464–65.

15. G. B. Sansom, *The Western World and Japan: A Study in the Interaction of European and Asiatic Cultures* (Rutland: Charles E. Tuttle Company, 1950), p. 255.

16. Sakamaki, "Japan and the United States," pp. 114–15.

17. Ibid., pp. 122–24.

18. Sakuma Shozan, *Reflections of My Errors (Seiken-roku)*, in de Bary et al., *Sources of Japanese Tradition*, II, p. 108.

19. For Tokugawa Ieyasu's biography, see Sadler, *The Maker of Modern Japan*; Conrad Totman, *Tokugawa Ieyasu: Shogun* (South San Francisco: Heian International, 1983); George Sansom, *A History of Japan, 1334–1615* (Stanford: Stanford University Press, 1963); and *A History of Japan, 1615–1867* (Stanford University Press, 1963). These three and John Whitney Hall, *Japan from Prehistory to Modern Times* (New York: Dell Publishing Company, 1970) and James Murdoch, *A History of Japan* (New York: Frederick Ungar Publishing Company, 1964), III: 1 and 2 provide the best overview of early Tokugawa history.

20. There are numerous accounts of the daimyo system. The most helpful were Sansom, *A History of Japan, 1334–1615*, pp. 396, 400, and Conrad Totman, *Politics in the Tokugawa Bakufu, 1600–1843* (Cambridge: Harvard University Press, 1967), pp. 13, 29, 32–40, 110–17.

21. Sadler, *The Maker of Modern Japan*, pp. 375–81; Totman, *Tokugawa Ieyasu*, p. 144; Herschel Webb, *The Japanese Imperial Institution in the Tokugawa Period* (New York: Columbia University Press, 1968), pp. 52–58.

22. For a sense of the extent of Japan's contact with the outside world in the sixteenth and seventeenth centuries, see the map in Martin Collcut et al., *Cultural Atlas of Japan* (New York: Facts on File, 1988), pp. 142–43.

23. Sansom, *A History of Japan, 1334–1615*, pp. 373–77.

24. Sansom, *A History of Japan, 1615–1867*, pp. 39–42.

25. Sadler, *The Maker of Modern Japan*, pp. 224–32; Totman, *Tokugawa Ieyasu*, pp. 66–67.

26. Log of the *Manhattan*, Old Dartmouth Historical Society, April 16–April 21, 1845.

27. *Hiroshige: One Hundred Views of Edo* (New York: George Braziller, Inc., 1986).

28. John Stevenson, *Yoshitoshi* (Boulder: Avery Press, 1986), pp. 12–13; John Whitney Hall, *Tanuma Okitsugu, 1719–1788* (Westport, Connecticut: Greenwood Press, Publishers, 1982), p. 113.

29. Totman, *Politics in the Tokugawa Bakufu*, pp. 95–97, 104–5, 180.

30. John W. Dower, ed., *Origins of the Modern Japanese State: Selected Writings of E. H. Norman* (New York: Pantheon Books, 1975), pp. 333.

31. Sansom, *A History of Japan, 1615–1867*, pp. 15, 99.

32. Herbert P. Bix, *Peasant Protest in Japan, 1590–1884* (New Haven: Yale University Press, 1986), pp. xxv–xxxii; Dower, ed., *Origins of the Modern Japanese State*, pp. 328–29.

33. Hall, *Tanuma Okitsugu*, p. 112.

34. Kokichi Katsu, *Musui's Story: The Autobiography of a Tokugawa Samurai* (Tucson: University of Arizona Press, 1988).

35. Bix, *Peasant Protest*, 109–26; Sansom, *A History of Japan, 1615–1867*, pp. 183–87.

36. Bix, *Peasant Protest*, pp. 149–58; Ivan Morris, *The Nobility of Failure: Tragic Heroes in the History of Japan* (New York: Farrar, Straus, Giroux, 1975), pp. 180–216; Tetsuo Najita, "Oshio Heihachiro (1793–1837)," in Albert M. Craig and Donald H. Shively, eds., *Personality in Japanese History* (Berkeley: University of California Press, 1970), pp. 155–79.

Chapter 8
THE BAKUFU CONFRONTS THE OUTER BARBARIANS

1. Aizawa Seishisai, *Shinron (New Theses)*, excerpted in William Theodore de Bary et al., eds., *Sources of Japanese Tradition* (New York: Columbia University Press, 1958), II, p. 89.

2. Watanabe Shujiro, *Abe Masahiro jiseki* (Tokyo: Tokyo University Press, 1910), I, p. 91.

3. Ibid., II, p. 414.

4. Conrad Totman, "Political Reconciliation in the Tokugawa Bakufu: Abe Masahiro and Tokugawa Nariaki, 1844–1852," in Albert M. Craig and Donald H. Shively, eds., *Peronality in Japanese History* (Berkeley: University of California Press, 1970), p. 190.

5. Harold Bolitho, *Treasures Among Men: The Fudai Daimyo in Tokugawa Japan* (New Haven: Yale University Press, 1974), pp. 98–99; Conrad D. Totman, "The Struggle for Control of the Shogunate (1853–1858)," *Papers on Japan* (Cambridge: East Asia Research Center, 1961), pp. 78–79; Watanabe, *Abe Masahiro jiseki*, I, p. 10.

6. Watanabe, ibid., pp. 13, 19–20.

7. Herbert P. Bix, *Peasant Protest in Japan, 1590–1884* (New Haven: Yale University Press, 1986), pp. 116–26.

8. Watanabe, *Abe Masahiro jiseki,* I, p. 33.

9. W. G. Beasley, *The Meiji Restoration* (Stanford: Stanford University Press, 1972), pp. 64–65; James Murdoch, *A History of Japan* (New York: Frederick Ungar Publishing Company, 1964), III, Part 2, pp. 460–62.

10. For Abe Masahiro's opposition to dealing with foreigners at the time of the *Morrison* visit in 1837, see Watanabe, *Abe Masahiro jiseki,* I, pp. 72–73; Murdoch, *A History of Japan,* III, Part 2, pp. 463–64.

11. J. Victor Koschmann, *The Mito Ideology: Discourse, Reform, and Insurrection in Late Tokugawa Japan, 1790–1864* (Berkeley: University of California Press, 1987), pp. 139–40; Murdoch, *A History of Japan,* III, Part 2, p. 462; Totman, "Political Reconciliation in the Tokugawa Bakufu," pp. 184–85; Totman, "The Struggle for Control of the Shogunate (1853–1858)," p. 79.

12. Beasley, *The Meiji Restoration,* p. 66; Richard T. Chang, *From Prejudice to Tolerance: A Study of the Japanese Image of the West, 1826–1864* (Tokyo: Sophia University, 1970), p. 24; Koschmann, *The Mito Ideology,* pp. 81–130; Murdoch, *A History of Japan,* III, Part 2, pp. 457–58; de Bary et al., *Sources of Japanese Tradition,* II, pp. 85–88.

13. E. W. Clement, "British Seamen and Mito Samurai in 1824," *Transactions of the Asiatic Society of Japan,* 1st Series, XXXIII (1905), pp. 91–97.

14. I have quoted from the excerpts from the *Shinron* in de Bary et al., *Sources of Japanese Tradition,* II, pp. 88–89. For a more complete translation, see Bob Tadashi Wakabayashi, *Anti-Foreignism and Western Learning in Early-Modern Japan: The New Theses of 1825* (Cambridge: Harvard University Press, 1986).

15. *Shinron,* p. 95.

16. Ibid., pp. 94, 88.

17. G. B. Sansom, *A History of Japan to 1334* (Stanford: Stanford University Press, 1963), pp. 30–33; excerpt from Motoori Norinaga's *Precious Comb-box (Tama kushige)* in de Bary et al., *Sources of Japanese Tradition,* II, pp. 15–18.

18. *Shinron,* p. 93.

19. Koschmann, *The Mito Ideology,* pp. 82, 85, 119.

20. For the best account of what Totman calls Abe's "restrained courtship" of Nariaki, see his "Political Reconciliation in the Tokugawa Bakufu."

21. *Meiji Japan through Contemporary Sources,* Vol. II: 1844–1882 (Tokyo: The Centre for East Asian Cultural Studies, 1970), pp. 6–8; Watanabe, *Abe Masahiro jiseki,* I, p. 176.

22. Robert K. Sakai, "Shimazu Nariakira and the Emergence of National Leadership in Satsuma" in Craig and Shively, *Personality in Japanese History,* pp. 216–17; Watanabe, *Abe Masahiro jiseki,* II, p. 444.

23. Sakai, "Shimazu Nariakira," pp. 218–19; Watanabe, *Abe Masahiro jiseki,* I, p. 95.

24. Watanabe, ibid., p. 79.

25. Ibid., p. 98.

26. Ibid., pp. 98–99.

27. For a firsthand account of Biddle's visit, see Charles Nordhoff, *Man-of-War Life* (Annapolis: Naval Institute Press, 1985), pp. 176–89. See also Biddle's report in *Official Documents Relative to the Empire of Japan*, U.S. Senate, 32nd Congress, 1st Session, Senate Executive Document 59, pp. 64–66, and the *Papers of Benajah Ticknor* (Surgeon aboard the *Columbia*), Sterling Library, Yale University, New Haven, Connecticut. For my understanding of Abe's struggles with key parts of the bureaucracy and his attempts to formulate a strategy for dealing with foreign incursions, I am indebted to Professor Mitani Hiroshi of the University of Tokyo. For an excellent critical study of the limits of Abe's accomplishments, see Harold Bolitho, "Abe Masahiro and the New Japan," in Jeffrey P. Mass and William B. Hauser, eds., *The Bakufu in Japanese History* (Stanford: Stanford University Press, 1985). Mitani Hiroshi, "Kaikoku Zenya," in Kindai Nihon Kenyukai, *Nihon Gaiko No Kiki Ninshiki*, 7 (1985), p. 1142.

28. Ibid., p. 1143.

29. Totman, "Political Reconciliation in the Tokugawa Bakufu," p. 190.

30. Watanabe, *Abe Masahiro jiseki*, I, pp. 62–64.

31. Ibid., II, p. 414.

32. Ibid., II, pp. 414–15.

33. Herschel Webb, *The Japanese Imperial Institution in the Tokugawa Period* (New York: Columbia University Press, 1968), pp. 231–33.

34. Sakamoto Kenichi, *Tenno to Meiji Ishin* (Tokyo: Akatsuki Shoba, 1983), p. 16.

35. Tokutomi Soho, *Kinsei Nihon Kokuminshi* (Tokyo: Minyusha, 1929), XXXI, p. 314.

36. Totman, "Political Reconciliation in the Tokugawa Bakufu," pp. 194–195; Totman, "The Struggle for Control of the Shogunate (1853–1858)," pp. 53–55.

37. Watanabe, *Abe Masahiro jiseki*, I, p. 100.

38. Ibid., pp. 99, 103.

39. Sakai, "Shimazu Nariakira," pp. 219–32.

40. Mitani, "Kaikoku Zenya," pp. 24–25.

41. Ibid., p. 25.

42. Totman, "Political Reconciliation in the Tokugawa Bakufu," pp. 198–99.

43. Ibid., pp. 200–1.

44. Kanbashi Norimasa, *Satsuma jin to Yoropa* (Kagoshima: Chosakusha, 1982), pp. 81–83.

45. Totman, "Political Reconciliation in the Tokugawa Bukufu," pp. 202–5.

46. Mitani, "Kaikoku Zenya," p. 39.

47. Ibid., pp. 38–39.

Chapter 9
THE COMING OF THE UNIVERSAL YANKEE NATION

1. J. W. Spalding, *The Japan Expedition: Japan and Around the World: An Account of Three Visits to the Japanese Empire* (New York: Redfield, 1855), p. 141.

2. S. Wells Williams, "A Journal of the Perry Expedition to Japan (1853–1854)," *Transactions of the Asiatic Society of Japan*, Vol. XXXVII, Part 2 (1910), p. 47.

3. Matthew Calbraith Perry, *The Japan Expedition, 1852–1854: The Personal Journal of Matthew C. Perry*, Roger Pineau, ed. (Washington: Smithsonian Institution Press, 1968), p. 92.

4. Williams, *Journal*, p. 47.

5. William H. Rutherford to Sarah Baldwin, July 17, 1853, *William H. Rutherford Papers*, Library of Congress.

6. Perry, *Journal*, p. 92.

7. Kayama Eizaemon, *Memorandum of Kayama Eizaemon, Yoriki on the Staff of the Uraga Governor*, p. 4. Typewritten translation by Muto Kiyoshi in the possession of Captain Roger Pineau, USNR Ret.

8. Ibid., p. 4.

9. Matthew Calbraith Perry, *Narrative of the Expedition of an American Squadron to the China Seas and Japan, performed in the years, 1852, 1853, and 1854, under the Command of Commodore M. C. Perry, United States Navy, by Order of the Government of the United States* (Washington: Beverley Tucker, Senate Printer, 1856), I, pp. 234–35; Williams, *Journal*, pp. 47–48.

10. Perry, *Narrative*, I, p. 237.

11. Tokyo Teikoku Daigaku, Bunka Daigaku, Shiryo Hensangakari, eds., *Dai Nihon Komonjo: Bakumatsu Gaikoku Kankei Monjo* (Tokyo: Imperial University, Shiryo Henan Kyoku, 1912), I, pp. 14–15.

12. Baba (Bunyi), *Genji yume monogatari* (Tokyo: Naigai Suppan Kyokai, 1905), p. 4.

13. Perry, *Journal*, p. 93.

14. Ibid., p. 91; Spalding, *Japan Expedition*, p. 130–31. Surprisingly, we could find no Japanese account of the meteor.

15. Kayama, *Memorandum*, pp. 6–7.

16. Perry, *Journal*, p. 95; Bayard Taylor, *A Visit to India, China, and Japan in the Year 1853* (London: Sampson Low, Son & Company, n.d.), p. 420.

17. Kayama, *Memorandum*, p. 8.

18. Ibid., pp. 9–10.

19. Kobayashi Tetsujiro, "Assorted News of the Visit of Foreign Ships," Nabeshima Archive, Saga Prefectural Library, pp. 1–2. Typewritten translation in the possession of Captain Roger Pineau, USNR Ret.

20. "A Doctor's Memorandum," Nabeshima Archive, Saga Prefectural Library, pp. 1–2. Typewritten translation in the possession of Captain Roger

Pineau, USNR Ret. The translator speculates that the author of this unsigned diary was Ito Genboku, a doctor attending the daimyo of Saga.

21. Tabohashi Kiyoshi, *Kindai Nihongaikoku Kankeishi* (Tokyo: Toeshin, 1943), p. 526.

22. Tokyo Teikoku Daigaku, *Dai Nihon Komonjo*, I, p. 144; Kayama, *Memorandum*, p. 10; Takashi Ishii, *Nihon Kaikokushi* (Tokyo: Yoshikawa Kobunsho, 1972), p. 48.

23. Tokutomi Soho, *Kinsei Nihon Kokuminshi* (Tokyo: Minyusha, 1929), XXXI, pp. 138–39.

24. Ibid., pp. 140–42.

25. Watanabe Shujiro, *Abe Masahiro jiseki* (Tokyo: Tokyo University Press, 1910), I, p. 146.

26. Williams, Journal, p. 53.

27. Perry, *Narrative*, I, p. 241.

28. Kayama, *Memorandum*, p. 11.

29. "A Doctor's Memorandum," pp. 2–4; Monbusho Ishin Shiryo Hensan Kai, *Ishinshi* (Tokyo: Meiji Shoin, 1940), I, pp. 563–64; Tokutomi, *Kinsei Nihon Kokuminshi*, XXXI, pp. 155–56.

30. Tokutomi, ibid., XXXI, pp. 163–64.

31. "A Doctor's Memorandum," p. 3.

32. *Ishinshi*, I, pp. 563–64; Tabohashi, *Kindai Nihongaikoku Kankeishi*, p. 527; Tokutomi, *Perry Raiko Oyoboi Sono Toji*, in *Kinsei Nihon Kokuminshi*, XXXI, pp. 153, 155–63.

33. Tokyo Teikoku Daigaku, *Dai Nihon Komonjo*, I, p. 153.

34. Kayama, *Memorandum*, pp. 11–14; Perry, *Narrative*, I, pp. 244–47.

35. Williams, "Journal," pp. 55–57.

36. Tabohashi, *Kindai Nihongaikoku Kankeishi*, p. 529.

37. "A Doctor's Memorandum," pp. 4–6.

38. Egami Teruhiko, *Kawaji Toshiakira* (Tokyo: Kyoikusha, 1987), p. 93; Tokutomi, *Kinsei Nihon Kokuminshi*, XXXI, pp. 148–49; Watanabe, *Abe Masahiro jiseki*, I, p. 140.

39. Perry, *Narrative*, I, p. 251.

40. Perry, *Journal*, p. 97.

41. Spalding, *The Japan Expedition*, p. 155.

42. Williams, "Journal," p. 58.

43. Perry, *Narrative*, I, p. 261.

44. Taylor, *A Visit to India, China and Japan*, p. 436.

45. Perry, *Journal*, p. 100.

46. Kayama, *Memorandum*, pp. 15–16.

47. Perry, *Journal*, p. 101.

48. Kayama, *Memorandum*, pp. 17–18.

49. Perry, *Narrative*, I, p. 268; Taylor, *A Visit to India, China and Japan*, p. 439.

Chapter 10
WAR AT HOME, PEACE ABROAD

1. Watanabe Shujiro, *Abe Masahiro jiseki* (Tokyo: Tokyo University Press, 1910), I, pp. 333–34.

2. W. G. Beasley, ed. *Selected Documents on Japanese Foreign Policy* (London: Oxford University Press, 1955), p. 107.

3. Beasley, ed., *Selected Documents*, pp. 117–18.

4. Watanabe, *Abe Masahiro jiseki*, I, pp. 331–36.

5. "A Doctor's Memorandum," Nabeshima Archive, Saga Prefectural Library, pp. 8–10.

6. Tokutomi Soho, *Kinsei Nihon Kokuminshi* (Tokyo: Minyusha, 1929), pp. 165–66.

7. For a description of the revolt, Herbert P. Bix, "Miura Meisuke, or Peasant Rebellion Under the Banner of 'Distress,'" *Bulletin of Concerned Asian Scholars*, X (April–June 1978), pp. 18–26.

8. There is no reference to the "white flag" letter in either Perry's journal or the official narrative. But it appears in the foremost Japanese collection of documents pertaining to foreign policy, Tokyo Teikoku Daigaku, Bunka Daigaku, Shiryo Hensangakari, eds., *Dai Nihon Komonjo: Bakumatsu Kaikoku Kankei Monjo* (Tokyo: Tokyo Imperial University, Shiryo Henan Kyoku, 1912), I, pp. 169–70, and is translated in *Meiji Japan Through Contemporary Sources*, Vol. II: 1844–1882 (Tokyo: The Centre for East Asian Cultural Studies, 1970), pp. 15–16. One can only speculate that Perry chose not to include the letter in his accounts of the expedition so as not to be portrayed as threatening the Japanese.

9. Matthew Calbraith Perry, *Narrative of the Expedition of an American Squadron to the China Seas and Japan, performed in the years, 1852, 1853, and 1854, under the Command of Commodore M. C. Perry, United States Navy, by Order of the Government of the United States* (Washington: Beverley Tucker, Senate Printer, 1856), I, pp. 256–57.

10. Ibid., p. 259.

11. Tokutomi, *Kinsei Nihon Kokuminshi*, XXXI, p. 191.

12. Ibid., pp. 195–96; Egami Teruhiko, *Kawaji Toshiakira* (Tokyo: Kyoikusha, 1987), p. 93; Watanabe, *Abe Masahiro jiseki*, II, pp. 690–91.

13. Watanabe, ibid., I, pp. 141–42.

14. Kanbashi Norimasa, *Satsuma jin to Yoropa* (Kagoshima: Chosakusha, 1982), pp. 395–96.

15. Tokutomi, *Kinsei Nihon Kokuminshi*, XXXI, p. 311.

16. Ibid., p. 233.

17. Watanabe, *Abe Masahiro jiseki*, I, p. 155.

18. Ibid., pp. 162–63, II, 691–700; Beasley, *Selected Documents*, pp. 102–7.

19. Beasley, ibid., p. 112–14.

20. Ibid., pp. 107–12.

21. Ibid., pp. 117–19.

22. Tokutomi, *Kinsei Nihon Kokuminshi*, XXXI, pp. 202–4; Yoshida Tsu-nekichi, *Ii Naosuke* (Tokyo: Yoshikawa Kobunkan, 1963), pp. 198–211.

23. Richard T. Chang, *From Prejudice to Tolerance: A Study of the Japanese Image of the West, 1826–1864* (Tokyo: Sophia University, 1970), p. 84; *Meiji Japan Through Contemporary Sources*, Vol. II: 1844–1882, pp. 25–26.

24. Watanabe, *Abe Masahiro jiseki*, I, p. 165.

25. Chang, *From Prejudice to Tolerance*, pp. 82–86.

26. George Alexander Lensen, *The Russian Push Toward Japan: Russo-Japanese Relations, 1697–1875* (Princeton: Princeton University Press, 1959), pp. 14–15, 25, 28, 32, 36–38, 49–54, 63–65, 78–82, 88–93, 96–120, 300–1.

27. See, for example, Donald Keene's discussion of Hayashi Shihei in *The Japanese Discovery of Europe, 1720–1830* (Stanford: Stanford University Press, 1969), pp. 39–45.

28. Warren Bartlett Walsh, *Russia and the Soviet Union: A Modern History* (Ann Arbor: The University of Michigan Press, 1968), pp. 215–23.

29. Ivan Goncharov, *The Frigate Pallada* (New York: St. Martin's Press, 1987), pp. 265–335; Lensen, *The Russian Push*, pp. 291–300; Lensen, *Russia's Japan Expedition of 1852 to 1855* (Gainesville: University of Florida Press, 1955), 14–15, 23, 29–34. Goncharov later became well known as the author of the celebrated novel *Oblomov*.

30. James Murdoch, *A History of Japan* (New York: Frederick Ungar Publishing Company, 1964), III, Part 2, p. 596; Seiho Arima, "The Western Influence on Japanese Military Science, Shipbuilding, and Navigation," *Monumenta Nipponica*, 19 (1964), p. 131.

31. *Mito-han Shiryo, Book of Inui* (Tokyo: Yoshikawa Kobunkan, 1970), I, pp. 94–95.

32. Watanabe, *Abe Masahiro jiseki*, I, p. 171.

33. Seiho Arima, "The Western Influence . . . ," p. 131; Harold Bolitho, "Abe Masahiro and the New Japan," in Jeffrey P. Mass and William B. Hauser, eds., *The Bakufu in Japanese History* (Stanford: Stanford University Press, 1985), pp. 180–81.

34. Watanabe, *Abe Masahiro jiseki*, I, pp. 388–89.

Chapter 11
CHINA OR JAPAN

1. J. W. Spalding, *The Japan Expedition: Japan and Around the World, an Account of Three Visits to the Japanese Empire* (New York: Redfield, 1855), p. 174.

2. *Correspondence between the State Department and the late Commissioner to China*, U.S. House of Representatives, 33rd Congress, 1st Session, Executive Document 123, pp. 176.

3. *A Report of the Secretary of the Navy . . . relative to the naval expedition to Japan,* U.S. Senate, 33rd Congress, 2nd Session, p. 60.

4. Ibid., p. 81.

5. Matthew Calbraith Perry, *The Japan Expedition, 1852–1854; The Personal Journal of Matthew C. Perry,* Roger Pineau, ed. (Washington: The Smithsonian Institution Press, 1968), p. 108; S. Wells Williams, "A Journal of the Perry Expedition to Japan, 1853–1854," *Transactions of the Asiatic Society of Japan,* XXXVII, Part 2 (1910), p. 72.

6. Perry, *Journal,* pp. 109–111; Williams, "Journal," pp. 74–77.

7. Tokyo Teikoku Daigaku, Bunka Daigaku, Shiryo Hensangakari, eds., *Dai Nihon Komonjo: Bakumatsu Kaikoku Kenkei Monjo* (Tokyo: Tokyo Imperial University, Shiryo Henan Kyoku, 1912), p. 679.

8. Perry to J. C. Dobbin, August 3, 1853, *Letters Received by the Secretary of the Navy from Commanding Officers of Squadrons,* National Archives, Washington, D.C. This letter, marked "Confidential," does not appear in *A Report of the Secretary of the Navy . . . relative to the naval expedition to Japan.*

9. Bayard Taylor, *A Visit to India, China, and Japan in the Year 1853* (London: Sampson Low, Son and Company, n.d.), p. 441.

10. Frederic Wakeman, Jr., *Strangers at the Gate: Social Disorder in South China, 1839–1861* (Berkeley: University of California Press, 1966), pp. 137–38; Williams to Frederick Wells Williams and Sarah Pond Williams, August 20, 1853, and Williams to William Frederick Williams, September 24, 1853, *S. Wells Williams Correspondence, Williams Family Papers,* Sterling Library, Yale University.

11. *Correspondence between the State Department and the late Commissioner to China,* p. 177; S. Y. Teng, *The Taiping Rebellion and the Western Powers* (London: Oxford University Press, 1971), p. 157.

12. *A Report of the Secretary of the Navy . . . relative to the naval expedition to Japan,* p. 61; *Correspondence between the State Department and the late Commissioner to China,* pp. 172–73.

13. *A Report of the Secretary of the Navy . . . relative to the naval expedition to Japan,* p. 62.

14. *Correspondence between the State Department and the late Commissioner to China,* pp. 163–69, 175–77.

15. Ibid., pp. 183–84, 266.

16. Ibid., pp. 189–98.

17. Ibid., pp. 203–5.

18. Ibid., pp. 206–9.

19. Ibid., p. 243.

20. Ibid., pp. 253–57.

21. *A Report of the Secretary of the Navy . . . relative to the naval expedition to Japan,* pp. 59–60, 64–65.

22. U.S. Department of State, *China Instructions,* National Archives, I, pp. 84–86.

23. *Correspondence between the State Department and the late Commissioner to China*, pp. 275–77.

24. *A Report of the Secretary of the Navy . . . relative to the naval expedition to Japan*, pp. 72–74.

25. *Correspondence between the State Department and the late Commissioner to China*, pp. 333–37.

26. Perry to Howland and Aspinwall, May 17, 1853, *Squadron Letters*.

27. Lieutenant John Contee to Perry, August 18, 1853, *Squadron Letters*.

28. Perry to Jane Slidell Perry, December 24, 1853, Houghton Library, Harvard University, Cambridge, Massachusetts; *A Report of the Secretary of the Navy . . . relative to the naval expedition to Japan*, pp. 75, 76.

29. *A Report of the Secretary of the Navy . . .*, ibid., p. 275; Henry F. Graff, ed., *Bluejackets in Japan: A Day-by-day Account Kept by Master's Mate John R. C. Lewis and Cabin Boy William B. Allen* (New York: New York Public Library, 1952), pp. 90–91; Perry to Dobbin, September 5, 1853; October 6, 1853; November 4, 1853, *Squadron Letters*; Deck logs of the *Lexington* and *Mississippi*.

30. Abbot to Laura Abbot, October 5, 1853, *Joel Abbot Papers*, Nimitz Library, U.S. Naval Academy; George Henry Preble, *The Opening of Japan: A Diary of Discovery in the Far East, 1853–1856*, Boleslaw Szczesniak, ed. (Norman: University of Oklahoma Press, 1962), p. 25.; Taylor, *A Visit to India, China, and Japan*, pp. 459–63; Steve Crowe, " 'To Do for My Children': The Father in Nineteenth-Century America." This biographical sketch of Abbot is a typewritten manuscript in the possession of Abbot Fletcher, Bath, Maine.

31. Perry to John Y. Mason, November 6, 1844; Abbot to Mason, November 4, 1846; Abbot to Daniel Webster, July 31, 1851; Abbot to Perry, March 29, 1852, *Abbot Papers*.

32. Abbot to John Abbot, June 2, 1853; Abbot to Laura Abbot, June 5, 1853; Abbot to Thomas Hambleton, June 21, 1853, *Abbot Papers*.

33. Preble, *The Opening of Japan*, p. 49.

34. Ibid., p. 54.

35. *China Mail*, September 22, 1853.

36. Samuel Eliot Morison, *"Old Bruin": The Life of Commodore Matthew C. Perry, 1794–1858* (Boston: Little, Brown and Company, 1967), pp. 349–50.

37. *A Report of the Secretary of the Navy . . . relative to the naval expedition to Japan*, p. 69.

38. D. W. Spooner to Perry, October 20, 1853; Perry to Dobbin, October 30, 1853; [Name scratched out] to Captain [no name], October 10, 1853; Edward Cunningham to J. S. Amory, October 12, 1853; Amory to Perry, October 13, 1853; Perry to Amory, October 26, 1853, *Squadron Letters*.

39. *A Report of the Secretary of the Navy . . . relative to the naval expedition to Japan*, pp. 80–83; Ivan Goncharov, *The Frigate Pallada* (New York: St. Martin's Press, 1987), pp. 340–58.

40. Perry, *Journal*, p. 136.

41. *A Report of the Secretary of the Navy . . . relative to the naval expedition to Japan*, pp. 82–87.

42. Ibid., pp. 80–81.

43. Ibid., pp. 88–90.

44. Ibid., pp. 90–101.

45. Ibid., p. 11.

46. Perry, *Journal*, pp. 138–139.

47. *Message of the President of the United States . . . Instructions to Mr. McLane*, U.S. Senate, 36th Congress, 1st Session, Senate Executive Document 39, pp. 2–4.

48. *A Report of the Secretary of the Navy . . . relative to the naval expedition to Japan*, pp. 106–8; Perry, *Journal*, p. 140.

Chapter 12
TO OUT-HEROD HEROD

1. George Alexander Lensen, *Russia's Japan Expedition of 1852 to 1855* (Gainesville: University of Florida Press, 1955), p. 42.

2. Matthew Calbraith Perry, *The Japan Expedition, 1852–1854: The Personal Journal of Matthew C. Perry*, Roger Pineau, ed. (Washington: Smithsonian Institution Press, 1968), p. 159.

3. Ishin Shiryo Hensan Kai, *Dai Nihon Ishin Shiryo* (Tokyo: Ishin Shiryo Hensan Jimukyoku, 1940), II-2, p. 490.

4. Ibid., p. 599.

5. Sarah Williams to Mrs. Williams, October 24, 1853, and September 9, 1853, *Samuel Wells Williams Family Papers*, Sterling Library, Yale University.

6. S. Wells Williams to William Frederick Williams, December 6, 1853, *Family Papers*.

7. "Journal of the Second Visit of Commodore Perry to Japan," in Matthew Calbraith Perry, *Narrative of the Expedition of an American Squadron to the China Seas and Japan, performed in the years, 1852, 1853, and 1854, under the Command of Commodore M. C. Perry, United States Navy, by Order of the Government of the United States* (Washington: Beverley Tucker, Senate Printer, 1856), II, pp. 395–96.

8. Ibid., p. 396; S. Wells Williams, "A Journal of the Perry Expedition to Japan (1853–1854)," *Transactions of the Asiatic Society of Japan*, XXXVII, Part 2, (1910), p. 88; Perry, *Narrative*, II, p. 396.

9. Perry, *Journal*, p. 147.

10. Perry, *Narrative*, I, p. 322.

11. Williams, Journal, p. 96; *Correspondence Relative to the Naval Expedition to Japan, 1853–1854*, U.S. Senate, 33rd Congress, 2nd Session, Executive Document 34, p. 109.

12. George Alexander Lensen, *Russia's Japan Expedition of 1852 to 1855* (Gainesville: University of Florida Press, 1955), pp. 40, 43, 49–56, 62–63.

13. Ivan Goncharov, *The Frigate Pallada* (New York: St. Martin's Press, 1987), p. 385.

14. Joel Abbot to Laura Abbot, March 21, 1854, *Joel Abbot Papers*, Nimitz Library, United States Naval Academy.

15. *Joel Abbot Diary*, February 12, 1854, *Abbot Papers*.

16. Watanabe Shujiro, *Abe Masahiro jiseki* (Tokyo: Tokyo University Press, 1910), I, p. 201.

17. Tokyo Teikoku Daigaku, Bunka Daigaku, Shiryo Hensangakari, eds., *Dai Nihon Komonjo: Bakumatsu Kaikoku Kankei Monjo* (Tokyo: Tokyo Imperial University, Shiryo Henan Kyoku, 1912), IV, pp. 89, 134, 137, 142–43, 162, 165, 171, 177, 236, 290.

18. Perry, *Narrative*, I, p. 328.

19. George Henry Preble, *The Opening of Japan: A Diary of Discovery in the Far East, 1853–1856*, Boleslaw Szczesniak, ed. (Norman: University of Oklahoma Press, 1962), pp. 123, 126.

20. Perry, *Journal*, pp. 159, 164.

21. Richard T. Chang, *From Prejudice to Tolerance: A Study of the Japanese Image of the West, 1826–1864* (Tokyo: Sophia University, 1970), pp. 81–82.

22. Watanabe, *Abe Masahiro jiseki*, I, p. 204.

23. Ishii Takashi, *Nihon Kaikokushi* (Tokyo: Yoshikawa Kobunsho, 1972), p. 85.

24. *Dai Nihon Ishin Shiryo*, II-2, p. 188; Emily V. Warriner, *Voyage to Destiny* (New York: Bobbs Merrill Company, 1956), pp. 151–53; Watanabe, *Abe Masahiro jiseki*, I, p. 205. For biographical material on Manjiro, see also Kaneko Hisakuza, *Manjiro, The Man Who Discovered America* (Boston: Houghton Mifflin Company, 1956); Katherine Plummer, *The Shogun's Reluctant Ambassadors: Sea Drifters* (Tokyo: The Lotus Press, 1985); Job C. Tripp, "A Japanese Student in Fairhaven," *Old Dartmouth Historical Sketches*, 40 (June and October 1914); and a translation of Manjiro's autobiographical notes that is deposited in the Brooklyn Museum.

25. *Dai Nihon Ishin Shiryo*, II-2, p. 490; Ishii, *Nihon Kaikokushi*, p. 85.

26. *Dai Nihon Ishin Shiryo*, II-2, pp. 582–83, 586; Ishii, *Nihon Kaikokushi*, p. 86; Watanabe, *Abe Masahiro jiseki*, I, p. 208.

27. *Dai Nihon Ishin Shiryo*, II-2, p. 599.

28. Perry, *Narrative*, I, pp. 337–38.

29. Watanabe, *Abe Masahiro jiseki*, I, p. 209.

30. *Dai Nihon Ishin Shiryo*, II-2, pp. 601–3.

31. Ishii, *Nihon Kaikokushi*, p. 106; Tabohashi Kyoshi, *Zotei Kindai Nihon Gaikoku Kankei Shi* (Tokyo: Toeshoin, 1953), pp. 598–99.

32. *Dai Nihon Ishin Shiryo*, III, p. 145–47; Tabohashi, *Zotei Kindai Nihon*, p. 599.

33. Tabohashi, ibid., p. 600.

34. *Dai Nihon Ishin Shiryo*, III, pp. 70–72; Tokyo Tokeiku Daigaku et al., eds., *Dai Nihon Komonjo*, IV, p. 474.

35. *Dai Nihon Ishin Shiryo*, III, pp. 70–72, 496.

36. Williams, "Journal," pp. 114, 119.

37. *Abbot Diary*, March 3, 1854.

38. Williams, "Journal," p. 123.

39. The substance of the conversations between Perry and the commissioners is reconstructed from a number of sources including the official *Narrative*; "Diary of an Official of the Bakufu," *Transactions of the Asiatic Society of Japan*, 2nd Series, VII, 1930; *Official Records: Flag Journal, U.S. Naval Expedition to Japan, 1852–1854*, Rutgers University Library; and Perry and Williams's journals. Also, Perry, *Narrative*, I, pp. 349–53.

40. Perry, *Narrative*, I, pp. 351–52.

41. "Diary of an Official of the Bakufu," p. 102.

42. Ibid., pp. 102–3; Perry, *Narrative*, I, pp. 353.

43. J. W. Spalding, *The Japan Expedition: Japan and Around the World, An Account of Three Visits to the Japanese Empire* (New York: Redfield, 1855), p. 232.

44. "Diary of an Official of the Bakufu," pp. 103–6. This exchange about the treatment of American sailors, commerce, and the value of human life is not reported in the official *Narrative*.

45. Ibid., p. 106.

46. Perry, *Journal*, p. 166.

47. Williams, "Journal," pp. 129–30.

48. *Dai Nihon Ishin Shiryo*, III, pp. 749–50.

49. Perry, *Narrative*, p. 356.

50. *Dai Nihon Ishin Shiryo*, IV, 37–38; Watanabe, *Abe Masahiro jiseki*, I, p. 234.

51. Watanabe, ibid., p. 212.

52. Preble, *The Opening of Japan*, p. 140; Spalding, *Japan Expedition*, p. 244.

53. Perry, *Narrative*, I, p. 361.

54. "Diary of an Official of the Bakufu," p. 107–10; Perry, *Narrative*, I, pp. 362–66.

55. *Dai Nihon Ishin Shiryo*, III, p. 803.

56. Ibid., IV, pp. 415–16, 483–84.

57. Ishii, *Nihon Kaikokushi*, p. 95.

58. Perry, *Journal*, p. 171.

59. Watanabe, *Abe Masahiro jiseki*, I, p. 222.

60. Ibid., pp. 249–50.

61. Williams, "Journal," p. 148.

62. Perry, *Narrative*, p. 377.

63. Williams, "Journal," p. 153.

64. Ibid., p. 151.

65. "Diary of an Official of the Bakufu," p. 115.

66. Ibid., p. 119.

67. Williams, "Journal," p. 162.

68. Perry, *Journal*, p. 182.

69. W. G. Beasley, ed., *Selected Documents on Japanese Foreign Policy* (London: Oxford University Press, 1955), pp. 122–27.

Chapter 13
TESTING THE TREATY

1. Yoshida Tsunekichi, *Tojin Okichi* (Tokyo: Chuokoronsha, 1966), pp. 15–16.

2. S. Wells Williams, "A Journal of the Perry Expedition to Japan (1853–1854)," *Transactions of the Asiatic Society of Japan*, XXXVII, Part 2 (1910), pp. 218–19.

3. J. W. Spalding, *The Japan Expedition: Japan and Around the World, An Account of Three Visits to the Japanese Empire* (New York: Redfield, 1855), p. 339.

4. Oliver Statler, *Shimoda Story* (Honolulu: University of Hawaii Press, 1969), p. 8.

5. Tabohashi Kyoshi, *Zotei Kindai Nihon Gaikoku Kankei Shi* (Tokyo: Toeshoin, 1953), p. 601.

6. Yoshida, *Tojin Okichi*, p. 6.

7. Matthew Calbraith Perry, *Narrative of the Expedition of an American Squadron to the China Seas and Japan, performed in the years, 1852, 1853, and 1854, under the Command of Commodore M. C. Perry, United States Navy, by Order of the Government of the United States* (Washington: Beverley Tucker, Senate Printer, 1856), I, p. 403.

8. Yoshida, *Tojin Okichi*, p. 14.

9. For biographical material on Yoshida Shoin, see Thomas M. Huber, *The Revolutionary Origins of Modern Japan* (Stanford: Stanford University Press, 1981), pp. 7–91; Naramoto Tatsuya, *Yoshida Shoin* (Tokyo: Shisakusha, 1971) and *Yoshida Shoin no Subete* (Tokyo: Jinbutsu Oraisha, 1984); and G. B. Sansom, *The Western World and Japan: A Study in the Interaction of European and Asiatic Cultures* (Rutland: Charles E. Tuttle Company, 1950), pp. 269–74.

10. Spalding, *The Japan Expedition*, pp. 282–85; Williams, "Journal," pp. 172–75.

11. Huber, *The Revolutionary Origins of Modern Japan*, pp. 20, 23, 39, 47–52, 79–91.

12. Perry, *Narrative*, I, pp. 419, 422.

13. Ibid., p. 424.

14. Williams, "Journal," p. 181.

15. Perry, *Narrative*, I, p. 423–24, 425.

16. Yoshida, *Tojin Okichi*, pp. 15–16.

17. Williams, "Journal," pp. 183–84.

18. *William Speiden Journal*, April 22, 1854, Naval Historical Foundation, Washington, D.C.

19. Oliver Statler, *The Black Ship Scroll* (Rutland: Charles E. Tuttle Company, 1964), pp. 75–77.

20. Williams, "Journal," p. 219.

21. Henry F. Graff, ed., *Bluejackets with Perry in Japan: A Day-by-day Account Kept by Master's Mate John R. C. Lewis and Cabin Boy William B. Allen* (New York: New York Public Library, 1952), pp. 146–48.

22. Perry, *Narrative*, I, p. 427.

23. Harold Bolitho, *Treasures Among Men: The Fudai Daimyo in Tokugawa Japan* (New Haven: Yale University Press, 1974), pp. 212–13; John A. Harrison, *Japan's Northern Frontier: A Preliminary Study in Colonization and Expansion with Special Reference to the Relations of Japan and Russia* (Gainesville: University of Florida Press, 1953), pp. 8–10, 29–31; Donald Keene, *The Japanese Discovery of Europe, 1720–1830* (Stanford: Stanford University Press, 1969), pp. 37, 136–37.

24. Williams, "Journal," p. 191.

25. Ibid., p. 192.

26. *A Report of the Secretary of the Navy ... relative to the naval expedition to Japan*, United States Senate, 33rd Congress, 2nd Session, Executive Document 34, pp. 151–52.

27. Williams, "Journal," p. 195.

28. George Alexander Lensen, *The Russian Push Toward Japan: Russo-Japanese Relations, 1697–1875* (Princeton: Princeton University Press, 1959), pp. 302–07; Tokutomi Soho, *Kinsei Nihon Kokuminshi* (Tokyo: Minyusha, 1929), XXXII, p. 305.

29. Perry, *Narrative*, I, pp. 472–75.

30. Tokutomi, *Kinsei Nihon Kokuminshi*, XXXII, p. 313.

31. Perry, *Narrative*, I, p. 426.

32. Tokutomi, *Kinsei Nihon Kokuminshi*, XXXII, pp. 321–22.

33. Williams, "Journal," p. 213.

34. Yoshida, *Tojin Okichi*, p. 24.

35. Perry, *Narrative*, I, p. 587.

36. Williams, "Journal," p. 235.

37. Spalding, *The Japan Expedition*, p. 336.

38. There are some indications that the Okinawan who attacked Board had been the Bettelheims' babysitter. Bettelheim convinced him to confess for the good of his fellow islanders. The Okinawan was banished until after Perry's departure, when he was brought back to a hero's welcome. Roger Pineau to Samuel Eliot Morison, April 20, 1970, *Samuel Eliot Morison Papers*, Harvard University Archives.

39. Spalding, *The Japan Expedition*, p. 339.

40. Ibid., p. 337; George Henry Preble, *The Opening of Japan: A Diary of Discovery in the Far East, 1853–1856*, Boleslaw Szczesniak, ed. (Norman: University of Oklahoma Press, 1962), p. 109; Williams, "Journal," p. 241.

Chapter 14
FILIBUSTERING TOWARD HEAVEN BY
THE GREAT WESTERN ROUTE

1. Matthew Calbraith Perry to S. Wells Williams, March 13, 1855, *Samuel Wells Williams Correspondence, Williams Family Papers*, Sterling Library, Yale University.

2. Matthew Calbraith Perry, *Narrative of the Expedition of an American Squadron to the China Seas and Japan, performed in the years, 1852, 1853, and 1854, under the Command of Commodore M. C. Perry, United States Navy, by Order of the Government of the United States* (Washington: Beverley Tucker, Senate Printer, 1856), II, p. 186.

3. F. B. Sanborn, ed., *The Writings of Henry David Thoreau* (New York and Boston: Houghton Mifflin Company, 1906), VI, p. 210.

4. W. G. Beasley, *The Meiji Restoration* (Stanford: Stanford University Press, 1972), p. 178.

5. Ibid., p. 107.

6. *A Report of the Secretary of the Navy . . . relative to the naval expedition to Japan*, U.S. Senate, 33rd Congress, 2nd Session, p. 116; Perry to J. C. Dobbin, December 8, 1853, April 3, 1854, *Letters Received by the Secretary of the Navy from Commanding Officers of Squadrons*, National Archives, Washington, D.C.

7. *A Report of the Secretary of the Navy . . . relative to the naval expedition to Japan*, pp. 108–10.

8. Ibid., pp. 176–78; S. Wells Williams, "A Journal of the Perry Expedition to Japan (1853–1854)," *Transactions of the Asiatic Society of Japan*, XXXVII, Part 2 (1910), pp. 256–57.

9. Williams to William Frederick Williams and Sarah Pond Williams, July 13, 1854 (P. S., August 19), *Samuel Wells Williams Correspondence, Williams Family Papers*, Sterling Library, Yale University, New Haven, Connecticut.

10. *The Correspondence of Messrs. McLane and Parker*, U.S. Senate, 35th Congress, 2nd Session, Senate Executive Document 22, pp. 2–55.

11. Perry to J. C. Dobbin, August 9, 1854, *Squadron Letters*; Robert Erwin Johnson, *Far China Station: The United States Navy in Asian Waters, 1800–1898* (Annapolis: Naval Institute Press, 1979), pp. 72–73.

12. *A Report of the Secretary of the Navy . . . relative to the naval expedition to Japan*, pp. 186–87.

13. Ibid., pp. 185–86.

14. David Black, *The King of Fifth Avenue: The Fortunes of August Belmont* (New York: The Dial Press, 1981), p. 130.

15. *Morning Courier and New York Enquirer*, July 14, 1854.

16. *New York Daily Tribune*, November 5, 8, and 9, 1854; *New York Herald*, September 4, 1853, November 1, 1853.

17. Perry to James Watson Webb, December 12, 1854, *James Watson Webb Collection*, Sterling Library, Yale University.

18. Samuel Eliot Morison, *"Old Bruin": The Life of Commodore Matthew C. Perry, 1794–1858* (Boston: Little, Brown and Company, 1967), p. 415.

19. *Morning Courier and New York Enquirer*, January 16, 1855.

20. Perry to Williams, March 13, 1855, *Williams Correspondence*.

21. David Hunter Miller, *Treaties and Other International Acts of the United States of America* (Washington: U.S. Government Printing Office, 1931), pp. 664–66.

22. *New York Daily Times*, September 24, 1854.

23. Perry to Williams, December 6, 1854, *Williams Correspondence*.

24. Perry to Webb, January 29, 1855, *Webb Collection*; *William Speiden Journal*, February 16, 1855, Naval Historical Foundation, Washington, D.C.

25. August Belmont to Perry, March 12, 1856, Houghton Library, Harvard University, Cambridge, Massachusetts.

26. Perry to Williams, March 13, 1855; Williams to James Dwight Dana, June 8, 1855; Perry to Williams, June 28, 1855, *Williams Correspondence*.

27. Perry to Williams, September 15, 1855, *Williams Correspondence*.

28. Morison, *"Old Bruin,"* pp. 419–21; Perry to Belmont, July 23, 1856, Houghton Library.

29. Perry, *Narrative*, I, p. 191.

30. Ibid., p. 326.

31. Ibid., p. 324.

32. Ibid., p. 212.

33. Ibid., pp. 358–59.

34. Morison, *"Old Bruin,"* p. 417.

35. J. W. Spalding, *The Japan Expedition: Japan and Around the World, An Account of Three Visits to the Japanese Empire* (New York: Redfield, 1855), pp. 353–54.

36. Perry, *Narrative*, I, pp. 380–90. Criticizing what he considered either willful or ignorant criticism of the Treaty of Kanagawa, Perry amplified these arguments in a special essay in the second volume of the *Narrative*. Ibid., II, pp. 185–87.

37. Perry, *Narrative*, II, p. 173.

38. Ibid., pp. 174–75.

39. Ibid., pp. 175–76.

40. Ibid., pp. 177–78, 179–80.

41. For Perry's instructions to Abbot and Abbot's report on what he found in Formosa, ibid., pp. 137–54. Tyler Dennett, *Americans in Eastern Asia* (New York: Octagon Books, 1979), pp. 284–91; Edward V. Gulick, *Peter Parker and the Opening of China* (Cambridge: Harvard University Press, 1973), pp. 189–93; Gideon Nye, Jr., to Perry, September 23, 1857, *The Archives of the Episcopal Church*, Austin, Texas.

42. George Henry Preble, *The Opening of Japan: A Diary of Discovery in the Far East, 1853–1856* (Norman: University of Oklahoma Press, 1962), p. 171.

43. Perry, *A Paper by Commodore M. C. Perry, U.S.N., Read Before the American Geographical and Statistical Society, at a meeting held March 6th,*

1856; Colonel Duncan S. Somerville, *The Aspinwall Empire* (Mystic: Mystic Seaport Museum, 1983), p. 99.

44. Abbot to Joseph Smith, September 9, 1854, *Joel Abbot Papers*, Nimitz Library, U.S. Naval Academy, Annapolis, Maryland.

45. Abbot to Laura Abbot, April 8, 1853, ibid.

46. Williams, "Journal," p. 222.

47. Ibid., pp. 224–26.

48. Perry, *Narrative*, I, p. 77.

49. Webb to Perry, May 1, 1857, *Webb Collection*.

50. *New York Herald*, March 7, 1858.

51. *Morning Courier and New York Enquirer*, March 5, 1858.

52. Perry, *Narrative*, II, pp. 201–10; Miller, *Treaties*, pp. 653–54.

53. George Alexander Lensen, *Russia's Japan Expedition of 1852 to 1855* (Gainesville: University of Florida Press, 1955), pp. 85–89, 111–26.

54. Yoshida Tsunekichi, *Tojin Okichi* (Tokyo: Chuokoronsha, 1966), p. 32.

55. For accounts of Harris's negotiations, see Mario E. Cosenza, ed., *The Complete Journal of Townsend Harris: The First American Consul and Minister to Japan* (Rutland: Charles E. Tuttle Company, 1959); Oliver Statler, *Shimoda Story* (Honolulu: University of Hawaii Press, 1969).

56. Beasley, *The Meiji Restoration*, pp. 99–100.

57. Ibid., p. 188.

58. Ibid., pp. 107–8.

59. Herbert P. Bix, *Peasant Protest in Japan, 1590–1884* (New Haven: Yale University Press, 1986), pp. 161–62, 167–72.

Chapter 15
THE BLACK SHIP METAPHOR, THE SECOND OPENING
OF JAPAN, AND GLOBAL HEGEMONY

1. Clyde V. Prestowitz, Jr., *Trading Places: How We Allowed Japan to Take the Lead* (New York: Basic Books, 1988), p. 105.

2. Douglas MacArthur, *Reminiscences* (New York: McGraw-Hill Book Company, 1964), p. 276.

3. Prestowitz, *Trading Places*, p. 277.

4. Theodore H. White, "The Danger from Japan," *The New York Times Magazine*, July 28, 1985.

5. Okita Saburo, "Japan's Quiet Strength," *Foreign Policy*, 75 (Summer 1989), p. 131.

6. *The New York Times*, June 28, 1989.

7. Morita Akio and Ishihara Shintaro, *The Japan That Can Say "No": The New U.S.-Japan Relations Card*, p. 67. Typewritten translation in author's possession.

8. John Dower, *War Without Mercy: Race and Power in the Pacific War* (New York: Pantheon Books, 1986), p. 316.

9. A. L. Sadler, *The Maker of Modern Japan: The Life of Tokugawa Ieyasu* (Rutland: Charles E. Tuttle Company, 1978), p. 7.

10. MacArthur, *Reminiscences*, pp. 272–77.

11. William Elliot Griffis, *Matthew Calbraith Perry: A Typical American Naval Officer* (Boston: Cupples and Hurd, 1887), p. 423.

12. Dorothy Borg and Okamoto Shimpei, eds., *Pearl Harbor as History: Japanese-American Relations, 1931–1941* (New York: Columbia University Press, 1973), p. 554.

13. Tyler Dennett, *Americans in Eastern Asia* (New York: Octagon Books, 1979), pp. 262, 272.

14. Stanley Karnow, *In Our Image: America's Empire in the Philippines* (New York: Random House, 1989), p. 125.

15. Akira Iriye, *Across the Pacific: An Inner History of American–East Asian Relations* (New York: Harcourt, Brace and World, 1967), pp. 201–2.

16. Samuel Eliot Morison, *"Old Bruin": The Life of Commodore Matthew C. Perry, 1794–1858* (Boston: Little, Brown and Company, 1967), p. 429. Actually, Morison could not make up his mind. At one point, he defended Perry against the charge of being an imperialist (ibid., p. 311). Finally he concluded that Perry was "an imperialist with a difference" (ibid., p. 429).

17. Peter Wiley, "Vietnam and the Pacific Rim Strategy," *Leviathan* (June 1969).

18. Peter Wiley, "The No Longer Pacific Pacific," *The Sacramento Bee*, February 24, 1985.

19. Jon Halliday, *A Political History of Japanese Capitalism* (New York: Pantheon Books, 1975), p. xxviii.

20. John Dower, *Empire and Aftermath: Yoshida Shigeru and the Japanese Experience 1878–1954* (Cambridge: Harvard University Press, 1979), pp. 312, 314.

21. Ibid., pp. 295, 317, 338–39, 345–46, 383.

22. William H. Davidson, *The Amazing Race: Winning the Technorivalry with Japan* (New York: John Wiley and Sons, 1984), p. 4.

23. Prestowitz, like many of Perry's contemporaries, misunderstands Perry's negotiating strategy with regard to opening the Japanese market. He did not, as Prestowitz claims, say, "Open your markets, or suffer the consequences." He in fact abandoned the idea of pressing for a trade agreement, knowing that the opening of the Japanese market was inevitable. Prestowitz, *Trading Places*, pp. 8, 77.

24. Dower, *War Without Mercy*, p. 314.

25. Prestowitz, *Trading Places*, p. 310.

26. For a telling recent analysis of the relationship between politics and economic development, see Karel van Wolferen, *The Enigma of Japanese Power* (New York: Alfred A. Knopf, 1989). See also Chalmers A. Johnson, *MITI and the Japanese Miracle: The Growth of Industrial Policy, 1925–1975* (Stanford: Stanford University Press, 1982).

27. Prestowitz, *Trading Places*, p. 268.

28. Ibid., pp. 250–71.

29. Ibid., pp. 161, 277, 290.

30. Okita Saburo, "Japan's Quiet Strength," *Foreign Policy*, 75 (Summer 1989), p. 131; Morita and Ishihara, *The Japan That Can Say "No,"* p. 69.

31. Okita, "Japan's Quiet Strength," p. 134.

32. *The New York Times*, June 28, 1989.

33. Morita and Ishihara, *The Japan That Can Say "No,"* p. 69.

BIBLIOGRAPHY

DOCUMENTS

Joel Abbot Papers. Nimitz Library, United States Naval Academy.

Belmont Family Collection. Houghton Library, Harvard University.

Blue, C. *Incidents of a Cruise to China, Loo Choo and Japan in the U.S. Sloop of War Vandalia.* Diary in the New York Public Library.

Franklin Buchanan Papers. Nimitz Library, United States Naval Academy.

"A Doctor's Memorandum." Nabeshima Archives, Saga Prefectural Library. A typewritten translation in the possession of Roger Pineau.

Thomas Dudley Collection. William L. Clements Library, University of Michigan.

Thomas Cochrane Dudley Papers. Smithsonian Institution.

Fleet Journal: U.S. Naval Expedition to Japan, 1852–1854. Rutgers University Library.

William E. Griffis Far East Collection. Rutgers University Library.

Kayama, Eizaemon. *Memorandum of Kayama Eizaemon, Yoriki in the Staff of the Uraga Governor.* Typewritten translation by Muto Kiyoshi in the possession of Roger Pineau.

John Pendleton Kennedy Papers. Enoch Pratt Free Library, Baltimore, Maryland.

Kobayashi, Tetsujiro. "Assorted News of the Visit of Foreign Ships." Nabeshima Archives, Saga Prefectural Library. Typewritten translation in the possession of Roger Pineau.

Deck Logs of the *Lexington* and *Mississippi.* National Archives.

Log of the *Manhattan.* Old Dartmouth Historical Society.

Autobiography of Manjiro Nakajima. Brooklyn Museum.

Samuel Eliot Morison Papers. Harvard University Archives.

*Matthew Calbraith Perry Papers.** Beinecke Library, Yale University.
Matthew Calbraith Perry Papers. Library of Congress.
Matthew Calbraith Perry Papers. U.S. Naval Academy Museum.
Oliver H. Perry Journal. Rutgers University Library.
Rodgers Family Naval Historical Foundation. Library of Congress.
William H. Rutherford Papers. Library of Congress.
William Speiden Journal. Naval Historical Foundation, Washington, D.C.
Papers of Benajah Ticknor. Sterling Library, Yale University.
U.S. Department of the Navy. *Letters Received by the Secretary of the Navy from Commanding Officers of Squadrons, 1841–1886.* National Archives.
U.S. Department of State. *China Instructions,* I. National Archives.
————. *Dispatches from U.S. Ministers to China,* VIII. National Archives.
James Watson Webb Collection. Sterling Library, Yale University.
Samuel Wells Williams Correspondence, Williams Family Papers. Sterling Library, Yale University.

GOVERNMENT DOCUMENTS

Correspondence between the State Department and the late Commissioner to China. U.S. House of Representatives, 33rd Congress, 1st Session, Executive Document 123.
The Correspondence of Messrs. McLane and Parker. U.S. Senate, 35th Congress, 2nd Session, Senate Executive Document 22.
Correspondence Relative to the Naval Expedition to Japan. U.S. Senate, 33rd Congress, 2nd Session, Senate Executive Document 34.
Message from the President of the United States. U.S. Senate, 32nd Congress, 1st Session, Executive Document 1.
Official Documents Relative to the Empire of Japan. U.S. Senate, 32nd Congress, 1st Session, Executive Document 59.
Report of Mr. Rusk. U.S. Senate, 31st Congress, 1st Session, Committee Report 202.
Report of the Committee on Naval Affairs on Naval Service. U.S. House of Representatives, 31st Congress, 2nd Session, House Report Number 35.
Report of the Committee on the Post Office and Roads. U.S. Senate, 31st Congress, 1st Session, Committee Report 202.
Report of the Navy Department. U.S. Senate, 29th Congress, 1st Session, Senate Document 187.

* There are also Perry letters and documents at the Alderman Library (University of Virginia), the Butler Library (Columbia University), the Franklin D. Roosevelt Library, the Historical Society of Pennsylvania, the Huntington Library, the National Archives, the New York Historical Society, the New York Public Library, the Chrysler Museum, the Smithsonian Institution, and the William L. Clements Library (University of Michigan).

Report of the Postmaster General. U.S. Senate, 31st Congress, 1st Session, Executive Document 77.

Report of the Secretary of the Navy. U.S. Senate, 31st Congress, 1st Session, Senate Executive Document 1.

———. U.S. Senate, 31st Congress, 2nd Session, Senate Document 1.

Report of the Secretary of the Navy: Information in Relation to Contracts . . . Steamships between New York and California. U.S. Senate, 32nd Congress, 1st Session, Executive Document 50.

Report of the Secretary of the Navy in Relation to the Contract with Howland and Aspinwall. U.S. Senate, Special Session (March 14, 1853), Executive Document 2.

Report of the Secretary of the Navy on the Subject of Corporal Punishment. U.S. Senate, 32nd Congress, 1st Session, Executive Document 10.

Report of the Secretary of the Navy . . . relative to the naval expedition to Japan. U.S. Senate, 33rd Congress, 2nd Session, Executive Document 34.

Report to Accompany Bills Senate Numbers 456 and 458. U.S. Senate, 32nd Congress, 1st Session, Committee Report 267.

Steam Communication with China and the Sandwich Islands. U.S. House of Representatives, 30th Congress, 1st Session, Committee Report 596.

Steamers Between California and China: Report of the House Committee on Naval Affairs. U.S. House of Representatives, 31st Congress, 2nd Session, Report 34.

BOOKS AND PERIODICALS

Albion, Robert Greenhalgh. *The Rise of the New York Port, 1815–1860.* Boston: Northeastern University Press, 1967.

Allard, Dean C., et al., eds. *United States Naval History Sources in the United States.* Washington: Department of the Navy, 1979.

Allen, Gardner W. *Our Navy and the West Indian Pirates.* Salem: Essex Institute, 1929.

Allen, H. C. *Great Britain and the United States: A History of Anglo-American Relations, 1783–1952.* New York: St. Martin's Press, 1955.

A.S. "Thoughts on the Navy." *The Naval Magazine,* Vol. II (January 1837), pp. 5–42.

Ashton, William George, trans. *Nihongi, Chronicles of Japan from the Earliest Times to A.D. 697.* Rutland: Charles E. Tuttle Company, 1972.

Baba (Bunyi). *Genji yume monogatari.* Tokyo: Naigai Suppan Kyokai, 1905.

Bain, Chester A. "Commodore Matthew Perry, Humphrey Marshall, and the Taiping Rebellion." *The Far East Quarterly,* X (May 1951), pp. 258–70.

Bartlett, Irving H. *Daniel Webster.* New York: W. W. Norton and Company, 1978.

Bauer, K. Jack. *A Maritime History of the United States: The Role of America's Seas and Waterways.* Columbia: University of South Carolina Press, 1988.

————. "Naval Shipbuilding Programs." *Military Affairs*, XXIX (Spring, 1965).

Beach, Edward L. *The United States Navy: 200 Years.* New York: Henry Holt and Company, 1986.

Beasley, William G. *Great Britain and the Opening of Japan, 1834–1858.* London: Luzac and Company, 1951.

————. *The Meiji Restoration.* Stanford: Stanford University Press, 1972.

————, ed. *Selected Documents on Japanese Foreign Policy.* London: Oxford University Press, 1955.

Beatty, Richmond Croom. *Bayard Taylor: Laureate of the Gilded Age.* Norman: University of Oklahoma Press, 1936.

Bellah, Robert. *Tokugawa Religion: The Cultural Roots of Modern Japan.* New York: The Free Press, 1985.

Bennett, Frank M. *Steam Navy of the United States.* Pittsburgh: Warren and Company, 1896.

Bix, Herbert P. "Miura Meisuke, or Peasant Rebellion Under the Banner of 'Distress.'" *Bulletin of Concerned Asian Scholars*, X (April–June 1978), pp. 18–26.

————. *Peasant Protest in Japan, 1590–1884.* New Haven: Yale University Press, 1986.

Black, David. *The King of Fifth Avenue: The Fortunes of August Belmont.* New York: The Dial Press, 1981.

Bockstoce, John R. *Whales, Ice, and Men: The History of Whaling in the Western Arctic.* Seattle: University of Washington Press, 1986.

Bohner, Charles H. *John Pendleton Kennedy.* Baltimore: Johns Hopkins Press, 1961.

Bolitho, Harold. "Abe Masahiro and the New Japan." In Jeffrey P. Mass and William B. Hauser, eds., *The Bakufu in Japanese History.* Stanford: Stanford University Press, 1985, pp. 173–88.

————. *Treasures Among Men: The Fudai Daimyo in Tokugawa Japan.* New Haven: Yale University Press, 1974.

Borg, Dorothy, and Okamoto Shumpei, eds. *Pearl Harbor as History: Japanese-American Relations, 1931–1941.* New York: Columbia University Press, 1973.

Borton, Hugh. "Peasant Uprisings in Japan of the Tokugawa Period." *Transactions of the Asiatic Society of Japan*, 2nd Series, Vol. 16 (1938).

Brown, Alexander Crosby. *Women and Children Last: The Loss of the Steamship "Arctic."* London: Frederick Muller Limited, 1962.

Chamberlain, Basil Hall, trans. *The Kojiki—Records of Ancient Matters.* Rutland: Charles E. Tuttle Company, 1981.

Chang, Richard T. *From Prejudice to Tolerance: A Study of the Japanese Image of the West, 1826–1864.* Tokyo: Sophia University, 1970.

Chesneaux, Jean, et al. *China from the Opium War to the 1911 Revolution.* New York: Pantheon Books, 1976.

Clark, Arthur H. *The Clipper Ship Era.* Riverside: 7 C's Press, 1970.

Clement, E. W. "British Seamen and Mito Samurai in 1824." *Transactions of the Asiatic Society of Japan*, 1st Series, XXXIII (1905), pp. 86–131.

Clyde, Paul Hibbert. *United States Policy Toward China: Diplomacy and Public Documents, 1839–1939*. Durham: Duke University Press, 1940.

Cole, Allen B., ed. "Captain David Porter's Proposed Expedition to the Pacific and Japan." *The Pacific Historical Review*, IX (March 1940), pp. 61–65.

——, ed. *A Scientist with Perry in Japan: The Journal of Dr. James Morrow*. Chapel Hill: University of North Carolina Press, 1947.

——, ed. *With Perry in Japan: The Diary of Edward Yorke McCauley*. Princeton: Princeton University Press, 1942.

——, ed. *Yankee Surveyors in the Shogun's Seas*. Princeton: Princeton University Press, 1947.

Collcut, Martin, et al. *Cultural Atlas of Japan*. New York: Facts on File, 1988.

Collis, Maurice. *Foreign Mud*. Singapore: Graham Brash, 1980.

Cooper, James Fenimore. *The Battle of Lake Erie; or, Answers to Messrs. Burges, Duer, and MacKenzie*. Cooperstown: H. and E. Phinney, 1843.

——. *Correspondence of James Fenimore Cooper*. New Haven: Yale University Press, 1922.

——. *Naval History of the United States*. Philadelphia: Lea and Blanchard, 1840.

——. *Proceedings of the Naval Court Martial in the Case of Alexander Slidell MacKenzie*. New York: Henry G. Langley, 1844.

Cosenza, Mario E., ed. *The Complete Journal of Townsend Harris: The First American Consul and Minister to Japan*. Rutland: Charles E. Tuttle Company, 1959.

Craig, Albert M. *Choshu in the Meiji Restoration*. Cambridge: Harvard University Press, 1961.

Craig, Albert M., and Donald H. Shively, eds. *Personality in Japanese History*. Berkeley: University of California Press, 1970.

Cranston, Earl. "Shanghai in the Taiping Rebellion." *Pacific Historical Review*, V (June 1936), pp. 147–60.

Cutler, Carl C. *Greyhounds of the Sea: The Story of the American Clipper Ship*. Annapolis: Naval Institute Press, 1930.

Davidson, William H. *The Amazing Race: Winning the Technorivalry with Japan*. New York: John Wiley and Sons, 1984.

de Bary, William Theodore, et al., eds. *Sources of Japanese Tradition*. New York: Columbia University Press, 1958.

Dennett, Tyler. *Americans in Eastern Asia*. New York: Octagon Books, 1979.

DeRoulhac, Hamilton, ed. *The Papers of William A. Graham*. Raleigh: North Carolina Department of Archives and History, 1957.

"Diary of an Official of the Bakufu." *Transactions of the Asiatic Society of Japan*, 2nd Series, VII (1930), pp. 98–119.

Dickens, Charles. *American Notes*. New York: Trade Publishing Company, n.d.

Doenhoff, Richard A. "Biddle, Perry, and Japan," *U.S. Naval Institute Proceedings*, XLII (November 1966), pp. 79–87.

Dower, John W. *Empire and Aftermath: Yoshida Shigeru and the Japanese*

Experience, 1878–1954. Cambridge: Harvard University Press, 1979.

————, ed. *Origins of the Modern Japanese State: Selected Writings of E. H. Norman.* New York: Pantheon Books, 1975.

————. *War Without Mercy: Race and Power in the Pacific War.* New York: Pantheon Books, 1986.

Downs, Jacques M. "American Merchants and Opium, 1815–1840." *Business History Review,* XLII (Winter 1968), pp. 418–442.

Dulles, Foster Rhea. *Yankees and Samurai: America's Rule in the Emergence of Modern Japan.* New York: Harper & Row, 1965.

Dupree, A. Hunter. "Science vs. The Military: Dr. James Morrow and the Perry Expedition." *Pacific Historical Review,* XXII (February 1953), pp. 29–37.

Dutton, Charles J. *Oliver Hazard Perry.* New York: Longmans, Green and Company, 1935.

Egami, Teruhiko. *Kawaji Toshiakira.* Tokyo: Kyoikusha, 1987.

Ellet, Elizabeth Fries. *Court Circles of the Republic.* Hartford: Hartford Publishing Company, 1870.

Fairbank, John King. *Trade and Diplomacy on the China Coast: The Opening of the Treaty Ports, 1842–1854.* Stanford: Stanford University Press, 1969.

Fay, Peter Ward. *The Opium War, 1840–1843.* New York: W. W. Norton and Company, 1976.

Forbes, Hildegarde B., ed. *Correspondence of Dr. Charles H. Wheelwright.* Boston: Privately Printed, 1958.

Forbes, Robert B. *Personal Reminiscences.* Boston: Little, Brown and Company, 1882.

Goncharov, Ivan. *The Frigate Pallada.* New York: St. Martin's Press, 1987.

Graff, Henry F., ed. *Bluejackets in Japan: A Day-by-day Account Kept by Master's Mate John R. C. Lewis and Cabin Boy William B. Allen.* New York: New York Public Library, 1952.

Green, Constance McLaughlin. *Washington.* Princeton: Princeton University Press, 1962.

Greene, D. C. "Osada's Life of Takano Nagahide [Choei]." *Transactions of the Asiatic Society of Japan,* 1st Series, XLI (August 1912), pp. 379–492.

Griffis, William Elliot. *Matthew Calbraith Perry: A Typical American Naval Officer.* Boston: Cupples and Hurd, 1887.

————. "Millard Fillmore and His Part in the Opening of Japan." Address Delivered to the Buffalo History Society, Rutgers University Library.

Gulick, Edward V. *Peter Parker and the Opening of China.* Cambridge: Harvard University Press, 1973.

Hall, John Whitney. *Japan from Prehistory to Modern Times.* New York: Dell Publishing Company, 1970.

————. *Tanuma Okitsugu, 1719–1788.* Westport: Greenwood Press, 1982.

Halliday, Jon. *A Political History of Japanese Capitalism.* New York: Pantheon Books, 1975.

Hansen-Taylor, Marie, and Horace E. Scudder, eds. *Life and Letters of Bayard Taylor.* Boston: Houghton Mifflin & Co., 1884.

Harrison, John A. *Japan's Northern Frontier: A Preliminary Study in Colonization and Expansion with Special Reference to the Relations of Japan and Russia.* Gainesville: University of Florida Press, 1953.

Haviland, E. K. "Early Steam Navigation to China." *American Neptune,* XXVI (1966), pp. 5–32.

Hayford, Harrison, ed. *The Somers Mutiny Affair.* Englewood Cliffs: Prentice Hall, 1962.

Heco, Joseph. *The Narrative of a Japanese.* Yokohama: Yokohama Printing and Publishing Company, n.d.

Heine, William. *With Perry to Japan: A Memoir by William Heine.* Honolulu: University of Hawaii Press, 1990.

Hiroshige: One Hundred Views of Edo. New York: George Braziller, 1986.

Horan, Leo. "Flogging in the United States Navy." *U.S. Naval Institute Proceedings,* LXXVI (August 1950), pp. 969–75.

Hsu, C. Y. *The Rise of Modern China.* New York: Oxford University Press, 1983.

Huber, Thomas M. *The Revolutionary Origins of Modern Japan.* Stanford: Stanford University Press, 1981.

Humphreys, Robert Arthur. *The Diplomatic History of British Honduras.* New York: Oxford University Press, 1961.

Hunter, William C. *Bits of Old China.* London: Kegan Paul, Trench and Company, 1885.

———. *The Fan Kwae at Canton.* London: Kegan Paul, Trench and Company, 1882.

Inoue, Kiyoshi. *Nihon No Rekishi* (Tokyo: Iwanami Shoten, 1965).

Iriye, Akira. *Across the Pacific: An Inner History of American–East Asia Relations.* New York: Harcourt, Brace and World, 1967.

———. "Minds Across the Pacific: Japan in American Writing, 1853–1883." *Papers on Japan.* Cambridge: Harvard University East Asian Research Center, 1961.

Irving, Washington. *Astoria.* New York: P. F. Collier & Son, 1864.

———. *Captain Bonneville.* New York: P. F. Collier & Son, 1864.

Ishii, Takashi. *Nihon Kaikokushi.* Tokyo: Yoshikawa Kobunsho, 1972.

Ishin, Shiryo Hensan Kai. *Dai Nihon Ishin Shiryo.* Tokyo: Ishin Shiryo Hensan Jimukyoku, 1940.

Jansen, Marius B. *Sakamoto Ryoma and the Meiji Restoration.* Princeton: Princeton University Press, 1961.

"Japan." *Democratic Review,* CLXVI (April 1852), pp. 319–32.

"Japan—the Expedition." *American Whig Revue,* XC (June 1852), pp. 507–15.

Johnson, Chalmers A. *MITI and the Japanese Miracle: The Growth of Industrial Policy, 1925–1975.* Stanford: Stanford University Press, 1982.

———, Laura D'Andrea Johnson, and John Zysman, eds. *Politics and Productivity.* Cambridge: Ballinger Publishing Company, 1989.

Johnson, Robert Erwin. *Far China Station: The United States Navy in Asian Waters, 1800–1898.* Annapolis: Naval Institute Press, 1979.

Junior League of Washington. *The City of Washington: An Illustrated History*. New York: Alfred A. Knopf, 1985.

Kaempfer, Englebert. *The History of Japan*. Glasgow: James MacLehose and Sons, 1906.

Kanbashi, Norimasa. *Satsuma jin to Yoropa*. Kagoshima: Chosakusha, 1982.

Kaneko, Hisakuza. *Manjiro, The Man Who Discovered America*. Boston: Houghton Mifflin Company, 1956.

Karnow, Stanley. *In Our Image: America's Empire in the Philippines*. New York: Random House, 1989.

Kato, Tetsuro. "The Age of 'JAPAMERICA'—Taking Japanese Development Seriously." *Hitotsubashi Journal of Social Studies*, XXI (August 1989), pp. 61–78.

Katsu, Kokichi. *Musui's Story: The Autobiography of a Tokugawa Samurai*. Tucson: University of Arizona Press, 1988.

Katz, Irving. *August Belmont: A Political Biography*. New York: Columbia University Press, 1968.

Keene, Donald. *The Japanese Discovery of Europe, 1720–1830*. Stanford: Stanford University Press, 1969.

Kelly, William W. *Deference and Defiance in Nineteenth-Century Japan*. Princeton: Princeton University Press, 1985.

Kemble, John Haskell. *The Panama Route, 1848–1869*. Berkeley: University of California Press, 1943.

Kerr, George H. *Okinawa: The History of an Island People*. Rutland: Charles E. Tuttle Company, 1958.

King, Charles. *The Claims of Japan and Malaysia upon Christendom*. New York: E. French, 1839.

Knox, Dudley W. *A History of the United States Navy*. New York: G. P. Putnam's Sons, 1948.

Komatsu, Kashiro. *Edojo*. Tokyo: Chosakusha, 1985.

Koschmann, J. Victor. *The Mito Ideology: Discourse, Reform, and Insurrection in Late Tokugawa Japan, 1790–1864*. Berkeley: The University of California Press, 1987.

Krout, Mary. "Perry's Expedition to Japan." *U.S. Naval Institute Proceedings*, XLVII (February 1921), pp. 215–29.

Kublin, Hyman. "Commodore Perry and the Bonin Islands." *U.S. Naval Institute Proceedings*, LXXVIII (March 1952), pp. 283–91.

Langley, Harold D. *Social Reform in the United States Navy, 1798–1862*. Urbana: University of Illinois Press, 1967.

Latourette, Kenneth Scott. *A History of Christian Missions in China*. New York: MacMillan Company, 1929.

Lawson, Will. *Pacific Steamers*. Glasgow: Brown, Son & Ferguson, 1927.

Lensen, George Alexander. *Russia's Japan Expedition of 1852 to 1855*. Gainesville: University of Florida Press, 1955.

———. *The Russian Push Toward Japan: Russo-Japanese Relations, 1697–1875*. Princeton: Princeton University Press, 1959.

Lewis, William S., and Murakami Naojiro, eds. *Ranald MacDonald: The Nar-*

rative of His Early Life. Spokane: The Eastern Washington State Historical Society, 1923.

Long, David F. *Sailor-Diplomat: A Biography of Commodore James Biddle*. Boston: Northeastern University Press, 1983.

Lovett, Robert W. "The Japan Expedition Press." *Harvard Library Bulletin*, XII (Spring, 1958), pp. 242–252.

Lubbock, Baird. *The Opium Clippers*. Glasgow: Brown, Son & Ferguson, 1933.

MacArthur, Douglas. *Reminiscences*. New York: McGraw-Hill Book Company, 1964.

MacFarlane, Charles. *Japan: An Account Geographical and Historical*. London: George Routledge & Company, 1852.

MacKenzie, Alexander Slidell. *The Life of Oliver Hazard Perry*. New York: Harper & Brothers, 1840.

Maruyama, Masao. *Studies in the Intellectual History of Tokugawa Japan*. Princeton: Princeton University Press, 1974.

Marvin, Winthrop L. *The American Merchant Marine: Its History and Romance from 1620 to 1902*. New York: Charles Scribner's Sons, 1916.

Meadows, Thomas Taylor. *The Chinese and Their Rebellion*. Stanford: Stanford University Press, 1953.

Meiji Japan Through Contemporary Sources. Tokyo: The Centre for East Asian Cultural Studies, 1970.

Melville, Herman. *Moby-Dick; or, The Whale*. New York: Hendricks House, 1952.

———. *White-Jacket; or, The World in a Man-of-War*. New York: New American Library, 1979.

Miller, David Hunter. *Treaties and Other International Acts of the United States of America*. Washington: U.S. Government Printing Office, 1931.

Mitani, Hiroshi. "On the Eve of the Opening of Japan: Tokugawa Foreign Policy in the Koka and Kaei Eras." In Kindai Nihon Kenyukai, *Nihon Gaiko No Kiki Ninshiki*, 7 (1985).

———. "Before Perry: Tokugawa Foreign Policy, 1846–1853." *Journal of Modern Japanese Studies* (in Japanese), 7, 1985.

Mito-han Shiryo. Book of Inui. Tokyo: Yoshikawa Kobunkan, 1970.

Monbusho Ishin Shiryo Hensan Kai. *Ishinshi*. Tokyo: Meiji Shoin, 1940.

Morison, Samuel Eliot. "Commodore Perry's Japan Expedition Press and Theatre." *American Antiquarian Society Proceedings*, LXXVII, Part I (1967).

———. *The Maritime History of Massachusetts, 1783–1860*. Boston: Northeastern University Press, 1979.

———. *"Old Bruin": The Life of Commodore Matthew C. Perry, 1794–1858*. Boston: Little, Brown and Company, 1967.

Morris, Ivan. *The Nobility of Failure: Tragic Heroes in the History of Japan*. New York: Farrar, Straus, Giroux, 1975.

Mooney, James L., ed. *The Dictionary of American Naval Fighting Ships*, 8 vols. Washington, D.C.: Naval Historical Center, 1981.

Moore, Barrington, Jr. "Japanese Peasant Protests and Revolts in Comparative Historical Perspective." *International Review of Social History*, XXIII:5 (1988), pp. 312–27.

——. *Social Origins of Dictatorship and Democracy*. Boston: Beacon Press, 1966.

Morita, Akio, and Ishihara, Shintaro. *The Japan That Can Say "No": The New U.S.–Japan Relations Card*. Typewritten translation in author's possession.

Morris, Jan. *Hong Kong*. New York: Random House, 1988.

Murdoch, James. *A History of Japan*. New York: Frederick Ungar Publishing Company, 1964.

Najita, Tetsuo. "Oshio Heihachiro (1793–1837)." In Albert M. Craig and Donald H. Shively, *Personality in Japanese History*. Berkeley: University of California Press, 1970, pp. 155–79.

Naramoto, Tatsuya. *Toshida Shoin no Subete*. Tokyo: Jinbutsu Oraisha, 1984.

——. *Yoshida Shoin*. Tokyo: Shisakusha, 1971.

Nevins, Allen, ed. *The Diary of Philip Hone*. New York: Kraus Reprint, 1969.

Newman, Peter C. *Caesars of the Wilderness*. Markham: Viking, 1987.

——. *Company of Adventurers: The Story of the Hudson's Bay Company*. Harmondsworth: Penguin Books, 1987.

Nitobe, Inazo. *The Intercourse Between the United States and Japan*. Wilmington: Scholarly Resources, 1973.

Nordhoff, Charles. *Man-of-War Life*. Annapolis: The Naval Institute Press, 1985.

Ohmae, Kenichi. *Beyond National Borders: Reflections on Japan and the World*. Homewood: Dow Jones–Irwin, 1987.

——. *Triad Power: The Coming Shape of Global Competition*. New York: The Free Press, 1985.

Okita, Saburo. "Japan's Quiet Strength." *Foreign Policy*, 75 (Summer 1989), pp. 128–145.

Olson, Charles. *Call Me Ishmael: A Study of Melville*. San Francisco: City Lights, 1947.

Palmer, Aaron Haight. *Documents and Facts Illustrating the Origin of the Mission to Japan*. Washington: Henry Polkhorn, 1857.

Paske-Smith, M. *Western Barbarians in Japan and Formosa in Tokugawa Days, 1603–1868*. Kobe: J. L. Thompson & Company, 1930.

Paullin, Charles O. *Commodore John Rodgers*. Cleveland: Arthur H. Clark Company, 1910.

Perry, Calbraith Bourn. *The Perrys of Rhode Island*. New York: Tobias A. Wright, 1913.

Perry, Matthew Calbraith. *Narrative of the Expedition of an American Squadron to the China Seas and Japan, performed in the years, 1852, 1853, and 1854, under the Command of Commodore M. C. Perry, United States Navy, by Order of the Government of the United States*. 3 vols. Washington: Beverley Tucker, Senate Printer, 1856. (Vols. 2 and 3 published in 1857.)

——. *The Japan Expedition, 1852–1854: The Personal Journal of Matthew*

C. Perry. Roger Pineau, ed. Washington: Smithsonian Institution Press, 1968.

———. *A Paper by Commodore M. C. Perry, U.S.N., Read Before the American Geographical and Statistical Society, at a meeting held March 6th, 1856.*

Plummer, Katherine. *The Shogun's Reluctant Ambassadors: Sea Drifters.* Tokyo: The Lotus Press, 1985.

Poore, Ben Perley. *Perley's Reminiscences of Sixty Years of the National Metropolis.* Philadelphia: Hubbard Brothers, 1886.

Preble, George Henry. *The Opening of Japan: A Diary of Discovery in the Far East, 1853–1856.* Boleslaw Szczesniak, ed. Norman: University of Oklahoma Press, 1962.

Prestowitz, Clyde V., Jr. *Trading Places: How We Allowed Japan to Take the Lead.* New York: Basic Books, 1988.

Railton, Stephen. *Fenimore Cooper: A Study of His Life and Imagination.* Princeton: Princeton University Press, 1978.

Rausch, Basil. *American Interest in Cuba, 1848–1855.* New York: Columbia University Press, 1948.

Rayback, Robert J. *Millard Fillmore: Biography of a President.* Buffalo: Henry Stewart, 1959.

Reynolds, Clark G. *History and the Sea: Essays on Maritime Strategy.* Columbia: University of South Carolina Press, 1989.

Ruby, Robert H. and John A. Brown. *The Chinook Indians: Traders of the Lower Columbia River.* Norman: University of Oklahoma Press, 1976.

Sadler, A. L. *The Maker of Modern Japan: The Life of Shogun Tokugawa Ieyasu.* Rutland: Charles E. Tuttle Company, 1937.

Sakai, Robert K. "The Ryukyu (liu-ch'iu) Islands as a Fief of Satsuma." In John King Fairbank, ed., *The Chinese World Order.* Cambridge: Harvard University Press, 1969, pp. 112–33.

———. "The Satsuma-Ryukyu Trade and the Tokugawa Seclusion Policy." *Journal of Asian Studies,* XXIII (1964), pp. 391–403.

———. "Shimazu Nariakira and the Emergence of National Leadership in Satsuma." In Albert M. Craig and Donald H. Shively, eds., *Personality in Japanese History.* Berkeley: University of California Press, 1970, pp. 209–233.

Sakamaki, Shunzo. "Japan and the United States, 1790–1853." *Transactions of the Asiatic Society of Japan,* 2nd Series, XVIII (1939).

Sakamoto, Kenichi. *Tenno to Meiji Ishin.* Tokyo: Akatsuki Shabo, 1983.

Sakanishi, Shio, ed. *A Private Journal of John Glendy Sproston.* Tokyo: Sophia University, 1940.

Sanborn, F. B. *The Writings of Henry David Thoreau.* New York and Boston: Houghton Mifflin Company, 1906.

Sansom, G. B. *A History of Japan to 1334; A History of Japan, 1334–1615; A History of Japan, 1615–1867.* Stanford: Stanford University Press, 1963.

———. *The Western World and Japan: A Study in the Interaction of Eu-*

ropean and Asiatic Cultures. Tokyo: Charles E. Tuttle Company, 1977.

Schaller, Michael. *The American Occupation of Japan: The Origins of the Cold War in Asia.* New York: Oxford University Press, 1985.

Scheiner, Irwin. "The Mindful Peasant: Sketches for a Study of Rebellion." *The Journal of Asian Studies,* XXXII:4 (August 1973), pp. 579–92.

———, and Najita Tetsuo, eds., *Japanese Thought in the Tokugawa Period, 1600–1868: Methods and Metaphors.* Chicago: The University of Chicago Press, 1978.

Schultz, John Richie, ed. *The Unpublished Letters of Bayard Taylor.* San Marino: The Huntington Library, 1937.

Schwartz, William Leonard. "Commodore Perry at Okinawa from the Unpublished Diary of a British Missionary." *American Historical Review,* LI (January 1946), pp. 262–76.

Sears, Louis Martin. *John Slidell.* Durham: Duke University Press, 1925.

Seiho, Arima. "The Western Influence on Japanese Military Science, Shipbuilding, and Navigation." *Monumenta Nipponica,* 19 (1964), pp. 118–34.

Sewall, John S. *The Logbook of the Captain's Clerk: Adventures in the China Seas.* Bangor: Charles H. Glass & Company, 1905.

Sheldon, G. W. "The Old Shipping Merchants of New York." *Harper's,* LXXXIV (1892), pp. 457–71.

Shimazu Nariakira Bunsho Kankokai Ken. *Shimazu Nariakira Bunsho.* Tokyo: Yashikawa Kobunkan, 1969.

Smith, Carl T. *Chinese Christians: Elites, Middlemen, and the Church in Hong Kong.* Oxford and New York: Oxford University Press, 1985.

Somerville, Colonel Duncan S. *The Aspinwall Empire.* Mystic: Mystic Seaport Museum, 1983.

Spalding, J. W. *The Japan Expedition: Japan and Around the World, An Account of Three Visits to the Japanese Empire.* New York: Redfield, 1855.

Sprout, Harold, and Margaret Sprout. *The Rise of American Naval Power, 1776–1918.* Princeton: Princeton University Press, 1939.

Stackpole, Edward. *The Sea-Hunters: The New England Whalers, 1635–1835.* Philadelphia: J. B. Lippincott Company, 1953.

Starbuck, Alexander. *History of the American Whaling Fishery.* New York: Argosy; Antiquarian, 1964.

Statler, Oliver. *The Black Ship Scroll.* Rutland: Charles E. Tuttle Company, 1964.

———. *The Shimoda Story.* Honolulu: University of Hawaii Press, 1969.

Stelle, Charles Clark. *Americans and the China Opium Trade in the Nineteenth Century.* New York: Arno Press, 1981.

Stevenson, John. *Yoshitoshi.* Boulder: Avery Press, 1986.

Swisher, Earl. *China's Management of the American Barbarians: A Study of Sino-American Relations, 1841–1861, with Documents.* New Haven: Far Eastern Publications, 1953.

Tabohashi Kiyoshi. *Kindai Nihongaikoku Kankeishi.* Tokyo: Toeshoin, 1943.
———. *Zotei Kindai Nihon Gaikoku Kankei Shi.* Tokyo: Toeshoin, 1953.
Taylor, Bayard. *El Dorado, or Adventures in the Path of Empire.* New York: Alfred A. Knopf, 1949.
———. *A Visit to India, China, and Japan in the Year 1853.* London: Sampson Low, Son & Company, n.d.
Te-kong, Tong. *United States Diplomacy in China, 1844–1860.* Seattle: University of Washington Press, 1964.
Teng, Yuan Chung. "Reverend Issachar Jacox Roberts and the Taiping Rebellion." *Journal of American Studies,* XXIII (November 1963), pp. 55–67.
Teng, S. Y. *The Taiping Rebellion and the Western Powers.* London: Oxford University Press, 1971.
Teruya, Yoshihiko. *Bernard J. Bettelheim and Okinawa: A Study of the First Protestant Missionary to the Island Kingdom, 1846–1854.* Master's thesis, University of the Ryukyus, 1954, University of Colorado, 1958.
Tokutomi, Soho. *Perry Raiko Oyobi Sono Toji.* In *Kinsei Nihon Kokuminshi.* Tokyo: Minyusha, 1929.
Tokyo Teikoku Daigaku, Bunka Daigaku, Shiryo Hensangakari, eds. *Dai Nihon Komonjo: Bakumatsu Kaikoku Kankei Monjo.* Tokyo: Tokyo Imperial University, Shiryo Henan Kyoku, 1912.
Totman, Conrad. "Political Reconciliation in the Tokugawa Bakufu: Abe Masahiro and Tokugawa Nariaki, 1844–1852." In Albert M. Craig and Donald H. Shively, eds., *Personality in Japanese History.* Berkeley: University of California Press, 1970, pp. 180–208.
———. *Politics in the Tokugawa Bakufu, 1600–1843.* Cambridge: Harvard University Press, 1967.
———. "The Struggle for Control of the Shogunate (1853–1858)." *Papers on Japan.* Cambridge: East Asia Research Center, 1961.
———. *Tokugawa Ieyasu: Shogun.* South San Francisco: Heian International, 1983.
Trautmann, Frederic, trans. *With Perry to Japan: A Memoir by William Heine.* Honolulu: University of Hawaii Press, 1990.
Treat, Payne, Jackson. *The Early Diplomatic Relations Between Japan and the United States.* Baltimore: The Johns Hopkins Press, 1917.
Tripp, Job C. "A Japanese Student in Fairhaven." *Old Dartmouth Historical Sketches,* 40 (June and October 1914), pp. 18–19.
Tyler, David Budlong. *Steam Conquers the Atlantic.* New York: D. Appleton-Century Company, 1939.
van Gulik, R. H. "*Kakkaron,* A Japanese Echo of the Opium War." *Monumenta Serica,* IV (1939–1940), pp. 478–545.
van Wolferen, Karel. *The Enigma of Japanese Power.* New York: Alfred A. Knopf, 1989.
Vernon, Manfred C. "The Dutch and the Opening of Japan by the United States." *Pacific Historical Review,* XXVIII (February 1959), pp. 39–48.

Vinton, P. "Japan." *Putnam's Monthly*, I (March 1853) pp. 241–51.

Vlastos, Stephen. *Peasant Protests and Uprisings in Tokugawa Japan*. Berkeley: University of California Press, 1986.

Wakabayashi, Bob Tadashi. *Anti-foreignism and Western Learning in Early-Modern Japan: The New Theses of 1825*. Cambridge: Harvard University Press, 1986.

Wakeman, Frederic, Jr. *Strangers at the Gate: Social Disorder in South China, 1839–1861*. Berkeley: University of California Press, 1966.

Waley, Arthur. *The Opium War through Chinese Eyes*. Stanford: Stanford University Press, 1968.

Walsh, Warren Bartlett. *Russia and the Soviet Union: A Modern History*. Ann Arbor: University of Michigan Press, 1968.

Walthall, Anne. *Social Protest and Popular Culture in Eighteenth-Century Japan*. Tucson: The University of Arizona Press, 1986.

Walworth, Arthur Clarence. *Black Ships Off Japan*. New York: Alfred A. Knopf, 1946.

Ward, Geoffrey C. *Before the Trumpet: Young Franklin Roosevelt*. New York: Harper & Row, 1945.

Warriner, Emily V. *Voyage to Destiny*. New York: Bobbs Merrill Company, 1956.

Watanabe, Shujiro. *Abe Masahiro jiseki*. 2 vols. Tokyo: Tokyo University Press, 1910. Reprinted in 1978.

Webb, Herschel. *The Japanese Imperial Institution in the Tokugawa Period*. New York: Columbia University Press, 1968.

Webster, Fletcher, ed. *The Private Correspondence of Daniel Webster*. Boston: Little, Brown and Company, 1875.

Wei, Betty Peh-T'i. *Shanghai: Crucible of Modern China*. Hong Kong: Oxford University Press, 1987.

Wermuth, Paul. *Bayard Taylor*. New York: Twayne Publishers, 1973.

Whipple, A. B. C. *The Challenge*. New York: William Morrow, 1987.

White, Theodore. "The Danger from Japan." *The New York Times Magazine*, July 28, 1985.

Whitlock, Francis B. *Two New Yorkers: Editor and Sea Captain, 1833*. New York: The Newcomen Society of England, 1945.

Wiley, Peter. "The No Longer Pacific Pacific." *The Sacramento Bee*, February 24, 1985.

————. "Vietnam and the Pacific Rim Strategy." *Leviathan*, I (June 1969).

Williams, Frederick Wells. *The Life and Letters of Samuel Wells Williams, LL.D., Missionary, Diplomatist, Sinologue*. New York: G. P. Putnam's Sons, 1889.

Williams, S. Wells. "A Journal of the Perry Expedition to Japan, 1853–1854." *Transactions of the Asiatic Society of Japan*, XXXVII, Part 2 (1910).

————. *The Middle Kingdom*. New York: Charles Scribner's Sons, 1914.

————. "Narrative of a Voyage of The Ship *Morrison*." *The Chinese Repository*, VI (September and December 1837), pp. 209–29, 355–81.

Winslow, F. C. "Captain Mercator Cooper's Voyage to Japan." *The Seamen's Friend*, Honolulu, February 2, 1846.

Yoshida, Tsunekichi. *Ii Naosuke*. Tokyo: Yoshikawa Kobunkan, 1963.

———. *Tojin Okichi*. Tokyo: Chuokoronsha, 1966.

Zennosuke, Tsuji. *Kaigai Kotsu ShiWa*. Tokyo: Toado Shobo, 1917.

INDEX

* Page numbers in italics refer to illustrations.

ILLUSTRATION CREDITS

From *Abe Masahiro jiseki*, p. 259
Bibliothèque Nationale, Paris, pp. 243, 245, 252
Brooklyn Museum, p. 247
Chrysler Museum, Norfolk, Virginia, pp. 150, 216, 319, 369
Hong Kong Museum of Art, p. 134
From *Inquiry into the Somers Mutiny* (1843), p. 61
Library of Congress, pp. 15, 20, 47, 55, 56, 74, 76, 106–7, 122, 130, 144,
    154, 157, 166, 184, 186, 188, 190, 196, 199, 208, 289, 291, 294, 305, 317,
    320, 356, 383, 389, 393, 399, 409, 411, 419, 421, 431, 436, 439, 441, 459,
    467
From *The Life and Letters of Samuel Wells Williams*, p. 150
Mariners Museum, Newport News, Virginia, p. 95
Massachusetts Historical Society, Boston, Massachusetts, p. 85
Mystic Seaport Museum, Mystic, Connecticut, p. 147
New York Historical Society, p. 9
Newsday, p. 484
Provincial Archives of British Columbia, Vancouver, p. 7
Roger Pineau Collection, Naval Historical Center, Washington, D.C., pp.
    143, 322, 337, 351
Shiryo Hensan-jo, Tokyo University, pp. 317, 391, 406, 416–17
Smithsonian Institution, p. 193
Tokugawa Remeikan Foundation, Tokyo, pp. 233, 262
Tokugawa Tunenari, p. 261
University of the Ryukyus, Okinawa, Japan, p. 171
U.S. Naval Academy Museum, Annapolis, Maryland, pp. 50, 127
U.S. Naval Historical Center, Washington, D.C., pp. 48, 59, 65